O9-AID-825

Praise for Ian Rankin's

THE BEAT GOES ON

"One of the great literary crime solvers of our time. The brooding Rebus of the dark novels never completely disappears.... But Rankin exposes other facets of this music-loving, pint-imbibing crazy diamond.... Rebus is a Van Morrison kind of detective. No guru, no method, for him, just sharp eyes, a good nose, and one foot in front of the other on an often-treacherous path. Put *The Beat Goes On* in your guest room for the pleasure of a traveler, weary or insomniac, who needs a stout companion for an evening's adventure."
—Jim Higgins, *Milwaukee Journal Sentinel*

"Crisply clever." —Colette Bancroft, *Tampa Bay Times*

"An enjoyable collection, frequently displaying the playfulness that is characteristic of the author."
—Barry Forshaw, *The Independent* (UK)

"Hugely satisfying.... Each tale—thanks to Rankin's skill at scene-setting and character—proceeds at an almost leisurely pace, until a pivotal paragraph produces a surprising conclusion. The sardonic humor shines brighter than in the complex novels too. However, it is Rankin's portrait of Edinburgh, a city with a split personality and a looming literary heritage, that is most impressive. No one mixes lightness and darkness better than him."
—Mark Sanderson, *Evening Standard* (UK)

"Sharply observed, economically written.... For Rankin fans used to a regular diet of Rebus, this collection makes up for the year off the author took after the 2013 novel *Saints of the Shadow Bible*. For the uninitiated with short attention spans interested in sampling one of the finest crime fiction practitioners going, it's an excellent place to start." —Dan DeLuca, *Philadelphia Inquirer*

"All of the stories are tightly wrought and entertaining. Rankin moves ahead at great speed to deliver work that is potently inspiring, bringing readers a gem in each one....His fans should add this tome to their other books in the series immediately."

—Barbara Lipkien Gershenbaum, *Bookreporter*

"It's a very welcome return for Rebus that should tide fans over—until his next full novel comes out."

—Laura DeMarco, *Cleveland Plain Dealer*

"Rebus is genuinely fun to read no matter how dark his cases become....*The Beat Goes On* is a deeply satisfying read and evokes the spirit of Edinburgh and Scotland in all its glory."

—Roisin O'Connor, *Independent on Sunday* (UK)

"Rewarding....A welcome addition to the Rankin canon."

—*Publishers Weekly*

"Neat, pleasing, inventive....They are well-made stories, a pleasure to read, one after the other, the work of a practiced and professional craftsman....If you are a fan of the novels, you won't be disappointed."

—Allan Massie, *The Scotsman* (UK)

THE BEAT GOES ON

Also by Ian Rankin

The Inspector Malcolm Fox Series
The Complaints
The Impossible Dead

The Detective Inspector Rebus Series
Knots & Crosses
Hide & Seek
Tooth & Nail (previously published as *Wolfman*)
A Good Hanging and Other Stories
Strip Jack
The Black Book
Mortal Causes
Let It Bleed
Black & Blue
The Hanging Garden
Death Is Not the End (a novella)
Dead Souls
Set in Darkness
The Falls
Resurrection Men
A Question of Blood
Fleshmarket Alley
The Naming of the Dead
Exit Music
Standing in Another Man's Grave
Saints of the Shadow Bible
Even Dogs in the Wild

Other Novels
Witch Hunt
Blood Hunt
Bleeding Hearts
Watchman
Doors Open
Dark Entries (graphic novel)

THE BEAT GOES ON

THE COMPLETE REBUS STORIES

IAN RANKIN

BACK BAY BOOKS

LITTLE, BROWN AND COMPANY

NEW YORK BOSTON LONDON

The characters and events in this book are fictitious. Any similarity to real persons, living or dead, is coincidental and not intended by the author.

Copyright © 2014 by John Rebus Ltd.
Copyright information for individual stories appears on page 471.
Excerpt from *Even Dogs in the Wild* copyright © 2015 by John Rebus Ltd.

Hachette Book Group supports the right to free expression and the value of copyright. The purpose of copyright is to encourage writers and artists to produce the creative works that enrich our culture.

The scanning, uploading, and distribution of this book without permission is a theft of the author's intellectual property. If you would like permission to use material from the book (other than for review purposes), please contact permissions@hbgusa.com. Thank you for your support of the author's rights.

Back Bay Books / Little, Brown and Company
Hachette Book Group
1290 Avenue of the Americas, New York, NY 10104
littlebrown.com

First United States Edition, August 2015
Originally published in Great Britain by Orion Publishing Group Ltd., October 2014
First Back Bay paperback edition, August 2016

Back Bay Books is an imprint of Little, Brown and Company, a division of Hachette Book Group, Inc. The Back Bay Books name and logo are trademarks of Hachette Book Group, Inc.

The publisher is not responsible for websites (or their content) that are not owned by the publisher.

The Hachette Speakers Bureau provides a wide range of authors for speaking events. To find out more, go to hachettespeakersbureau.com or call (866) 376-6591.

ISBN 978-0-316-29683-0 (hc) / 978-0-316-29680-9 (pb)
LCCN 2015940040

10 9 8 7 6 5 4 3 2 1

RRD-C

Printed in the United States of America

CONTENTS

A few words about these stories.

'Dead and Buried', which opens this collection, is one of the most recent stories I've written. We've placed it at the very start because it takes place in the mid-1980s, when Rebus was learning the ropes at Summerhall police station (as featured in my novel *Saints of the Shadow Bible*). There then follow the twelve stories from my collection *A Good Hanging and Other Stories*. These were written to comprise a chronological year in Rebus's life, so 'Playback' is set in March, 'A Good Hanging' in August (while the Festival Fringe is in full swing – as it were), and 'Auld Lang Syne' in December. After this come seven stories from *Beggars Banquet* along with the novella 'Death Is Not the End' (part of which ended up 'cannibalised' in my novel *Dead Souls*). Additionally, we've included six uncollected stories – these were mostly written for magazines and newspapers, sometimes for the Christmas edition, which is why the festive season crops up. Then there are two brand new stories – 'The Passenger' and 'A Three-Pint Problem'. The final story in the collection, 'The Very Last Drop', is set immediately after Rebus's retirement at the end of *Exit Music* and was written to be read aloud at a charity night at Edinburgh's Caledonian Brewery – you'll see why when you reach it.

I hope you get as much fun reading these stories as I had writing them.

Ian Rankin

PS: After the first edition of this book appeared, we found an old story lurking in the files – 'My Shopping Day'. It is included here, as is a new story, 'Cinders', written for Christmas 2014.

THE BEAT GOES ON

Dead and Buried

'Colder than an ex-wife's kiss,' Detective Inspector Stefan Gilmour muttered, shuffling his feet and rubbing his hands.

'I wouldn't know,' Rebus replied. His own hands were pushed deep into the pockets of his coat. It was 3 p.m. on a winter afternoon, and the lights in the prison yard had already been switched on. Faces sometimes appeared at the barred windows, accompanied by curious looks and gestures. The mechanical digger was making slow progress, workmen with pickaxes standing ready.

'I keep forgetting you're still married,' Gilmour commented. 'That'll be for the sake of your daughter, eh?'

Rebus glowered at him, but Gilmour was focusing his attention on the unmarked grave. They were in an unused corner of the grounds of HMP Saughton, close by its high sheer walls. The guards who had brought them to the spot had vanished indoors again sharpish. In place of a hearse, the undertaker had provided a pale blue van pockmarked with rust. It carried a cheap, plain coffin, since nobody reckoned much would remain of the original. Twenty years back Joseph Blay had been hanged not fifty yards away, one of the last men to be executed in Scotland. Rebus had been shown the hanging shed on a previous visit to the prison. It was still, he'd been informed, in full working order should capital punishment make a comeback.

The digger scraped at the ground again, and this time threw up some long splinters of wood. One of the workmen gestured for the driver to lift the arm away, before climbing into the hole, accompanied – with some apparent reluctance – by his younger colleague. As they worked with their pickaxes, more of the coffin was revealed, some sections intact. There was no smell at all, not that Rebus could pick up. The first he saw of Joseph Blay was a shank of hair with the skull below. The fresh coffin had been produced from the back of the van. Nobody was here to loiter. Blay wore a dark suit. Rebus didn't know what he'd expected from the exhumation: worms emerging from eye sockets maybe, or the stench of putrefaction. He had been steeling himself all morning, forgoing breakfast and lunch so there'd be nothing for him to bring up. But all he was looking at was a skeleton in a cheap suit, resembling the prop from some medical students' prank.

'Afternoon, Joe,' Gilmour said, giving a little salute.

After a few more minutes, the workmen were ready to lift the body. Blay's trousers and suit jacket seemed stuck to the ground beneath, but eventually came free. The remains were treated with neither great reverence nor any disrespect. The deceased was a job, and that job would be carried out with brisk efficiency before any of the living participants froze to death.

'What's that?' Rebus asked, nodding towards the hole. Gilmour narrowed his eyes, then clambered into the trench, crouching to pick up a pocket watch on a chain.

'Probably in his jacket,' he said, offering his free hand to Rebus so he could be helped back up. The lid had already been placed on the new coffin and it was being loaded into the van.

'Where will he end up?' Rebus asked.

Gilmour shrugged. 'Nowhere worse than this,' he offered, returning the sombre stare of one of the old lags at a second-storey window.

'Hard to disagree,' Rebus said. The digger's engine had started up again. There was a hole to be refilled.

At a pub near Haymarket Station, Gilmour ordered Irish coffees. The coffee was instant and the cream UHT, but with an extra slug of Grouse in each mug it might just do the job. There was no fire as such, but radiator pipes hissed away under the row of bench seats, so they sat side by side and slurped. Rebus had lit a cigarette and could feel his whole face tingling as he began to thaw.

'Remind me,' he said eventually. 'What the hell just happened?'

'It's how they did it back then,' Gilmour obliged. 'When you were hanged, you went to a grave inside the prison grounds. Joseph Blay killed a man who owed him money. Went to his house and stabbed him. Found guilty and sentenced to the scaffold.'

'And this was in '63?'

Gilmour nodded. 'Twenty years back. Charlie Cruikshank was in charge of the case. He's dead now, too – heart attack a couple of years ago.'

'I've heard of him.'

'Taught me everything I know. Man was a legend in the Edinburgh Police.'

'Did he attend the execution?'

Gilmour nodded again. 'He always did. When he used to talk about them, you could tell he thought we'd made a big mistake doing away with them. Not that he thought it was a deterrent. I've not met many killers who paused beforehand to consider the consequences.'

'So for him it was what? A vengeance sort of thing.'

'Well, it stopped them getting into any more bother, didn't it? And saved all of us the cost of their upkeep in the nick.'

'I suppose.'

Gilmour drained his glass and told Rebus it was his round.

'Same again?'

'Aye, but without the coffee and the cream,' Gilmour responded with a wink.

When Rebus returned from the bar with their whiskies, he saw that Gilmour was playing with the pocket watch, trying to prise it open.

'I thought you handed it over,' Rebus commented.

'You think he'll miss it?'

'All the same ...'

'Hell's teeth, John, it's not like it's worth anything. Case looks like pewter. Here, you have a go.' He handed the watch to Rebus and went to ask the barman for a knife. The timepiece had very little weight to it and no markings that Rebus could see. He worked at it with his thumbnail without success. Meantime, the barman had offered up a small screwdriver. Gilmour took back the watch and eventually got it open. The glass was opaque, the face discoloured and water damaged. The hands had stopped at quarter past six.

'No inscription,' Gilmour said.

'Must have had sentimental value at least,' Rebus offered. 'For him to be buried with it. His dad's maybe, or even his granddad's?'

Gilmour rubbed his thumb across the glass, turning the watch in his hand. Then he got busy with the screwdriver again, until the mechanism came free from its casing. An inch-long cardboard rectangle was stuck there. It came apart in the process, adhering to both the workings of the watch and the inner case. If there had been any writing on it, the words had long faded.

'What do you reckon?' Gilmour asked.

'Is there something I'm not seeing here, Stefan?' Rebus asked in return.

'You're the detective, John.' Gilmour placed the watch on the table between them. 'You tell me.'

*

The watch sat on Gilmour's desk at Summerhall police station for the rest of the week. The old building felt like it might not survive till spring. Two of the windows in the CID office wouldn't shut properly, and strips of newspaper had been stuffed into the gaps. An unlagged water pipe in the roof space had burst a fortnight back, bringing down part of the ceiling in a storeroom. Rebus had only been stationed there for a month and a half, but the mood of the place had managed to seep into his bones. He felt he was still being tested by his new colleagues, and that somehow the pocket watch was part of it. DS Dod Blantyre had offered to have it looked at by a watchmaker of his acquaintance, but Gilmour had shaken his head. There was a photo one day in the *Scotsman*, showing the construction work at HMP Saughton. New workshops were being built – the reason for Joseph Blay's exhumation. It still wasn't clear to Rebus why Gilmour had taken him there – or even why Gilmour himself had felt the need to be present. He hadn't joined the force until '65, two years after Blay's execution. When Rebus found himself alone in the office with Dod Blantyre, he asked if Blantyre had known Charlie Cruikshank.

'Oh aye,' Blantyre said with a chuckle. 'Some boy, Charlie.'

'He seems to have taken Stefan under his wing.'

Blantyre nodded. 'They were close,' he agreed. 'But then Charlie wasn't someone you wanted to get on the wrong side of.'

'Did he work at Summerhall?'

Blantyre shook his head. 'Leith – that was Stefan's first posting. Pair of them used to go to watch Hearts play. And here's the thing: Stefan grew up supporting *Hibs*. Could never admit as much to Charlie though. Had to keep gritting his teeth and joining in whenever a goal was scored.'

'Would it have meant a falling out between them if Cruikshank had found out?'

'You planning on writing Stefan's biography, John? What's with all the questions anyway?'

'Just curious.'

'I tend to find that's a dangerous trait in CID. You might want to get shot of it.' There was an edge to Blantyre's voice. For the rest of the afternoon, Rebus could feel the man's eyes on him, the mood lightening only when, at quarter past five, Stefan Gilmour announced that he could hear the siren call of the local bar. As the group left Summerhall, however, Rebus realised he had left his pools coupon in the office.

'I'll catch you up,' he said.

The coupon was in his desk drawer, filled out and ready to be handed in at the pub. He'd often asked himself what he would do if he ever did get a big win. Retire to warmer climes? He doubted his wife would want to give up her job. Nor, for that matter, would he. Pausing by Gilmour's desk, he scooped up the watch and turned it in his hand, the chain dangling. It was easier to open now, the mechanism sliding onto his palm. But it still wasn't about to tell him anything.

'Sixty-three?' the clerk said. 'That counts as recent history.'

The man was bald and cadaverous, his glasses horn-rimmed and greasy. The warehouse in Granton was his fiefdom, and he obviously knew every inch of it.

'How far back do records go?' Rebus inquired.

'I've got some dating from the 1940s – they're not complete sets though.'

'You sound disappointed.'

The man peered at him, then gestured towards a desk. 'You can wait here while I fetch what you need.'

'Thanks.' Rebus sat down and, seeing an ashtray, decided to get a cigarette lit. It was nine in the morning and he'd warned the office he had a dentist's appointment. Running his tongue around his mouth, he realised he really should make an appointment, having cancelled the last one. It was five minutes before the clerk returned. He placed a manila folder in front of Rebus, then produced a notebook from his pocket.

'Just need to sign you in,' he said. 'Warrant card, please.'

Rebus handed it over and watched as the man began to enter his details onto a page.

'You always do that?' Rebus asked.

'It's important to keep a record.'

'Anyone else requested this file recently?'

The clerk offered a thin smile. 'I wondered if you'd twig.'

'I'm guessing it was a DI called Gilmour.'

The clerk nodded. 'Just three weeks back. Our hanged man is suddenly a popular figure ...'

Frazer Spence was the only one in the office when Rebus returned to Summerhall.

'Must have been quite a procedure,' he said.

'What do you mean?'

Spence patted his cheek with a finger. 'The dentist. I'm usually in and out in half an hour.'

'That's because you brush your teeth.'

'Twice a day,' Spence confirmed.

'How's your bike, by the way?' Spence had come off his motorcycle the previous weekend.

'Garage says it'll take a week or so.'

'You need to be more careful on that thing.'

Spence just shrugged. 'Hit a patch of oil. Could have happened to anyone.'

'Still, sliding along a road on your backside at fifty miles an hour – maybe a lesson there, eh?'

'My leathers bore the brunt.'

'All the same.' Rebus paused and looked around the office. 'Where are the others?'

'Meeting one of Stefan's snitches. He might have something on the hold-up at that jeweller's on George Street.'

'Bit of progress would be welcome.'

'Definitely.'

Rebus was standing next to Gilmour's desk. The watch was no longer sitting there, so he opened the drawer. It lay on top of a stack of betting slips. Rebus lifted it out and slipped it into his pocket. 'I'm off out again,' he told Spence.

'So what do I tell Stefan when he gets back?'

'Tell him he's not the only cop in town with informants to keep sweet.'

'So which pub can he find you in if he needs you?'

Rebus pressed a finger to his lips and gave a wink.

'What's on your mind, John?'

It was mid-evening. A park bench next to Bruntsfield Links. Rebus had been waiting twenty minutes for Stefan Gilmour to arrive. Gilmour sat down, hands in coat pockets, legs splayed. Rebus had just stubbed a cigarette out under his heel and was resisting the urge to light another.

'I've not been at Summerhall as long as the rest of you,' Rebus began.

'You're still one of the Saints though.'

'All the same, I keep wondering if I'm still on probation.' Rebus held the watch out towards Gilmour.

'I knew you'd taken it,' his boss said with a smile. 'So what did you do with it?'

'The forensics lab. They've got some kind of camera there hooked up to a computer.'

Gilmour shook his head slowly. 'Isn't technology amazing?'

'Getting better all the time,' Rebus agreed. 'But sometimes the old ways work, too. Your name's on the list at the storage unit in Granton – three weeks ago, you pulled the file on Joseph Blay. This was after news broke that his remains would have to be moved.'

'True enough.'

'Your old mentor's doing?'

Gilmour was staring out across the links. The street-lamps were lit and a haar was encroaching from the coast. 'Charlie Cruikshank told me to keep an eye on Blay. At the time, I'd no idea what he meant – Blay was long dead.'

'But you kept to your word.'

'I usually do.'

'Did you expect something to turn up in the coffin?'

Gilmour offered a shrug. 'I'd really no idea. Poring over the case-notes didn't offer any clues.'

'Until after the body was dug up,' Rebus said.

Gilmour half-turned towards him. 'On you go then, hot-shot. The stage is all yours.'

'The evidence against Blay was flimsy. Yes, he was owed money by Jim Chivers, but he was by no means the only enemy Chivers had. You could have filled the courtroom with them. Blay's finger-prints were found in the victim's home, but then he'd been a regular visitor, so they couldn't be said to be conclusive. Added to which, the knife was never found and there didn't seem to be any traces of blood on Blay's clothes or shoes. His story was that he'd spent the evening of the stabbing at the flicks in Morningside, seeing *The Man Who Shot Liberty Valance*. Problem was, no one could verify it. Staff at the picture house knew him for a regular but weren't able to say which shows he'd been to. He hadn't gone with anyone or spoken to anyone – took the bus home straight after, and again, no driver would admit to seeing him. One thing I *did* glean was that there was history between Blay and your old boss. Cruikshank had tried a few times to put Blay away and had always fallen short.'

'We all end up with at least one of those.'

'If we stay in the job long enough,' Rebus agreed.

'Having second thoughts, John? That would be a pity. Seems to me you're shaping up to be a good detective.'

'Meaning what?'

'Meaning someone who goes the extra mile. Someone who's conscientious.' Gilmour paused. 'And someone with a clear sense of good guys and bad.'

'You could have gone to Saughton alone. That would have been the safe move. But instead you took me. You needed to see what I'd do, how I'd react.'

'I had no idea there'd be anything worth a reaction.'

'But there was.' Rebus nodded towards the pocket watch, still resting in Gilmour's hand.

'It's just a keepsake, John.'

'A keepsake with a little scrap of cardboard hidden inside. You know what they told me at the forensics lab? They told me it's a cinema ticket, one of those old-fashioned stubs they used to give you. They can't make out any of the details. My guess is, the date and time would have been legible at one time, maybe even the title of the film.'

'You're thinking *Liberty Valance*?'

'Seems to fit the bill. A tiny bit of evidence that would have helped Joseph Blay's case. Probably emptied out his pockets when he was arrested, and Charlie Cruikshank palmed it. Knew he couldn't have it being found. So Blay's found guilty and Cruikshank is there to watch him hanged. He still has the ticket stub so he hides it inside the watch, just because he can. That's why he needed you to keep an eye on Joseph Blay – because that stub could have proved a man's innocence. Your boss was content to see someone go to the scaffold, no matter whether they'd committed the crime or not.'

'We can't know that, John. Who's to say how that stub ended up where it did?'

'You know I'm right though.'

'Good luck proving it.'

Rebus shook his head. 'We both know I can't do that.'

'But do you *want* to do it? See, being a cop isn't just about getting to the truth – it's knowing what to do with it when you arrive. Making judgement calls, some of them at a moment's notice.'

'That's not what Cruikshank did though, is it?'

'Maybe it is. He knows Blay's guilty. That ticket could have come from anywhere – Blay could have picked it up off the pavement or from the floor of a bus. Charlie took it out of circulation so as not to confuse the jury.'

'He wanted a guilty verdict at all costs.'

'He didn't want a guilty man to get off, John. That's the story here.'

'And you'd do the exact same thing, Stefan? That's what your old mentor taught you?'

'He gave his whole life to the job, John, heart and soul.' Gilmour rose to his feet and stood in front of Rebus. He held out the pocket watch. 'Do you want this?' he asked.

'What would I do with it?'

'You'd take it to The Complaints, lay out your version of events.'

'And what good would that do?' Rebus stared at the watch, then averted his gaze and shook his head. Gilmour waited a few more beats, then stuffed the watch into his coat.

'That's us then,' he said, reaching out his hand. 'Welcome to the Saints of the Shadow Bible, John.'

After only a moment's hesitation, Rebus stood up and returned the handshake.

Playback

It was the perfect murder.

Perfect, that is, so far as the Lothian and Borders Police were concerned. The murderer had telephoned in to confess, had then panicked and attempted to flee, only to be caught leaving the scene of the crime. End of story.

Except that now he was pleading innocence. Pleading, yelling and screaming it. And this worried Detective Inspector John Rebus, worried him all the way from his office to the four-storey tenement in Leith's trendy dockside area. The tenements here were much as they were in any working-class area of Edinburgh, except that they boasted colour-splashed roller blinds or Chinese-style bamboo affairs at their windows, and their grimy stone façades had been power-cleaned, their doors now boasting intruder-proof intercoms. A far cry from the greasy Venetian blinds and kicked-in passage-ways of the tenements in Easter Road or Gorgie, or even in nearby parts of Leith itself, the parts the developers were ignoring as yet.

The victim had worked as a legal secretary, this much Rebus knew. She had been twenty-four years old. Her name was Moira Bitter. Rebus smiled at that. It was a guilty smile, but at this hour of the morning any smile he could raise was something of a miracle.

He parked in front of the tenement, guided by a uniformed officer who had recognised the badly dented front bumper of Rebus's car. It was rumoured that the dent had come from knocking down too many old ladies, and who was Rebus to deny it? It was the stuff of legend and it gave him prominence in the fearful eyes of the younger recruits.

A curtain twitched in one of the ground-floor windows and Rebus caught a glimpse of an elderly lady. Every tenement, it seemed, tarted up or not, boasted its elderly lady. Living alone, with one dog or four cats for company, she was her building's eyes and ears. As Rebus entered the hallway, a door opened and the old lady stuck out her head.

'He was going to run for it,' she whispered. 'But the bobby caught him. I saw it. Is the young lass dead? Is that it?' Her lips were pursed in keen horror. Rebus smiled at her but said nothing. She would know soon enough. Already she seemed to know as much as he did himself. That was the trouble with living in a city the size of a town, a town with a village mentality.

He climbed the four flights of stairs slowly, listening all the while to the report of the constable who was leading him inexorably towards the corpse of Moira Bitter. They spoke in an undertone: stairwell walls had ears.

'The call came at about 5 a.m., sir,' explained PC MacManus. 'The caller gave his name as John MacFarlane and said he'd just murdered his girlfriend. He sounded distressed by all accounts, and I was radioed to investigate. As I arrived, a man was running down the stairs. He seemed in a state of shock.'

'Shock?'

'Sort of disorientated, sir.'

'Did he say anything?' asked Rebus.

'Yes, sir, he told me, "Thank God you're here. Moira's dead." I then asked him to accompany me upstairs to the flat in question, called in for assistance, and the gentleman was arrested.'

Rebus nodded. MacManus was a model of efficiency, not a word out of place, the tone just right. Everything by rote and without the interference of too much thought. He would go far as a uniformed officer, but Rebus doubted the young man would ever make CID. When they reached the fourth floor, Rebus paused for breath then walked into the flat.

The hall's pastel colour scheme extended to the living-room and bedroom. Mute colours, subtle and warming. There was nothing subtle about the blood though. The blood was copious. Moira Bitter lay sprawled across her bed, her chest a riot of colour. She was wearing apple-green pyjamas, and her hair was silky blonde. The police pathologist was examining her head.

'She's been dead about three hours,' he informed Rebus. 'Stabbed three or four times with a small sharp instrument, which, for the sake of convenience, I'm going to term a knife. I'll examine her properly later on.'

Rebus nodded and turned to MacManus, whose face had a sickly grey tinge to it.

'Your first time?' Rebus asked. The constable nodded slowly. 'Never mind,' Rebus continued. 'You never get used to it anyway. Come on.'

He led the constable out of the room and back into the small hallway. 'This man we've arrested, what did you say his name was?'

'John MacFarlane, sir,' said the constable, taking deep breaths. 'He's the deceased's boyfriend apparently.'

'You said he seemed in a state of shock. Was there anything else you noticed?'

The constable frowned, thinking. 'Such as, sir?' he said at last.

'Blood,' said Rebus coolly. 'You can't stab someone in the heat of the moment without getting blood on you.'

MacManus said nothing. Definitely not CID material and perhaps realising it for the very first time. Rebus turned from him and entered the living-room. It was almost neurotically tidy. Magazines and newspapers in their rack beside the sofa. A chrome and glass coffee table bearing nothing more than a clean ashtray and a paperback romance. It could have come straight from an Ideal Home exhibition. No family photographs, no clutter. This was the lair of an individualist. No ties with the past, a present ransacked wholesale from Habitat and Next. There was no evidence of a struggle. No evidence of an encounter of any kind: no glasses or coffee cups. The killer had not loitered, or else had been very tidy about his business.

Rebus went into the kitchen. It, too, was tidy. Cups and plates stacked for drying beside the empty sink. On the draining-board were knives, forks, teaspoons. No murder weapon. There were spots of water in the sink and on the draining-board itself, yet the cutlery and crockery were dry. Rebus found a dishtowel hanging up behind the door and felt it. It was damp. He examined it more closely. There was a small smudge on it. Perhaps gravy or chocolate. Or blood. Someone had dried something recently, but what?

He went to the cutlery drawer and opened it. Inside, amidst the various implements was a short-bladed chopping knife with a heavy black handle. A quality knife, sharp and gleaming. The other items in the drawer were bone dry, but this chopping knife's wooden handle was damp to the touch. Rebus was in no doubt: he had found his murder weapon.

Clever of MacFarlane though to have cleaned and put away the knife. A cool and calm action. Moira Bitter had been dead three hours. The call to the police station had come an hour ago. What had MacFarlane done during the intervening two hours? Cleaned the flat? Washed and dried the dishes? Rebus looked in the kitchen's swing-bin, but found no other clues, no broken ornaments, nothing that might hint at a struggle. And if there had been no struggle, if the murderer had gained access to the tenement and to Moira Bitter's flat without forcing an entry ... if all this were true, Moira had known her killer.

Rebus toured the rest of the flat, but found no other clues. Beside the telephone in the hall stood an answering machine. He played the tape, and heard Moira Bitter's voice.

'Hello, this is Moira. I'm out, I'm in the bath, or I'm otherwise engaged.' (A giggle.) 'Leave a message and I'll get back to you, unless you sound boring.'

There was only one message. Rebus listened to it, then wound back the tape and listened again.

'Hello, Moira, it's John. I got your message. I'm coming over. Hope you're not "otherwise engaged". Love you.'

John MacFarlane: Rebus didn't doubt the identity of the caller. Moira sounded fresh and fancy-free in her message. But did MacFarlane's response hint at jealousy? Perhaps she *had* been otherwise engaged when he'd arrived. He lost his temper, blind rage, a knife lying handy. Rebus had seen it before. Most victims knew their attackers. If that were not the case, the police wouldn't solve so many crimes. It was a blunt fact. You double bolted your door against the psychopath with the chainsaw, only to be stabbed in the back by your lover, husband, son or neighbour.

John MacFarlane was as guilty as hell. They would find blood on his clothes, even if he'd tried cleaning it off. He had stabbed his girlfriend, then calmed down and called in to report the crime, but had grown frightened at the end and had attempted to flee.

The only question left in Rebus's mind was the why? The why and those missing two hours.

Edinburgh through the night. The occasional taxi rippling across setts and lone shadowy figures slouching home with hands in pockets, shoulders hunched. During the night hours, the sick and the old died peacefully, either at home or in some hospital ward. Two in the morning until four: the dead hours. And then some died horribly, with terror in their eyes. The taxis still rumbled past, the night people kept moving. Rebus let his car idle at traffic lights, missing the change to green, only coming to his senses as amber turned red again. Glasgow Rangers were coming to town on Saturday. There would be casual violence. Rebus felt comfortable with the thought. The worst football hooligan could probably not have stabbed with the same ferocity as Moira Bitter's killer. Rebus lowered his eyebrows. He was rousing himself to fury, keen for confrontation. Confrontation with the murderer himself.

*

John MacFarlane was crying as he was led into the interrogation room, where Rebus had made himself look comfortable, cigarette in one hand, coffee in the other. Rebus had expected a lot of things, but not tears.

'Would you like something to drink?' he asked. MacFarlane shook his head. He had slumped into the chair on the other side of the desk, his shoulders sagging, head bowed, and the sobs still coming from his throat. He mumbled something.

'I didn't catch that,' said Rebus.

'I said I didn't do it,' MacFarlane answered quietly. 'How could I do it? I love Moira.'

Rebus noted the present tense. He gestured towards the tape machine on the desk. 'Do you have any objections to my making a recording of this interview?' MacFarlane shook his head again. Rebus switched on the machine. He flicked ash from his cigarette onto the floor, sipped his coffee, and waited. Eventually, MacFarlane looked up. His eyes were stinging red. Rebus stared hard into those eyes, but still said nothing. MacFarlane seemed to be calming. Seemed, too, to know what was expected of him. He asked for a cigarette, was given one, and started to speak.

'I'd been out in my car. Just driving, thinking.'

Rebus interrupted him. 'What time was this?'

'Well,' said MacFarlane, 'ever since I left work, I suppose. I'm an architect. There's a competition on just now to design a new art gallery and museum complex in Stirling. Our partnership's going in for it. We were discussing ideas most of the day, you know, brainstorming.' He looked up at Rebus again, and Rebus nodded. Brainstorm: now there was an interesting word.

'And after work,' MacFarlane continued, 'I was so fired up I just felt like driving. Going over the different options and plans in my head. Working out which was strongest—'

He broke off, realising perhaps that he was talking in a rush, without thought or caution. He swallowed and inhaled some smoke. Rebus was studying MacFarlane's clothes. Expensive leather brogues, brown corduroy trousers, a thick white cotton shirt, the kind cricketers wore, open at the neck, a tailor-made tweed jacket. MacFarlane's 3-Series BMW was parked in the police garage, being searched. His pockets had been emptied, a Liberty print tie confiscated in case he had ideas about hanging himself. His brogues, too, were without their laces, these having been confiscated along with the tie. Rebus had gone through the belongings. A wallet, not exactly bulging with money but containing a fair spread of credit cards. There were more cards, too, in MacFarlane's personal organiser.

Rebus flipped through the diary pages, then turned to the sections for notes and for addresses. MacFarlane seemed to lead a busy but quite normal social life.

Rebus studied him now, across the expanse of the old table. MacFarlane was well-built, handsome if you liked that sort of thing. He looked strong, but not brutish. Probably he would make the local news headlines as 'Secretary's Yuppie Killer'. Rebus stubbed out his cigarette.

'We know you did it, John. That's not in dispute. We just want to know why.'

MacFarlane's voice was brittle with emotion. 'I swear I didn't, I swear.'

'You're going to have to do better than that.' Rebus paused again. Tears were dripping onto MacFarlane's corduroys. 'Go on with your story,' he said.

MacFarlane shrugged. 'That's about it,' he said, wiping his nose with the sleeve of his shirt.

Rebus prompted him. 'You didn't stop off anywhere for petrol or a meal or anything like that?' He sounded sceptical. MacFarlane shook his head.

'No, I just drove until my head was clear. I went all the way to the Forth Road Bridge. Turned off and went into Queensferry. Got out of the car to have a look at the water. Threw a few stones in for luck.' He smiled at the irony. 'Then drove round the coast road and back into Edinburgh.'

'Nobody saw you? You didn't speak to anyone?'

'Not that I can remember.'

'And you didn't get hungry?' Rebus sounded entirely unconvinced.

'We'd had a business lunch with a client. We took him to The Eyrie. After lunch there, I seldom need to eat until the next morning.'

The Eyrie was Edinburgh's most expensive restaurant. You didn't go there to eat, you went there to spend money. Rebus was feeling peckish himself. The canteen did a fine bacon buttie.

'When did you last see Miss Bitter alive?'

At the word 'alive', MacFarlane shivered. It took him a long time to answer. Rebus watched the tape revolving. 'Yesterday morning,' MacFarlane said at last. 'She stayed the night at my flat.'

'How long have you known her?'

'About a year. But I only started going out with her a couple of months ago.'

'Oh? And how did you know her before that?'

MacFarlane paused. 'She was Kenneth's girlfriend,' he said at last.

'Kenneth being—'

MacFarlane's cheeks reddened before he spoke. 'My best friend,' he said. 'Kenneth was my best friend. You could say I stole her from him. These things happen, don't they?'

Rebus raised an eyebrow. 'Do they?' he said. MacFarlane bowed his head again.

'Can I have a coffee?' he asked quietly. Rebus nodded, then lit another cigarette.

MacFarlane sipped the coffee, holding it in both hands like a shipwreck survivor. Rebus rubbed his nose and stretched, feeling tired. He checked his watch. Eight in the morning. What a life. He had eaten two bacon rolls and a string of rind curled across the plate in front of him. MacFarlane had refused food, but finished the first cup of coffee in two gulps and gratefully accepted a second.

'So,' Rebus said, 'you drove back into town.'

'That's right.' MacFarlane took another sip of coffee. 'I don't know why, but I decided to check my answering machine for calls.'

'You mean when you got home?'

MacFarlane shook his head. 'No, from the car. I called home from my car-phone and got the answering machine to play back any messages.'

Rebus was impressed. 'That's clever,' he said.

MacFarlane smiled again, but the smile soon vanished. 'One of the messages was from Moira,' he said. 'She wanted to see me.'

'At that hour?' MacFarlane shrugged. 'Did she say why she wanted to see you?'

'No. She sounded ... strange.'

'Strange?'

'A bit ... I don't know, distant maybe.'

'Did you get the feeling she was on her own when she called?'

'I've no idea.'

'Did you call her back?'

'Yes. Her answering machine was on. I left a message.'

'Would you say you're the jealous type, Mr MacFarlane?'

'What?' MacFarlane sounded surprised by the question. He seemed to give it serious thought. 'No more so than the next man,' he said at last.

'Why would anyone want to kill her?'

MacFarlane stared at the table, shaking his head slowly.

'Go on,' said Rebus, sighing, growing impatient. 'You were saying how you got her message.'

'Well, I went straight to her flat. It was late, but I knew if she was asleep I could always let myself in.'

'Oh?' Rebus was interested. 'How?'

'I had a spare key,' MacFarlane explained.

Rebus got up from his chair and walked to the far wall and back, deep in thought.

'I don't suppose,' he said, 'you've got any idea *when* Moira made that call?'

MacFarlane shook his head. 'But the machine will have logged it,' he said. Rebus was more impressed than ever. Technology was a wonderful thing. What's more, he was impressed by MacFarlane. If the man was a murderer, then he was a very good one, for he had fooled Rebus into thinking him innocent. It was crazy. There was nothing to point to him not being guilty. But all the same, a feeling was a feeling, and Rebus most definitely had a feeling.

'I want to see that machine,' he said. 'And I want to hear the message on it. I want to hear Moira's last words.'

It was interesting how the simplest cases could become so complex. There was still no doubt in the minds of those around Rebus – his superiors and those below him – that John MacFarlane was guilty of murder. They had all the proof they needed, every last bit of it circumstantial.

MacFarlane's car was clean: no bloodstained clothes stashed in the boot. There were no prints on the chopping-knife, though MacFarlane's prints were found elsewhere in the flat, not surprising given that he'd visited that night, as well as on many a previous one. No prints either on the kitchen sink and taps, though the murderer had washed a bloody knife. Rebus thought that curious. And as for motive: jealousy, a falling-out, a past indiscretion discovered. The CID had seen them all.

Murder by stabbing was confirmed and the time of death narrowed down to a quarter of an hour either side of three in the morning. MacFarlane claimed that at that time he was driving towards Edinburgh, but had no witnesses to corroborate the claim. There was no blood to be found on MacFarlane's clothing, but, as Rebus himself knew, that didn't mean the man wasn't a killer.

More interesting, however, was that MacFarlane denied making the call to the police. Yet someone – in fact, whoever murdered Moira Bitter – *had* made it. And more interesting even than this was the telephone answering machine.

Rebus went to MacFarlane's flat in Liberton to investigate. The traffic was busy coming into town, but quiet heading out. Liberton was one of Edinburgh's many anonymous middle-class districts, substantial houses, small shops, a busy thoroughfare. It looked innocuous at midnight, and was even safer by day.

What MacFarlane had termed a 'flat' comprised, in fact, the top two storeys of a vast, detached house. Rebus roamed the building, not sure if he was looking for anything in particular. He found little. MacFarlane led a rigorous and regimented life and had the home to accommodate such a lifestyle. One room had been turned into a makeshift gymnasium, with weightlifting equipment and the like. There was an office for business use, a study for private use. The main bedroom was decidedly masculine in taste, though a framed painting of a naked woman had been removed from one wall and tucked behind a chair. Rebus thought he detected Moira Bitter's influence at work.

In the wardrobe were a few pieces of her clothing and a pair of her shoes. A snapshot of her had been framed and placed on MacFarlane's bedside table. Rebus studied the photograph for a long time, then sighed and left the bedroom, closing the door after him. Who knew when John MacFarlane would see his home again?

The answering machine was in the living-room. Rebus played the tape of the previous night's calls. Moira Bitter's voice was clipped and confident, her message to the point: 'Hello.' Then a pause. 'I need to see you. Come round as soon as you get this message. Love you.'

MacFarlane had told Rebus that the display unit on the machine showed time of call. Moira's call registered at 3.50 a.m., about forty-five minutes after her death. There was room for some discrepancy, but not three-quarters of an hour's worth. Rebus scratched his chin and pondered. He played the tape again. 'Hello.' Then the pause. 'I need to see you.' He stopped the tape and played it again, this time with the volume up and his ear close to the machine. That pause was curious and the sound quality on the tape was poor. He rewound and listened to another call from the same evening. The quality was better, the voice much clearer. Then he listened to Moira again. Were these recording machines infallible? Of course not. The time displayed could have been tampered with. The recording itself could be a fake. After all, whose word did he have that this *was* the voice of Moira Bitter? Only John MacFarlane's. But John MacFarlane had been caught leaving the scene of a murder. And now Rebus was being presented with a sort of an alibi for the man. Yes, the tape could well be a fake, used by MacFarlane to substantiate his story, but stupidly not put into use until after the time of death. Still, from what Rebus had heard from Moira's own answering machine, the voice was certainly similar to her own. The lab boys could sort it out with their clever machines. One technician in particular owed him a rather large favour.

Rebus shook his head. This still wasn't making much sense. He played the tape again and again.

'Hello.' Pause. 'I need to see you.'

'Hello.' Pause. 'I need to see you.'

'Hello.' Pause. 'I need—'

And suddenly it became a little clearer in his mind. He ejected the tape and slipped it into his jacket pocket, then picked up the telephone and called the station. He asked to speak to Detective Constable Brian Holmes. The voice, when it came on the line, was tired but amused.

'Don't tell me,' Holmes said, 'let me guess. You want me to drop everything and run an errand for you.'

'You must be psychic, Brian. Two errands really. Firstly, last night's calls. Get the recording of them and search for one from John MacFarlane, claiming he'd just killed his girlfriend. Make a copy of it and wait there for me. I've got another tape for you, and I want them both taken to the lab. Warn them you're coming—'

'And tell them it's priority, I know. It's *always* priority. They'll say what they always say: give us four days.'

'Not this time,' Rebus said. 'Ask for Bill Costain and tell him Rebus is collecting on his favour. He's to shelve what he's doing. I want a result today, not next week.'

'What's the favour you're collecting on?'

'I caught him smoking dope in the lab toilets last month.'

Holmes laughed. 'The world's going to pot,' he said. Rebus groaned at the joke and put down the receiver. He needed to speak with John MacFarlane again. Not about lovers this time, but about friends.

Rebus rang the doorbell a third time and at last heard a voice from within.

'Jesus, hold on! I'm coming.'

The man who answered the door was tall, thin, with wire-framed glasses perched on his nose. He peered at Rebus and ran his fingers through his hair.

'Mr Thomson?' Rebus asked. 'Kenneth Thomson?'

'Yes,' said the man, 'that's right.'

Rebus flipped open his ID. 'Detective Inspector John Rebus,' he said by way of introduction. 'May I come in?'

Kenneth Thomson held open the door. 'Please do,' he said. 'Will a cheque be all right?'

'A cheque?'

'I take it you're here about the parking tickets,' said Thomson. 'I'd have got round to them eventually, believe me. It's just that I've been hellish busy, and what with one thing and another ...'

'No, sir,' said Rebus, his smile as cold as a church pew, 'nothing to do with parking fines.'

'Oh?' Thomson pushed his glasses back up his nose and looked at Rebus. 'Then what's the problem?'

'It's about Miss Moira Bitter,' said Rebus.

'Moira? What about her?'

'She's dead, sir.'

Rebus had followed Thomson into a cluttered room overflowing with bundles of magazines and newspapers. A hi-fi sat in one corner, and covering the wall next to it were shelves filled with cassette tapes. These had an orderly look to them, as though they had been indexed, each tape's spine carrying an identifying number.

Thomson, who had been clearing a chair for Rebus to sit on, froze at the detective's words.

'Dead?' he gasped. 'How?'

'She was murdered, sir. We think John MacFarlane did it.'

'John?' Thomson's face was quizzical, then sceptical, then resigned. 'But why?'

'We don't know that yet, sir. I thought you might be able to help.'

'Of course I'll help if I can. Sit down, please.'

Rebus perched on the chair, while Thomson pushed aside some newspapers and settled himself on the sofa.

'You're a writer, I believe,' said Rebus.

Thomson nodded distractedly. 'Yes,' he said. 'Freelance journalism, food and drink, travel, that sort of thing. Plus the occasional commission to write a book. That's what I'm doing now, actually. Writing a book.'

'Oh? I like books myself. What's it about?'

'Don't laugh,' said Thomson, 'but it's a history of the haggis.'

'The haggis?' Rebus couldn't disguise a smile in his voice, warmer this time: the church pew had been given a cushion. He cleared his throat noisily, glancing around the room, noting the piles of books leaning precariously against walls, the files and folders and newsprint cuttings. 'You must do a lot of research,' he said appreciatively.

'Sometimes,' said Thomson. Then he shook his head. 'I still can't believe it. About Moira, I mean. About John.'

Rebus took out his notebook, more for effect than anything else. 'You were Miss Bitter's lover for a while,' he stated.

'That's right, Inspector.'

'But then she went off with Mr MacFarlane.'

'Right again.' A hint of bitterness had crept into Thomson's voice. 'I was very angry at the time, but I got over it.'

'Did you still see Miss Bitter?'

'No.'

'What about Mr MacFarlane?'

'No again. We spoke on the telephone a couple of times. It always seemed to end in a shouting match. We used to be like, well, it's a cliché, I suppose, but we used to be like brothers.'

'Yes,' said Rebus, 'so Mr MacFarlane told me.'

'Oh?' Thomson sounded interested. 'What else did he say?'

'Not much really.' Rebus rose from his perch and went to the window, holding aside the net curtain to stare out onto the street below. 'He said you'd known each other for years.'

'Since school,' Thomson added.

Rebus nodded. 'And he said you drove a black Ford Escort. That'll be it down there, parked across the street?'

Thomson came to the window. 'Yes,' he agreed, uncertainly, 'that's it. But I don't see what—'

'I noticed it as I was parking my own car,' Rebus continued, brushing past Thomson's interruption. He let the curtain fall and turned back into the room. 'I noticed you've got a car alarm. I suppose you must get a lot of burglaries around here.'

'It's not the most salubrious part of town,' Thomson said. 'Not all writers are like Jeffrey Archer.'

'Did money have anything to do with it?' Rebus asked. Thomson paused.

'With what, Inspector?'

'With Miss Bitter leaving you for Mr MacFarlane. He's not short of a bob or two, is he?'

Thomson's voice rose perceptibly. 'Look, I really can't see what this has to do with—'

'Your car was broken into a few months ago, wasn't it?' Rebus was examining a pile of magazines on the floor now. 'I saw the report. They stole your radio and your car phone.'

'Yes.'

'I notice you've replaced the car phone.' He glanced up at Thomson, smiled, and continued browsing.

'Of course,' said Thomson. He seemed confused now, unable to fathom where the conversation was leading.

'A journalist would need a car phone, wouldn't he?' Rebus observed. 'So people could keep in touch, contact him at any time. Is that right?'

'Absolutely right, Inspector.'

Rebus threw the magazine back onto the pile and nodded slowly. 'Great things, car phones.' He walked over towards Thomson's desk. It was a small flat. This room obviously served a double purpose as study and living-room. Not that Thomson entertained many visitors. He was too aggressive for many people, too secretive for others. So John MacFarlane had said.

On the desk there was more clutter, though in some appearance of organisation. There was also a neat word processor, and beside it a telephone. And next to the telephone sat an answering machine.

'Yes,' Rebus repeated. 'You need to be in contact.' Rebus smiled towards Thomson. 'Communication, that's the secret. And I'll tell you something else about journalists.'

'What?' Unable to comprehend Rebus's direction, Thomson's tone had become that of someone bored with a conversation. He shoved his hands deep into his pockets.

'Journalists are hoarders.' Rebus made this sound like some great wisdom. His eyes took in the room again. 'I mean, near-pathological hoarders. They can't bear to throw things away, because they never know when something might become useful. Am I right?'

Thomson shrugged.

'Yes,' said Rebus, 'I bet I am. Look at these cassettes, for example.' He went to where the rows of tapes were neatly displayed. 'What are they? Interviews, that sort of thing?'

'Mostly, yes,' Thomson agreed.

'And you still keep them, even though they're years old?'

Thomson shrugged again. 'So I'm a hoarder.'

But Rebus had noticed something on the top shelf, some brown cardboard boxes. He reached up and lifted one down. Inside were more tapes, marked with months and years. But these tapes were smaller. Rebus gestured with the box towards Thomson, his eyes seeking an explanation.

Thomson smiled uneasily. 'Answering machine messages,' he said.

'You keep these, too?' Rebus sounded amazed.

'Well,' Thomson said, 'someone may agree to something over the phone, an interview or something, then deny it later. I need them as records of promises made.'

Rebus nodded, understanding now. He replaced the brown box on its shelf. He still had his back to Thomson when the telephone rang, a sharp electronic sound.

'Sorry,' Thomson apologised, going to answer it.

'Not at all.'

Thomson picked up the receiver. 'Hello?' He listened, then frowned. 'Of course,' he said finally, holding the receiver out towards Rebus. 'It's for you, Inspector.'

Rebus raised a surprised eyebrow and accepted the receiver. It was, as he had known it would be, Detective Constable Holmes.

'Okay,' Holmes said. 'Costain no longer owes you that favour. He's listened to both tapes. He hasn't run all the necessary tests yet, but he's pretty convinced.'

'Go on.' Rebus was looking at Thomson, who was sitting, hands clasping knees, on the arm of the chair.

'The call we received last night,' said Holmes, 'the one from John MacFarlane admitting to the murder of Moira Bitter, originated from a portable telephone.'

'Interesting,' said Rebus, his eyes on Thomson. 'And what about the other one?'

'Well, the tape you gave me seems to be twice-removed.'

'What does that mean?'

'It means,' said Holmes, 'that according to Costain it's not just a recording, it's the recording of a recording.' Rebus nodded, satisfied.

'Okay, thanks, Brian.' He put down the receiver.

'Good news or bad?' Thomson asked.

'A bit of both,' answered Rebus thoughtfully. Thomson had risen to his feet.

'I feel like a drink, Inspector. Can I get you one?'

'It's a bit early for me, I'm afraid,' Rebus said, looking at his watch. It was eleven o'clock: opening time. 'All right,' he said, 'just a small one.'

'The whisky's in the kitchen,' Thomson explained. 'I'll just be a moment.'

'Fine, sir, fine.'

Rebus listened as Thomson left the room and headed off towards the kitchen. He stood beside the desk, thinking through what he now knew. Then, hearing Thomson returning from the kitchen, floor-boards bending beneath his weight, he picked up the waste-paper basket from below the desk, and, as Thomson entered the room, proceeded to empty the contents in a heap on the sofa.

Thomson stood in the doorway, a glass of whisky in each hand, dumbstruck. 'What on earth are you doing?' he spluttered at last. But Rebus ignored him and started to pick through the now strewn contents of the bin, talking as he searched.

'It was pretty close to being fool-proof, Mr Thomson. Let me explain. The killer went to Moira Bitter's flat and talked her into letting him in despite the late hour. He murdered her quite callously, let's make no mistake about that. I've never seen so much premeditation in a case before. He cleaned the knife and returned it to its drawer. He was wearing gloves, of course, knowing John MacFarlane's fingerprints would be all over the flat, and he cleaned the knife precisely to disguise the fact that he *had* worn gloves. MacFarlane, you see, had not.'

Thomson took a gulp from one glass, but otherwise seemed rooted to the spot. His eyes had become vacant, as though picturing Rebus's story in his mind.

'MacFarlane,' Rebus continued, still rummaging, 'was summoned to Moira's flat. The message did come from her. He knew her voice well enough not to be fooled by someone else's voice. The killer sat outside Moira's flat, sat waiting for MacFarlane to arrive. Then the killer made one last call, this one to the police, in the guise of an hysterical MacFarlane. We know this last call was made on a car phone. The lab boys are very clever that way. The police are hoarders, too, you see, Mr Thomson. We make recordings of emergency calls made to us. It won't be hard to voice-print that call and try to match it to John MacFarlane. But it won't be John MacFarlane, will it?' Rebus paused for effect. 'It'll be you.'

Thomson gave a thin smile, but his grip on the two glasses had grown less steady, and whisky was dribbling from the angled lip of one of them.

'Ah-ha.' Rebus had found what he was looking for in the contents of the bin. With a pleased-as-punch grin on his unshaven, sleepless face, he pinched forefinger and thumb together and lifted them for his own and Thomson's inspection. He was holding a tiny sliver of brown recording tape.

'You see,' he continued, 'the killer had to lure MacFarlane to the murder scene. Having killed Moira, he went to his car, as I've said. There he had his portable telephone and a cassette recorder. He was a hoarder. He had kept all his answering machine tapes, including messages left by Moira at the height of their affair. He found the message he needed and he spliced it. He played this message to John MacFarlane's answering machine. All he had to do after that was wait. The message MacFarlane received was "Hello. I need to see you." There was a pause after the "hello". And that pause was where the splice was made in the tape, excising this.' Rebus looked at the sliver of tape. 'The one word "Kenneth". "Hello, Kenneth, I need to see you." It was Moira Bitter talking to you, Mr Thomson, talking to you a long time ago.'

Thomson hurled both glasses at once, so that they arrowed in towards Rebus, who ducked. The glasses collided above his head, shards raining down on him. Thomson had reached the front door, had hauled it open even, before Rebus was on him, lunging, pushing the younger man forwards through the doorway and onto the tenement landing. Thomson's head hit the metal rails with a muted chime and he let out a single moan before collapsing. Rebus shook himself free of glass, feeling one or two tiny pieces nick him as he brushed a hand across his face. He brought a hand to his nose and inhaled deeply. His father had always said whisky would put hairs on his chest. Rebus wondered if the same miracle might be effected on his temples and the crown of his head ...

It had been the perfect murder.

Well, almost. But Kenneth Thomson had reckoned without Rebus's ability actually to believe someone innocent despite the evidence against him. The case against John MacFarlane had been overwhelming. Yet Rebus, feeling it to be wrong, had been forced to invent other scenarios, other motives and other means to the fairly chilling end. It wasn't enough that Moira had died – died at the hands of someone she knew. MacFarlane had to be implicated in her murder. The killer had been out to tag them both. But it was Moira the killer hated, hated because she had broken a friendship as well as a heart.

Rebus stood on the steps of the police station. Thomson was in a cell somewhere below his feet, somewhere below ground level. Confessing to everything. He would go to jail, while John MacFarlane, perhaps not realising his luck, had already been freed.

The streets were busy now. Lunchtime traffic, the reliable noises of the everyday. The sun was even managing to burst from its slumber. All of which reminded Rebus that his day was over. Time, all in all he felt, for a short visit home, a shower and a change of clothes, and, God and the Devil willing, some sleep.

The Dean Curse

The locals in Barnton knew him either as 'the Brigadier' or as 'that Army type who bought the West Lodge'. West Lodge was a huge but until recently neglected detached house set in a walled acre and a half of grounds and copses. Most locals were relieved that its high walls hid it from general view, the house itself being too angular, too gothic for modern tastes. Certainly, it was very large for the needs of a widower and his unsmiling daughter. Mrs MacLennan, who cleaned for the Brigadier, was pumped for information by curious neighbours, but could say only that Brigadier-General Dean had had some renovations done, that most of the house was habitable, that one room had become a library, another a billiard-room, another a study, another a makeshift gymnasium and so on. The listeners would drink this in deeply, yet it was never enough. What about the daughter? What about the Brigadier's background? What happened to his wife?

Shopkeepers too were asked for their thoughts. The Brigadier drove a sporty open-topped car which would pull in noisily to the side of the road to allow him to pop into this or that shop for a few things, including, each day at the same time, a bottle of something or other from the smarter of the two off-licences.

The grocer, Bob Sladden, reckoned that Brigadier-General Dean had been born nearby, even that he had lived for a few childhood years in West Lodge and so had retired there because of its carefree connections. But Miss Dalrymple, who at ninety-three was as old as anyone in that part of Barnton, could not recall any family named Dean living at West Lodge. Could not, indeed, recall any Deans ever living in this 'neck' of Barnton, with the exception of Sam Dean. But when pressed about Sam Dean, she merely shook her head and said, 'He was no good, that one, and got what he deserved. The Great War saw to him.' Then she would nod slowly, thoughtfully, and nobody would be any further forward.

Speculation grew wilder as no new facts came to light, and in

The Claymore public bar one afternoon, a bar never patronised by the Brigadier (and who'd ever heard of an Army man not liking his drink?), a young out-of-work plasterer named Willie Barr came up with a fresh proposition.

'Maybe Dean isn't his real name.'

But everyone around the pool table laughed at that and Willie just shrugged, readying to play his next shot. 'Well,' he said, 'real name or not, I wouldn't climb over that daughter of his to get to any of you lot.'

Then he played a double off the cushion, but missed. Missed not because the shot was difficult or he'd had too many pints of Snakebite, but because his cue arm jerked at the noise of the explosion.

It was a fancy car all right, a Jaguar XJS convertible, its bodywork a startling red. Nobody in Barnton could mistake it for anyone else's car. Besides, everyone was used to it revving to its loud roadside halt, was used to its contented ticking-over while the Brigadier did his shopping. Some complained – though never to his face – about the noise, about the fumes from the exhaust. They couldn't say why he never switched off the ignition. He always seemed to want to be ready for a quick getaway. On this particular afternoon, the getaway was quicker even than usual, a squeal of tyres as the car jerked out into the road and sped past the shops. Its driver seemed ready actually to disregard the red stop light at the busy junction. He never got the chance. There was a ball of flames where the car had been and the heart-stopping sound of the explosion. Twisted metal flew into the air, then down again, wounding passers-by, burning skin. Shop windows blew in, shards of fine glass finding soft targets. The traffic lights turned to green, but nothing moved in the street.

For a moment, there was a silence punctuated only by the arrival on terra firma of bits of speedometer, headlamp, even steering-wheel. Then the screaming started, as people realised they'd been wounded. More curdling still though were the silences, the dumb horrified faces of people who would never forget this moment, whose shock would disturb each wakeful night.

And then there was a man, standing in a doorway, the doorway of what had been the wine merchant's. He carried a bottle with him, carefully wrapped in green paper, and his mouth was open in surprise. He dropped the bottle with a crash when he realised his car was not where he had left it, realising that the roaring he had heard and thought he recognised was that of his own car being driven away. At his feet, he saw one of his driving gloves lying on the pavement in front of him. It was still smouldering. Only five minutes before, it had been lying on the leather of his passenger seat. The wine merchant was standing beside him now, pale and shaking, looking in dire need of a drink. The Brigadier nodded towards the carcass of his sleek red Jaguar.

'That should have been me,' he said. Then: 'Do you mind if I use your telephone?'

John Rebus threw *The Dain Curse* up in the air, sending it spinning towards his living-room ceiling. Gravity caught up with it just short of the ceiling and pulled it down hard, so that it landed open against the uncarpeted floor. It was a cheap copy, bought secondhand and previously much read. But not by Rebus; he'd got as far as the beginning of the third section, 'Quesada', before giving up, before tossing what many regard as Hammett's finest novel into the air. Its pages fell away from the spine as it landed, scattering chapters. Rebus growled. The telephone had, as though prompted by the book's demise, started ringing. Softly, insistently. Rebus picked up the apparatus and studied it. It was six o'clock on the evening of his first rest-day in what seemed like months. Who would be phoning him? Pleasure or business? And which would he prefer it to be? He put the receiver to his ear.

'Yes?' His voice was non-committal.

'DI Rebus?' It was work then. Rebus grunted a response. 'DC Coupar here, sir. The Chief thought you'd be interested.' There was a pause for effect. 'A bomb's just gone off in Barnton.'

Rebus stared at the sheets of print lying all around him. He asked the Detective Constable to repeat the message.

'A bomb, sir. In Barnton.'

'What? A World War Two leftover you mean?'

'No, sir. Nothing like that. Nothing like that at all.'

There was a line of poetry in Rebus's head as he drove out towards one of Edinburgh's many quiet middle-class districts, the sort of place where nothing happened, the sort of place where crime was measured in a yearly attempted break-in or the theft of a bicycle. That was Barnton. The line of poetry hadn't been written about Barnton. It had been written about Slough.

It's my own fault, Rebus was thinking, for being disgusted at how far-fetched that Hammett book was. Entertaining, yes, but you could strain credulity only so far, and Dashiell Hammett had taken that strain like the anchor-man on a tug-o'-war team, pulling with all his might. Coincidence after coincidence, plot after plot, corpse following corpse like something off an assembly line.

Far-fetched, definitely. But then what was Rebus to make of his telephone call? He'd checked: it wasn't 1st April. But then he wouldn't put it past Brian Holmes or one of his other colleagues to pull a stunt on him just because he was having a day off, just because he'd carped on about it for the previous few days. Yes, this had Holmes' fingerprints all over it. Except for one thing.

The radio reports. The police frequency was full of it; and when Rebus switched on his car radio to the local commercial channel, the news was there, too. Reports of an explosion in Barnton, not far from the roundabout. It is thought a car has exploded. No further details, though there are thought to be many casualties. Rebus shook his head and drove, thinking of the poem again, thinking of anything that would stop him focussing on the truth of the news. A car bomb? *A car bomb?* In Belfast, yes, maybe even on occasion in London. But here in Edinburgh? Rebus blamed himself. If only he hadn't cursed Dashiell Hammett, if only he hadn't sneered at his book, at its exaggerations and its melodramas, if only ... Then none of this would have happened.

But of course it would. It had.

The road had been blocked off. The ambulances had left with their cargo. Onlookers stood four deep behind the orange and white tape of the hastily erected cordon. There was just the one question: how many dead? The answer seemed to be: just the one. The driver of the car. An Army bomb disposal unit had materialised from somewhere and, for want of anything else to do, was checking the shops either side of the street. A line of policemen, aided so far as Rebus could judge by more Army personnel, was moving slowly up the road, mostly on hands and knees, in what an outsider might regard as some bizarre slow-motion race. They carried with them polythene bags, into which they dropped anything they found. The whole scene was one of brilliantly organised confusion and it didn't take Rebus longer than a couple of minutes to detect the mastermind behind it all – Superintendent 'Farmer' Watson. 'Farmer' only behind his back, of course, and a nickname which matched both his north-of-Scotland background and his at times agricultural methods. Rebus decided to skirt around his superior officer and glean what he could from the various less senior officers present.

He had come to Barnton with a set of preconceptions and it took time for these to be corrected. For example, he'd premised that the person in the car, the as-yet-unidentified deceased, would be the car's owner and that this person would have been the target of the bomb attack (the evidence all around most certainly pointed to a bomb, rather than spontaneous combustion, say, or any other more likely explanation). Either that or the car might be stolen or borrowed, and the driver some sort of terrorist, blown apart by his own device before he could leave it at its intended destination. There were certainly Army installations around Edinburgh: barracks, armouries, listening posts. Across the Forth lay what was left of Rosyth naval dockyard, as well as the underground installation at Pitreavie. There were targets. Bomb meant terrorist meant target. That was how it always was.

But not this time. This time there was an important difference. The apparent target escaped, by dint of leaving his car for a couple of minutes to nip into a shop. But while he was in the shop someone had tried to steal his car, and that person was now drying into the tarmac beneath the knees of the crawling policemen. This much Rebus learned before Superintendent Watson caught sight of him, caught sight of him smiling wryly at the car thief's luck. It wasn't every day you got the chance to steal a Jaguar XJS ... but what a day to pick.

'Inspector!' Farmer Watson beckoned for Rebus to join him, which Rebus, ironing out his smile, did.

Before Watson could start filling him in on what he already knew, Rebus himself spoke.

'Who was the target, sir?'

'A man called Dean.' Meaningful pause. 'Brigadier-General Dean, retired.'

Rebus nodded. 'I thought there were a lot of Tommies about.'

'We'll be working with the Army on this one, John. That's how it's done, apparently. And then there's Scotland Yard, too. Their anti-terrorist people.'

'Too many cooks if you ask me, sir.'

Watson nodded. 'Still, these buggers are supposed to be special-ised.'

'And we're only good for solving the odd drunk driving or domestic, eh, sir?'

The two men shared a smile at this. Rebus nodded towards the wreck of the car. 'Any idea who was behind the wheel?'

Watson shook his head. 'Not yet. And not much to go on either. We may have to wait till a mum or girlfriend reports him missing.'

'Not even a description?'

'None of the passers-by is fit to be questioned. Not yet anyway.'

'So what about Brigadier-General Whassisname?'

'Dean.'

'Yes. Where is he?'

'He's at home. A doctor's been to take a look at him, but he seems all right. A bit shocked.'

'A bit? Someone rips the arse out of his car and he's a *bit* shocked?' Rebus sounded doubtful. Watson's eyes were fixed on the advancing line of debris collectors.

'I get the feeling he's seen worse.' He turned to Rebus. 'Why don't you have a word with him, John? See what you think.'

Rebus nodded slowly. 'Aye, why not,' he said. 'Anything for a laugh, eh, sir?'

Watson seemed stuck for a reply, and by the time he'd formed one Rebus had wandered back through the cordon, hands in trouser pockets, looking for all the world like a man out for a stroll on a balmy summer's evening. Only then did the Superintendent remember that this was Rebus's day off. He wondered if it had been such a bright idea to send him off to talk to Brigadier-General Dean. Then he smiled, recalling that he had brought John Rebus out here precisely because something didn't quite feel right. If he could feel it, Rebus would feel it too, and would burrow deep to find its source – as deep as necessary and, perhaps, deeper than was seemly for a Superintendent to go.

Yes, there were times when even Detective Inspector John Rebus came in useful.

It was a big house. Rebus would go further. It was bigger than the last hotel he'd stayed in, though of a similar style: closer to Hammer Films than *House and Garden*. A hotel in Scarborough it had been; three days of lust with a divorced school-dinner lady. School-dinner ladies hadn't been like that in Rebus's day ... or maybe he just hadn't been paying attention.

He paid attention now. Paid attention as an Army uniform opened the door of West Lodge to him. He'd already had to talk his way past a mixed guard on the gate – an apologetic PC and two uncompromising squaddies. That was why he'd started thinking back to Scarborough – to stop himself punching those squaddies in their square-chinned faces. The closer he came to Brigadier-General Dean, the more aggressive and unlovely the soldiers seemed. The two on the gate were like lambs compared to the one on the main door of the house, yet he in his turn was meekness itself compared to the one who led Rebus into a well-appointed living-room and told him to wait.

Rebus hated the Army – with good reason. He had seen the soldier's lot from the inside and it had left him with a resentment so huge that to call it a 'chip on the shoulder' was to do it an injustice. Chip? Right now it felt like a whole transport cafe! There was only one thing for it. Rebus made for the sideboard, sniffed the contents of the decanter sitting there and poured himself an inch of whisky. He was draining the contents of the glass into his mouth when the door opened.

Rebus had brought too many preconceptions with him today. Brigadier-Generals were squat, ruddy-faced men, with stiff moustaches and VSOP noses, a few silvered wisps of Brylcreemed hair and maybe even a walking stick. They retired in their seventies and babbled of campaigns over dinner.

Not so Brigadier-General Dean. He looked to be in his mid- to late-fifties. He stood over six feet tall, had a youthful face and vigorous dark hair. He was slim too, with no sign of a retirement gut or a port drinker's red-veined cheeks. He looked twice as fit as Rebus felt and for a moment the policeman actually caught himself straightening his back and squaring his shoulders.

'Good idea,' said Dean, joining Rebus at the sideboard. 'Mind if I join you?' His voice was soft, blurred at the edges, the voice of an educated man, a civilised man. Rebus tried hard to imagine Dean giving orders to a troop of hairy-fisted Tommies. Tried, but failed.

'Detective Inspector Rebus,' he said by way of introduction. 'Sorry to bother you like this, sir, but there are a few questions—'

Dean nodded, finishing his own drink and offering to replenish Rebus's.

'Why not?' agreed Rebus. Funny thing though: he could swear this whisky wasn't whisky at all but whiskey – Irish whiskey. Softer than the Scottish stuff, lacking an edge.

Rebus sat on the sofa, Dean on a well-used armchair. The Brigadier-General offered a toast of *slainte* before starting on his second drink, then exhaled noisily.

'Had to happen sooner or later, I suppose,' he said.

'Oh?'

Dean nodded slowly. 'I worked in Ulster for a time. Quite a long time. I suppose I was fairly high up in the tree there. I always knew I was a target. The Army knew, too, of course, but what can you do? You can't put bodyguards on every soldier who's been involved in the conflict, can you?'

'I suppose not, sir. But I assume you took precautions?'

Dean shrugged. 'I'm not in *Who's Who* and I've got an unlisted telephone number. I don't even use my rank much, to be honest.'

'But some of your mail might be addressed to Brigadier-General Dean?'

A wry smile. 'Who gave you that impression?'

'What impression, sir?'

'The impression of rank. I'm not a Brigadier-General. I retired with the rank of Major.'

'But the—'

'The what? The locals? Yes, I can see how gossip might lead to exaggeration. You know how it is in a place like this, Inspector. An incomer who keeps himself to himself. A military air. They put two and two together then multiply it by ten.'

Rebus nodded thoughtfully. 'I see.' Trust Watson to be wrong even in the fundamentals. 'But the point I was trying to make about your mail still stands, sir. What I'm wondering, you see, is how they found you.'

Dean smiled quietly. 'The IRA are quite sophisticated these days, Inspector. For all I know, they could have hacked into a computer, bribed someone in the know, or maybe it was just a fluke, sheer chance.' He shrugged. 'I suppose we'll have to think of moving somewhere else now, starting all over again. Poor Jacqueline.'

'Jacqueline being?'

'My daughter. She's upstairs, terribly upset. She's due to start university in October. It's her I feel sorry for.'

Rebus looked sympathetic. He felt sympathetic. One thing about Army life and police life – both could have a devastating effect on your personal life.

'And your wife, sir?'

'Dead, Inspector. Several years ago.' Dean examined his now empty glass. He looked his years now, looked like someone who needed a rest. But there was something other about him, something cool and hard. Rebus had met all types in the Army – and since. Veneers could no longer fool him, and behind Major Dean's sophisticated veneer he could glimpse something other, something from the man's past. Dean hadn't just been a good soldier. At one time he'd been lethal.

'Do you have any thoughts on how they might have found you, sir?'

'Not really.' Dean closed his eyes for a second. There was resignation in his voice. 'What matters is that they *did* find me.' His eyes met Rebus's. 'And they can find me again.'

Rebus shifted in his seat. Christ, what a thought. What a, well, time-bomb. To always be watching, always expecting, always fearing. And not just for yourself.

'I'd like to talk to Jacqueline, sir. It may be that she'll have some inkling as to how they were able to—'

But Dean was shaking his head. 'Not just now, Inspector. Not yet. I don't want her – well, you understand. Besides, I'd imagine that this will all be out of your hands by tomorrow. I believe some people from the Anti-Terrorist Branch are on their way up here. Between them and the Army … well, as I say, it'll be out of your hands.'

Rebus felt himself prickling anew. But Dean was right, wasn't he? Why strain yourself when tomorrow it would be someone else's weight? Rebus pursed his lips, nodded, and stood up.

'I'll see you to the door,' said the Major, taking the empty glass from Rebus's hand.

As they passed into the hallway, Rebus caught a glimpse of a young woman – Jacqueline Dean presumably. She had been hovering by the telephone-table at the foot of the staircase, but was now starting up the stairs themselves, her hand thin and white on the bannister. Dean, too, watched her go. He half-smiled, half-shrugged at Rebus.

'She's upset,' he explained unnecessarily. But she hadn't looked upset to Rebus. She had looked like she was moping.

The next morning, Rebus went back to Barnton. Wooden boards had been placed over some of the shop windows, but otherwise there were few signs of yesterday's drama. The guards on the gate to West Lodge had been replaced by beefy plainclothes men with London accents. They carried portable radios, but otherwise might have been bouncers, debt collectors or bailiffs. They radioed the house. Rebus couldn't help thinking that a shout might have done the job for them, but they were in love with technology; you could see that by the way they held their radio-sets. He'd seen soldiers holding a new gun the same way.

'The guvnor's coming down to see you,' one of the men said at last. Rebus kicked his heels for a full minute before the man arrived.

'What do you want?'

'Detective Inspector Rebus. I talked with Major Dean yesterday and—'

The man snapped. 'Who told you his rank?'

'Major Dean himself. I just wondered if I might—'

'Yes, well there's no need for that, Inspector. We're in charge now. Of course you'll be kept informed.'

The man turned and walked back through the gates with a steady, determined stride. The guards were smirking as they closed the gates behind their 'guvnor'. Rebus felt like a snubbed schoolboy, left out of the football game. Sides had been chosen and there he stood, unwanted. He could smell London on these men, that cocky superiority of a self-chosen elite. What did they call themselves? C13 or somesuch, the Anti-Terrorist Branch. Closely linked to Special Branch, and everyone knew the trade name for Special Branch – Smug Bastards.

The man had been a little younger than Rebus, well-groomed and accountant-like. More intelligent, for sure, than the gorillas on the gate, but probably well able to handle himself. A neat pistol might well have been hidden under the arm of his close-fitting suit. None of that mattered. What mattered was that the captain was leaving Rebus out of his team. It rankled; and when something rankled, it rankled hard.

Rebus had walked half a dozen paces away from the gates when he half-turned and stuck his tongue out at the guards. Then, satisfied with this conclusion to his morning's labours, he decided to make his own inquiries. It was eleven-thirty. If you want to find out about someone, reasoned a thirsty Rebus, visit his local.

The reasoning, in this case, proved false: Dean had never been near The Claymore.

'The daughter came in though,' commented one young man. There weren't many people in the pub at this early stage of the day, save a few retired gentlemen who were in conversation with three or four reporters. The barman, too, was busy telling his life story to a young female hack, or rather, into her tape recorder. This made getting served difficult, despite the absence of a lunchtime scrum. The young man had solved this problem, however, reaching behind the bar to refill his glass with a mixture of cider and lager, leaving money on the bartop.

'Oh?' Rebus nodded towards the three-quarters full glass. 'Have another?'

'When this one's finished I will.' He drank greedily, by which time the barman had finished with his confessions – much (judging by her face) to the relief of the reporter. 'Pint of Snakebite, Paul,' called the young man. When the drink was before him, he told Rebus that his name was Willie Barr and that he was unemployed.

'You said you saw the daughter in here?' Rebus was anxious to have his questions answered before the alcohol took effect on Barr.

'That's right. She came in pretty regularly.'

'By herself?'

'No, always with some guy.'

'One in particular, you mean?'

But Willie Barr laughed, shaking his head. 'A different one every time. She's getting a bit of a name for herself. And,' he raised his voice for the barman's benefit, 'she's not even eighteen, I'd say.'

'Were they local lads?'

'None I recognised. Never really spoke to them.' Rebus swirled his glass, creating a foamy head out of nothing.

'Any Irish accents among them?'

'In here?' Barr laughed. 'Not in here. Christ, no. Actually, she hasn't been in for a few weeks, now that I think of it. Maybe her father put a stop to it, eh? I mean, how would it look in the Sunday papers? Brigadier's daughter slumming it in Barnton.'

Rebus smiled. 'It's not exactly a slum though, is it?'

'True enough, but her boyfriends ... I mean, there was more of the car mechanic than the estate agent about them. Know what I mean?' He winked. 'Not that a bit of rough ever hurt *her* kind, eh?' Then he laughed again and suggested a game or two of pool, a pound a game or a fiver if the detective were a betting man.

But Rebus shook his head. He thought he knew now why Willie Barr was drinking so much: he was flush. And the reason he was flush was that he'd been telling his story to the papers – for a price. *Brigadier's Daughter Slumming It*. Yes, he'd been telling tales all right, but there was little chance of them reaching their intended audience. The Powers That Be would see to that.

Barr was helping himself to another pint as Rebus made to leave the premises.

It was late in the afternoon when Rebus received his visitor, the Anti-Terrorist accountant.

'A Mr Matthews to see you,' the Desk Sergeant had informed Rebus, and 'Matthews' he remained, giving no hint of rank or proof of identity. He had come, he said, to 'have it out' with Rebus.

'What were you doing in The Claymore?'

'Having a drink.'

'You were asking questions. I've already told you, Inspector Rebus, we can't have—'

'I know, I know.' Rebus raised his hands in a show of surrender. 'But the more furtive you lot are, the more interested I become.'

Matthews stared silently at Rebus. Rebus knew that the man

was weighing up his options. One, of course, was to go to Farmer Watson and have Rebus warned off. But if Matthews were as canny as he looked, he would know this might have the opposite effect from that intended. Another option was to talk to Rebus, to ask him what he wanted to know.

'What do you want to know?' Matthews said at last.

'I want to know about Dean.'

Matthews sat back in his chair. 'In strictest confidence?' Rebus nodded. 'I've never been known as a clipe.'

'A clipe?'

'Someone who tells tales,' Rebus explained. Matthews was thoughtful.

'Very well then,' he said. 'For a start, Dean is an alias, a very necessary one. During his time in the Army Major Dean worked in Intelligence, mostly in West Germany but also for a time in Ulster. His work in both spheres was very important, crucially important. I don't need to go into details. His last posting was West Germany. His wife was killed in a terrorist attack, almost certainly IRA. We don't think they had targeted her specifically. She was just in the wrong place with the wrong number plates.'

'A car bomb?'

'No, a bullet. Through the windscreen, point-blank. Major Dean asked to be ... he was invalided out. It seemed best. We provided him with a change of identity, of course.'

'I thought he looked a bit young to be retired. And the daughter, how did she take it?'

'She was never told the full details, not that I'm aware of. She was in boarding school in England.' Matthews paused. 'It was for the best.'

Rebus nodded. 'Of course, nobody'd argue with that. But why did – Dean – choose to live in Barnton?'

Matthews rubbed his left eyebrow, then pushed his spectacles back up his sharply sloping nose. 'Something to do with an aunt of his,' he said. 'He spent holidays there as a boy. His father was Army, too, posted here, there and everywhere. Never the most stable upbringing. I think Dean had happy memories of Barnton.'

Rebus shifted in his seat. He couldn't know how long Matthews would stay, how long he would continue to answer Rebus's questions. And there were so many questions.

'What about the bomb?'

'Looks like the IRA, all right. Standard fare for them, all the hall-marks. It's still being examined, of course, but we're pretty sure.'

'And the deceased?'

'No clues yet. I suppose he'll be reported missing sooner or later. We'll leave that side of things to you.'

'Gosh, thanks.' Rebus waited for his sarcasm to penetrate, then, quickly: 'How does Dean get on with his daughter?'

Matthews was caught off-guard by the question. He blinked twice, three times, then glanced at his wristwatch.

'All right, I suppose,' he said at last, making show of scratching a mark from his cuff. 'I can't see what ... Look, Inspector, as I say, we'll keep you fully informed. But meantime—'

'Keep out of your hair?'

'If you want to put it like that.' Matthews stood up. 'Now I really must be getting back—'

'To London?'

Matthews smiled at the eagerness in Rebus's voice. 'To Barnton. Don't worry, Inspector, the more *you* keep out of *my* hair, the quicker I can get out of yours. Fair enough?' He shot a hand out towards Rebus, who returned the almost painful grip.

'Fair enough,' said Rebus. He ushered Matthews from the room and closed the door again, then returned to his seat. He slouched as best he could in the hard, uncomfortable chair and put his feet up on the desk, examining his scuffed shoes. He tried to feel like Sam Spade, but failed. His legs soon began to ache and he slid them from the surface of the desk. The coincidences in Dashiell Hammett had nothing on the coincidence of someone nicking a car seconds before it exploded. Someone must have been watching, ready to detonate the device. But if they were watching, how come they didn't spot that Dean, the intended victim, wasn't the one to drive off?

Either there was more to this than met the eye, or else there was less. Rebus was wary – very wary. He'd already made far too many prejudgements, had already been proved wrong too many times. Keep an open mind, that was the secret. An open mind and an inquiring one. He nodded his head slowly, his eyes on the door.

'Fair enough,' he said quietly. 'I'll keep out of your hair, Mr Matthews, but that doesn't necessarily mean I'm leaving the barber's.'

The Claymore might not have been Barnton's most salubrious establishment, but it was as Princes Street's Caledonian Hotel in comparison with the places Rebus visited that evening. He began with the merely seedy bars, the ones where each quiet voice seemed to contain a lifetime's resentment, and then moved downwards, one rung of the ladder at a time. It was slow work; the bars tended to be in a ring around Edinburgh, sometimes on the outskirts or in the distant housing schemes, sometimes nearer the centre than most of the population would dare to think.

Rebus hadn't made many friends in his adult life, but he had his network of contacts and he was as proud of it as any grandparent would be of their extended family. They were like cousins, these contacts; mostly they knew each other, at least by reputation, but Rebus never spoke to one about another, so that the extent of the chain could only be guessed at. There were those of his colleagues who, in Major Dean's words, added two and two, then multiplied by ten. John Rebus, it was reckoned, had as big a net of 'snitches' as any copper on the force bar none.

It took four hours and an outlay of over forty pounds before Rebus started to catch a glimpse of a result. His basic question, though couched in vague and imprecise terms, was simple: have any car thieves vanished off the face of the earth since yesterday?

One name was uttered by three very different people in three distinct parts of the city: Brian Cant. The name meant little to Rebus.

'It wouldn't,' he was told. 'Brian only shifted across here from the west a year or so ago. He's got form from when he was a nipper, but he's grown smart since then. When the Glasgow cops started sniffing, he moved operations.' The detective listened, nodded, drank a watered-down whisky, and said little. Brian Cant grew from a name into a description, from a description into a personality. But there was something more.

'You're not the only one interested in him,' Rebus was told in a bar in Gorgie. 'Somebody else was asking questions a wee while back. Remember Jackie Hanson?'

'He used to be CID, didn't he?'

'That's right, but not any more ...'

Not just any old banger for Brian Cant: he specialised in 'quality motors'. Rebus eventually got an address: a third-floor tenement flat near Powderhall race-track. A young man answered the door. His name was Jim Cant, Brian's younger brother. Rebus saw that Jim was scared, nervous. He chipped away at the brother quickly, explaining that he was there because he thought Brian might be dead. That he knew all about Cant's business, but that he wasn't interested in pursuing this side of things, except insofar as it might shed light on the death. It took a little more of this, then the brother opened up.

'He said he had a customer interested in a car,' Jim Cant explained. 'An Irishman, he said.'

'How did he know the man was Irish?'

'Must have been the voice. I don't think they met. Maybe they did. The man was interested in a specific car.'

'A red Jaguar?'

'Yeah, convertible. Nice cars. The Irishman even knew where there was one. It seemed a cinch, that's what Brian kept saying. A cinch.'

'He didn't think it would be hard to steal?'

'Five seconds' work, that's what he kept saying. I thought it sounded too easy. I told him so.' He bent over in his chair, grabbing at his knees and sinking his head between them. 'Ach, Brian, what the hell have you done?'

Rebus tried to comfort the young man as best he could with brandy and tea. He drank a mug of tea himself, wandering through the flat, his mind thrumming. Was he blowing things up out of all proportion? Maybe. He'd made mistakes before, not so much errors of judgement as errors of jumping the gun. But there was something about all of this ... Something.

'Do you have a photo of Brian?' he asked as he was leaving. 'A recent one would be best.' Jim Cant handed him a holiday snap.

'We went to Crete last summer,' he explained. 'It was magic.' Then, holding the door open for Rebus: 'Don't I have to identify him or something?'

Rebus thought of the scrapings which were all that remained of what may or may not have been Brian Cant. He shook his head. 'I'll let you know,' he said. 'If we need you, we'll let you know.'

The next day was Sunday, day of rest. Rebus rested in his car, parked fifty yards or so along the road from the gates to West Lodge. He put his radio on, folded his arms and sank down into the driver's seat. This was more like it. The Hollywood private eye on a stakeout. Only in the movies, a stakeout could be whittled away to a few minutes' footage. Here, it was measured in a slow ticking of seconds ... minutes ... quarter hours.

Eventually, the gates opened and a figure hurried out, fairly trotting along the pavement as though released from bondage. Jacqueline Dean was wearing a denim jacket, short black skirt and thick black tights. A beret sat awkwardly on her cropped dark hair and she pressed the palm of her hand to it from time to time to stop it sliding off altogether. Rebus locked his car before following her. He kept to the other side of the road, wary not so much from fear that she might spot him but because C13 might have put a tail on her, too.

She stopped at the local newsagent's first and came out heavy-laden with Sunday papers. Rebus, making to cross the road, a Sunday-morning stroller, studied her face. What was the expression he'd thought of the first time he'd seen her? Yes, *moping*. There was still something of that in her liquid eyes, the dark shadows beneath. She was making for the corner shop now. Doubtless she would appear with rolls or bacon or butter or milk. All the things Rebus seemed to find himself short of on a Sunday, no matter how hard he planned.

He felt in his jacket pockets, but found nothing of comfort there, just the photograph of Brian Cant. The window of the corner shop, untouched by the blast, contained a dozen or so personal ads, felt-tipped onto plain white postcards. He glanced at these, and past them, through the window itself to where Jacqueline was making her purchases. Milk and rolls: elementary, my dear Conan Doyle. Waiting for her change, she half-turned her head towards the window. Rebus concentrated on the postcards. 'Candy, Masseuse' vied for attention with 'Pram and carry-cot for sale', 'Babysitting considered', and 'Lada, seldom used'. Rebus was smiling, almost despite himself, when the door of the shop tinkled open.

'Jacqueline?' he said. She turned towards him. He was holding open his ID. 'Mind if I have a word, Miss Dean?'

Major Dean was pouring himself a glass of Irish whiskey when the drawing-room door opened.

'Mind if I come in?' Rebus's words were directed not at Dean but at Matthews, who was seated in a chair by the window, one leg crossed over the other, hands gripping the arm-rests. He looked like a nervous businessman on an airplane, trying not to let his neighbour see his fear.

'Inspector Rebus,' he said tonelessly. 'I thought I could feel my scalp tingle.'

Rebus was already in the room. He closed the door behind him. Dean gestured with the decanter, but Rebus shook his head.

'How did you get in?' Matthews asked.

'Miss Dean was good enough to escort me through the gate. You've changed the guard detail again. She told them I was a friend of the family.'

Matthews nodded. 'And are you, Inspector? Are you a friend of the family?'

'That depends on what you mean by friendship.'

Dean had seated himself on the edge of his chair, steadying the glass with both hands. He didn't seem quite the figure he had been on the day of the explosion. A reaction, Rebus didn't doubt. There had been a quiet euphoria on the day; now came the aftershock.

'Where's Jacqui?' Dean asked, having paused with the glass to his lips.

'Upstairs,' Rebus explained. 'I thought it would be better if she didn't hear this.'

Matthews' fingers plucked at the arm-rests. 'How much does she know?'

'Not much. Not yet. Maybe she'll work it out for herself.'

'So, Inspector, we come to the reason why you're here.'

'I'm here,' Rebus began, 'as part of a murder inquiry. I thought that's why you were here, too, Mr Matthews. Maybe I'm wrong. Maybe you're here to cover up rather than bring to light.'

Matthews' smile was momentary. But he said nothing.

'I didn't go looking for the culprits,' Rebus went on. 'As you said, Mr Matthews, that was *your* department. But I did wonder who the victim was. The accidental victim, as I thought. A young car thief called Brian Cant, that would be my guess. He stole cars to order. A client asked him for a red open-top Jag, even told him where he might find one. The client told him about Major Dean. Very specifically about Major Dean, right down to the fact that every day he'd nip into the wine-shop on the main street.' Rebus turned to Dean. 'A bottle of Irish a day, is it, sir?'

Dean merely shrugged and drained his glass.

'Anyway, that's what your daughter told me. So all Brian Cant had to do was wait near the wine-shop. You'd get out of your car, leave it running, and while you were in the shop he could drive the car away. Only it bothered me that the client – Cant's brother tells me he spoke with an Irish accent – knew so much, making it easy for Cant. What was stopping this person from stealing the car himself?'

'And the answer came to you?' Matthews suggested, his voice thick with irony.

Rebus chose to avoid his tone. He was still watching Dean. 'Not straight away, not even then. But when I came to the house, I couldn't help noticing that Miss Dean seemed a bit strange. Like she was waiting for a phone call from someone and that someone had let her down. It's easy to be specific now, but at the time it just struck me as odd. I asked her about it this morning and she admitted it's because she's been jilted. A man she'd been seeing, and seeing regularly, had suddenly stopped calling. I asked her about him, but she couldn't be very helpful. They never went to his flat, for example. He drove a flashy car and had plenty of money, but she was vague about what he did for a living.'

Rebus took a photograph from his pocket and tossed it into Dean's lap. Dean froze, as though it were some hair-trigger grenade.

'I showed her a photograph of Brian Cant. Yes, that was the name of her boyfriend – Brian Cant. So you see, it was small wonder she hadn't heard from him.'

Matthews rose from the chair and stood before the window itself, but nothing he saw there seemed to please him, so he turned back into the room. Dean had found the courage to lift the photograph from his leg and place it on the floor. He got up too, and made for the decanter.

'For Christ's sake,' Matthews hissed, but Dean poured regardless.

Rebus's voice was level. 'I always thought it was a bit of a coincidence, the car being stolen only seconds before exploding. But then the IRA use remote control devices, don't they? So that someone in the vicinity could have triggered the bomb any time they liked. No need for all these long-term timers and what have you. I was in the SAS once myself.'

Matthews raised an eyebrow. 'Nobody told me that,' he said, sounding impressed for the first time.

'So much for Intelligence, eh?' Rebus answered. 'Speaking of which, you told me that Major Dean here was in Intelligence. I think I'd go further. Covert operations, that sort of thing? Counter-intelligence, subversion?'

'Now you're speculating, Inspector.'

Rebus shrugged. 'It doesn't really matter. What matters is that someone had been spying on Brian Cant, an ex-policeman called Jackie Hanson. He's a private detective these days. He won't say anything about his clients, of course, but I think I can put two and two together without multiplying the result. He was working for you, Major Dean, because you were interested in Brian Cant. Jacqueline was serious about him, wasn't she? So much so that she might have forsaken university. She tells me they were even talking of moving in together. You didn't want her to leave. When you found out what Cant did for a ... a living, I suppose you'd call it, you came up with a plan.' Rebus was enjoying himself now, but tried to keep the pleasure out of his voice.

'You contacted Cant,' he went on, 'putting on an Irish accent. Your Irish accent is probably pretty good, isn't it, Major? It would need to be, working in counter-intelligence. You told him all about a car – your car. You offered him a lot of money if he'd steal it for you and you told him precisely when and where he might find it. Cant was greedy. He didn't think twice.' Rebus noticed that he was sitting very comfortably in his own chair, whereas Dean looked ... the word that sprang to mind was 'rogue'. Matthews, too, was sparking internally, though his surface was all metal sheen, cold bodywork.

'You'd know how to make a bomb, that goes without saying. Wouldn't you, Major? Know thine enemy and all that. Like I say, I was in the SAS myself. What's more, you'd know how to make an IRA device, or one that looked like the work of the IRA. The remote was in your pocket. You went into the shop, bought your whiskey, and when you heard the car being driven off, you simply pressed the button.'

'Jacqueline.' Dean's voice was little more than a whisper. 'Jacqueline.' He rose to his feet, walked softly to the door and left the room. He appeared to have heard little or nothing of Rebus's speech. Rebus felt a pang of disappointment and looked towards Matthews, who merely shrugged.

'You cannot, of course, prove any of this, Inspector.'

'If I put my mind to it I can.'

'Oh, I've no doubt, no doubt.' Matthews paused. 'But will you?'

'He's mad, you've got to see that.'

'Mad? Well, he's unstable. Ever since his wife ...'

'No reason for him to murder Brian Cant.' Rebus helped himself to a whisky now, his legs curiously shaky. 'How long have you known?'

Matthews shrugged again. 'He tried a similar trick in Germany, apparently. It didn't work that time. So what do we do now? Arrest him? He'd be unfit to plead.'

'However it happens,' Rebus said, 'he's got to be made safe.'

'Absolutely.' Matthews was nodding agreement. He came to the sideboard. 'A hospital, somewhere he can be treated. He was a good soldier in his day. I've read his record. A good soldier. Don't worry, Inspector Rebus, he'll be "made safe" as you put it. He'll be taken care of.' A hand landed on Rebus's forearm. 'Trust me.'

Rebus trusted Matthews – about as far as he could spit into a Lothian Road headwind. He had a word with a reporter friend, but the man wouldn't touch the story. He passed Rebus on to an investigative journalist who did some ferreting, but there was little or nothing to be found. Rebus didn't know Dean's real name. He didn't know Matthews' first name or rank or even, to be honest, that he had been C13 at all. He might have been Army, or have inhabited that indefinite smear of operations somewhere between Army, Secret Service and Special Branch.

By the next day, Dean and his daughter had left West Lodge and a fortnight later it appeared in the window of an estate agent on George Street. The asking price seemed surprisingly low, if your tastes veered towards *The Munsters*. But the house would stay in the window for a long time to come.

Dean haunted Rebus's dreams for a few nights, no more. But how did you make safe a man like that? The Army had designed a weapon and that weapon had become misadjusted, its sights all wrong. You could dismantle a weapon. You could dismantle a man, too, come to that. But each and every piece was still as lethal as the whole. Rebus put aside fiction, put aside Hammett and the rest and of an evening read psychology books instead. But then they too, in their way, were fiction, weren't they? And so, too, in time became the case that was not a case of the man who had never been.

Being Frank

It wasn't easy, being Frank.

That's what everybody called him, when they weren't calling him a dirty old tramp or a scrounger or a layabout. Frank, they called him. Only the people at the hostel and at the Social Security bothered with his full name: Francis Rossetti Hyslop. Rossetti, he seemed to remember, not after the painter but after his sister the poet, Christina. Most often, a person – a person in authority – would read that name from the piece of paper they were holding and then look up at Frank, not quite in disbelief, but certainly wondering how he'd come so low.

He couldn't tell them that he was climbing higher all the time. That he preferred to live out of doors. That his face was weather-beaten, not dirty. That a plastic bag was a convenient place to keep his possessions. He just nodded and shuffled his feet instead, the shuffle which had become his trademark.

'Here he comes,' his companions would cry. 'Here comes The Shuffler!' Alias Frank, alias Francis Rossetti Hyslop.

He spent much of the spring and autumn in Edinburgh. Some said he was mad, leaving in the summer months. That, after all, was when the pickings were richest. But he didn't like to bother the tourists, and besides, summer was for travelling. He usually walked north, through Fife and into Kinross or Perthshire, setting up camp by the side of a loch or up in the hills. And when he got bored, he'd move on. He was seldom moved on by gamekeepers or the police. Some of them he knew of old, of course. But others he encountered seemed to regard him more and more as some rare species, or, as one had actually said, a 'national monument'.

It was true, of course. Tramp meant to walk and that's what tramps used to do. The term 'gentleman of the road' used to be accurate. But the tramp was being replaced by the beggar: young, fit men who didn't move from the city and who were unrelenting in their search for spare change. That had never been Frank's way. He had his regulars of course, and often he only had to sit on a bench in The Meadows, a huge grassy plain bordered by tree-lined paths, and wait for the money to appear in his lap.

That's where he was when he heard the two men talking. It was a bright day, a lunchtime and there were few spaces to be had on the meagre supply of Meadows' benches. Frank was sitting on one, arms folded, eyes closed, his legs stretched out in front of him with one foot crossed over the other. His three carrier bags were on the ground beside him, and his hat lay across his legs – not because he was hot especially, but because you never knew who might drop a coin in while you were dozing, or pretending to doze.

Maybe his was the only bench free. Maybe that's why the men sat down beside him. Well, 'beside him' was an exaggeration. They squeezed themselves onto the furthest edge of the bench, as far from him as possible. They couldn't be comfortable, squashed up like that and the thought brought a moment's smile to Frank's face.

But then they started to talk, not in a whisper but with voices lowered. The wind, though, swept every word into Frank's right ear. He tried not to tense as he listened, but it was difficult. Tried not to move, but his nerves were jangling.

'It's war,' one said. 'A council of war.'

War? He remembered reading in a newspaper recently about terrorists. Threats. A politician had said something about vigilance. Or was it vigilantes? A council of war: it sounded ominous. Maybe they were teasing him, trying to scare him from the bench so that they could have it for themselves. But he didn't think so. They were speaking in undertones; they didn't think he could hear. Or maybe they simply knew that it didn't matter whether an old tramp heard them or not. Who would believe him?

This was especially true in Frank's case. Frank believed that there was a worldwide conspiracy. He didn't know who was behind it, but he could see its tentacles stretching out across the globe. Everything was connected, that was the secret. Wars were connected by arms manufacturers, the same arms manufacturers who made the guns used in robberies, who made the guns used by crazy people in America when they went on the rampage in a shopping-centre or hamburger restaurant. So already you had a connection between hamburgers and dictators. Start from there and the thing just grew and grew.

And because Frank had worked this out, he wondered from time to time if *they* were after him. The dictators, the arms industry, or maybe even the people who made the buns for the hamburger chains. Because he *knew*. He wasn't crazy; he was sure of that.

'If I was,' he told one of his regulars, 'I wouldn't wonder if I was or not, would I?'

And she'd nodded, agreeing with him. She was a student at the university. A lot of students became regulars. They lived in Tollcross, Marchmont, Morningside, and had to pass through The Meadows on their way to the university buildings in George Square. She was studying psychology, and she told Frank something.

'You've got what they call an active fantasy life.'

Yes, he knew that. He made up lots of things, told himself stories. They whiled away the time. He pretended he'd been an RAF pilot, a spy, minor royalty, a slave-trader in Africa, a poet in Paris. But he *knew* he was making all these stories up, just as he knew that there really was a conspiracy.

And these two men were part of it.

'Rhodes,' one of them was saying now.

A council of war in Rhodes. So there was a Greek connection, too. Well, that made sense. He remembered stories about the generals and their junta. The terrorists were using Greece as their base. And Edinburgh was called the 'Athens of the north'. Yes! Of course! That's why they were basing themselves in Edinburgh too. A symbolic gesture. Had to be.

But who would believe him? That was the problem, being Frank. He'd told so many stories in the past, given the police so much information about the conspiracy, that now they just laughed at him and sent him on his way. Some of them thought he was looking for a night in the cells and once or twice they'd even obliged, despite his protests.

No, he didn't want to spend another night locked up. There was only one thing for it. He'd follow the men and see what he could find. Then he'd wait until tomorrow. They were talking about tomorrow, too, as if it was the start of their campaign. Well, tomorrow was Sunday and with a bit of luck if Frank hung around The Meadows, he'd bump into another of his regulars, one who might know exactly what to do.

Sunday morning was damp, blustery. Not the sort of day for a constitutional. This was fine by John Rebus: it meant there'd be fewer people about on Bruntsfield Links. Fewer men chipping golf-balls towards his head with a wavering cry of 'Fore!' Talk about crazy golf! He knew the Links had been used for this purpose for years and years, but all the same there were so many paths cutting through that it was a miracle no one had been killed.

He walked one circuit of the Links, then headed as usual across Melville Drive and into The Meadows. Sometimes he'd stop to watch a kickabout. Other times, he kept his head down and just walked, hoping for inspiration. Sunday was too close to Monday for his liking and Monday always meant a backlog of work. Thinking about it never did any good, of course, but he found himself thinking of little else.

'Mr Rebus!'

But then The Meadows offered other distractions, too.

'Mr Rebus!'

'Hello, Frank.'

'Sit yourself down.'

Rebus lowered himself onto the bench. 'You look excited about something.'

Frank nodded briskly. Though he was seated, he shuffled his feet on the earth, making little dance movements. Then he looked around him, as though seeking interlopers.

Oh no, thought Rebus, here we go again.

'War,' Frank whispered. 'I heard two men talking about it.'

Rebus sighed. Talking to Frank was like reading one of the Sunday rags – except sometimes the stories *he* told were more believable. Today didn't sound like one of those days.

'Talking about war? Which war?'

'Terrorism, Mr Rebus. Has to be. They've had a council of war at Rhodes. That's in Greece.'

'They were Greek, were they?'

Frank wrinkled his face. 'I don't think so. I can give you a description of them though. They were both wearing suits. One was short and bald, the other one was young, taller, with black hair.'

'You don't often see international terrorists wearing suits these days, do you?' Rebus commented. Actually, he thought to himself, that's a lie: they're becoming more smartly dressed all the time.

In any case, Frank had an answer ready. 'Need a disguise though, don't they? I followed them.'

'Did you?' A kickabout was starting nearby. Rebus concentrated on the kick-off. He liked Frank, but there were times ...

'They went to a bed and breakfast near the Links.'

'Did they now?' Rebus nodded slowly.

'And they said it was starting *today*. Today, Mr Rebus.'

'They don't hang about, do they? Anything else?'

Frank frowned, thinking. 'Something about lavatories, or laboratories. Must have been laboratories, mustn't it? And money, they talked about that. Money they needed to set it up. That's about it.'

'Well, thanks for letting me know, Frank. I'll keep my ears open, see if I can hear any whispers. But listen, don't go following people in future. It could be dangerous, understand?'

Frank appeared to consider this. 'I see what you mean,' he said at last, 'but I'm tougher than I look, Mr Rebus.'

Rebus was standing now. 'Well, I'd better be getting along.' He slipped his hands into his pockets. The right hand emerged again holding a pound note. 'Here you go, Frank.' He began to hand the money over, then withdrew it again. Frank knew what was coming and grinned.

'Just one question,' Rebus said, as he always did. 'Where do you go in the winter?'

It was a question a lot of his cronies asked him. 'Thought you were dead,' they'd say each spring as he came walking back into their lives. His reply to Rebus was the same as ever: 'Ah, that would be telling, Mr Rebus. That's *my* secret.'

The money passed from one hand to the other and Rebus sauntered off towards Jawbone Walk, kicking a stone in front of him. Jawbone because of the whale's jawbone which made an arch at one end of the path. Frank knew that. Frank knew lots of things. But he knew, too, that Rebus hadn't believed him. Well, more fool him. For over a year now they'd played this little game: where did Frank go in the winter? Frank wasn't sure himself why he didn't just say, I go to my sister's place in Dunbar. Maybe because it was the truth. Maybe because it *was* a secret.

Rebus looked to him like a man with secrets, too. Maybe one day Rebus would set out for a walk and never return home, would just keep on walking the way Frank himself had done. What was it the girl student had said?

'Sometimes I think we're *all* gentlemen of the road. It's just that most of us haven't got the courage to take that first step.'

Nonsense: that first step was the easiest. It was the hundredth, the thousandth, the millionth that was hard. But not as hard as going back, never as hard as that.

Rebus had counted the steps up to his second-floor flat many, many times. It always added up to the same number. So how come with the passing years there seemed to be more? Maybe it was the height of each step that was changing. Own up, John. For once, own up: it's *you* that's changing. You're growing older and stiffer. You never used to pause on the first-floor landing, never used to linger outside

Mrs Cochrane's door, breathing in that smell unique to blackcurrant bushes and cat-pee.

How could one cat produce that amount of odour? Rebus had seen it many a time: a fat, smug-looking creature with hard eyes. He'd caught it on his own landing, turning guiltily to look at him before sprinting for the next floor up. But it was inside Mrs Cochrane's door just now. He could hear it mewling, clawing at the carpet, desperate to be outside. He wondered. Maybe Mrs Cochrane was ill? He'd noticed that recently her brass nameplate had become tarnished. She wasn't bothering to polish it any more. How old was she anyway? She seemed to have come with the tenement, almost as if they'd constructed the thing around her. Mr and Mrs Costello on the top floor had been here nigh-on twenty-five years, but they said she'd been here when they arrived. Same brass nameplate on her door. Different cat, of course, and a husband, too. Well, he'd been dead by the time Rebus and his wife – now ex-wife – had moved here, what, was it ten years ago now?

Getting old, John. Getting old. He clamped his left hand onto the bannister and somehow managed the last flight of steps to his door.

He started a crossword in one of the newspapers, put some jazz on the hi-fi, drank a pot of tea. Just another Sunday. Day of rest. But he kept catching glimpses of the week ahead. No good. He made another pot of tea and this time added a dollop of J&B to the mixture in his mug. Better. And then, naturally, the doorbell rang.

Jehovah's Witnesses. Well, Rebus had an answer ready for them. A friend in the know had said that Roman Catholics are taught how to counter the persuasive arguments of the JWs. Just tell them you're a Catholic and they'll go away.

'I'm Catholic,' he said. They didn't go away. There were two of them, dressed in dark suits. The younger one stood a little behind the older one. This didn't matter, since he was a good foot taller than his elder. He was holding a briefcase. The chief, however, held only a piece of paper. He was frowning, glancing towards this. He looked at Rebus, sizing him up, then back to the paper. He didn't appear to have heard what Rebus said.

'I'm Catholic,' Rebus repeated, but hollowly.

The man shook his head. Maybe they were foreign missionaries, come to convert the heathen. He consulted his scrap of paper again.

'I think this is the wrong address,' he said. 'There isn't a Mr Bakewell here?'

'Bakewell?' Rebus started to relax. A simple mistake; they weren't JWs. They weren't salesmen or cowboy builders or tinkers. Simply, they'd got the wrong flat. 'No,' he said. 'No Mr Bakewell here. And his tart's not here either.'

Oh, they laughed at that. Laughed louder than Rebus had expected. They were still laughing as they made their apologies and started back downstairs. Rebus watched them until they were out of sight. He'd stopped laughing almost before they'd begun. He checked that his keys were in his pocket, then slammed shut his door – but with himself still out on the landing.

Their footsteps sent sibilant echoes up towards the skylight. What was it about them? If pressed, he couldn't have said. There was just *something*. The way the smaller, older man had seemed to weigh him up in a moment, then mentioned Bakewell. The way the younger man had laughed so heartily, as if it were such a release. A release of what? Tension, obviously.

The footsteps had stopped. Outside Mrs Cochrane's door. Yes, that was the ting-ting-ting of her antiquated doorbell, the kind you pulled, tightening and releasing the spring on a bell inside the door. The door which was now being pulled open. The older man spoke.

'Mrs Cochrane?' Well, they'd got that name right. But then it was on her nameplate, wasn't it? *Anyone* could have guessed at it.

'Aye.' Mrs Cochrane, Rebus knew, was not unique in making this sound not only questioning but like a whole sentence. Yes, I'm Mrs Cochrane, and who might you be and what do you want?

'Councillor Waugh.'

Councillor! No, no, there was no problem: Rebus had paid his Poll Tax, always put his bin-bags out the night before, never earlier. They might be after Bakewell, but Rebus was in the clear.

'It's about the roadworks.'

'Roadworks?' echoed Mrs Cochrane.

Roadworks? thought Rebus.

'Yes, roadworks. Digging up the roads. You made a complaint about the roads. I've come to talk to you about it.'

'Roadworks? Here, you mean?'

He was patient, Rebus had to grant him that. 'That's right, Mrs Cochrane. The road outside.'

There was a bit more of this, then they all went indoors to talk over Mrs Cochrane's grievances. Rebus opened his own door and went in, too. Then, realising, he slapped his hand against his head. These were the two men Shuffling Frank had been talking about! Of course they were, only Frank had misheard: council of war was Councillor Waugh; Rhodes was roads. What else had Frank said? Something about money: well, that might be the money for the repairs. That it was all planned to start on Sunday: and here they were, on Sunday, ready to talk to the residents about roadworks.

What roadworks? The road outside was clear, and Rebus hadn't heard any gossip concerning work about to start. Something else Frank had heard them say. Lavatories or laboratories. Of course, his own cherished conspiracy theory had made him plump for 'laboratories', but what if he'd misheard again? Where did lavatories fit into the scheme? And if, as seemed certain, these were the two men, what was a local councillor doing staying at a bed and breakfast? Maybe he owned it, of course. Maybe it was run by his wife.

Rebus was a couple of paces further down his hall when it hit him. He stopped dead. Slow, John, slow. Blame the whisky, maybe. And Jesus, wasn't it so obvious when you thought of it? He went back to his door opened it quietly, and slipped out onto the landing.

There was no such thing as silent movement on an Edinburgh stairwell. The sound of shoe on stone, a sound like sandpaper at work, was magnified and distorted, bouncing off the walls upwards and downwards. Rebus slipped off his shoes and left them on his landing, then started downstairs. He listened outside Mrs Cochrane's door. Muffled voices from the living-room. The layout of her flat was the same as Rebus's own: a long hallway off which were half a dozen doors, the last of which – actually around a corner – led to the living-room. He crouched down and pushed open the letterbox. The cat was just inside the door and it swiped at him with its paw. He let the hinge fall back.

Then he tried the doorhandle, which turned. The door opened. The cat swept past him and down the stairs. Rebus began to feel that the odds were going his way. The door was open just wide enough to allow him to squeeze inside. Open it an inch or two further, he knew, and it creaked with the almightiest groan. He tiptoed into the hallway. Councillor Waugh's voice boomed from the living-room.

'Bowel trouble. Terrible in a man so young.'

Yes, he'd no doubt be explaining why his assistant was taking so long in the lavatory: that was the excuse they always made. Well, either that or a drink of water. Rebus passed the toilet. The door wasn't locked and the tiny closet was empty. He pushed open the next door along – Mrs Cochrane's bedroom. The young man was closing the wardrobe doors.

'Well,' said Rebus, 'I hope you didn't think *that* was the toilet.'

The man jerked around. Rebus filled the doorway. There was no way past him; the only way to get out was to go through him, and that's what the man tried, charging at the doorway, head low. Rebus stood back a little, giving himself room and time, and brought his knee up hard, aiming for the bridge of the nose but finding mouth instead. Well, it was an imprecise science, wasn't it? The man flew backwards like a discarded ragdoll and fell onto the bed. Flat out, to Rebus's satisfaction.

They'd heard the noise of course, and the 'councillor' was already on his way. But he, too, would need to get past Rebus to reach the front door. He stopped short. Rebus nodded slowly.

'Very wise,' he said. 'Your colleague's going to need some new teeth when he wakes up. I'm a police officer by the way. And you, "councillor", are under arrest.'

'Arresting the councillor?' This from Mrs Cochrane, who had appeared in the hall.

'He's no more a councillor than I am, Mrs Cochrane. He's a con-man. His partner's been raking through your bedroom.'

'What?' She went to look.

'Bakewell,' Rebus said, smiling. They would try the same ruse at every door where they didn't fancy their chances. Sorry, wrong address, and on to the next potential sucker until they found someone old enough or gullible enough. Rebus was trying to remember if Mrs Cochrane had a telephone. Yes, there was one in her living-room, wasn't there? He gestured to his prisoner.

'Let's go back into the living-room,' he said. Rebus could call the station from there ...

Mrs Cochrane was back beside him. 'Blood on my good quilt,' she muttered. Then she saw that Rebus was in his stocking-soles. 'You'll get chilblains, son,' she said. 'Mark my words. You should take better care of yourself. Living on your own like that. You need somebody to look after you. Mark my words. He told me he was a councillor. Would you credit it? And me been wanting to talk to them for ages about the dogs' mess on the Links.'

'Hello, Shuffler.'

'Mr Rebus! Day off is it? Don't usually see you around here during the week.'

Frank was back on his bench, a newspaper spread out on his lap. One of yesterday's papers. It contained a story about some black magic conspiracy in the United States. Wealthy people, it was reckoned, influential people, taking part in orgies and rituals. Yes, and the arms manufacturers would be there, too. That's how they got to know the politicians and the bankers. It all connected.

'No, I'm off to work in a minute. Just thought I'd stop by. Here.' He was holding out a ten-pound note. Frank looked at it suspiciously, moved his hand towards it, and took it. What? Didn't Rebus even want to ask him the question?

'You were right,' Rebus was saying. 'What you told me about those two men, dead right. Well, nearly dead right. Keep your ears open, Frank. And in future, I'll try to keep *my* ears open when you talk to me.'

And then he turned and was walking away, back across the grass towards Marchmont. Frank stared at the money. Ten pounds. Enough to finance another long walk. He needed a long walk to clear his head. Now that they'd had the council of war at Rhodes, the laboratories would be making potions for satanic rituals. They'd put the politicians in a trance, and ... No, no, it didn't bear thinking about.

'Mr Rebus!' he called. 'Mr Rebus! I go to my sister's! She lives in Dunbar! That's where I go in the winter!'

But if the distant figure heard him, it made no sign. Just kept on walking. Frank shuffled his feet. Ten pounds would buy a transistor radio, or a pair of shoes, a jacket, or a new hat, maybe a little camping stove. That was the problem with having money: you ended up with decisions to make. And if you bought anything, where would you put it? He'd need either to ditch something, or to start on another carrier-bag.

That was the problem, being Frank.

Concrete Evidence

'It's amazing what you find in these old buildings,' said the contractor, a middle-aged man in safety helmet and overalls. Beneath the overalls lurked a shirt and tie, the marks of his station. He was the chief, the gaffer. Nothing surprised him any more, not even unearthing a skeleton.

'Do you know,' he went on, 'in my time, I've found everything from ancient coins to a pocket-watch. How old do you reckon he is then?'

'We're not even sure it *is* a he, not yet. Give us a chance, Mr Beesford.'

'Well, when can we start work again?'

'Later on today.'

'Must be gey old though, eh?'

'How do you make that out?'

'Well, it's got no clothes on, has it? They've perished. Takes time for that to happen, plenty of time ...'

Rebus had to concede, the man had a point. Yet the concrete floor beneath which the bones had been found ... *it* didn't look so old, did it? Rebus cast an eye over the cellar again. It was situated a storey or so beneath road-level, in the basement of an old building off the Cowgate. Rebus was often in the Cowgate; the mortuary was just up the road. He knew that the older buildings here were a veritable warren, long narrow tunnels ran here, there and, it seemed, everywhere, semi-cylindrical in shape and just about high enough to stand up in. This present building was being given the full works – gutted, new drainage system, rewiring. They were taking out the floor in the cellar to lay new drains and also because there seemed to be damp – certainly there was a fousty smell to the place – and its cause needed to be found.

They were expecting to find old drains, open drains perhaps. Maybe even a trickle of a stream, something which would lead to damp. Instead, their pneumatic drills found what remained of a corpse, perhaps hundreds of years old. Except, of course, for that concrete floor. It couldn't be more than fifty or sixty years old, could it? Would clothing deteriorate to a visible nothing in so short a time? Perhaps the damp could do that. Rebus found the cellar oppressive. The smell, the shadowy lighting provided by portable lamps, the dust.

But the photographers were finished, and so was the pathologist, Dr Curt. He didn't have too much to report at this stage, except to comment that he preferred it when skeletons were kept in cupboards, not confined to the cellar. They'd take the bones away, along with samples of the earth and rubble around the find, and they'd see what they would see.

'Archaeology's not really my line,' the doctor added. 'It may take me some time to bone up on it.' And he smiled his usual smile.

It took several days for the telephone call to come. Rebus picked up the receiver.

'Hello?'

'Inspector Rebus? Dr Curt here. About our emaciated friend.'

'Yes?'

'Male, five feet ten inches tall, probably been down there between thirty and thirty-five years. His left leg was broken at some time, long before he died. It healed nicely. But the little finger on his left hand had been dislocated and it did *not* heal so well. I'd say it was crooked all his adult life. Perfect for afternoon tea in Morningside.'

'Yes?' Rebus knew damned well Curt was leading up to something. He knew, too, that Curt was not a man to be hurried.

'Tests on the soil and gravel around the skeleton show traces of human tissue, but no fibres or anything which might have been clothing. No shoes, socks, underpants, nothing. Altogether, I'd say he was buried there in the altogether.'

'But did he die there?'

'Can't say.'

'All right, what did he die *of*?'

There was an almost palpable smile in Curt's voice. 'Inspector, I thought you'd never ask. Blow to the skull, a blow of considerable force to the back of the head. Murder, I'd say. Yes, definitely murder.'

There were, of course, ways of tracing the dead, of coming to a near-infallible identification. But the older the crime, the less likely this outcome became. Dental records, for example. They just weren't *kept* in the 50s and 60s the way they are today. A dentist practising then would most probably be playing near-full-time golf by now. And the record of a patient who hadn't been in for his check-up since 1960? Discarded, most probably. Besides, as Dr Curt pointed out, the man's teeth had seen little serious work, a few fillings, a single extraction.

The same went for medical records, which didn't stop Rebus from checking. A broken left leg, a dislocated left pinkie. Maybe some aged doctor would recall? But then again, maybe not. Almost certainly not. The local papers and radio were interested, which was a bonus. They were given what information the police had, but no memories seemed to be jogged as a result.

Curt had said he was no archaeologist; well, Rebus was no historian either. He knew other cases – contemporary cases – were yammering for his attention. The files stacked up on his desk were evidence enough of that. He'd give this one a few days, a few hours of his time. When the dead ends started to cluster around him, he'd drop it and head back for the here and now.

Who owned the building back in the 1950s? That was easy enough to discover: a wine importer and merchant. Pretty much a one-man operation, Hillbeith Vintners had held the premises from 1948 until 1967. And yes, there was a Mr Hillbeith, retired from the trade and living over in Burntisland, with a house gazing out across silver sands to the grey North Sea.

He still had a cellar, and insisted that Rebus have a 'wee taste' from it. Rebus got the idea that Mr Hillbeith liked visitors – a socially acceptable excuse for a drink. He took his time in the cellar (there must have been over 500 bottles in there) and emerged with cobwebs hanging from his cardigan, holding a dusty bottle of something nice. This he opened and sat on the mantelpiece. It would be half an hour or so yet at the very least before they could usefully have a glass.

Mr Hillbeith was, he told Rebus, seventy-four. He'd been in the wine trade for nearly half a century and had 'never regretted a day, not a day, nor even an hour'. Lucky you, Rebus thought to himself.

'Do you remember having that new floor laid in the cellar, Mr Hillbeith?'

'Oh, yes. That particular cellar was going to be for best claret. It was just the right temperature, you see, and there was no vibration from passing buses and the like. But it was damp, had been ever since I'd moved in. So I got a building firm to take a look. They suggested a new floor and some other alterations. It all seemed fairly straightforward and their charges seemed reasonable, so I told them to go ahead.'

'And when was this, sir?'

'1960. The spring of that year. There you are, I've got a great memory where business matters are concerned.' His small eyes beamed at Rebus through the thick lenses of their glasses. 'I can even tell you how much the work cost me ... and it was a pretty penny at the time. All for nothing, as it turned out. The cellar was still damp, and there was always that *smell* in it, a very unwholesome smell. I couldn't take a chance with the claret, so it became the general stock-room, empty bottles and glasses, packing-cases, that sort of thing.'

'Do you happen to recall, Mr Hillbeith, was the smell there *before* the new floor was put in?'

'Well, certainly there was *a* smell there before the floor was laid, but the smell afterwards was different somehow.' He rose and fetched two crystal glasses from the china cabinet, inspecting them for dust. 'There's a lot of nonsense talked about wine, Inspector. About decanting, the type of glasses you must use and so on. Decanting can help, of course, but I prefer the feel of the bottle. The bottle, after all, is part of the wine, isn't it?' He handed an empty glass to Rebus. 'We'll wait a few minutes yet.'

Rebus swallowed drily. It had been a long drive. 'Do you recall the name of the firm, sir, the one that did the work?'

Hillbeith laughed. 'How could I forget? Abbot & Ford, they were called. I mean, you just don't forget a name like that, do you? Abbot & Ford. You see, it sounds like Abbotsford, doesn't it? A small firm they were, mind. But you may know one of them, Alexander Abbot.'

'Of Abbot Building?'

'The same. He went on to make quite a name for himself, didn't he? Quite a fortune. Built up quite a company, too, but he started out small like most of us do.'

'How small, would you say?'

'Oh, small, small. Just a few men.' He rose and stretched an arm towards the mantelpiece. 'I think this should be ready to taste, Inspector. If you'll hold out your glass—'

Hillbeith poured slowly, deliberately, checking that no lees escaped into the glass. He poured another slow, generous measure for himself. The wine was reddish-brown. 'Robe and disc not too promising,' he muttered to himself. He gave his glass a shake and studied it. 'Legs not promising either.' He sighed. 'Oh dear.' Finally, Hillbeith sniffed the glass anxiously, then took a swig.

'Cheers,' said Rebus, indulging in a mouthful. A mouthful of vinegar. He managed to swallow, then saw Hillbeith spit back into the glass.

'Oxidisation,' the old man said, sounding cruelly tricked. 'It happens. I'd best check a few more bottles to assess the damage. Will you stay, Inspector?' Hillbeith sounded keen.

'Sorry, sir,' said Rebus, ready with his get-out clause. 'I'm still on duty.'

Alexander Abbot, aged fifty-five, still saw himself as the force behind the Abbot Building Company. There might be a dozen executives working furiously beneath him, but the company had grown from *his* energy and from *his* fury. He was Chairman, and a busy man too. He made this plain to Rebus at their meeting in the executive offices of ABC. The office spoke of business confidence, but then in Rebus's experience this meant little in itself. Often, the more dire straits a company was in, the healthier it tried to look. Still, Alexander Abbot seemed happy enough with life.

'In a recession,' he explained, lighting an overlong cigar, 'you trim your workforce pronto. You stick with regular clients, good payers, and don't take on too much work from clients you don't know. They're the ones who're likely to welch on you or go bust, leaving nothing but bills. Young businesses ... they're always hit hardest in a recession, no back-up you see. Then, when the recession's over for another few years, you dust yourself off and go touting for business again, re-hiring the men you laid off. That's where we've always had the edge over Jack Kirkwall.'

Kirkwall Construction was ABC's main competitor in the Lowlands, when it came to medium-sized contracts. Doubtless Kirkwall was the larger company. It, too, was run by a 'self-made' man, Jack Kirkwall. A larger-than-life figure. There was, Rebus quickly realised, little love lost between the two rivals.

The very mention of Kirkwall's name seemed to have dampened Alexander Abbot's spirits. He chewed on his cigar like it was a debtor's finger.

'You started small though, didn't you, sir?'

'Oh aye, they don't come much smaller. We were a pimple on the bum of the construction industry at one time.' He gestured to the walls of his office. 'Not that you'd guess it, eh?'

Rebus nodded. 'You were still a small firm back in 1960, weren't you?'

'1960. Let's think. We were just starting out. It wasn't ABC then, of course. Let's see. I think I got a loan from my dad in 1957, went into partnership with a chap called Hugh Ford, another self-employed builder. Yes, that's right. 1960, it was Abbot & Ford. Of course it was.'

'Do you happen to remember working at a wine merchant's in the Cowgate?'

'When?'

'The spring of 1960.'

'A wine merchant's?' Abbot furrowed his brow. 'Should be able to remember that. Long time ago, mind. A wine merchant's?'

'You were laying a new floor in one of his cellars, amongst other work. Hillbeith Vintners.'

'Oh, aye, Hillbeith, it's coming back now. I remember him. Little funny chap with glasses. Gave us a case of wine when the job was finished. Nice of him, but the wine was a bit off as I remember.'

'How many men were working on the job?'

Abbot exhaled noisily. 'Now you're asking. It was over thirty years ago, Inspector.'

'I appreciate that, sir. Would there be any records?'

Abbot shook his head. 'There might have been up to about ten years ago, but when we moved into this place a lot of the older stuff got chucked out. I regret it now. It'd be nice to have a display of stuff from the old days, something we could set up in the reception. But no, all the Abbot & Ford stuff got dumped.'

'So you don't remember how many men were on that particular job? Is there anyone else I could talk to, someone who might—'

'We were small back then, I can tell you that. Mostly using casual labour and part-timers. A job that size, I wouldn't think we'd be using more than three or four men, if that.'

'You don't recall anyone going missing? Not turning up for work, that sort of thing?'

Abbot bristled. 'I'm a stickler for time-keeping, Inspector. If anyone had done a bunk, I'd remember, I'm pretty sure of that. Besides, we were careful about who we took on. No lazy buggers, nobody who'd do a runner halfway through a job.'

Rebus sighed. Here was one of the dead ends. He rose to his feet. 'Well, thanks anyway, Mr Abbot. It was good of you to find time to see me.' The two men shook hands, Abbot rising to his feet.

'Not at all, Inspector. Wish I could help you with your little mystery. I like a good detective story myself.' They were almost at the door now.

'Oh,' said Rebus, 'just one last thing. Where could I find your old partner Mr Ford?'

Abbot's face lost its animation. His voice was suddenly that of an old man. 'Hugh died, Inspector. A boating accident. He was drowned. Hell of a thing to happen. Hell of a thing.'

Two dead ends.

Mr Hillbeith's telephone call came later that day, while Rebus was ploughing through the transcript of an interview with a rapist. His head felt full of foul-smelling glue, his stomach acid with caffeine.

'Is that Inspector Rebus?'

'Yes, hello, Mr Hillbeith. What can I do for you?' Rebus pinched the bridge of his nose and screwed shut his eyes.

'I was thinking all last night about that skeleton.'

'Yes?' In between bottles of wine, Rebus didn't doubt.

'Well, I was trying to think back to when the work was being done. It might not be much, but I definitely recall that there were four people involved. Mr Abbot and Mr Ford worked on it pretty much full-time, and there were two other men, one of them a teenager, the other in his forties. They worked on a more casual basis.'

'You don't recall their names?'

'No, only that the teenager had a nickname. Everyone called him by that. I don't think I ever knew his real name.'

'Well, thanks anyway, Mr Hillbeith. I'll get back to Mr Abbot and see if what you've told me jogs his memory.'

'Oh, you've spoken to him then?'

'This morning. No progress to report. I didn't realise Mr Ford had died.'

'Ah, well, that's the other thing.'

'What is?'

'Poor Mr Ford. Sailing accident, wasn't it?'

'That's right.'

'Only I remember that, too. You see, that accident happened just after they'd finished the job. They kept talking about how they were going to take a few days off and go fishing. Mr Abbot said it would be their first holiday in years.'

Rebus's eyes were open now. 'How soon was this after they'd finished your floor?'

'Well, directly after, I suppose.'

'Do you remember Mr Ford?'

'Well, he was very quiet. Mr Abbot did all the talking, really. A very quiet man. A hard worker though, I got that impression.'

'Did you notice anything about his hands? A misshapen pinkie?'

'Sorry, Inspector, it *was* a long time ago.'

Rebus appreciated that. 'Of course it was, Mr Hillbeith. You've been a great help. Thank you.'

He put down the receiver. A long time ago, yes, but still murder, still calculated and cold-blooded murder. Well, a path had opened in front of him. Not much of a path perhaps, a bit overgrown and treacherous. Nevertheless ... Best foot forward, John. Best foot forward.

Of course, he kept telling himself, he was still ruling possibilities out rather than ruling them in, which was why he wanted to know a little more about the boating accident. He didn't want to get the information from Alexander Abbot.

Instead, the morning after Hillbeith's phone-call, Rebus went to the National Library of Scotland on George IV Bridge. The doorman let him through the turnstile and he climbed an imposing staircase to the reading room. The woman on the desk filled in a one-day reader's card for him, and showed him how to use the computer. There were two banks of computers, being used by people to find the books they needed. Rebus had to go into the reading room and find an empty chair, note its number and put this on his slip when he'd decided which volume he required. Then he went to his chair and sat, waiting.

There were two floors to the reading room, both enveloped by shelves of reference books. The people working at the long desks downstairs seemed bleary. Just another morning's graft for them; but Rebus found it all fascinating. One person worked with a card index in front of him, to which he referred frequently. Another seemed asleep, head resting on arms. Pens scratched across countless sheets of paper. A few souls, lost for inspiration, merely chewed on their pens and stared at the others around them, as Rebus was doing.

Eventually, his volume was brought to him. It was a bound edition of the *Scotsman*, containing every issue for the months from January to June, 1960. Two thick leather buckles kept the volume closed. Rebus unbuckled these and began to turn the pages.

He knew what he was looking for, and pretty well where to find it, but that didn't stop him browsing through football reports and front page headlines. 1960. He'd been busy trying to lose his virginity and supporting Hearts. Yes, a long time ago.

The story hadn't quite made the front page. Instead, there were two paragraphs on page three. 'Drowning Off Lower Largo.' The victim, Mr Hugh Ford, was described as being twenty-six years of age (a year older than the survivor, Mr Alex Abbot) and a resident of Duddingston, Edinburgh. The men, on a short fishing-holiday, had taken a boat out early in the morning, a boat hired from a local man, Mr John Thomson. There was a squall, and the boat capsized. Mr Abbot, a fair swimmer, had made it back to the shore. Mr Ford, a poor swimmer, had not. Mr Ford was further described as a 'bachelor, a quiet man, shy according to Mr Abbot, who was still under observation at the Victoria Hospital, Kirkcaldy'. There was a little more, but not much. Apparently, Ford's parents were dead, but he had a sister, Mrs Isabel Hammond, somewhere out in Australia.

Why hadn't Abbot mentioned any of this? Maybe he wanted to forget. Maybe it still gave him the occasional bad dream. And of course he would have forgotten all about the Hillbeith contract precisely because this tragedy happened so soon afterwards. So soon. Just the one line of print really bothered Rebus; just that one sentence niggled.

'Mr Ford's body has still not been recovered.'

Records might get lost in time, but not by Fife Police. They sent on what they had, much of it written in fading ink on fragile paper, some of it typed – badly. The two friends and colleagues, Abbot and Ford, had set out on Friday evening to the Fishing-Net Hotel in Largo, arriving late. As arranged, they'd set out early next morning on a boat they'd hired from a local man, John Thomson. The accident had taken place only an hour or so after setting out. The boat was recovered. It had been overturned, but of Ford there was no sign. Inquiries were made. Mr Ford's belongings were taken back to Edinburgh by Mr Abbot, after the latter was released from hospital, having sustained a bump to the head when the boat went over. He was also suffering from shock and exhaustion. Mr Ford's sister, Mrs Isabel Hammond, was never traced.

They had investigated a little further. The business run jointly by Messrs Abbot and Ford now became Mr Abbot's. The case-notes contained a good amount of information and suspicion – between the lines, as it were. Oh yes, they'd investigated Alexander Abbot, but there had been no evidence. They'd searched for the body, had found none. Without a body, they were left with only their suspicions and their nagging doubts.

'Yes,' Rebus said quietly to himself, 'but what if you were looking for the body in the wrong place?' The wrong place at the wrong time. The work on the cellar had ended on Friday afternoon and by Saturday morning Hugh Ford had ceased to exist.

The path Rebus was on had become less overgrown, but it was still rock-strewn and dangerous, still a potential dead-end.

*

The Fishing-Net Hotel was still in existence, though apparently much changed from its 1960 incarnation. The present owners told Rebus to arrive in time for lunch if he could and it would be on the house. Largo was north of Burntisland but on the same coastline. Alexander Selkirk, the original of Defoe's *Robinson Crusoe*, had a connection with the fishing village. There was a small statue of him somewhere which Rebus had been shown as a boy (but only after much hunting, he recalled). Largo was picturesque, but then so were most, if not all, of the coastal villages in Fife's 'East Neuk'. But it was not yet quite the height of the tourist season and the customers taking lunch at the Fishing-Net Hotel were businessmen and locals.

It was a good lunch, as picturesque as its surroundings but with a bit more flavour. And afterwards, the owner, an Englishman for whom life in Largo was a long-held dream come true, offered to show Rebus round, including 'the very room your Mr Ford stayed in the night before he died'.

'How can you be sure?'

'I looked in the register.'

Rebus managed not to look too surprised. The hotel had changed hands so often since 1960, he despaired of finding anyone who would remember the events of that weekend.

'The register?'

'Yes, we were left a lot of old stuff when we bought this place. The store-rooms were choc-a-bloc. Old ledgers and what have you going back to the 1920s and '30s. It was easy enough to find 1960.'

Rebus stopped in his tracks. 'Never mind showing me Mr Ford's room, would you mind letting me see that register?'

He sat at a desk in the manager's office with the register open in front of him, while Mr Summerson's finger stabbed the line. 'There you are, Inspector, H. Ford. Signed in at 11.50 p.m., address given as Duddingston. Room number seven.'

It wasn't so much a signature as a blurred scrawl and above it, on a separate line, was Alexander Abbot's own more flowing signature.

'Bit late to arrive, wasn't it?' commented Rebus.

'Agreed.'

'I don't suppose there's anyone working here nowadays who worked in the hotel back then?'

Summerson laughed quietly. 'People do retire in this country, Inspector.'

'Of course, I just wondered.' He remembered the newspaper story. 'What about John Thomson? Does the name mean anything to you?'

'Old Jock? Jock Thomson? The fisherman?'

'Probably.'

'Oh, yes, he's still about. You'll almost certainly find him down by the dockside or else in the Harbour Tavern.'

'Thanks. I'd like to take this register with me if I may?'

Jock Thomson sucked on his pipe and nodded. He looked the archetype of the 'old salt', from his baggy cord trousers to his chiselled face and silvery beard. The only departure from the norm was, perhaps, the Perrier water in front of him on a table in the Harbour Tavern.

'I like the fizz,' he explained after ordering it, 'and besides, my doctor's told me to keep off the alcohol. Total abstinence, he said, total abstinence. Either the booze goes, Jock, or the pipe does. No contest.'

And he sucked greedily on the pipe. Then complained when his drink arrived without 'the wee slice of lemon'. Rebus returned to the bar to fulfil his mission.

'Oh aye,' said Thomson, 'remember it like it was yesterday. Only there's not much to remember, is there?'

'Why do you say that?'

'Two inexperienced laddies go out in a boat. Boat tips. End of story.'

'Was the weather going to be bad that morning?'

'Not particularly. But there *was* a squall blew up. Blew up and blew out in a matter of minutes. Long enough though.'

'How did the two men seem?'

'How do you mean?'

'Well, were they looking forward to the trip?'

'Don't know, I never saw them. The younger one, Abbot was it? He phoned to book a boat from me, said they'd be going out early, six or thereabouts. I told him he was daft, but he said there was no need for me to be on the dockside, if I'd just have the boat ready and tell him which one it was. And that's what I did. By the time I woke up that morning, he was swimming for the shore and his pal was food for the fish.'

'So you never actually saw Mr Ford?'

'No, and I only saw the lad Abbot afterwards, when the ambulance was taking him away.'

It was fitting into place almost too easily now. And Rebus thought, sometimes these things are only visible with hindsight, from a space of years. 'I don't suppose,' he ventured, 'you know anyone who worked at the hotel back then?'

'Owner's moved on,' said Thomson, 'who knows where to. It might be that Janice Dryman worked there then. Can't recall if she did.'

'Where could I find her?'

Thomson peered at the clock behind the bar. 'Hang around here ten minutes or so, you'll bump into her. She usually comes in of an afternoon. Meantime, I'll have another of these if you're buying.'

Thomson pushed his empty glass over to Rebus. Rebus, most definitely, was buying.

Miss Dryman – 'never married, never really saw the point' – was in her early fifties. She worked in a gift-shop in town and after her stint finished usually nipped into the Tavern for a soft drink and 'a bit of gossip'. Rebus asked what she would like to drink.

'Lemonade, please,' she said, 'with a drop of whisky in it.' And she laughed with Jock Thomson, as though this were an old and cherished joke between them. Rebus, not used to playing the part of straight-man, headed yet again for the bar.

'Oh yes,' she said, her lips poised above the glass. 'I was working there at the time all right. Chambermaid and general dogsbody, that was me.'

'You wouldn't see them arrive though?'

Miss Dryman looked as though she had some secret to impart. '*Nobody* saw them arrive, I know that for a fact. Mrs Dennis who ran the place back then, she said she'd be buggered if she'd wait up half the night for a couple of fishermen. They knew what rooms they were in and their keys were left at reception.'

'What about the front door?'

'Left unlocked, I suppose. The world was a safer place back then.'

'Aye, you're right there,' added Jock Thomson, sucking on his sliver of lemon.

'And Mr Abbot and Mr Ford knew this was the arrangement?'

'I suppose so. Otherwise it wouldn't have worked, would it?'

So Abbot knew there'd be nobody around at the hotel, not if he left it late enough before arriving.

'And what about in the morning?'

'Mrs Dennis said they were up and out before she knew anything about it. She was annoyed because she'd already cooked the kippers for their breakfast before she realised.'

So nobody saw them in the morning either. In fact ...

'In fact,' said Rebus, 'nobody saw Mr Ford at all. Nobody at the hotel, not you, Mr Thomson, nobody.' Both drinkers conceded this.

'I saw his stuff though,' said Miss Dryman.

'What stuff?'

'In his room, his clothes and stuff. That morning. I didn't know anything about the accident and I went in to clean.'

'The bed had been slept in?'

'Looked like it. Sheets all rumpled. And his suitcase was on the floor, only half unpacked. Not that there was much *to* unpack.'

'Oh?'

'A single change of clothes, I'd say. I remember them because they seemed mucky, you know, not fresh. Not the sort of stuff *I'd* take on holiday with me.'

'What? Like he'd been working in them?'

She considered this. 'Maybe.'

'No point wearing clean clothes for fishing,' Thomson added. But Rebus wasn't listening.

Ford's clothes, the clothes he had been working in while laying the floor. It made sense. Abbot bludgeoned him, stripped him and covered his body in fresh cement. He'd taken the clothes away with him and put them in a case, opening it in the hotel room, ruffling the sheets. Simple, but effective. Effective these past thirty years. The motive? A falling out perhaps, or simple greed. It was a small company, but growing, and perhaps Abbot hadn't wanted to share. Rebus placed a five-pound note on the table.

'To cover the next couple of rounds,' he said, getting to his feet. 'I'd better be off. Some of us are still on duty.'

There were things to be done. He had to speak to his superior, Chief Inspector Lauderdale. And that was for starters. Maybe Ford's Australian sister could be traced this time round. There had to be someone out there who could acknowledge that Ford had suffered from a broken leg in his youth, and that he had a crooked finger. So far, Rebus could think of only one person – Alexander Abbot. Somehow, he didn't think Abbot could be relied on to tell the truth, the whole truth.

Then there was the hotel register. The forensics lab could ply their cunning trade on it. Perhaps they'd be able to say for certain that Ford's signature was merely a bad rendition of Abbot's. But again, he needed a sample of Ford's handwriting in order to substantiate that the signature was not genuine. Who did he know who might possess such a document? Only Alexander Abbot. Or Mr Hillbeith, but Mr Hillbeith had not been able to help.

'No, Inspector, as I told you, it was Mr Abbot who handled all the paperwork, all that side of things. If there is an invoice or a receipt, it will be in his hand, not Mr Ford's. I don't recall ever seeing Mr Ford writing anything.'

No through road.

Chief Inspector Lauderdale was not wholly sympathetic. So far all Rebus had to offer were more suppositions to add to those of the Fife Police at the time. There was no proof that Alexander Abbot had killed his partner. No proof that the skeleton was Hugh Ford. Moreover, there wasn't even much in the way of circumstantial evidence. They could bring in Abbot for questioning, but all he had to do was plead innocence. He could afford a good lawyer; and even bad lawyers weren't stupid enough to let the police probe too deeply.

'We need proof, John,' said Lauderdale, 'concrete evidence. The simplest proof would be that hotel signature. If we prove it's not Ford's, then we have Abbot at that hotel, Abbot in the boat and Abbot shouting that his friend has drowned, *all* without Ford having been there. That's what we need. The rest of it, as it stands, is rubbish. You know that.'

Yes, Rebus knew. He didn't doubt that, given an hour alone with Abbot in a darkened alley, he'd have his confession. But it didn't work like that. It worked through the law. Besides, Abbot's heart might not be too healthy. BUSINESSMAN, 55, DIES UNDER QUESTIONING. No, it had to be done some other way.

The problem was, there *was* no other way. Alexander Abbot was getting away with murder. Or was he? Why did his story have to be false? Why did the body have to be Hugh Ford's? The answer was: because the whole thing seemed to fit. Only, the last piece of the jigsaw had been lost under some sofa or chair a long time ago, so long ago now that it might remain missing for ever.

He didn't know why he did it. If in doubt, retrace your steps ... something like that. Maybe he just liked the atmosphere. Whatever, Rebus found himself back in the National Library, waiting at his desk for the servitor to bring him his bound volume of old news. He mouthed the words of 'Yesterday's Papers' to himself as he waited. Then, when the volume appeared, he unbuckled it with ease and pulled open the pages. He read past the April editions, read through into May and June. Football results, headlines – and what was this? A snippet of business news, barely a filler at the bottom right-hand corner of a page. About how the Kirkwall Construction Company was swallowing up a couple of smaller competitors in Fife and Midlothian.

'The 1960s will be a decade of revolution in the building industry,' said Managing Director Mr Jack Kirkwall, 'and Kirkwall Construction aims to meet that challenge through growth and quality. The bigger we are, the better we are. These acquisitions strengthen the company, and they're good news for the workforce, too.'

It was the kind of sentiment which had lasted into the 1980s. Jack Kirkwall, Alexander Abbot's bitter rival. Now there was a man Rebus ought to meet ...

The meeting, however, had to be postponed until the following week. Kirkwall was in hospital for a minor operation.

'I'm at that age, Inspector,' he told Rebus when they finally met, 'when things go wrong and need treatment or replacing. Just like any bit of well-used machinery.'

And he laughed, though the laughter, to Rebus's ears, had a hollow centre. Kirkwall looked older than his sixty-two years, his skin saggy, complexion wan. They were in his living-room, from where, these days, he did most of his work.

'Since I turned sixty, I've only really wandered into the company headquarters for the occasional meeting. I leave the daily chores to my son, Peter. He seems to be managing.' The laughter this time was self-mocking.

Rebus had suggested a further postponement of the meeting, but when Jack Kirkwall knew that the subject was to be Alexander Abbot, he was adamant that they should go ahead.

'Is he in trouble then?'

'He might be,' Rebus admitted. Some of the colour seemed to reappear in Kirkwall's cheeks and he relaxed a little further into his reclining leather chair. Rebus didn't want to give Kirkwall the story. Kirkwall and Abbot were still business rivals, after all. Still, it seemed, enemies. Given the story, Kirkwall might try some underhand tactic, some rumour in the media, and if it got out that the story originally came from a police inspector, well. Hello, being sued and goodbye, pension.

No, Rebus didn't want that. Yet he did want to know whether Kirkwall knew anything, knew of any reason why Abbot might wish, might *need* to kill Ford.

'Go on, Inspector.'

'It goes back quite a way, sir. 1960, to be precise. Your firm was at that time in the process of expansion.'

'Correct.'

'What did you know about Abbot & Ford?'

Kirkwall brushed the palm of one hand over the knuckles of the other. 'Just that they were growing, too. Of course, they were younger than us, much smaller than us. ABC still is much smaller than us. But they were cocky, they were winning some contracts ahead of us. I had my eye on them.'

'Did you know Mr Ford at all?'

'Oh yes. Really, he was the cleverer of the two men. I've never had much respect for Abbot. But Hugh Ford was quiet, hardworking. Abbot was the one who did the shouting and got the firm noticed.'

'Did Mr Ford have a crooked finger?'

Kirkwall seemed bemused by the question. 'I've no idea,' he said at last. 'I never actually met the man, I merely knew *about* him. Why? Is it important?'

Rebus felt at last that his meandering, narrowing path had come to the lip of a chasm. Nothing for it but to turn back.

'Well,' he said, 'it would have clarified something.'

'You know, Inspector, my company *was* interested in taking Abbot & Ford under our wing.'

'Oh?'

'But then with the accident, that tragic accident. Well, Abbot took control and he wasn't at all interested in any offer we had to make. Downright rude, in fact. Yes, I've always thought that it was such a *lucky* accident so far as Abbot was concerned.'

'How do you mean, sir?'

'I mean, Inspector, that Hugh Ford was on our side. He wanted to sell up. But Abbot was against it.'

So, Rebus had his motive. Well, what did it matter? He was still lacking that concrete evidence Lauderdale demanded.

'... Would it show up from his handwriting?'

Rebus had missed what Kirkwall had been saying. 'I'm sorry, sir, I didn't catch that.'

'I said, Inspector, if Hugh Ford had a crooked finger, would it show from his handwriting?'

'Handwriting?'

'Because I had his agreement to the takeover. He'd written to me personally to tell me. Had gone behind Abbot's back, I suppose. I bet Alex Abbot was mad as hell when he found out about that.' Kirkwall's smile was vibrant now. 'I always thought that accident was a bit too lucky where Abbot was concerned. A bit too neat. No proof though. There was never any proof.'

'Do you still have the letter?'

'What?'

'The letter from Mr Ford, do you still have it?'

Rebus was tingling now, and Kirkwall caught his excitement. 'I never throw anything away, Inspector. Oh yes, I've got it. It'll be upstairs.'

'Can I see it? I mean, can I see it now?'

'If you like,' Kirkwall made to stand up, but paused. '*Is* Alex Abbot in trouble, Inspector?'

'If you've still got that letter from Hugh Ford, then, yes, sir, I'd say Mr Abbot could be in very grave trouble indeed.'

'Inspector, you've made an old man very happy.'

It was the letter against Alex Abbot's word, of course, and he denied everything. But there was enough now for a trial. The entry in the hotel, while it was *possibly* the work of Alexander Abbot was *certainly* not the work of the man who had written the letter to Jack Kirkwall. A search warrant gave the police the powers to look through Abbot's home and the ABC headquarters. A contract, drawn up between Abbot and Ford when the two men had gone into partnership, was discovered to be held in a solicitor's safe. The signature matched that on the letter to Jack Kirkwall. Kirkwall himself appeared in court to give evidence. He seemed to Rebus a different man altogether from the person he'd met previously: sprightly, keening, enjoying life to the full.

From the dock, Alexander Abbot looked on almost reproachfully, as if this were just one more business trick in a life full of them. Life, too, was the sentence of the judge.

Seeing Things

To be honest, if you were going to see Christ anywhere in Edinburgh, the Hermitage was perfect.

Or, to give it its full title, the Hermitage of Braid, named after the Braid Burn which trickled through the narrow, bushy wilderness between Blackford Hill and Braid Hills Road. Across this road, the Hermitage became a golf course, its undulations cultivated and well-trodden, but on sunny weekend afternoons, the Hermitage itself was as wild a place as your imagination wished it to be. Children ran in and out of the trees or threw sticks into the burn. Lovers could be seen hand-in-hand as they tackled the tricky descent from Blackford Hill. Dogs ran sniffing to stump and post, watched, perhaps, by punks seated atop an outcrop. Can would be tipped to mouth, the foam savoured. Picnic parties would debate the spot most sheltered from the breeze.

It was sometimes hard to believe that the place was in Edinburgh, that the main entrance to the Hermitage was just off the busy Comiston Road at the southern reach of Morningside. The protesters – such as they were – had held vigil at these gates for a couple of days, singing songs and handing out their 'No Popery' pamphlets. Occasionally a megaphone would appear, so that they could deliver their rant. A seller of religious nick-nacks and candles had set up his pitch across the road from the protesters, and at a canny distance along the road from them. The megaphone was most often directed towards him, there being no other visible target.

A rant was occurring as Inspector John Rebus arrived. Would the day of judgement be like this, he wondered, accepting a leaflet. Would the loudest voices belong to the saved? *Megaphones will be provided*, he thought to himself as he passed through the gates. He studied the leaflet. No Popery, indeed.

'Why ever not?' And so asking, he crumpled the paper and tossed it into the nearest wastepaper-bin. The voice followed him as though it had a mission and he was it.

'There must be NO idolatry! There is but ONE God and it is HE ye should worship! Do not turn YOUR face to graven IMAGES! The Good Book is the ONLY truth ye NEED!'

Rave on ...

They were a minority of course, far outweighed by the curious who came to see. But they in their turn looked as though they might be outnumbered very soon by the shrine-builders. Rebus liked to think of himself as a Christian, albeit with too many questions and doubts to ally himself with either side, Catholic or Protestant. He could not escape the fact that he had been born a Protestant; but his mother, a religious woman, had died young, and his father had been indifferent.

Rebus hadn't even been aware of any difference between Catholic and Protestant until he'd started school. His pre-school-days best friend was a Catholic, a boy called Miles Skelly. Come their first day at school, the boys had been split up, sent to schools on different sides of town. Parted like this daily, they soon grew to have new friends and stopped playing together.

That had been Rebus's first lesson in 'the divide'. But he had nothing against Catholics. The Protestant community might call them 'left-footers', but Rebus himself kicked a ball with his left foot. He did, however, mistrust the shrine mentality. It made him uneasy: statues which wept or bled or moved. Sudden visions of the Virgin Mary. A face imprinted on a shroud.

A faith should be just that, Rebus reasoned. And if you held belief, what need had you of miracles, especially ones that seemed more the province of the Magic Circle than of the divine? So the closer he came to the spot itself, the shakier became his legs. There was a tangle of undergrowth, and in front of it a stunted tree. Around this tree had been arranged candles, small statues, photographs, written prayers, flowers, all in the last two or three days. It was quite a transformation. A knot of people knelt nearby, but at a respectful distance. Their heads were bowed in prayer. Others sat, arms out behind them, supporting themselves on the grass. They wore beatific smiles, as though they could hear or see something Rebus couldn't. He listened hard, but heard only whispers of prayer, the distant barking of dogs. He looked, but saw only a tree, though it had to be admitted that the sunlight seemed to catch it in a particularly striking way, picking it out from the undergrowth behind it.

There was a rustling from beyond the tree itself. Rebus moved around the congregation – there was no other word for the gathering – towards the undergrowth, where several police cadets were on their hands and knees, not in worship this time but searching the ground.

'Anything?'

One of the figures straightened up, pressing his fingers into his spine as he exhaled. Rebus could hear the vertebrae crackling.

'Nothing, sir, not a blasted thing.'

'Language, Holmes, language. Remember, this is a holy site.'

Detective Constable Brian Holmes managed a wry smile. He'd been smiling a lot this morning. For once he'd been put in charge and it didn't matter to him that he was in a damp copse, or that he was in charge of a shower of disgruntled cadets, or that he had twigs in his hair. He was in charge. Not even John Rebus could take that away from him.

Except that he could. And did.

'All right,' Rebus said, 'that's enough. We'll have to make do with what we've got. Or rather, what the lab boys have got.'

The cadets rose mercifully to their feet. One or two brushed white chalky powder from their knees, others scraped at dirt and grass stains. 'Well done, lads,' Rebus admitted. 'Not very exciting, I know, but that's what police work is all about. So if you're joining for thrills and spills, think again.'

That should have been *my* speech, Holmes thought to himself as the cadets grinned at Rebus's words. They would agree with anything he said, anything he did. He was an Inspector. He was *the* Inspector Rebus. Holmes felt himself losing height and density, becoming like a patch of low mist or a particularly innocuous shadow. Rebus was in charge now. The cadets had all but forgotten their former leader. They had eyes for only one man, and that man was ordering them to go and drink some tea.

'What's up, Brian?'

Holmes, watching the cadets shuffle away, realised Rebus was speaking to him. 'Sorry?'

'You look like you've found a tanner and lost a shilling.'

Holmes shrugged. 'I suppose I'm thinking about how I could have had one-and-six. No news yet on the blood?'

'Just that it's every bit as messianic as yours and mine.'

'What a surprise.'

Rebus nodded towards the clearing. 'Try telling them that. They'll have an answer for you.'

'I know. I've already been ticked off for desecration. You know they've started posting an all-night guard?'

'What for?'

'In case the Wee Frees chop down the tree and run away with it.'

They stared at one another, then burst out laughing. Hands quickly went to mouths to stifle the sound. Desecration upon desecration.

'Come on,' said Rebus, 'you look like you could do with a cuppa yourself. My treat.'

'Now that *is* a miracle,' said Holmes, following his superior out of the trees. A tall, muscled man was approaching. He wore denims and a white T-shirt. A large wooden cross swung from his neck, around which was also tied a red kerchief. His beard was as thick and black as his hair.

'Are you police officers?'

'Yes,' Rebus said.

'Then I think you should know, they're trying to steal the tree.'

'Steal it, sir?'

'Yes, steal it. We've got to keep watch twenty-four hours. Last night, one of them had a knife, but there were too many of us, thank God.'

'And you are?'

'Steven Byrne.' He paused. 'Father Steven Byrne.'

Rebus paused too, digesting this new information. 'Well, Father, would you recognise this man again? The one with the knife?'

'Yes, probably.'

'Well, we could go down to the station and have a look at some photographs.'

Father Byrne seemed to be appraising Rebus. Acknowledging that he was being taken seriously, he nodded slowly. 'Thank you, I don't think that'll be necessary. But I thought you ought to know. Things might turn nasty.'

Rebus bit back a comment about turning the other cheek. 'Not if we can help it,' he said instead. 'If you see the man again, Father, let us know straight away. Don't try anything on your own.'

Father Byrne looked around him. 'There aren't so many telephones around here.' His eyes were twinkling with humour. An attractive man, thought Rebus. Even a touch charismatic.

'Well,' he said, 'we'll try to make sure a patrol car comes by and checks on things. How would that be?'

Father Byrne nodded. Rebus made to move away. 'Bless you,' he heard the man saying. Rebus kept walking, but for some reason his cheeks had turned deep red. But it was right and proper, after all, wasn't it? Right that he should be blessed.

'Blessed are the peacemakers,' he quoted, as the megaphone came back into range.

The story was a simple one. Three girls had been in the Hermitage one late afternoon. School over, they'd decided to cut through the park, climb Blackford Hill and come down the other side towards their homes. A long way round for a short-cut, as Rebus had put it at the time.

They were sensible girls, from good Catholic homes. They were fifteen and all had future plans that included university and a career as well as marriage. They didn't seem inclined to fantasy or exaggeration. They stuck to the same story throughout. They'd been about thirty yards or so from the tree when they'd seen a man. One second he wasn't there, the next he was. Dressed in white and with a glow all around him. Long wavy dark hair and a beard. A very pale face, they were definite about that. He leaned with one hand against the tree, the other to his side. His right side – again, all three concurred on this. Then he took the hand away, and they saw that there was blood on his side. A dark red patch. They gasped. They looked to each other for confirmation that they'd seen what they had seen. When they looked again, the figure had vanished.

They ran to their separate homes, but over dinner the story came out in each of the three households. Disbelieved, perhaps, for a moment. But then why would the girls lie? The parents got together and went to the Hermitage. They were shown the place, the tree. There was no sign of anyone. But then one of the mothers shrieked before crossing herself.

'Look at that!' she cried. 'Just look at it!'

It was a smeared red mark, still wet on the bark of the tree. Blood.

The parents went to the police and the police made an initial search of the area, but in the meantime, the neighbour of one of the families telephoned a friend who was a stringer on a Sunday newspaper. The paper ran the story of the 'Hermitage Vision' and the thing began to grow. The blood, it was said, hadn't dried. And this was true, though as Rebus knew it could well have something to do with the reaction of blood and bark. Footprints were found, but so many and so varied that it was impossible to say when they'd been made or by whom. The parents, for example, had searched the area thoroughly, destroying a lot of potential evidence. There were no bloodstains on the ground. No patients with side wounds had been treated in any of the city's hospitals or by any doctor.

The description of the figure was vague: tallish, thinnish, the long hair and beard of course – but was the hair brown or black? The girls couldn't be sure. Dressed in white – 'like a gown', one of them remembered later. But by then the story had become public property; how far would that distort her memories of the evening? And as for the glow. Well, Rebus had seen how the sun hit that particular spot. Imagine a lowish sun, creeping towards evening. That would explain the glow – to a rational man.

But then the zealous – of both sides – appeared. The believers and the doubters, carrying candles or toting megaphones. It was a quiet time for news: the media loved it. The girls photographed well. When they appeared on TV, the trickle of visitors to the site became a flood. Coach-loads headed north from Wales and England. Organised parties were arriving from Ireland. A Parisian magazine had picked up on the mystery; so, it was rumoured, had a Bible-thumping cable channel from the USA.

Rebus wanted to raise his hands and turn back the tide. Instead of which that tide rolled straight over him. Superintendent Watson wanted answers.

'I don't like all this hocus-pocus,' he said, with Presbyterian assuredness and an Aberdonian lilt. 'I want something tangible. I want an explanation, one I can *believe*. Understood?'

Understood. Rebus understood it; so did Chief Inspector Lauderdale. Chief Inspector Lauderdale understood that *he* wanted Rebus to do something about it. Rebus understood that hands were being washed; that his alone were to work on the case. If in doubt, delegate. That was where Brian Holmes and his cadets entered the picture. Having found no new clues – no clues *period* – Rebus decided to back off. Media interest was already dying. Some local historian would now and again come up with a 'fact' or a 'theory' and these would revive the story for a while – the hermit who'd lived in the Hermitage, executed for witchcraft in 1714 and said still to haunt the place, that sort of thing, but it couldn't last. It was like poking at embers without feeding them. A momentary glow, no more. When the media interest died, so would that of the fringe lunatics. There had already been copycat 'visions' in Cornwall, Caerphilly and East Croydon. The Doubting Thomases were appearing. What's more, the blood had gone, washed away in an overnight deluge which also extinguished the candles around the tree.

A recurrence of the 'vision' was needed if the thing were not to die. Rebus prayed each night for a quick and merciful release. It didn't come. Instead there was a 4 a.m. phone call.

'This better be worth it.'

'It is.'

'Go on then.'

'How soon can you get to the Hermitage?'

Rebus sat up in bed. 'Talk to me.'

'They've found a body. Well, that's putting it a bit strongly. Let's say they've found a trunk.'

*

A trunk it was, and not the sort you stuck travel labels on either.

'Dear God in heaven,' Rebus whispered, staring at the thing. 'Who found it?'

Holmes didn't look too good himself. 'One of the tree people,' he said. 'Wandered over here looking for a place to do his number twos. Had a torch with him. Found this. I think you could say he's in a state of shock. Apparently, so are his trousers.'

'I can't say I blame them.' A generator hummed in the background, providing juice for the three tall halogen lamps which lit the clearing. Some uniformed officers were cordoning off the area with strips of orange tape. 'So nobody's touched it?'

'Nobody's been near it.'

Rebus nodded, satisfied. 'Better keep it that way till forensics get here. Where the hell's the pathologist?'

Holmes nodded over Rebus's shoulder. 'Speak of the devil,' he said.

Rebus turned. Two men in sombre Crombie-style coats were walking briskly towards the scene. One carried a black surgeon's bag, the other had his hands firmly in his pockets, protection from the chill air. The halogen had fooled a few of the local birds, who were chirping their hearts out. But morning wasn't far away.

Chief Inspector Lauderdale nodded curtly towards Rebus, reckoning this greeting enough under the circumstances. The pathologist, Dr Curt, was, however (and despite his name), as voluble as ever.

'Top of the morning to you, Inspector.' Rebus, knowing Dr Curt of old, waited for the inevitable joke. The doctor obliged, gesturing towards the body. 'Not often I get a trunk call these days.'

Rebus, as was expected of him, groaned. The doctor beamed. Rebus knew what came next: the corny newspaper headlines. Again, Dr Curt obliged. 'Corpse in the coppice baffles cops,' he mused brightly, donning overshoes and coveralls before making for the corpse itself.

Chief Inspector Lauderdale looked stunned. He shuffled closer to Rebus. 'Is he always like this?'

'Always.'

The doctor had crouched down to inspect the body. He asked for the position of the lamps to be changed, then started his examination. But there was time for a last twist of the head towards Rebus.

'I'm afraid we're too late,' Dr Curt called out. 'Poor chap's dead.'

Chuckling to himself, he set to work, bringing a tape-recorder out of his case and mumbling into it from time to time.

Lauderdale watched for a minute. It was about fifty-nine seconds too long. He turned to Rebus again. 'What can you tell me?'

'About Dr Curt? Or about the deceased?'

'About the deceased.'

Rebus pushed his fingers through his hair, scratching at the scalp. He was mentally listing the bad puns still available to Dr Curt – he got legless, he's out of 'arm's way, lost his head, hadn't paid his bills so got cut off, was for the chop anyway, had no bleeding right, worked as a hack, take a butcher's at him ...

'Inspector?'

Rebus started. 'What?'

Lauderdale stared at him hard.

'Oh,' Rebus said, remembering. 'Well, he's naked of course. And they haven't severed *every* limb, so we know for sure that it *is* a he. Nothing else yet, sir. Come first light, we'll search the area for the missing appendages. One thing I'm pretty sure of, he wasn't butchered here.'

'Oh?'

'No blood, sir. Not that I can see.'

'Gentlemen!' It was Curt, calling to them, waving his arm for them to join him. They, too, had to slip on the elastic shoes, like ill-fitting polythene bags, and the coveralls. The forensics people would want to cover every inch of the ground around the victim's body. It didn't do to leave erroneous 'clues' like fibres from your jacket or a dropped coin.

'What is it, Doctor?'

'First, let me tell you that he's male, aged anywhere between thirty-five and fifty. Either dissolute thirty-five or a fairly well-preserved fifty. Stocky, too, unless the legs are in ridiculous propor-tion to the trunk. I can give a better guesstimate once we've had him on the slab.' His smile seemed directed at Lauderdale especially. 'Been dead a day or more. He was brought here in this condition, of course.'

'Of course,' said Lauderdale. 'No blood.'

The doctor nodded, still smiling. 'But there's something else. Look here.' He pointed to what was left of the right shoulder. 'Do you see this damage?' He circled the shoulder with his finger. They had to bend closer to see what he was talking about. The shoulder had been attacked with a knife, like someone had tried to peel it. It all looked clumsy and amateurish compared to the other neat examples.

'A tattoo,' Rebus said. 'Got to be.'

'Quite right, Inspector. They've tried removing it. *After* they dumped the trunk here. They must have spotted that there was still part of the tattoo left, enough to help us identify the victim.

So ...' He moved his finger from the shoulder stump to the ground beneath it. Rebus could just make out the shreds of skin.

'We can piece it back together,' Rebus stated.

'Of course we can!' The doctor stood up. 'They must think we're stupid. They go to all this trouble, then leave something like that.' He shook his head slowly. Rebus held his breath, waiting. The doctor's face brightened. 'It's years since I last did a jigsaw,' he said, opening his bag, placing his things back in it, and closing it with a loud snap. 'An open and shut case,' he said, moving back towards the cordon.

After he'd gone, off to his slab to await delivery of the body, Lauderdale lingered to see that everything was running smoothly. It was, as Rebus assured him. Lauderdale then bid him goodnight. Rebus didn't think anyone had ever 'bid' him goodnight before; wasn't sure anyone had *ever* bid anyone goodnight, outside of books and plays. It was especially strange to be bid goodnight at dawn. He could swear there was a cock crowing in the distance, but who in Morningside would keep chickens?

He looked for Holmes and found him over beside the tree-dwellers. Overnight, a guard-duty worked in shifts, two or three people at a time for two hours at a stretch. Holmes was chatting, seeming casual. He shifted his weight from foot to foot, as though cramp or cold were seeping through his socks.

Hadn't a leg to stand on: that was another one Dr Curt could have used.

'You seem very cheerful this morning, Inspector. But then each morning is a cause for celebration in itself.' Intent on Holmes, Rebus hadn't noticed the other figure who, like him, was making his way towards the tree. Dressed in jeans, tartan shirt and lumber jacket, but with the same wooden cross. It was Father Byrne. Sky-blue eyes, piercing eyes, the pupils like tiny points of ink. The smile spreading from the lips and mouth towards the eyes and cheeks. The man's very beard seemed to take part in the process.

'I don't know about cheerful, Father Byrne—'

'Please, call me Steven.'

'Well, as I was saying, I don't know about cheerful. You know there was a murder last night?'

Now the eyes opened wide. 'A murder? Here?'

'Well, not strictly speaking, no. But the body was dumped here. We'll need to talk to anyone who was here yesterday. They may have seen something.'

Holmes waved a notebook. 'I've already collected some names and addresses.'

'Good lad. Have there been any more threats, Father?'

'Threats?'

'You remember, the man with the knife.'

'No, not that I know of.'

'Well, I really would like you to come down to the station and see if you can pick him out from some photographs.'

'Now?'

'Sometime today.' Rebus paused. 'At your convenience.'

Father Byrne caught the meaning of the pause. 'Well, of course. If you think it will help. I'll come this morning. But you don't think ...? Surely not.'

Rebus shrugged. 'Probably just a coincidence, Father. But you have to admit, it *is* quite a coincidence. Someone comes down here with a knife. Some days later, a body appears not three hundred yards away. Yes, coincidence.' That pause again. 'Wouldn't you say?'

But Father Byrne didn't seem to have an answer for that.

No, it was no coincidence, Rebus was sure of that. Fine, if you were going to dump a body the Hermitage was as good a spot as any. But not in a clearing, where it would be stumbled upon sooner rather than later. And not so close to the famous tree, where, as everyone knew, people were to be found round-the-clock, making dumping a body nearby a risky procedure. Too risky. There had to be a reason. There had to be some meaning. Some message.

Yes, some *message*.

And wasn't three hundred yards a long way to go for number twos? Well, that one was cleared up quickly. The man admitted that he hadn't gone off alone. He'd gone with his girlfriend. After finding the body, the man had sent her home. Partly because she was in shock; partly to avoid any 'slur on her character'. Father Byrne passed this news on to Rebus when he came to the station to look through the mug-shots – without success.

A new sort of tourist now visited the Hermitage, to view a new kind of 'shrine'. They wanted to see the spot where the trunk had been discovered. Locals still brought their dogs, and lovers still followed the route of the burn; but they wore fixed looks on their faces, as though unwilling to accept that the Hermitage, *their* Hermitage, had become something else, something they never believed it could be.

Rebus, meantime, played with a jigsaw. The tattoo was coming together, though it was a slow business. Errors were made. And one error, once made, led to more pieces being placed incorrectly, until the whole thing had to be broken up and started again. Blue was the predominant colour, along with some patches of red. The dark, inked lines tended to be straight. It looked like a professional job. Tattoo parlours were visited, but the description given was too vague as yet. Rebus showed yet another configuration of the pieces to Brian Holmes: it was the fifth such photograph in a week. The lab had provided their own dotted outline of how they thought the design might continue. Holmes nodded.

'It's a Kandinsky,' he said. 'Or one of his followers. Solid bars of colour. Yes, definitely a Kandinsky.'

Rebus was amazed. 'You mean Kandinsky did this tattoo?'

Holmes looked up from the photograph, grinned sheepishly. 'Sorry, I was making a joke. Or trying to. Kandinsky was a painter.'

'Oh,' Rebus sounded disappointed. 'Yes,' he said, 'yes, of course he was. Right.'

Feeling guilty at having raised his superior's hopes, Holmes concentrated all the harder on the photo. 'Could be a swastika,' he offered. 'Those lines ...'

'Yes.' Rebus turned the photograph towards him, then slapped a hand against it. 'No!' Holmes flinched. 'No, Brian, not a swastika ... a Union Jack! It's a bloody Union Jack!'

Once the lab had the design in front of them, it was a straight-forward job of following it in their reconstruction. Not just a Union Jack, though, as they found. A Union Jack with the letters UFF slurred across it, and a machine gun half-hidden behind the letters.

'Ulster Freedom Fighters,' Rebus murmured. 'Right, let's get back to those tattoo parlours.'

A CID officer in Musselburgh came up with the break. A tat-tooist there thought he recognised the design as the work of Tam Finlayson, but Finlayson had retired from the business some years ago, and tracing him was hard work. Rebus even feared for a moment that the man might be dead and buried. He wasn't. He was living with his daughter and son-in-law in Brighton.

A Brighton detective visited the address and telephoned Edinburgh with details. Shown the photograph, Finlayson had flinched, then had taken, as the daughter put it, 'one of his turns'. Pills were administered and finally Finlayson was in a state to talk. But he was scared, there was no doubt of that. Reassured, though, by the information that the tattoo belonged to a corpse, the tattooist owned up. Yes, it was his work. He'd done it maybe fifteen years before. And the customer? A young man called Philips. Rab Philips. Not a terrorist, just a tearaway looking for a cause.

'Rab Philips?' Rebus stared at his telephone. '*The* Rab Philips?'

Who else? A dim, small-time villain who'd spent enough time in prison, that university of life, to become a clever small-time villain. And who had grown, matured, if you like, into a big-game player. Well, not quite Premier League, but not Sunday kickabout either. He'd certainly been keeping himself to himself these past couple of years. No gossip on the street about him; no dirt; no news at all really.

Well, there was news now. Pubs and clubs were visited, drinks bought, occasionally an arm twisted and the information began to trickle in. Philips's home was searched, his wife questioned. Her story was that he'd told her he was going to London for a few days on a business trip. Rebus nodded calmly and handed her a photograph.

'Is that Rab's tattoo?'

She went pale. Then she went into hysterics.

Meanwhile, Philips's cronies and 'associates' had been rounded up and questioned. One or two were released and picked up again, released and picked up. The message was clear: CID thought they knew more than they were telling and unless they told what they knew, this process would go on indefinitely. They were nervous, of course, and who could blame them? They couldn't know who would now take over their ex-boss's terrain. There were people out there with grudges and knives. The longer they hung about in police stations, the more of a liability they would appear.

They told what they knew, or as much as CID needed to know. That was fine by Rebus. Rab Philips, they said, had started shifting drugs. Nothing serious, mostly cannabis, but in hefty quantities. Edinburgh CID had done much to clear up the hard drug problem in the city, mainly by clearing out the dealers. New dealers would always appear, but they were small-fry. Rab Philips, though, had been so quiet for so long that he was not a suspect. And besides, the drugs were merely passing through Edinburgh; they weren't staying there. Boats would land them on the Fife coast or further north. They would be brought to Edinburgh and from there transferred south. To England. Which meant, in effect, to London. Rebus probed for an Ulster connection, but nobody had anything to tell him.

'So who are the drugs going to in London?'

Again, nobody knew. Or nobody was saying. Rebus sat at his desk, another jigsaw to work on now, but this time in his head – a jigsaw of facts and possibilities. Yes, he should have known from the start. Dismemberment equals gangland. A betrayal, a double-cross. And the penalty for same. Rebus reached for his telephone again and this time put in a call to London.

'Inspector George Flight, please.'

Trust Flight to make it all seem so easy. Rebus gave him the description and an hour later Flight came back with a name. Rebus added some details and Flight went visiting. This time, the phone call came to Rebus's flat. It was late evening and he was lying half-asleep in his chair, the telephone waiting on his lap.

Flight was in good humour. 'I'm glad you told me about the wound,' he said. 'I asked him a few questions, noticed he was a bit stiff. As he stood up to show me out, I slapped him on his right side. I made it seem sort of playful. You know, not malicious like.' He chuckled. 'You should have seen him, John. Doubled over like a bloody pen-knife. It started bleeding again, of course. The silly sod hadn't had it seen to. I wouldn't wonder if it's gone septic or something.'

'When did he get back from Edinburgh?'

'Couple of days ago. Think we can nail him?'

'Maybe. We could do with some evidence though. But I think I can do something about that.'

As Rebus explained to Brian Holmes, it had been more than a 'hunch'. A hunch was, as Dr Curt himself might put it, a stab in the dark. Rebus had a little more light to work by. He told the story as they drove through early-morning Edinburgh towards the Hermitage. The three girls had seen a man appearing from the trees. A wounded man. It seemed clear now that he'd been stabbed in some skirmish nearer to, or by the side of, Braid Hills Road. A switch of drugs from one car to another. An attempted double-cross. He'd been wounded and had fled down the hill into the Hermitage itself, coming into the clearing at the same time as the girls, making himself scarce when he saw them.

Because, of course, he had something to hide: his wound. He had patched himself up, but had stuck around Edinburgh, looking for revenge. Rab Philips had been grabbed, dismembered and his body dumped in the Hermitage as a message to Philips's gang. The message was: you don't mess with London.

Then the wounded villain had finally headed back south. But he was the antithesis of Philips; he wore flashy clothes. 'Probably a white coat,' Rebus had told George Flight. 'White trousers. He's got long hair and a beard.'

Flight had bettered the description. 'It's a white trench-coat,' he'd said. 'And yellow trousers, would you believe. A real old ex-hippy this one.' His name was Shaun McLafferty. 'Everyone on the street knows Shaun,' Flight went on. 'I didn't know he'd started pushing dope though. Mind you, he'd try anything, that one.'

McLafferty. 'He wouldn't,' Rebus asked, 'be Irish by any chance?'

'London Irish,' said Flight. 'I wouldn't be surprised if the IRA was creaming ten per cent off his profits. Maybe more. After all, he either pays up or they take over. It happens.'

Maybe it was as simple as that then. An argument over 'the divide'. An IRA supporter finding himself doing business with a UFF tattoo. The kind of mix old Molotov himself would have appreciated.

'So,' Brian Holmes said, having digested all this, 'Inspector Flight paid a visit to McLafferty?'

Rebus nodded. 'And he was wounded in his right side. Stab wound, according to George.'

'So why,' Holmes said, 'are we here?'

They had parked the car just outside the gates and were now walking into the Hermitage.

'Because,' Rebus said, 'we still lack evidence.'

'What evidence?'

But Rebus wasn't saying; perhaps because he didn't know the answer himself. They were approaching the tree. There was no sign of the once ubiquitous guard, but a familiar figure was kneeling before the tree.

'Morning, Father.'

Father Byrne looked up. 'Good morning, Inspector. You too, Constable.'

Rebus looked around him. 'All alone?'

Byrne nodded. 'Enthusiasm seems to have waned, Inspector. No more megaphones, or coach parties, or cameras.'

'You sound relieved.'

'Believe me, I am.' Father Byrne held out his arms. 'I much prefer it like this, don't you?'

Rebus was obliged to nod his agreement. 'Anyway,' he said, 'we think we can explain what the girls saw.'

Father Byrne merely shrugged.

'No more guard-duties?' Rebus asked.

'The men stopped bothering us.'

Rebus nodded thoughtfully. His eyes were on the tree. 'It wasn't you they were after, Father. It was the tree. But not for the reason you think. Brian, give me a hand, will you?'

A literal hand. Rebus wanted Holmes to form a stirrup from his hands, so that Rebus could place a foot on them and be hoisted up into the tree. Holmes steadied himself against the tree and complied, not without a silent groan. It was feasible that Rebus weighed a good three and a half stones more than him. Still, ours is not to reason why ... and *heave!*

Rebus scrabbled with his hands, finding knot-holes, moss, but nothing else, nothing hidden. He peered upwards, seeking any fissure in the bark, any cranny. Nothing.

'All right, Brian.'

Gratefully, Holmes lowered Rebus groundwards. 'Anything?'

Rebus shook his head. He was gnawing his bottom lip.

'Are you going to tell me what we're looking for?'

'McLafferty had something else to hide from the girls, something on top of the fact that he'd been stabbed. Let's think.' McLafferty had come through the copse, the undergrowth, had rested for a second against the tree, fled back through the copse.

'Chalk!' Rebus thumped the tree with his fist.

'Pardon?'

'Chalk! That morning I came to check on you. When the cadets got up, their knees had white, powdery chalk on them.'

'Yes?'

'Well look!' Rebus led Holmes into the copse. 'There's no white rock here. No bits of chalky stone. That wasn't bloody chalk.' He fell to his knees and began to burrow furiously, raking his hands through the earth.

The girls' parents had messed up the ground, making the white powder inconspicuous. Enough to mark a trouser-knee, but hardly noticeable otherwise. Certainly, nothing a cadet would bother with. And besides, they'd been looking for something *on* the ground, not below it.

'Ah!' He paused, probed a spot with his fingers, then began to dig around it. 'Look,' he said, 'just the one packet and it's burst. That's what it was. Must have burst when McLafferty was burying it. Better call for forensics, Brian. His blood and his prints will be all over it.'

'Right, sir.' Stunned, Brian Holmes sprinted from the clearing, then stopped and turned back. 'Keys,' he explained. Rebus fished his car-keys from his pocket and tossed them to him. Father Byrne, who had been a spectator throughout, came a little closer.

'Heroin, Father. Either that or cocaine. Bigger profits than cannabis, you see. It all comes down to money in the end. They were doing a deal. McLafferty got himself stabbed. He was holding a packet when it happened. Got away somehow, ran down here before he had time to think. He knew he'd better get rid of the stuff, so he buried it. The men who were bothering you, McLafferty's men, it was *this* they were after. Then they got Rab Philips instead and went home satisfied. If it wasn't for your all-night vigil, they'd've had this stuff too.'

Rebus paused, aware that he couldn't be making much sense to the priest. Father Byrne seemed to read his mind and smiled.

'For a minute there, Inspector,' he said, 'I thought you were speaking in tongues.'

Rebus grinned, too, feeling breathless. With McLafferty's prints on the bag, they would have the evidence they needed. 'Sorry you didn't get your miracle,' he said.

Father Byrne's smile broadened. 'Miracles happen every day, Inspector. I don't need to have them invented for me.'

They turned to watch as Holmes came wandering back towards them. But his eyes were concentrating on an area to the left of them. 'They're on their way,' he said, handing Rebus's keys back to him.

'Fine.'

'Who was that by the way?'

'Who?'

'The other man.' Holmes looked from Rebus to Byrne back to Rebus again. 'The other man,' he repeated. 'The one who was standing here with you. When I was coming back, he was ...' He was pointing now, back towards the gate, then over towards the left of the tree. But his voice died away.

'No, never mind,' he said. 'I thought ... I just, no never mind. I must be—'

'Seeing things?' Father Byrne suggested, his fingers just touching the wooden cross around his neck.

'That's right, yes. Yes, seeing things.'

Ghosts, thought Rebus. Spirits of the wood. Rab Philips maybe, or the Hermitage Witch. My God, those two would have a lot to talk about, wouldn't they?

A Good Hanging

I

It was quite some time since a scaffold had been seen in Parliament Square. Quite some time since Edinburgh had witnessed a hanging, too, though digging deeper into history the sight might have been common enough. Detective Inspector John Rebus recalled hearing some saloon-bar story of how criminals, sentenced to hang, would be given the chance to run the distance of the Royal Mile from Parliament Square to Holyrood, a baying crowd hot on their heels. If the criminal reached the Royal Park before he was caught, he would be allowed to remain there, wandering in safety so long as he did not step outside the boundary of the park itself. True or not, the tale conjured up the wonderful image of rogues and vagabonds trapped within the confines of Arthur's Seat, Salisbury Crags and Whinny Hill. Frankly, Rebus would have preferred the noose.

'It's got to be a prank gone wrong, hasn't it?'

A prank. Edinburgh was full of pranks at this time of year. It was Festival time, when young people, theatrical people, flooded into the city with their enthusiasm and their energy. You couldn't walk ten paces without someone pressing a handbill upon you or begging you to visit their production. These were the 'Fringe lunatics' as Rebus had not very originally, but to his own satisfaction, termed them. They came for two or three or four weeks, mostly from London and they squeezed into damp sleeping-bags on bedsit floors throughout the city, going home much paler, much more tired and almost always the poorer. It was not unusual for the unlucky Fringe shows, those given a venue on the outskirts, those with no review to boast of, starved of publicity and inspiration, for those unfortunate shows to play to single-figure audiences, if not to an audience of a single figure.

Rebus didn't like Festival time. The streets became clogged, there seemed a despair about all the artistic fervour and, of course, the crime rate rose. Pickpockets loved the festival. Burglars found easy pickings in the overpopulated, underprotected bedsits. And, finding their local pub taken over by the 'Sassenachs', the natives were inclined to throw the occasional punch or bottle or chair. Which was why Rebus avoided the city centre during the Festival, skirting around it in his car, using alleyways and half-forgotten routes. Which was why he was so annoyed at having been called here today, to Parliament Square, the heart of the Fringe, to witness a hanging.

'Got to be a prank,' he repeated to Detective Constable Brian Holmes. The two men were standing in front of a scaffold, upon which hung the gently swaying body of a young man. The body swayed due to the fresh breeze which was sweeping up the Royal Mile from the direction of Holyrood Park. Rebus thought of the ghosts of the royal park's inmates. Was the wind of their making? 'A publicity stunt gone wrong,' he mused.

'Apparently not, sir,' Holmes said. He'd been having a few words with the workmen who were trying to erect a curtain of sorts around the spectacle so as to hide it from the view of the hundreds of inquisitive tourists who had gathered noisily outside the police cordon. Holmes now consulted his notebook, while Rebus, hands in pockets, strolled around the scaffold. It was of fairly ramshackle construction, which hadn't stopped it doing its job.

'The body was discovered at four-fifty this morning. We don't think it had been here long. A patrol car passed this way at around four and they didn't see anything.'

'That doesn't mean much,' Rebus interrupted in a mutter.

Holmes ignored the remark. 'The deceased belonged to a Fringe group called Ample Reading Time. They come from the University of Reading, thus the name.'

'It also makes the acronym ART,' Rebus commented.

'Yes, sir,' said Holmes. His tone told the senior officer that Holmes had already worked this out for himself. Rebus wriggled a little, as though trying to keep warm. In fact, he had a summer cold.

'How did we discover his identity?' They were in front of the hanging man now, standing only four or so feet below him. Early twenties, Rebus surmised. A shock of black curly hair.

'The scaffold has a venue number pinned to it,' Holmes was saying. 'A student hall of residence just up the road.'

'And that's where the ART show's playing?'

'Yes, sir.' Holmes consulted the bulky Fringe programme which he had been holding behind his notebook. 'It's a play of sorts called "Scenes from a Hanging".' The two men exchanged a look at this.

'The blurb,' Holmes continued, consulting the company's entry near the front of the programme, 'promises "thrills, spills and a live hanging on stage".'

'A live hanging, eh? Well, you can't say they didn't deliver. So, he takes the scaffold from the venue, wheels it out here – I notice it's on wheels, presumably to make it easier to trundle on and off the stage – and in the middle of the night he hangs himself, without anyone hearing anything or seeing anything.' Rebus sounded sceptical.

'Well,' said Holmes, 'be honest, sir.' He was pointing towards and beyond the crowd of onlookers. 'Does anything look suspicious in Edinburgh at this time of year?'

Rebus followed the direction of the finger and saw that a twelve-foot-high man was enjoying a grandstand view of the spectacle, while somewhere to his right someone was juggling three saucepans high into the air. The stilt-man walked towards the pans, grabbed one from mid-air and set it on his head, waving down to the crowd before moving off. Rebus sighed.

'I suppose you're right, Brian. Just this once you may be right.'

A young DC approached, holding a folded piece of paper towards them. 'We found this in his trousers back-pocket.'

'Ah,' said Rebus, 'the suicide note.' He plucked the sheet from the DC's outstretched hand and read it aloud.

'"Pity it wasn't *Twelfth Night*".'

Holmes peered at the line of type. 'Is that it?'

'Short but sweet,' said Rebus. '*Twelfth Night*. A play by Shakespeare and the end of the Christmas season. I wonder which one he means?' Rebus refolded the note and slipped it into his pocket. 'But is it a suicide note or not? It could just be a bog-standard note, a reminder or whatever, couldn't it? I still think this is a stunt gone wrong.' He paused to cough. He was standing beside the cobblestone inset of the Heart of Midlothian, and like many a Scot before him, he spat for luck into the centre of the heart-shaped stones. Holmes looked away and found himself gazing into the dead man's dulled eyes. He turned back as Rebus was fumbling with a handkerchief.

'Maybe,' Rebus was saying between blows, 'we should have a word with the rest of the cast. I don't suppose they'll have much to keep them occupied.' He gestured towards the scaffold. 'Not until they get back their prop. Besides, we've got a job to do, haven't we?'

II

'Well, I say we keep going!' the voice yelled. 'We've got an important piece of work here, a play people should *see*. If anything, David's death will bring audiences *in*. We shouldn't be pushing them away. We shouldn't be packing our bags and crawling back south.'

'You sick bastard.'

Rebus and Holmes entered the makeshift auditorium as the speaker of these last three words threw himself forwards and landed a solid punch against the side of the speech-maker's face. His glasses flew from his nose and slid along the floor, stopping an inch or two short of Rebus's scuffed leather shoes. He stooped, picked up the spectacles and moved forward.

The room was of a size, and had an atmosphere, that would have suited a monastery's dining-hall. It was long and narrow, with a stage constructed along its narrow face and short rows of chairs extending back into the gloom. What windows there were had been blacked-out and the hall's only natural light came from the open door through which Rebus had just stepped, to the front left of the stage itself.

There were five of them in the room, four men and a woman. All looked to be in their mid- to late-twenties. Rebus handed over the glasses.

'Not a bad right-hook that,' he said to the attacker, who was looking with some amazement at his own hand, as though hardly believing it capable of such an action. 'I'm Inspector Rebus, this is Detective Constable Holmes. And you are?'

They introduced themselves in turn. Sitting on the stage was Pam, who acted. Beside her was Peter Collins, who also acted. On a chair in front of the stage, legs and arms crossed and having obviously enjoyed tremendously the one-sided bout he had just witnessed, sat Marty Jones.

'I don't act,' he said loudly. 'I just design the set, build the bloody thing, make all the props and work the lights and the music during the play.'

'So it's your scaffold then?' commented Rebus. Marty Jones looked less confident.

'Yes,' he said. 'I made it a bit too bloody well, didn't I?'

'We could just as easily blame the rope manufacturer, Mr Jones,' Rebus said quietly. His eyes moved to the man with the spectacles, who was nursing a bruised jaw.

'Charles Collins,' the man said sulkily. He looked towards where Peter Collins sat on the stage. 'No relation. I'm the director. I also wrote "Scenes from a Hanging".'

Rebus nodded. 'How have the reviews been?'

Marty Jones snorted.

'Not great,' Charles Collins admitted. 'We've only had four,' he went on, knowing if he didn't say it someone else would. 'They weren't exactly complimentary.'

Marty Jones snorted again. Stiffening his chin, as though to take another punch, Collins ignored him.

'And the audiences?' Rebus asked, interested.

'Lousy.' This from Pam, swinging her legs in front of her as though such news was not only quite acceptable, but somehow humorous as well.

'Average, I'd say,' Charles Collins corrected. 'Going by what other companies have been telling me.'

'That's the problem with staging a new play, isn't it?' Rebus said knowledgeably, while Holmes stared at him. Rebus was standing in the midst of the group now, as though giving them a preproduction pep talk. 'Trying to get audiences to watch new work is always a problem. They prefer the classics.'

'That's right,' Charles Collins agreed enthusiastically. 'That's what I've been telling—' with a general nod in everyone's direction, 'them. The classics are "safe". That's why we need to challenge people.'

'To excite them,' Rebus continued, 'to shock them even. Isn't that right, Mr Collins? To give them a spectacle?'

Charles Collins seemed to see where Rebus's line, devious though it was, was leading. He shook his head.

'Well, they got a spectacle all right,' Rebus went on, all enthusiasm gone from his voice. 'Thanks to Mr Jones's scaffold, the people got a shock. Someone was hanged. I think his name's David, isn't it?'

'That's right.' This from the attacker. 'David Caulfield.' He looked towards the writer/director. 'Supposedly a friend of ours. Someone we've known for three years. Someone we never thought could ...'

'And you are?' Rebus was brisk. He didn't want anyone breaking down just yet, not while there were still questions that needed answers.

'Hugh Clay.' The young man smiled bitterly. 'David always said it sounded like "ukulele".'

'And you're an actor?'

Hugh Clay nodded.

'And so was David Caulfield?'

Another nod. 'I mean, we're not really professionals. We're students. That's all. Students with pretensions.'

Something about Hugh Clay's voice, its tone and its slow rhythms, had made the room darken, so that everyone seemed less animated, more reflective, remembering at last that David Caulfield was truly dead.

'And what do you think happened to him, Hugh? I mean, how do you think he died?'

Clay seemed puzzled by the question. 'He killed himself, didn't he?'

'Did he?' Rebus shrugged. 'We don't know for certain. The pathologist's report may give us a better idea.' Rebus turned to Marty Jones, who was looking less confident all the time. 'Mr Jones, could David have operated the scaffold by himself?'

'That's the way I designed it,' Jones replied. 'I mean, David worked it himself every night. During the hanging scene.'

Rebus pondered this. 'And could someone else have worked the mechanism?'

Jones nodded. 'No problem. The neck noose we used was a dummy. The real noose was attached around David's chest, under his arms. He held a cord behind him and at the right moment he pulled the cord, the trapdoor opened and he fell about a yard. It looked pretty bloody realistic. He had to wear padding under his arms to stop bruising.' He glanced at Charles Collins. 'It was the best bit of the show.'

'But,' said Rebus, 'the scaffold could easily be rejigged to work properly?'

Jones nodded. 'All you'd need is a bit of rope. There's plenty lying around backstage.'

'And then you could hang yourself? Really hang yourself?'

Jones nodded again.

'Or someone could hang you,' said Pam, her eyes wide, voice soft with horror.

Rebus smiled towards her, but seemed to be thinking about something else. In fact, he wasn't thinking of anything in particular: he was letting them stew in the silence, letting their minds and imaginations work in whatever way they would.

At last, he turned to Charles Collins. 'Do you think David killed himself?'

Collins shrugged. 'What else?'

'Any particular reason why he would commit suicide?'

'Well,' Collins looked towards the rest of the company. 'The show,' he said. 'The reviews weren't very complimentary about David's performance.'

'Tell me a little about the play.'

Collins tried not to sound keen as he spoke. Tried, Rebus noticed, but failed. 'It took me most of this year to write,' he said. 'What we have is a prisoner in a South American country, tried and found guilty, sentenced to death. The play opens with him standing on the scaffold, the noose around his neck. Scenes from his life are played out around him, while his own scenes are made up of soliloquies dealing with the larger questions. What I'm asking the audience to do is to ask themselves the same questions he's asking himself on the scaffold. Only the answers are perhaps more urgent, more important for him, because they're the last things he'll ever know.'

Rebus broke in. The whole thing sounded dreadful. 'And David would be on stage the entire time?' Collins nodded. 'And how long was that?'

'Anywhere between two hours and two and a half—' with a glance towards the stage, 'depending on the cast.'

'Meaning?'

'Sometimes lines were forgotten, or a scene went missing.' (Peter and Pam smiled in shared complicity.) 'Or the pace just went.'

'"Never have I prayed so ardently for a death to take place", as one of the reviews put it,' Hugh Clay supplied. 'It was a problem of the play. It didn't have anything to do with David.'

Charles Collins looked ready to protest. Rebus stepped in. 'But David's mentions weren't exactly kind?' he hinted.

'No,' Clay admitted. 'They said he lacked the necessary *gravitas* whatever that means.'

'"Too big a part for too small an actor",' interrupted Marty Jones, quoting again.

'Bad notices then,' said Rebus. 'And David Caulfield took them to heart?'

'David took everything to heart,' explained Hugh Clay. 'That was part of the problem.'

'The other part being that the notices were true,' sniped Charles Collins. But Clay seemed prepared for this.

'"Overwritten and messily directed by Charles Collins",' he quoted. Another fight seemed to be on the cards. Rebus blew his nose noisily.

'So,' he said. 'Notices were bad, audiences were poor. And you didn't decide to remedy this situation by staging a little publicity stunt? A stunt that just happened – nobody's fault necessarily – to go wrong?'

There were shakes of the head, eyes looked to other eyes, seemingly innocent of any such plans.

'Besides,' said Marty Jones, 'you couldn't hang yourself accidentally on that scaffold. You either had to mean to do it yourself, or else someone had to do it for you.'

More silence. An impasse seemed to have been reached. Rebus collapsed noisily into a chair. 'All things considered,' he said with a sigh, 'you might have been better off sticking to *Twelfth Night*.'

'That's funny,' Pam said.

'What is?'

'That's the play we did last year,' she explained. 'It went down very well, didn't it?' She had turned to Peter Collins, who nodded agreement.

'We got some good reviews for that,' he said. 'David was a brilliant Malvolio. He kept the cuttings pinned to his bedroom wall, didn't he, Hugh?'

Hugh Clay nodded. Rebus had the distinct feeling that Peter Collins was trying to imply something, perhaps that Hugh Clay had seen more of David Caulfield's bedroom walls than was strictly necessary.

He fumbled in his pocket, extracting the note from below the handkerchief. Brian Holmes, he noticed, was staying very much in the wings, like the minor character in a minor scene. 'We found a note in David's pocket,' Rebus said without preamble. 'Maybe your success last year explains it.' He read it out to them. Charles Collins nodded.

'Yes, that sounds like David all right. Harking back to past glories.'

'You think that's what it means?' Rebus asked conversationally.

Collins nodded. 'You should know, Inspector, that actors are conceited. The greater the actor, the greater the ego. And David was, I admit, on occasion a very gifted actor.' He was speechifying again, but Rebus let him go on. Perhaps it was the only way a director could communicate with his cast.

'It would be just like David to get depressed, suicidal even, by bad notices, and just like him to decide to stage as showy an exit as he could, something to hit the headlines. I happen to think he succeeded splendidly.'

No one seemed about to contradict him on this, not even David Caulfield's stalwart defender, Hugh Clay. It was Pam who spoke, tears in her eyes at last.

'I only feel sorry for Marie,' she said.

Charles Collins nodded. 'Yes, Marie's come into her own in "Scenes from a Hanging".'

'She means,' Hugh Clay said through gritted teeth, 'she feels sorry for Marie because Marie's lost David, not because Marie can no longer act in your bloody awful play.'

Rebus felt momentary bemusement, but tried not to show it. Marty Jones, however, had seen all.

'The other member of ART,' he explained to Rebus. 'She's back at the flat. She wanted to be left on her own for a bit.'

'She's pretty upset,' Peter Collins agreed.

Rebus nodded slowly. 'She and David were ...?'

'Engaged,' Pam said, the tears falling now, Peter Collins's arm snaking around her shoulders. 'They were going to be married after the Fringe was finished.'

Rebus stole a glance towards Holmes, who raised his eyebrows in reply. Just like every good melodrama, the raised eyebrows said. A twist at the end of every bloody act.

III

The flat the group had rented, at what seemed to Rebus considerable expense, was a dowdy but spacious second-floor affair on Morrison Street, just off Lothian Road. Rebus had been to the block before, during the investigation of a housebreaking. That had been years ago, but the only difference in the tenement seemed to be the installation of a communal intercom at the main door. Rebus ignored the entry-phone and pushed at the heavy outside door. As he had guessed, it was unlocked anyway.

'Bloody students,' had been one of Rebus's few voiced comments during the short, curving drive down the back of the Castle towards the Usher Hall and Lothian Road. But then Holmes, driving, had been a student, too, hadn't he? So Rebus had not expanded on his theme. Now they climbed the steep winding stairwell until they arrived at the second floor. Marty Jones had told them that the name on the door was BLACK. Having robbed the students of an unreasonable rent (though no doubt the going rate), Mr and Mrs Black had departed for a month-long holiday on the proceeds. Rebus had borrowed a key from Jones and used it to let Holmes and himself in. The hall was long, narrow and darker than the stairwell. Off it were three bedrooms, a bathroom, a kitchen and the living-room. A young woman, not quite out of her teens, came out of the kitchen carrying a mug of coffee. She was wearing a long baggy T-shirt and nothing else, and there was a sleepy, tousled look to her, accompanying the red streakiness of her eyes.

'Oh,' she said, startled. Rebus was quick to respond.

'Inspector Rebus, miss. This is Detective Constable Holmes. One of your friends lent us a key. Could we have a word?'

'About David?' Her eyes were huge, doe-like, her face small and round. Her hair was short and fair, the body slender and brittle. Even in grief – perhaps especially in grief – she was mightily attractive, and Holmes raised his eyebrows again as she led them into the living-room.

Two sleeping bags lay on the floor, along with paperback books, an alarm clock, mugs of tea. Off the living-room was a box-room, a large walk-in cupboard. These were often used by students to make an extra room in a temporary flat and light coming from the half-open door told Rebus that this was still its function. Marie went into the room and switched off the light, before joining the two policemen.

'It's Pam's room,' she explained. 'She said I could lie down there. I didn't want to sleep in our ... in my room.'

'Of course,' Rebus said, all understanding and sympathy.

'Of course,' Holmes repeated. She signalled for them to sit, so they did, sinking into a sofa the consistency of marshmallow. Rebus feared he wouldn't be able to rise again without help and struggled to keep himself upright. Marie meantime had settled, legs beneath her, with enviable poise on the room's only chair. She placed her mug on the floor, then had a thought.

'Would you like ...?'

A shake of the head from both men. It struck Rebus that there was something about her voice. Holmes beat him to it.

'Are you French?'

She smiled a pale smile, then nodded towards the Detective Constable. 'From Bordeaux. Do you know it?'

'Only by the reputation of its wine.'

Rebus blew his nose again, though pulling the hankie from his pocket had been a struggle. Holmes took the hint and closed his mouth. 'Now then, Miss ...?' Rebus began.

'Hivert, Marie Hivert.'

Rebus nodded slowly, playing with the hankie rather than trying to replace it in his pocket. 'We're told that you were engaged to Mr Caulfield.'

Her voice was almost a whisper. 'Yes. Not officially, you understand. But there was – a promise.'

'I see. And when was this promise made?'

'Oh, I'm not sure exactly. March, April. Yes, early April I think. Springtime.'

'And how were things between David and yourself?' She seemed not quite to understand. 'I mean,' said Rebus, 'how did David seem to you?'

She shrugged. 'David was David. He could be—' she raised her eyes to the ceiling, seeking words, 'impossible, nervous, exciting, foul-tempered.' She smiled. 'But mostly exciting.'

'Not suicidal?'

She gave this serious thought. 'Oh yes, I suppose,' she admitted. 'Suicidal, just as actors can be. He took criticism to heart. He was a perfectionist.'

'How long had you known him?'

'Two years. I met him through the theatre group.'

'And you fell in love?'

She smiled again. 'Not at first. There was a certain … competitiveness between us, you might say. It helped our acting. I'm not sure it helped our relationship altogether. But we survived.' Realising what she had said, she grew silent, her eyes dimming. A hand went to her forehead as, head bowed, she tried to collect herself.

'I'm sorry,' she said, collapsing into sobs. Holmes raised his eyebrows: someone should be here with her. Rebus shrugged back: she can handle it on her own. Holmes's eyebrows remained raised: can she? Rebus looked back at the tiny figure, engulfed by the armchair. Could actors always tell the real world from the illusory?

We survived. It was an interesting phrase to have used. But then she was an interesting young woman.

She went to the bathroom to splash water on her face and while she was gone Rebus took the opportunity to rise awkwardly to his feet. He looked back at the sofa.

'Bloody thing,' he said. Holmes just smiled.

When she returned, composed once more, Rebus asked if David Caulfield might have left a note somewhere. She shrugged. He asked if she minded them having a quick look round. She shook her head. So, never men to refuse a gift, Rebus and Holmes began looking.

The set-up was fairly straightforward. Pam slept in the box-room, while Marty Jones and Hugh Clay had sleeping-bags on the living-room floor. Marie and David Caulfield had shared the largest of the three bedrooms, with Charles and Peter Collins having a single room each. Charles Collins's room was obsessively tidy, its narrow single bed made up for the night and on the quilt an acting-copy of 'Scenes from a Hanging', covered in marginalia and with several long speeches, all Caulfield's, seemingly excised. A pencil lay on the typescript, evidence that Charles Collins was taking the critics' view to heart himself and attempting to shorten the play as best he could.

Peter Collins's room was much more to Rebus's personal taste, though Holmes wrinkled his nose at the used underwear underfoot, the contents of the hastily unpacked rucksack scattered over every surface. Beside the unmade bed, next to an overflowing ashtray, lay another copy of the play. Rebus flipped through it. Closing it, his attention was caught by some doodlings on the inside cover. Crude heart shapes had been constructed around the words 'I love Edinburgh'. His smile was quickly erased when Holmes held the ashtray towards him.

'Not exactly Silk Cut,' Holmes was saying. Rebus looked. The butts in the ashtrays were made up of cigarette papers wrapped around curled strips of cardboard. They were called 'roaches' by those who smoked dope, though he couldn't remember why. He made a tutting sound.

'And what were we doing in here when we found these?' he asked. Holmes nodded, knowing the truth: they probably couldn't charge Peter Collins even if they'd wanted to, since there was no reason for their being in his room. *We were looking for someone else's suicide note* probably wouldn't impress a latter-day jury.

The double room shared by Marie Hivert and David Caulfield was messiest of all. Marie helped them sift through a few of Caulfield's things. His diary proved a dead end, since he had started it faithfully on 1st January but the entries ceased on 8th January. Rebus, having tried keeping a diary himself, knew the feeling.

But in the back of the diary were newspaper clippings, detailing Caulfield's triumph in the previous year's *Twelfth Night*. Marie, too, had come in for some praise as Viola, but the glory had been Malvolio's. She wept again a little as she read through the reviews. Holmes said that he'd make another cup of coffee. Did he want her to fetch Pam from the theatre? She shook her head. She'd be all right. She promised she would.

While Marie sat on the bed and Holmes filled the kettle, Rebus wandered back into the living-room. He peered into the box-room, but saw little there to interest him. Finally, he came back to the sleeping-bags on the floor. Marie was coming back into the room as he bent to pick up the paperback book from beside one sleeping-bag. It was Tom Wolfe's *Bonfire of the Vanities*. Rebus had a hardback copy at home, still unopened. Something fell from the back of the book, a piece of card. Rebus retrieved it from the floor. It was a photograph of Marie, standing on the Castle ramparts with the Scott

Monument behind her. The wind blew her hair fiercely against her face and she was attempting to sweep the hair out of her eyes as she grinned towards the camera. Rebus handed the picture to her.

'Your hair was longer then,' he said.

She smiled and nodded, her eyes still moist. 'Yes,' she said. 'That was in June. We came to look at the venue.'

He waved the book at her. 'Who's the Tom Wolfe fan?'

'Oh,' she said, 'it's doing the rounds. I think Marty's reading it just now.' Rebus flipped through the book again, his eyes lingering a moment on the inside cover. 'Tom Wolfe's had quite a career,' he said before placing the book, face down as it had been, beside the sleeping-bag. He pointed towards the photograph. 'Shall I put it back?' But she shook her head.

'It was David's,' she said. 'I think I'd like to keep it.'

Rebus smiled an avuncular smile. 'Of course,' he said. Then he remembered something. 'David's parents. Have you been in touch at all?'

She shook her head, horror growing within her. 'Oh God,' she said, 'they'll be devastated. David was very close to his mother and father.'

'Well,' said Rebus, 'give me the details and I'll phone them when I get back to the station.'

She frowned. 'But I don't ... No, sorry,' she said, 'all I know is that they live in Croydon.'

'Well, never mind,' said Rebus, knowing, in fact, that the parents had already been notified, but interested that Caulfield's apparent fiancée should know their address only vaguely. If David Caulfield had been so close to his mother and father, wouldn't they have been told of the engagement? And once told, wouldn't they have wanted to meet Marie? Rebus's knowledge of English geography wasn't exactly Mastermind material, but he was fairly sure that Reading and Croydon weren't at what you would call opposite ends of the country.

Interesting, all very interesting. Holmes came in carrying three mugs of coffee, but Rebus shook his head, suddenly the brisk senior officer.

'No time for that, Holmes,' he said. 'There's plenty of work waiting for us back at the station.' Then, to Marie: 'Take care of yourself, Miss Hivert. If there's anything we can do, don't hesitate.'

Her smile was winning. 'Thank you, Inspector.' She turned to Holmes, taking a mug from him. 'And thank you, too, constable,' she said. The look on Holmes's face kept Rebus grinning all the way back to the station.

IV

There the grin promptly vanished. There was a message marked URGENT from the police pathologist asking Rebus to call him. Rebus pressed the seven digits on his new-fangled telephone. The thing had a twenty-number memory and somewhere in that memory was the single-digit number that would connect him with the pathologist, but Rebus could never remember which number was which and he kept losing the sheet of paper with all the memory numbers on it.

'It's four,' Holmes reminded him, just as he'd come to the end of dialling. He was throwing Holmes a kind of half-scowl when the pathologist himself answered.

'Oh, yes, Rebus. Hello there. It's about this hanging victim of yours. I've had a look at him. Manual strangulation, I'd say.'

'Yes?' Rebus, his thoughts on Marie Hivert, was waiting for some punch-line.

'I don't think you understand me, Inspector. *Manual* strangulation. From the Latin *manus*, meaning the hand. From the deep body temperature, I'd say he died between midnight and two in the morning. He was strung up on that contraption some time thereafter. Bruising around the throat is definitely consistent with thumb-pressure especially.'

'You mean someone strangled him?' Rebus said, really for Holmes's benefit.

'I *think* that's what I've been telling you, yes. If I find out anything more, I'll let you know.'

'Are the forensics people with you?'

'I've contacted the lab. They're sending someone over with some bags, but to be honest, we started off on this one thinking it was simple suicide. We may have inadvertently destroyed the tinier scraps of evidence.'

'Not to worry,' Rebus said, a father-confessor now, easing guilt. 'Just get what you can.'

He put down the receiver and stared at his Detective Constable. Or, rather, stared *through* him. Holmes knew that there were times for talking and times for silence, and that this fell into the latter category. It took Rebus a full minute to snap out of his reverie.

'Well I'll be buggered,' he said. 'We've been talking with a murderer this morning, Brian. A cold-blooded one at that. And we didn't even know it. I wonder whatever happened to the famous police "nose" for a villain. Any idea?'

Holmes frowned. 'About what happened to the famous police "nose"?'

'No,' cried Rebus, exasperated. 'I mean, any idea who did it?'

Holmes shrugged, then brought the Fringe programme back out from where it had been rolled up in his jacket pocket. He started turning pages. 'I think,' he said, 'there's an Agatha Christie playing somewhere. Maybe we could get a few ideas?'

Rebus's eyes lit up. He snatched the programme from Holmes's hands. 'Never mind Agatha Christie,' he said, starting through the programme himself. 'What we want is Shakespeare.'

'What, *Macbeth*? *Hamlet*? *King Lear*?'

'No, not a tragedy, a good comedy, something to cheer the soul. Ah, here we go.' He stabbed the open page with his finger. '*Twelfth Night*. That's the play for us, Brian. That's the very play for us.'

The problem, really, in the end was: which *Twelfth Night*? There were three on offer, plus another at the Festival proper. One of the Fringe versions offered an update to gangster Chicago, another played with an all-female cast and the third boasted futuristic stage-design. But Rebus wanted traditional fare, and so opted for the Festival performance. There was just one hitch: it was a complete sell-out.

Not that Rebus considered this a hitch. He waited while Holmes called his girlfriend, Nell Stapleton, and apologised to her about some evening engagement he was breaking, then the two men drove to the Lyceum, tucked in behind the Usher Hall so as to be almost invisible to the naked eye.

'There's a five o'clock performance,' Rebus explained. 'We should just make it.' They did. There was a slight hold-up while Rebus explained to the house manager that this really was police business and not some last-minute culture beano, and a place was found for them in a dusty corner to the rear of the stalls. The lights were dimming as they entered.

'I haven't been to a play in years,' Rebus said to Holmes, excited at the prospect. Holmes, bemused, smiled back, but his superior's eyes were already on the stage, where the curtain was rising, a guitar was playing and a man in pale pink tights lay across an ornate bench, looking as cheesed off with life as Holmes himself felt. Why did Rebus always have to work from instinct, and always alone, never letting anyone in on whatever he knew or thought he knew? Was it because he was afraid of failure? Holmes suspected it was. If you kept your ideas to yourself, you couldn't be proved wrong. Well, Holmes had his own ideas about this case, though he was damned if he'd let Rebus in on them.

'If music be the food of love ...' came the voice from the stage. And that was another thing – Holmes was starving. It was odds-on the back few rows would soon find his growling stomach competition for the noises from the stage.

'Will you go hunt, my lord?'

'What, Curio?'

'The hart.'

'Why, so I do, the noblest that I have ...'

Holmes sneaked a glance towards Rebus. To say the older man's attention was rapt would have been understating the case. He'd give it until the end of Act One, then sneak out to the nearest chip shop. Leave Rebus to his Shakespeare; Holmes was a nationalist when it came to literature. A pity Hugh MacDiarmid had never written a play.

In fact, Holmes went for a wander, up and down Lothian Road as far as the Caledonian Hotel to the north and Tollcross to the south. Lothian Road was Edinburgh's fast-food centre and the variety on offer brought with it indecision. Pizza, burgers, kebabs, Chinese, baked potatoes, more burgers, more pizza and the once-ubiquitous fish and chip shop (more often now an offshoot of a kebab or burger restaurant). Undecided, he grew hungrier, and stopped for a pint of lager in a noisy barn of a pub before finally settling for a fish supper, naming himself a nationalist in cuisine as well as in writing.

By the time he returned to the theatre, the players were coming out to take their applause. Rebus was clapping as loudly as anyone, enjoyment evident on his face. But when the curtain came down, he turned and dragged Holmes from the auditorium, back into the foyer and out onto the street.

'Fish and chips, eh?' he said. 'Now there's an idea.'

'How did you know?'

'I can smell the vinegar coming off your hands. Where's the chippie?'

Holmes nodded in the direction of Tollcross. They started walking. 'So did you learn anything?' Holmes asked. 'From the play, I mean?'

Rebus smiled. 'More than I'd hoped for, Brian. If you'd been paying attention, you'd have noticed it, too. The only speech that mattered was way back in Act One. A speech made by the Fool, whose name is Feste. I wonder who played Feste in ART's production last year? Actually, I think I can guess. Come on then, where's this chip shop? A man could starve to death on Lothian Road looking for something even remotely edible.'

'It's just off Tollcross. It's nothing very special.'

'So long as it fills me up, Brian. We've got a long evening ahead of us.'

'Oh?'

Rebus nodded vigorously. 'Hunting the heart, Brian.' He winked towards the younger man. 'Hunting the heart.'

V

The door of the Morrison Street flat was opened by Peter Collins. He looked surprised to see them.

'Don't worry, Peter,' Rebus said, pushing past him into the hall. 'We're not here to put the cuffs on you for possession.' He sniffed the air in the hall, then tutted. 'Already? At this rate you'll be stoned before *News at Ten*.'

Peter blushed.

'All right if we come in?' Rebus asked, already sauntering down the hall towards the living-room. Holmes followed him indoors, smiling an apology. Peter closed the door behind them.

'They're mostly out,' Peter called.

'So I see,' said Rebus, in the living-room now. 'Hello, Marie, how are you feeling?'

'Hello again, Inspector. I'm a little better.' She was dressed, and seated primly on the chair, hands resting on her knees. Rebus looked towards the sofa, but thought better of sitting down. Instead he rested himself on the sofa's fairly rigid arm. 'I see you're all getting ready to go.' He nodded towards the two rucksacks parked against the living-room wall. The sleeping-bags from the floor had been folded away, as had books and alarm clocks.

'Why bother to stay?' Peter said. He flopped onto the sofa and pushed a hand through his hair. 'We thought we'd drive down through the night. Be back in Reading by dawn with any luck.'

Rebus nodded at this. 'So the show does *not* go on?'

'It'd be a bit bloody heartless, don't you think?' This from Peter Collins, with a glance towards Marie.

'Of course,' Rebus agreed. Holmes had stationed himself between the living-room door and the rucksacks. 'So where is everyone?'

Marie answered. 'Pam and Marty have gone for a last walk around.'

'And Charles is almost certainly off getting drunk somewhere,' added Collins. 'Rueing his failed show.'

'And Hugh?' asked Rebus. Collins shrugged.

'I think,' Marie said, 'Hugh went off to get drunk, too.'

'But for different reasons, no doubt,' Rebus speculated.

'He was David's best friend,' she answered quietly.

Rebus nodded thoughtfully. 'Actually, we just bumped into him – literally.'

'Who?' asked Peter.

'Mr Clay. He seems to be in the middle of a pub crawl the length of Lothian Road. We were coming out of a chip shop and came across him weaving his way to the next watering-hole.'

'Oh?' Collins didn't sound particularly interested.

'I told him where the best pubs in this neighbourhood are. He didn't seem to know.'

'That was good of you,' Collins said, voice heavy with irony.

'Nice of them all to leave you alone, isn't it though?'

The question hung in the air. At last, Marie spoke. 'What do you mean?'

But Rebus shifted on his perch and left the comment at that. 'No,' he said instead, 'only I thought Mr Clay might have had a better idea of the pubs, seeing how he was here last year, and then again in June to look at the venue. But of course, as he was good enough to explain, he *wasn't* here in June. There were exams. Some people had to study harder than others. Only three of you came to Edinburgh in June.' Rebus raised a finger shiny with chip-fat. 'Pam, who has what I'd call a definite crush on you, Peter.' Collins smiled at this, but weakly. Rebus raised a second and then third finger. 'And you two. Just the three of you. That, I presume, is where it started.'

'What?' The blood had drained from Marie's face, making her somehow more beautiful than ever. Rebus shifted again, seeming to ignore her question.

'It doesn't really matter who took that photo of you, the one I found in *Bonfire of the Vanities*.' He was staring at her quite evenly now. 'What matters is that it was there. And on the inside cover someone had drawn a couple of hearts, very similar to some I happened to see on Peter's copy of the play. It matters that on his copy of the play, Peter has also written the words "I love Edinburgh".' Peter Collins was ready to protest, but Rebus studiously ignored him, keeping his eyes on Marie's, fixing her, so that there might only have been the two of them in the room.

'You told me,' he continued, 'that you'd come to Edinburgh to check on the venue. I took that "you" to mean all of you, but Hugh Clay has put me right on that. You came without David, who was too busy studying to make the trip. And you told me something else earlier. You said your relationship with him had "survived". Survived what? I asked myself afterwards. The answer seems pretty straightforward. Survived a brief fling, a fling that started in Edinburgh and lasted the summer.'

Now, only now, did he turn to Peter Collins. 'Isn't that right, Peter?'

Collins, his face mottled with anger, made to rise.

'Sit down,' Rebus ordered, standing himself. He walked towards the fireplace, turned and faced Collins, who looked to be disappearing into the sofa, reducing in size with the passing moments. 'You love Edinburgh,' he went on, 'because that's where your little fling with Marie started. Fair enough, these things are never anyone's fault, are they? You managed to keep it fairly secret. The Tom Wolfe book belongs to you, though, and that photo you'd kept in it – maybe forgetting it was there – that photo might have been a giveaway, but then again it could all be very innocent, couldn't it?

'But it's hard to keep something like that so secret when you're part of a very small group. There were sixteen of you in ART last year; that might have made it manageable. But not when there were only seven of you. I'm not sure who else knows about it. But I am sure that David Caulfield found out.' Rebus didn't need to turn round to know that Marie was sobbing again. He kept staring at Peter Collins. 'He found out, and last night, late and backstage, perhaps drunk, the two of you had a fight. Quite dramatic in its way, isn't it? Fighting over the heroine and all that. But during the fight you just happened to strangle the life out of David Caulfield.' He paused, waiting for a denial which didn't come.

'Perhaps,' he continued, 'Marie wanted to go to the police. I don't know. But if she did, you persuaded her not to. Instead, you came up with something more dramatic. You'd make it look like suicide. And by God, what a suicide, the kind that David himself might just have attempted.' Rebus had been moving forward without seeming to, so that now he stood directly over Peter Collins.

'Yes,' he went on, 'very dramatic. But the note was a mistake. It was a bit too clever, you see. You thought everyone would take it as a reference to David's success in last year's production, but you knew yourself that there was a double meaning in it. I've just been to see *Twelfth Night*. Bloody good it was, too. You played Feste last year, didn't you, Peter? There's one speech of his ... how does it go?' Rebus seemed to be trying to remember. 'Ah yes: "Many a good hanging prevents a bad marriage." Yes, that's it. And that's when I knew for sure.'

Peter Collins was smiling thinly. He gazed past Rebus towards Marie, his eyes full and liquid. His voice when he spoke was tender. '"Many a good hanging prevents a bad marriage; and for turning away, let summer bear it out."'

'That's right,' Rebus said, nodding eagerly. 'Summer bore it out, all right. A summer fling. That's all. Not worth killing someone for, was it, Peter? But that didn't stop you. And the hanging was so apt, so neat. When you recalled the Fool's quote, you couldn't resist putting that note in David's pocket.' Rebus was shaking his head. 'More fool you, Mr Collins. More fool you.'

Brian Holmes went home from the police station that night in sombre mood. The traffic was slow, too, with theatre-goers threading in and out between the near-stationary cars. He rolled down the driver's-side window, trying to make the interior less stuffy, less choked, and instead let in exhaust fumes and balmy late-evening air. Why did Rebus have to be such a clever bugger so much of the time? He seemed always to go into a case at an odd angle, like someone cutting a paper shape which, apparently random, could then be folded to make an origami sculpture, intricate and recognisable.

'Too clever for his own good,' he said to himself. But what he meant was that his superior was too clever for Holmes's own good. How was he expected to shine, to be noticed, to push forwards towards promotion, when it was always Rebus who, two steps ahead, came up with the answers? He remembered a boy at school who had always beaten Holmes in every subject save History. Yet Holmes had gone to university; the boy to work on his father's farm. Things could change, couldn't they? Though all he seemed to be learning from Rebus was how to keep your thoughts to yourself, how to be devious, how to, well, how to *act*. Though all this were true, he would still be the best understudy he possibly could be. One day, Rebus wouldn't be there to come up with the answers, or – occasion even more to be relished – would be unable to find the answers. And when that time came, Holmes would be ready to take the stage. He felt ready right now, but then he supposed every understudy must feel that way.

A flybill was thrown through his window by a smiling teenage girl. He heard her pass down the line of cars, yelling 'Come and see our show!' as she went. The small yellow sheet of paper fluttered onto the passenger seat and stayed there, face up, to haunt Holmes all the way back to Nell. Growing sombre again, it occurred to him how different things might have been if only Priestley had called the play *A Detective Constable Calls* instead.

Tit for Tat

Before he'd arrived in Edinburgh in 1970, Inspector John Rebus had fixed in his mind an image of tenement life. Tenements were things out of the Gorbals in the early years of the century, places of poverty and despair, safe havens for vermin and disease. They were the enforced homes of the poorest of the working class, a class almost without a class, a sub-class. Though tenements rose high into the air, they might as well have been dug deep into the ground. They were society's replacement for the cave.

Of course, in the 1960s the planners had come up with something even more outrageous – the tower-block. Even cities with plenty of spare land started to construct these space-saving horrors. Perhaps the moral rehabilitation of the tenement had something to do with this new contender. Nowadays, a tenement might contain the whole of society in microcosm – the genteel spinster on the ground floor, the bachelor accountant one floor above, then the barkeeper, and above the barkeeper, always it seemed right at the top of the house, the students. This mix was feasible only because the top two floors contained flats rented out by absentee landlords. Some of these landlords might own upwards of one hundred separate flats – as was spectacularly the case in Glasgow, where the figure was even rumoured, in one or two particulars, to rise into four figures.

But in Edinburgh, things were different. In Edinburgh, the New Town planners of the nineteenth century had come up with streets of fashionable houses, all of them, to Rebus's latter-day eyes, looking like tenements. Some prosperous areas of the city, such as Marchmont where Rebus himself lived, boasted almost nothing *but* tenements. And with the price of housing what it was, even the meaner streets were seeing a kind of renaissance, stone-blasted clean by new owner-occupiers who kept the cooking-range in the living-room as an 'original feature'.

The streets around Easter Road were as good an example as any. The knock-on effect had reached Easter Road late. People had to decide first that they couldn't afford Stockbridge, then that they couldn't quite afford any of the New Town or its immediate surroundings, and at last they might arrive in Easter Road, not by chance but somehow through fate. Soon, an enterprising soul saw his or her opportunity and opened a delicatessen or a slightly upmarket café, much to the bemusement of the 'locals'. These were quiet, accepting people for the most part, people who liked to see the tenement buildings being restored even if they couldn't understand why anyone would pay good money for bottled French water. (After all, you were always told to steer clear of the water on foreign holidays, weren't you?)

Despite this, the occasional Alfa Romeo or Golf GTi might find itself scratched maliciously, as might a too-clean 2CV or a coveted Morris Minor. But arson? Attempted murder? Well, that was a bit more serious. That was a very serious turn of events indeed. The trick was one perfected by racists in mixed areas. You poured petrol through the letter-box of a flat, then you set light to a rag and dropped it through the letter-box, igniting the hall carpet and ensuring that escape from the resulting fire was made difficult if not impossible. Of course, the noise, the smell of petrol meant that usually someone inside the flat was alerted early on, and mostly these fires did not spread. But sometimes ... sometimes.

'His name's John Brodie, sir,' the police constable informed Rebus as they stood in the hospital corridor. 'Age thirty-four. Works for an insurance company in their accounts department.'

None of which came as news to Rebus. He had been to the second-floor flat, just off Easter Road, reeking of soot and water now; an unpleasant clean-up ahead. The fire had spread quickly along the hall. Some jackets and coats hanging from a coat-stand had caught light and sent the flames licking along the walls and ceiling. Brodie, asleep in bed (it all happened around one in the morning) had been wakened by the fire. He'd dialled 999, then had tried putting the fire out himself, with a fair degree of success. A rug from the living-room had proved useful in snuffing out the progress of the fire along the hall and some pans of water had dampened things down. But there was a price to pay – burns to his arms and hands and face, and smoke inhalation. Neighbours, alerted by the smoke, had broken down the door just as the fire engine was arriving. CID, brought to the scene by a police constable's suspicions, had spoken with some of the neighbours. A quiet man, Mr Brodie, they said. A decent man. He'd only moved in a few months before. Worked for an insurance company. Nobody thought he smoked, but they seemed to assume he'd left a cigarette burning somewhere.

'Careless that. Even supposing we *do* live in Auld Reekie.' And the first-floor occupier had chuckled to himself, until his wife yelped from their flat that there was water coming in through the ceiling. The man looked helpless and furious.

'Insurance should cover it,' Rebus commented, pouring oil on troubled ... no, not the best image that. The husband went off to investigate further and the other tenement dwellers began slouching off to bed, leaving Rebus to head into the burnt-out hallway itself.

But even without the Fire Officer, the cause of the fire had been plain to Rebus. Chillingly plain. The smell of petrol was everywhere.

He took a look round the rest of the flat. The kitchen was tiny, but boasted a large sash-window looking down onto back gardens and across to the back of the tenement over the way. The bathroom was smaller still, but kept very neat. No ring of grime around the bath, no strewn towels or underpants, nothing steeping in the sink. A very tidy bachelor was Mr Brodie. The living-room, too, was uncluttered. A series of framed prints more or less covered one wall. Detailed paintings of birds. Rebus glanced at one or two: willow warbler, bearded tit. The rooms would need to be redecorated, of course, otherwise the charred smell would always be there. Insurance would probably cover it. Brodie was an insurance man, wasn't he? He'd know. Maybe he'd even squeeze a cheque out of the company without too much haggling.

Finally, Rebus went into the bedroom. Messier here, mostly as a result of the hurriedly flung-back bedclothes. Pyjama bottoms lying crumpled on the bed itself. Slippers and a used mug sitting on the floor beside the bed, and in one corner, next to the small wardrobe, a tripod atop which was fixed a good make of SLR camera. On the floor against the wall was a large-format book, *Better Zoom Pictures*, with a photograph of an osprey on the front. Probably one of the Loch Garten ospreys, thought Rebus. He'd taken his daughter there a couple of times in the past. Tourists, plenty of them, he had seen, but ospreys were there none.

If anyone had asked him what he thought most odd about the flat, he would have answered: there's no television set. What did Mr Brodie do for company then of an evening?

For no real reason, Rebus bent down and peered beneath the bed itself, and was rewarded with a pile of magazines. He pulled one out. Soft porn, a 'readers' wives' special. He pushed it back into place. The tidy bachelor's required bedtime companion. And, partly, an answer to his earlier question.

He left the flat and sought out one or two of the still wakeful neighbours. No one had seen or heard anything. Access to the tenement itself was easy; you just pushed open the communal front door, the lock of which had broken recently and was waiting to be fixed.

'Any reason,' Rebus asked, 'why anyone would bear Mr Brodie a grudge?'

That gave them pause. No smouldering cigarette then, but arson. But there were shakes of rumpled heads. No reason. A very quiet man. Kept himself to himself. Worked in insurance. Always stopped for a chat if you met him on the stairs. Always cleaned the stairs promptly when his turn came, not like some they could mention. Probably paid his rent promptly, too. Tea was being provided in the kitchen of one of the first-floor flats, where the 'Auld Reekie' wag was being consoled.

'I only painted that ceiling three months back. Do you know how much textured paint costs?'

Soon enough everyone found the answer. The man's wife looked bored. She smiled towards the tea-party's hostess.

'Wasn't that first fireman dishy?' she said.

'Which one?'

'The one with the blue eyes. The one who told us not to worry. He could give me a fireman's lift anytime.'

The hostess snorted into her tea. Rebus made his excuses and left.

Rebus had dealt with racist arson attacks before. He'd even come across 'anti-yuppie' attacks, usually in the form of graffiti on cars or the outside walls of property. A warehouse conversion in Leith had been sprayed with the slogan HOUSES FOR THE NEEDY, NOT THE GREEDY. The attack on Brodie seemed more personal, but it was worth considering all the possible motives. He was crossing things off from a list in his mind as he drove to the hospital. Once there, he talked to the police constable in the corridor and, after nodding his head a few times, he entered the ward where John Brodie had been 'made comfortable'. Despite the hour, Brodie was far from asleep. He was propped up against a pillow, his arms lying out in front of him on top of the sheets. Thick creamy white cotton pads and delicate-looking bandages predominated. Part of his hair had been shaved away, so that burns to the scalp could be treated. He had no eyebrows, and only remnants of eyelashes. His face was round and shiny; easy to imagine it breaking into a chuckle, but probably not tonight.

Rebus picked a chair out from a pile against the far wall and sat down, only then introducing himself.

Brodie's voice was shaky. 'I know who did it.'

'Oh?' Rebus kept his voice low, in deference to the sleeping bodies around him. This was not quite how he'd expected the conversation to begin.

Brodie swallowed. 'I know who did it and I know *why* she did it. But I don't want to press charges.'

Rebus wasn't about to say that this decision was not up to Brodie himself. He didn't want the man clamming up. He wanted jaw-jaw. He nodded as if in agreement. 'Is there anything I can get you?' he said, inviting further confessions, as though from one friend to another.

'She must be a bit cracked,' Brodie went on, as though Rebus hadn't spoken at all. 'I told the police that at the time. She's doolally, I said. Must be. Well, this proves it, doesn't it?'

'You think she needs help?'

'Maybe. Probably.' He seemed deep in thought for a moment. 'Yes, almost certainly. I mean, it's going a bit far, isn't it? Even if you think you've got grounds. But she didn't have grounds. The police *told* her that.'

'But they didn't manage to convince her.'

'That's right.'

Rebus thought he was playing this fairly well. Obviously, Brodie was in shock. Maybe he was even babbling a bit, but as long as he was kept talking, Rebus would be able to piece together whatever the story was that he was trying to tell. There was a wheezy, dry laugh from the bed.

Brodie's eyes twinkled. 'You don't know what I'm talking about, do you?' Rebus was obliged to shake his head. 'Of course you don't. Well, I'll have a sip of water and then I'll tell you.'

And he did.

The morning was bright but grey: 'sunshine and showers', the weatherman would term it. It wasn't quite autumn yet. The too-short summer might yet have some surprises. Rebus waited in his room – his desk located not too far from the radiator – until the two police constables could be found. They were uneasy when they came in, until he reassured them. Yes, as requested, they had brought their notebooks with them. And yes, they remembered the incident very well indeed.

'It started with anonymous phone calls,' one of them began. 'They seemed to be genuine enough. Miss Hooper told us about one of them in particular. Her phone rings. Man on the other end identifies himself as a police inspector and tells her there's an anonymous caller who's going through the Edinburgh directory trying number after number. He says her number might come up soon, but the police have put a trace on her line. So can she keep the man talking for as long as possible.'

'Oh yes.' Really, Rebus didn't need to hear the rest. But he listened patiently to the constable's story.

'Later on that day, a man did ring. He asked her some very personal questions and she kept him talking. Afterwards, she rang the police station to see if they'd caught him. Only, of course, the name the so-called inspector had given wasn't known to the station. It was the anonymous caller himself, setting her up.'

Rebus shook his head slowly. It was old, but clever. 'So she complained about anonymous calls?'

'Yes, sir. But then the calls stopped. So that didn't seem too bad. No need for an operator to intercept or a change of number or anything.'

'How did Miss Hooper seem at the time?'

The constable shrugged and turned to his colleague, who now spoke. 'A bit nervy, sir. But that was understandable, wasn't it? A very nice lady, I'd say. Not married. I don't think she even had a boyfriend.' He turned his head towards his colleague. 'Didn't she say something like that, Jim?'

'I think so, yes.'

'So then what happened?' asked Rebus.

'A few weeks later, this would be just over a week ago, we had another call from Miss Hooper. She said a man in the tenement across the back from her was a peeping Tom. She'd seen him at a window, aiming his binoculars towards her building. More particularly, she thought, towards her own flat. We investigated and spoke to Mr Brodie. He appeared quite concerned about the allegations. He showed us the binoculars and admitted using them to watch from his kitchen window. But he assured us that he was bird-watching.'

The other constable smiled at this. '"Bird-watching," he said.'

'Ornithology,' said Rebus.

'That's right, sir. He said he was very interested in birds, a bird-fancier sort of thing.' Another smile. They were obviously hoping Rebus would come to enjoy the joke with them. They were wrong, though they didn't seem to sense this just yet.

'Go on,' he said simply.

'Well, sir, there did seem to be a lot of pictures of birds in his flat.'

'You mean the prints in the living-room?'

'That's right, sir, pictures of an ornithological nature.'

Now the other constable interrupted. 'You won't believe it, sir. He said he was watching the tenement and the garden because he'd seen some. ...' pause for effect ... 'bearded tits.'

Now both the young constables were grinning.

'I'm glad you find your job so amusing,' Rebus said. 'Because I don't think frightening phone calls, peeping Toms and arson attacks are material for jokes!'

The grins disappeared.

'Get on with it,' Rebus demanded. The constables looked at one another.

'Not much more to tell, sir,' said the one called Jim. 'The gentleman, Mr Brodie, seemed genuine enough. But he promised to be a bit more careful in future. Like I say, he seemed genuinely concerned. We informed Miss Hooper of our findings. She didn't seem entirely convinced.'

'Obviously not,' said Rebus, but he did not go on to clarify. Instead, he dismissed the two officers and sat back in his chair. Brodie suspected Hooper of the arson attack, not, it would appear, without reason. What was more, Brodie had said he couldn't think of any other enemies he might have made. Either that or he wasn't about to tell Rebus about them. Rebus leaned back in his chair and rested his arm along the radiator, enjoying its warmth. The next person to speak to, naturally, was Miss Hooper herself. Another day, another tenement.

'Bearded tits,' Rebus said to himself. This time, he allowed himself a smile.

'It's your lucky day,' Miss Hooper told him. 'Normally I don't come home for lunch, but today I just felt like it.'

Lucky indeed. Rebus had knocked on the door of Miss Hooper's first-floor flat but received no answer. Eventually, another door on the landing had opened, revealing a woman in her late forties, stern of face and form.

'She's not in,' the woman had stated, unnecessarily.

'Any idea when she'll be back?'

'Who are you then?'

'Police.'

The woman pursed her lips. The nameplate above her doorbell, to the left of the door itself, read McKAY. 'She works till four o'clock. She's a schoolteacher. You'll catch her at school if you want her.'

'Thank you. Mrs McKay, is it?'

'It is.'

'Could I have a word?'

'What about?'

By now, Rebus was standing at Mrs McKay's front door. Past her, he caught sight of a dark entrance hall strewn with bits and pieces of machinery, enough to make up most, but not quite all, of a motorbike.

'About Miss Hooper,' he said.

'What about her?'

No, she was not about to let him in. He could hear her television blaring. Lunchtime game-show applause. The resonant voice of the questionmaster. Master of the question.

'Have you known her long?'

'Ever since she moved in. Three, four years. Aye, four years.' She had folded her arms now, and was resting one shoulder against the door-jamb. 'What's the problem?'

'I suppose you must know her quite well, living on the same landing?'

'Well enough. She comes in for a cuppa now and again.' She paused, making it quite clear to Rebus that this was not an honour *he* was about to receive.

'Have you heard about the fire?'

'Fire?'

'Across the back.' Rebus gestured in some vague direction with his head.

'Oh aye. The fire engine woke me right enough. Nobody hurt though, was there?'

'What makes you say that?'

She shuffled now, unfolding her arms so one hand could rub at another. 'Just ... what I heard.'

'A man was injured, quite seriously. He's in hospital.'

'Oh.'

And then the main door opened and closed. Sound of feet on stone echoing upwards.

'Oh, here's Miss Hooper now,' said Mrs McKay. Said with relief, Rebus thought to himself. Said with relief ...

Miss Hooper let him in and immediately switched on the kettle. She hoped he wouldn't mind if she made herself a sandwich? And would he care for one himself? Cheese and pickle or peanut butter and apple? No, on second thoughts, she'd make some of both, and he could choose for himself.

A teacher? Rebus could believe it. There was something in her tone, in the way she seemed to have to utter all of her thoughts aloud, and in the way she asked questions and then answered them herself. He could see her standing in her classroom, asking her questions and surrounded by silence.

Alison Hooper was in her early thirties. Small and slim, almost schoolboyish. Short straight brown hair. Tiny earrings hooked into tiny ears. She taught in a primary school only ten minutes' walk from her flat. The flat itself was scattered with books and magazines, from many of which had been cut illustrations, clearly intended to find their way into her classroom. Mobiles hung from her living-room ceiling: some flying pigs, an alphabet, teddy bears waving from aeroplanes. There were colourful rugs on her walls, but no rugs at all on the stripped floor. She had a breathy, nervous way with her and an endearing twitch to her nose. Rebus followed her into the kitchen and watched her open a loaf of brown sliced bread.

'I usually take a packed lunch with me, but I slept in this morning and didn't have time to make it. I could have eaten in the canteen, of course, but I just felt like coming home. Your lucky day, Inspector.'

'You had trouble sleeping last night then?'

'Well, yes. There was a fire in the tenement across the back.' She pointed through her window with a buttery knife. 'Over there. I heard sirens and the fire-engine's motor kept rumbling away, so I couldn't for the life of me get back to sleep.'

Rebus went across to the window and looked out. John Brodie's tenement stared back at him. It could have been any tenement anywhere in the city. Same configuration of windows and drainpipes, same railing-enclosed drying-green. He angled his head further to look into the back garden of Alison Hooper's tenement. Movement there. What was it? A teenager working on his motorbike. The motorbike standing on the drying-green, and all the tools and bits and pieces lying on a piece of plastic which had been spread out for the purpose. The nearby garden shed stood with its door propped open by a wooden stretcher. Through the doorway Rebus could see yet more motorbike spares and some oil cans.

'The fire last night,' he said, 'it was in a flat occupied by Mr John Brodie.'

'Oh!' she said, her knife-hand pausing above the bread. 'The peeping Tom?' Then she swallowed, not slow on the uptake. 'That's why you're here then.'

'Yes. Mr Brodie gave us your name, Miss Hooper. He thought perhaps—'

'Well, he's right.'

'Oh?'

'I mean, I do have a grudge. I do think he's a pervert. Not that I seem able to convince the police of that.' Her voice was growing shriller. She stared at the slices of bread in a fixed, unblinking way. 'No, the police don't seem to think there's a problem. But I know. I've talked to the other residents. We *all* know.' Then she relaxed, smiled at the bread. She slapped some peanut butter onto one slice. Her voice was calm. 'I do have a grudge, Inspector, but I did not set fire to that man's flat. I'm even pleased that he wasn't injured.'

'Who says he wasn't?'

'What?'

'He's in hospital.'

'Is he? I thought someone said there'd been no—'

'Who said?'

She shrugged. 'I don't know. One of the other teachers. Maybe they'd heard something on the radio. I don't know. Tea or coffee?'

'Whatever you're having.'

She made two mugs of decaffeinated instant. 'Let's go through to the living-room,' she said.

There, she gave him the story of the phone calls, and the story of the man with the binoculars.

'Bird-watching my eye,' she said. 'He was looking into people's windows.'

'Hard to tell, surely.'

She twitched her nose. 'Looking into people's windows,' she repeated.

'Did anyone else see him?'

'He stopped after I complained. But who knows? I mean, it's easy enough to see someone during the day. But at night, in that room of his with the lights turned off. He could sit there all night watching us. Who would know?'

'You say you spoke to the other residents?'

'Yes.'

'All of them?'

'One or two. That's enough, word gets round.'

I'll bet, thought Rebus. And he had another thought, which really was just a word: tenementality. He ate the spicy sandwich and the sickly sandwich quickly, drained his mug and said he'd leave her to finish her lunch in peace. ('Finish your piece in peace,' he'd nearly said, but hadn't, just in case she didn't get the joke.) He walked downstairs, but instead of making along the passage to the front door, turned right and headed towards the tenement's back door.

Outside, the biker was fitting a bulb to his brake-light. He took the new bulb from a plastic box and tossed the empty box onto the sheet of plastic.

'Mind if I take that?' asked Rebus. The youth looked round at him, saw where he was pointing, then shrugged and returned to his work. There was a small cassette recorder playing on the grass beside him. Heavy Metal. The batteries were low and the sound was tortuous.

'Can if you like,' he said.

'Thanks.' Rebus lifted the box by its edges and slipped it into his jacket pocket. 'I use them to keep my flies in.'

The biker turned and grinned.

'Fishing flies,' Rebus explained, smiling himself. 'It's just perfect for keeping my fishing flies in.'

'No flies on you, eh?' said the youth.

Rebus laughed. 'Are you Mrs McKay's son?' he asked.

'That's right.' The bulb was fitted, the casing was being screwed back into place.

'I'd test that before you put the casing on. Just in case it's a dud. You'd only have to take it apart again.'

The boy looked round again. 'No flies on you,' he repeated. He took the casing off again.

'I've just been up seeing your mum.'

'Oh aye?' The tone told Rebus that the boy's parents were either separated, or else the father was dead. You're her latest, are you? the tone implied. Mum's latest fancy-man.

'She was telling me about the fire.'

The boy examined the casing closely. 'Fire?'

'Last night. Have you noticed any of your petrol-cans disappearing? Or maybe one's got less in than you thought?'

Now, the red see-through casing might have been a gem under a microscope. But the boy was saying nothing.

'My name's Rebus, by the way, Inspector Rebus.'

Rebus had a little courtroom conversation with himself on the way back to the station.

And did the suspect drop anything when you revealed your identity to him?

Yes, he dropped his jaw.

Dropped his jaw?

That's right. He looked like a hairless ape with a bad case of acne. And he lost his nut.

Lost his nut?

A nut he'd been holding. It fell into the grass. He was still looking for it when I left.

What about the plastic box, Inspector, the one in which the new brake-light bulb had been residing? Did he ask for it back?

I didn't give him the chance. It's my intention *never* to give a sucker an even chance.

Back at the station, comfortable in his chair, the desk solid and reliable in front of him, the heater solid and reliable behind, Rebus thought about fire, the easy assassin. You didn't need to get your hands on a gun. Didn't even need to buy a knife. Acid, poison, again, difficult to find. But fire ... fire was everywhere. A disposable lighter, a box of matches. Strike a match and you had fire. Warming, nourishing, dangerous fire. Rebus lit a cigarette, the better to help him think. There wouldn't be any news from the lab for some time yet. Some time. Something was niggling. Something he'd heard. What was it? A saying came to mind: prompt payment will be appreciated. You used to get that on the bottom of invoices. Prompt payment.

Probably pays his rent promptly, too.

Well, well. Now there was a thing. Owner-occupier. Not every owner *did* occupy, and not every occupier was an owner. Rebus recalled that Detective Sergeant Hendry of Dunfermline CID was a keen bird-watcher. Once or twice, on courses or at conferences, he'd collared Rebus and bored him with tales of the latest sighting of the Duddingston bittern or the Kilconquhar red-head smew. Like all hobbyists, Hendry was keen to have others share his enthusiasm. Like all anti-hobbyists, Rebus would yawn with more irony than was necessary.

Still, it was worth a phone-call.

'I'll have to call you back, John,' said a busy DS Hendry. 'It's not the sort of thing I could tell you offhand. Give me your number at home and I'll ring you tonight. I didn't know you were interested.'

'I'm not, believe me.'

But his words went unheeded. 'I saw siskins and twite earlier in the year.'

'Really?' said Rebus. 'I've never been one for country and western music. Siskins and twite, eh? They've been around for years.'

By the following morning, he had everything he needed. He arrived as Mrs McKay and her son were eating a late breakfast. The television was on, providing the noise necessary to their lives. Rebus had come accompanied by two other officers, so that there could be no doubting he meant business. Gerry McKay's jaw dropped again as Rebus began to speak. The tale itself was quickly told. John Brodie's front door had been examined, the metal letterbox checked for fingerprints. Some good, if oily, prints had been found, and these matched those found on the plastic box Rebus had taken from Gerry McKay. There could be no doubting that Gerry McKay had pushed open John Brodie's letterbox. If Gerry would accompany the officers to the station.

'Mum!' McKay was on his feet, yelling, panicky. 'Mum, tell them! Tell them!'

Mrs McKay had a face as dark as ketchup. Rebus was glad he had brought the other officers. Her voice trembled when she spoke. 'It wasn't Gerry's idea,' she said. 'It was mine. If there's anyone you want to talk to about it, it should be me. It was my idea. Only, I knew Gerry'd be faster getting in and out of the stairwell. That's all. He's got nothing to do with it.' She paused, her face turning even nastier. 'Besides, that wee shite deserved all he got. Dirty, evil little runt of a man. You didn't see the state Alison was in. Such a nice wee girl, wouldn't say boo to a goose, and to be got into a state like that. I couldn't let him get away with it, hell. And if it were up to you lot, he'd have gotten off scot-free, wouldn't he? It's nothing to do with Gerry.'

'It'll be taken into account at the trial,' Rebus said quietly.

John Brodie looked not to have moved since Rebus had left him. His arms still lay on the top of the bed-cover, and he was still propped up against a pillow.

'Inspector Rebus,' he said. 'Back again.'

'Back again,' said Rebus, placing a chair by the bed and seating himself. 'The doctor says you're doing fine.'

'Yes,' said Brodie.

'Anything I can get you?' Brodie shook his head. 'No? Juice? A bit of fruit maybe? How about something to read? I notice you like girlie mags. I saw one in your flat. I could get you a few of those if you like.' Rebus winked. 'Readers' wives, eh? Amateurs. That's your style. All those blurry Polaroid shots, heads cut off. That's what you like, eh, John?'

But John Brodie was saying nothing. He was looking at his arms. Rebus drew the chair closer to the bed. Brodie flinched, but could not move.

'*Panurus biarmicus*,' Rebus hissed. Now Brodie looked blankly at him. Rebus repeated the words. Still Brodie looked blank. 'Go on,' Rebus chided, 'take a guess.'

'I don't know what you're talking about.'

'No?' Rebus was wide-eyed. 'Curious that. Sounds like the name of a disease, doesn't it? Maybe you know it better as the bearded tit.'

'Oh.' Brodie smiled shyly, and nodded. 'Yes, the bearded tit.'

Rebus smiled too, but coldly. 'You didn't know, you didn't have a clue. Shall I tell you something about the bearded tit? No, better yet, Mr Brodie, you tell *me* something about it.' He sat back and folded his arms expectantly.

'What?'

'Go on.'

'Look, what's all this about?'

'It's quite simple, you see.' Rebus sat forward again. 'The bearded tit isn't commonly found in Scotland. I got that from an expert. Not commonly found, that's what he said. More than that, its habitat – and I'm quoting here – is "extensive and secluded reed-beds". Do you see what I'm getting at? You'd hardly call Easter Road a reed-bed, would you?'

Brodie raised his head a little, his thin lips very straight and wide. He was thinking, but he wasn't talking.

'You see what I'm getting at, don't you? You told those two constables that you were watching bearded tits from your window. But that's just not true. It couldn't possibly be true. You said the name of the first bird that came into your head, and it came into your head because there was a drawing on your living-room wall. I saw it myself. But it's not you that's the bird-watcher, John. It's your landlord and landlady. You rented the place furnished and you haven't changed anything. It's their drawings on the wall. They got in touch about the insurance, you see. Wondering whether the fire was accidental. They saw a bit about it in the newspaper. They could appreciate that they hadn't heard from you, what with you being in hospital and all, but they wanted to sort out the insurance. So I was able to ask them about the birds on the wall. *Their* birds, John, not yours. It was quick thinking of you to come up with the story. It even fooled those two PCs. It might have fooled me. That book about zoom photography, even that had a picture of birds on the front.' He paused. 'But you're a peeper, John, that's all. That's what you are, a nasty little voyeur. Miss Hooper was right all the time.'

'Was it her who—?'

'You'll find out soon enough.'

'It's all lies, you know. Hearsay, circumstantial. You've no proof.'

'What about the photos?'

'What photos?'

Rebus sighed. 'Come on, John. All that gear in your bedroom. Tripod, camera, zoom lenses. Photographing birds, were you? I'd be interested to see the results. Because it wasn't just binoculars, was it? You took piccies, too. In your wardrobe, are they?' Rebus checked his watch. 'With luck I'll have the search warrant inside the hour. Then I intend to take a good look round your flat, John. I intend taking a *very* good look.'

'There's nothing there.' He was shaking now, his arms moving painfully in their gauze bandages. 'Nothing. You've no right. Someone tried to kill ... No right. They tried to kill me.'

Rebus was willing to concede a point. 'Certainly they tried to scare you. We'll see what the courts decide.' He rose to his feet. Brodie was still twittering on. Twit, twit, twit. It would be a while before he'd be able to use a camera again.

'Do you want to know something else, John?' Rebus said, unable to resist one of his parting shots. 'Something about the bearded tit? It's classified as a *babbler*.' He smiled a smile of warm sunshine. 'A babbler!' he repeated. 'Looks to me like you're a bit of a babbler yourself. Well,' he picked up the chair and pretended to be considering something, 'at any rate, I'd certainly classify you as a tit.'

He returned that evening to his own tenement and his roaring gas fire. But there was a surprise awaiting him on the doorhandle of his flat. A reminder from Mrs Cochrane downstairs. A reminder that it was his week for washing the stairs and that he hadn't done it yet and it was nearly the end of the week and when was he going to do it? Rebus sent a roar into the stairwell before slamming shut the door behind him. It was only a moment before other doors started to open, faces peering out, and another Edinburgh tenement conversation began, multi-storeyed, undertone and echoing.

Not Provan

How badly did Detective Inspector John Rebus want to nail Willie Provan? Oh, badly, very badly indeed. Rebus visualised it as a full-scale crucifixion, each nail going in slowly, the way Willie liked to put the boot and the fist slowly, methodically, into the victims of his violence.

Rebus had first encountered Willie Provan five years before, as a schoolkid spiralling out of control. Both parents dead, Willie had been left in the charge of a dotty and near-deaf aunt. He had taken charge of her house, had held wild parties there, parties to which the police were eventually, habitually called by neighbours at the end of their tether.

Entering the house had been like stepping into an amateur production of *Caligula*: naked, under-aged couples so drunk or drugged they could not complete the act which so interested them; emptied tins of solvent, polythene bags encrusted with the dregs of the stuff. A whiff of something animal, something less-than-human in the air. And, in a small back room upstairs, the aunt, locked in and sitting up in her bed, a cold cup of tea and a half-eaten sandwich on the table beside her.

By the time he left school, Willie was already a legend. Four years on the dole had benefited him little. But he had learned cunning, and so far the police had been unable to put him away. He remained a thorn in Rebus's side. Today, Rebus felt someone might just come along and pluck that thorn out.

He sat in the public gallery and watched the court proceedings. Near him were a few of Willie Provan's friends, members of his gang. They called themselves the Tiny Alice, or T-Alice. No one knew why. Rebus glanced over towards them. Sleeves rolled up, sporting tattoos and unshaven grins. They were the city's sons, the product of an Edinburgh upbringing, but they seemed to belong to another culture, another civilisation entirely, reared on Schwarzenegger videos and bummed cigarettes. Rebus shivered, feeling he understood them better than he liked to admit.

The case against Provan was solid and satisfying. On a cup-tie evening several months ago, a football fan had been heading towards the Heart of Midlothian ground. He was late, his train from Fife having been behind time. He was an away supporter and he was on his own in Gorgie.

An arm snaked around his neck, yanked him into a tenement stairwell, and there Willie Provan had kicked and punched him into hospitalisation. For what reason? Rebus could guess. It had nothing to do with football, nothing with football hooliganism. Provan pretended a love of Hearts, but had never, to Rebus's knowledge, attended a game. Nor could he name more than two or three players in the current team's line-up.

Nevertheless, Gorgie was his patch, his territory. He had spotted an invader and had summarily executed him, in his own terms. But his luck had run out. A woman had heard some sounds from the stairwell and had opened her door to investigate. Provan saw her and ran off. But she had given the police a good description and had later identified Provan as the attacker. Moreover, a little while after the attack, a constable, off duty and happening to pass Tynecastle Park, had spotted a young man, apparently disorientated. He had approached the man and asked him if he was all right, but at that point some members of T-Alice had appeared from their local pub, directly opposite the Hearts ground and had taken the man inside.

The constable thought little of it, until he heard about the assault and was given a description of the attacker. The description matched that of the disorientated man, and that man turned out to be Willie Provan. With Provan's previous record, this time he would go down, Rebus was sure of that. So he sat and he watched and he listened.

He watched the jurors, too. They winced, perceptibly as they were told of the injuries to the victim, injuries which still, several months on, kept him in hospital, unable to walk and with respiratory difficulties to boot. To boot. Ha! Rebus let a short-lived smile wrinkle his face. Yes, the jury would convict. But Rebus was most interested in one juror in particular, an intense young man who was taking copious notes, sending intelligent written questions to the judge, studying photographs and diagrams with enthusiasm. The model juror, ready to see that justice was done and all was fair and proper. At one point, the young man looked up and caught Rebus watching him. After that, he gave Rebus some of his attention, but still scribbled his notes and checked and rechecked what he had written.

The other jurors were solemn, looked bored even. Passive spectators at a one-horse race. Guilty. Probably by the end of the day. Rebus would sit it out. The prosecution had finished its case, and the defence case had already begun. The usual stuff when an obviously guilty party pleaded not guilty: trying to catch out prosecution witnesses, instilling mistrust, trying to persuade the jury that things were not as cut and dried as they seemed, that there was probable cause for doubt. Rebus sat back and let it wash over him. Provan would go down.

Then came the iceberg, ripping open the bow of Rebus's confidence.

The defence counsel had called the off-duty constable, the one who had spotted Provan outside the Hearts ground. The constable was young, with a bad case of post-juvenile acne. He tried to stand to attention as the questions were put to him, but when flustered would raise a hand towards his scarred cheeks. Rebus remembered his own first time on the witness stand. A Glasgow music hall stage could not have been more terrifying.

'And what time do you say it was when you first saw the accused?' The defence counsel had a slight Irish brogue, and his eyes were dark from want of sleep. His cheap ballpoint pen had burst, leaving black stains across his hands. Rebus felt a little sorry for him.

'I'm not sure, sir.'

'You're not sure?' The words came slowly. The inference was: this copper is a bit thick, isn't he? How can you the jury trust him? For the counsel was staring at the jury as he spoke and this seemed to unnerve the constable further. A hand rubbed against a cheek.

'Roughly then,' continued the defence counsel. 'Roughly what time was it?'

'Sometime between seven-thirty and eight, sir.'

The counsel nodded, flipping through a sheaf of notes. 'And what did you say to the accused?' As the constable was about to reply, the counsel interrupted, still with his face towards the jury. 'I say "the accused" because there's no disagreement that the person the constable saw outside the football ground was my client.' He paused. 'So constable, what did you say?'

'"Are you all right?" Something like that.'

Rebus glanced towards where Provan sat in the dock. Provan was looking terribly confident. His clear blue eyes were sparkling and he sat forwards in his chair, keen to catch the dialogue going on before him. For the first time, Rebus felt an uneasy stab: the thorn again, niggling him. What was going on?

'You asked him if he was all right.' It was a statement. The counsel paused again. Now the prosecution counsel was frowning: he too was puzzled by this line of questioning. Rebus felt his hands forming into fists.

'You asked him if he was all right, and he replied? What exactly *did* he reply?'

'I couldn't really make it out, sir.'

'Why was that? Were his words slurred perhaps?'

The constable shrugged. 'A little, maybe.'

'A little? Mmm.' The counsel looked at his notes again. 'What about the noise from the stadium?'

'Sir?'

'You were directly outside the ground. There was a cup-tie being played in front of thousands of spectators. It was noisy, wasn't it?'

'Yes, sir,' agreed the constable.

'In fact, it was *very* noisy, wasn't it, Constable Davidson? It was *extraordinarily* noisy. That was why you couldn't hear my client's reply. Isn't that the case?'

The constable shrugged again, not sure where any of this was leading, happy enough to agree with the defence. 'Yes, sir,' he said.

'In fact, as you approached my client, you may remember that there was a sudden upsurge in the noise from the ground.'

The constable nodded, seeming to remember. 'That's right, yes. I think a goal had just been scored.'

'Indeed, a goal had been scored. Just after you had first spotted my client, as you were walking towards him. A goal was scored, the noise was terrific. You shouted your question to my client, and he replied, but his words were drowned out by the noise from the ground. His friends saw him from the Goatfell public house and came to his aid, leading him inside. The noise was still very great, even then. They were shouting to you to let you know they would take care of him. Isn't that right?'

Now, the counsel turned to the constable, fixing him with his dark eyes.

'Yes, sir.'

The counsel nodded, seeming satisfied. Willie Provan, too, looked satisfied. Rebus's nerves were jangling. He was reminded of a song lyric: *there's something happening here, but you don't know what it is*. Something was most definitely happening here, and Rebus didn't like it. The defence counsel spoke again.

'Do you know what the score was that night?'

'No, sir.'

'It was one–nil. The home team won by a single goal, the single goal you heard from outside the ground. A single goal scored—'

picking up the notes for effect, turning again to face the jury, 'in the fifteenth minute of the game, a game that kicked off ... when? Do you happen to recall?'

The constable knew now, knew where this was leading. His voice when he spoke had lost a little of its life. 'It was a seven-thirty kick-off.'

'That's right, it was. So you see, Police Constable Davidson, it was seven forty-five when you saw my client outside the ground. I don't think you would contest that now, would you? And yet we heard Mrs McClintock say that it was twenty to eight when she heard a noise on her stairwell and went to her door. She was quite specific because she looked at her clock before she went to the door. Her call to the police was timed at seven forty-two, just two minutes later.'

Rebus didn't need to hear any more, tried to shut his ears to it. The tenement where the assault had taken place was over a mile from Tynecastle Park and the Goatfell pub. To have been where he was when the constable had approached him, Provan would have had to run, in effect, a four-minute mile. Rebus doubted he was capable of it, doubted everything now. But looking at Provan he could *see* the little prick was guilty. He was as guilty as hell and he was about to get away scot bloody free. Rebus's knuckles were white, his teeth were gritted. Provan looked up at him and smiled. The thorn was in Rebus's side again, working away relentlessly, bleeding the policeman to death.

It couldn't be true. It just couldn't. The trial wasn't over yet. Things had been strung out over the afternoon, the prosecution clearly flustered and playing for time, wondering what tactic to try next, what question to ask. He had lasted the afternoon and court had been adjourned after the summings up. It was all to do with time, as the defence counsel contended. The prosecution tried to negate the time factor and rely instead on the one and only witness. He asked: can we be certain a goal had been scored at that precise moment when PC Davidson approached the accused? Is it not better to trust the identification of the witness, Mrs McClintock, who had actually disturbed the attacker in the course of the assault? And so on. But Rebus knew the case was doomed. There was too much doubt now, way too much. Not guilty, or maybe that Scots get-out clause of 'not proven', whatever. If only the victim had caught a glimpse of Provan, if only. If, if, if. The jury would assemble again tomorrow at ten-thirty, retire to their room and emerge before lunch with a decision which would make Provan a free man. Rebus shook his head.

He was sitting in his car, not up to driving. Just sitting there, the key in the ignition, trying to think things through. But going around in circles, no clear direction, his mind filled with Provan's smile, a smile he would happily tear from that face. Illegal thoughts coursed through his head, ways of fixing Provan, ways of putting him inside. But no: it had to be clean, it had to be *right*. Justification was only part of the process; justice demanded more.

At last, he gave an audible growl, the sound of a caged animal, and turned the ignition, starting the car, heading nowhere in particular. At home he would only brood. A pub might be an idea. There were a few pubs, their clientele almost silent, where a man might drink in solitude and quiet. A kind of a wake for The Law. Damn it, no, he knew where he was headed. Tried not to know, but knew all the same. He was driving towards Gorgie, driving deep into Willie Provan's territory, into the gangland ruled by Tiny Alice. He was heading into the Wild West End of Edinburgh.

The streets were narrow, tenements rising on either side. A cold October wind was blowing, forcing people to angle their walk into the wind, giving them the jack-knife look of a Lowry painting. They were all coming home from work. It was dark, the headlamps of cars and buses like torches in a cave. Gorgie always seemed dark. Even on a summer's day it seemed dark. It had something to do with the narrowness of the streets and the height of the tenements; they seemed like trees in the Amazon, blocking out the light to the pallid vegetation beneath.

Rebus found Cooper Road and parked on the opposite side of the street from number 42. He switched off his engine and wondered what to do now. He was treading dangerously: not the physical danger of the T-Alice, but the more enveloping danger of involvement in a case. If he spoke with Mrs McClintock and the defence counsel were to learn of it, Rebus might be in serious trouble. He wasn't even sure he should be in the vicinity of the crime. Should he turn back? No. Provan was going to get off anyway, whether because of an unconvinced jury or a procedural technicality. Besides, Rebus wasn't getting involved. He was just in the area, that was all.

He was about to get out of the car when he saw a man dressed in duffel coat and jeans shuffle towards the door of number 42 and stop there, studying it. The man pushed at the door and it opened. He looked around before entering the stairwell, and Rebus recognised with a start the intent face of the keen juror from Provan's trial.

Now *this* might be trouble. This might be very bad indeed. What the hell was the juror doing here anyway? The answer seemed simple enough: he was becoming involved, the same as Rebus.

Because he, too, could not believe Provan's luck. But what was he doing at number 42? Was he going to talk to Mrs McClintock? If so, he faced certain disqualification from the jury. Indeed, it was Rebus's duty as a police officer, having seen the juror enter that stairwell, to report this fact to the court officials.

Rebus gnawed at his bottom lip. He could go in and warn the juror, of course, but then he, a policeman, would be guilty of approaching a juror on the very evening prior to a judgment. That could mean more than a slapped wrist and a few choice words from the Chief Super. That could mean the end of his career.

Suddenly, Rebus's mind was made up for him. The door of the tenement was heaved open and out ran the juror, an eye on his watch as he turned left and sprinted towards Gorgie Road. Rebus smiled with relief and shook his head.

'You little bugger,' he murmured in appreciation. The juror was timing the whole thing. It was all a matter of time, so the defence had said, and the juror wanted to time things for himself. Rebus started the car and drove off, following behind the juror until the young man discovered a short cut and headed off down an alleyway. Unable to follow, Rebus fed into the traffic on the main road and found himself in the rush hour jams, heading west out of town. It didn't matter: he knew the juror's destination.

Turning down a sidestreet, Rebus rounded a bend and came immediately upon Tynecastle Park. The Goatfell was ahead of him on the other side of the street. Rebus stopped the car on some double yellow lines by the stadium side of the road. Opposite the Goatfell, the juror was doubled over on the pavement, hands pressing into his sides, exhausted after the run and trying to regain his breath. Rebus examined his watch. Eight minutes since the juror had started off from the tenement. The only witness placed the attack at seven-forty, absolutely certain in her mind that this had been the time. The goal had been scored at seven forty-five. Perhaps Mrs McClintock's clock had been wrong? It could be that simple, couldn't it? But they'd have a hell of a job proving it in court, and no jury would convict on the possibility of a dodgy clock.

Besides, her call to the police had been logged, hadn't it? There was no room for manoeuvre on the time, unless … Rebus tapped his fingers against the steering wheel. The juror had recovered some of his equilibrium, and was now staring at the Goatfell. *Don't do it, son*, Rebus intoned mentally. *Don't.*

The juror looked both ways as he crossed the road and, once across, he looked both ways again before pushing open the door of

the Goatfell and letting it rattle shut behind him. Rebus groaned
and screwed shut his eyes.

'Stupid little ...' He pulled the keys from the ignition, and leaned
across the passenger seat to lock the passenger side door. You
couldn't be too careful around these parts. He stared at his radio.
He could call for back-up, *should* call for back-up, but that would
involve explanations. No, he was in this one alone.

He opened his own door and swivelled out of his seat, closing the
door after him. Pausing to lock the door, he hesitated. After all,
you never knew when a quick getaway might be needed. He left
the door unlocked. Then, having taken three steps in the direction
of the Goatfell, he stopped again and returned to the car, this time
unlocking the passenger-side door, too.

You can't afford to get involved, John, he told himself. But his
feet kept moving forwards. The front of the Goatfell was uninviting,
its bottom half a composition of large purple and black tiles, some
missing, the others cracked and chipped and covered in graffiti.
The top half was constructed from glass panels, some frosted, some
bottle glass. From the fact that there seemed no rhyme or reason
to the pattern of these different panels, Rebus guessed that many a
fight or thrown stone had seen most of the original panels replaced
over time with whatever was available and cheap. He stopped for
a moment at the solid wooden door, considering his madness, his
folly. Then he pushed open the door and went inside.

The interior was, if anything, less prepossessing than the exterior.
Red stubbled linoleum, plastic chairs and long wooden benches, a
pool table, its green baize torn in several places. The lone gaming
machine coughed up a few coins for an unshaven man who looked
as though he had spent most of his adult life battling with it. At one
small table sat three thick-set men and a dozing greyhound. Behind
the pool table, three more men, younger, shuffling, were arguing
over selections from the jukebox. And at the bar stood a solitary
figure – the juror – being served with a half pint of lager by the
raw-faced barman.

Rebus went to the far end of the bar, as far from the juror as
he could get and, keeping his face towards the optics, waited to be
served.

'What'll it be?' The barman's question was not unfriendly.

'Half of special and a Bell's,' replied Rebus. This was his gambit
in any potentially rough pub. He could think of no good reason why;
somehow it just seemed like the right order. He remembered the
roughest drinking den he'd ever encountered, deep in a Niddrie
housing scheme. He'd given his order and the barman asked, in all

seriousness, whether he wanted the two drinks in the same glass. That had shaken Rebus, and he hadn't lingered.

Served with two glasses this evening, one foaming, the other a generous measure of amber, he thanked the barman with a nod and the exact money. But the barman was already turning away, walking back to the conversation he had been having at the other end of the bar before Rebus had walked in, the conversation he'd been having with the juror.

'Aye, that was some game all right. Pity you missed it.' 'Well,' explained the juror, 'what with being away for so long. I've kind of lost touch with their fortunes.'

'Fortune had nothing to do with that night. Cracker of a goal. I must've seen it on the telly a dozen times. Should have been goal of the season.'

The juror sighed. 'Wish I'd been here to see it.'

'Where did you say you'd been again?'

'Europe mostly. Working. I'm only back for a few weeks, then I'm off again.'

Rebus had to admit that the juror made a convincing actor. Of course, there might be a grain of truth in his story, but Rebus doubted it. All the same, good actor or no, he was digging too deep too soon into the barman's memory of that night.

'When did you say the goal was scored?'

'Eh?' The barman seemed puzzled.

'How far into the game,' explained the juror.

'I don't know. Fifteen, twenty minutes, something like that. What difference does it make?'

'Oh, nothing, no, no difference. I was just wondering.'

But the barman was frowning, suspicious now. Rebus felt his grip on the whisky glass tightening.

There's no need for this, son. I know the answer now. It was you that led me to it, but I know now. Just drink your drink and let's get out of here.

Then, as the question and answer session between the juror and barman began again, Rebus glanced into a mirror and his heart dipped fast. The three young men had turned from the wall-mounted jukebox and were now in the process of starting a game of pool. Rebus recognised one of them from the public gallery. Tattoos. Tattoos had sat in the public gallery most of the morning and a little of the afternoon. He seemed not to have recognised Rebus. More to the point, he had not yet recognised the juror – but he would. Rebus had no doubt in his mind about that. Tattoos had spent a long portion of the day staring at fifteen faces, fifteen individuals who, collectively, could put his good friend Willie Provan away for a stretch. Tattoos would recognise the juror, and God alone could tell what would happen then.

God was in a funny mood. Tattoos, standing back while one of the other two T-Alice members played a thunderous break-shot, glanced towards the bar and saw the juror. Perhaps because Rebus was much further away, and partly hidden from view by the juror, Tattoos gave him no heed. But his eyes narrowed as he spotted the juror and Rebus could feel the young man trying to remember where he'd seen the drinker at the bar before. Where and when. Not too long ago. But not to speak to; just a face, a face in a crowd. On a bus? No. In a shop? No. But just a short time ago.

A grunt from one of the other players told Tattoos it was his turn. He lifted a cue from against the wall and bent low over the table, potting an easy ball. Meantime, Rebus had missed the low-voiced conversation between the juror and the barman. From the look on the juror's face, however, it was clear he had discovered something of import: the same 'something' Rebus had deduced while sitting in his car. Keen to leave now that he had his answer, the juror finished his drink.

Tattoos was walking around the table to his next shot. He looked again towards the bar, then towards the table. Then towards the bar again. Rebus, watching this in the wall mirror, saw Tattoos's jaw visibly drop open. Damn him, he had finally placed the juror. He placed his cue on the table and started slowly towards the bar. Rebus felt the tide rising around him. Here he was, where he shouldn't be, following a jury member on the eve of a retiral for verdict and now said juror was about to be approached by a friend of the accused.

For 'approached' read 'nobbled', or at the very least 'scared off'.

There was nothing for it. Rebus finished off the whisky and pushed the half pint away.

Tattoos had reached his quarry, who was just turning to go. Tattoos pointed an unnecessary finger.

'It's you, isn't it? You're on my pal's case. One of the jury. Christ, it *is* you.' Tattoos sounded as though he would have been less surprised to have encountered the entire Celtic team supping in his local. He grabbed hold of the juror's shoulder. 'Come on, I want a wee word.'

The juror's face, once red from running, had drained of all colour. Tattoos was hauling him towards the pub door.

'Easy, Dobbs!' called the barman.

'Not your concern, shite-face!' Tattoos, aka Dobbs, growled, tugging the door open and propelling the juror through it, out onto the street.

The bar fell quiet again. The dog, who had awakened at the noise, rested its head back on its paws. The pool game continued. A record came on the jukebox.

'Turn it up a bit!' yelled one of the pool players. 'I can hardly hear it!'

Rebus nodded to the barman in a gesture of farewell. Then he, too, made for the door.

Outside, he knew he must act quickly. At any sign of trouble, members of T-Alice would crawl out of the woodwork like so many termites. Tattoos had pinned the juror to a shop-front window between the Goatfell and Rebus's car. Rebus's attention was drawn from the conflict to the car itself. Its doors were open! He could see two kids playing inside it, crawling over its interior, pretending they were at the wheel of a racing car. Rebus hissed and moved forwards. He was almost passing Tattoos and the juror when he yelled:

'Get out of my bloody car!'

Even Tattoos turned at this and as he did so Rebus hammered a clenched fist into his nose. It had to be fast: Rebus didn't want Tattoos to be able ever to identify him. The sound of the nose flattening was dull and unmistakable. Tattoos let go of the juror and held his hands to his face. Rebus hit him again, this time in proper boxing fashion, knuckles against the side of the jaw. Tattoos fell against the glass shop-front and sank to the pavement.

It was Rebus's turn to grab the juror's shoulder, marching him towards the car with no words of explanation. The juror went quietly, glancing back just the once towards the prone body.

Seeing Rebus approach, brimstone in his eyes, the two boys ran from the car. Rebus watched them go, committing their faces to memory. Future Willie Provans.

'Get in,' he said to the juror, shoving him towards the passenger side. They both shut the car doors after them. Rebus's police radio was missing, and wires protruded from beneath the dashboard, evidence of an attempted hot-wiring. Rebus was relieved the attempt hadn't worked. Otherwise he would be trapped in Gorgie, surrounded by hostile natives. It didn't bear thinking about.

The car started first time and Rebus revved it hard as he drove off, never looking back.

'I know you,' said the juror. 'You were in the public gallery, too.'

'That's right.'

The juror grew quiet. 'You're not one of ...?'

'I want to see Willie Provan behind bars. That's all you need to know, and I don't want to know anything about you. I just want you to go home, go back to court tomorrow, and do your duty.'

'But I know how he—'

'So do I.' Rebus stopped at a red traffic light and checked in the mirror. No one was following. He turned to the juror. 'It was a cup-tie, a big crowd,' he said. 'And ever since Hillsborough, the football bosses and the police have been careful about big crowds.'

'That's right.' The juror was bursting to come out with it first. 'So they held up the game for ten minutes to let everybody in. The barman told me.'

Rebus nodded. The game had been a seven-thirty kick-off all right, but that intended kick-off time had been delayed. The goal, scored fifteen minutes into the game, had been scored at seven fifty-five, *not* seven forty-five, giving Provan plenty of time to make the one-mile trip from Cooper Road to the Goatfell. The truth would have come out eventually, but it might have taken a little time. The situation, however, was still dangerous. The light turned green, and Rebus moved off.

'So you think Provan is guilty?' he asked the juror.

'I know he is. It's obvious.'

Rebus nodded. 'He could still get away with it.'

'How?'

'If,' Rebus explained carefully, 'it comes to light that you and I have been doing a little snooping. You'll be thrown off the jury. It could go to a retrial, or some technicality might arise which would see Provan go free. We can't let that happen, can we?'

Rebus heard his own words. They sounded calm. Yet inside him the adrenalin was racing and his fist was pleasantly sore from use.

'No,' answered the juror, as Rebus had hoped he would.

'So,' continued Rebus, 'what I propose is that I have a quiet word with the prosecution counsel. Let's let him stand up in court and come out with the solution. That way no problems or technicalities arise. You just stay quiet and let the process work through.'

The juror seemed disheartened. This was his feat, after all, his sleuthing had turned things around. And for what?

'There's no glory in it, I'm afraid,' said Rebus. 'But at least you'll have the satisfaction of knowing Provan is inside, not out there, waiting to pick off another victim.' Rebus nodded through the wind-screen and the juror stared at the city streets, thinking it over.

'Okay,' he said at last. 'Yes, you're right.'

'So we keep it quiet?'

'We keep it quiet,' the juror agreed. Rebus nodded slowly. This might shape up all right after all. The whisky was warming his veins. A quiet word to the prosecution, maybe by way of a typed and anonymous note, something that would keep Rebus out of the case. It was a pity he couldn't be in court tomorrow for the revelation. But the last thing he wanted was to encounter a broken-nosed Tattoos. A pity though; he wanted to see Provan's face and he wanted to catch Provan's eyes and he wanted to give him a great big pitiless smile.

'You can stop here,' said the juror, waking Rebus from his reverie. They were approaching Princes Street. 'I just live down Queens—'

'Don't tell me,' Rebus said abruptly. The juror looked at him.

'Technicalities?' he ventured. Rebus smiled and nodded. He pulled the car over to the side of the road. The juror opened his door, got out, but then bent down into the car again.

'I don't even know who you are,' he said.

'That's right,' said Rebus, reaching across and pulling shut the door. 'You don't.'

He drove off into the Edinburgh evening. No thorn jabbed him now. By tomorrow there would be another. And then he'd have to report the theft of his radio. There would be smiles at that, smiles and, behind his back if not to his face, laughter.

John Rebus could laugh, too.

Sunday

Where was that light coming from? Bright, hot light. Knives in the night. Last night, was it? No, the night before. Just another Friday in Edinburgh. A drug haul at a dance hall. A few of the dealers trying to run for it. Rebus cornering one. The man, sweating, teeth bared, turning before Rebus's eyes into an animal, something wild, predatory, scared. And cornered. The glint of a knife ...

But that was Friday, the night before last. So this was Sunday. Yes! Sunday morning. (Afternoon, maybe.) Rebus opened his eyes and squinted into the sunshine, streaming through his uncurtained window. No, not sunshine. His bedside lamp. Must have been on all night. He had come to bed drunk last night, drunk and tired. Had forgotten to close the curtains. And now warming light, birds resting on the window-ledge. He stared into a small black eye, then checked his watch. Ten past eight. Morning then, not afternoon. Early morning.

His head was the consistency of syrup, his limbs stiff. He'd been fit as a young man; not fitness daft, but fit all the same. But one day he had just stopped caring. He dressed quickly, then checked and found that he was running out of clean shirts, clean pants, clean socks. Today's chore then: doing the laundry. Ever since his wife had left him, he had taken his dirty washing to a public laundrette at the top of Marchmont Road, where a service wash cost very little and the manageress always used to fold his clean clothes away very neatly, a smile on her scrupulous lips. But in a fit of madness one Saturday afternoon, he had walked calmly into an electrical shop and purchased a washer/dryer for the flat.

He pressed the dirty bundle into the machine and found he was down to one last half-scoop of washing powder. What the hell, it would have to do. There were various buttons and controls on the machine's fascia, but he only ever used one programme: Number 5 (40 degrees), full load, with ten minutes' tumble dry at the end. The results were satisfactory, if never perfect. He switched the machine on, donned his shoes and left the flat, double-locking the door behind him.

His car, parked directly outside the main entrance to the tenement, scowled at him. *I need a wash, pal.* It was true, but Rebus shook his head. Not today, today was his day off, the only day this week. Some other time, some other free time. Who was he kidding? He'd drive into a car wash one afternoon between calls. His car could like it or lump it.

The corner shop was open. Rebus had seldom seen it closed. He bought ground coffee, rolls, milk, margarine, a packet of bacon. The bacon, through its plastic wrapping, had an oily, multicoloured look to it, but its sell-by date seemed reasonable. Pigs: very intelligent creatures. How could one intelligent creature eat another? Guilty conscience, John? It must be Sunday. Presbyterian guilt, Calvinist guilt. *Mea culpa*, he thought to himself, taking the bacon to the checkout till. Then he turned back and bought some washing powder, too.

Back in the flat, the washing machine was churning away. He put Coleman Hawkins on the hi-fi (not too loud; it was only quarter to nine). Soon the church bells would start ringing, calling the faithful. Rebus would not answer. He had given up churchgoing. Any day but Sunday he might have gone. But Sunday, Sunday was the only day off he had. He remembered his mother, taking him with her to church every Sunday while his father stayed at home in bed with tea and the paper. Then one Sunday, when he was twelve or thirteen, his mother had said he could choose: go with her or stay with his father. He stayed and saw his little brother's jealous eyes glance at him, desperate to be of an age where he would be given the same choice.

Ah me, John, Sunday morning. Rubbedy-rrub of the washing machine, the coffee's aroma wafting up from the filter. (Getting short on filters, but no panic: he only used them on Sunday.) He went into the bathroom. Suddenly, staring at the bath itself, he felt an overwhelming urge to steep himself in hot water. Wednesdays and Saturdays: those were his usual days for a bath. Go on, break the rules. He turned on the hot tap, but it was a mere trickle. Damn! the washing machine was being fed all the flat's hot water. Oh well. Bath later. Coffee now.

At five past nine, the Sunday papers thudded through the letterbox. *Sunday Post, Mail*, and *Scotland on Sunday*. He seldom read them, but they helped the day pass. Not that he got bored on a Sunday. It was the day of rest, so he rested. A nice lazy day. He refilled his coffee mug, went back into the bathroom and walked over to the toilet to examine a roughly circular patch on the wall beside it, a couple of feet up from floor level. The patch was slightly discoloured and he touched it with the palm of his hand. Yes, it was damp. He had first noticed the patch a week ago. Damp, slightly damp. He couldn't think why. There was no dampness anywhere else, no apparent source of the damp. Curious, he had peeled away the paper from the patch, had scratched at the plaster wall. But no answer had emerged. He shook his head. That would irritate him for the rest of the day. As before, he went to the bedroom and returned with an electric hairdryer and an extension flex. He plugged the hairdryer into the flex, and rested the dryer on the toilet seat, aimed towards the patch, then switched on the hairdryer and tested that it was hitting the spot. That would dry things out a bit, but he knew the patch would return.

Washing machine rumbling. Hairdryer whirring. Coleman Hawkins in the living-room. He went into the living-room. Could do with a tidy, couldn't it? Hoover, dust. Car sitting outside waiting to be washed. Everything could wait. There were the papers to be read. There they were on the table, just next to his briefcase. The briefcase full of documents for his attention, half-completed case-notes, reminders of appointments, all the rubbish he hadn't found time for during the week at the station. All the so-important paperwork, without which his life would be milk and honey. Some toast perhaps? Yes, he would eat some toast.

He checked his watch: ten past eleven. He had switched off the hairdryer, but left it sitting on the toilet, the extension lead snaking across the floor to the wall-socket in the hall. The washing machine was silent, spent. One more cup of coffee left in the pot. He had flicked through the papers, looking for the interesting, the unusual. Same old stories: court cases, weekend crime, sport. There was even a paragraph on Friday night's action. He skipped that, but remembered all the same. Bright knife's flat edge, caught in the lamplight. Sour damp smell in the alleyway. Feet standing in something soft. Don't look down, look at him, look straight at him, the cornered animal. Look at him, talk to him with your eyes, try to calm him, or quell him.

There were birds on the window sill, chirping, wanting some crumbled up crusts of bread, but he had no bread worth the name left in the flat; just fresh rolls, too soft to be thrown out. Ach, he'd never eat six rolls though, would he? One or two would go stale and then he'd give them to the birds. So why not give them some in advance, while the rolls are soft and sweet?

In the kitchen he prepared the broken pieces of bread on a plate, then took it to the birds on the window-ledge. Hell: what about lunch? Sunday afternoon lunch. In the freezer compartment, he found a steak. How long would it take to defrost? Damn! he meant to pick up the microwave during the week. The shop had called him to say they'd fixed the fault. He was supposed to have collected it on Friday, but he'd been too busy. So: defrost in a low oven. And wine. Yes, open a bottle. He could always drink just one or two glasses, then keep the rest of the bottle for some other occasion. Last Christmas, a friend had given him a vacuum-tube. It was supposed to keep wine fresh after opening. Where had he put it? In the cupboard beside the wine: that would make sense. But there was no gadget to be found.

He chose a not-bad bottle, bought from a reliable wine merchant in Marchmont and stood it on the table in the living-room. Beside his briefcase. Let the sediment settle. That's what Sunday was all about, wasn't it? Maybe he could try one of the crosswords. It was ages since he'd done a crossword. A glass of wine and a crossword while he waited for the meat to thaw. Sediment wouldn't be settled yet, but what the hell. He opened the bottle and poured an inch into his glass. Glanced at his watch again. It was half past eleven. A bit early to be drinking. Cheers.

You could break the rules on a Sunday, couldn't you?

Christ, what a week it had been at work. Everything from a senile rapist to a runaway blind boy. A shotgun robbery at a bookmaker's shop and an apparently accidental drowning at the docks. Drunk, the victim had been. Dead drunk. Fished about a bottle of whisky and a recently dismembered kebab from his stomach. Annual crime figures for the Lothians were released: murder slightly up on the previous year, sexual assaults well up, burglaries up, street crime down a little, motoring offences significantly reduced. The clear-up rate for housebreakings in some parts of Edinburgh was standing at less than five per cent. Rebus was not exactly a fascist, not quite a totalitarian, but he knew that given wider powers of entry and search, that final figure could be higher. There were high-rise blocks where a flat on the twelfth floor would be broken into time after time. Was someone climbing twelve flights to break in? Of course not: someone in the block was responsible, but without the powers of immediate and indiscriminate search, they'd never find the culprit.

And that was the tip of the whole polluted iceberg. Maniacs were put back on the streets by institutions unable or unwilling to cope. Rebus had never seen so many beggars in Edinburgh as in this past year. Teenagers (and younger) up to grandparents, dossing, cadging the occasional quid or cigarette. Christ, it depressed him to think of it almost as much as it did to pretend he could ignore it. He stalked through to the kitchen and felt the steak. It was still solid at its core. He lifted the nearly dry clothes out of the machine and draped them over the cold radiators throughout the flat. More music on the hi-fi. Art Pepper this time, a little louder, the hour being respectable. Not that the neighbours ever complained. Sometimes he could see in their eyes that they wanted to complain – complain about his noise, his irregular comings and goings, the way he revved his car or coughed his way up the stairwell. They wanted to complain, but they daren't, for fear that he would somehow 'stitch them up' or would prove not to be amenable to some favour they might ask one day. They all watched the TV police dramas and thought they must know their neighbour pretty well. Rebus shook his head and poured more wine: two inches deep in the glass this time. They knew nothing about him. Nothing. He didn't have a TV, hated all the game shows and the cop shows and the news programmes. Not having a TV had set him apart from his colleagues at the station: he found he had little to discuss with them of a morning. His mornings were quieter and saner for it.

He checked the damp patch in the bathroom again, letting his hand rest against it for half a minute. Mmm: it still wasn't completely dry. But then maybe his hands were damp from the washing he had been carrying. What the hell. Back in the bedroom, he picked up some books from the floor and stacked them against a wall, beside other columns of paperbacks and hardbacks, read and unread. One day he would get time to read them. They were like contraband: he couldn't stop himself buying them, but then he never really did anything with them once he'd bought them. The buying was the thing, that sense of ownership. Perhaps somewhere in Britain someone had exactly the same collection of books as him, but he doubted it. The range was too eclectic, everything from secondhand rugby yearbooks to dense philosophical works. Meaningless, really; without pattern. So much of his working life was spent to a pattern, a modus operandi. A series of rules for the possible (not probable) solving of crimes. One of the rules would have it that he get through the briefcase full of work before Monday morning and, preferably, while still sober.

Bell. Bell?

Bell. Someone at his front door. Jesus, on a *Sunday*? Not on a Sunday, please, God. The wrong door: they'd got the wrong door. Give them a minute and they would realise their mistake. Bell again. Bloody hell's bells. Right then, he would answer it.

He pulled the door open slowly, peering around it. Detective Constable Brian Holmes was standing on the tenement landing.

'Brian?'

'Hello, sir. Hope you don't mind. I was in the neighbourhood and thought I'd ... you know.'

Rebus held open the door. 'Come in.'

He led Holmes through the hall, stepping over the electric flex. Holmes stared at the flex, an alarmed look on his face.

'Don't worry,' said Rebus, pausing at the threshold of the living-room. 'I'm not going to jump in the bath with an electric fire. Just drying out a damp patch.'

'Oh.' Holmes sounded unconvinced. 'Right.'

'Sit down,' said Rebus. 'I've just opened a bottle of wine. Would you like some?'

'Bit early for me,' Holmes said, glancing towards Rebus's glass.

'Well, coffee then. I think there's still some in the pot.'

'No thanks, I'm fine.'

They were both seated, Rebus in his usual chair, Holmes perched on the edge of the sofa. Rebus knew why the younger officer was here, but he was damned if he would make it easy for him.

'In the neighbourhood you say?'

'That's right. I was at a party last night in Mayfield. Afterwards, I stopped the night.'

'Oh?'

Holmes smiled. 'No such luck, I slept on the sofa.'

'It's still off with Nell then?'

'I don't know. Sometimes she ... let's change the subject.'

He flipped one of the newspapers over so that he could study the back page. 'Did you see the boxing last night?'

'I don't have a television.'

Holmes looked around the room, then smiled again. 'Neither you do. I hadn't noticed.'

'I'll bear that in mind when you come up for promotion, Constable.' Rebus took a large gulp of wine, watching Holmes over the rim of the glass. Holmes was looking less comfortable by the second.

'Any plans for the day?'

'Such as?'

Holmes shrugged. 'I don't know. I thought maybe you had a Sunday routine. You know: clean the car, that sort of thing.'

Rebus nodded towards the briefcase on the table. 'Paperwork. That'll keep me busy most of the day.'

Holmes nodded, flicking through the paper until he came, as Rebus knew he would, to the piece about the nightclub bust.

'It's at the bottom of the page,' Rebus said. 'But then you know that, don't you? You've already seen it.' He rose from his chair sharply and walked to the hi-fi, turning the record over. Alto sax bloomed from the speakers. Holmes still hadn't said anything. He was pretending to read the paper, but his eyes weren't moving. Rebus returned to his seat.

'Was there really a party, Brian?'

'Yes.' Holmes paused. 'No.'

'And you weren't just passing?'

'No. I wanted to see how you were.'

'And how am I?'

'You look fine.'

'That's because I *am* fine.'

'Are you sure?'

'Perfectly.'

Holmes sighed and threw aside the paper. 'I'm glad to hear it. I was worried, John. We were all a bit shaken up.'

'I've killed someone before, Brian. It wasn't the first time.'

'Yes, but Christ, I mean ...' Holmes got up and walked to the window, looking down on the street. A nice quiet street in a quiet part of town. Net curtains and trim front gardens, the gardens of professional people, lawful people, people who smiled at you in shops or chatted in a bus queue.

But Rebus's mind flashed again to the dark alleyway, a distant streetlamp, the cornered drug dealer. He had thrown packets from his pockets onto the ground as he had run. Like sowing seed.

Small polythene bags of drugs soft and hard. Sowing them in the soft mud, every year a new crop.

Then the blinding light. The flat steel of a knife. Not a huge knife, but how big did a knife need to be? An inch of blade would be enough. Anything more was excess. It was a very excessive knife indeed, curved, serrated edge, a commando special. The kind you could buy from a camping shop. The kind *anybody* could buy from a camping shop. A serious knife for outdoor pursuits. Rebus had the idea they called them 'survival' knives.

The man – not much more than a boy in reality, eighteen or nineteen – had not hesitated. He slid the knife out from the waistband of his trousers. He lunged, one swipe, two swipes. Rebus wasn't fit, but his reactions were fast. On the third swipe, he snapped out a hand and caught the wrist, twisting it all the way. The knife fell to the ground. The dealer cried out in pain and dropped to one knee. No words had passed between the two men. There was no real need for words.

But then Rebus had realised that his opponent was not on his knees as a sign of defeat. He was scrabbling around for the knife and found it with his free hand. Rebus let go of the dead wrist and pinned the man's left arm to his body, but the arm was strong and the blade sheared through Rebus's trousers, cutting a red line up across his thigh. Rebus brought his knee up hard into his adversary's crotch and felt the body go limp. He repeated the action, but the dealer wasn't giving up. The knife was rising again. Rebus grabbed the wrist with one hand, the other going for the man's throat. Then he felt himself being spun and pushed hard up against the wall of the alley. The wall was damp, smelling of mould. He pressed a thumb deep into the dealer's larynx, still wrestling with the knife. His knee thudded into the man's groin again. And then, as the strength in the knife-arm eased momentarily, Rebus yanked the wrist and pushed.

Pushed hard, driving the dealer across the alley and against the other wall. Where the man gasped, gurgled, eyes bulging. Rebus stood back and released his grasp on the wrist, the wrist which held the knife, buried up to the hilt in the young man's stomach.

'Oh shit,' he whispered. 'Oh shit, oh shit, oh shit.'

The dealer was staring in surprise at the handle of the knife. His hand fell away from it, but the knife itself stayed put. He shuffled forward, walking past Rebus, who could only stand and watch, making for the entrance to the alleyway. The tip of the knife was protruding through the back of the dealer's jacket. He made it to the mouth of the alley before falling to his knees.

'Sir?'

'Mmm?' Rebus looked up and saw that Holmes was studying him from the window. 'What is it, Brian?'

'Are you okay?'

'I told you, I'm fine.' Rebus tipped the last of the wine down his throat and placed the glass on the floor, trying to control the trembling in his hand.

'It's just that ... well, I've never—'

'You've never killed anyone.'

'That's right,' Holmes came back to the sofa. 'I haven't.' He sat down, hands pressed between his knees, leaning slightly forwards as he spoke. 'What does it feel like?'

'Feel like?' Rebus smiled with half his mouth. 'It doesn't feel like anything. I don't even think about it. That's the best way.'

Holmes nodded slowly. Rebus was thinking: *get to the point.* And then Holmes came to the point.

'Did you mean to do it?' he asked.

Rebus had no hesitation. 'It was an accident. I didn't know it had happened until it did happen. We got into a clinch and somehow the knife ended up where it ended up. That's all. That's what I told them back at the station and that's what I'll tell any inquiry they shove at me. It was an accident.'

'Yes,' said Holmes quietly, nodding. 'That's what I thought.'

Accidents will happen, won't they?

Like burning the steak. Like finishing the bottle when you'd meant to have just a couple of glasses. Like punching a dent in the bathroom wall. Accidents happened and most of them happened in the home.

Holmes refused the offer of lunch and left. Rebus sat in the chair for a while, just listening to jazz, forgetting all about the steak. He only remembered it when he went to open another bottle of wine. The corkscrew had found its way back into the cutlery drawer, and he plucked out a knife by mistake. A small sharp-bladed knife with a wooden handle. He kept this knife for steaks especially.

It was good of Holmes to look in, no matter what the motive. And it was good of him not to stay, too. Rebus needed to be alone, needed time and space enough to think. He had told Holmes he never thought about it, never thought about death. That was a lie; he thought about it all the time. This weekend he was replaying Friday night, going over the scene time and time again in his head. Trying to answer the question Holmes himself had asked: was it an accident? But every time Rebus went through it, the answer became more and more vague. The hand was holding the knife, and then Rebus was angling that hand away from himself, propelling the hand and the body behind it backward into the wall of the alley. Angling the hand ... That was the vital moment. When he grabbed the wrist so that the knife was pointing towards the dealer, what had been going through his mind then? The thought that he was saving himself? Or that he was about to kill the dealer?

Rebus shook his head. It was no clearer now than it had been at the time. The media had chalked it up yesterday as self-defence and the internal inquiry would come to the same conclusion. Could he have disarmed the young man? Probably. Would the man have killed Rebus, given the chance? Certainly. Had he lived, would he have become Prime Minister, or fascist dictator, or Messiah? Would he have seen the error of his ways, or would he have gone on dispensing the only thing he had to sell? What about his parents, his family, his friends who had known him at school, who had known him as a child: what would they be thinking now? Were the photograph albums and the paper hankies out? Pictures of the dealer as a boy, dressed up as a cowboy on his birthday, pictures of him splashing in the bath as a baby. Memories of someone John Rebus had never known.

He shook his head again. Thinking about it would do no good, but it was the only way to deal with it. And yes, he felt guilty. He felt soiled and defeated and bad. But he would stop feeling bad, and then eventually he would stop feeling anything at all. He had killed before; it might be he would kill again. You never knew until the moment itself.

And sometimes even then, you still didn't know, and would continue not to know. Holmes mentioned Mayfield. Rebus knew of a church in Mayfield with an evening service on a Sunday. A church with a restrained congregation and a minister not overly keen on prying into one's affairs. Maybe he would go there later. Meantime, he felt like a walk. He would walk through The Meadows and back across Bruntsfield Links, with a diversion towards the ice-cream shop near Tollcross. Maybe he'd bump into his friend Frank.

For this was Sunday, his day off, and he could do whatever he liked, couldn't he? After all, Sunday was a day for breaking the rules. It was the only day he could afford.

Auld Lang Syne

Places Detective Inspector John Rebus did not want to be at midnight on Hogmanay: number one, the Tron in Edinburgh.

Which was perhaps, Rebus decided, why he found himself at five minutes to midnight pushing his way through the crowds which thronged the area of the Royal Mile outside the Tron Kirk. It was a bitter night, a night filled with the fumes of beer and whisky, of foam licking into the sky as another can was opened, of badly sung songs and arms around necks and stooped, drunken proclamations of undying love, proclamations which would be forgotten by morning.

Rebus had been here before, of course. He had been here the previous Hogmanay, ready to root out the eventual troublemakers, to break up fights and crunch across the shattered glass covering the setts. The best and worst of the Scots came out as another New Year approached: the togetherness, the sharpness, the hugging of life, the inability to know when to stop, so that the hug became a smothering stranglehold. These people were drowning in a sea of sentiment and sham. *Flower of Scotland* was struck up by a lone voice for the thousandth time, and for the thousandth time a few more voices joined in, all falling away at the end of the first chorus.

'Gawn yirsel there, big man.'

Rebus looked around him. The usual contingent of uniformed officers was going through the annual ritual of having hands shaken by a public suddenly keen to make friends. It was the WPCs Rebus felt sorry for, as another slobbering kiss slapped into the cheek of a young female officer. The police of Edinburgh knew their duty: they always offered one sacrificial lamb to appease the multitude. There was actually an orderly queue standing in front of the WPC waiting to kiss her. She smiled and blushed. Rebus shivered and turned away. Four minutes to midnight. His nerves were like struck chords. He hated crowds. Hated drunken crowds more. Hated the fact that another year was coming to an end. He began to push through the crowd with a little more force than was necessary.

People Detective Inspector John Rebus would rather not be with at midnight on Hogmanay: number one, detectives from Glasgow CID.

He smiled and nodded towards one of them. The man was standing just inside a bus shelter, removed from the general scrum of the road itself. On top of the shelter, a Mohican in black leather did a tribal dance, a bottle of strong lager gripped in one hand. A police constable shouted for the youth to climb down from the shelter. The punk took no notice. The man in the bus shelter smiled back at John Rebus. He's not waiting for a bus, Rebus thought to himself, he's waiting for a bust.

Things Detective Inspector John Rebus would rather not be doing at midnight on Hogmanay: number one, working.

So he found himself working, and as the crowd swept him up again, he thought of Dante's *Inferno*. Three minutes to midnight. Three minutes away from hell. The Scots, pagan at their core, had always celebrated New Year rather than Christmas. Back when Rebus was a boy, Christmases were muted. New Year was the time for celebration, for first-footing, black bun, Madeira cake, coal wrapped in silver foil, stovies during the night and steak pie the following afternoon. Ritual after ritual. Now he found himself observing another ritual, another set of procedures. A meeting was about to take place. An exchange would be made: a bag filled with money for a parcel full of dope. A consignment of heroin had entered Scotland via a west coast fishing village. The CID in Glasgow had been tipped off, but failed to intercept the package. The trail had gone cold for several days, until an informant came up with the vital information. The dope was in Edinburgh. It was about to be handed on to an east coast dealer. The dealer was known to Edinburgh CID, but they'd never been able to pin a major possession charge on him. They wanted him badly. So did the west coast CID.

'It's to be a joint operation,' Rebus's boss had informed him, with no trace of irony on his humourless face. So now here he was, mingling with the crowds, just as another dozen or so undercover officers were doing. The men about to make the exchange did not trust one another. One of them had decided upon the Tron as a public enough place to make the deal. With so many people around, a double-cross was less likely to occur. The Tron at midnight on Hogmanay: a place of delirium and riot. No one would notice a discreet switch of cases, money for dope, dope for money. It was perfect.

Rebus, pushing against the crowd again, saw the money-man

for the very first time. He recognised him from photographs. Alan Lyons, 'Nal' to his friends. He was twenty-seven years old, drove a Porsche 911 and lived in a detached house on the riverside just outside Haddington. He had been one of Rab Philips's men until Philips's demise. Now he was out on his own. He listed his occupation as 'entrepreneur'. He was sewerage.

Lyons was resting his back against a shop window. He smoked a cigarette and gave the passers-by a look that said he was not in the mood for handshakes and conversation. A glance told Rebus that two of the Glasgow crew were keeping a close watch on Lyons, so he did not linger. His interest now was in the missing link, the man with the package. Where was he? A countdown was being chanted all around him. A few people reckoned the New Year was less than ten seconds away; others, checking their watches, said there was a minute left. By Rebus's own watch, they were already into the New Year by a good thirty seconds. Then, without warning, the clock chimes rang and a great cheer went up. People were shaking hands, hugging, kissing. Rebus could do nothing but join in.

'Happy New Year.'

'Happy New Year, pal.'

'Best of luck, eh?'

'Happy New Year.'

'All the best.'

'Happy New Year.'

Rebus shook a Masonic hand, and looked up into a face he recognised. He returned the compliment – 'Happy New Year' – and the man smiled and moved on, hand already outstretched to another well-wisher, another stranger. But this man had been no stranger to Rebus. Where the hell did he know him from? The crowd had rearranged itself, shielding the man from view. Rebus concentrated on the memory of the face. He had known it younger, less jowly, but with darker eyes. He could hear the voice: a thick Fife accent. The hands were like shovels, miner's hands. But this man was no miner.

He had his radio with him, but trapped as he was in the midst of noise there was no point trying to contact the others on the surveillance. He wanted to tell them something. He wanted to tell them he was going to follow the mystery man. Always supposing, that was, he could find him again in the crowd.

And then he remembered: Jackie Crawford. Dear God, it was Jackie Crawford!

People Rebus did not want to shake hands with as the old year became the new: number one, Jackie 'Trigger' Crawford.

Rebus had put Crawford behind bars four years ago for armed

robbery and wounding. The sentence imposed by the judge had been a generous stretch of ten years. Crawford had headed north from court in a well-guarded van. He had not gained the nickname 'Trigger' for his quiet and homely outlook on life. The man was a headcase of the first order, gun happy and trigger happy. He'd taken part in a series of bank and building society robberies; short, violent visits to High Streets across the Lowlands. That nobody had been killed owed more to strengthened glass and luck than to Crawford's philanthropy. He'd been sent away for ten, he was out after four. What was going on? Surely, the man could not be out and walking the streets *legally*? He had to have broken out, or at the very least cut loose from some day-release scheme. And wasn't it a coincidence that he should bump into Rebus, that he should be here in the Tron at a time when the police were waiting for some mysterious drug pedaller?

Rebus believed in coincidence, but this was stretching things a bit too far. Jackie Crawford was somewhere in this crowd, somewhere shaking hands with people whom, a scant four years before, he might have been terrorising with a sawn-off shotgun. Rebus had to do something, whether Crawford was the 'other man' or not. He began squeezing through the crowd again, this time ignoring proffered hands and greetings. He moved on his toes, craning his head over the heads of the revellers, seeking the square-jawed, wiry-haired head of his prey. He was trying to recall whether there was some tradition in Scotland that ghosts from your past came to haunt you at midnight on Hogmanay. He thought not. Besides, Crawford was no ghost. His hands had been meaty and warm, his thumb pressing speculatively against Rebus's knuckles. The eyes which had glanced momentarily into Rebus's eyes had been clear and blue, but uninterested.

Had Crawford recognised his old adversary? Rebus couldn't be sure. There had been no sign of recognition, no raising of eyebrows or opening of the mouth. Just three mumbled words before moving on to the next hand. Was Crawford drunk? Most probably: few sane and sober individuals visited the Tron on this night of all nights. Good: a drunken Crawford would have been unlikely to recognise him. Yet the voice had been quiet and unslurred, the eyes focussed. Crawford had not seemed drunk, had not acted drunk. Sober as a judge, in fact. This, too, worried Rebus.

But then, *everything* worried him this evening. He couldn't afford any slip-ups from the operation's Edinburgh contingent. It would give too much ammo to the Glasgow faction: there was a certain competitive spirit between the two forces. For 'competitive spirit' read 'loathing'. Each would want to claim any arrest as *its* victory; and each would blame any foul-up on the other.

This had been explained to him very clearly by Chief Inspector Lauderdale.

'But surely, sir,' Rebus had replied, 'catching these men is what's most important.'

'Rubbish, John,' Lauderdale had replied. 'What's important is that we don't look like arseholes in front of McLeish and his men.'

Which, of course, Rebus had already known: he just liked winding his superior up a little the better to watch him perform. Superintendent Michael McLeish was an outspoken and devout Catholic, and Rebus's chief did not like Catholics. But Rebus hated bigots, and so he wound up Lauderdale whenever he could and had a name for him behind his back: the Clockwork Orangeman.

The crowd was thinning out as Rebus headed away from the Tron and uphill towards the castle. He was, he knew, moving away from the surveillance and should inform his fellow officers of the fact, but if his hunch was right, he was also following the man behind the whole deal. Suddenly he caught sight of Crawford, who seemed to be moving purposefully out of the crowd, heading onto the pavement and giving a half-turn of his head, knowing he was being followed.

So he had recognised Rebus, and now had seen him hurrying after him. The policeman exhaled noisily and pushed his way through the outer ring of the celebrations. His arms ached, as though he had been swimming against a strong current, but now that he was safely out of the water, he saw that Crawford had vanished. He looked along the row of shops, separated each from the other by narrow, darkened closes. Up those closes were the entrances to flats, courtyards surrounded by university halls of residence, and many steep and worn steps leading from the High Street down to Cockburn Street. Rebus had to choose one of them. If he hesitated, or chose wrongly, Crawford would make good his escape. He ran to the first alley and, glancing down it, listening for footsteps, decided to move on. At the second close, he chose not to waste any more time and ran in, passing dimly-lit doorways festooned with graffiti, dank walls and frozen cobbles. Until, launching himself down a flight of steps into almost absolute darkness, he stumbled. He flailed for a hand-rail to stop him from falling, and found his arm grabbed by a powerful hand, saving him.

Crawford was standing against the side of the alley, on a platform between flights of steps. Rebus sucked in air, trying to calm himself. There was a sound in his ears like the aftermath of an explosion.

'Thanks,' he spluttered.

'You were following me.' The voice was effortlessly calm.

'Was I?' It was a lame retort and Crawford knew it. He chuckled. 'Yes, Mr Rebus, you were. You must have gotten a bit of a shock.'

Rebus nodded. 'A bit, yes, after all these years, Jackie.'

'I'm surprised you recognised me. People tell me I've changed.'

'Not that much.' Rebus glanced down at his arm, which was still in Crawford's vice-like grip. The grip relaxed and fell away. 'Sorry.'

Rebus was surprised at the apology, but tried not to let it show. He was busy covertly studying Crawford's body, looking for any bulge big enough to be a package or a gun.

'So what were you doing back there?' he asked, not particularly interested in the answer, but certainly interested in the time it might buy him.

Crawford seemed amused. 'Bringing in the New Year, of course. What else would I be doing?'

It was a fair question, but Rebus chose not to answer it. 'When did you get out?'

'A month back.' Crawford could sense Rebus's suspicion. 'It's legit. Honest to God, Sergeant, as He is my witness. I haven't done a runner or anything.'

'You ran from *me*. And it's Inspector now, by the way.'

Crawford smiled again. 'Congratulations.'

'Why did you run?'

'Was I running?'

'You know you were.'

'The reason I was running was because the last person I wanted to see tonight of all nights was you, Inspector Rebus. You spoilt it for me.'

Rebus frowned. He was *looking* at Trigger Crawford, but felt he was talking to somebody else, someone calmer and less dangerous, someone, well, *ordinary*. He was confused, but still suspicious. 'Spoilt what exactly?'

'My New Year resolution. I came here to make peace with the world.'

It was Rebus's turn to smile, though not kindly. 'Make peace, eh?'

'That's right.'

'No more guns? No more armed robberies?'

Crawford was shaking his head slowly. Then he held open his coat. 'No more shooters, Inspector. That's a promise. You see, I've made my own peace.'

Peace or piece? Rebus couldn't be sure. He was reaching into his own jacket pocket, from which he produced a police radio. Crawford looked on the level. He even sounded on the level, but facts had to be verified. So he called in and asked for a check to be made on John Crawford, nickname 'Trigger'. Crawford smiled shyly at the mention of that name. Rebus held onto the radio, waiting for the computer to do its stuff, waiting for the station to respond.

'It's been a long time since anyone called me Trigger,' Crawford said. 'Quite some time.'

'How come they released you after four?'

'A bit less than four, actually,' corrected Crawford. 'They released me because I was no longer a threat to society. You'll find that hard to believe. In fact, you'll find it *impossible* to believe. That's not my fault, it's yours. You think men like me can never go straight. But we can. You see, something happened to me in prison. I found Jesus Christ.'

Rebus knew the look on his face was a picture, and it caused Crawford to smile again, still shyly. He looked down at the tips of his shoes.

'That's right, Inspector. I became a Christian. It wasn't any kind of blinding light. It took a while. I got bored inside and I started reading books. One day I picked up the Bible and just opened it at random. What I read there seemed to make sense. It was the Good News Bible, written in plain English. I read bits and pieces, just flicked through it. Then I went to one of the Sunday services, mainly because there were a few things I couldn't understand and I wanted to ask the minister about them. And he helped me a bit. That's how it started. It changed my life.'

Rebus could think of nothing to say. He thought of himself as a Christian, too, a sceptical Christian, a little like Crawford himself perhaps. Full of questions that needed answering. No, this couldn't be right. He was *nothing* like Crawford. Nothing at all like him. Crawford was an animal; his kind never changed. Did they? Just because he had never met a 'changed man', did that mean such a thing did not exist? After all, he'd never met the Queen or the Prime Minister either. The radio crackled to life in his hand.

'Rebus here,' he said, and then listened.

It was all true. The details from Crawford's file were being read to him. Model prisoner. Bible class. Recommended for early release. Personal tragedy.

'Personal tragedy?' Rebus looked at Crawford.

'Ach, my son died. He was only in his twenties.'

Rebus, having heard enough, had already switched off the radio. 'I'm sorry,' he said. Crawford just shrugged, shrugged shoulders beneath which were tucked no hidden shotguns, and slipped his hands into his pockets, pockets where no pistols lurked. But Rebus held out a hand towards him.

'Happy New Year,' he said.

Crawford stared at the hand, then brought out his own right hand. The two men shook warmly, their grips firm.

'Happy New Year,' said Crawford. Then he glanced back up the close. 'Look, Inspector, if it's all right with you I think I'll go back up the Tron. It was daft of me to run away in the first place. There are plenty of hands up there I've not shaken yet.'

Rebus nodded slowly. He understood now. For Crawford, the New Year was something special, a new start in more ways than one. Not everyone was given that chance.

'Aye,' he said. 'On you go.'

Crawford had climbed three steps before he paused. 'Incidentally,' he called, 'what were *you* doing at the Tron?'

'What else would I be doing there on New Year?' replied Rebus. 'I was working.'

'No rest for the wicked, eh?' said Crawford, climbing the slope back up to the High Street.

Rebus watched until Crawford disappeared into the gloom. He knew he should follow him. After all, he *was* still working. He was sure now that Crawford had been speaking the truth, that he had nothing to do with the drug deal. Their meeting had been coincidence, nothing more. But who would have believed it? Trigger Crawford a 'model prisoner'. And they said mankind no longer lived in an age of miracles.

Rebus climbed slowly. There seemed more people than ever on the High Street. He guessed things would be at their busiest around half past midnight, with the streets emptying quickly after that. If the deal was going to go through, it would take place before that time. He recognised one of the Glasgow detectives heading towards him. As he spotted Rebus, the detective half-raised his arms.

'Where have you been? We thought you'd buggered off home.'

'Nothing happening then?'

The detective sighed. 'No, nothing at all. Lyons looks a bit impatient. I don't think he's going to give it much longer himself.'

'I thought your informant was air-tight?'

'As a rule. Maybe this will be the exception.' The detective smiled, seemingly used to such disappointments in his life. Rebus had noticed earlier that the young man possessed badly chewed fingernails and even the skin around the nails was torn and raw-looking. A stressed young man. In a few years he would be overweight and then would become heart attack material. Rebus knew that he himself was heart attack material: h.a.m., they called it back at the station. You were lean (meaning fit) or you were ham. Rebus was decidedly the latter.

'So anyway, where were you?'

'I bumped into an old friend. Well, to be precise an old adversary. Jackie Crawford.'

'Jackie Crawford? You mean Trigger Crawford?' The young detective was rifling through his memory files. 'Oh yes, I heard he was out.'

'Did you? Nobody bothered to tell me.'

'Yes, something about his son dying. Drug overdose. All the fire went out of Crawford after that. Turned into a Bible basher.'

They were walking back towards the crowd. Back towards where Alan Lyons waited for a suitcase full of heroin. Rebus stopped dead in his tracks.

'Drugs? Did you say his son died from drugs?'

The detective nodded. 'The big H. It wasn't too far from my patch. Somewhere in Partick.'

'Did Crawford's son live in Glasgow then?'

'No, he was just visiting. He stayed here in Edinburgh.' The detective was not as slow as some. He knew what Rebus was thinking. 'Christ, you don't mean ...?'

And then they were both running, pushing their way through the crowd, and the detective from Glasgow was shouting into his radio, but there was noise all around him, yelling and cheering and singing, smothering his words. Their progress was becoming slower. It was like moving through water chest-high. Rebus's legs felt useless and sore and there was a line of sweat trickling down his spine. Crawford's son had died from heroin, heroin purchased most probably in Edinburgh, and the man behind most of the heroin deals in Edinburgh was waiting somewhere up ahead. Coincidence? He had never really believed in coincidences, not really. They were convenient excuses for shrugging off the unthinkable.

What had Crawford said? Something about coming here tonight to make peace. Well, there were ways and ways of making peace, weren't there? 'If any mischief should follow, then thou shalt give life for life.' That was from Exodus. A dangerous book, the Bible. It could be made to say anything, its meaning in the mind of the beholder.

What was going through Jackie Crawford's mind? Rebus dreaded to think. There was a commotion up ahead, the crowd forming itself into a tight semi-circle around a shop-front. Rebus squeezed his way to the front.

'Police,' he shouted. 'Let me through, please.'

Grudgingly, the mass of bodies parted just enough for him to make progress. Finally he found himself at the front, staring at the slumped body of Alan Lyons. A long smear ran down the shop window to where he lay and his chest was stained dark red. One of the Glasgow officers was trying unsuccessfully to stem the flow of blood, using his own rolled-up coat, now sopping wet. Other officers were keeping back the crowd. Rebus caught snatches of what they were saying.

'Looked like he was going to shake hands.'

'Looked like he was hugging him.'

'Then the knife ...'

'Pulled out a knife.'

'Stabbed him twice before we could do anything.'

'Couldn't do anything.'

A siren had started nearby, inching closer. There were always ambulances on standby near the Tron on Hogmanay. Beside Lyons, still gripped in his left hand, was the bag containing the money for the deal.

'Will he be all right?' Rebus said to nobody in particular, which was just as well since nobody answered. He was remembering back a month to another dealer, another knife ... Then he saw Crawford. He was being restrained on the edge of the crowd by two more plainclothes men. One held his arms behind him while the other frisked him for weapons. On the pavement between where Crawford stood and Alan Lyons lay dying or dead there was a fairly ordinary looking knife, small enough to conceal in a sock or a waistband, but enough for the job required. More than an inch of blade was excess. The other detective was beside Rebus.

'Aw, Christ,' he said. But Rebus was staring at Crawford and Crawford was staring back, and in that moment they understood one another well enough. 'I don't suppose,' the detective was saying, 'we'll be seeing the party with the merchandise. Always supposing he was going to turn up in any event.'

'I'm not so sure about that,' answered Rebus, turning his gaze from Crawford. 'Ask yourself this: how did Crawford know Lyons would be in the High Street tonight?' The detective did not answer. Behind them, the crowd was pressing closer for a look at the body and then making noises of revulsion before opening another can of lager or half-bottle of vodka. The ambulance was still a good fifty yards away. Rebus nodded towards Crawford.

'He knows where the stuff is, but he's probably dumped it some-where. Somewhere nobody can ever touch it. It was just bait, that's all. Just bait.'

And as bait it had worked. Hook, line and bloody sinker. Lyons had swallowed it, while Rebus, equally fooled, had swallowed something else. He felt it sticking in his throat like something cancerous, something no amount of coughing would dislodge. He glanced towards the prone body again and smiled involuntarily. A headline had come to mind, one that would never be used.

LYONS FED TO THE CHRISTIAN.

Someone was being noisily sick somewhere behind him. A bottle shattered against a wall. The loudest voices in the crowd were growing irritable and hard-edged. In fifteen minutes or so, they would cease to be revellers and would be transformed into troublemakers. A woman shrieked from one of the many darkened closes. The look on Jackie Crawford's face was one of calm and righteous triumph. He offered no resistance to the officers. He had known they were watching Lyons, had known he might kill Lyons but he would never get away. And still he had driven home the knife. What else was he to do with his freedom?'

The night was young and so was the year. Rebus held out his hand towards the detective.

'Happy New Year,' he said. 'And many more of them.'

The young man stared at him blankly. 'Don't think you're blaming us for this,' he said. 'This was your fault. You let Crawford go. It's Edinburgh's balls-up, not ours.'

Rebus shrugged and let his arm fall to his side. Then he started to walk along the pavement, moving further and further from the scene. The ambulance moved past him. Someone slapped him on the back and offered a hand. From a distance, the young detective was watching him retreat.

'Away to hell,' said Rebus quietly, not sure for whom the message was intended.

The Gentlemen's Club

It was the most elegant of all Edinburgh's elegant Georgian circuses, a perfect circle in design and construction, the houses themselves as yet untouched by the private contractors who might one day renovate and remove, producing a dozen tiny flats from each.

A perfect circle surrounding some private gardens, the gardens a wash of colour despite the January chill: violet, pink, red, green and orange. A tasteful display, though. No flower was allowed to be too vibrant, too bright, too inelegant.

The gate to the gardens was locked, of course. The keyholders paid a substantial fee each year for the privilege of that lock. Everyone else could look, could peer through the railings as he was doing now, but entrance was forbidden. Well, that was Edinburgh for you, a closed circle within a closed circle.

He stood there, enjoying the subtle smells in the air now that the flurry of snowflakes had stopped. Then he shifted his attention to the houses, huge three- and four-storey statements of the architect's confidence. He found himself staring at one particular house, the one outside which the white police Sierra was parked. It was too ripe a day to be spoiled, but duty was duty. Taking a final deep breath, he turned from the garden railings and walked towards number 16, with its heavy closed curtains but its front door ajar.

Once inside, having introduced himself, John Rebus had to climb three large flights of stairs to 'the children's floor', as his guide termed it. She was slender and middle-aged and dressed from head to toe in grey. The house was quiet, only one or two shafts of sunlight penetrating its gloom. The woman walked near-silently and quickly, while Rebus tugged on the bannister, breathing hard.

It wasn't that he was unfit, but somehow all the oxygen seemed to have been pumped out of the house.

Arriving at last at the third floor, the woman passed three firmly closed doors before stopping at a fourth. This one was open, and inside Rebus could make out the gleaming tiles of a large bathroom and the shuffling, insect-like figures of Detective Constable Brian Holmes and the police pathologist, not the lugubrious Dr Curt but the one everybody called – though not to his face, never to his face – Dr Crippen. He turned to his guide.

'Thank you, Mrs McKenzie.' But she had already averted her eyes and was making back for the safety of the stairs. She was a brave one though, to bring him all the way up here in the first place. And now there was nothing for it but to enter the room. 'Hello, Doctor.'

'Inspector Rebus, good morning. Not a pretty sight, is it?'

Rebus forced himself to look. There was not much water in the bath, and what water there was had been dyed a rich ruby colour by the girl's blood. She was undressed and as white as a statue. She had been very young, sixteen or seventeen, her body not yet quite fully formed. A late developer.

Her arms lay peacefully by her sides, wrists turned upwards to reveal the clean incisions. Holmes used a pair of tweezers to hold up a single razor blade for Rebus's inspection. Rebus winced and shook his head.

'What a waste,' he said. He had a daughter himself, not much older than this girl. His wife had taken their daughter with her when she left him. Years ago now. He'd lost touch, the way you do sometimes with family, though you keep in contact with friends.

He was moving around the bath, committing the scene to memory. The air seemed to glow, but the glow was already fading.

'Yes,' said Holmes. 'It's a sin.'

'Suicide, of course,' Rebus commented after a silence. The pathologist nodded, but did not speak. They were not usually so awkward around a corpse, these three men. Each thought he had seen the worst, the most brutal, the most callous. Each had anecdotes to relate which would make strangers shudder and screw shut their eyes. But this, this was different. Something had been taken quietly, deliberately and ruinously from the world.

'The question,' Rebus said, for the sake of filling the void, 'is why.'

Why indeed. Here he was, standing in a bathroom bigger than his own living-room, surrounded by powders and scents, thick towels, soaps and sponges. But here was this gruesome and unnecessary death. There had to be a reason for it. Silly, stupid child. What had she been playing at? Mute anger turned to frustration, and he almost staggered as he made his way out to the landing.

There had to be a reason. And he was just in the mood now to track it down.

*

'I've told you already,' said Thomas McKenzie irritably, 'she was the happiest girl in Christendom. No, we didn't spoil her, and no, we never forbade her seeing anyone. There is no reason in the world, Inspector, why Suzanne should have done what she did. It just doesn't make sense.'

McKenzie broke down again, burying his face in his hands. Rebus loathed himself, yet the questions had to be asked.

'Did she,' he began, 'did she have a boyfriend, Mr McKenzie?'

McKenzie got up from his chair, walked to the sideboard and poured himself another whisky. He motioned to Rebus who, still cradling a crystal inch of the stuff, shook his head. Mrs McKenzie was upstairs resting. She had been given a sedative by her doctor, an old friend of the family who had seemed in need of similar treatment himself.

But Thomas McKenzie had not needed anything. He was sticking to the old remedies, sloshing a fresh measure of malt into his glass.

'No,' he said, 'no boyfriends. They've never really been Suzanne's style.'

Though he would not be travelling to his office today, McKenzie had still dressed himself in a dark blue suit and tie. The drawing-room in which Rebus sat had about it the air of a commercial office, not at all homely or lived-in. He couldn't imagine growing up in such a place.

'What about school?' he asked.

'What do you mean?'

'I mean, was she happy there?'

'Very.' McKenzie sat down with his drink. 'She gets good reports, good grades. She ... she *was* going to the University in October.'

Rebus watched him gulp at the whisky. Thomas McKenzie was a tough man, tough enough to make his million young and then canny enough not to lose it. He was forty-four now, but looked younger. Rebus had no idea how many shops McKenzie now owned, how many company directorships he held along with all his other holdings and interests. He was new money trying to look like old money, making his home in Stockbridge, convenient for Princes Street, rather than further out in bungalow land.

'What was she going to study?' Rebus stared past McKenzie towards where a family portrait sat on a long, polished sideboard. No family snapshot, but posed, a sitting for a professional photographer. Daughter gleaming in the centre, sandwiched by grinning parents. A mock-up cloudscape behind them, the clouds pearl-coloured, the sky blue.

'Law,' said McKenzie. 'She had a head on her shoulders.'

Yes, a head of mousy-brown hair. And her father had found her early in the morning, already cold. McKenzie hadn't panicked. He'd made the phone calls before waking his wife and telling her. He always rose first, always went straight to the bathroom. He had remained calm, most probably from shock. But there was a stiffness to McKenzie, too, Rebus noticed. He wondered what it would take really to rouse the man.

Something niggled. Suzanne had gone to the bathroom, run some water into the bath, lain down in it, and slashed her wrists. Fine, Rebus could accept that. Maybe she had expected to be found and rescued. Most failed suicides were cries for help, weren't they? If you *really* wanted to kill yourself, you went somewhere quiet and secret, where you couldn't possibly be found in time. Suzanne hadn't done that. She had almost certainly expected her father to find her in time. Her timing had been a little awry.

Moreover, she must have known her father always rose before her mother, and therefore that he would be the first to find her. This notion interested Rebus, though no one around him seemed curious about it.

'What about friends at school,' Rebus went on. 'Did Suzanne have many friends?'

'Oh yes, lots.'

'Anyone in particular?'

McKenzie was about to answer when the door opened and his wife walked in, pale from her drugged sleep.

'What time is it?' she asked, shuffling forwards.

'It's eleven, Shona,' her husband said, rising to meet her. 'You've only been asleep half an hour.' They embraced one another, her arms tight around his body. Rebus felt like an intruder on their grief, but the questions still had to be asked.

'You were about to tell me about Suzanne's friends, Mr McKenzie.'

Husband and wife sat down together on the sofa, hands clasped.

'Well,' said McKenzie, 'there were lots of them, weren't there, Shona?'

'Yes,' said his wife. She really was an attractive woman. Her face had the same smooth sheen as her daughter's. She was the sort of woman men would instinctively feel protective towards, whether protection was needed or not. 'But I always liked Hazel best,' she went on.

McKenzie turned to Rebus and explained. 'Hazel Frazer, daughter of Sir Jimmy Frazer, the banker. A peach of a girl. A real peach.' He paused, staring at his wife, and then began, softly, with dignity, to cry. She rested his head against her shoulder and stroked his hair, talking softly to him. Rebus averted his eyes and drank his whisky. Then bit his bottom lip, deep in thought. In matters of suicide, just who was the victim, who the culprit?

Suzanne's room was a cold and comfortless affair. No posters on the walls, no teenage clutter or signs of an independent mind. There was a writing-pad on the dressing table, but it was blank. A crumpled ball of paper sat in the bottom of an otherwise empty bin beside the wardrobe. Rebus carefully unfolded the sheet. Written on it, in a fairly steady hand, was a message: 'Told you I would.'

Rebus studied the sentence. Told whom? Her parents seemed to have no inkling their daughter was suicidal, yet the note had been meant for someone. And having written it, why had she discarded it? He turned it over. The other side, though blank was slightly tacky. Rebus sniffed the paper, but could find no smell to identify the stickiness. He carefully folded the paper and slipped it into his pocket.

In the top drawer of the dressing-table was a leather-bound diary. But Suzanne had been no diarist. Instead of the expected teenage outpourings, Rebus found only one-line reminders, every Tuesday for the past six months or so, 'The Gentlemen's Club – 4.00'. Curiouser and curiouser. The last entry was for the previous week, with nothing in the rest of the diary save blank pages.

The Gentlemen's Club – what on earth could she have meant? Rebus knew of several clubs in Edinburgh, dowdy remnants of a former age, but none was called simply The Gentlemen's Club. The diary went into his pocket along with the note.

Thomas McKenzie saw him to the door. The tie around his neck was hanging loosely now and his voice was sweet with whisky.

'Just two last questions before I go,' Rebus said.

'Yes?' said McKenzie, sighing.

'Do you belong to a club?'

McKenzie seemed taken aback, but shrugged. 'Several, actually. The Strathspey Health Club. The Forth Golf Club. And Finlay's as was.'

'Finlay's Gentlemen's Club?'

'Yes, that's right. But it's called Thomson's now.'

Rebus nodded. 'Final question,' he said. 'What did Suzanne do on Tuesdays at four?'

'Nothing special. I think she had some drama group at school.'

'Thank you, Mr McKenzie. Sorry to have troubled you. Goodbye.'

'Goodbye, Inspector.'

Rebus stood on the top step, breathing in lungfuls of fresh air. Too much of a good thing could be stifling. He wondered if Suzanne McKenzie had felt stifled. He still wondered why she had died. And, knowing her father would be the first to find her, why had she lain down *naked* in the bath? Rebus had seen suicides before – lots of them – but whether they chose the bathroom or the bedroom, they were always clothed.

'Naked I came,' he thought to himself, remembering the passage from the Book of Job, 'and naked shall return.'

On his way to Hawthornden School for Girls, Rebus received a message from Detective Constable Holmes, who had returned to the station.

'Go ahead,' said Rebus. The radio crackled. The sky overhead was the colour of a bruise, the static in the air playing havoc with the radio's reception.

'I've just run McKenzie's name through the computer,' said Holmes, 'and come up with something you might be interested in.'

Rebus smiled. Holmes was as thorough as any airport sniffer dog. 'Well?' he said. 'Are you going to tell me, or do I have to buy the paperback?'

There was a hurt pause before Holmes began to speak and Rebus remembered how sensitive to criticism the younger man could be. 'It seems,' Holmes said at last, 'that Mr McKenzie was arrested several months back for loitering outside a school.'

'Oh? Which school?'

'Murrayfield Comprehensive. He wasn't charged, but it's on record that he was taken to Murrayfield police station and questioned.'

'That *is* interesting. I'll talk to you later.' Rebus terminated the call. The rain had started to fall in heavy drops. He picked up the radio again and asked to be put through to Murrayfield police station. His luck was in. A colleague there remembered the whole incident.

'We kept it quiet, of course,' the Inspector told Rebus. 'And McKenzie swore he'd just stopped there to call into his office. But the teachers at the school were adamant he'd parked there before, during the lunch-break. It's not the most refined area of town after all, is it? A Daimler does tend to stand out from the crowd around there, especially when there isn't a bride in the back of it.'

'I take your point,' said Rebus, smiling. 'Anything else?'

'Yes, one of the kids told a teacher he'd seen someone get into McKenzie's Daimler once, but we couldn't find any evidence of that.'

'Vivid imaginations, these kids,' Rebus agreed. This was all his colleague could tell him, but it was enough to muddy the water. Had Suzanne discovered her father's secret and, ashamed, killed herself? Or perhaps her schoolfriends had found out and teased her about it? If McKenzie liked kids, there might even be a tang of incest about the whole thing. That would at least go some way towards explaining Suzanne's nudity: she wasn't putting on show anything her father hadn't seen before. But what about The Gentlemen's Club? Where did it fit in? At Hawthornden School, Rebus hoped he might find some answers.

It was the sort of school fathers sent their daughters to so that they might learn the arts of femininity and ruthlessness. The headmistress, as imposing a character as the school building itself, fed Rebus on cakes and tea before leading him to Suzanne's form mistress, a Miss Selkirk, who had prepared more tea for him in her little private room.

Yes, she told him, Suzanne had been a very popular girl and news of her death came as quite a shock. She had run around with Hazel Frazer, the banker's daughter. A very vivacious girl, Hazel, head of school this year, though Suzanne hadn't been far behind in the running. A competitive pair, their marks for maths, English, languages almost identical. Suzanne the better at sciences; Hazel the better at economics and accounts. Splendid girls, the pair of them.

Biting into his fourth or fifth cake, Rebus nodded again. These women were all so commanding that he had begun to feel like a schoolboy himself. He sat with knees primly together, smiling, asking his questions almost apologetically.

'I don't suppose,' he said, 'the name The Gentlemen's Club means anything to you?'

Miss Selkirk thought hard. 'Is it,' she said at last, 'the name of a discotheque?'

Rebus smiled. 'I don't think so. Why do you ask?'

'Well, it's just that I do seem to recall having heard it before from one of the girls, quite recently, but only in passing.'

Rebus looked disappointed.

'I am sorry, Inspector.' She tapped her skull. 'This old head of mine isn't what it used to be.'

'That's quite all right,' said Rebus quietly. 'One last thing, do you happen to know who takes the school's drama classes?'

'Ah,' said Miss Selkirk, 'that's young Miss Phillips, the English teacher.'

Miss Phillips, who insisted that Rebus call her Jilly, was not only young but also very attractive. Waves of long auburn hair fell over her shoulders and down her back. Her eyes were dark and moist with recently shed tears. Rebus felt more awkward than ever.

'I believe,' he said, 'that you run the school's drama group.'

'That's right.' Her voice was fragile as porcelain.

'And Suzanne was in the group?'

'Yes. She was due to play Celia in our production of *As You Like It*.'

'Oh?'

'That's Shakespeare, you know.'

'Yes,' said Rebus, 'I do know.'

They were talking in the corridor, just outside her classroom, and through the panes of glass in the door, Rebus could see a class of fairly mature girls, healthy and from well-ordered homes, whispering together and giggling. Odd that, considering they'd just lost a friend.

'Celia,' he said, 'is Duke Frederick's daughter, isn't she?'

'I'm impressed, Inspector.'

'It's not my favourite Shakespeare play,' Rebus explained, 'but I remember seeing it at the Festival a few years back. Celia has a friend, doesn't she?'

'That's right, Rosalind.'

'So who was going to play Rosalind?'

'Hazel Frazer.'

Rebus nodded slowly at this. It made sense. 'Is Hazel in your classroom at the moment?'

'Yes, she's the one with the long black hair. Do you see her?'

Oh yes, Rebus could see her. She sat, calm and imperturbable, at the still centre of a sea of admirers. The other girls giggled and whispered around her, hoping to catch her attention or a few words of praise, while she sat oblivious to it all.

'Yes,' he said, 'I see her.'

'Would you care to speak with her, Inspector?'

He knew Hazel was aware of him, even though she averted her eyes from the door. Indeed, he knew precisely *because* she refused to look, while the other girls glanced towards the corridor from time to time, interested in this interruption to their classwork. Interested and curious. Hazel pretended to be neither, which in itself interested Rebus.

'No,' he said to Jilly Phillips, 'not just now. She's probably upset, and it wouldn't do much good for me to go asking her questions under the circumstances. There was one thing, though.'

'Yes, Inspector?'

'This after-school drama group of yours, the one that meets on Tuesdays, it doesn't happen to have a nickname, does it?'

'Not that I know of.' Jilly Phillips furrowed her brow. 'But, Inspector?'

'Yes?'

'You're under some kind of misapprehension. The drama group meets on Fridays, not Tuesdays. And we meet before lunch.'

Rebus drove out of the school grounds and parked by the side of the busy main road. The drama group met during school hours, so what had Suzanne done on Tuesdays after school, while her parents thought she was there? At least, McKenzie had said he'd thought that's what she'd done on Tuesdays. Suppose he'd been lying? Then what?

A maroon-coloured bus roared past Rebus's car. A 135, on its way to Princes Street. He started up the car again and followed it along its route, all the time thinking through the details of Suzanne's suicide. Until suddenly, with blinding clarity, he saw the truth of the thing, and bit his bottom lip fiercely, wondering just what on earth he could – should – do about it.

Well, the longer he thought about doing something, the harder it would become to do it. So he called Holmes and asked him for a large favour, before driving over to the house owned by Sir Jimmy Frazer.

Frazer was not just part of the Edinburgh establishment – in many ways he *was* that establishment. Born and educated in the city, he had won hard-earned respect, friendship and awe on his way to the top. The nineteenth-century walled house in which his family made its home was part of his story. It had been about to be bought by a company, an English company, and knocked down to make way for a new apartment block. There were public protests about this act of vandalism and in had stepped Sir Jimmy Frazer, purchasing the house and making it his own.

That had been years ago, but it was a story still heard told by hard men to other hard men in watering holes throughout the city. Rebus examined the house as he drove in through the open gates. It was an ugly near-Gothic invention, mock turrets and spires, hard, cold and uninviting. A maid answered the door. Rebus introduced himself and was ushered into a large drawing-room, where Sir Jimmy's wife, tall and dark haired like her daughter, waited.

'I'm sorry to trouble you, Lady—' Rebus was cut short by an imperious hand, but an open smile.

'Just Deborah, please.' And she motioned for Rebus to sit.

'Thank you,' he said. 'I'm sorry to trouble you, but—'

'Yes, your call *was* intriguing, Inspector. Of course, I'll do what I can. It's a tragedy, poor Suzanne.'

'You knew her then?'

'Of course. Why ever shouldn't we know her? She visited practically every Tuesday.'

'Oh?' Rebus had suspected as much, but was keen to learn more.

'After school,' Lady Deborah continued. 'Hazel and Suzanne and a few other chums would come back here. They didn't stay late.'

'But what exactly did they do?'

She laughed. 'I've no idea. What do girls of that age do? Play records? Talk about boys? Try to defer growing up?' She gave a wry smile, perhaps thinking of her own past. Rebus checked his wristwatch casually. Five to four. He had a few minutes yet.

'Did they,' he asked, 'confine themselves to your daughter's room?'

'More or less. Not her bedroom, of course. There's an old playroom upstairs. Hazel uses that as a kind of den.'

Rebus nodded. 'May I see it?'

Lady Deborah seemed puzzled. 'I suppose so, though I can't see—'

'It would help,' Rebus interrupted, 'to give me an overall picture of Suzanne. I'm trying to work out the kind of girl she was.'

'Of course,' said Lady Deborah, though she sounded unconvinced.

Rebus was shown to a small, cluttered room at the end of a long corridor. Inside, the curtains were closed. Lady Deborah switched on the lights.

'Hazel won't allow the maid in here,' Lady Deborah explained, apologising for the untidiness. '*Secrets*, I suppose,' she whispered.

Rebus did not doubt it. There were two small sofas, piles of pop and teenage magazines scattered on the floor, an ashtray full of dog-ends (which Lady Deborah pointedly chose to ignore), a stereo against one wall and a desk against another, on which sat a personal computer, its screen switched on but blank.

'She always forgets to turn that thing off,' said Lady Deborah. Rebus could hear the telephone ringing downstairs. The maid answered it and then called up to Lady Deborah.

'Oh dear. Please excuse me, Inspector.'

Rebus smiled and bowed slightly as she left. His watch said four o'clock. As prearranged, it would be Holmes on the phone. Rebus had told him to pretend to be anybody, to say *anything*, so long as he kept Lady Deborah occupied for five minutes. Holmes had suggested he be a journalist seeking some quotes for a magazine feature. Rebus smiled now. Yes, there was probably vanity enough in Lady Deborah to keep her talking with a reporter for at least five minutes, maybe more.

Still, he couldn't waste time. He had expected to have to do a lot of searching, but the computer seemed the obvious place to start. There were floppy discs stored in a plastic box beside the monitor. He flipped through them until he came to one labelled GC DISC. There could be no doubt. He slipped the disc into the computer and watched as the display came up. He had found the records of The Gentlemen's Club.

He read quickly. Not that there was much to read. Members must attend every week, at four o'clock on Tuesday. Members must wear a tie. (Rebus looked quickly in a drawer of the desk and found five ties. He recognised them as belonging to various clubs in the city: the Strathspey, the Forth Golf Club, Finlay's Club. Stolen from the girls' fathers of course, and worn to meetings of a secret little clique, itself a parody of the clubs their fathers frequented.)

In a file named 'Exploits of the Gentlemen's Club', Rebus found lists of petty thefts, acts of so-called daring, and lies. Members had stolen from city centre shops, had carried out practical jokes against teachers and pupils alike, had been, in short, malicious.

There were many exploits attributed to Suzanne, including lying to her parents about what she did on Tuesday after school. Twenty-eight exploits in all. Hazel Frazer's list totalled thirty at the bottom, yet Rebus could count only twenty-nine entries on the screen. And in a separate file, the agenda for a meeting yet to be held, was a single item, recorded as 'New Business: can suicide be termed an exploit of the Gentlemen's Club?'

Rebus heard steps behind him. He turned, but it was not Lady Deborah. It was Hazel Frazer. Her eyes looked past him to the screen, firstly in fear and disbelief, then in scorn.

'Hello, Hazel.'

'You're the policeman,' she said in a level tone. 'I saw you at the school.'

'That's right.' Rebus studied her as she came into the room. She was a cool one, all right. That was Hawthornden for you, breeding strong, cold women, each one her father's daughter. 'Are you jealous of her?'

'Of whom? Suzanne?' Hazel smiled cruelly. 'Why should I be?'

'Because,' answered Rebus, 'Suzanne's is the ultimate exploit. For once, she beat you.'

'You think that's why she did it?' Hazel sounded smug. When Rebus shook his head, a little of her confidence seeped away.

'I know why she did it, Hazel. She did it because she found out about you and her father. She found out because you told her. I notice it's too much of a secret for you to put on your computer, but you've added it to the list, haven't you? As an exploit. I expect you were having an argument, bragging, being competitive. And it just slipped out. You told Suzanne you were her father's lover.'

Her cheeks were becoming a deep strawberry red, while her lips drained of colour. But she wasn't about to speak, so Rebus went on at her.

'You met him at lunchtime. You couldn't meet near Hawthornden. That would be too risky. So you'd take a bus to Murrayfield. It's only ten minutes ride away. He'd be waiting in his car. You told Suzanne and she couldn't bear to know. So she killed herself.' Rebus was becoming angry. 'And all you can be bothered to do is write about her on your files and wonder whether suicide is an "exploit".' His voice had risen and he hardly registered the fact that Lady Deborah was standing in the doorway, looking on in disbelief.

'No!' yelled Hazel. 'She did it first! She slept with Daddy months ago! So I did it back to her. *That's* what she couldn't live with! That's why she—'

Then it happened. Hazel's shoulders fell forward and, eyes closed, she began to cry, silently at first, but then loudly. Her mother ran to comfort her and told Rebus to leave. Couldn't he see what the girl was going through? He'd pay, she told him. He'd pay for upsetting her daughter. But she was crying too, crying like Hazel, mother and child. Rebus could think of nothing to say, so he left.

Descending the stairs, he tried not to think about what he had just unleashed. Two families broken now instead of one, and to what end? Merely to prove, as he had always known anyway, that a pretty face was no mirror of the soul and that the spirit of competition still flourished in Scotland's well-respected education system. He dug his hands deep into his jacket pockets, felt something there and drew out Suzanne's note. The crumpled note, found discarded in her bin, sticky on one side. He stopped halfway down the stairs, staring at the note without really seeing it. He was visualising something else, something almost too horrible, too unbelievable.

Yet he believed it.

Thomas McKenzie was surprised to see him. Mrs McKenzie had, he said, gone to stay with a sister on the other side of the city. The body had been taken away, of course, and the bathroom cleaned. McKenzie was without jacket and tie and had rolled up his shirt-sleeves. He wore half-moon glasses and carried a pen with him as he opened the door to Rebus.

In the drawing-room, there were signs that McKenzie had been working. Papers were strewn across a writing desk, a briefcase open on the floor. A calculator sat on the chair, as did a telephone.

'I'm sorry to disturb you again, sir,' Rebus said, taking in the scene. McKenzie had sobered up since the morning. He looked like a businessman rather than a grieving father.

McKenzie seemed to realise that the scene before Rebus created a strange impression.

'Keeping busy,' he said. 'Keeping the mind occupied, you know. Life can't stop because ...' He fell silent.

'Quite, sir,' Rebus said, seating himself on the sofa. He reached into his pocket. 'I thought you might like this.' He held the paper towards McKenzie, who took it from him and glanced at it. Rebus stared hard at him, and McKenzie twitched, attempting to hand back the note.

'No, sir,' said Rebus, 'you keep it.'

'Why?'

'It will always remind you,' said Rebus, his voice cold and level, 'that you could have saved your daughter.'

McKenzie was aghast. 'What do you mean?'

'I mean,' said Rebus, his voice still lacking emotion, 'that Suzanne wasn't intending to kill herself, not really. It was just something to attract your attention, to shock you into ... I don't know, action I suppose, a *re*action of some kind.'

McKenzie positioned himself slowly so that he rested on the armrest of one of the upholstered chairs.

'Yes,' Rebus went on, 'a reaction. That's as good a way of putting it as any. Suzanne knew what time you got up every morning. She wasn't stupid. She timed the slashing of her wrists so that you would find her while there was still time to save her. She also had a sense of the dramatic, didn't she? So she stuck her little note to the bathroom door. You saw the note and you went into the bathroom. And she wasn't dead, was she?'

McKenzie had screwed shut his eyes. His mouth was open, the teeth gritted in remembrance.

'She wasn't dead,' Rebus continued, 'not quite. And you knew damned well why she'd done it. Because she'd warned you she would. She had told you she would. Unless you stopped seeing Hazel, unless you owned up to her mother. Perhaps she had a lot of demands, Mr McKenzie. You never really got on with her anyway, did you? You didn't know what to do. Help her, or leave her to die? You hesitated. You waited.'

Rebus had risen from his seat now. His voice had risen, too. The tears were streaming down McKenzie's face, his whole body shuddering. But Rebus was relentless.

'You walked around a bit, you walked into her room. You threw her note into the waste-bin. And eventually, *eventually* you reached for a telephone and made the calls.'

'It was already too late,' McKenzie bawled. 'Nobody could have saved her.'

'They could have tried!' Rebus was yelling now, yelling close to McKenzie's own twisted face. '*You* could have tried, but you didn't. You wanted to keep your secret. Well by God your secret's out.' The last words were hissed and with them Rebus felt his fury ebb. He turned and started to walk away.

'What are you going to do?' McKenzie moaned.

'What can I do?' Rebus answered quietly. 'I'm not going to do anything, Mr McKenzie. I'm just going to leave you to get on with the rest of your life.' He paused. 'Enjoy it,' he said, closing the doors of the drawing-room behind him.

He stood on the steps of the house, trembling, his heart pounding. In a suicide, who was to blame, who the victim? He still couldn't answer the question. He doubted he ever would. His watch told him it was five minutes to five. He knew the pub near the circus, a quiet bar frequented by thinkers and amateur philosophers, a place where nothing happened and the measures were generous. He felt like having one drink, maybe two at most. He would raise his glass and make a silent toast: to the lassies.

Monstrous Trumpet

John Rebus went down onto his knees.

'I'm begging you,' he said, 'don't do this to me, please.'

But Chief Inspector Lauderdale just laughed, thinking Rebus was clowning about as per usual. 'Come on, John,' he said. 'It'll be just like Interpol.'

Rebus got back to his feet. 'No it won't,' he said. 'It'll be like a bloody escort service. Besides, I can't speak French.'

'Apparently he speaks perfect English, this Monsieur ...' Lauderdale made a show of consulting the letter in front of him on his desk.

'Don't say it again, sir, please.'

'Monsieur Cluzeau.' Rebus winced. 'Yes,' Lauderdale continued, enjoying Rebus's discomfort, 'Monsieur Cluzeau. A fine name for a member of the *gendarmerie*, don't you think?'

'It's a stunt,' Rebus pleaded. 'It's got to be. DC Holmes or one of the other lads ...'

But Lauderdale would not budge. 'It's been verified by the Chief Super,' he said. 'I'm sorry about this, John, but I thought you'd be pleased.'

'*Pleased?*'

'Yes. Pleased. You know, showing a bit of Scots hospitality.'

'Since when did the CID job description encompass "tourist guide"?'

Lauderdale had had enough of this: Rebus had even stopped calling him 'sir'. 'Since, Inspector, I ordered you to do it.'

'But why *me*?'

Lauderdale shrugged. 'Why not you?' He sighed, opened a drawer of his desk and dropped the letter into it. 'Look, it's only a day, two at most. Just do it, eh? Now if you don't mind, Inspector, I've got rather a lot to do.'

But the fight had gone out of Rebus anyway. His voice was calm, resigned. 'When does he get here?'

Again, there was a pause while that missing 'sir' hung motionless in the air between them. Well, thought Lauderdale, the sod deserves this. 'He's already here.'

'What?'

'I mean, he's in Edinburgh. The letter took a bit of a time to get here.'

'You mean it sat in someone's office for a bit of time.'

'Well, whatever the delay, he's here. And he's coming to the station this afternoon.'

Rebus glanced at his watch. It was eleven-fifty. He groaned.

'*Late* afternoon, I'd imagine,' said Lauderdale, trying to soften the blow now that Rebus was heading for the canvas. This had been a bit of a mess all round. He'd only just received final confirmation himself that Monsieur Cluzeau was on his way. 'I mean,' he said, 'the French like to take a long lunch, don't they? Notorious for it. So I don't suppose he'll be here till after three.'

'Fine, he can take us as he finds us. What am I supposed to do with him anyway?'

Lauderdale tried to retain his composure: *just say it once, damn you! Just once so I know that you recognise me for what I am!* He cleared his throat. 'He wants to see how we work. So show him. As long as he can report back to his own people that we're courteous, efficient, diligent, scrupulous, and that we always get our man, well, I'll be happy.'

'Right you are, sir,' said Rebus, opening the door, making ready to leave Lauderdale's newly refurbished office. Lauderdale sat in a daze: *he'd said it! Rebus had actually ended a sentence with 'sir'!*

'That should be easy enough,' he was saying now. 'Oh, and I might as well track down Lord Lucan and catch the Loch Ness monster while I'm at it. I'm sure to have a spare five minutes.'

Rebus closed the door after him with such ferocity that Lauderdale feared for the glass-framed paintings on his walls. But glass was more resilient than it looked. And so was John Rebus.

Cluzeau had to be an arse-licker, hell-bent on promotion. What other reason could there be? The story was that he was coming over for the Scotland–France encounter at Murrayfield. Fair enough, Edinburgh filled with Frenchmen once every two years for a weekend in February, well-behaved if boisterous rugby fans whose main pleasure seemed to be dancing in saloon bars with ice-buckets on their heads.

Nothing out of the ordinary there. But imagine a Frenchman who, having decided to take a large chunk of his annual leave so as to coincide with the international season, then has another idea: while in Scotland he'll invite himself to spend a day with the local police force. His letter to his own chief requesting an introduction so impresses the chief that *he* writes to the Chief Constable. By now, the damage is done, and the boulder starts to bounce down the hillside – Chief Constable to Chief Super, Chief Super to Super, Super to Chief Inspector – and Chief Inspector to Mr Muggins, aka John Rebus.

Thank you and *bonne nuit*. Ha! There, he did remember a bit of French after all. Rhona, his wife, had done one of those teach-yourself French courses, all tapes and repeating phrases. It had driven Rebus bonkers, but some of it had stuck. And all of it in preparation for a long weekend in Paris, a weekend which hadn't come off because Rebus had been drawn into a murder inquiry. Little wonder she'd left him in the end.

Bonne nuit. Bonjour. That was another word. *Bonsoir.* What about *Bon accord*? Was that French, too? Bo'ness sounded French. Hadn't Bonnie Prince Charlie been French? And dear God, what was he going to do with the Frenchman?

There was only one answer: get busy. The busier he was, the less time there would be for small-talk, xenophobia and falling-out. With the brain and the body occupied, there would be less temptation to mention Onion Johnnies, frogs'-legs, the war, French letters, French kissing and *French and Saunders*. Oh dear God, what had he done to deserve this?

His phone buzzed.

'*Oui?*' said Rebus, smirking now because he remembered how often he'd managed to get away with not calling Lauderdale 'sir'.

'Eh?'

'Just practising, Bob.'

'You must be bloody psychic then. There's a French gentleman down here says he's got an appointment.'

'What? Already?' Rebus checked his watch again. It was two minutes past twelve. Christ, like sitting in a dentist's waiting-room and being called ahead of your turn. Would he really look like Peter Sellers? What if he didn't speak English?

'John?'

'Sorry, Bob, what?'

'What do you want me to tell him?'

'Tell him I'll be right down.' Right down in the dumps, he thought to himself, letting the receiver drop like a stone.

There was only one person in the large, dingy reception. He wore a biker's leather jacket and had a spider's-web tattoo creeping up out of his soiled T-shirt and across his throat. Rebus stopped in his tracks. But then he saw another figure, over to his left against the wall. This man was studying various Wanted and Missing posters. He was tall, thin, and wore an immaculate dark blue suit with a tightly-knotted red silk tie. His shoes looked brand new, as did his haircut.

Their eyes met, forcing Rebus into a smile. He was suddenly aware of his own rumpled chain-store suit, his scuffed brogues, the shirt with a button missing on one cuff.

'Inspector Rebus?' The man was coming forward, hand held out.

'That's right.' They shook. He was wearing after-shave too, not too strong but certainly noticeable. He had the bearing of someone much further up the ladder, yet Rebus had been told they were of similar ranks. Having said which, there was no way Rebus was going to say 'Inspector Cluzeau' out loud. It would be too ... too ...

'For you.'

Rebus saw that he was being handed a plastic carrier-bag. He looked inside. A litre of duty-free malt, a box of chocolates and a small tin of something. He lifted out the chocolates.

'Escargots,' Cluzeau explained. 'But made from chocolate.'

Rebus studied the picture on the box. Yes, chocolates in the shape of snails. And as for the tin ...

'Foie gras. It is a pâté made from fatted goose liver. A local delicacy. You spread it on your toast.'

'Sounds delicious,' Rebus said, with just a trace of irony. In fact, he was overwhelmed. None of this stuff looked as though it came cheap, meat paste or no. 'Thank you.'

The Frenchman shrugged. He had the kind of face which, shaved twice a day, still sported a five o'clock shadow. Hirsute: that was the word. What was that joke again, the one that ended with someone asking 'Hirsute?' and the guy replying 'No, the suit's mine, but the knickers are hers'? Hairy wrists, too, on one of which sat a thin gold wristwatch. He was tapping this with his finger.

'I am not too early, I hope.'

'What?' It was Rebus's curse to remember the endings of jokes but never their beginnings. 'No, no. You're all right. I was just, er, hold on a second, will you?'

'Sure.'

Rebus walked over to the reception desk, behind which stood the omnipresent Bob Leach. Bob nodded towards the bag.

'Not a bad haul,' he said.

Rebus kept his voice low, but not so low, he hoped, as to arouse Cluzeau's suspicions. 'Thing is, Bob, I wasn't expecting him for a

few hours yet. What the hell am I going to do with him? I don't
suppose you've got any calls?'

'Nothing you'd be interested in, John.' Leach examined the pad
in front of him. 'Couple of car smashes. Couple of break-ins. Oh,
and the art gallery.'

'Art gallery?'

'I think young Brian's on that one. Some exhibition down the
High Street. One of the pieces seems to have walked.'

Well, it wasn't too far away, and it *was* a tourist spot. St Giles.
John Knox's House. Holyrood.

'The very dab,' said Rebus. 'That'll do us nicely. Give me the
address, will you?'

Leach scribbled onto a pad of paper and tore off the sheet, handing it across the counter.

'Thanks, Bob.'

Leach was nodding towards the bag. Not only omnipresent,
thought Rebus, but omniscrounging too. 'What else did you get
apart from the whisky?'

Rebus bent towards him and hissed: 'Meat paste and snails!'

Bob Leach looked disheartened. 'Bloody French,' he said. 'You'd
think he'd bring you something decent.'

Rebus didn't bother with back-street shortcuts as they drove towards the Royal Mile. He gave Cluzeau the full tour. But the French
policeman seemed more interested in Rebus than in the streets of
his city.

'I was here before,' he explained. 'Two years ago, for the rugby.'

'Do they play a lot of rugby down your way then?'

'Oh yes. It is not so much a game, more a love affair.'

Rebus assumed Cluzeau would be Parisian. He was not. Parisians,
he said, were – his phrase – 'cold fish'. And in any case the city was
not representative of the real France. The countryside – that was
the real France, and especially the countryside of the south-west.
Cluzeau was from Périgueux. He had been born there and now lived
and worked there. He was married, with four children. And yes,
he carried a family photo in his wallet. The wallet itself he carried
inside a black leather pouch, almost like a clutch-purse. The pouch
also contained identity documents, passport, chequebook, diary, a
small English–French dictionary. No wonder he looked good in a
suit: no bulges in the pockets, no wear on the material.

Rebus handed back the photograph.

'Very nice,' he said.

'And you, Inspector?'

So it was Rebus's turn to tell his tale. Born in Fife. Out of school and into the Army. Paras eventually and from there to the SAS. Breakdown and recovery. Then the police. Wife, now ex-wife, and one daughter living with her mother in London. Cluzeau, Rebus realised, had a canny way of asking questions, making them sound more like statements. So that instead of answering, you were merely acknowledging what he already seemed to know. He'd remember that for future use.

'And now we are going where?'

'The High Street. You might know it better as the Royal Mile.'

'I've walked along it, yes. You say separated, not divorced?'

'That's right.'

'Then there is a chance ...?'

'What? Of us getting back together? No, no chance of that.'

This elicited another huge shrug from Cluzeau. 'It was another man ...?'

'No, just *this* man.'

'Ah. In my part of France we have many crimes of passion. And here in Edinburgh?'

Rebus gave a wry grin. 'Where there's no passion ...'

The Frenchman seemed to make hard work of understanding this.

'French policemen carry guns, don't they?' Rebus asked, filling the silence.

'Not on vacation.'

'I'm glad to hear it.'

'Yes, we have guns. But it is not like in America. We have respect for guns. They are a way of life in the country. Every Frenchman is a hunter at heart.'

Rebus signalled, and drew in to the roadside. 'Scotsmen, too,' he said, opening his door. 'And right now I'm going to hunt down a sandwich. This cafe does the best boiled ham in Edinburgh.'

Cluzeau looked dubious. 'The famous Scottish cuisine,' he murmured, unfastening his seatbelt.

They ate as they drove – ham for Rebus, salami for Cluzeau – and soon enough arrived outside the Heggarty Gallery. In fact, they arrived outside a wools and knitwear shop, which occupied the street-level. The gallery itself was up a winding stairwell, the steps worn and treacherous. They walked in through an unprepossessing door and found themselves in the midst of an argument. Fifteen or so women were crowded around Detective Constable Brian Holmes.

'You can't keep us here, you know!'

'Look, ladies—'

'Patronising pig.'

'Look, I need to get names and addresses first.'

'Well, go on then, what are you waiting for?'

'Bloody cheek, like we're criminals or something.'

'Maybe he wants to strip-search us.'

'Chance would be a fine thing.' There was some laughter at this.

Holmes had caught sight of Rebus and the look of relief on his face told Rebus all he needed to know. On a trellis table against one wall stood a couple of dozen wine bottles, mostly empty, and jugs of orange juice and water, mostly still full. Cluzeau lifted a bottle and wrinkled his nose. He sniffed the neck and the nose wrinkled even further.

The poster on the gallery door had announced an exhibition of paintings and sculpture by Serena Davies. The exhibition was entitled 'Hard Knox' and today was its opening. By the look of the drinks table, a preview had been taking place. Free wine all round, glasses replenished. And now a squabble, which might be about to turn ugly.

Rebus filled his lungs. 'Excuse me!' he cried. The faces turned from Brian Holmes and settled on him. 'I'm Inspector Rebus. Now, with a bit of luck we'll have you all out of here in five minutes. Please bear with us until then. I notice there's still some drink left. If you'll fill your glasses and maybe have a last look round, by the time you finish you should be able to leave. Now, I just need a word with my colleague.'

Gratefully, Holmes squeezed his way out of the scrum and came towards Rebus.

'You've got thirty seconds to fill me in,' Rebus said.

Holmes took a couple of deep breaths. 'A sculpture in bronze, male figure. It was sitting in the middle of one of the rooms. Preview opens. Somebody starts yelling that it's disappeared. The artist goes up the wall. She won't let anybody in or out, because if somebody's nicked it, that somebody's still in the gallery.'

'And that's the state of play? Nobody in or out since it went missing?'

Holmes nodded. 'Of course, as I tried telling her, they could have high-tailed it *before* she barricaded everyone else in.' Holmes was looking at the man who had come to stand beside Rebus. 'Can we help you, sir?'

'Oh,' said Rebus. 'You haven't been introduced. This is ...' But no, he still couldn't make himself say the name. Instead, he nodded towards Holmes. 'This is Detective Constable Holmes.' Then, as Cluzeau shook hands with Holmes: 'The inspector here has come over from France to see how we do things in Edinburgh.' Rebus turned to Cluzeau. 'Did you catch what Brian was saying? Only I know his accent's a bit thick.'

'I understood perfectly.' He turned to Holmes. 'Inspector Rebus forgot to say, but my name is Cluzeau.' Somehow it didn't sound so funny when spoken by a native. 'How big is the statue? Do we know what it looks like?'

'There's a picture of it in the catalogue.' Holmes took the small glossy booklet from his pocket and handed it to Cluzeau. 'That's it at the top of the page.'

While Cluzeau studied this, Holmes caught Rebus's eye, then nodded down to the Frenchman's pouch.

'Nice handbag.'

Rebus gave him a warning look, then glanced at the catalogue. His eyes opened wide. 'Good Christ!'

Cluzeau read from the catalogue. '"Monstrous Trumpet. Bronze and multi-media. Sixteen—" what do these marks mean?'

'Inches.'

'Thank you. "Sixteen inches. Three thousand five hundred pounds." *C'est cher*. It's expensive.'

'I'll say,' said Rebus. 'You could buy a car for that.' Well, he thought, you could certainly buy *my* car for that.

'It is an interesting piece, don't you think?'

'Interesting?' Rebus studied the small photograph of the statue called 'Monstrous Trumpet'. A nude male, his face exaggeratedly spiteful, was sticking out his tongue, except that it wasn't a tongue, it was a penis. And where that particular organ should have been, there was what looked like a piece of sticking-plaster. Because of the angle of the photo, it was just possible to discern something protruding from the statue's backside. Rebus guessed it was meant to be a tongue.

'Yes,' said Cluzeau, 'I should very much like to meet the artist.'

'Doesn't look as though you've got any choice,' said Holmes, seeming to retreat though in fact he didn't move. 'Here she comes.'

She had just come into the room, of that Rebus was certain. If she'd been there before, he'd have noticed her. And even if he hadn't Cluzeau certainly would have. She was just over six feet tall, dressed in long flowing white skirt, black boots, puffy white blouse and a red satin waistcoat. Her eye make-up was jet black, matching her long straight hair, and her wrists fairly jangled with bangles and bracelets. She addressed Holmes.

'No sign of it. I've had a thorough look.' She turned towards Rebus and Cluzeau. Holmes started making the introductions.

'This is Inspector Rebus, and Inspector Cl ...' he stumbled to a halt. Yes, thought Rebus, it's a problem, isn't it, Brian? But Cluzeau appeared not to have noticed. He was squeezing Serena Davies's hand.

'Pleased to meet you.'

She looked him up and down without embarrassment, gave a cool smile, and passed to Rebus. 'Well, thank goodness the grown-ups are here at last.' Brian Holmes reddened furiously. 'I hope we didn't interrupt your lunch, Inspector. Come on, I'll show you where the piece was.'

And with that she turned and left. Some of the women offered either condolences over her loss, or else praise for what works remained, and Serena Davies gave a weak smile, a smile which said: I'm coping, but don't ask me how.

Rebus touched Holmes's shoulder. 'Get the names and addresses, eh, Brian?' He made to follow the artist, but couldn't resist a parting shot. 'You've got your crayons with you, have you?'

'And my marbles,' Holmes retorted. By God, thought Rebus, he's learning fast. But then, he had a good teacher, hadn't he?

'Magnificent creature,' Cluzeau hissed into his ear as they passed through the room. A few of the women glanced towards the Frenchman. I'm making him look too good, Rebus thought. Pity I had to be wearing this old suit today.

The small galleries through which they passed comprised a maze, an artful configuration of angles and doorways which made more of the space than there actually was. As to the works on display, well, Rebus couldn't be sure, of course, but there seemed an awful lot of violence in them, violence acted out upon a particular part of the masculine anatomy. Even the Frenchman was quiet as they passed red splashes of colour, twisted statues, great dollops of paint. There was one apparent calm centre, an extremely large and detailed drawing of the vulva. Cluzeau paused for a moment.

'I like this,' he said. Rebus nodded towards a red circular sticker attached to the wall beside the portrait.

'Already sold.'

Cluzeau tapped the relevant page of the catalogue. 'Yes, for one thousand five hundred pounds.'

'In here!' the artist's voice commanded. 'When you've stopped gawping.' She was in the next room of the gallery, standing by the now empty pedestal. The sign beneath it showed no red blob. No sale. 'It was right here.' The room was about fifteen feet by ten, in the corner of the gallery: only one doorway and no windows. Rebus looked up at the ceiling, but saw only strip lighting. No trapdoors.

'And there were people in here when it happened?'

Serena Davies nodded. 'Three or four of the guests. Ginny Elyot, Margaret Grieve, Helena Mitchison and I think Lesley Jameson.'

'Jameson?' Rebus knew two Jamesons in Edinburgh, one a doctor and the other ...

'Tom Jameson's daughter,' the artist concluded.

The other a newspaper editor called Tom Jameson. 'And who was it raised the alarm?' Rebus asked.

'That was Ginny. She came out of the room shouting that the statue had vanished. We all rushed into the room. Sure enough.' She slapped a hand down on the pedestal.

'Time, then,' Rebus mused, 'for someone to sneak away while everyone else was occupied?'

But the artist shook her mane of hair. 'I've already told you, there's nobody missing. Everyone who was here *is* here. In fact, I think there are a couple more bodies now than there were at the time.'

'Oh?'

'Moira Fowler was late. As usual. She arrived a couple of minutes after I'd barred the door.'

'You let her in?'

'Of course. I wasn't worried about letting people *in*.'

'You said "a couple of bodies"?'

'That's right. Maureen Beck was in the loo. Bladder trouble, poor thing. Maybe I should have hung a couple of paintings in there.'

Cluzeau frowned at this. Rebus decided to help him. 'The toilets being where exactly?'

'Next flight up. A complete pain really. The gallery shares them with the shop downstairs. Crammed full of cardboard boxes and knitting patterns.'

Rebus nodded. The Frenchman coughed, preparing to speak. 'So,' he said, 'you have to leave the gallery actually to use the ... loo?'

Serena Davies nodded. 'You're French,' she stated. Cluzeau gave a little bow. 'I should have guessed from the *pochette*. You'd never find a Scotsman carrying one of those.'

Cluzeau seemed prepared for this point. 'But the sporran serves the same purpose.'

'I suppose it does,' the artist admitted, 'but its primary function is as a signifier.' She looked to both men. Both men looked puzzled. 'It's hairy and it hangs around your groin,' she explained.

Rebus stayed silent, but pursed his lips. Cluzeau nodded to himself, frowning.

'Maybe,' said Rebus, 'you could explain your exhibition to us, *Ms* Davies?'

'Well, it's a comment on Knox of course.'

'Knocks?' asked Cluzeau.

'John Knox,' Rebus explained. 'We passed by his old house a little way back.'

'John Knox,' she went on, principally for the Frenchman's benefit, but perhaps too, she thought, for that of the Scotsman, 'was a Scottish preacher, a follower of Calvin. He was also a misogynist, hence the title of one of his works – *The First Blast of the Trumpet Against the Monstrous Regiment of Women.*'

'He didn't mean all women,' Rebus felt obliged to add. Serena Davies straightened her spine like a snake rising up before its kill.

'But he did,' she said, 'by association. And, also by association, these works are a comment on *all* Scotsmen. And all men.'

Cluzeau could feel an argument beginning. Arguments, to his knowledge, were always counter-productive even when enjoyable. 'I think I see,' he said. 'And your exhibition responds to this man's work. Yes.' He tapped the catalogue. '"Monstrous Trumpet" is a pun then?'

Serena Davies shrugged, but seemed pacified. 'You could call it that. I'm saying that Knox talked with one part of his anatomy – *not* his brain.'

'And,' added Rebus, 'that at the same time he talked out of his arse?'

'Yes,' she said.

Cluzeau was chuckling. He was still chuckling when he asked: 'And who could have reason for stealing your work?'

The mane rippled again. 'I've absolutely no idea.'

'But you suspect one of your guests,' Cluzeau continued. 'Of course you do: you have already stated that there was no one else here. You were among friends, yet one of them is the Janus figure, yes?'

She nodded slowly. 'Much as I hate to admit it.'

Rebus had taken the catalogue from Cluzeau and seemed to be studying it. But he'd listened to every word. He tapped the missing statue's photo.

'Do you work from life?'

'Mostly, yes, but not for "Monstrous Trumpet".'

'It's a sort of ... ideal figure then?'

She smiled at this. 'Hardly ideal, Inspector. But in that it comes from up here—' she tapped her head, 'from an idea rather than from life, yes, I suppose it is.'

'Does that go for the face, too?' Rebus persisted. 'It seems so life-like.'

She accepted the compliment, studying the photo with him. 'It's not any one man's face,' she said. 'At most it's a composite of men I know.' Then she shrugged. 'Maybe.'

Rebus handed the catalogue to Cluzeau. 'Did you search anyone?' he asked the artist.

'I asked them to open their bags. Not very subtle of me, but I was – *am* – distraught.'

'And did they?'

'Oh yes. Pointless really, there were only two or three bags big enough to hide the statue in.'

'But they were empty?'

She sighed, pinching the bridge of her nose between two fingers. The bracelets were shunted from wrist to elbow. 'Utterly empty,' she said. 'Just as I feel.'

'Was the piece insured?'

She shook her head again, her forehead lowered. A portrait of dejection, Rebus thought. Lifelike, yet not quite real. He noticed too that, now her eyes were averted, the Frenchman was appraising her. He caught Rebus watching him and raised his eyebrows, then shrugged, then made a gesture with his hands. Yes, thought Rebus, I know what you mean. Only don't let *her* catch you thinking what I know you're thinking.

And, he supposed, what he was thinking too.

'I think we'd better go through,' he said. 'The other women will be getting impatient.'

'Let them!' she cried.

'Actually,' said Rebus, 'perhaps you could go ahead of us? Warn them that we may be keeping them a bit longer than we thought.'

She brightened at the news, then sneered. 'You mean you want me to do your dirty work for you?'

Rebus shrugged innocently. 'I just wanted a moment to discuss the case with my colleague.'

'Oh,' she said. Then nodded: 'Yes, of course. Discuss away. I'll tell them they've to stay put.'

'Thank you,' said Rebus, but she'd already left the room.

Cluzeau whistled silently. 'What a creature!'

It was meant as praise, of course, and Rebus nodded assent. 'So what do you think?'

'Think?'

'About the theft.'

'Ah.' Cluzeau scraped at his chin with his fingers. 'A crime of passion,' he said at last and with confidence.

'How do you work that out?'

Cluzeau gave another of his shrugs. 'The process of elimination. We eliminate money: there are more expensive pieces here and besides, a common thief would burgle the premises when they were empty, no?'

Rebus nodded, enjoying this, so like his own train of thought was it. 'Go on.'

'I do not think this piece is so precious that a collector would have it stolen. It is not insured, so there is no reason for the artist herself to have it stolen. It seems logical that someone invited to the exhibition stole it. So we come to the figure of the Janus. Someone the artist herself knows. Why should such a person – a supposed friend – steal this work?' He paused before answering his own question. 'Jealousy. Revenge, *et voilà*, the crime of passion.'

Rebus applauded silently. 'Bravo. But there are thirty-odd suspects out there and no sign of the statue.'

'Ah, I did not say I could solve the crime; all I offer is the "why".'

'Then follow me,' Rebus said, 'and we'll encounter the "who" and the "how" together.'

In the main gallery, Serena Davies was in furious conversation with one knot of women. Brian Holmes was trying to take names and addresses from another group. A third group stood, bored and disconsolate, by the drinks table, and a fourth group stood beside a bright red gash of a painting, glancing at it from time to time and talking among themselves.

Most of the women in the room either carried clutch-purses tucked safely under their arms, or else let neat shoulder-bags swing effortlessly by their sides. But there were a few larger bags and these had been left in a group of their own between the drinks table and another smaller table on which sat a small pile of catalogues and a visitors' book. Rebus walked across to this spot and studied the bags. There was one large straw shopping-bag, apparently containing only a cashmere cardigan and a folded copy of the *Guardian*. There was one department store plastic carrier-bag, containing an umbrella, a bunch of bananas, a fat paperback and a copy of the *Guardian*. There was one canvas shopping-bag, containing an empty crisp packet, a copy of the *Scotsman* and a copy of the *Guardian*.

All this Rebus could see just by standing over the bags. He reached down and picked up the carrier-bag.

'Can I ask whose bag this is?' he said loudly.

'It's mine.'

A young woman stepped forward from the drinks table, starting to blush furiously.

'Follow me, please,' said Rebus, walking off to the next room along. Cluzeau followed and so, seconds later, did the owner of the bag, her eyes terrified.

'Just a couple of questions, that's all,' Rebus said, trying to put her at ease. The main gallery was hushed; he knew people would be straining to hear the conversation. Brian Holmes was repeating an address to himself as he jotted it down.

Rebus felt a little bit like an executioner, walking up to the bags, picking them up in turn and wandering off with the owner towards the awaiting guillotine. The owner of the carrier-bag was Trish Poole, wife of a psychology lecturer at the university. Rebus had met Dr Poole before, and told her so, trying to help her relax a little. It turned out that a lot of the women present today were either academics in their own right, or else were the wives of academics. This latter group included not only Trish Poole, but also Rebecca Eiser, wife of the distinguished Professor of English Literature. Listening to Trish Poole tell him this, Rebus shivered and could feel his face turn pale. But that had been a long time ago.

After Trish Poole had returned for a whispered confab with her group, Rebus tried the canvas bag. This belonged to Margaret Grieve, a writer and, as she said herself, 'one of Serena's closest friends'. Rebus didn't doubt this, and asked if she was married. No, she was not, but she did have a 'significant other'. She smiled broadly as she said this. Rebus smiled back. She'd been in the room with the statue when it was noticed to be missing? Yes, she had. Not that she'd seen anything. She'd been intent on the paintings. So much so that she couldn't be sure whether the statue had been in the room when she'd entered, or whether it had already gone. She thought perhaps it had already gone.

Dismissed by Rebus, she returned to her group in front of the red gash and they too began whispering. An elegant older woman came forward from the same group.

'The last bag is mine,' she said haughtily, her vowels pure Morningside. Perhaps she'd been Jean Brodie's elocution mistress; but no, she wasn't even quite Maggie Smith's age, though to Rebus there were similarities enough between the two women.

Cluzeau seemed quietly cowed by this grand example of Scottish womanhood. He stood at a distance, giving her vowels the necessary room in which to perform. And, Rebus noticed, he clutched his pouch close to his groin, as though it were a lucky charm. Maybe that's what sporrans were?

'I'm Maureen Beck,' she informed them loudly. There would be no hiding *this* conversation from the waggling ears.

Maureen Beck told Rebus that she was married to the architect

Robert Beck and seemed surprised when this name meant nothing to the policeman. She decided then that she disliked Rebus and turned to Cluzeau, answering to his smiling countenance every time Rebus asked her a question. She was in the loo at the time, yes, and returned to pandemonium. She'd only been out of the room a couple of minutes, and hadn't seen anyone ...

'Not even *Ms* Fowler?' Rebus asked. 'I believe she was late to arrive?'

'Yes, but that was a minute or two *after* I came back in.'

Rebus nodded thoughtfully. There was a teasing piece of ham wedged between two of his back teeth and he pushed it with his tongue. A woman put her head around the partition.

'Look, Inspector, some of us have got appointments this afternoon. Isn't there at least a telephone we can use?'

It was a good point. Who was in charge of the gallery itself? The gallery director, it turned out, was a timid little woman who had burrowed into the quietest of the groups. She was only running the place for the real owner, who was on a well-deserved holiday in Paris. (Cluzeau rolled his eyes at this. 'No one,' he said with a shudder, 'deserves such torture.') There was a cramped office, and in it an old Bakelite telephone. If the women could leave twenty pence for each call. A line started to form outside the office. ('Ah, how you love queuing!') Mrs Beck, meantime, had returned to her group. Rebus followed her, and was introduced to Ginny Elyot, who had raised the alarm, and to Moira Fowler the latecomer.

Ginny Elyot kept patting her short auburn hair as though searching it for misplaced artworks. A nervous habit, Rebus reasoned. Cluzeau quickly became the centre of attention, with even the distant and unpunctual Moira becoming involved in the interrogation. Rebus sidled away and touched Brian Holmes's arm.

'That's all the addresses noted, sir.'

'Well done, Brian. Look, slip upstairs, will you? Give the loo a recce.'

'What am I looking for exactly – suspiciously shaped bundles of four-ply?'

Rebus actually laughed. 'We should be so lucky. But yes, you never know what you might find. And check any windows, too. There might be a drainpipe.'

'Okay.'

As Holmes left, a small hand touched Rebus's arm. A girl in her late-teens, eyes gleaming behind studious spectacles, jerked her head towards the gallery's first partitioned room. Rebus followed her. She was so small, and spoke so quietly, he actually had to grasp hands to knees and bend forward to listen.

'I want the story.'

'Pardon?'

'I want the story for my dad's paper.'

Rebus looked at her. His voice too was a dramatic whisper. 'You're Lesley Jameson?'

She nodded.

'I see. Well, as far as I'm concerned the story's yours. But we haven't *got* a story yet.'

She looked around her, then dropped her voice even lower. 'You've seen her.'

'Who?'

'Serena, of course. She's ravishing, isn't she?' Rebus tried to look non-committal. 'She's terribly attractive to men.' This time he attempted a Gallic shrug. He wondered if it looked as stupid as it felt. Her voice died away almost completely, reducing Rebus to lip-reading. 'She has loads of men after her. Including Margaret's.'

'Ah,' said Rebus, 'right.' He nodded, too. So Margaret Grieve's boyfriend was ...

The lips made more movements: 'He's Serena's lover.'

Yes, well, now things began to make more sense. Maybe the Frenchman was right: a crime of passion. The one thing missing thus far had been the passion itself; but no longer. And it was curious, when he came to think of it, how Margaret Grieve had said she couldn't recall whether the statue had been in the room or not. It wasn't the sort of thing you could miss, was it? Not for a bunch of samey paintings of pink bulges and grey curving masses. The newspapers in her bag would have concealed the statue quite nicely, too. There was just one problem.

Cluzeau's head appeared around the partition. 'Ah! Here you are. I'm sorry if I interrupt—'

But Lesley Jameson was already making for the main room. Cluzeau watched her go, then turned to Rebus.

'Charming women.' He sighed. 'But all of them either married or else with lovers. And one of them, of course, is the thief.'

'Oh?' Rebus sounded surprised. 'You mean one of the women you've just been talking with?'

'Of course.' Now he, too, lowered his voice. 'The statue left the gallery in a bag. You could not simply hide it under your dress, could you? But I don't think a plastic bag would have been strong enough for this task. So, we have a choice between Madame Beck and Mademoiselle Grieve.'

'Grieve's boyfriend has been carrying on with our artist.'

Cluzeau digested this. But he too knew there was a problem. 'She did not leave the gallery. She was shut in with the others.' Rebus nodded. 'So there has to have been an accomplice. I think I'd better have another word with Lesley Jameson.'

But Brian Holmes had appeared. He exhaled noisily. 'Thank Christ for that,' he said. 'For a minute there I thought you'd buggered off and left me.'

Rebus grinned. 'That might not have been such a bad idea. How was the loo?'

'Well, I didn't find any solid evidence,' Holmes replied with a straight face. 'No skeins of wool tied to the plumbing and hanging out of the windows for a burglar to shimmy down.'

'But there is a window?'

'A small one in the cubicle itself. I stood on the seat and had a squint out. A two-storey drop to a sort of back yard, nothing in it but a rusting Renault Five and a skip full of cardboard boxes.'

'Go down and take a look at that skip.'

'I thought you might say that.'

'And take a look at the Renault,' ordered Cluzeau, his face set. 'I cannot believe a French car would rust. Perhaps you are mistaken and it is a Mini Cooper, no?'

Holmes, who prided himself on knowing a bit about cars, was ready to argue, then saw the smile spread across the Frenchman's face. He smiled, too.

'Just as well you've got a sense of humour,' he said. 'You'll need it after the match on Saturday.'

'And you will need your Scottish stoicism.'

'Save it for the half-time entertainment, eh?' said Rebus, but with good enough humour. 'The sooner we get this wrapped up, the more time we'll have left for sightseeing.'

Cluzeau seemed about to argue, but Rebus held up a hand. 'Believe me,' he said, 'you'll want to see these sights. Only the locals know the *very* best pubs in Edinburgh.'

Holmes went to investigate the skip and Rebus spoke in whispers with Lesley Jameson – when he wasn't fending off demands from the detainees. What had seemed to most of them something unusual and thrilling at first, a story to be repeated across the dining-table, had now become merely tiresome. Though they had asked to make phone calls, Rebus couldn't help overhearing some of those conversations. They weren't warning of a late arrival or cancelling an appointment: they were spreading the news.

'Look, Inspector, I'm really tired of being kept here.'

Rebus turned from Lesley Jameson to the talker. His voice lacked emotion. 'You're not being kept here.'

'What?'

'Who said you were? Only *Ms* Davies as I understand. You're free to leave whenever you want.'

There was hesitation at this. To leave and taste freedom again? Or to stay, so as not to miss anything? Muttered dialogues took place and eventually one or two of the guests did leave. They simply walked out, closing the door behind them.

'Does that mean we can go?'

Rebus nodded. Another woman left, then another, then a couple.

'I hope you're not thinking of kicking me out,' Lesley Jameson warned. She wanted desperately to be a journalist, and to do it the hard way, *sans* nepotism. Rebus shook his head.

'Just keep talking,' he said.

Cluzeau was in conversation with Serena Davies. When Rebus approached them, she was studying the Frenchman's strong-looking hands. Rebus waved his own nail-bitten paw around the gallery.

'Do you,' he asked, 'have any trouble getting people to pose for all these paintings?'

She shook her head. 'No, not really. It's funny you should ask, Monsieur Cluzeau was just saying—'

'Yes, I'll bet he was. But Monsieur Cluzeau—' testing the words, not finding them risible any more, 'has a wife and family.'

Serena Davies laughed; a deep growl which seemed to run all the way up and down the Frenchman's spine. At last, she let go his hand. 'I thought we were talking about modelling, Inspector.'

'We were,' said Rebus drily, 'but I'm not sure Mrs Cluzeau would see it like that ...'

'Inspector ...?' It was Maureen Beck. 'Everyone seems to be leaving. Do I take it we're free to go?'

Rebus was suddenly businesslike. 'No,' he said. 'I'd like you to stay behind a little longer.' He glanced towards the group – Ginny Elyot, Moira Fowler, Margaret Grieve – 'all of you, please. This won't take long.'

'That's what my husband says,' commented Moira Fowler, raising a glass of water to her lips. She placed a tablet on her tongue and washed it down.

Rebus looked to Lesley Jameson, then winked. 'Fasten your seatbelt,' he told her. 'It's going to be a bumpy ride.'

The gallery was now fast emptying and Holmes, having battled against the tide on the stairwell, entered the room on unsteady legs, his eyes seeking out Rebus.

'Jeez!' he cried. 'I thought you'd decided to bugger off after all. What's up? Where's everyone going?'

'Anything in the skip?' But Holmes shrugged: nothing. 'I've sent everyone home,' Rebus explained.

'Everyone except us,' Maureen Beck said sniffily.

'Well,' said Rebus, facing the four women, 'that's because nobody but *you* knows anything about the statue.'

The women themselves said nothing at this, but Cluzeau gave a small gasp – perhaps to save them the trouble. Serena Davies, however, had replaced her growl with a lump of ice.

'You mean one of *them* stole my work?'

Rebus shook his head. 'No, that's not what I mean. One person couldn't have done it. There had to be an accomplice.' He nodded towards Moira Fowler. '*Ms* Fowler, why don't you take DC Holmes down to your car? He can carry the statue back upstairs.'

'Moira!' Another change of tone, this time from ice to fire. For a second, Rebus thought Serena Davies might be about to make a lunge at the thief. Perhaps Moira Fowler thought so too, for she moved without further prompting towards the door.

'Okay,' she said, 'if you like.'

Holmes watched her pass him on her way to the stairwell.

'Go on then, Brian,' ordered Rebus. Holmes seemed undecided. He knew he was going to miss the story. What's more, he didn't fancy lugging the bloody thing up a flight of stairs.

'*Vite!*' cried Rebus, another word of French suddenly coming back to him. Holmes moved on tired legs towards the door. Up the stairs, down the stairs, up the stairs. It would, he couldn't help thinking, make good training for the Scottish pack.

Serena Davies had put her hand to her brow. Clank-a-clank-clank went the bracelets. 'I can't believe it of Moira. Such treachery.'

'Hah!' This from Ginny Elyot, her eyes burning. 'Treachery? You're a good one to speak. Getting Jim to "model" for you. Neither of you telling her about it. What the hell do you think she thought when she found out?'

Jim being, as Rebus knew from Lesley, Moira Fowler's husband. He kept his eyes on Ginny.

'And you, too, *Ms* Elyot. How did you feel when you found out about ... David, is it?'

She nodded. Her hand went towards her hair again, but she caught herself, and gripped one hand in the other. 'Yes, David,' she said quietly. 'That statue's got David's eyes, his hair.' She wasn't looking at Rebus. He didn't feel she was even replying to his question.

She was remembering.

'And Gerry's nose and jawline. I'd recognise them anywhere.'

This from Margaret Grieve, she of the significant other. 'But Gerry can't keep secrets, not from me.'

Maureen Beck, who had been nodding throughout, never taking her moist eyes off the artist, was next. Her husband too, Robert, the architect, had modelled for Serena Davies. On the quiet, of course. It had to be on the quiet: no knowing what passions might be aroused otherwise. Even in a city like Edinburgh, even in women as seemingly self-possessed and cool-headed as these. Perhaps it had all been very innocent. Perhaps.

'He's got Robert's figure,' Maureen Beck was saying. 'Down to the scar on his chest from that riding accident.'

A crime of passion, just as Cluzeau had predicted. And after Rebus telling him that there was no such thing as passion in the city. But there was; and there were secrets too. Locked within these paintings, fine so long as they were abstract, so long as they weren't modelled from life. But for all that 'Monstrous Trumpet' was, in Serena Davies's words, a 'composite', its creation still cut deep. For each of the four women, there was something recognisable there, something modelled from life, from husband or lover. Something which burned and humiliated.

Unable to stand the thought of public display, of visitors walking into the gallery and saying 'Good God, doesn't that statue look like ...?' Unable to face the thought of this, and of the ridicule (the detailed penis, the tongue, and that sticking-plaster) they had come together with a plan. A clumsy, almost unworkable plan, but the only plan they had.

The statue had gone into Margaret Grieve's roomy bag, at which point Ginny Elyot had raised the alarm – hysterically so, attracting all the guests towards that one room, unaware as they pressed forwards that they were passing Margaret Grieve discreetly moving the other way. The bag had been passed to Maureen Beck, who had then slipped upstairs to the toilet. She had opened the window and dropped the statue down into the skip, from where Moira Fowler had retrieved it, carrying it out to her own car. Beck had returned, to find Serena Davies stopping people from leaving; a minute or two later, Moira Fowler had arrived.

She now walked in, followed by a red-faced Holmes, the statue cradled in his arms. Serena Davies, however, appeared not to notice. She had her eyes trained on the parquet floor and, again, she was being studied by Cluzeau. 'What a creature,' he had said of her. What a creature indeed. The four thieves would certainly be in accord in calling her 'creature'.

Who knows, thought Rebus, they might even be in *bon accord*.

The artist was neither temperamental nor stupid enough to insist on pressing charges and she bent to Rebus's suggestion that the piece be withdrawn from the show. The pressure thereafter was on Lesley Jameson not to release the story to her father's paper. Female solidarity won in the end, but it was a narrow victory.

Not much female solidarity elsewhere, thought Rebus. He made up a few mock headlines, the sort that would have pleased Dr Curt. Feminist Artist's Roll Models; Serena's Harem of Husbands; The Anti-Knox Knocking Shop. All as he sat squeezed into a corner of the Sutherland Bar. Somewhere along the route, Cluzeau – now insisting that Rebus call him Jean-Pierre – had found half a dozen French fans, in town for the rugby and already in their cups. Then a couple of the Scottish fans had tagged along too and now there were about a dozen of them, standing at the bar and singing French rugby songs. Any minute now someone would tip an ice-bucket onto their heads. He prayed it wouldn't be Brian Holmes, who, shirt-tail out and tie hanging loose, was singing as lustily as anyone, despite the language barrier – or even, perhaps, because of it.

Childish, of course. But then that was men for you. Simple pleasures and simple crimes. Male revenge was simple almost to the point of being infantile: you went up to the bastard and you stuck your fist into his face or kneed him in the nuts. But the revenge of the female. Ah, that was recondite stuff. He wondered if it was finished now, or would Serena Davies face more plots, plots more subtle, or better executed, or more savage? He didn't really want to think about it. Didn't want to think about the hate in the four women's voices, or the gleam in their eyes. He drank to forget. That was why men joined the Foreign Legion too, wasn't it? To forget. Or was it?

He was buggered if he could remember. But something else niggled too. The women had laid claim to a lover's jawline, a husband's figure. But whose, he couldn't help wondering, was the penis?

Someone was tugging at his arm, pulling him up. The glasses flew from the table and suddenly he was being hugged by Jean-Pierre.

'John, my friend, John, tell me who this man Peter Zealous is that everyone is talking to me about?'

'It's Sellers,' Rebus corrected. To tell or not to tell? He opened his mouth. There was the machine-gun sound of things spilling onto the bar behind him. Small, solid things. Next thing he knew, it was dark and his head was very cold and very wet.

'I'll get you for this, Brian,' he said, removing the ice-bucket from his head. 'So help me I will.'

My Shopping Day

Two things about being a good-looking guy who dresses well: one, you tend to get noticed; two, nobody thinks you capable of a naughty deed. In my line of work – necessarily peripatetic – there's a trade-off between the two. I'm hoping people will be looking at my face and not my hands. And I'm hoping they'll wander off in blissful ignorance afterwards.

I'm a pickpocket, only the term has lost its meaning – fine for Oliver Twist, but not for the 1990s. We're dippers, lifters. I specialise in handbags, shopping-bags, carriers. I'm not a weight-lifter or a big dipper – a little but often, that's me. I saw a stage act once, he could have your wristwatch off your hand, the belt off your trousers, and you wouldn't notice. He'd have your wallet, your glasses, your wife, your kids, and you'd take a look around and be naked and shivering in a dark alley.

He was that good. I'm not. But I look better than he did; I take care of myself. I went backstage after the show and he was pouring whisky into a glass that wasn't too clean. I got him to go through a couple of moves, thinking I could maybe incorporate them into *my* act, but nothing came of it. I asked him why, when he could make a fortune in train stations, airports and cinema foyers, he was wasting his time on the stage of a working-men's club in Leven. He said the problem was he needed to show off. He had this gift, and he couldn't keep it quiet. He knew damned well that if he lifted a wallet, he'd want the victim to know about it.

Theatrical types, I've met a few.

I'm a bit of an actor myself of course; have to be. My face is smiling, giving a come-on, and my mouth is saying all this 'pardon-me-all-my-fault' stuff, but my mind is on what my hands are doing, slipping in and out of bags and baskets, palming the purse or the wallet or whatever of value happens to be lying there in plain view or just beyond. I wear expensive aftershave – not that cloying crap you see shagged to death on TV just before Christmas – and when

I get close they get a good waft of it. It all helps to keep them occupied – preoccupied – during the performance. That was one lesson
the old stooge in Leven taught me: preoccupation. Persuade them
they're part of a certain scenario and they'll go along with it. Simple
really.

I frequent the big supermarkets and shopping centres. I see
young women kicking their heels and holding clipboards, ready to
collar some brain-fried shopper into taking part in their 'consumer
survey'. Right, only what they're really doing is easing you into a
pitch for double glazing, new kitchen, conservatory. And people
keep taking the bait. I want to scream at them: come *on*! Wakey-
wakey! But what use would it do? A trawl up and down those aisles
and your head is mush.

I know shopping centres don't want you doing it, but just walk
in some day and position yourself on the safe side of the check-outs.
Now stand there and watch the show. Watch a shopper breeze into
the shop with head held high, trolley buzzing. Then watch them at
the check-out, watch them as they leave. Their skin's turned grey,
eyes dark. They frown, their jaw moves, there's almost drool there
at the corners. Shoulders slumped, head sagging. These people have
been beaten, pummelled. They've been hijacked, gagged, throttled,
stymied, shaken and stirred. On the way home, they'll be argu-
mentative, downright rude, and once home they'll collapse, fight
with spouse and kids, maybe have a little weep in the privacy of the
toilet. And inside their head will be some shocking refrain, something they can't seem to shrug off without the aid of hard drink.
It'll be some synthesised, sanitised, la-la-la singalong hit from the
'60s or '70s. The music they shopped to, music you don't so much
hear as ingest. While you're standing at the check-out, watching the
sorry parade, you might want to try *listening* to that music. Believe
me, it's hard to do: the music doesn't want you to listen to it. It
wants you to feel it, which is a different thing altogether.

Okay, so you're thinking: the best time to lift those purses and
wallets is when the shoppers come stumbling out with their trolleys laden, right? Wrong: I take them *inside* the shop, while their
minds are at the same time filling with junk and jangling with a
mental shopping list. They're seeing novelties they didn't know
they needed – chocolate-flavoured pasta; canned caffeine with a
free colour-change straw – and almost forgetting washing-up liquid
and the kids' dinner. Boom: that's when I bump into them. That's
when I brush against their cheap coats as I lean past for that perfect
tomato towards the back of the display. That's when I half-turn my
head, give them the smile, and say something about how crowded

the shop is today. Caught a little off-guard, they're open to the full effect: dental work, jawline, groomed hair, expensive clothes, sweetened breath and aftershave. My blue eyes sparkle with the same drops TV presenters use. The hand I've reached past their own wears a Breitling wristwatch, all bells and whistles and 2k of Swiss whatever. I'm working now. See, I don't just have to hold this woman – nearly always a woman – in thrall; I have at the same time to hide what my other hand is doing from other shoppers in the vicinity, some of whom, attracted to the show, will be watching me, watching her, and thinking they'd like to be over by the tomatoes right now instead.

It can take ten or fifteen minutes to size up the punter. They need to be a certain type – that goes without saying – and there has to be something worth nicking from them. I have to make sure nobody knows I'm shadowing them as I pass down the aisles with my handbasket (one or two items in it which I'll ditch later: I don't want to be standing in a check-out queue while my victim finds out she's missing cash and credit cards). So many variables, it's a juggling act really. And I have to be a good psychologist. And I have to get away.

So you can see, it's not easy money when all's said and done.

But it beats clerical work, no?

Edinburgh had produced a good haul that Saturday. I'd hit three edge-of-town superstores. Saturday afternoons in those places are like hell on earth. Plus, they're either shrewd or tight-fisted on the east coast: no really easy pickings. They keep their money close to them and are suspicious of any stranger – *any* stranger. I blame those market researchers; you never know who's going to turn out to be one. Best-looking man I've ever seen came to my door one night with the old clipboard and pen. Turned out he was trying to sell carpets. Looked like he was wearing one, too.

And in the morning, just to show I'm not a bad bloke, I'd rejected a wallet which had been held out to me on a plate. There was a blind guy in the first shopping centre, walking the marbled and mirrored halls with confidence and a guide-dog. The guide-dog was a beauty of a Labrador: I love dogs, always have done. It was early in the day and I was just limbering up, sizing the place and its level of security. So I asked the old guy if I could pat his dog, gave me a chance to take a surreptitious look around. Gorgeous dog it was, come-hither eyes, all that. Nice and solid with a good coat. Liked to be stroked, too. So me and the old guy got talking. He was wearing some tatty old tweed jacket with greasy elbows – mind, I can see that smartness of appearance is problematical when you're blind. Anyway, the jacket was all baggy and worn, and when it swung open as the man leaned down to stroke his Lab, I saw his wallet inside, swinging from a loose pocket. And I could have had it, but he was blind for Christ's sake, and maybe I just wasn't ready. So I'd decided to leave it alone and guess what? He leaned a bit further down and the bloody thing slipped out onto the floor. He didn't seem to have heard it, too busy murmuring sweet nothings to the dog, whose name was 'Sabre'. I picked up the wallet, gave its contents a once-over. Sabre's eyes were on me, but he wasn't saying anything. Seemed like he was on my side.

'You dropped this,' I told the old fellow, wedging the wallet into his hand.

Temptation is a terrible thing though ...

Anyway, afternoon shift over, I'd returned to my car and driven it to the furthest corner of the car park to count my haul. I always choose the quietest corner, usually round by the loading bays. Saturday afternoons these aren't usually in use, unless someone's bought a bed or a bike and has driven round to load it into the car. Today, there was a transit van parked nearby, but nobody was in it, and when I looked around I didn't see anyone. So I spread the stuff on the passenger seat and got to work.

There was a guy I knew once called Playtex, partnered him a couple of times. He was called Playtex because he could lift and separate – as in lift people's money and separate them from it. Anyway, his advice was to get away from the scene pronto. But then one day while driving out of the car park, he smacked into a disabled car. There was a cop car nearby, and of course Playtex didn't just have cash and plastic in his own car, he had the purses and wallets too, spread all over the place after the impact.

Now me, I like to take my time, not panic. Go through everything then and there, that way I can ditch the unnecessaries as soon as possible. The purses and wallets go into a bottle bank if there is one: stick them in a bin and they might be found too soon. ID cards, photo-cards, that sort of thing – same place. Cash and credit cards, cash cards, stuff like that I keep, plus any little things like stamps. These days, of course, nobody's supposed to carry cash, but you'd be surprised. First thing a lot of people do before they start their shopping is visit the bank or the machine: they might need cash for a restaurant, a cup of coffee or a double gin, a taxi home, the TV papers ... I get a lot of nice fresh tens and twenties. The plastic I offload to a guy I meet three times a week in a pub in Glasgow. It's a hassle, meeting him this often, but he says we have to 'strike while the iron is hot'. In other words, he needs the cards before they get too old. Some people, so he tells me, will wait up to a week before reporting missing cards, on the chance that they might turn up. Or they simply won't notice they're missing. But all the same, he needs them pronto, so he can maximise their shelf-life. He can use cash cards too, though I don't know how. He bypasses the code or something; works a couple of times then you throw the card away or the machine swallows it.

I'd made not too bad a showing that afternoon. The bottle bank was about ten yards away, so I got out of the car and walked over to it, pushing the leatherware inside. I could smell sour wine and beer slops, and knew I'd be drinking better than either that evening.

I was just getting back into my car when I heard the squeal. It was coming from the transit. I heard it again. There was no one in the front of the van, so the sound had to be coming from the back. No windows, so I couldn't be sure. But yes: the whole van rocked suddenly and I heard a thudding sound. Then a voice – definitely a voice this time – a man's, hissing something that sounded very much like, 'You won't do that again, you bitch!'

I got back into my car and just sat there, hands resting on the steering-wheel. Then I put my window down. I didn't hear anything else. The van was white mostly, but with a black roof. It looked like a respray. The front grille was crimson and the wing-mirror nearest me was missing. There was a partition behind the seats, blocking off the back. I licked my lips, wondering what was happening in there, wondering what to do about it. This last was easy to answer: nothing. Get the hell away from there and forget about it. I started my engine and slipped into first, crawling from the scene.

I'd got as far as the bottle bank when, eyes on the rearview, I saw the transit's back doors swing open. I couldn't see inside: the van had been backed close to a wall. I watched a man jump down and slam the doors shut. He wiped his mouth with the back of his hand, then put his wrist to his mouth and sucked on it. He was over six feet, black T-shirt, black denims and a black leather waistcoat. He looked in his forties, long hair thinning badly. When he looked up, he saw my car and seemed interested in it. I started off again, hoping he'd think I'd been paying a visit to the bottle bank – which, after all, was the truth.

I circled the car park, but ignored the arrows to the exit, instead coming back round to where, from a safe distance, I could again see the transit. The man was moving now, walking towards the superstore's front entrance. He had an awkward, gangling gait, arms swinging low. He reminded me of a guy I'd known years back who'd been the roadie with a third-rate rock band. Same straggly brown hair and overdone sideburns, same sleepless eyes. It wasn't him, it just looked like him.

He disappeared through the automatic doors. I stared towards the van. From this distance, I couldn't see any movement, couldn't hear anything. But I knew there was someone in there, a woman. I didn't like to think about what she was doing there. Had he locked the doors after him? I could hare over there and maybe let her out ...

If he didn't come back out and find me there. He'd seen me by the bottle bank. Maybe he was standing in the shop doorway, waiting for me to make a move. A car was moving slowly towards the bottle bank. It was a shiny black BMW, tinted windows. It didn't stop at the bottle bank; it made for the van, stopped dead in front of it.

Christ, now what?

A man got out. He wore a cream-coloured suit, well-cut, and a pink polo shirt, plus sunglasses – and I'd bet they were Ray-Bans. His hair was light brown, neatly trimmed, and his jaw made chewing motions. He walked to the back of the transit and, without hesitating, pulled open the doors and jumped in. The doors closed after him.

I sat there frowning, conjuring innocent scenarios. The only one that seemed even remotely feasible was that the roadie-lookalike was a pimp, the BMW a punter, and the woman in the back a prossie. But in all honesty I didn't believe that, not for one minute.

Then the doors of the superstore opened and this time it was a security guard who came out, two-way held to his mouth. He seemed to be scanning the car park. I knew the score: he wasn't looking for anyone in a transit van. Chances were, he was looking for *me*. This time, I followed the exit arrows.

I was staying in a bed & breakfast, nicely anonymous on the Dalkeith Road. The front garden had been paved over to create three parking spaces, but mine was the only car there. It was out of season. I'd been asked if I was in town on business, and had answered that I was, the proprietor not seeming to notice that the weekend was a funny time to be conducting business.

There was a bathroom along the hall, and I soaked in a bath for half an hour, eyes closed. My jacket hung from a hook on the back of the door, its inside pocket padded with cash. The plastic was in a brown A4 envelope – sealed – beneath my car's passenger seat. Hotel and B&B rooms were public property. You never knew who'd come traipsing through, or how curious they'd be, so I preferred to keep the stuff in my locked car. The car itself was not worth stealing, not even worth breaking into. There was a yawning gap where a radio should be, and the upholstery was torn and frayed. There were times when it paid not to be showy.

I was reasoning with myself: there was nothing you could do; it would have been too risky; what if there'd been some innocent explanation? Do you want to see yourself in the clink? There was nothing you could do.

I kept coming back to that, trying to convince myself. *You won't do that again, you bitch!* And he'd come out of the van wiping his mouth and sucking his wrist. Had he tried something and she'd bitten him? The squeal I'd heard had been the sound of someone in pain. Maybe the man. Maybe her.

Probably her.

The bath was cold before I got out.

That evening, I tried eating Indian, but couldn't summon up an appetite. Instead I drove through the city, wishing I had a radio, something that might take my mind off things. A radio would have been cheap at the price.

I found myself back at the 'retail park'. It looked different at night, eerie, otherworldly. The interiors of the buildings were well-lit, so you could see a lot of merchandise, only no one was buying.

The car park was empty, sodium lights overhead deterring ne'er-do-wells. But I drove into the car park anyway. These places used private security firms, but they'd be tucked up inside the stores, and probably wouldn't venture out except in the direst emergency. I saw that there was a single car parked in the car park, a nice-looking Volvo, surrounded by a sea of spaces and the occasional island of metal trolleys. But there was no transit van. I stopped my car in front of where it had been, and, headlights full-beam, got out to examine the ground.

I didn't know what I was doing, what I was looking for. Clues? Clues to what? Something that might put my mind at rest perhaps, but I wasn't sure what would do that. There was nothing, of course, not the least sign that any vehicle had ever been there. Just a wad of gum lying next to the wall. I remembered the man in the BMW had been chewing something; this was probably his. Could I take it to the police? Look at this valuable piece of evidence, officers! Can you test the saliva for DNA? Will it lead you to a house of slaughter, an evil trade in sex-slaves?

Thank you, sir, and could we have your name and profession ...?

What was I doing? There had been a noise from a van. A man had yelled something and come out of the van. Another man had gone into the van. So what? I would be leaving town the following day.

By tomorrow night, it would all be forgotten. I got back into my car and reversed from the scene.

But as I passed the solitary Volvo, I slowed, then stopped. If someone had been in that van against their will, then maybe they'd been abducted. Abducted from where? From this very car park perhaps. Which meant their car would still be here, unclaimed at the end of the day.

I got out of my car once more and walked around the Volvo. Could have been dumped by joy-riders of course, except how many joy-riders opted for Volvos? Again, I didn't know what I was looking for. I glanced around, saw nobody, and took a closer look at the car. No keys in the ignition. Something lying on the passenger seat. What was it? Looked like a letter. I tried to read the name on the envelope, but couldn't. Then I did something crazy – I tried the driver's door. And it wasn't locked. It opened with a soft click, no alarm. An unlocked Volvo: now I knew something was wrong. I took out the envelope and held it under lamplight. There was a man's name on it – Mr Roger Masson – but no address.

The woman's husband? The car didn't seem about to yield any other clues. I heard a lorry revving, and closed the door to the Volvo, heading back to my own car. I was behind the steering-wheel before the lorry came into view. It seemed to be collecting rubbish from one of the other shops. I was driving out of the car park before I realised I still had the envelope in my hand.

I stopped at a pub on Corstorphine Road and asked for the phone book. Saturday night: the place was mobbed. Plenty of good-looking young women, a few giving me interested looks as I stood at the bar. Under normal circumstances, I'd have stayed for a drink, flashed around a bit of money. Maybe I'd have found someone for the night. But tonight, all I wanted was an address. Roger Masson: Barnton Avenue West. Back in my car I checked my A-Z, found the street, and drove there.

Ask me why. Go on, do it. I couldn't give you an answer now, couldn't have done then. It just seemed ... it seemed a thing to do; maybe not *the* thing to do – certainly not the *sensible* thing to do – but a thing to do. And I did it.

Big houses next to a golf course. Very big houses actually, detached, modern, big gardens. Very nice, and completely silent. It wasn't the sort of street where you'd nip next door for the loan of some coffee: you'd phone the stuff in instead. I stopped the car at the bottom of the drive. The gates were open, and I could see the house clearly. There were lights on inside. Someone walked across a window: a man. He looked worried. He was holding a portable

phone to his ear. He held it away from his ear and broke the connection, then rubbed at his forehead. A very worried man. He let his
shoulders slump. It was hard to tell from a distance, but he looked
in his fifties, if well-preserved. Nice greying hair, open-necked shirt.
He seemed to be staring into space, but I realised finally that he
wasn't. He was looking out of the window.

He was looking at me.

He turned and walked from the room. The anxious husband,
wondering where his wife was. What could I tell him? Nothing. All
he'd done was satisfy me that something was wrong. And now that
I'd seen his home, I had the feeling that maybe the reason why Mrs
Masson had taken her Volvo to the shops this afternoon and not
come back was that she'd been unavoidably detained.

By kidnappers.

I watched the front door open, and Masson come running out. He
didn't have anything but socks on his feet, and consequently ran on
tiptoe down the gravel drive.

'Hey, you!' he was shouting. 'I want to talk to you!'

I started the car and moved off.

'Wait a minute! Help, somebody! Help!'

I tore away from there like I had something to fear. Up onto
Queensferry Road and back towards town, missing at least one red
light in the process and decidedly ignoring the speed limit.

Which is why the cops caught me.

Flashing blue lights in my rearview, and headlamps flicking to
full-beam to tell me to pull over. So what else could I do? I pulled
over, easing two wheels up onto the pavement to make room for
passing traffic – ever the courteous driver.

I can wing this, I thought. I've not been drinking, and I've no
unpaid fines. I can wing this.

'Step out of the car, please, sir.'

I stepped out of the car. There were two of them, uniformed, one
– the elder – talking to me, the other walking around the car like I
was planning to sell it.

'Something wrong, officers?' The elder blinked at me like I'd been
watching too many films.

'Does a red light mean "go faster"?' he asked, while his partner
smirked. I tried a shy grin.

'It was on me before I saw it."

'Been drinking this evening, sir?'

'Not a drop.' The younger cop was peering in through the front
passenger window. I was all too aware of the plastic in the envelope
under the seat. But the envelope was *sealed:* they couldn't open it

even if they found it, not without reasonable suspicion. That might not stop them opening it, of course, but at least my lawyer would have a stick to beat them with.

'No?'

I shook my head, breathed out hard, remembered I'd tried eating a curry.

'Was that a madras or a vindaloo?' the older cop asked, not bothering to wait for an answer. His car had a computer on board; a lot of them do these days. Depends where you are; whether the regional force has had enough money in the kitty. He could go and put my licence plate through his machine: it would come up clean. Never buy a dodgy car.

'Just wait there,' the youngster said, going to join his partner. So I stood by my car, arms folded, trying not to look guilty as a parade of motorists slowed to watch. The old guy was on his radio. I had a sudden thought: Masson has called a 999 with my description. Would he do that? No telling what a man will do when he's desperate. The cops were looking at me through their windscreen, maybe trying to sweat me, get me to run for it. No way, not with the envelope under the passenger seat.

So I stood and waited, and at last they came back, both of them.

'We'd like you to come down the station,' the elder said.

'What? Am I being arrested?'

'Just a routine matter.'

'For not stopping at a red light?'

'Routine, sir. If you'll come with us.'

I tried to look disgruntled, appalled – it wasn't hard. 'What about my car?'

'My colleague will drive it, sir. If you'll come with me ...'

I sat mute in the passenger seat all the way to the cop shop.

Police stations are not designed to make you feel like the driven snow, even if the worst thing you've done in your life is try peeping at your sister while she was in the bath. They are like black holes. Once you're in there, to the outside world you've ceased to exist, and the outside world itself ceases to have meaning for you.

That can be frightening. It can loosen tongues. Suddenly you remember about your sister, and blurt it out, dredging up a memory from ten or twenty years ago. You'd tell them anything, these quiet listeners, these stone faces. You'd tell them you once waded through her underwear drawer too, even if this were a downright lie.

I don't have a sister. I wasn't about to tell them anything.

The CID office was big and needed a lick of paint. There were large cracks snaking across the ceiling towards the flickering lengths of centred strip-lighting. There were six desks, big old bulky things, like school surplus from the Billy Bunter era. And there were detectives, wearing suits and ties and looking like they couldn't wait to knock off. I was seated in front of one of the tables. There was no one sitting across from me. I'd been asked if I wanted a cup of coffee. I'd declined. They didn't want to breath-test me, that much was clear. Nothing else was.

Then the detective came and sat down, pulling his chair in inch by inch till he was happy with the arrangement. He lined three ballpoint pens in a row in front of him. There was a clean pad of paper below the pens.

'Do you know why we've asked you here, Mr ...' He looked at a slip of paper in his paw. 'Mr Croft?'

He was not especially tall, but had bulk and confidence. His temples were turning grey; the rest of his hair looked like it would follow soon enough. His eyes were dark, sceptical. He watched me shake my head, then searched his in-tray, at last pulling out a sheet of paper.

'"Six feet one or two",' he read, '"dark hair, well-groomed, well-dressed, blue eyes, squarish face, good teeth. A nice manner".' He looked up. 'Sound familiar, Mr Croft?'

'I might know a few women like that.'

He allowed a smile. 'It could be you, Mr Croft.'

'Could be a lot of people, Sergeant.'

'It's Inspector. Inspector Rebus.'

'Look,' I sat forward, 'what is this all about?'

'It's about someone lifting purses out of bags, Mr Croft.'

'Ridiculous.' I half-laughed. 'Good God, where's this supposed to have happened?'

'All over the city. You live here, Mr Croft?'

'Visiting.'

'When did you arrive?'

'Yesterday evening.'

The detective nodded to himself. 'Two women came up with this description, Mr Croft. Two women in two different supermarkets, two different areas of the city.'

'I did go to *one* supermarket this afternoon.'

'Which one?'

I shrugged. 'Cameron Toil, was that it? Somewhere near my hotel.'

'Foot of Dalkeith Road?'

I nodded.

'What did you want?'

'Razors, deodorant ...' I lowered my voice. 'Contraceptives.'

He ignored my man-to-man admission. 'Got the receipt by any chance?'

I laughed again. 'Threw it away.'

'What line of work are you in?'

'I'm a photographer.' I am too: there's an SLR in the boot of my car. One thing about travelling around the country, I get to take some wonderful photographs. Twice now I've won my camera club's annual prize.

'For a company?'

I shook my head. 'Freelance. I can show you my portfolio.'

'Don't be disgusting,' someone called from across the room. The Inspector smiled at that, and I smiled, too. We were beginning to get along just fine.

'There's been some sort of mistake,' I said. 'Check my hotel room, my car.' I gave him my most honest look, dewy eyes and all.

'Why were you in such a rush?'

'Sorry?'

'On Queensferry Road.'

'I wasn't in any hurry. But when that road's quiet ... you can build up a head of steam without noticing.'

'Lucky you,' the same voice called.

'So you've no objections to us searching your hotel room or your car?'

'None.'

He nodded again. 'So where's the stuff stashed?'

Bluff! my brain yelled. I stared him out, made sure my smile wasn't wavering. 'Look, Inspector ...'

Someone had answered a phone. Now they called across the room. 'John, someone called Masson for you.'

My heart dropped like a stone.

The Inspector picked up his receiver, pushed a button, and leaned back in his chair. 'Mr Masson? What can I do for you, sir?' The way he spoke, I knew this Masson had clout to spare. Rebus's face hardened as he listened. 'What?' He began writing on his notepad. For the moment, I'd been forgotten. 'A pet? When was this?' He listened some more, scribbling furiously. 'Why didn't you come to us straight away? What make of car?' His writing was appalling, but I read the words 'Volvo' and 'car park'. 'And there was no note? Where's your wife now? Can I speak to her, please, sir?'

He put his hand over the mouthpiece. 'Be with you in a minute.'

I nodded, feeling like my head might actually fall off. Mrs Masson was coming to the phone! Her husband was bringing her! So she hadn't been in the van. She was nothing to do with it. What had he said about a pet and a note ...? My hand went to my jacket pocket. The envelope was still there.

'Mrs Masson?' Rebus said now. 'How are you? Yes, must be terrible. They were supposed to leave a note? Have you seen these men?' He listened, started scribbling again. 'You've only spoken to one man? But he spoke in the plural? Well, it might be important, Mrs Masson. When was this?' He began writing again. I could feel sweat trickling down my back. 'No, it's serious all right, I just wish you'd come to us right at the start. I'd like to come out there and see you.' He listened again, scribbled – by now the top sheet of the pad looked like a blackboard at the end of a school day. When he put the receiver down he did so slowly, still writing. Then he got up abruptly and went to talk with someone at the far end of the room.

I slipped my hand into my pocket and felt the envelope. It hadn't been stuck down. I felt inside. Sure enough there was a sheet of paper there. I eased it out, my face blank, unfolded it on my knee and read the pencilled capitals.

£2,000 TO GET THE BITCH BACK. GET MONEY READY, WE'LL CALL.

The squeal I'd heard had been human, but it had been the roadie's voice. He'd just been bitten by Mrs Masson's pet dog: *You won't do that again, you bitch!* Maybe he'd muzzled her, tied her up, knocked her cold. Maybe he'd done worse. If there's one thing I abhor more than the cruelty we inflict on each other, it's cruelty inflicted on animals.

Especially dogs.

It was as clear as day now. Mrs Masson had been instructed to leave her car in the car park, and to return some time later, when she'd find a ransom note on the passenger seat. Only I'd chanced by and lifted the bloody note. So now she didn't know what was expected of her and was going up the wall. And her husband, driven by this, had at last called the police – perhaps against her wishes. All she wanted was her dog back. Meantime, I had the note *and* a description of the dognappers. I had more than any of them.

And I was stuck here.

Rebus came back and tore the sheet from his pad, folded it into his pocket. By now the other note was safe in my pocket. He looked at me for a long time, as if trying to place me. I went dewy-eyed again.

'I've got your licence plate, your name and your address,' he said quietly. 'I've got everything I need – for the moment. I'll want to talk to you again tomorrow. Be here at ten-thirty, understood?'

Two choices: stick with innocent bewilderment, or nod. I nodded. Not that I'd be here tomorrow morning: I'd be packed and gone by midnight.

He gave me another long stare. 'Your car's outside, get the keys from the desk.' He moved away, but paused and turned. 'See you tomorrow, Mr Croft.' He made it sound like a threat

It didn't bother me, I knew I was off and running. That was the only sensible course, I kept telling myself. And I believed it, too.

I sat in my car, hands trembling as they ran over the steering-wheel. I didn't know whether to laugh or cry. In the end, I think I did both simultaneously. I leaned down and felt beneath the passenger seat. The envelope was still there. Everyone deserves a lucky break, I thought, starting the engine.

I'd go back to the B&B, pack my things, and never come back.

Wouldn't that be a callous ending?

But as I drove, I thought of the two men and wondered what kind of dog Mrs Masson owned: something small and snapping, or a big, hearty beast fit for walks across the golf course? I hoped for the latter, for something like the blind man's Labrador. I heard the squeal again. It could have been a dog squealing. And the thump I'd heard: had the roadie smashed its head? My hands tightened on the steering-wheel and, first pub I saw, I pulled over and went looking for another phone book.

This time I had a whisky – a good-sized one. Well, they weren't going to stop me twice in the same night, were they? And I needed the courage. I looked up Masson's address and took down his telephone number. I couldn't call from the bar: too noisy. But there was a box fifty yards along the road, and I used that. A man answered, Masson himself I presumed.

'Inspector Rebus, please."

I heard the man say 'someone for you' as he handed the phone over. 'Hello?'

'Just listen. You're looking for two men.' I gave my descriptions, eyes squeezed shut as I tried to make them as accurate and telling as I could. Then I described the van and the BMW. 'And they want two grand. They'll probably be phoning later.'

Rebus had listened to this in silence. Now he spoke.

'Mr Croft, is that you?'

This time my heart sank like something altogether more massive than a mere stone. A block of city granite maybe.

'Was it your car Mr Masson saw?' Rebus went on.

I licked dry lips. 'Yes,' I said.

'Are you mixed up in this?'

'Only as a ... well, I saw the van. I thought I heard something. I was worried, so I went back tonight.'

'You found the note?' He sounded amused.

'Yes.'

'Why didn't you come forward?' He caught himself. 'No, stupid question. Thanks for your call.'

'Do you still want me at the station tomorrow?'

'Were you planning on coming?'

'It doesn't really fit with my schedule.'

'Get out of the city, Mr Croft. Don't ever come back.'

'Inspector, one question – what breed is she?'

There was a pause while the detective checked. 'Persian Blue,' he said at last.

'What?'

'Persian Blue.'

'But that's a cat.'

'Sorry?'

'A cat.'

'That's right.'

'I *hate* cats!'

I slammed the phone down, went back to the B&B and packed my suitcase in a blind fury. I had paid till noon Sunday, so there was no problem. I just left my key behind, got back into the car and drove.

I was heading down Dalkeith Road, making for the city by-pass, when I saw the van. I blinked, shook my head, but it was definitely the van. I knew not only from the black roof, the missing wing-mirror, but because it was being shadowed by a black BMW. They were going around a roundabout as I approached it. I watched them turn off, then followed. Cameron Toll Shopping Precinct. They were driving into the car park, the only vehicles around at that time of night. I switched off my lights and hung back, watching as they came to a stop.

The roadie got out of the van, and was joined by Mr Smooth, who checked his watch. There was a wall-mounted telephone close by. The roadie opened the back of the van and got in. After checking his watch again, rocking on the balls of his feet, Mr Smooth got in too, closing the doors after him. I kept my lights off and lifted my foot from the brake, rolling down the slight incline towards them, keeping going until my front bumper touched their rear. My car's a big old Merc, same axle-height as a transit. They felt the impact and tried opening the doors, only they were jammed shut by my radiator grille. I got out and jumped up onto my bonnet, my face close to the inch-wide gap in the transit's rear doors.

'A female cat isn't called a bitch!' I screamed at them.

I might have screamed it more than once actually, before getting down and going to the telephone.

Talk Show

Lowland Radio was a young but successful station broadcasting to lowland Scotland. It was said that the station owed its success to two very different personalities. One was the DJ on the midmorning slot, an abrasive and aggressive Shetland Islander, called Hamish MacDiarmid. MacDiarmid hosted a phone-in, supposedly concerning the day's headlines, but in fact these were of relatively minor importance. People did not listen to the phone-in for opinion and comment: they listened for the attacks MacDiarmid made on just about every caller. There were occasional fierce interchanges, interchanges the DJ nearly always won by dint of severing the connection with anyone more intelligent, better informed, or more rational than himself.

Rebus knew that there were men in his own station who would try to take a break between ten-forty-five and eleven-fifteen just to listen. The people who phoned the show knew what they'd get, of course: that was part of the fun. Rebus wondered if they were masochists, but in fact he knew they probably saw themselves as challengers. If they could best MacDiarmid, they would have 'won'. And so MacDiarmid himself became like some raging bull, entering the ring every morning for another joust with the picadors. So far he'd been goaded but not wounded, but who knew how long the luck would last ...?

The other 'personality' – always supposing personality could be applied to someone so ethereal – was Penny Cook, the softly spoken, seductive voice on the station's late-night slot. Five nights a week, on her show *What's Cookin'*, she offered a mix of sedative music, soothing talk, and calming advice to those who took part in her own phone-in segment. These were very different people from those who chose to confront Hamish MacDiarmid. They were quietly worried about their lives, insecure, timid; they had home problems, work problems, personal problems. They were the kind of people, Rebus mused, who got sand kicked in their faces. MacDiarmid's callers, on the other hand, were probably the ones doing the kicking ...

Perhaps it said something about the lowlands of Scotland that Penny Cook's show was said to be the more popular of the two. Again, people at the station talked about it with the fervour usually reserved for TV programmes.

'Did you hear yon guy with the bend in his tackle ...?'

'That woman who said her husband didn't satisfy her ...'

'I felt sorry for that hooker though, wantin' out o' the game ...'

And so on. Rebus had listened to the show himself a few times, slumped on his chair after closing-time. But never for more than a few minutes; like a bedtime story, a few minutes of Penny Cook sent John Rebus straight to the land of Nod. He'd wondered what she looked like. Husky, comfortable, come-to-bed: the picture of her he'd built up was all images, but none of them exactly physical. Sometimes she sounded blonde and tiny, sometimes statuesque with flowing raven hair. His picture of Hamish MacDiarmid was much more vivid: bright red beard, caber-tossing biceps and a kilt.

Well, the truth would out. Rebus stood in the cramped reception area of Lowland Radio and waited for the girl on the switchboard to finish her call. On the wall behind her, a sign said WELCOME:. That colon was important. This seemed to be Lowland Radio's way of greeting the personalities who'd come to the station, perhaps to give interviews. Today, below the WELCOME:, written in felt tip were the names JEZ JENKS and CANDY BARR. Neither name meant anything to Rebus, though they probably would to his daughter. The receptionist had finished her call.

'Have you come for some stickers?'

'Stickers?'

'Car-stickers,' she explained. 'Only we're all out of them. Just temporary, we'll be getting more next week if you'd like to call back.'

'No, thanks anyway. I'm Inspector Rebus. I think Miss Cook's expecting me.'

'Oh, sorry.' The receptionist giggled. 'I'll see if she's around. It was Inspector ...?'

'Rebus.'

She scribbled the name on a pad and returned to her switchboard. 'An Inspector Reeves to see you, Penny ...'

Rebus turned to another wall and cast an eye over Lowland Radio's small display of awards. Well, there was stiff competition these days, he supposed. And not much advertising revenue to go round. Another local station had countered the challenge posed by Hamish MacDiarmid, hiring what they called 'The Ranter', an anonymous individual who dished out insult upon insult to anyone foolish enough to call his show.

It all seemed a long way from the Light Programme, a long way from glowing valves and Home Counties diction. Was it true that the BBC announcers used to wear dinner jackets? DJs in DJs, Rebus thought to himself and laughed.

'I'm glad somebody's cheerful.' It was Penny Cook's voice; she was standing right behind him. Slowly he turned to be confronted by a buxom lady in her early forties – only a year or two younger than Rebus himself. She had permed light brown hair and wore round glasses – the kind popularised by John Lennon on one hand and the NHS on the other.

'I know, I know,' she said. 'I'm never what people expect.' She held out a hand, which Rebus shook. Not only did Penny Cook sound unthreatening, she *looked* unthreatening.

All the more mysterious then that someone, some anonymous caller, should be threatening her life ...

They walked down a corridor towards a sturdy-looking door, to the side of which had been attached a push-button array.

'Security,' she said, pressing four digits before pulling open the door. 'You never know what a lunatic might do given access to the airwaves.'

'On the contrary,' said Rebus, 'I've heard Hamish MacDiarmid.'

She laughed. He didn't think he'd heard her laugh before. 'Is Penny Cook your real name?' he asked, thinking the ice sufficiently broken between them.

'Afraid so. I was born in Nairn. To be honest, I don't think my parents had heard of Penicuik. They just liked the name Penelope.'

They were passing studios and offices. Loudspeakers placed in the ceiling of the corridor relayed the station's afternoon show.

'Ever been inside a radio station before, Inspector?'

'No, never.'

'I'll show you around if you like.'

'If you can spare the time ...'

'No problem.' They were approaching one studio outside which a middle-aged man was in quiet conversation with a spiky-headed teenager. The teenager looked sullen and in need of a wash. Rebus wondered if he were the man's son. If so, a lesson in parental control was definitely needed.

'Hi, Norman,' Penny Cook said in passing. The man smiled towards her. The teenager remained sullen: a controlled pose,

Rebus decided. Further along, having passed through another combination-lock door, Penny herself cleared things up.

'Norman's one of our producers.'

'And the kid with him?'

'Kid?' She smiled wryly. 'That was Jez Jenks, the singer with Leftover Lunch. He probably makes more a day than you and I make in a good year.'

Rebus couldn't remember ever having a 'good year' – the curse of the honest copper. A question came to him.

'And Candy Barr?'

She laughed at this. 'I thought my own name took some beating. Mind you, I don't suppose it's her real name. She's an actress or a comedienne or something. From across the water, of course.'

'Doesn't sound like an Irish name,' Rebus said as Penny Cook held open her office door.

'I wouldn't make jokes around here, Inspector,' she said. 'You'll probably find yourself being signed up for a spot on one of our shows.'

'The Laughing Policeman?' Rebus suggested. But then they were in the office, the door was closed, and the atmosphere cooled appropriately. This was business, after all. Serious business. She sat at her desk. Rebus sat down on the chair across from her.

'Do you want a coffee or anything, Inspector?'

'No thanks. So, when did these calls start, Miss Cook?'

'About a month ago. The first time he tried it, he actually got through to me on-air. That takes some doing. The calls are filtered through two people before they get to me. Efficient people, too. They can usually tell a crank caller from the real thing.'

'How does the system work? Somebody calls in ... then what?'

'Sue or David takes the call. They ask a few questions. Basically, they want to know the person's name, and what it is they want to talk to me about. Then they take a telephone number, tell the caller to stay by his or her telephone, and if we want to put the person on-air, they phone the caller back and prepare them.'

'Fairly rigorous then.'

'Oh yes. And even supposing the odd crank does get through, we've got a three-second delay on them when they're on-air. If they start cussing or raving, we cut the call before it goes out over the ether.'

'And is that what happened with this guy?'

'Pretty much.' She shook a cassette box at him. 'I've got the tape here. Do you want to hear?'

'Please.'

She started to load a cassette player on the ledge behind her. There were no windows in the office. From the number of steps they'd descended to get there, Rebus reckoned this whole floor of the building was located beneath ground-level.

'So you got a phone number for this guy?'

'Only it turned out to be a phone box in some housing scheme. We didn't know that at the time. We never usually take calls from phone boxes. But it was one of those ones that use the phone cards. No beeps, so nobody could tell.' She had loaded the tape to her satisfaction, but was now waiting for it to rewind. 'After he tried getting through again, we phoned his number. It rang and rang, and then some old girl picked it up. She explained where the box was. That was when we knew he'd tricked us.' The tape thumped to a stop. She hit the play button, and sat down again. There was a hiss as the tape began, and then her voice filled the room. She smiled in embarrassment, as if to say: yes, it's a pose, this husky, sultry, late-night me. But it's a living ...

'And now we've got Peter on line one. Peter, you're through to Penny Cook. How are things with you this evening?'

'Not so good, Penny.'

She interrupted the tape for a moment: 'This is where we cut him off.'

The man's voice had been sleepy, almost tranquillised. Now it erupted. 'I know what you're up to! I know what's going on!' The tape went dead. She leaned back in her chair and switched off the machine.

'It makes me shiver every time I hear it. That anger ... such a sudden change in the voice. Brr.' She reached into her drawer and brought out cigarettes and a lighter. Rebus accepted a cigarette from her.

'Thanks,' he said. Then: 'The name'll be false, of course, but did he give a surname?'

'A surname, an address, even a profession. He said he lived in Edinburgh, but we looked up the street name in the *A to Z* and it doesn't exist. From now on, we check that addresses are real before we call back. His surname was Gemmell. He even spelt it out for Sue. She couldn't believe he was a crank, he sounded so genuine.'

'What did he tell her his problem was?'

'Drinking too much ... how it was affecting his work. I like that sort of problem. The advice is straightforward, and it can be helping a lot of people too scared to phone in.'

'What did he say his job was?'

'Bank executive. He gave Sue the bank's name and everything, and he kept saying it wasn't to be broadcast.' She smiled, shook her head. 'I mean, this nut really was *good*.'

Rebus nodded. 'He seems to have known the set-up pretty well.'

'You mean he got to the safe without triggering any of the alarms?' She smiled still. 'Oh yes, he's a real pro.'

'And the calls have persisted?'

'Most nights. We've got him tagged now though. He's tried using different accents ... dialects ... always a different name and job. But he hasn't managed to beat the system again. When he knows he's been found out, he does that whole routine again. "I know what you've done." Blah, blah. We put the phone down on him before he can get started.'

'And what *have* you done, Miss Cook?'

'Absolutely nothing, Inspector. Not that I know of.'

Rebus nodded slowly. 'Can I hear the tape again?'

'Sure.' She wound it back, and they listened together. Then she excused herself – 'to powder my nose' – and Rebus listened twice more. When she returned, she was carrying two plastic beakers of coffee.

'Thought I might tempt you,' she said. 'Milk, no sugar ... I hope that's all right.'

'Thank you, yes, that's just the job.'

'So, Inspector, what do you think?'

He sipped the lukewarm liquid. 'I think,' he said, 'you've got an anonymous phone-caller.'

She raised her cup, as though to toast him. 'God bless CID,' she said. 'What would we do without you?'

'The problem is that he's probably mobile, not sticking to the same telephone kiosk every time. That's supposing he's as clever as he seems. We can get BT to put a trace on him, but for that you'd have to keep him talking. Or, if he gives his number, we can trace him from that. But it takes time.'

'And meanwhile he could be slipping off into the night?'

'I'm afraid so. Still, apart from continuing to fend him off and hoping he gets fed up, I can't see what else can be done. You don't recognise the voice? Someone from your past ... an ex-lover ... someone with a grudge?'

'I don't make enemies, Inspector.'

Looking at her, listening to her voice, he found that easy to believe. Maybe not personal enemies ...

'What about the other radio stations? They can't be too thrilled about your ratings.'

Her laughter was loud. 'You think they've put out a contract on me, is that it?'

Rebus smiled and shrugged. 'Just a thought. But yours *is* the most popular show Lowland has got, isn't it?'

'I think I'm still just about ahead of Hamish, yes. But then Hamish's show is just ... well, Hamish. My show's all about the people themselves, the ones who call in. Human interest, you could say.'

'And there's plenty of interest.'

'Suffering is always interesting, isn't it? It appeals to the voyeur. We *do* get our fair share of crank calls. Maybe that's why. All those lonely, slightly deranged people out there ... listening to me. Me, pretending I've got all the answers.' Her smile this time was rueful. 'The calls recently have been getting ... I don't know whether to say "better" or "worse". Worse problems, better radio.'

'Better for your ratings, you mean?'

'Most advertisers ignore the late-night slots. That's common knowledge. Not a big enough audience. But it's never been a problem on my show. We did slip back for a little while, but the figures picked up again. Up and up and up ... Don't ask me what sort of listeners we're attracting. I leave all that to market research.'

Rebus finished his coffee and clasped both knees, preparing to rise. 'I'd like to take the tape with me, is that possible?'

'Sure.' She ejected the tape.

'And I'd like to have a word with ... Sue, is it?'

She checked her watch. 'Sue, yes, but she won't be in for a few hours yet. Night shift, you see. Only us poor disc jockeys have to be here twenty-four hours. I exaggerate, but it feels like it sometimes.' She patted a tray on the ledge beside the cassette player. The tray was filled with correspondence. 'Besides, I have my fan mail to deal with.'

Rebus nodded, glanced at the cassette tape he was now holding. 'Let me have a think about this, Miss Cook. I'll see what we can do.'

'OK, Inspector.'

'Sorry I can't be more constructive. You were quite right to contact us.'

'I didn't suppose there was much you could—'

'We don't know that yet. As I say, give me a little time to think about it.'

She rose from her chair. 'I'll see you out. This place is a maze, and we can't have you stumbling in on the *Afternoon Show*, can we? You might end up doing your Laughing Policeman routine after all ...'

*

As they were walking down the long, hushed corridor, Rebus saw two men in conversation at the bottom of the stairwell. One was a beefy, hearty-looking man with a mass of rumpled hair and a good growth of beard. His cheeks seemed veined with blood. The other man proved a significant contrast, small and thin with slicked-back hair. He wore a grey suit and white shirt, the latter offset by a bright red paisley-patterned tie.

'Ah,' said Penny Cook quietly, 'a chance to kill two birds. Come on, let me introduce you to Gordon Prentice – he's the station chief – and to the infamous Hamish MacDiarmid.'

Well, Rebus had no trouble deciding which man was which. Except that, when Penny did make the introductions, he was proved utterly wrong. The bearded man pumped his hand.

'I hope you're going to be able to help, Inspector. There are some sick minds out there.' This was Gordon Prentice. He wore baggy brown cords and an open-necked shirt from which protruded tufts of wiry hair. Hamish MacDiarmid's hand, when Rebus took it, was limp and cool, like something lifted from a larder. No matter how hard he tried, Rebus couldn't match this ... for want of a better word, *yuppie* ... couldn't match him to the combative voice. But then MacDiarmid spoke.

'Sick minds is right, and stupid minds too. I don't know which is worse, a deranged audience or an educationally subnormal one.' He turned to Penny Cook. 'Maybe you got the better bargain, Penelope.' He turned back to Prentice. So that's what a sneer looks like, Rebus thought. But MacDiarmid was speaking again. 'Gordon, how about letting Penny and me swap shows for a day? She could sit there agreeing with every bigoted caller I get, and I could get stuck in about her social cripples. What do you think?'

Prentice chuckled and placed a hand on the shoulder of both his star DJs. 'I'll give it some thought, Hamish. Penny might not be too thrilled though. I think she has a soft spot for her "cripples".'

Penny Cook certainly didn't look 'too thrilled' by the time Rebus and she were out of earshot.

'Those two,' she hissed. 'Sometimes they act like I'm not even there! Men ...' She glanced towards Rebus. 'Present company ex- cluded, of course.'

'I'll take that as a compliment.'

'I shouldn't be so hard on Gordon actually. I know I joke about being here twenty-four hours a day, but I really think he *does* spend all day and all night at the station. He's here from early morning, but each night he comes into the studio to listen to a bit of my show. Beyond the call of duty, wouldn't you say?'

Rebus merely shrugged.

'I bet,' she went on, 'when you saw them you thought it was Hamish with the beard.'

Rebus nodded. She giggled. 'Everybody does,' she said. 'Nobody's what they seem in this place. I'll let you into a secret. The station doesn't keep any publicity shots of Hamish. They're afraid it would hurt his image if everyone found out he looks like a wimp.'

'He's certainly not *quite* what I expected.'

She gave him an ambiguous look. 'No, well, *you're* not quite what *I* was expecting either.' There was a moment's stillness between them, broken only by some coffee commercial being broadcast from the ceiling: '... but Camelot Coffee is no myth, and mmm ... it tastes *so* good.' They smiled at one another and walked on.

Driving back into Edinburgh, Rebus listened, despite himself, to the drivel on Lowland Radio. Advertising was tight, he knew that. Maybe that was why he seemed to hear the same dozen or so adverts over and over again. Lots of air-time to fill and so few advertisers to fill it ...

'... and mmm ... it tastes *so* good.'

That particular advert was beginning to get to him. It careered around in his head, even when it wasn't being broadcast. The actor's voice was so ... what was the word? It was like being force-fed a tablespoon of honey. Cloying, sickly, altogether too much.

'Was Camelot a myth or is it real? Arthur and Guinevere, Merlin and Lancelot. A dream, or—'

Rebus switched off the radio. 'It's only a jar of bloody coffee,' he told his radio set. Yes, he thought, a jar of coffee ... and mmm ... it tastes *so* good. Come to think of it, he needed coffee for the flat. He'd stop off at the corner shop, and whatever he bought it wouldn't be Camelot.

But, as a promotional gimmick, there was a fifty-pence refund on Camelot, so Rebus did buy it, and sat at home that evening drinking the vile stuff and listening to Penny Cook's tape. Tomorrow evening, he was thinking, he might go along to the station to catch her show live. He had an excuse after all: he wanted to speak with Sue, the telephonist. That was the excuse; the truth was that he was intrigued by Penny Cook herself.

You're not quite what I was expecting.

Was he reading too much into that one sentence? Maybe he was. Well, put it another way then: he had a *duty* to return to Lowland Radio, a duty to talk to Sue. He wound the tape back for the umpteenth time. That ferocious voice. Sue had been surprised by its ferocity, hadn't she? The man had seemed so quiet, so polite in their initial conversation. Rebus was stuck. Maybe the caller *would* simply get fed up. When it was a question of someone's home being called, there were steps you could take: have someone intercept all calls, change the person's number and keep it ex-directory. But Penny Cook needed her number to be public. She couldn't hide, except behind the wall provided by Sue and David.

Then he had an idea. It wasn't much of an idea, but it was better than nothing. Bill Costain at the Forensic Science Lab was keen on sound recording, tape recorders, all that sort of stuff. Maybe he could do something with Mr Anonymous. Yes, he'd call him first thing tomorrow. He sipped his coffee, then squirmed.

'Tastes more like camel than Camelot,' he muttered, hitting the play button.

The morning was bright and clear, but Bill Costain was dull and overcast.

'I was playing in a darts match last night,' he explained. 'We won for a change. The amount of drink we put away, you'd think Scotland had just done the Grand Slam.'

'Never mind,' said Rebus, handing over the cassette tape. 'I've brought you something soothing ...'

'Soothing' wasn't the word Costain himself used after listening to the tape. But he enjoyed a challenge, and the challenge Rebus had laid down was to tell him anything at all about the voice. He listened several times to the tape, and put it through some sort of analyser, the voice becoming a series of peaks and troughs.

Costain scratched his head. 'There's too big a difference between the voice at the beginning and the voice when hysterical.'

'How do you mean?' Costain always seemed able to baffle Rebus.

'The hysterical voice is so much higher than the voice at the beginning. It's hardly ... natural.'

'Meaning?'

'I'd say one of them's a put-on. Probably the initial voice. He's disguising his normal tone, speaking in a lower register than usual.'

'So can we get back to his *real* voice?'

'You mean can we retrieve it? Yes, but the lab isn't the best place for that. A friend of mine has a recording studio out Morningside way. I'll give him a bell ...'

They were in luck. The studio's facilities were not in use that morning. Rebus drove them to Morningside and then sat back as Costain and his friend got busy at the mixing console. They slowed the hysteric part of the tape; then managed somehow to take the pitch of the voice down several tones. It began to sound more than slightly unnatural, like a Dalek or something electronic. But then they started to build it back up again, until Rebus was listening to a slow, almost lifeless vocal over the studio's huge monitor speakers.

'I ... know ... what ... you've ... done.'

Yes, there was life there now, almost a hint of personality. After this, they switched to the caller's first utterance – 'Not so good, Penny' – and played around with it, heightening the pitch slightly, even speeding it up a bit.

'That's about as good as it gets,' Costain said at last.

'It's brilliant, Bill, thanks. Can I get a copy?'

Having dropped Costain back at the lab, Rebus wormed his way back through the lunchtime traffic to Great London Road police station. He played this new tape several times, then switched from tape to radio. Christ, he'd forgotten: it was still tuned to Lowland.

'... and mmm ... it tastes *so* good.'

Rebus fairly growled as he reached for the off button. But the damage, the delirious, wonderful damage, had already been done ...

The wine bar was on the corner of Hanover Street and Queen Street. It was a typical Edinburgh affair in that though it might have started with wine, quiche and salad in mind, it had reverted to beer – albeit mainly of the 'designer' variety – and pies. Always supposing you could call something filled with chickpeas and spices a 'pie'. Still, it had an IPA pump, and that was good enough for Rebus. The place had just finished its lunchtime peak, and tables were still cluttered with plates, glasses and condiments. Having paid over the odds for his drink, Rebus felt the barman owed him a favour. He gave the young man a name. The barman nodded towards a table near the window. The table's sole occupant looked just out of his teens. He flicked a lock of hair back from his forehead and gazed out of the window. There was a newspaper folded into quarters on his knee. He tapped his teeth with a ballpoint, mulling over some crossword clue.

Without asking, Rebus sat down opposite him. 'It whiles away the time,' he said. The tooth-tapper seemed still intent on the window.

Maybe he could see his reflection there. The modern Narcissus. Another flick of the hair.

'If you got a haircut, you wouldn't need to keep doing that.'

This achieved a smile. Maybe he thought Rebus was trying to chat him up. Well, after all, this was known as an actors' bar, wasn't it? Half a glass of orange juice sat on the table, the ubiquitous ice-cube having melted away to a sliver.

'Aye,' Rebus mused, 'passes the time.'

This time the eyes turned from the window and were on him. Rebus leaned forward across the table. When he spoke, he spoke quietly, confidently.

'I know what you've done,' he said, not sure even as he said it whether he were quoting or speaking for himself.

The lock of hair fell forward and stayed there. A frozen second, then another, and the man rose quickly to his feet, the chair tipping back. But Rebus, still seated, had grabbed at an arm and held it fast.

'Let go of me!'

'Sit down.'

'I said let go!'

'And I said sit down!' Rebus pulled him back on to his chair. 'That's better. We've got a lot to talk about, you and me. We can do it here or down at the station, and by "station" I don't mean Scotrail. OK?'

The head was bowed, the careful hair now almost completely dishevelled. It was that easy ... Rebus found the tiniest grain of pity. 'Do you want something else to drink?' The head shook from side to side. 'Not even a cup of coffee?'

Now the head looked up at him.

'I saw the film once,' Rebus went on. 'Bloody awful it was, but not half as bad as the coffee. Give me Richard Harris's singing any day.'

Now, finally, the head grinned. 'That's better,' said Rebus. 'Come on, son. It's time, if you'll pardon the expression, to spill the beans.'

The beans spilled ...

Rebus was there that night for *What's Cookin'*. It surprised him that Penny Cook herself, who sounded so calm on the air, was, before the programme, a complete bundle of nerves. She slipped a small yellow tablet on to her tongue and washed it down with a beaker of water.

'Don't ask,' she said, cutting off the obvious question. Sue and David were stationed by their telephones in the production room;

which was separated from Penny's studio by a large glass window. Her producer did his best to calm things down. Though not yet out of his thirties, he looked to be an old pro at this. Rebus wondered if he shouldn't have his own counselling show ...

Rebus chatted with Sue for ten minutes or so, and watched as the production team went through its paces. Really, it was a two-man operation – producer and engineer. There was a last-minute panic when Penny's microphone started to play up, but the engineer was swift to replace it. By five minutes to eleven, the hysteria seemed over. Everyone was calm now, or was so tense it didn't show. Like troops just before a battle, Rebus was thinking. Penny had a couple of questions about the running order of the night's musical pieces. She held a conversation with her producer, communicating via mikes and headphones, but looking at one another through the window.

Then she turned her eyes towards Rebus, winked at him, and crossed her fingers. He crossed his fingers back at her.

'Two minutes everyone ...'

At the top of the hour there was news, and straight after the news ...

A tape played. The show's theme music. Penny leaned towards her microphone, which hung like an anglepoise over her desk. The music faded.

'Hello again. This is Penny Cook, and this is *What's Cookin'*. I'll be with you until three o'clock, so if you've got a problem, I'm just a phone call away. And if you want to ring me the number as ever is ...'

It was extraordinary, and Rebus could only marvel at it. Her eyes were closed, and she looked so brittle that a shiver might turn her to powder. Yet that voice ... so controlled ... no, not controlled; rather, it was as though it were apart from her, as though it possessed a life of its own, a personality ... Rebus looked at the studio clock. Four hours of this, five nights a week? All in all, he thought, he'd rather be a policeman.

The show was running like clockwork. Calls were taken by the two operators, details scribbled down. There was discussion with the producer about suitable candidates, and during the musical interludes or the commercials – '... and mmm ... it tastes *so* good' – the producer would relay details about the callers to Penny.

'Let's go with that one,' she might say. Or: 'I can't deal with that, not tonight.' Usually, her word was the last, though the producer might demur.

'I don't know, it's quite a while since we covered adultery ...'
Rebus watched. Rebus listened. But most of all, Rebus waited ...

'OK, Penny,' the producer told her, 'it's line two next. His name's Michael.'

She nodded. 'Can somebody get me a coffee?'

'Sure.'

'And next,' she said, 'I think we've got Michael on line two. Hello, Michael?'

It was quarter to midnight. As usual, the door of the production room opened and Gordon Prentice stepped into the room. He had nods and smiles for everyone, and seemed especially pleased to see Rebus.

'Inspector,' he said shaking Rebus's hand. 'I see you take your work seriously, coming here at this hour.' He patted the producer's shoulder. 'How's the show tonight?'

'Been a bit tame so far, but this looks interesting.'

Penny's eyes were on the dimly lit production room. But her voice was all for Michael.

'And what do you do for a living, Michael?'

The caller's voice crackled out of the loudspeakers. 'I'm an actor, Penny.'

'Really? And are you working just now?'

'No, I'm what we call "resting".'

'Ah well, they say there's no rest for the wicked. I suppose that must mean you *haven't* been wicked.'

Gordon Prentice, running his fingers through his beard, smiled at this, turning to Rebus to see how he was enjoying himself. Rebus smiled back.

'On the contrary,' the voice was saying. 'I've been really quite wicked. And I'm ashamed of it.'

'And what is it you're so ashamed of, Michael?'

'I've been telephoning you anonymously, Penny. Threatening you. I'm sorry. You see, I thought you knew about it. But the policeman tells me you don't. I'm sorry.'

Prentice wasn't smiling now. His eyes had opened wide in disbelief.

'Knew about what, Michael?' Her eyes were staring at the window. Light bounced off her spectacles, sending flashes like laser beams into the production room.

'Knew about the fix. When the ratings were going down, the station head, Gordon Prentice, started rigging the shows, yours and Hamish MacDiarmid's. MacDiarmid might even be in on it.'

'What do you mean, rigging?'

'Kill it!' shouted Prentice. 'Kill transmission! He's raving mad! Cut the line someone. Here, I'll do it—'

But Rebus had come up behind Prentice and now locked his own arms around Prentice's. 'I think you'd better listen,' he warned.

'Out of work actors,' Michael was saying, the way he'd told Rebus earlier in the day. 'Prentice put together a ... you could call it a cast, I suppose. Half a dozen people. They phone in using different voices, always with a controversial point to make or some nice juicy problem. One of them told me at a party one night. I didn't believe her until I started listening for myself. An actor can tell that sort of thing, when a voice isn't quite right, when something's an act rather than for real.'

Prentice was struggling, but couldn't break Rebus's hold. 'Lies!' he yelled. 'Complete rubbish! Let go of me, you—'

Penny Cook's eyes were on Prentice now, and on no one but Prentice.

'So what you're saying, Michael, if I understand you, is that Gordon Prentice is rigging our phone-ins so as to boost audience figures?'

'That's right.'

'Michael, thank you for your call.'

It was Rebus who spoke, and he spoke to the producer.

'That'll do.'

The producer nodded through the glass to Penny Cook, then flipped a switch. Music could be heard over the loudspeakers. The producer started to fade the piece out. Penny spoke into her microphone.

'A slightly longer musical interlude there, but I hope you enjoyed it. We'll be going back to your calls very shortly, but first we've got some commercials.'

She slipped off her glasses and rubbed the bridge of her nose.

'A private performance,' Rebus explained to Prentice. 'For our benefit only. The listeners were hearing something else.' Rebus felt Prentice's body soften, the shoulders slump. He was caught, and knew it for sure. Rebus relaxed his hold on the man: he wouldn't try anything now.

The Camelot Coffee ad was playing. It had been easy really. Recognising the voice on the commercial as that of the phone caller, Rebus had contacted the ad agency involved, who had given him the name and address of the actor concerned: Michael Barrie, presently resting and to be found most days in a certain city-centre wine bar ...

Barrie knew he was in trouble, but Rebus was sure it could be smoothed out. But as for Gordon Prentice ... ah, that was different altogether.

'The station's ruined!' he wailed. 'You must know that!' He pleaded with the producer, the engineer, but especially with the hate-filled eyes of Penny Cook who, behind glass, could not even hear him. 'Once this gets out, you'll *all* be out of a job! All of you! That's why I—'

'Back on in five seconds, Penny,' said the producer, as though it was just another night on *What's Cookin'*. Penny Cook nodded, resting her glasses back on her nose. The stuffing looked to have been knocked out of her. With one final baleful glance towards Prentice, she turned to her microphone.

'Welcome back. A change of direction now, because I'd like to say a few words to you about the head of Lowland Radio, Gordon Prentice. I hope you'll bear with me for a minute or two. It shouldn't take much longer than that …'

It didn't, but what she said was tabloid news by morning, and Lowland Radio's licence was withdrawn not long after that. Rebus went back to Radio Three for when he was driving, and no radio at all in his flat. Hamish MacDiarmid, as far as he could ascertain, went back to a croft somewhere, but Penny Cook stuck around, going freelance and doing some journalism as well as the odd radio programme.

It was very late one night when the knock came at Rebus's door. He opened it to find Penny standing there. She pretended surprise at seeing him.

'Oh, hello,' she said. 'I didn't know you lived here. Only, I've run out of coffee and I was wondering …'

Laughing, Rebus led her inside. 'I can let you have the best part of a jar of Camelot,' he said. 'Or alternatively we could get drunk and go to bed …'

They got drunk.

Trip Trap

Blame it on patience.

Patience, coincidence, or fate. Whatever, Grace Gallagher came downstairs that morning and found herself sitting at the dining table with a cup of strong brown tea (there was just enough milk in the fridge for one other cup), staring at the pack of cards. She sucked cigarette smoke into her lungs, feeling her heart beat the faster for it. This cigarette she enjoyed. George did not allow her to smoke in his presence, and in his presence she was for the best part of each and every day. The smoke upset him, he said. It tasted his mouth, so that food took on a funny flavour. It irritated his nostrils, made him sneeze and cough. Made him giddy. George had written the book on hypochondria.

So the house became a no-smoking zone when George was up and about. Which was precisely why Grace relished this small moment by herself, a moment lasting from seven fifteen until seven forty-five. For the forty years of their married life, Grace had always managed to wake up thirty clear minutes before her husband. She would sit at the table with a cigarette and tea until his feet forced a creak from the bedroom floorboard on his side of the bed. That floorboard had creaked from the day they'd moved into 26 Gillan Drive, thirty-odd years ago. George had promised to fix it; now he wasn't even fit to fix himself tea and toast.

Grace finished the cigarette and stared at the pack of cards. They'd played whist and rummy the previous evening, playing for stakes of a penny a game. And she'd lost as usual. George hated losing, defeat bringing on a sulk which could last the whole of the following day, so to make her life a little easier Grace now allowed him to win, purposely throwing away useful cards, frittering her trumps. George would sometimes notice and mock her for her stupidity. But more often he just clapped his hands together after another win, his puffy fingers stroking the winnings from the table top.

Grace now found herself opening the pack, shuffling, and laying out the cards for a hand of patience, a hand which she won without effort. She shuffled again, played again, won again. This, it seemed, was her morning. She tried a third game, and again the cards fell right, until four neat piles stared back at her, black on red on black on red, all the way from king to ace. She was halfway through a fourth hand, and confident of success, when the floorboard creaked, her name was called, and the day – her real day – began. She made tea (that was the end of the milk) and toast, and took it to George in bed. He'd been to the bathroom, and slipped slowly back between the sheets.

'Leg's giving me gyp today,' he said. Grace was silent, having no new replies to add to this statement. She placed his tray on the bed and pulled open the curtains. The room was stuffy, but even in summer he didn't like the windows open. He blamed the pollution, the acid rain, the exhaust fumes. They played merry hell with his lungs, making him wheezy, breathless. Grace peered out on to the street. Across the road, houses just like hers seemed already to be wilting from the day's ordinariness. Yet inside her, despite everything, despite the sour smell of the room, the heavy breath of her unshaven husband, the slurping of tea, the grey heat of the morning, Grace could feel something extraordinary. Hadn't she won at patience? Won time and time again? Paths seemed to be opening up in front of her.

'I'll go fetch you your paper,' she said.

George Gallagher liked to study racing form. He would pore over the newspaper, sneering at the tipsters' choices, and would come up with a 'super yankee' – five horses which, should they all romp home as winners, would make them their fortune. Grace would take his betting slip to the bookie's on the High Street, would hand across the stake money – less than £1.50 per day – and would go home to listen on the radio as horse after horse failed in its mission, the tipsters' choices meantime bringing in a fair return. But George had what he called 'inside knowledge', and besides, the tipsters were all crooked, weren't they? You couldn't trust them. Grace was a bloody fool if she thought she could. Often a choice of George's would come in second or third, but despite her efforts he refused to back any horse each way. All or nothing, that's what he wanted.

'You never win big by betting that way.'

Grace's smile was like a nail file: *we never win at all.*

George wondered sometimes why it took his wife so long to fetch the paper. After all, the shop was ten minutes' walk away at most, yet Grace would usually be out of the house for the best part of an hour. But there was always the story of a neighbour met, gossip exchanged, a queue in the shop, or the paper not having arrived, entailing a longer walk to the newsagent's further down the road ...

In fact, Grace took the newspaper to Lossie Park, where, weather permitting, she sat on one of the benches and, taking a ballpoint pen (free with a woman's magazine, refilled twice since) from her handbag, proceeded to attempt the newspaper's crossword. At first, she'd filled in the 'quick' clues, but had grown more confident with the years so that she now did the 'cryptic', often finishing it, sometimes failing for want of one or two answers, which she would ponder over the rest of the day. George, his eyes fixed on the sports pages, never noticed that she'd been busy at the crossword. He got his news, so he said, from the TV and the radio, though in fact Grace had noticed that he normally slept through the television news, and seldom listened to the radio.

If the weather was dreich, Grace would sit on a sheltered bench, where one day a year or so back she had been joined by a gentleman of similar years (which was to say, eight or nine years younger than George). He was a local, a widower, and his name was Jim Malcolm. They talked, but spent most of the time just watching the park itself, studying mothers with prams, boys with their dogs, games of football, lovers' tiffs, and, even at that early hour, the occasional drunk. Every day they met at one bench or another, seeming to happen upon one another by accident, never seeing one another at any other time of the day, or any other location, other than those truly accidental meetings in a shop or on the pavement.

And then, a few weeks back, springtime, standing in the butcher's shop, Grace had overheard the news of Jim Malcolm's death. When her turn came to be served, Grace asked for half a pound of steak mince, instead of the usual 'economy' stuff. The butcher raised an eyebrow.

'Something to celebrate, Mrs Gallagher?'

'Not really,' Grace had said quietly. That night, George had eaten the expensive mince without comment.

Today she completed the crossword in record time. It wasn't that the clues seemed easier than usual; it was more that her brain seemed to be working faster than ever before, catching that inference or this anagram. Anything, she decided, was possible on a day like this. Simply anything. The sun was appearing from behind a bank of cloud. She closed the newspaper, folded it into her bag alongside the pen, and stood up. She'd been in the park barely ten minutes. If she returned home so quickly, George might ask questions. So instead she walked a slow circuit of the playing fields, her thoughts on patience, and crosswords and creaking floorboards, and much more besides.

Blame it on Patience.

Detective Inspector John Rebus had known Dr Patience Aitken for several years, and not once during their working relationship had he been able to refuse her a favour. Patience seemed to Rebus the kind of woman his parents, if still alive, would have been trying to marry him off to, were he still single. Which, in a sense, he was, being divorced. On finding he *was* divorced, Patience had invited Rebus round to her surprisingly large house for what she had called 'dinner'. Halfway through a home-baked fruit pie, Patience had admitted to Rebus that she was wearing no underwear. Homely but smouldering: that was Patience. Who could deny such a woman a favour? Not John Rebus. And so it was that he found himself this evening standing on the doorstep of 26 Gillan Drive, and about to intrude on private grief.

Not that there was anything very private about a death, not in this part of Scotland, or in any part of Scotland come to that. Curtains twitched at neighbouring windows, people spoke in lowered voices across the divide of a garden fence, and fewer televisions than usual blared out the ubiquitous advertising jingles and even more ubiquitous game show applause.

Gillan Drive was part of an anonymous working-class district on the south-eastern outskirts of Edinburgh. The district had fallen on hard times, but there was still the smell of pride in the air. Gardens were kept tidy, the tiny lawns clipped like army haircuts, and the cars parked tight against the kerbs were old – W and X registrations predominated – but polished, showing no signs of rust. Rebus took it all in in a moment. In a neighbourhood like this, grief was for sharing. Everybody wanted their cut. Still something stopped him lifting the door knocker and letting it fall. Patience Aitken had been vague, wary, ambivalent: that was why she was asking him for a favour, and not for his professional help.

'I mean,' she had said over the telephone, 'I've been treating George Gallagher on and off – more *on* than off – for years. I think about the only complaints I've ever not known him to think he had are beri-beri and elephantiasis, and then only because you never read about them in the "Doc's Page" of the *Sunday Post*.'

Rebus smiled. GPs throughout Scotland feared their Monday morning surgeries, when people would suddenly appear in droves suffering from complaints read about the previous morning in the *Post*. No wonder people called the paper an 'institution' ...

'And all the while,' Patience Aitken was saying, 'Grace has been by his bedside. Always patient with him, always looking after him. The woman's been an angel.'

'So what's the problem?' Rebus nursed not only the telephone, but a headache and a mug of black coffee as well. (Black coffee because he was dieting; a headache for not unconnected reasons.)

'The problem is that George fell downstairs this morning. He's dead.'

'I'm sorry to hear it.'

There was a silence at the other end of the line.

'I take it,' Rebus said, 'that you don't share my feelings.'

'George Gallagher was a cantankerous old man, grown from a bitter younger man and most probably a fairly unsociable teenager. I don't think I ever heard him utter a civil word, never mind a "please" or a "thank you".'

'Fine,' said Rebus, 'so let's celebrate his demise.'

Silence again.

Rebus sighed and rubbed his temples. 'Out with it,' he ordered.

'He's supposed to have fallen downstairs,' Patience Aitken explained. 'He did go downstairs in the afternoon, sometimes to watch racing on the telly, sometimes just to stare at a different set of walls from the bedroom. But he fell at around eleven o'clock, which is a bit early for him ...'

'And you think he was pushed?' Rebus tried not to sound cynical. Her reply was blunt. 'Yes, I do.'

'By this angel who's managed to put up with him all these years?'

'That's right.'

'OK, Doc, so point me to the medical evidence.'

'Well, it's a narrow staircase, pretty steep, about eleven or twelve steps, say. If you weighed around thirteen stone, and happened to slip at the top, you'd sort of be bounced off the sides as you fell, wouldn't you?'

'Perhaps.'

'And you'd try to grab hold of something to stop your fall. There's a banister on one wall. They were waiting for the council to come and fit an extra banister on the other wall.'

'So you'd reach out to grab something, fair enough.' Rebus drained the sour black coffee and studied the pile of work in his in-tray.

'Well, you'd have bruising, wouldn't you?' said Patience Aitken. 'Grazes on your elbows or knees, there'd be marks where you'd clawed at the walls.'

Rebus knew that she was surmising, but could not disagree thus far. 'Go on,' he said.

'George Gallagher only has significant marks on his head, where he hit the floor at the bottom of the stairs, breaking his neck in the process. No real bruising or grazing to the body, no marks on the wall as far as I can see.'

'So you're saying he flew from the top landing with a fair bit of momentum, and the first thing he touched was the ground?'

'That's how it looks. Unless I'm imagining it.'

'So he either jumped, or he was pushed?'

'Yes.' She paused again. 'I know it sounds tenuous, John. And Christ knows I don't want to accuse Grace of anything ...'

Rebus picked up a ballpoint pen from beside the telephone and scrabbled on the surface of his desk until he found the back of an envelope upon which to write.

'You're only doing your job, Patience,' he said. 'Give me the address and I'll go pay my respects.'

The door of 26 Gillan Drive opened slowly, and a man peered out at Rebus, then ushered him quickly inside, laying a soft hand on his arm.

'In ye come, son. In ye come. The women are in the living-room. The kitchen's through here.' He nodded his head, then led Rebus through a narrow hallway past a closed door, from behind which came tearful sounds, towards a half-open door at the back of the house. Rebus had not even glanced at the stairs as they'd passed them, the stairs which had faced him at the open front door of the house. The kitchen door was now opened from within, and Rebus saw that seven or eight men had squeezed into the tiny back room. There were stale smells of cooking fat and soup, stew and fruit cake, but above them wafted a more recent smell: whisky.

'Here ye are, son.' Someone was handing him a tumbler with a good inch of amber liquid in it. Everyone else had just such a glass nestling in their hand. They all shuffled from one foot to another, awkward, hardly daring to speak. They had nodded at Rebus's entrance, but now gave him little heed. Glasses were replenished. Rebus noticed the Co-op price label on the bottle.

'You've just moved into Cashman Street, haven't you?' someone was asking someone else.

'Aye, that's right. A couple of months ago. The wife used to meet Mrs Gallagher at the shops, so we thought we'd drop in.'

'See this estate, son, it was miners' rows once upon a time. It used to be that you lived here and died here. But these days there's that much coming and going ...'

The conversation continued at the level of a murmur. Rebus was standing with his back to the sink's draining board, next to the back door. A figure appeared in front of him.

'Have another drop, son.' And the inch in his glass rose to an inch and a half. Rebus looked around him in vain, seeking out a relative of the deceased. But these men looked like neighbours, like the sons of neighbours, the male half of the community's heart. Their wives, sisters, mothers would be in the living-room with Grace Gallagher. Closed curtains blocking out any light from what was left of the day: handkerchiefs and sweet sherry. The bereaved in an armchair, with someone else perched on an arm of the chair, offering a pat of the hand and well-meant words. Rebus had seen it all, seen it as a child with his own mother, and as a young man with his father, seen it with aunts and uncles, with the parents of friends and more recently with friends themselves. He wasn't so young now. The odd contemporary was already falling victim to the Big C or an unexpected heart attack. Today was the last day of April. Two days ago, he'd gone to Fife and laid flowers on his father's grave. Whether it was an act of remembrance or of simple contrition, he couldn't have said ...

His guide pulled him back to the present. 'Her daughter-in-law's already here. Came over from Falkirk this afternoon.'

Rebus nodded, trying to look wise. 'And the son?'

Eyes looked at him. 'Dead these past ten years. Don't you know that?'

There was suspicion now, and Rebus knew that he had either to reveal himself as a policeman, or else become more disingenuous still. These people, authentically mourning the loss of someone they had known, had taken him as a mourner too, had brought him in here to share with them, to be part of the remembering group.

'I'm just a friend of a friend,' he explained. 'They asked me to look in.'

It looked from his guide's face, however, as though an interrogation might be about to begin. But then somebody else spoke.

'Terrible crash it was. What was the name of the town again?'

'Methil. He'd been working on building a rig there.'

'That's right,' said the guide knowledgeably. 'Pay night it was. They'd been out for a few drinks, like. On their way to the dancing. Next thing ...'

'Aye, terrible smash it was. The lad in the back seat had to have both legs taken off.'

Well, thought Rebus, I bet he didn't go to any more hops. Then he winced, trying to forgive himself for thinking such a thing. His guide saw the wince and laid the hand back on his arm.

'All right, son, all right.' And they were all looking at him again, perhaps expecting tears. Rebus was growing red in the face.

'I'll just ...' he said, motioning towards the ceiling with his head. 'You know where it is?'

Rebus nodded. He'd seen all there was to see downstairs, and so knew the bathroom must lie upstairs, and upstairs was where he was heading. He closed the kitchen door behind him and breathed deeply. There was sweat beneath his shirt, and the headache was reasserting itself. That'll teach you, Rebus, it was saying. That'll teach you for taking a sip of whisky. That'll teach you for making cheap jokes to yourself. Take all the aspirin you like. They'll dissolve your stomach lining before they dissolve me.

Rebus called his headache two seven-letter words before beginning to climb the stairs.

He gave careful scrutiny to each stair as he climbed, and to the walls either side of each stair. The carpet itself was fairly new, with a thickish pile. The wallpaper was old, and showed a hunting scene, horse-riders and dogs with a fox panting and worried in the distance. As Patience Aitken had said, there were no scrapes or claw-marks on the paper itself. What's more, there were no loose edges of carpet. The whole thing had been tacked down with a professional's skill. Nothing for George Gallagher to trip over, no threads or untacked sections; and no smooth threadbare patches for him to slip on.

He gave special attention to where the upstairs landing met the stairs. George Gallagher probably fell from here, from this height. Further down the stairs, his chances of survival would have been much greater. Yes, it was a steep and narrow staircase all right. A trip and a tumble would certainly have caused bruising. Immediate death at the foot of the stairs would doubtless have arrested much of the bruising, the blood stilling in the veins and arteries, but bruising there would have been. The post-mortem would be specific; so far Rebus was trading on speculation, and well he knew it.

Four doors led off the landing: a large cupboard (what Rebus as a child would have called a 'press'), filled with sheets, blankets, two ancient suitcases, a black-and-white television lying on its side; a musty spare bedroom, its single bed made up ready for the visitor who never came; the bathroom, with a battery-operated razor lying on the cistern, never to be used again by its owner; and the bedroom. Nothing interested Rebus in either the spare bedroom or the bathroom, so he slipped into the main bedroom, closing the door behind him, then opening it again, since to be discovered behind a closed door would be so much more suspicious than to be found inside an open one.

The sheets, blanket and quilt had been pulled back from the bed, and three pillows had been placed on their ends against the headboard so that one person could sit up in bed. He'd seen a breakfast tray in the kitchen, still boasting the remnants of a morning meal: cups, toast crumbs on a greasy plate, an old coffee jar now holding the remains of some home-made jam. Beside the bed stood a walking-frame. Patience Aitken had said that George Gallagher usually wouldn't walk half a dozen steps without his walking-frame (a Zimmer she'd called it, but to Rebus Zimmer was the German for 'room'...). Of course, if Grace were helping him, he could walk without it, leaning on her the way he'd lean his weight on a stick. Rebus visualised Grace Gallagher coaxing her husband from his bed, telling him he wouldn't be needing his walking-frame, she'd help him down the stairs. He could lean on her ...

On the bed rested a newspaper, dotted with tacky spots of jam. It was today's paper, and it was open at the racing pages. A blue pen had been used to ring some of the runners – Gypsy Pearl, Gazumpin, Lot's Wife, Castle Mallet, Blondie – five in total, enough for a super yankee. The blue pen was sitting on a bedside table, beside a glass half filled with water, some tablets (the label made out to Mr G. Gallagher), a pair of reading spectacles in their case, and a paperback cowboy novel – large print – borrowed from the local library. Rebus sat on the edge of the bed and flipped through the newspaper. His eyes came to rest on a particular page, the letters and cartoons page. At bottom right was a crossword, a completed crossword at that. The pen used to fill in the squares seemed different to that used for the racing form further on in the paper, and the hand seemed different too: more delicate, more feminine. Thin faint marks rather than the robust lines used to circle the day's favoured horses. Rebus enjoyed the occasional crossword, and, impressed to find this one completed, was more impressed to find that the answers were those to the cryptic clues rather than the quick clues most people favoured. He began to read, until at some point in his reading his brow furrowed, and he blinked a couple of times before closing the paper, folding it twice, and rolling it into his jacket pocket. A second or two's reflection later, he rose from the bed and walked slowly to the bedroom door, out on to the landing where, taking careful hold of the banister, he started downstairs.

*

He stood in the kitchen with his whisky, pondering the situation. Faces came and went. A man would finish his drink with a sigh or a clearing of the throat.

'Ay well,' he'd say, 'I suppose I'd better ...' And with these words, and a bow of the head, he would move out of the kitchen, timidly opening the living-room door so as to say a few words to the widow before leaving. Rebus heard Grace Gallagher's voice, a high, wavering howl: 'Thanks for coming. It was good of you. Cheerio.'

The women came and went, too. Sandwiches appeared from somewhere and were shared out in the kitchen. Tongue, corned beef, salmon paste. White 'half-pan' bread sliced in halves. Despite his diet, Rebus ate his fill, saying nothing. Though he only half knew it, he was biding his time, not wishing to create a disturbance. He waited as the kitchen emptied. Once or twice someone had attempted to engage him in conversation, thinking they knew him from a neighbouring street or from the public bar of the local. Rebus just shook his head, the friend of a friend, and the enquiries usually ended there.

Even his guide left, again patting Rebus's arm and giving him a nod and a wink. It was a day for universal gestures, so Rebus winked back. Then, the kitchen vacant now, muggy with the smell of cheap cigarettes, whisky and body odour, Rebus rinsed out his glass and stood it end-up on the draining board. He walked into the hallway, paused, then knocked and pushed open the living-room door.

As he had suspected, Grace Gallagher, as frail-looking as he'd thought, dabbing behind her fifties-style spectacles, was seated in an armchair. On the arm of the chair sat a woman in her forties, heavy-bodied but not without presence. The other chairs were vacant. Teacups sat on a dining table, alongside an unfinished plate of sandwiches, empty sherry glasses, the bottle itself, and, curiously, a pack of playing cards, laid out as though someone had broken off halfway through a game of patience.

Opposite the television set sat another sunken armchair, looking as if it had not been sat in this whole afternoon. Rebus could guess why: the deceased's chair, the throne to his tiny kingdom. He smiled towards the two women. Grace Gallagher only half looked towards him.

'Thanks for dropping by,' she said, her voice slightly revived from earlier. 'It was good of you. Cheerio.'

'Actually, Mrs Gallagher,' said Rebus, stepping into the room, 'I'm a police officer, Detective Inspector Rebus. Dr Aitken asked me to look in.'

'Oh.' Grace Gallagher looked at him now. Pretty eyes sinking into crinkly white skin. A dab of natural colour on each cheek. Her silvery hair hadn't seen a perm in quite a while, but someone had combed it, perhaps to enable her to face the rigours of the afternoon. The daughter-in-law – or so Rebus supposed the woman on the arm of the chair to be – was rising.

'Would you like me to ...?'

Rebus nodded towards her. 'I don't think this'll take long. Just routine really, when there's been an accident.' He looked at Grace, then at the daughter-in-law. 'Maybe if you could go into the kitchen for five minutes or so?'

She nodded keenly, perhaps a little too keenly. Rebus hadn't seen her all evening, and so supposed she'd felt duty bound to stay cooped up in here with her mother-in-law. She seemed to relish the prospect of movement.

'I'll pop the kettle on,' she said, brushing past Rebus. He watched the door close, waited as she padded down the short hallway, listened until he heard water running, the sounds of dishes being tidied. Then he turned back to Grace Gallagher, took a deep breath, and walked over towards her, dragging a stiff-backed dining chair with him. This he sat on, only a foot or two from her. He could feel her growing uneasy. She writhed a little in the armchair, then tried to disguise the reaction by reaching for another paper hankie from a box on the floor beside her.

'This must be a very difficult time for you, Mrs Gallagher,' Rebus began. He wanted to keep things short and clear cut. He had no evidence, had nothing to play with but a little bit of psychology and the woman's own state of mind. It might not be enough; he wasn't sure whether or not he *wanted* it to be enough. He found himself shifting on the chair. His arm touched the newspaper in his pocket. It felt like a talisman.

'Dr Aitken told me,' he continued, 'that you'd looked after your husband for quite a few years. It can't have been easy.'

'I'd be lying if I said that it was.'

Rebus tried to find the requisite amount of iron in her words. Tried but failed.

'Yes,' he said, 'I believe your husband was, well, a bit *difficult* at times.'

'I won't deny that either. He could be a real bugger when he wanted to.' She smiled, as if in memory of the fact. 'But I'll miss him. Aye, I'll miss him.'

'I'm sure you will, Mrs Gallagher.'

He looked at her, and her eyes fixed on to his, challenging him.

He cleared his throat again. 'There's something I'm not absolutely sure about, concerning the accident. I wonder if maybe you can help me?'

'I can try.'

Rebus smiled his appreciation. 'It's just this,' he said. 'Eleven o'clock was a bit early for your husband to be coming downstairs. What's more, he seemed to be trying to come down without his walking-frame, which is still beside the bed.' Rebus's voice was becoming firmer, his conviction growing. 'What's more, he seems to have fallen with a fair amount of force.'

She interrupted him with a snap. 'How do you mean?'

'I mean he fell straight down the stairs. He didn't just slip and fall, or stumble and roll down them. He went flying off the top step and didn't hit anything till he hit the ground.' Her eyes were filling again. Hating himself, Rebus pressed on. 'He didn't fall, Mrs Gallagher. He was helped to the top of the stairs, and then he was helped down them with a push in the back, a pretty vigorous push at that.' His voice grew less severe, less judgemental. 'I'm not saying you meant to kill him. Maybe you just wanted him hospitalised, so you could have a rest from looking after him. Was that it?'

She was blowing her nose, her small shoulders squeezed inwards towards a brittle neck. The shoulders twitched with sobs. 'I don't know what you're talking about. You think I ... How could you? Why would you say anything like that? No, I don't believe you. Get out of my house.' But there was no power to any of her words, no real enthusiasm for the fight. Rebus reached into his pocket and brought out the newspaper.

'I notice you do crosswords, Mrs Gallagher.'

She glanced up at him, startled by this twist in the conversation. 'What?'

He motioned with the paper. 'I like crosswords myself. That's why I was interested when I saw you'd completed today's puzzle. Very impressive. When did you do that?'

'This morning,' she said through another handkerchief. 'In the park. I always do the crossword after I've bought the paper. Then I bring it home so George can look at his horses.'

Rebus nodded, and studied the crossword again. 'You must have been preoccupied with something this morning then,' he said. 'What do you mean?'

'It's quite an easy one, really. I mean, easy for someone who does crosswords like this and finishes them. Where is it now?' Rebus seemed to be searching the grid. 'Yes,' he said. 'Nineteen across. You've got the down solutions, so that means the answer to nineteen across must be something R something P. Now, what's the clue?' He looked for it, found it. 'Here it is, Mrs Gallagher. "Perhaps deadly in part." Four letters. Something R something P. Something deadly. Or deadly in part. And you've put TRIP. 'What were you thinking about, I wonder? I mean, when you wrote that? I wonder what your mind was on?'

'But it's the right answer,' said Grace Gallagher, her face creasing in puzzlement. Rebus was shaking his head.

'No,' he said. 'I don't think so. I think the "in part" means the letters of "part" make up the word you want. The answer's TRAP, Mrs Gallagher. "Perhaps deadly in part": TRAP. Do you see? But you were thinking of something else when you filled in the answer. You were thinking about how if your husband tripped down the stairs you might be rid of him. Isn't that right, Grace?'

She was silent for a moment, the silence broken only by the ticking of the mantelpiece clock and the clank of dishes being washed in the kitchen. Then she spoke, quite calmly.

'Myra's a good lass. It was terrible when Billy died. She's been like a daughter to me ever since.' Another pause, then her eyes met Rebus's again. He was thinking of his own mother, of how old she'd be today had she lived. Much the same age as this woman in front of him. He took another deep breath, but stayed silent, waiting.

'You know, son,' she said, 'if you look after an invalid, people think you're a martyr. I was a martyr all right, but only because I put up with him for forty years.' Her eyes strayed to the empty armchair, and focused on it as though her husband were sitting there and hearing the truth for the very first time. 'He was a sweet talker back then, and he had all the right moves. None of that once Billy came along. None of that ever again.' Her voice, which had been growing softer, now began hardening again. 'They shut the pit, so he got work at the bottle factory. Then they shut that, and all he could get was part-time chalking up the winners at the bookie's. A man gets gey bitter, Inspector. But he didn't have to take it out on me, did he?' She moved her eyes from the chair to Rebus. 'Will they lock me up?' She didn't sound particularly interested in his answer.

'That's not for me to say, Grace. Juries decide that sort of thing.'

She smiled. 'I thought I'd done the crossword in record time. Trust me to get one wrong.' And she shook her head slowly, the smile falling from her face as the tears came again, and her mouth opened in a near-silent bawl.

The door swung open, the daughter-in-law entering with a tray full of crockery.

'There now,' she called. 'We can all have a nice cup of—' She saw the look on Grace Gallagher's face, and she froze.

'What have you done?' she cried accusingly. Rebus stood up.

'Mrs Gallagher,' he said to her, 'I'm afraid I've got a bit of bad news ...'

She had known of course. The daughter-in-law had known. Not that Grace had said anything, but there had been a special bond between them. Myra's parting words to Rebus's retreating back had been a vicious 'That bugger deserved all he got!' Net curtains had twitched; faces had appeared at darkened windows. Her words had echoed along the street and up into the smoky night air.

Maybe she was right at that. Rebus couldn't judge. All he could be was fair. So why was it that he felt so guilty? So ashamed? He could have shrugged it off, could have reported back to Patience that there was no substance to her fears. Grace Gallagher had suffered; would continue to suffer. Wasn't that enough? OK, so the law demanded more, but without Rebus there was no case, was there?

He felt right, felt vindicated, and at the same time felt a complete and utter bastard. More than that, he felt as though he'd just sentenced his own mother. He stopped at a late-night store and stocked up on beer and cigarettes. As an afterthought, he bought six assorted packets of crisps and a couple of bars of chocolate. This was no time to diet. Back home, he could conduct his own post-mortem, could hold his own private wake. On his way out of the shop, he bought the final edition of the evening paper, and was reminded that this was 30 April. Tomorrow morning, before dawn, crowds of people would climb up Arthur's Seat and, at the hill's summit, would celebrate the rising of the sun and the coming of May. Some would dab their faces with dew, the old story being that it would make them more beautiful, more handsome. What exactly was it they were celebrating, all the hungover students and the druids and the curious? Rebus wasn't sure any more. Perhaps he had never known in the first place.

Later that night, much later, as he lay along his sofa, the hi-fi blaring some jazz music from the sixties, his eye caught the day's racing results on the paper's back page. Gypsy Pearl had come home first at three-to-one. In the very next race, Gazumpin had won at seven-to-two on. Two races further on, Lot's Wife had triumphed at a starting price of eight-to-one. At another meeting, Castle Mallet had won the two thirty. Two-to-one joint favourite. That left only Blondie. Rebus tried to focus his eyes, and finally found the horse, its name misprinted to read 'Bloodie'. Though three-to-one favourite, it had come home third in a field of thirteen.

Rebus stared at the misspelling, wondering what had been going through the typist's mind when he or she had made that one small but no doubt meaningful slip ...

Castle Dangerous

Sir Walter Scott was dead.

He'd been found at the top of his namesake's monument in Princes Street Gardens, dead of a heart attack and with a new and powerful pair of binoculars hanging around his slender, mottled neck.

Sir Walter had been one of Edinburgh's most revered QCs until his retirement a year ago. Detective Inspector John Rebus, climbing the hundreds (surely it must be hundreds) of spiralling steps up to the top of the Scott Monument, paused for a moment to recall one or two of his run-ins with Sir Walter, both in and out of the courtrooms on the Royal Mile. He had been a formidable character, shrewd, devious and subtle. Law to him had been a challenge rather than an obligation. To John Rebus, it was just a day's work.

Rebus ached as he reached the last incline. The steps here were narrower than ever, the spiral tighter. Room for one person only, really. At the height of its summer popularity, with a throng of tourists squeezing through it like toothpaste from a tube, Rebus reckoned the Scott Monument might be very scary indeed.

He breathed hard and loud, bursting through the small doorway at the top, and stood there for a moment, catching his breath. The panorama before him was, quite simply, the best view in Edinburgh. The castle close behind him, the New Town spread out in front of him, sloping down towards the Firth of Forth, with Fife, Rebus's birthplace, visible in the distance. Calton Hill ... Leith ... Arthur's Seat ... and round to the castle again. It was breathtaking, or would have been had the breath not already been taken from him by the climb.

The parapet upon which he stood was incredibly narrow; again, there was hardly room enough to squeeze past someone. How crowded did it get in the summer? Dangerously crowded? It seemed dangerously crowded just now, with only four people up here. He looked over the edge upon the sheer drop to the gardens below, where a massing of tourists, growing restless at being barred from the monument, stared up at him. Rebus shivered.

Not that it was cold. It was early June. Spring was finally late-blooming into summer, but that cold wind never left the city, that wind which never seemed to be warmed by the sun. It bit into Rebus now, reminding him that he lived in a northern climate. He looked down and saw Sir Walter's slumped body, reminding him why he was here.

'I thought we were going to have another corpse on our hands there for a minute.' The speaker was Detective Sergeant Brian Holmes. He had been in conversation with the police doctor, who himself was crouching over the corpse.

'Just getting my breath back,' Rebus explained.

'You should take up squash.'

'It's squashed enough up here.' The wind was nipping Rebus's ears. He began to wish he hadn't had that haircut at the weekend. 'What have we got?'

'Heart attack. The doctor reckons he was due for one anyway. A climb like that in an excited state. One of the witnesses says he just doubled over. Didn't cry out, didn't seem in pain ...'

'Old mortality, eh?' Rebus looked wistfully at the corpse. 'But why do you say he was excited?'

Holmes grinned. 'Think I'd bring you up here for the good of your health? Here.' He handed a polythene bag to Rebus. Inside the bag was a badly typed note. 'It was found in the binocular case.'

Rebus read the note through its clear polythene window: GO TO TOP OF SCOTT MONUMENT. TUESDAY MIDDAY. I'LL BE THERE. LOOK FOR THE GUN.

'The gun?' Rebus asked, frowning.

There was a sudden explosion. Rebus started, but Holmes just looked at his watch, then corrected its hands. One o'clock. The noise had come from the blank charge fired every day from the castle walls at precisely one o'clock.

'The gun,' Rebus repeated, except now it was a statement. Sir Walter's binoculars were lying beside him. Rebus lifted them – 'He wouldn't mind, would he?' – and fixed them on the castle. Tourists could be seen walking around. Some peered over the walls. A few fixed their own binoculars on Rebus. One, an elderly Asian, grinned and waved. Rebus lowered the binoculars. He examined them. 'These look brand new.'

'Bought for the purpose, I'd say, sir.'

'But what exactly *was* the purpose, Brian? What was he supposed to be looking at?' Rebus waited for an answer. None was forthcoming. 'Whatever it was,' Rebus went on, 'it as good as killed him. I suggest we take a look for ourselves.'

'Where, sir?'

Rebus nodded towards the castle. 'Over there, Brian. Come on.'

'Er, Inspector ...?' Rebus looked towards the doctor, who was upright now, but pointing downwards with one finger. 'How are we going to get him down?'

Rebus stared at Sir Walter. Yes, he could see the problem. It would be hard graft taking him all the way back down the spiral stairs. What's more, damage to the body would be unavoidable. He supposed they could always use a winch and lower him straight to the ground ... Well, it was a job for ambulancemen or undertakers, not the police. Rebus patted the doctor's shoulder.

'You're in charge, Doc,' he said, exiting through the door before the doctor could summon up a protest. Holmes shrugged apologetically, smiled, and followed Rebus into the dark. The doctor looked at the body, then over the edge, then back to the body again. He reached into his pocket for a mint, popped it into his mouth, and began to crunch on it. Then he, too, made for the door.

Splendour was falling on the castle walls. Wrong poet, Rebus mused, but right image. He tried to recall if he'd ever read any Scott, but drew a blank. He thought he might have picked up *Waverley* once. As a colleague at the time had said, 'Imagine calling a book after the station.' Rebus hadn't bothered to explain; and hadn't read the book either, or if he had it had left no impression ...

He stood now on the ramparts, looking across to the Gothic exaggeration of the Scott Monument. A cannon was almost immediately behind him. Anyone wanting to be seen from the top of the monument would probably have been standing right on this spot. People did not linger here though. They might wander along the walls, take a few photographs, or pose for a few, but they would not stand in the one spot for longer than a minute or two.

Which meant, of course, that if someone *had* been standing here longer, they would be conspicuous. The problem was twofold: first, conspicuous to whom? Everyone else would be in motion, would not notice that someone was lingering. Second, all the potential witnesses would by now have gone their separate ways, in tour buses or on foot, down the Royal Mile or on to Princes Street, along George the Fourth Bridge to look at Greyfriars Bobby ... The people milling around just now represented a fresh intake, new water flowing down the same old stream.

Someone wanted to be seen by Sir Walter, and Sir Walter wanted to see him – hence the binoculars. No conversation was needed, just the sighting. Why? Rebus couldn't think of a single reason. He turned away from the wall and saw Holmes approaching. Meeting his eyes, Holmes shrugged his shoulders.

'I've talked to the guards on the gate. They don't remember seeing anyone suspicious. As one of them said, "All these bloody tourists look the same to me."'

Rebus smiled at this, but then someone was tugging at his sleeve, a small handbagged woman with sunglasses and thick lipstick.

'Sorry, could I ask you to move over a bit?' Her accent was American, her voice a nasal sing-song. 'Lawrence wants a picture of me with that gorgeous skyline behind me.'

Rebus smiled at her, even made a slight bow, and moved a couple of yards out of the way, Holmes following suit.

'Thanks!' Lawrence called from behind his camera, freeing a hand so that he could wave it towards them. Rebus noticed that the man wore a yellow sticker on his chest. He looked back to the woman, now posing like the film star she so clearly wasn't, and saw that she too had a badge, her name – Diana – felt-tipped beneath some package company's logo.

'I wonder ...' Rebus said quietly.

'Sir?'

'Maybe you were asking the wrong question at the gate, Brian. Yes, the right idea but the wrong question. Come on, let's go back and ask again. We'll see how eagle-eyed our friends really are.'

They passed the photographer – his badge called him Larry rather than Lawrence – just as the shutter clicked.

'Great,' he said to nobody in particular. 'Just one more, sweetheart.' As he wound the film, Rebus paused and stood beside him, then made a square from the thumb and forefinger of both hands and peered through it towards the woman Diana, as though assessing the composition of the picture. Larry caught the gesture.

'You a professional?' he asked, his tone just short of awe.

'Only in a manner of speaking, Larry,' said Rebus, turning away again. Holmes was left standing there, staring at the photographer. He wondered whether to shrug and smile again, as he had done with the doctor. What the hell. He shrugged. He smiled. And he followed Rebus towards the gate.

Rebus went alone to the home of Sir Walter Scott, just off the Corstorphine Road near the zoo. As he stepped out of his car, he could have sworn he detected a faint wafting of animal dung. There was another car in the driveway, one which, with a sinking heart, he recognised. As he walked up to the front door of the house, he saw that the curtains were closed in the upstairs windows, while downstairs, painted wooden shutters had been pulled across to block out the daylight.

The door was opened by Superintendent 'Farmer' Watson.

'I thought that was your car, sir,' Rebus said as Watson ushered him into the hall. When he spoke, the superintendent's voice was a whispered growl.

'He's still up there, you know.'

'Who?'

'Sir Walter, of course!' Flecks of saliva burst from the corners of Watson's mouth. Rebus thought it judicious to show not even the mildest amusement.

'I left the doctor in charge.'

'Dr Jameson couldn't organise a brewery visit. What the hell did you think you were doing?'

'I had ... *have* an investigation on my hands, sir. I thought I could be more usefully employed than playing undertaker.'

'He's stiff now, you know,' Watson said, his anger having diminished. He didn't exactly know why it was that he could never stay angry with Rebus; there was something about the man. 'They don't think they can get him down the stairs. They've tried twice, but he got stuck both times.'

Rebus pursed his lips, the only way he could prevent them spreading into a wide grin. Watson saw this and saw, too, that the situation was not without a trace of humour.

'Is that why you're here, sir? Placating the widow?'

'No, I'm here on a personal level. Sir Walter and Lady Scott were friends of mine. That is, Sir Walter was, and Lady Scott still is.'

Rebus nodded slowly. Christ, he was thinking, the poor bugger's only been dead a couple of hours and here's old Farmer Watson already trying to ... But no, surely not. Watson was many things, but not callous, not like that. Rebus rebuked himself silently, and in so doing missed most of what Watson was saying.

'—in here.'

And a door from the hallway was being opened. Rebus was being shown into a spacious living-room – or were they called drawing-rooms in houses like this? Walking across to where Lady Scott sat by the fireside was like walking across a dance hall.

'This is Inspector Rebus,' Watson was saying. 'One of my men.'

Lady Scott looked up from her handkerchief. 'How do you do?'

She offered him a delicate hand, which he lightly touched with his own, in place of his usual firm handshake. Lady Scott was in her mid fifties, a well-preserved monument of neat lines and precise movements. Rebus had seen her accompanying her husband to various functions in the city, had come across her photograph in the paper when he had received his knighthood. He saw, too, from the corner of his eye, the way Watson looked at her, a mixture of pity and something more than pity, as though he wanted at the same time to pat her hand and hug her to him.

Who would want Sir Walter dead? That was, in a sense, what he had come here to ask. Still the question itself was valid. Rebus could think of adversaries – those Scott had crossed in his professional life, those he had helped put behind bars, those, perhaps, who resented everything from his title to the bright blue socks that had become something of a trademark after he admitted on a radio show that he wore no other colour on his feet ...

'Lady Scott, I'm sorry to intrude on you at a time like this. I know it's difficult, but there are a couple of questions ...'

'Please, ask your questions.' She gestured for him to sit on the sofa – the sofa on which Farmer Watson had already made himself comfortable. Rebus sat down awkwardly. This whole business was awkward. He knew the chess player's motto: if in doubt, play a pawn. Or as the Scots themselves would say, ca' canny. But that had never been his style, and he couldn't change now. As ever, he decided to sacrifice his queen.

'We found a note in Sir Walter's binocular case.'

'He didn't own a pair of binoculars.' Her voice was firm.

'He probably bought them this morning. Did he say where he was going?'

'No, just out. I was upstairs. He called that he was "popping out for an hour or two", and that was all.'

'What note?' This from Watson. What note indeed. Rebus wondered why Lady Scott hadn't asked the same thing.

'A typed note, telling Sir Walter to be at the top of the Scott Monument at midday.' Rebus paused, his attention wholly on Sir Walter's widow. 'There have been others, haven't there? Other notes?'

She nodded slowly. 'Yes. I found them by accident. I wasn't prying, I'm not like that. I was in Walter's office – he always called it that, his "office", never his study – looking for something, an old newspaper I think. Yes, there was an article I wanted to reread, and I'd searched high and low for the blessed paper. I was looking in Walter's office, and I found some ... letters.' She wrinkled her nose.

'He'd kept them quiet from me. Well, I suppose he had his reasons. I never said anything to him about finding them.' She smiled ruefully. 'I used to think sometimes that the unsaid was what kept our marriage alive. That may seem cruel. Now he's gone, I wish we'd told one another more ...'

She dabbed at a liquid eye with the corner of her handkerchief, wrapped as it was around one finger, her free hand twisting and twisting the corners. To Rebus, it looked as if she were using it as a tourniquet.

'Do you know where these other notes are?' he asked.

'I don't know. Walter may have moved them.'

'Shall we see?'

The office was untidy in the best legal tradition: any available flat surface, including the carpet, seemed to be fair game for stacks of brown folders tied with ribbon, huge bulging manilla envelopes, magazines and newspapers, books and learned journals. Two walls consisted entirely of bookcases, from floor to near the ornate but flaking ceiling. One bookcase, glass-fronted, contained what Rebus reckoned must be the collected works of the other Sir Walter Scott. The glass doors looked as though they hadn't been opened in a decade; the books themselves might never have been read. Still, it was a nice touch – to have one's study so thoroughly infiltrated by one's namesake.

'Ah, they're still here.' Lady Scott had slid a concertina-style folder out from beneath a pile of similar such files. 'Shall we take them back through to the morning-room?' She looked around her. 'I don't like it in here ... not now.'

Her Edinburgh accent, with its drawn vowels, had turned 'morning' into 'mourning'. Either that, thought Rebus, or she'd said 'mourning-room' in the first place. He would have liked to have stayed a little longer in Sir Walter's office, but was compelled to follow. Back in her chair, Lady Scott untied the ribbon around the file and let it fall open. The file itself was made up of a dozen or more compartments, but only one seemed to contain any paperwork. She pulled out the letters and handed them to Watson, who glanced through them wordlessly before handing them to Rebus.

Sir Walter had taken each note from its envelope, but had paper-clipped the envelopes to the backs of their respective notes. So Rebus was able to ascertain that the notes had been posted between three weeks and one week ago, and all bore a central London postmark. He read the three notes slowly to himself, then reread them. The first came quickly to its point.

I ENCLOSE A LETTER. THERE ARE PLENTY MORE

WHERE IT CAME FROM. YOU WILL HEAR FROM ME
AGAIN.

The second fleshed out the blackmail.

I HAVE ELEVEN MORE LETTERS. IF YOU'D LIKE
THEM BACK, THEY WILL COST £2,000. GET THE MONEY.

The third, posted a week ago, finalised things.

PUT THE MONEY IN A CARRIER BAG. GO TO THE
CAFE ROYAL AT 9 P.M. FRIDAY. STAND AT THE BAR
AND HAVE A DRINK. LEAVE THE BAG THERE AND GO
MAKE A PHONE CALL. SPEND TWO MINUTES AWAY
FROM THE BAR. WHEN YOU COME BACK, THE LETTERS
WILL BE THERE.

Rebus looked up at Lady Scott. 'Did he pay?'

'I've really no idea.'

'But you could check?'

'If you like, yes.'

Rebus nodded. 'I'd like to be sure.' The first note said that a
letter was enclosed, obviously a letter concerning Sir Walter – but
what kind of letter? Of the letter itself there was no sign. Twelve apparently incriminating or embarrassing letters for £2,000. A small
price to pay for someone of Sir Walter's position in society. What's
more, it seemed to Rebus a small price to *ask*. And if the exchange
had taken place as arranged, what was the point of the last note,
the one found in Sir Walter's binocular case? Yes, that was a point.

'Did you see the mail this morning, Lady Scott?'

'I was first to the door, yes.'

'And was there an envelope like these others?'

'I'm sure there wasn't.'

Rebus nodded. 'Yes, if there had been, I think Sir Walter would
have kept it, judging by these.' He shook the notes – all with envelopes attached.

'Meaning, John?' Superintendent Watson sounded puzzled. To
Rebus's ears, it was his natural voice.

'Meaning,' he explained, 'that the last note, the one we found on
Sir Walter, was as it arrived at the house. No envelope. It must have
been pushed through the letterbox. I'd say sometime yesterday or
this morning. The blackmail started in London, but the blackmailer
came up here for the payoff. And he or she is still here – or was until
midday. Now, I'm not so certain. If Sir Walter paid the money' – he
nodded towards Lady Scott – 'and I *would* like you to check on that,
please, today if possible. *If*, as I say, Sir Walter paid, *if* he got the
letters back, then what was this morning's little game all about?'

Watson nodded, arms folded, looking down into his lap as though seeking answers. Rebus doubted they'd be found so close to home. He rose to his feet.

'We could do with finding those letters, too. Perhaps, Lady Scott, you might have another look in your husband's ... office.'

She nodded slowly. 'I should tell you, Inspector, that I'm not sure I *want* to find them.'

'I can understand that. But it would help us track down the blackmailer.'

Her voice was as low as the light in the room. 'Yes, of course.'

'And in the meantime, John?' Watson tried to sound like a man in charge of something. But there was a pleading edge to his voice.

'Meantime,' said Rebus, 'I'll be at the Castellain Hotel. The number will be in the book. You can always have me paged.'

Watson gave Rebus one of his dark looks, the kind that said: I don't know what you're up to, but I can't let anyone else know that I *don't* know. Then he nodded and almost smiled.

'Of course,' he said. 'Yes, off you go. I may stay on a little longer ...' He looked to Lady Scott for her assent. But she was busy with the handkerchief again, twisting and twisting and twisting ...

The Castellain Hotel, a minute's walk from Princes Street, was a chaos of tourists. The large pot-planted lobby looked as though it was on someone's tour itinerary, with one large organised party about to leave, milling about as their luggage was taken out to the waiting bus by hard-pressed porters. At the same time, another party was arriving, the holiday company's representative conspicuous by being the only person who looked like he knew what was going on.

Seeing that a group was about to leave, Rebus panicked. But their lapel badges assured him that they were part of the Seascape Tours package. He walked up to the reception desk and waited while a harassed young woman in a tartan two-piece tried to take two telephone calls at the same time. She showed no little skill in the operation, and all the time she was talking her eyes were on the scrum of guests in front of her. Finally, she found a moment and a welcoming smile for him. Funny how at this time of year there were so many smiles to be found in Edinburgh ...

'Yes, sir?'

'Detective Inspector Rebus,' he announced. 'I'd like a word with the Grebe Tours rep if she's around.'

'She's a he,' the receptionist explained. 'I think he might be in his room, hold on and I'll check.' She had picked up the telephone. 'Nothing wrong, is there?'

'No, nothing, just want a word, that's all.'

Her call was answered quickly. 'Hello, Tony? There's a gentleman in reception to see you.' Pause. 'Fine, I'll tell him. 'Bye.' She put down the receiver. 'He'll be down in a minute.'

Rebus nodded his thanks and, as she answered another telephone call, moved back into the reception hall, dodging the bags and the worried owners of the bags. There was something thrilling about holidaymakers. They were like children at a party. But at the same time there was something depressing, too, about the herd mentality. Rebus had never been on a package holiday in his life. He mistrusted the production-line cheerfulness of the reps and the guides. A walk along a deserted beach: now *that* was a holiday. Finding a pleasant out-of-the-way pub ... playing pinball so ruthlessly that the machine 'tilted' ... wasn't he due for a holiday himself?

Not that he would take one: the loneliness could be a cage as well as a release. But he would never, he hoped, be as caged as these people around him. He looked for a Grebe Tours badge on any passing lapel or chest, but saw none. The Edinburgh Castle gatekeepers had been eagle-eyed all right, or one of them had. He'd recalled not only that a Grebe Tours bus had pulled in to the car park at around half past eleven that morning, but also that the rep had mentioned where the tour party was staying – the Castellain Hotel.

A small, balding man came out of the lift and fairly trotted to the reception desk, then, when the receptionist pointed towards Rebus, trotted over towards him, too. Did these reps take pills? potions? laughing gas? How the hell did they manage to keep it up?

'Tony Bell at your service,' the small man said. They shook hands. Rebus noticed that Tony Bell was growing old. He had a swelling paunch and was a little breathless after his jog. He ran a hand over his babylike head and kept grinning.

'Detective Inspector Rebus.' The grin subsided. In fact, most of Tony Bell's face seemed to subside.

'Oh Jesus,' he said, 'what is it? A mugger, pickpocket, what? Is somebody hurt? Which hospital?'

Rebus raised a hand. 'No need to panic,' he reassured him. 'Your charges are all quite safe.'

'Thank Christ for that.' The grin returned. Bell nodded towards a door, above which was printed the legend Dining-Room and Bar. 'Fancy a drink?'

'Anything to get out of this war zone,' Rebus said.

'You should see the bar after dinner,' said Tony Bell, leading the way, 'now *that's* a war zone ...'

As Bell explained, the Grebe Tours party had a free afternoon. He checked his watch and told Rebus that they would probably start returning to the hotel fairly soon. There was a meeting arranged for before dinner, when the next day's itinerary would be discussed. Rebus told the rep what he wanted, and Bell himself suggested he stay put for the meeting. Yes, Rebus agreed, that seemed sensible, and meantime would Tony like another drink?

This particular Grebe Tours party was American. They'd flown in almost a month ago for what Bell called the 'Full British Tour' – Canterbury, Salisbury, Stonehenge, London, Stratford, York, the Lake District, Trossachs, Highlands, and Edinburgh.

'This is just about the last stop,' he said. 'For which relief much thanks, I can tell you. They're nice people mind, I'm not saying they're not, but ... demanding. Yes, that's what it is. If a Brit doesn't quite understand what's been said to him, or if something isn't *quite* right, or whatever, they tend to keep their gobs shut. But Americans ...' He rolled his eyeballs. 'Americans,' he repeated, as though it explained all.

It did. Less than an hour later, Rebus was addressing a packed, seated crowd of forty American tourists in a room off the large dining-room. He had barely given them his rank when a hand shot into the air.

'Er ... yes?'

The elderly woman stood up. 'Sir, are you from Scotland Yard?'

Rebus shook his head. 'Scotland Yard's in London.'

She was still standing. 'Now why is that?' she asked. Rebus had no answer to this, but someone else suggested that it was because that part of London was called Scotland Yard. Yes, but why was it called Scotland Yard in the first place? The woman had sat down now, but all around her was discussion and conjecture. Rebus looked towards Tony Bell, who rose from his own seat and succeeded in quietening things down.

Eventually, Rebus was able to make his point. 'We're interested', he said, 'in a visitor to Edinburgh Castle this morning. You may have seen someone while you were there, someone standing by the walls, looking towards the Scott Monument. He or she might have been standing there for some time. If that means something to anybody, I'd like you to tell me about it. At the same time, it's possible that those of you who took photographs of your visit may have by chance snapped the person we're looking for. If any of you have cameras, I'd like to see the photos you took this morning.'

He was in luck. Nobody remembered seeing anyone suspicious – they were too busy looking at the sights. But two photographers had used polaroids, and another had taken his film into a same-day processor at lunchtime and so had the glossy photographs with him. Rebus studied these while Tony Bell went over the next day's arrangements with the group. The polaroid photos were badly taken, often blurry, with people in the background reduced to matchstick men. But the same-day photos were excellent, sharply focused 35 mm jobs. As the tour party left the room, en route for dinner, Tony Bell came over to where Rebus was sitting and asked the question he knew he himself would be asked more than once over dinner.

'Any joy?'

'Maybe,' Rebus admitted. 'These two people keep cropping up.' He spread five photographs out in front of him. In two, a middle-aged woman was caught in the background, staring out over the wall she was leaning on. Leaning on, or hiding behind? In another two, a man in his late twenties or early thirties stood in similar pose, but with a more upright stance. In one photo, they could both be seen half turning with smiles on their faces towards the camera.

'No.' Tony Bell was shaking his head. 'They might look like wanted criminals, but they're in our party. I think Mrs Eglinton was sitting in the back row near the door, beside her husband. You probably didn't see her. But Shaw Berkely was in the second row, over to one side. I'm surprised you didn't see him. Actually, I take that back. He has this gift of being innocuous. Never asks questions or complains. Mind you, I think he's seen most of this before.'

'Oh?' Rebus was gathering the photos together.

'He told me he'd been to Britain before on holiday.'

'And there's nothing between him and—?' Rebus was pointing to the photograph of the man and woman together.

'Him and Mrs Eglinton?' Bell seemed genuinely amused. 'I don't know – maybe. She certainly mothers him a bit.'

Rebus was still studying the print. 'Is he the youngest person on the tour?'

'By about ten years. Sad story really. His mother died, and after the funeral he said he just had to get away. Went into the travel agent's and we were offering a reduction for late bookings.'

'His father's dead too, then?'

'That's right. I got his life story one night late in the bar. On a tour, I get everyone's story sooner or later.'

Rebus flipped through the sheaf of photos a final time. Nothing new presented itself to him. 'And you were at the castle between about half past eleven and quarter to one?'

'Just as I told you.'

'Oh well.' Rebus sighed. 'I don't think—'

'Inspector?' It was the receptionist, her head peering around the door. 'There's a call for you.'

It was Superintendent Watson. He was concise, factual. 'Withdrew five hundred pounds from each of four accounts, all on the same day, and in plenty of time for the rendezvous at the Café Royal.'

'So presumably he paid up.'

'But did he get the letters back?'

'Mmm. Has Lady Scott had a look for them?'

'Yes, we've been through the study – not thoroughly, there's too much stuff in there for that. But we've had a look.' That 'we' sounded comfortable, sounded as though Watson had already got his feet under the table. 'So what now, John?'

'I'm coming over, if you've no objection, sir. With respect, I'd like a look at Sir Walter's office for myself ...'

He went in search of Tony Bell, just so he could say thanks and goodbye. But he wasn't in the musty conference room, and he wasn't in the dining-room. He was in the bar, standing with one foot on the bar rail as he shared a joke with the woman he had called Mrs Eglinton. Rebus did not interrupt, but he did wink at the phone-bound receptionist as he passed her, then pushed his way out of the Castellain Hotel's double doors just as the wheezing of a bus's air brakes signalled the arrival of yet more human cargo.

There was no overhead lighting in Sir Walter Scott's study, but there were numerous floor lamps, desk lamps, and anglepoises. Rebus switched on as many as worked. Most were antiquated, with wiring to match, but there was one newish anglepoise attached to the bookcase, pointing inwards towards the collection of Scott's writings. There was a comfortable chair beside this lamp, and an ashtray on the floor between chair and bookcase.

When Watson put his head around the door, Rebus was seated in this chair, elbows resting on his knees, and chin resting between the cupped palms of both hands.

'Margaret – that is, Lady Scott – she wondered if you wanted anything.'

'I want those letters.'

'I think she meant something feasible – like tea or coffee.'

Rebus shook his head. 'Maybe later, sir.'

Watson nodded, made to retreat, then thought of something. 'They got him down in the end. Had to use a winch. Not very dignified, but what can you do? I just hope the papers don't print any pictures.'

'Why don't you have a word with the editors, just to be on the safe side?'

'I might just do that, John.' Watson nodded. 'Yes, I might just do that.'

Alone again, Rebus rose from his chair and opened the glass doors of the bookcase. The position of chair, ashtray and lamp was interesting. It was as though Sir Walter had been reading volumes from these shelves, from his namesake's collected works. Rebus ran a finger over the spines. A few he had heard of; the vast majority he had not. One was titled *Castle Dangerous*. He smiled grimly at that. Dangerous, all right; or in Sir Walter's case, quite lethal. He angled the light farther into the bookcase. The dust on a row of books had been disturbed. Rebus pushed with one finger against the spine of a volume, and the book slid a good two inches back until it rested against the solid wall behind the bookcase. Two uniform inches of space for the whole of this row. Rebus reached a hand down behind the row of books and ran it along the shelf. He met resistance, and drew the hand out again, now clutching a sheaf of papers. Sir Walter had probably thought it as good a hiding place as any – a poor testament to Scott the novelist's powers of attraction. Rebus sat down in the chair again, brought the anglepoise closer, and began to sift through what he'd found.

There were, indeed, twelve letters, ornately fountain-penned promises of love with honour, of passion until doomsday. As with all such youthful nonsense, there was a lot of poetry and classical imagery. Rebus imagined it was standard private boys' school stuff, even today. But these letters had been written half a century ago, sent from one schoolboy to another a year younger than himself. The younger boy was Sir Walter, and from the correspondence it was clear that Sir Walter's feelings for the writer had been every bit as inflamed as those of the writer himself.

Ah, the writer. Rebus tried to remember if he was still an MP. He had the feeling he had either lost his seat, or else had retired. Maybe he was still on the go; Rebus paid little attention to politics. His attitude had always been: don't vote, it only encourages them. So, here was the presumed scandal. Hardly a scandal, but just about enough to cause embarrassment. At worst a humiliation. But then Rebus was beginning to suspect that humiliation, not financial profit, was the price exacted here.

And not even necessarily public humiliation, merely the private knowledge that someone knew of these letters, that someone had possessed them. Then the final taunt, the taunt Sir Walter could not resist: come to the Scott Monument, look across to the castle, and you will see who has been tormenting you these past weeks. You will know.

But now that same taunt was working on Rebus. He knew so much, yet in effect he knew nothing at all. He now possessed the 'what', but not the 'who'. And what should he do with the old love letters? Lady Scott had said she wasn't sure she wanted to find them. He could take them away with him – destroy them. Or he could hand them over to her, tell her what they were. It would be up to her either to destroy them unread or to discover this silly secret. He could always say: It's all right, it's nothing really ... Mind you, some of the sentences were ambiguous enough to disturb, weren't they? Rebus read again. 'When you scored 50 n.o. and afterwards we showered ...' 'When you stroke me like that ...' 'After rugger practice ...'

Ach. He got up and opened the bookcase again. He would replace them. Let time deal with them; he could not. But in placing his hand back down behind the line of books, he brushed against something else, not paper but stiff card. He hadn't noticed it before because it seemed stuck to the wall. He peeled it carefully away and brought it into the light. It was a photograph, black and white, ten inches by eight and mounted on card. A man and woman on an esplanade, arm in arm, posing for the photographer. The man looked a little pensive, trying to smile but not sure he actually wanted to be caught like this. The woman seemed to wrap both her arms round one of his, restraining him; and she was laughing, thrilled by this moment, thrilled to be with him.

The man was Sir Walter. A Sir Walter twenty years older than the schoolboy of the love letters, mid thirties perhaps. And the woman? Rebus stared long and hard at the woman. Put the photograph down and paced the study, touching things, peering through the shutters. He was thinking and not thinking. He had seen the woman before somewhere ... but where? She was not Lady Scott, of that he was certain. But he'd seen her recently, seen that face ... that face.

And then he knew. Oh yes, he knew.

He telephoned the Castellain, half listening as the story was given to him. Taken ill suddenly ... poorly ... decided to go home ... airport ... flying to London and catching a connection tonight ... Was there a problem? Well, of course there was a problem, but no one at the hotel could help with it, not now. The blackmail over, Rebus himself had inadvertently caused the blackmailer to flee. He had gone to the hotel hoping – such a slim hope – for help, not realising that one of the Grebe Tours party was his quarry. Once again, he had sacrificed his queen too early in the game.

He telephoned Edinburgh Airport, only to be told that the flight had already taken off. He asked to be rerouted to Security, and asked them for the name of the security chief at Heathrow. He was calling Heathrow when Watson appeared in the hall.

'Making quite a few calls, aren't you, John? Not personal, I hope.'

Rebus ignored his superior as his call was connected. 'Mr Masterson in Security, please,' he said. And then: 'Yes, it is urgent. I'll hold.' He turned to Watson at last. 'Oh, it's personal all right, sir. But it's nothing to do with me. I'll tell you all about it in a minute. Then we can decide what to tell Lady Scott. Actually, seeing as you're a friend of the family and all, *you* can tell her. That'd be best, wouldn't it, sir? There are some things only your friends can tell you, after all, aren't there?'

He was through to Heathrow Security, and turned away from Watson the better to talk with Masterson. The superintendent stood there, dimly aware that Rebus was going to force him to tell Margaret something she would probably rather not hear. He wondered if she would ever again have time for the person who would tell her ... And he cursed John Rebus, who was so good at digging yet never seemed to soil his own hands. It was a gift, a terrible, destructive gift. Watson, a staunch believer in the Christian God, doubted Rebus's gift had come down from on high. No, not from on high.

The phone call was ending. Rebus put down the receiver and nodded towards Sir Walter's study.

'If you'll step into the office, sir,' he said, 'there's something I'd like to show you ...'

Shaw Berkely was arrested at Heathrow, and, despite protestations regarding his health and cries for consular aid, was escorted back to Edinburgh, where Rebus was waiting, brisk and definitive, in Interview Room A of Great London Road police station.

Berkely's mother had died two months before. She had never told him the truth about his birth, spinning instead some story about his father being dead. But in sorting through his mother's papers, Shaw discovered the truth – several truths, in fact. His mother had been in love with Walter Scott, had become pregnant by him, but had been, as she herself put it in her journal, 'discarded' in favour of the 'better marriage' provided by Margaret Winton-Addams.

Shaw's mother accepted some money from Scott and fled to the United States, where she had a younger sister. Shaw grew up believing his father dead. The revelation not only that he was alive, but that he had prospered in society after having caused Shaw's mother misery and torment, led to a son's rage. But it was impotent rage, Shaw thought, until he came across the love letters. His mother must at some point have stolen them from Scott, or at least had come out of the relationship in possession of them. Shaw decided on a teasing revenge, knowing Scott would deduce that any blackmailer in possession of the letters was probably also well informed about his affair and the bastard son.

He used the tour party as an elaborate cover (and also, he admitted, because it was a cheap travel option). He brought with him to Britain not only the letters, but also the series of typed notes. The irony was that he had been to Edinburgh before, had studied there for three months as part of some exchange with his American college. He knew now why his mother, though proud of the scholarship, had been against his going. For three months he had lived in his father's city, yet hadn't known it.

He sent the notes from London – the travel party's base for much of its stay in England. The exchange – letters for cash – had gone ahead in the Café Royal, the bar having been a haunt of his student days. But he had known his final note, delivered by hand, would tempt Sir Walter, would lead him to the top of the Scott Monument. No, he said, he hadn't just wanted Sir Walter to see him, to see the son he had never known. Shaw had much of the money on him, stuffed into a money belt around his waist. The intention had been to release wads of money, Sir Walter's money, down on to Princes Street Gardens.

'I didn't mean for him to die ... I just wanted him to know how I felt about him ... I don't know. But Jesus' – he grinned – 'I still wish I'd let fly with all that loot.'

Rebus shuddered to think of the ramifications. Stampede in Princes Street! Hundreds dead in lunchtime spree! Biggest *scoo-root* ever! No, best not to think about it. Instead, he made for the Café Royal himself. It was late morning, the day after Berkely's arrest. The pub was quiet as yet, but Rebus was surprised to see Dr Jameson standing at the bar, fortifying himself with what looked suspiciously like a double whisky. Remembering how he had left the doctor in the lurch regarding Sir Walter's body, Rebus grinned broadly and offered a healthy slap on the back.

'Morning, Doc, fancy seeing you in here.' Rebus leaned his elbows on the bar. 'We mustn't be keeping you busy enough.' He paused. There was a twinkle in his eye as he spoke. 'Here, let me get you a stiff one ...' And he laughed so hard even the waiters from the Oyster Bar came to investigate. But all they saw was a tall, well-built man leaning against a much smaller, more timid man, and saying as he raised his glass: 'Here's to mortality, to old mortality!'

So all in all it was just another day in the Café Royal.

In the Frame

Inspector John Rebus placed the letters on his desk.

There were three of them. Small, plain white envelopes, locally franked, the same name and address printed on each in a careful hand. The name was K. Leighton. Rebus looked up from the envelopes to the man sitting on the other side of the desk. He was in his forties, frail-looking and restless. He had started talking the moment he'd entered Rebus's office, and didn't seem inclined to stop.

'The first one arrived on Tuesday, last Tuesday. A crank, I thought, some sort of malicious joke. Not that I could think of anyone who might do that sort of thing.' He shifted in his seat. 'My neighbours over the back from me ... well, we don't always see eye to eye, but they wouldn't resort to this.' His eyes glanced up towards Rebus for a second. 'Would they?'

'You tell me, Mr Leighton.'

As soon as he'd said this, Rebus regretted the choice of words. Undoubtedly, Kenneth Leighton *would* tell him. Rebus opened the first envelope's flap, extracted the sheet of writing-paper and unfolded it. He did the same with the second and third letters and laid all three before him.

'If it had been only the one,' Kenneth Leighton was saying, 'I wouldn't have minded, but it doesn't look as though they're going to stop. Tuesday, then Thursday, then Saturday. I spent all weekend worrying about what to do ...'

'You did the right thing, Mr Leighton.'

Leighton wriggled pleasurably. 'Well, they always say you should go to the police. Not that I think there's anything serious. I mean, *I've* not got anything to hide. My life's an open book ...'

An open book and an unexciting one, Rebus would imagine. He tried to shut out Leighton's voice and concentrated instead on the first letter.

> *Mr Leighton,*
> *We've got photos you wouldn't want your wife to see, believe us.*
> *Think about it. We'll be in touch.*

Then the second:

> *Mr Leighton,*
> *£2,000 for the photos. That seems fair, doesn't it? You really*
> *wouldn't want your wife to see them. Get the money. We'll be in*
> *touch.*

And the third:

> *Mr Leighton,*
> *We'll be sending one reprint to show we mean business. You'd*
> *better get to it before your wife does. There are plenty more copies.*

Rebus looked up, and caught Leighton staring at him. Leighton immediately looked away. Rebus had the feeling that if he stood behind the man and said 'boo' quite softly in his ear, Leighton would melt all down the chair. He looked like the sort of person who might make an enemy of his neighbours, complaining too strenuously about a noisy party or a family row. He looked like a crank.

'You haven't received the photo yet?'

Leighton shook his head. 'I'd have brought it along, wouldn't I?'

'And you've no idea what sort of photo it might be?'

'None at all. The last time somebody took my picture was at my niece's wedding.'

'And when was that?'

'Three years ago. You see what I'm saying, Inspector? This doesn't make any sense.'

'It must make sense to at least one person, Mr Leighton.' Rebus nodded towards the letters.

They had been written in blue ball-point, the same pen which had been used to address the envelopes. A cheap blue ball-point, leaving smears and blots of ink. It was anything but professional-looking. The whole thing looked like a joke. Since when did blackmailers use their own handwriting? Anyone with a rudimentary education in films, TV cop shows and thriller novels knew that you used a typewriter or letters cut out of newspapers, or whatever; anything that would produce a dramatic effect. These letters were too personal to look dramatic. Polite, too: that use of 'Mr Leighton' at the start of each one. A particular word caught Rebus's attention and held it. But then Leighton said something interesting.

'I don't even have a wife, not now.'

'You're not married?'

'I was. Divorced six years ago. Six years and one month.'

'And where's your wife now, Mr Leighton?'

'Remarried, lives in Glenrothes. I got an invite to the wedding, but I didn't go. Can't remember what I sent them for a present ...' Leighton was lost in thought for a moment, then collected himself. 'So you see, if these letters are written by someone I know, how come they *don't* know I'm divorced?'

It was a good question. Rebus considered it for a full five seconds. Then he came to his conclusion.

'Let's leave it for now, Mr Leighton,' he said. 'There's not much we can do till this photo arrives ... *if* it arrives.'

Leighton looked numb, watching Rebus fold the letters and replace them in their envelopes. Rebus wasn't sure what the man had expected. Fingerprints lifted from the envelopes by forensic experts? A tell-tale fibre leading to an arrest? Handwriting identified ... saliva from the stamps and the envelope-flaps checked ... psychologists analysing the wording of the messages themselves, coming up with a profile of the blackmailer? It was all good stuff, but not on a wet Monday morning in Edinburgh. Not with CID's case-load and budget restrictions.

'Is that it?'

Rebus shrugged. That was it. We're only human, Mr Leighton. For a moment, Rebus thought he'd actually voiced his thoughts. He had not. Leighton still sat there, pale and disappointed, his mouth set like the bottom line of a balance sheet.

'Sorry,' said Rebus, rising.

'I've just remembered,' said Leighton.

'What?'

'Six wine glasses, that's what I gave them. Caithness glass they were too.'

'Very nice I'm sure,' said Rebus, stifling a post-weekend yawn as he opened the office door.

But Rebus was certainly intrigued.

No wife these past six years, and the last photograph of Leighton dated back three years to a family wedding. Where was the material for blackmail? Where the motive? Means, motive and opportunity. Means: a photograph, apparently. Motive: unknown. Opportunity

... Leighton was a nobody, a middle-aged civil servant. He earned enough, but not enough to make him blackmail material. He had confided to Rebus that he barely had £2,000 in his building society account.

'Hardly enough to cover their demand,' he had said, as though he were considering actually paying off the blackmailers, even though he had nothing to hide, nothing to fear. Just to get them off his back? Or because he *did* have something to hide? Most people did, if it came to it. The guilty secret or two (or more, many more) stored away just below the level of consciousness, the way suitcases were stored under beds. Rebus wondered if he himself were blackmail material. He smiled: was the Pope a Catholic? Was the Chief Constable a Mason? Leighton's words came back to him: *Hardly enough to cover their demand.* What sort of civil servant was Leighton anyway? Rebus sought out the day-time telephone number Leighton had left along with his home address and phone number. Seven digits, followed by a three-figure extension number. He punched the seven digits on his receiver, waited, and heard a switchboard operator say, 'Good afternoon, Inland Revenue.' Rebus replaced the receiver with a guilty silence.

On Tuesday morning, Leighton phoned the station. Rebus got in first.

'You didn't tell me you were a taxman, Mr Leighton.'

'What?'

'A taxman.'

'What does it matter?'

What did it matter? How many enemies could one taxman make? Rebus swallowed back the question. He could always use a friend in Her Majesty's Inland Revenue, for personal as well as strictly professional use ...

'I know what you're thinking,' Leighton was saying, though Rebus doubted it. 'And it's true that I work in the Collector's office, sending out the demands. But my name's never on the demands. The Inspector of Taxes might be mentioned by name, but I'm a lowly cog, Inspector.'

'Even so, you must write to people sometimes. There might be somebody out there with a grudge.'

'I've given it some thought, Inspector. It was my *first* thought. But in any case I don't deal with Edinburgh.'

'Oh?'

'I deal with south London.'

Rebus noted that, phoning from his place of work, Leighton was less nervous-sounding. He sounded cool, detached. He sounded like a tax collector. South London: but the letters had local postmarks – another theory sealed under cover and posted into eternity, no return address.

'The reason I'm calling,' Leighton was saying, 'is that I had another letter this morning.'

'With a photo?'

'Yes, there's a photo.'

'And?'

'It's difficult to explain. I could come to the station at lunchtime.'

'Don't bother yourself, Mr Leighton. I'll come to the tax office. All part of the service.'

Rebus was thinking of back-handers, gifts from grateful members of the public, all the pubs where he could be sure of a free drink, chip shops that wouldn't charge for a feed, all the times he'd helped out for a favour, the way those favours accumulated and were paid off ... Tax forms asked you about tips received. Rebus always left the box blank. Had he always been accurate about amounts of bank interest? More crucially, several months ago he had started renting his flat to three students while he lived rent-free with Dr Patience Aitken. He had no intention of declaring ... well, maybe he would. It helped to know a friendly taxman, someone who might soon owe him a favour.

'That's very good of you, Inspector,' Leighton was saying.

'Not at all, sir.'

'Only it all seems to have been a mistake anyway.'

'A mistake?'

'You'll see when I show you the photograph.'

Rebus saw.

He saw a man and a woman. In the foreground was a coffee table, spread with bottles and glasses and cans, an ashtray full to over-flowing. Behind this, a sofa, and on the sofa a man and a woman. Lying along the sofa, hugging one another. The photographer had caught them like this, their faces just beginning to turn towards the camera, grinning and flushed with that familiar mix of alcohol and passion. Rebus had been to these sorts of party, parties where the alcohol was necessary before there could be any passion. Behind the couple, two men stood in animated conversation. It was a good clear photo, the work of a 35 mm camera with either a decent flash-gun or else no necessity for one.

'And here's the letter,' said Leighton. They were seated on an uncomfortable, spongy sofa in the tax office's reception area. Rebus had been hoping for a sniff behind the scenes, but Leighton worked in an open-plan office with less privacy even than the reception area. Few members of the public ever visited the building, and the receptionist was at the other end of the hallway. Staff wandered through on their way to the coffee machine or the snack dispenser, the toilets or the post-room, but otherwise this was as quiet as it got.

'A bit longer than the others,' Leighton said, handing the letter over.

Mr Leighton,
Here is the photo. We have plenty more, plus negatives. Cheap at £2,000 the lot, and your wife will never know. The money should be in fives and tens, nothing bigger. Put it in a William Low's carrier-bag and go to Greyfriars Kirkyard on Friday at 3 p.m. Leave the bag behind Greyfriars Bobby's gravestone. Walk away. Photos and negatives will be sent to you.

'Not exactly the quietest spot for a handover,' Rebus mused. Although the actual statue of Greyfriars Bobby, sited just outside the kirkyard, was more popular with tourists, the gravestone was a popular enough stop-off. The idea of leaving a bagful of money there surreptitiously was almost laughable. But at least now the extortion was serious. A time and place had been mentioned as well as a sum, a sum to be left in a Willie Low's bag. Rebus more than ever doubted the blackmailer's professionalism.

'You see what I mean?' Leighton said. 'I can only think that if it isn't a joke, then it's a case of mistaken identity.'

True enough, Leighton wasn't any of the three men in the photo, not by any stretch of the will or imagination. Rebus concentrated on the woman. She was small, heavy, somehow managing to fit into a dress two sizes too small for her. It was black and short, rumpled most of the way to her bum, with plenty of cleavage at the other end. She also wore black tights and black patent-leather shoes. But somehow Rebus didn't think he was looking at a funeral.

'I don't suppose', he said, 'this is your wife?'

Leighton actually laughed, the sound of paper shredding.

'Thought not,' Rebus said quietly. He turned his attention to the man on the sofa, the man whose arms were trapped beneath the weight of the smirking woman. There was something about that face, that hairstyle. Then it hit Rebus, and things started to make a little more sense.

'I didn't recognise him at first,' he said, thinking out loud.

'You mean you know him?'

Rebus nodded slowly. 'Only I've never seen him smile before, that's what threw me.' He studied the photo again, then stabbed it with a finger. The tip of his finger was resting on the face of one of the other men, the two behind the sofa. 'And I know him,' he said. 'I can place him now.' Leighton looked impressed. Rebus moved his finger on to the recumbent woman. 'What's more, I know her too. I know her quite well.'

Leighton didn't look impressed now, he looked startled, perhaps even disbelieving.

'Three out of four,' Rebus said. 'Not a bad score, eh?' Leighton didn't answer, so Rebus smiled reassuringly. 'Don't you worry, sir. I'll take care of this. You won't be bothered any more.'

'Well ... thank you, Inspector.'

Rebus got to his feet. 'All part of the service, Mr Leighton. Who knows, maybe *you'll* be able to help *me* one of these days ...'

Rebus sat at his desk, reading the file. Then, when he was satisfied, he tapped into the computer and checked some details regarding a man who was doing a decent stretch in Peterhead jail. When he'd finished, there was a broad grin on his face, an event unusual enough in itself to send DC Siobhan Clarke sauntering over in Rebus's direction, trying not to get too close (fear of being hooked), but close enough to register interest. Before she knew it, Rebus was reeling her in anyway.

'Get your coat,' he said.

She angled her head back towards her desk. 'But I'm in the middle of—'

'You're in the middle of *my* catchment, Siobhan. Now fetch your coat.'

Never be nosy, and always keep your head down: somehow Siobhan Clarke hadn't yet learned those two golden rules of the easy life. Not that anything was easy when John Rebus was in the office. Which was precisely why she liked working near him.

'Where are we going?' she said.

Rebus told her on the way. He also handed the file to her so she could read it through.

'Not guilty,' she said at last.

'And I'm Robbie Coltrane,' said Rebus. They were both talking about a case from a few months before. A veteran hard man had been charged with the attempted armed hold-up of a security van. There had been evidence as to his guilt – just about enough evidence – and his alibi had been shaky. He'd told police of having spent the day in question in a bar near his mother's home in Muirhouse, probably the city's most notorious housing scheme. Plenty of witnesses came forward to agree that he had been there all day. These witnesses boasted names like Tam the Bam, Big Shug, the Screwdriver, and Wild Eck. The look of them in the witness-box, police reasoned, would be enough to convince the jury of the defendant's guilt. But there had been one other witness ...

'Miss June Redwood,' quoted DC Clarke, rereading the case-notes.

'Yes,' said Rebus, 'Miss June Redwood.'

An innocent, dressed in a solemn two-piece as she gave her evidence at the trial. She was a social worker, caring for the most desperate in Edinburgh's most desperate area. Needing to make a phone call, and sensing she'd have no luck with Muirhouse's few public kiosks, she had walked into the Castle Arms, probably the first female the regulars had seen in the saloon bar since the land-lord's wife had walked out on him fifteen years before. She'd asked to use the phone, and a man had wandered over to her from a table and, with a wink, had asked if she'd like a drink. She'd refused. She could see he'd had a few – more than a few. His table had the look of a lengthy session about it – empty pint glasses placed one inside another to form a leaning tower, ashtray brimming with butts and empty packets, the newspaper's racing page heavily marked in biro.

Miss Redwood had given a quietly detailed account, at odds with the loud, confident lies of the other defence witnesses. And she was sure that she'd walked into the bar at 3 p.m., five minutes before the attack on the security van took place. The prosecution counsel had tried his best, gaining from the social worker the acknowledgement that she knew the accused's mother through her work, though the old woman was not actually her client. The prosecutor had stared out at the fifteen jury members, attempting without success to plant doubt in their minds. June Redwood was a rock-solid witness. Solid enough to turn a golden prosecution case into a verdict of 'not guilty'. The accused had walked free. Close, as the fairground saying went, but definitely no goldfish.

Rebus had been in court for the verdict, and had left with a shrug and a low growl. A security guard lay in hospital suffering from shotgun wounds. Now the case would have to be looked at again, if not by Rebus then by some other poor bugger who would go through the same old steps, knowing damned fine who the main suspect was, and knowing that he was walking the streets and drinking in pubs, and chuckling at his luck.

Except that it wasn't luck: it was planning, as Rebus now knew.

DC Clarke finished her second reading of the file. 'I suppose you checked on Redwood at the time?'

'Of course we did. Not married, no boyfriends. No proof – not even the faintest rumour – that she knew Keith.'

Clarke looked at the photo. 'And this is her?'

'It's her, and it's him – Keith Leyton.'

'And it was sent to …?'

'It was addressed to a Mr K. Leighton. They didn't get the spelling right. I checked in the phone book. Keith Leyton's ex-directory. Either that or he doesn't have a phone. But our little tax collector is in there under K. Leighton.'

'And they sent the letters to him by mistake?'

'They must know Keith Leyton hangs out in Muirhouse. His mum lives in Muirhouse Crescent.'

'Where does Kenneth Leighton live?'

Rebus grinned at the windscreen. 'Muir*wood* Crescent – only it's not in Muirhouse, it's in Currie.'

Siobhan Clarke smiled too. 'I don't believe it,' she said.

Rebus shrugged. 'It happens. They looked in the phone book, thought the address looked right, and started sending the letters.'

'So they've been trying to blackmail a criminal …'

'And instead they've found a taxman.' Now Rebus laughed outright. 'They must be mad, naïve, or built like a hydro-electric station. If they'd *really* tried this bampot caper on with Leyton, he'd have dug a fresh grave or two in Greyfriars for them. I'll give them one thing, though.'

'What's that?'

'They know about Keith's wife.'

'His wife?'

Rebus nodded. 'She lives near the mum. Big woman. Jealous. That's why Keith would keep any girlfriend secret – that's why he'd *want* to keep her a secret. The blackmailers must have thought that gave them a chance that he'd cough up.'

Rebus stopped the car. He had parked outside a block of flats in Oxgangs. The block was one of three, each one shaped like a capital H lying on its face. Caerketton Court: Rebus had once had a fling with a school-dinner lady who lived on the second floor …

'I checked with June Redwood's office,' he said. 'She's off sick.' He craned his neck out of the window. 'Tenth floor apparently, let's hope the lift's working.' He turned to Siobhan. 'Otherwise we'll have to resort to the telephone.'

The lift was working, though barely. Rebus and Siobhan ignored the wrapped paper parcel in one corner. Neither liked to think what it might contain. Still, Rebus was impressed that he could hold his breath for as long as the lift took to crackle its way up ten flights. The tenth floor seemed all draughts and high-pitched winds. The building had a perceptible sway, not quite like being at sea. Rebus pushed the bell of June Redwood's flat and waited. He pushed again. Siobhan was standing with her arms folded around her, shuffling her feet.

'I'd hate to see you on a football terrace in January,' said Rebus.

There was a sound from inside the door, then the door itself was opened by a woman with unwashed hair, a tissue to her nose, and wrapped in a thick dressing-gown.

'Hello there, Miss Redwood,' said Rebus brightly. 'Remember me?' Then he held up the photograph. 'Doubtless you remember him too. Can we come in?'

They went in. As they sat in the untidy living-room, it crossed Siobhan Clarke's mind that they had no way of proving *when* the photo was taken. And without that, they had nothing. Say the party had taken place after the trial – it could well be that Leyton and June Redwood had met then. In fact, it made sense. After his release, Leyton probably *would* want to throw a party, and he would certainly want to invite the woman who had been his saviour. She hoped Rebus had thought of this. She hoped he wasn't going to go too far ... as usual.

'I don't understand,' said June Redwood, wiping her nose again.

'Come on, June,' said Rebus. 'Here's the proof. You and Keith together in a clinch. The man you claimed at his trial was a complete stranger. Do you often get this comfortable with strangers?'

This earned a thin smile from June Redwood.

'If so,' Rebus continued, 'you must invite me to one of your parties.'

Siobhan Clarke swallowed hard. Yes, the Inspector was going to go too far. Had she ever doubted it?

'You'd be lucky,' said the social worker.

'It's been known,' said Rebus. He relaxed into his chair. 'Doesn't take a lot of working out, does it?' he went on. 'You must have met Keith through his mum. You became ... friends, let's call it. I don't know what his wife will call it.' Blood started to tinge June

Redwood's neck. 'You look better already,' said Rebus. 'At least I've put a bit of colour in your cheeks. You met Keith, started going out with him. It had to be kept secret though. The only thing Keith Leyton fears is *Mrs* Keith Leyton.'

'Her name's Joyce,' said Redwood.

Rebus nodded. 'So it is.'

'I could know that from the trial,' she snapped. 'I wouldn't have to know him to know that.'

Rebus nodded again. 'Except that you were a witness, June. You weren't in court when Joyce Leyton was mentioned.'

Her face now looked as though she'd been lying out too long in the non-existent sun. But she had a trump card left. 'That photo could have been taken any time.'

Siobhan held her breath: yes, this was the crunch. Rebus seemed to realise it too. 'You're right there,' he said. 'Any time at all ... up to a month before Keith's trial.'

The room was quiet for a moment. The wind found a gap somewhere and rustled a spider-plant near the window, whistling as though through well-spaced teeth.

'What?' said June Redwood. Rebus held the photograph up again.

'The man behind you, the one with long hair and the tattoo. Ugly-looking loon. He's called Mick McKelvin. It must have been some party, June, when bruisers like Keith and Mick were invited. They're not exactly your cocktail crowd. They think a canapé's something you throw over a stolen car to keep it hidden.' Rebus smiled at his own joke. Well, someone had to.

'What are you getting at?'

'Mick went inside four weeks before Keith's trial. He's serving three years in Peterhead. Persistent B and E. So you see, there's no way this party could have taken place *after* Keith's trial. Not unless Peterhead's security has got a bit lax. No, it had to be before, meaning you *had* to know him before the trial. Know what that means?' Rebus sat forward. June Redwood wasn't wiping her nose with the tissue now; she was hiding behind it, and looking frightened. 'It means you stood in the witness-box and you lied, just like Keith told you to. Serious trouble, June. You might end up with your own social worker, or even a prison visitor.' Rebus's voice had dropped in volume, as though June and he were having an intimate tête-à-tête over a candlelit dinner. 'So I really think you'd better help us, and you can start by talking about the party. Let's start with the photograph, eh?'

'The photo?' June Redwood looked ready to weep.

'The photo,' Rebus echoed. 'Who took it? Did he take any other pics of the two of you? After all, at the moment you're looking at a jail sentence, but if any photos like this one get to Joyce Leyton, you might end up collecting signatures.' Rebus waited for a moment, until he saw that June didn't get it. 'On your plaster casts,' he explained.

'Blackmail?' said Rab Mitchell.

He was sitting in the interview room, and he was nervous. Rebus stood against one wall, arms folded, examining the scuffed toes of his black Dr Martens. He'd only bought them three weeks ago. They were hardly broken in – the tough leather heel-pieces had rubbed his ankles into raw blisters – and already he'd managed to scuff the toes. He knew how he'd done it too: kicking stones as he'd come out of June Redwood's block of flats. Kicking stones for joy. That would teach him not to be exuberant in future. It wasn't good for your shoes.

'Blackmail?' Mitchell repeated.

'Good echo in here,' Rebus said to Siobhan Clarke, who was standing by the door. Rebus liked having Siobhan in on these interviews. She made people nervous. Hard men, brutal men, they would swear and fume for a moment before remembering that a young woman was present. A lot of the time, she discomfited them, and that gave Rebus an extra edge. But Mitchell, known to his associates as 'Roscoe' (for no known reason), would have been nervous anyway. A man with a proud sixty-a-day habit, he had been stopped from lighting up by a tutting John Rebus.

'No smoking, Roscoe, not in here.'

'What?'

'This is a non-smoker.'

'What the f— what are you blethering about?'

'Just what I say, Roscoe. No smoking.'

Five minutes later, Rebus had taken Roscoe's cigarettes from where they lay on the table, and had used Roscoe's Scottish Bluebell matches to light one, which he inhaled with great delight.

'Non-smoker!' Roscoe Mitchell fairly yelped. 'You said so yourself!' He was bouncing like a kid on the padded seat. Rebus exhaled again.

'Did I? Yes, so I did. Oh well ...' Rebus took a third and final puff from the cigarette, then stubbed it out underfoot, leaving the longest, most extravagant stub Roscoe had obviously ever seen in his life. He stared at it with open mouth, then closed his mouth tight and turned his eyes to Rebus.

'What is it you want?' he said.

'Blackmail,' said John Rebus.

'Blackmail?'

'Good echo in here.'

'Blackmail? What the hell do you mean?'

'Photos,' said Rebus calmly. 'You took them at a party four months ago.'

'Whose party?'

'Matt Bennett's.'

Roscoe nodded. Rebus had placed the cigarettes back on the table. Roscoe couldn't take his eyes off them. He picked up the box of matches and toyed with it. 'I remember it,' he said. A faint smile. 'Brilliant party.' He managed to stretch the word 'brilliant' out to four distinct syllables. So it really had been a good party.

'You took some snaps?'

'You're right. I'd just got a new camera.'

'I won't ask where from.'

'I've got a receipt.' Roscoe nodded to himself. 'I remember now. The film was no good.'

'How do you mean?'

'I put it in for developing, but none of the pictures came out. Not one. They reckoned I'd not put the film in the right way, or opened the case or something. The negatives were all blank. They showed me them.'

'They?'

'At the shop. I got a consolation free film.'

Some consolation, thought Rebus. Some swap, to be more accurate. He placed the photo on the table. Roscoe stared at it, then picked it up the better to examine it.

'How the—?' Remembering there was a woman present, Roscoe swallowed the rest of the question.

'Here,' said Rebus, pushing the pack of cigarettes in his direction. 'You look like you need one of these.'

Rebus sent Siobhan Clarke and DS Brian Holmes to pick up Keith Leyton. He also advised them to take along a back-up. You never could tell with a nutter like Leyton. Plenty of back-up, just to be on the safe side. It wasn't just Leyton after all; there might be Joyce to deal with too.

Meantime, Rebus drove to Tollcross, parked just across from the traffic lights, tight in at a bus stop, and, watched by a frowning queue, made a dash for the photographic shop's doorway. It was chucking it down, no question. The queue had squeezed itself so tightly under the metal awning of the bus shelter that vice might have been able to bring them up on a charge of public indecency. Rebus shook water from his hair and pushed open the shop's door.

Inside it was light and warm. He shook himself again and approached the counter. A young man beamed at him.

'Yes, sir?'

'I wonder if you can help,' said Rebus. 'I've got a film needs developing, only I want it done in an hour. Is that possible?'

'No problem, sir. Is it colour?'

'Yes.'

'That's fine then. We do our own processing.'

Rebus nodded and reached into his pocket. The man had already begun filling in details on a form. He printed the letters very neatly, Rebus noticed with pleasure.

'That's good,' said Rebus, bringing out the photo. 'In that case, you must have developed this.'

The man went very still and very pale.

'Don't worry, son, I'm not from Keith Leyton. In fact, Keith Leyton doesn't know anything about you, which is just as well for you.'

The young man rested the pen on the form. He couldn't take his eyes off the photograph.

'Better shut up shop now,' said Rebus. 'You're coming down to the station. You can bring the rest of the photos with you. Oh, and I'd wear a cagoule, it's not exactly fair, is it?'

'Not exactly.'

'And take a tip from me, son. Next time you think of blackmailing someone, make sure you get the right person, eh?' Rebus tucked the photo back into his pocket. 'Plus, if you'll take my advice, don't use words like "reprint" in your blackmail notes. Nobody says reprint except people like you.' Rebus wrinkled his nose. 'It just makes it too easy for us, you see.'

'Thanks for the warning,' the man said coolly.

'All part of the service,' said Rebus with a smile. The clue had actually escaped him throughout. Not that he'd be admitting as much to Kenneth Leighton. No, he would tell the story as though he'd been Sherlock Holmes and Philip Marlowe rolled into one. Doubtless Leighton would be impressed. And one day, when Rebus was needing a favour from the taxman, he would know he could put Kenneth Leighton in the frame.

Facing the Music

An unmarked police car.

Interesting phrase, that. Inspector John Rebus's car, punch-drunk and weather-beaten, scarred and mauled, would still merit description as 'unmarked', despite the copious evidence to the contrary. Oily-handed mechanics stifled grins whenever he waddled into a forecourt. Garage proprietors adjusted the thick gold rings on their fingers and reached for the calculator.

Still, there were times when the old war-horse came in handy. It might or might not be 'unmarked'; unremarkable it certainly was. Even the most cynical law-breaker would hardly expect CID to spend their time sitting around in a breaker's-yard special. Rebus's car was a must for undercover work, the only problem coming if the villains decided to make a run for it. Then, even the most elderly and infirm could outpace it.

'But it's a stayer,' Rebus would say in mitigation.

He sat now, the driving-seat so used to his shape that it formed a mould around him, stroking the steering-wheel with his hands. There was a loud sigh from the passenger seat, and Detective Sergeant Brian Holmes repeated his question.

'Why have we stopped?'

Rebus looked around him. They were parked by the side of Queensferry Street, only a couple of hundred yards from Princes Street's west end. It was early afternoon, overcast but dry. The gusts of wind blowing in from the Firth of Forth were probably keeping the rain away. The corner of Princes Street, where Fraser's department store and the Caledonian Hotel tried to outstare one another, caught the winds and whipped them against unsuspecting shoppers, who could be seen, dazed and numb, making their way afterwards along Queensferry Street, in search of coffee and shortcake. Rebus gave the pedestrians a look of pity. Holmes sighed again. He could murder a pot of tea and some fruit scones with butter.

'Do you know, Brian,' Rebus began, 'in all the years I've been in Edinburgh, I've never been called to any sort of a crime on this street.' He slapped the steering-wheel for emphasis. 'Not once.'

'Maybe they should put up a plaque,' suggested Holmes.

Rebus almost smiled. 'Maybe they should.'

'Is that why we're sitting here? You want to break your duck?' Holmes glanced into the tea-shop window, then away again quickly licking dry lips. 'It might take a while, you know,' he said.

'It might, Brian. But then again ...'

Rebus tapped out a tattoo on the steering-wheel. Holmes was beginning to regret his own enthusiasm. Hadn't Rebus tried to deter him from coming out for this drive? Not that they'd driven much. But anything, Holmes reasoned, was better than catching up on paperwork. Well, just about anything.

'What's the longest time you've been on a stake-out?' he asked, making conversation.

'A week,' said Rebus. 'Protection racket run from a pub down near Powderhall. It was a joint operation with Trading Standards. We spent five days pretending to be on the broo, playing pool all day.'

'Did you get a result?'

'We beat them at pool,' Rebus said.

There was a yell from a shop doorway, just as a young man was sprinting across the road in front of their car. The young man was carrying a black metal box. The person who'd called out did so again.

'Stop him! Thief! Stop him!'

The man in the shop doorway was waving, pointing towards the sprinter. Holmes looked towards Rebus, seemed about to say something, but decided against it. 'Come on then!' he said.

Rebus started the car's engine, signalled, and moved out into the traffic. Holmes was focusing through the windscreen. 'I can see him. Put your foot down!'

'"Put your foot down, *sir*",' Rebus said calmly. 'Don't worry, Brian.'

'Hell, he's turning into Randolph Place.'

Rebus signalled again, brought the car across the oncoming traffic, and turned into the dead end that was Randolph Place. Only, while it was a dead end for cars, there were pedestrian passages either side of West Register House. The young man, carrying the narrow box under his arm, turned into one of the passages. Rebus pulled to a halt. Holmes had the car door open before it had stopped, and leapt out, ready to follow on foot.

'Cut him off!' he yelled, meaning for Rebus to drive back on to Queensferry Street, around Hope Street and into Charlotte Square, where the passage emerged.

'"Cut him off, *sir*",' mouthed Rebus.

He did a careful three-point turn, and just as carefully moved back out into traffic held to a crawl by traffic lights. By the time he reached Charlotte Square and the front of West Register House, Holmes was shrugging his shoulders and flapping his arms. Rebus pulled to a stop beside him.

'Did you see him?' Holmes asked, getting into the car.

'No.'

'Where have you been anyway?'

'A red light.'

Holmes looked at him as though he were mad. Since when had Inspector John Rebus stopped for a red light? 'Well, I've lost him anyway.'

'Not your fault, Brian.'

Holmes looked at him again. 'Right,' he agreed. 'So, back to the shop? What was it anyway?'

'Hi-fi shop, I think.'

Holmes nodded as Rebus moved off again into the traffic. Yes, the box had the look of a piece of hi-fi, some slim rack component. They'd find out at the shop. But instead of doing a circuit of Charlotte Square to take them back into Queensferry Street, Rebus signalled along George Street. Holmes, still catching his breath, looked around disbelieving.

'Where are we going?'

'I thought you were fed up with Queensferry Street. We're going back to the station.'

'*What?*'

'Back to the station.'

'But what about—?'

'Relax, Brian. You've got to learn not to fret so much.'

Holmes examined his superior's face. 'You're up to something,' he said at last.

Rebus turned and smiled. 'Took you long enough,' he said.

But whatever it was, Rebus wasn't telling. Back at the station, he went straight to the main desk.

'Any robberies, Alec?'

The desk officer had a few. The most recent was a snatch at a specialist hi-fi shop.

'We'll take that,' said Rebus. The desk officer blinked.

'It's not much, sir. Just a single item, thief did a runner.'

'Nevertheless, Alec,' said Rebus. 'A crime has been committed, and it's our duty to investigate it.' He turned to head back out to the car.

'Is he all right?' Alec asked Holmes.

Holmes was beginning to wonder, but decided to go along for the ride anyway.

'A cassette deck,' the proprietor explained. 'Nice model, too. Not top of the range, but nice. Top-of-the-range stuff isn't kept out on the shop floor. We keep it in the demonstration rooms.'

Holmes was looking at the shelf where the cassette deck had rested. There were other decks either side of the gap, more expensive decks at that.

'Why would he choose that one?' Holmes asked.

'Eh?'

'Well, it's not the dearest, is it? And it's not even the closest to the door.'

The dealer shrugged. 'Kids these days, who can tell?' His thick hair was still tousled from where he had stood in the Queensferry Street wind-tunnel, yelling against the elements as passers-by stared at him.

'I take it you've got insurance, Mr Wardle?' The question came from Rebus, who was standing in front of a row of loudspeakers.

'Christ yes, and it costs enough.' Wardle shrugged. 'Look, it's okay. I know how it works. Points system, right? Anything under a four-point crime, and you lads don't bother. You just fill out the forms so I can claim from the insurance. What does this rate? One point? Two at the most?'

Rebus blinked, perhaps stunned by the use of the word 'lads' in connection with him.

'You've got the serial number, Mr Wardle,' he said at last. 'That'll give us a start. Then a description of the thief – that's more than we usually get in cases of shop-snatching. Meantime, you might move your stock a bit further back from the door and think about a common chain or circuit alarm so they can't be taken off their shelves. Okay?'

Wardle nodded.

'And be thankful,' mused Rebus. 'After all, it could've been worse. It could have been a ram-raider.' He picked up a CD case from where it sat on top of a machine: Mantovani and his Orchestra. 'Or even a critic,' said Rebus.

*

Back at the station, Holmes sat fuming like a readying volcano. Or at least like a tin of something flammable left for too long in the sun.

Whatever Rebus was up to, as per usual he wasn't saying. It infuriated Holmes. Now Rebus was off at a meeting in the Chief Super's office: nothing very important, just routine ... like the snatch at the hi-fi shop.

Holmes played the scene through in his mind. The stationary car, causing an obstruction to the already slow movement of traffic. Then Wardle's cry, and the youth running across the road, jinking between cars. The youth had half turned, giving Holmes a moment's view of a cheek speckled with acne, cropped spiky hair. A skinny runt of a sixteen-year-old in faded jeans and trainers. Pale blue windcheater with a lumberjack shirt hanging loose below its hemline.

And carrying a hi-fi component that was neither the easiest piece in the shop to steal, nor the dearest. Wardle had seemed relaxed about the whole affair. The insurance would cover it. An insurance scam: was that it? Was Rebus working on some insurance diddle on the q.t., maybe as a favour to some investigator from the Pru? Holmes hated the way his superior worked, like a greedy if talented footballer hogging the ball, dribbling past man after man, getting himself trapped beside the by-line but still refusing to pass the ball. Holmes had known a boy at school like that. One day, fed up, Holmes had scythed the smart-arse down, even though they'd been on the same side ...

Rebus had known the theft would take place. Therefore, he'd been tipped off. Therefore, the thief had been set up. There was just one big *but* to the whole theory – Rebus had let the thief get away. It didn't make sense. It didn't make any sense at all.

'Right,' Holmes said, nodding to himself. 'Right you are, sir.' And with that, he went off to find the young offender files.

That evening, just after six, Rebus thought that since he was in the area anyway, he'd drop into Mr Wardle's home and report the lack of progress on the case. It might be that, time having passed, Wardle would remember something else about the snatch, some crucial detail. The description he'd been able to give of the thief had been next to useless. It was almost as though he didn't want the hassle, didn't want the thief caught. Well, maybe Rebus could jog his memory.

The radio came to life. It was a message from DS Holmes. And when Rebus heard it, he snarled and turned the car back around towards the city centre.

It was lucky for Holmes, so Rebus said, that the traffic had been heavy, the fifteen-minute journey back into town being time enough for him to calm down. They were in the CID room. Holmes was seated at his desk, hands clasped behind his head. Rebus was standing over him, breathing hard. On the desk sat a matt-black cassette deck.

'Serial numbers match,' Holmes said, 'just in case you were wondering.'

Rebus couldn't quite sound disinterested. 'How did you find him?'

With his hands still behind his head, Holmes managed a shrug. 'He was on file, sir. I just sat there flipping through them till I spotted him. That acne of his is as good as a tattoo. James Iain Bankhead, known to his friends as Jib. According to the file, you've arrested him a couple of times yourself in the past.'

'Jib Bankhead?' said Rebus, as though trying to place the name. 'Yes, rings a bell.'

'I'd have thought it'd ring a whole fire station, sir. You last arrested him three months ago.' Holmes made a show of consulting the file on his desk. 'Funny, you not recognising him ...' Holmes kept his eyes on the file.

'I must be getting old,' Rebus said.

Holmes looked up. 'So what now, sir?'

'Where is he?'

'Interview Room B.'

'Let him stay there then. Can't do any harm. Has he said anything?'

'Not a word. Mind you, he *did* seem surprised when I paid him a visit.'

'But he kept his mouth shut?'

Holmes nodded. 'So what now?' he repeated.

'Now,' said Rebus, 'you come along with me, Brian. I'll tell you all about it on the way ...'

Wardle lived in a flat carved from a detached turn-of-the-century house on the south-east outskirts of the city. Rebus pressed the bell on the wall to the side of the substantial main door. After a moment, there was the muffled sound of footsteps, three clicks as locks were undone, and the door opened from within.

'Good evening, Mr Wardle,' said Rebus. 'I see you're security-conscious at home at least.' Rebus was nodding towards the door, with its three separate keyholes, spy-hole and security chain.

'You can't be too—' Wardle broke off as he saw what Brian Holmes was carrying. 'The deck!'

'Good as new,' said Rebus, 'apart from a few fingerprints.' Wardle opened the door wide. 'Come in, come in.'

They entered a narrow entrance hall which led to a flight of stairs. Obviously the ground floor of the house did not belong to Wardle. He was dressed much as he had been in the shop: denims too young for his years, an open-necked shirt louder than a Wee Free sermon, and brown moccasins.

'I can't believe it,' he said, leading them towards the stairs. 'I really can't. But you could have brought it round to the shop ...'

'Well, sir, we were going to be passing anyway.' Rebus closed the door, noting the steel plate on its inner face. The door-surround too was reinforced with metal plates. Wardle turned and noticed Rebus's interest.

'Wait till you see the hi-fi, Inspector. It'll all become clear.' They could already hear the music. The bass was vibrating each step of the stairs.

'You must have sympathetic neighbours,' Rebus remarked.

'She's ninety-two,' said Wardle. 'Deaf as a post. I went round to explain to her about the hi-fi just after I moved in. She couldn't hear a word I was saying.'

They were at the top of the stairs now, where a smaller hallway led into a huge open-plan living-room and kitchen. A sofa and two chairs had been pushed hard back against one wall, and there was nothing but space between them and the opposite wall, where the hi-fi system sat, with large floor-standing speakers either side of it. One rack comprised half a dozen black boxes, boasting nothing to Rebus's eye but a single red light.

'Amplifiers,' Wardle explained, turning down the music.

'What, all of them?'

'Pre-amp and power supply, plus an amp for each driver.' Holmes had rested the cassette deck on the floor, but Wardle moved it away immediately.

'Spoils the sound,' he said, 'if there's an extra piece of gear in the room.'

Holmes and Rebus stared at one another. Wardle was in his element now. 'Want to hear something? What's your taste?'

'Rolling Stones?' Rebus asked.

'*Sticky Fingers, Exile, Let It Bleed*?'

'That last one,' said Rebus.

Wardle went over to where a twenty-foot row of LPs was standing against the wall beneath the window.

'I thought those went out with the Ark,' said Holmes.

Wardle smiled. 'You mean with the CD. No, vinyl's still the best. Sit down.' He went over to the turntable and took off the LP he'd been playing. Rebus and Holmes sat. Holmes looked to Rebus, who nodded. Holmes got up again.

'Actually, could I use your loo?' he asked.

'First right out on the landing,' said Wardle. Holmes left the room. 'Any particular track, Inspector?'

'"Gimme Shelter",' stated Rebus. Wardle nodded agreement, set the needle on the disc, rose to his feet, and turned up the volume. 'Something to drink?' he asked. The room exploded into a wall of sound. Rebus had heard the phrase 'wall of sound' before. Well, here he was with his nose pressed against it.

'A whisky, please,' he yelled. Wardle tipped his head towards the hall. 'Same for him.' Wardle nodded and went off towards the kitchen area. Pinned to the sofa as he was, Rebus looked around the room. He had eyes for everything but the hi-fi. Not that there was much to see. A small coffee table whose surface seemed to be covered with arcana to do with the hi-fi system, cleaning-brushes and such like. There were some nice-looking prints on the wall. Actually, one looked like a real painting rather than a print: the surface of a swimming-pool, someone moving through the depths. But no TV, no shelves, no books, no knick-knacks, no family photos. Rebus knew Wardle was divorced. He also knew Wardle drove a Y-registered Porsche 911. He knew quite a lot about Wardle, but not yet enough ...

A healthy glass of whisky was handed to him. Wardle placed another on the floor for Holmes, then returned to the kitchen and came back with a glass for himself. He sat down next to Rebus.

'What do you think?'

'Fantastic,' Rebus called back.

Wardle grinned.

'How much would this lot cost me?' Rebus asked, hoping Wardle wouldn't notice how long Holmes had been out of the room.

'About twenty-five K.'

'You're joking. My flat didn't cost that.'

Wardle just laughed. But he was glancing towards the living-room door. He looked as though he might be about to say something, when the door opened and Holmes came in, rubbing his hands as though drying them off. He smiled, sat, and toasted Wardle with his glass. Wardle went over to the amplifier to turn down the volume. Holmes nodded towards Rebus. Rebus toasted no one in particular and finished his drink. The volume dipped.

'What was that?' Holmes asked.

'*Let It Bleed.*'

'I thought my ears would.'

Wardle laughed. He seemed to be in a particularly good mood. Maybe it was because of the cassette deck.

'Listen,' he said, 'how the hell did you get that deck back so quickly?'

Holmes was about to say something, but Rebus beat him to it. 'It was abandoned.'

'Abandoned?'

'At the bottom of a flight of stairs on Queen Street,' Rebus went on. He had risen to his feet. Holmes took the hint and, eyes twisted shut, gulped down his whisky. 'So you see, sir, we were just lucky, that's all. Just lucky.'

'Well, thanks again,' said Wardle. 'If you ever want some hi-fi, drop into the shop. I'm sure a discount might be arranged.'

'We'll bear that in mind, sir,' said Rebus. 'Just don't expect me to put my flat on the market ...'

Back at the station, Rebus first of all had Jib released, then went to his office, where he spread the files out across his desk, while Holmes pulled over a chair. Then they both sat, reading aloud from lists. The lists were of stolen goods, high-quality stuff stolen in the dead of night by real professionals. The hauls – highly selective hauls – came from five addresses, the homes of well-paid middle-class people, people with things well worth the stealing.

Five robberies, all at dead of night, alarm systems disconnected. Art objects had been taken, antiques, in one case an entire collection of rare European stamps. The housebreakings had occurred at more or less monthly intervals, and all within a twenty-mile radius of central Edinburgh. The connection between them? Rebus had explained it to Holmes on their way to Wardle's flat.

'Nobody could see *any* connection, apart from the fact that the five victims worked in the west end. The Chief Super asked me to take a look. Guess what I found? They'd all had smart new hi-fi systems installed. Up to six months before the break-ins. Systems bought from Queensferry Audio and installed by Mr Wardle.'

'So he'd know what was in each house?' Holmes had said.

'And he'd be able to give the alarm system a look-over while he was there, too.'

'Could just be coincidence.'

'I know.'

Oh yes, Rebus knew. He knew he had only the hunch, the coincidence. He had no proof, no evidence of any kind. Certainly nothing that would gain him a search warrant, as the Chief Super had been good enough to confirm, knowing damned well that Rebus would take it further anyway. Not that this concerned the Chief Super, so long as Rebus worked alone, and didn't tell his superiors what he was up to. That way, it was Rebus's neck in the noose, Rebus's pension on the line.

Rebus guessed his only hope was that Wardle had kept some of the stolen pieces, that some of the stuff was still on his premises. He'd already had a young DC go into Queensferry Audio posing as a would-be buyer. The DC had gone in four times in all, once to buy some tapes, then to look at hi-fi, then to spend an hour in one of the demo rooms, and finally just for a friendly chat ... He'd reported back to Rebus that the place was clean. No signs of any stolen merchandise, no locked rooms or cupboards ...

So then Rebus had persuaded a uniformed constable to pose as a Neighbourhood Watch supervisor. He had visited Wardle at home, not getting past the downstairs hallway. But he'd been able to report that the place was 'like Fort Knox, metal door and all'. Rebus had had experience of steel-reinforced doors: they were favoured by drug dealers, so that when police came calling with a sledgehammer for invitation, the dealers would have time enough to flush everything away.

But a hi-fi dealer with a steel door ... Well, that was a new one. True, twenty-five grand's worth of hi-fi was an investment worth protecting. But there were limits. Not that Rebus suspected Wardle of actually doing the breaking and entering himself. No, he just passed the information on to the men Rebus really wanted, the gang. But Wardle was the only means of getting at them ...

Finally, in desperation, Rebus had turned to Jib. And Jib had done what he was told, meaning Rebus now owed him a large favour. It was all highly irregular; unlawful, if it came to it. If anyone found out ... well, Rebus would be making the acquaintance of his local broo office. Which was why, as he explained to Holmes, he'd been keeping so quiet about it.

The plan was simple. Jib would run off with something, anything, watched by Rebus to make sure nothing went wrong – such as a daring citizen's arrest by one or more passers-by. Later, Rebus would turn up at the shop to investigate the theft. Then later still, he would arrive at Wardle's flat, ostensibly to report the lack of progress. If a further visit was needed, the cassette deck would be found. But now he had Holmes's help, so one visit only should suffice, one man keeping Wardle busy while the other sniffed around the rooms in the flat.

They sat now, poring over the lists, trying to match what Holmes had seen in Wardle's two bedrooms with what had been reported stolen from the five luxury homes.

'Carriage clock,' read Rebus, 'nineteenth-century Japanese cigar box, seventeenth-century prints of Edinburgh by James Gordon, a Swarbreck lithograph ...'

Holmes shook his head at the mention of each, then read from one of his own lists. 'Ladies' and gents' Longines watches, a Hockney print, Cartier pen, first-edition set of the Waverley novels, Ming vase, Dresden pieces ...' He looked up. 'Would you believe, there's even a case of champagne.' He looked down again and read: 'Louis Roederer Cristal 1985. Value put at six hundred pounds. That's a hundred quid a bottle.'

'Bet you're glad you're a lager man,' said Rebus. He sighed. 'Does none of this mean anything to you, Brian?'

Holmes shook his head. 'Nothing like any of this in either of the bedrooms.'

Rebus cursed under his breath. 'Hold on,' he said. 'What about that print?'

'Which one? The Hockney?'

'Yes, have we got a photo of it?'

'Just this,' said Holmes, extracting from the file a page torn from an art gallery's catalogue. He handed it to Rebus, who studied the picture. 'Why?'

'Why?' echoed Rebus. 'Because you sat with this painting in front of your nose on Wardle's living-room wall. I thought it was a real painting, but this is it all right.' He tapped the sheet of paper. 'It says here the print's limited to fifty impressions. What number is the stolen one?'

Holmes looked down the list. 'Forty-four.'

'Right,' said Rebus. 'That should be easy enough to confirm.' He checked his watch. 'What time are you expected home?'

Holmes was shaking his head. 'Never mind that. If you're going back to Wardle's flat, I'm coming too.'

'Come on then.'

It was only as they were leaving the office that Holmes thought to ask: 'What if it isn't the same number on the print?'

'Then we'll just have to face the music,' said Rebus.

But as it turned out, the only one facing the music was Wardle, and he sang beautifully. A pity, Rebus mused later, that he hadn't arranged for a discount on a new hi-fi system first. He'd just have to wait for Queensferry Audio's closing-down sale ...

Window of Opportunity

Bernie Few's jailbreaks were an art.

And over the years he had honed his art. His escapes from prison, his shrugging off of guards and prison officers, his vanishing acts were the stuff of lights-out stories in jails the length and breadth of Scotland. He was called 'The Grease-Man', 'The Blink', and many other names, including the obvious 'Houdini' and the not-so-obvious 'Claude' (Claude Rains having starred as the original *Invisible Man*).

Bernie Few was beautiful. As a petty thief he was hopeless, but after capture he started to show his real prowess. He wasn't made for being a housebreaker; but he surely did shine as a jailbreaker. He'd stuffed himself into rubbish bags and mail sacks, taken the place of a corpse from one prison hospital, squeezed his wiry frame out of impossibly small windows (sometimes buttering his naked torso in preparation), and crammed himself into ventilation shafts and heating ducts.

But Bernie Few had a problem. Once he'd scaled the high walls, waded through sewers, sprinted from the prison bus, or cracked his guard across the head, once he'd done all this and was outside again, breathing free air and melting into the crowd ... his movements were like clockwork. All his ingenuity seemed to be exhausted. The prison psychologists put it differently. They said he wanted to be caught, really. It was a game to him.

But to Detective Inspector John Rebus, it was more than a game. It was a chance for a drink.

Bernie would do three things. One, he'd go throw a rock through his ex-wife's living-room window. Two, he'd stand in the middle of Princes Street telling everyone to go to hell (and other places besides). And three, he'd get drunk in Scott's Bar. These days, option one was difficult for Bernie, since his ex-wife had not only moved without leaving a forwarding address but had, at Rebus's suggestion, gone to live on the eleventh floor of an Oxgangs tower block.

No more rocks through the living-room window, unless Bernie was handy with ropes and crampons.

Rebus preferred to wait for Bernie in Scott's Bar, where they refused to water down either the whisky or the language. Scott's was a villain's pub, one of the ropiest in Edinburgh. Rebus recognised half the faces in the place, even on a dull Wednesday afternoon. Bail faces, appeal faces. They recognised him, too, but there wasn't going to be any trouble. Every one of them knew why he was here. He hoisted himself on to a barstool and lit a cigarette. The TV was on, showing a satellite sports channel. Cricket, some test between England and the West Indies. It is a popular fallacy that the Scots don't watch cricket. Edinburgh pub drinkers will watch *anything*, especially if England are involved, more especially if England are odds on to get a drubbing. Scott's, as depressing a watering hole as you could ever imagine, had transported itself to the Caribbean for the occasion.

Then the door to the toilets opened with a nerve-jarring squeal, and a man loped out. He was tall and skinny, loose-limbed, hair falling over his eyes. He had a hand on his fly, just checking prior to departure, and his eyes were on the floor.

'See youse then,' he said to nobody, opening the front door to leave. Nobody responded. The door stayed open longer than it should. Someone else was coming in. Eyes flashed from the TV for a moment. Rebus finished his drink and rose from the stool. He knew the man who'd just left the bar. He knew him well. He knew, too, that what had just happened was impossible.

The new customer, a small man with a handful of coins, had a voice hoarse from shouting as he croakily ordered a pint. The barman didn't move. Instead, he looked to Rebus, who was looking at Bernie Few.

Then Bernie Few looked at Rebus.

'Been down to Princes Street, Bernie?' Rebus asked.

Bernie Few sighed and rubbed his tired face. 'Time for a short one, Mr Rebus?'

Rebus nodded. He could do with another himself anyway. He had a couple of things on his mind, neither of them Bernie Few.

Police officers love and hate surveillance operations in more or less equal measure. There's the tedium, but even that beats being tied to a CID desk. Often on a stakeout there's a good spirit, plus there's that adrenal rush when something eventually happens.

The present surveillance was based in a second-floor tenement flat, the owners having been packed off to a seaside caravan for a fortnight. If the operation needed longer than a fortnight, they'd be sent to stay with relations.

The watchers worked in two-man teams and twelve-hour shifts. They were watching the second-floor flat of the tenement across the road. They were keeping tabs on a bandit called Ribs Mackay. He was called Ribs because he was so skinny. He had a heroin habit, and paid for it by pushing drugs. Only he'd never been caught at it, a state of affairs Edinburgh CID were keen to rectify.

The problem was, since the surveillance had begun, Ribs had been keeping his head down. He stayed in the flat, nipping out only on brief sorties to the corner shop. He'd buy beer, vodka, milk, cigarettes, sometimes breakfast cereal or a jar of peanut butter, and he'd always top off his purchases with half a dozen bars of chocolate. That was about it. There had to be more, but there wasn't any more. Any day now, the operation would be declared dead in the water.

They tried to keep the flat clean, but you couldn't help a bit of untidiness. You couldn't help nosy neighbours either: everyone on the stairwell wondered who the strangers in the Tully residence were. Some asked questions. Some didn't need to be told. Rebus met an old man on the stairs. He was hauling a bag of shopping up to the third floor, stopping for a breather at each step.

'Help you with that?' Rebus offered.

'I can manage.'

'It wouldn't be any bother.'

'I said I can manage.'

Rebus shrugged. 'Suit yourself.' Then he climbed to the landing and gave the recognised knock on the door of the Tullys' flat.

DC Jamphlar opened the door a crack, saw Rebus, and pulled it all the way open. Rebus nipped inside.

'Here,' he said, handing over a paper bag, 'doughrings.'

'Thank you, sir,' said Jamphlar.

In the cramped living-room, DC Connaught was sitting on a dining chair at the net curtain, peering through the net and out of the window. Rebus joined him for a moment. Ribs Mackay's window was grimy, but you could see through the grime into an ordinary-looking living-room. Not that Ribs came to the window much. Connaught wasn't concentrating on the window. He was ranging between the second-floor window and the ground-floor door. If Ribs left the flat, Jamphlar went haring after him, while Connaught followed Ribs's progress from the window and reported via radio to his colleague.

Initially, there'd been one man in the flat and one in a car at street level. But the man at street level hadn't been needed, and looked suspicious anyway. The street was no main thoroughfare, but a conduit between Clerk Street and Buccleuch Street. There were a few shops at road level, but they carried the look of permanent closure.

Connaught glanced up from the window. 'Afternoon, sir. What brings you here?'

'Any sign of him?' Rebus said.

'Not so much as a tweet.'

'I reckon I know why that is. Your bird's already flown.'

'No chance,' said Jamphlar, biting into a doughring.

'I saw him half an hour ago in Scott's Bar. That's a fair hike from here.'

'Must've been his double.'

But Rebus shook his head. 'When was the last time you saw him?'

Jamphlar checked the notebook. 'We haven't seen him this shift. But this morning Cooper and Sneddon watched him go to the corner shop and come back. That was seven-fifteen.'

'And you come on at eight?'

'Yes, sir.'

'And you haven't seen him since?'

'There's someone in there,' Connaught persisted. 'I've seen movement.'

Rebus spoke slowly. 'But you haven't seen Ribs Mackay, and I have. He's out on the street, doing whatever he does.' He leaned closer to Connaught. 'Come on, son, what is it? Been skiving off? Half an hour down the pub, a bit of a thirst-quencher? Catching some kip on the sofa? Looks comfortable, that sofa.'

Jamphlar was trying to swallow a mouthful of dough which had become suddenly dry. 'We've been doing our job!' he said, spraying crumbs.

Connaught just stared at Rebus with burning eyes. Rebus believed those eyes.

'All right,' he conceded, 'so there's another explanation. A back exit, a convenient drainpipe.'

'The back door's been bricked up,' Connaught said stiffly. 'There's a drainpipe, but Ribs couldn't manage down it.'

'How do you know?'

'I know.' Connaught stared out through the curtain.

'Something else then. Maybe he's using a disguise.'

Jamphlar, still chewing, flicked through the notebook. 'Everyone who comes out and goes in is checked off.'

'He's a druggie,' said Connaught. 'He's not bright enough to fool us.'

'Well, son, that's just what he's doing. You're watching an empty flat.'

'TV's just come on,' said Connaught. Rebus looked out through the curtain. Sure enough, he could see the animated screen. 'I hate this programme,' Connaught muttered. 'I wish he'd change the channel.'

'Maybe he can't,' said Rebus, making for the door.

He returned to the surveillance that evening, taking someone with him. There'd been a bit of difficulty, getting things arranged. Nobody was keen for him to walk out of the station with Bernie Few. But Rebus would assume full responsibility.

'Damned right you will,' said his boss, signing the form.

Jamphlar and Connaught were off, Cooper and Sneddon were on.

'What's this I hear?' Cooper said, opening the door to Rebus and his companion.

'About Ribs?'

'No,' said Cooper, 'about you bringing the day shift a selection of patisseries.'

'Come and take a look,' Sneddon called. Rebus walked over to the window. The light was on in Ribs's living-room, and the blinds weren't shut. Ribs had opened the window and was looking down on to the night-time street, enjoying a cigarette. 'See?' Sneddon said.

'I see,' said Rebus. Then he turned to Bernie Few. 'Come over here, Bernie.' Few came shuffling over to the window, and Rebus explained the whole thing to him. Bernie thought about it, rasping a hand over his chin, then asked the same questions Rebus had earlier asked Jamphlar and Connaught. Then he thought about it some more, staring out through the curtain.

'You keep an eye on the second-floor window?' he asked Cooper.

'That's right.'

'And the main door?'

'Yes.'

'You ever think of looking anywhere else?'

Cooper didn't get it. Neither did Sneddon.

'Go on, Bernie,' said Rebus.

'Look at the top floor,' Bernie Few suggested. Rebus looked. He saw a cracked and begrimed window, covered with ragged bits of cardboard. 'Think anyone lives there?' Bernie asked.

'What are you saying?'

'I think he's done a proper switch on you. Turned the tables, like.' He smiled. 'You're not watching Ribs Mackay. *He's* watching *you*.'

Rebus nodded, quick to get it. 'The change of shifts.' Bernie was nodding too. 'There's that minute or two when one shift's going off and the other's coming on.'

'A window of opportunity,' Bernie agreed. 'He watches, sees the new shift arrive, and skips downstairs and out the door.'

'And twelve hours later,' said Rebus, 'he waits in the street till he sees the next shift clocking on. Then he nips back in.'

Sneddon was shaking his head. 'But the lights, the telly ...'

'Timer switches,' Bernie Few answered casually. 'You think you see people moving about in there. Maybe you do, but not Ribs. Could just be shadows, a breeze blowing the curtains.'

Sneddon frowned. 'Who *are* you?'

'An expert witness,' Rebus said, patting Bernie Few's shoulder. Then he turned to Sneddon. 'I'm going over there. Keep an eye on Bernie here. And I *mean* keep an eye on him. As in, don't let him out of your sight.'

Sneddon blinked, then stared at Bernie. 'You're Buttery Bernie.' Bernie shrugged, accepting the nickname. Rebus was already leaving.

He went to the bar at the street's far corner and ordered a whisky. He sluiced his mouth out with the stuff, so that it would be heavy on his breath, then came out of the bar and weaved his way towards Ribs Mackay's tenement, just another soak trying to find his way home. He tugged his jacket over to one side, and undid a couple of buttons on his shirt. He could do this act. Sometimes he did it too well. He got drunk on the method.

He pushed open the tenement door and was in a dimly lit hallway, with worn stone steps curving up. He grasped the banister and started to climb. He didn't even pause at the second floor, but he could hear music from behind Ribs's door. And he saw the door was reinforced, just the kind dealers fitted. It gave them those vital extra seconds when the drug squad came calling, sledgehammers and axes their invitations. Seconds were all you needed to flush evidence away, or to swallow it. These days, prior to a house raid, the drugs squad opened up the sewers and had a man stationed there, ready for the flush ...

On the top-floor landing, Rebus paused for breath. The door facing him looked hard done by, scarred and chipped and beaten. The nameplate had been hauled off, leaving deep screw holes in the wood. Rebus knocked on the door, ready with excuses and his drunk's head-down stance. He waited, but there was no answer.

He listened, then put his eyes to the letterbox. Darkness. He tried the door handle. It turned, and the door swung inwards. When he thought about it, an unlocked door made sense. Ribs would need to come and go in a hurry, and locks took time.

Rebus stepped quietly into the short hallway. Some of the interior doors were open, bringing with them chinks of streetlight. The place smelt musty and damp, and it was cold. There was no furniture, and the wallpaper had peeled from the walls. Long strips now lay in wrinkled piles, like an old woman's stockings come to rest at her ankles. Rebus walked on tiptoe. He didn't know how good the floors were, and he didn't want anyone below to hear him. He didn't want Ribs Mackay to hear him.

He went into the living-room. It was identical in shape to the surveillance living-room. There were newspapers on the floor, a carpet rolled up against one wall. Tufts of carpet lay scattered across the floor. Mice had obviously been taking bits for nesting. Rebus went to the window. There was a small gap where two pieces of cardboard didn't quite meet. Through this gap he had a good view of the surveillance flat. And though the lights were off, the streetlight illuminated the net curtain, so that anyone behind the curtain who moved became a shadow puppet. Someone, Sneddon or Cooper or Bernie Few, was moving just now.

'You clever little runt,' Rebus whispered. Then he picked something up off the floor. It was a single-lens reflex camera, with telephoto lens attached. Not the sort of thing you found lying in abandoned flats. He picked it up and focused on the window across the street. There was absolutely no doubt in his mind now. It was so simple. Ribs sneaked up here, watched the surveillance through the telephoto while they thought they were watching him, and at eight o'clock walked smartly out of the tenement and went about his business.

'You're as good as gold, Bernie,' said Rebus. Then he put the camera back just the way he'd found it and tiptoed back through the flat.

'Where is he?'

Stupid question, considering. Sneddon just shrugged. 'He had to use the bathroom.'

'Of course he did,' said Rebus.

Sneddon led him through to the bathroom. It had a small window high on one wall. The window was open. It led not to the outside, but merely back into the hall near the flat's stairwell door.

'He was in here a while, so I came looking. Banged on the door, no answer, managed to force the thing open, but he wasn't here.' Sneddon's face and neck were red with embarrassment; or maybe it was just the exercise. 'I ran downstairs, but there was no sign of him.'

'I don't believe he could have squeezed out of that window,' Rebus said sceptically. 'Not even Bernie Few.' The window was about twelve inches by nine. It could be reached by standing on the rim of the bath, but the walls were white tile, and Rebus couldn't see any signs of scuff marks. He looked at the toilet. Its lid was down, but didn't sit level with the pan. Rebus lifted the lid and found himself staring at towels, several of them, stuffed down into the pan.

'What the ...?' Sneddon couldn't believe his eyes. But Rebus could. He opened the small airing cupboard beneath the sink. It was empty. A shelf had been lifted out and placed upright in the back of the cupboard. There was just about room inside to make for a hiding place. Rebus smiled at the disbelieving Sneddon.

'He waited till you'd gone downstairs.'

'Then what?' said Sneddon. 'You mean he's still in the flat?'

Rebus wondered. 'No,' he said at last, shaking his head. 'But think of what he just told us, about how Ribs was tricking us.'

He led Sneddon out of the flat, but instead of heading down, he climbed up a further flight to the top floor. Set into the ceiling was a skylight, and it too was open.

'A walk across the rooftops,' said Rebus.

Sneddon just shook his head. 'Sorry, sir,' he offered.

'Never mind,' said Rebus, knowing, however, that his boss would.

At seven next morning, Ribs Mackay left his flat and walked jauntily to the corner shop, followed by Sneddon. Then he walked back again, enjoying a cigarette, not a care in the world. He'd shown himself to the surveillance team, and now they had something to tell the new shift, something to occupy them during the changeover.

As usual the changeover happened at eight. And exactly a minute after Jamphlar and Connaught entered the tenement, the door across the street opened and Ribs Mackay flew out.

Rebus and Sneddon, snug in Rebus's car, watched him go. Then Sneddon got out to follow him. He didn't look back at Rebus, but he did wave an acknowledgement that his superior had been right. Rebus hoped Sneddon was better as a tail than he was as a watcher. He hoped they'd catch Ribs with the stuff on him, dealing it out perhaps, or taking delivery from his own supplier. That was the plan. That had been the plan throughout.

He started the ignition and drove out on to Buccleuch Street. Scott's Bar was an early opener, and John Rebus had an appointment there.

He owed Bernie Few a drink.

Death is Not the End

I

Is loss redeemed by memory? Or does memory merely swell the sense of loss, becoming the enemy? The language of loss is the language of memory: remembrance, memorial, momento. People leave our lives all the time: some we met only briefly, others we'd known since birth. They leave us memories – which become skewed through time – and little more.

The silent dance continued. Couples writhed and shuffled, threw back their heads or ran hands through their hair, eyes darting around the dance floor, seeking out future partners maybe, or past loves to make jealous. The TV monitor gave a greasy look to everything.

No sound, just pictures, the tape cutting from dance floor to main bar to second bar to toilet hallway, then entrance foyer, exterior front and exterior back. Exterior back was a puddled alley, full of rubbish bins and a Merc belonging to the club's owner. Rebus had heard about the alley: a punter had been knifed there the previous summer. Mr Merc had complained about the bloody smear on his passenger-side window. The victim had lived.

The club was called Gaitanos, nobody knew why. The owner just said it sounded American and a bit jazzy. The larger part of the clientele had decided on the nickname 'Guisers', and that was what you heard in the pubs on a Friday and Saturday night – 'Going down Guisers later?' The young men would be dressed smart-casual, the women scented from heaven and all stations south. They left the pubs around ten or half past – that's when it would be starting to get lively at Guisers.

Rebus was seated in a small uncomfortable chair which itself sat in a stuffy dimly lit room. The other chair was filled by an audio-visual technician, armed with two remotes. His occasional belches – of which he seemed blissfully ignorant – bespoke a recent snack of spring onion crisps and Irn-Bru.

'I'm really only interested in the main bar, foyer and out front,' Rebus said.

'I could edit them down to another tape, but we'd lose definition. The recording's duff enough as it is.' The technician scratched inside the sagging armpit of his black T-shirt.

Rebus leaned forward a little, pointing at the screen. 'Coming up now.' They waited. The view jumped from back alley to dance floor. 'Any second.' Another cut: main bar, punters queuing three deep. The technician didn't need to be told, and froze the picture. It wasn't so much black and white as sepia, the colour of dead photographs. Interior light, the audio-visual wizard had explained. He was adjusting the tracking now, and moving the action along one frame at a time. Rebus moved in on the screen, bending so one knee rested on the floor. His finger was touching a face. He took out the assortment of photos from his pocket and held them against the screen.

'It's him,' he said. 'I was pretty sure before. You can't go in a bit closer?'

'For now, this is as good as it gets. I can work on it later, stick it on the computer. The problem is the source material, to wit: one shitty security video.'

Rebus sat back on his chair. 'All right,' he said. 'Let's run forward at half-speed.'

The camera stayed with the main bar for another fifteen seconds, then switched to the second bar and all points on the compass. When it returned to the main bar, the crush of drinkers seemed not to have moved. Unbidden, the technician froze the tape again.

'He's not there,' Rebus said. Again he approached the screen, touched it with his finger. 'He should be there.'

'Next to the sex goddess.' The technician belched again.

Yes. Spun silver hair, almost like a cloud of candy-floss, dark eyes and lips. While those around her were either intent on catching the eyes of the bar staff or on the dance floor, she was looking off to one side. There were no shoulders to her dress.

'Let's check the foyer,' Rebus said.

Twenty seconds later, there showed a steady stream entering the club, but no one leaving. Exterior front showed a queue awaiting admittance by the brace of bouncers, and a few passers-by.

'In the toilet maybe,' the technician suggested. But Rebus had studied the tape a dozen times already, and though he watched just once more he knew he wouldn't see the young man again, not at the bar, not on the dance floor, and not back around the table where his mates were waiting – with increasing disbelief and impatience – for him to get his round in.

The young man's name was Damon Mee and, according to the timer running at the bottom right-hand corner of the screen, he had vanished from the world sometime between 11.44 and 11.45 p.m. on Friday 22 April.

'Where is this place anyway? I don't recognise it.'

'Kirkcaldy,' Rebus said.

The technician looked at him. 'How come it ended up here?'

Good question, Rebus thought, but not one he was about to answer. 'Go back to that bar shot,' he said. 'Take it nice and slow again.'

The technician aimed his right-hand remote. 'Yes, sir, Mr DeMille,' he said.

April meant still not quite spring in Edinburgh. A few sunny days to be sure, buds getting twitchy, wondering if winter had been paid the ransom. But there was snow still hanging in a sky the colour of chicken bones. Office talk: how Rangers were going to retain the championship; why Hearts and Hibs would never win it – was it finally time for the two local sides to become friends, form one team which might – *might* – stand half a chance? As someone said, their rivalry was part and parcel of the city's make-up. Hard to imagine Rangers and Celtic thinking of marriage in the same way, or even of a quick poke on the back stairs.

After years of following football only on pub televisions and in the back of the daily tabloid, Rebus was starting to go to matches again. DC Siobhan Clarke was to blame, coaxing him to a Hibs game one dreary afternoon. The men on the green sward weren't half as interesting as the spectators, who proved by turns sharp-witted, vulgar, perceptive and incorrigible. Siobhan had taken him to her usual spot. Those in the vicinity seemed to know her pretty well. It was a good-humoured afternoon, even if Rebus couldn't have said who scored the eventual three goals. But Hibs had won: the final-whistle hug from Siobhan was proof of that.

It was interesting to Rebus that, for all the barriers around the ground, this was a place where shields were dropped. After a while, it felt like one of the safest places he'd ever been. He re-called fixtures his father had taken him to in the fifties and early sixties – Cowdenbeath home games, and a crowd numbered in the hundreds; getting there necessitated a change of buses, Rebus and his younger brother fighting over who could hold the roll of tickets. Their mother was dead by then and their father was trying to carry on much as before, like they might not notice she was missing. Those Saturday trips to the football were supposed to fill a gap. You saw a lot of fathers and sons on the terraces but not many mothers, and that in itself was reminder enough. There was a boy of Rebus's age who stood near them. Rebus had walked over to him one day and blurted out the truth.

'I don't have a mum at home.'

The boy had stared at him, saying nothing.

Ever since, football had reminded him of those days and of his mother. He stood on the terraces alone these days and followed the game mostly – movements which could be graceful as ballet or as jagged as free association – but sometimes found that he'd drifted elsewhere, to a place not at all unpleasant, and all the time surrounded by a community of bodies and wills.

'I'll tell you how to beat Rangers,' he said now, addressing the whole office.

'How?' Siobhan Clarke offered.

'Clone Stevie Scoular half a dozen times.'

There were murmurs of agreement, and then the Farmer put his head around the door.

'John, my office.'

The Farmer – Chief Superintendent Watson to his face – was pouring a mug of coffee from his machine when Rebus knocked at the open door.

'Sit down, John.' Rebus sat. The Farmer motioned with an empty mug, but he turned down the offer and waited for his boss to get to his chair and the point both.

'My birthday's coming up,' the Farmer said. This was a new one on Rebus, who kept quiet. 'I'd like a present.'

'Not just a card this year then?'

'What I want, John, is Topper Hamilton.'

Rebus let that sink in. 'I thought Topper was Mr Clean these days?'

'Not in my books.' The Farmer cupped his hands around his coffee mug. 'He got a fright last time and, granted, he's been keeping a low profile, but we both know the best villains have got little or no profile at all.'

'So what's he been up to?'

'I heard a story he's the sleeping partner in a couple of clubs and casinos. I also hear he bought a taxi firm from Big Ger Cafferty when Big Ger went into Barlinnie.'

Rebus was thinking back three years to their big push against Topper Hamilton: they'd set up surveillance, used a bit of pressure here and there, got a few people to talk. In the end, it hadn't so much amounted to a hill of beans as to a fart in an empty can. The procurator fiscal had decided not to proceed to trial. But then God or Fate, call it what you like, had provided a spin to the story. Not a plague of boils or anything for Topper Hamilton, but a nasty little cancer which had given him more grief than the whole of the Lothian and Borders Police. He'd been in and out of hospital, endured chemo and the whole works, and had emerged a more slender figure in every sense.

The Farmer – who'd once settled an office argument by reeling off the books in both Old and New Testaments – wasn't yet content that God and life had done their worst to Topper, or that retribution had been meted out in some mysterious divine way. He wanted Topper in court, even if they had to wheel him there on a trolley.

It was a personal thing.

'Last time I looked,' Rebus said now, 'it wasn't illegal to invest in a casino.'

'It is if your name hasn't come up during the vetting procedure. Think Topper could get a gaming licence?'

'Fair point. But I still don't see—'

'Something else I heard. You've got a snitch works as a croupier.'

'So?'

'Same casino Topper has a finger in.'

Rebus saw it all and started shaking his head. 'I made him a promise. He'll tell me about punters, but nothing on the management.'

'And you'd rather keep that promise than give me a birthday present?'

'A relationship like that … it's eggshells.'

The Farmer's eyes narrowed. 'You think ours isn't? Talk to him, John. Get him to do some ferreting.'

'I could lose a good snitch.'

'Plenty more bigmouths out there.' The Farmer watched Rebus get to his feet. 'I was looking for you earlier. You were in the video room.'

'A missing person.'

'Suspicious?'

Rebus shrugged. 'Could be. He went up to the bar for a round of drinks, never came back.'

'We've all done that in our time.'

'His parents are worried.'

'How old is he?'

'Twenty-three.'

The Farmer thought about it. 'Then what's the problem?'

II

The problem was the past. A week before, he'd received a phone call from a ghost.

'Inspector John Rebus, please.'

'Speaking.'

'Oh, hello there. You probably won't remember me.' A short laugh. 'That used to be a bit of a joke at school.'

Rebus, immune to every kind of phone call, had this pegged a crank. 'Why's that?' he asked, wondering which punchline he was walking into.

'Because it's my name: Mee.' The caller spelt it for him. 'Brian Mee.'

Inside Rebus's head, a fuzzy photograph took sudden shape – a mouth full of prominent teeth, freckled nose and cheeks, a kitchen-stool haircut. 'Barney Mee?' he said.

More laughter on the line. 'Aye, they used to call me Barney. I'm not sure I ever knew why.'

Rebus could have told him: after Barney Rubble in *The Flintstones*. He could have added, because you were a dense wee bastard. But instead he asked how this ghost from his past was doing.

'No' bad, no' bad.' The laugh again; Rebus recognised it now as a sign of nerves.

'So what can I do for you, Brian?'

'Well, me and Janis, we thought … Well, it was my mum's idea actually. She knew your dad. Both my mum and dad knew him, only my dad passed away, like. They all used to drink at the Goth.'

'Are you still in Bowhill?'

'Never quite escaped. Ach, it's all right really. I work in Glenrothes though. Lucky to have a job these days, eh? Mind, you've done well for yourself, Johnny. Do you still get called that?'

'I prefer John.'

'I remember you hated it when anyone called you Jock.' Another wheezing laugh. The photo was even sharper now, bordered with a white edge the way photos always were in the past. A decent footballer, a bit of a terrier, the hair reddish-brown. Dragging his satchel along the ground until the stitching rubbed away. Always with some huge hard sweet in his mouth, crunching down on it, his nose running. And one incident: he'd lifted some nude mags from under his dad's side of the bed and brought them to the toilets next to the Miners' Institute, there to be pored over like textbooks. Afterwards, half a dozen twelve-year-old boys had looked at each other, minds fizzing with questions.

'So what can I do for you, Brian?'

'Like I say, it was my mum's idea. Only, she remembered you were in the police in Edinburgh – saw your name in the paper a while back – and she thought you could maybe help.'

'With what?'

'Our son. I mean, mine and Janis's. He's called Damon.'

'What's he done?' Rebus thought: something minor, and way outside his territory anyway.

'He's vanished.'

'Run away?'

'More like in a puff of smoke. He was in this club with his pals, see, and he went—'

'Have you tried calling the police?' Rebus caught himself. 'I mean Fife Constabulary.'

'Oh aye.' Mee sounded dismissive. 'They asked a few questions, like, sniffed around a bit, then said there was nothing they could do. Damon's twenty-three. They say he's got a right to bugger off if he wants.'

'They've got a point. People run away all the time, Brian. Girl trouble maybe.'

'He was engaged.'

'Maybe he got scared?'

'Helen's a lovely girl. Never a raised voice between them.'

'Did he leave a note?'

'Nothing. I went through this with the police. He didn't take any clothes or anything. He didn't have any reason to go.'

'So you think something's happened to him?'

'I know what those buggers are thinking. They say we should give him another week or so to come back, or at least get in touch, but I know they'll only start doing something about it when the body turns up.'

Again, Rebus could have confirmed that this was only sensible. Again, he knew Mee wouldn't want to hear it.

'The thing is, Brian,' he said, 'I work in Edinburgh. Fife's not my patch. I mean, I can make a couple of phone calls, but it's hard to know what else to do.'

The voice was close to despair. 'Well, if you could just do *some-thing*. Like, anything. We'd be very grateful. It would put our minds at rest.' A pause. 'My mum always speaks well of your dad. He's remembered in this town.'

And buried there, too, Rebus thought. He picked up a pen. 'Give me your phone number, Brian.' And, almost an afterthought, 'Better give me the address, too.'

That evening, he drove north out of Edinburgh, paid his toll at the Forth Bridge, and crossed into Fife. It wasn't as if he never went there – he had a brother in Kirkcaldy. But though they spoke on the phone every month or so, there were seldom visits. He couldn't think of any other family he still had in Fife. The place liked to call itself 'the Kingdom' and there were those who would agree that it was another country, a place with its own linguistic and cultural currency. For such a small place it seemed almost endlessly complex – had seemed that way to Rebus even when he was growing up. To outsiders the place meant coastal scenery and St Andrew's, or a stretch of motorway between Edinburgh and Dundee, but the west-central Fife of Rebus's childhood had been very different, ruled by coal mines and linoleum, dockyards and chemical plants, an industrial landscape shaped by basic needs, and producing people who were wary and inward-looking with the blackest humour you'd ever find.

They'd built new roads since Rebus's last visit, and knocked down a few more landmarks, but the place didn't feel so very different from thirty-odd years before. It wasn't such a great span of time after all, except in human terms; maybe not even then. Entering Cardenden – Bowhill had disappeared from road signs in the 1960s, even if locals still knew it as a village distinct from its neighbour – Rebus slowed to see if the memories would turn out sweet or sour. Then he caught sight of a Chinese takeaway and thought: both, of course.

Brian and Janis Mee's house was easy enough to find: they were standing by the gate waiting for him. Rebus had been born in a prefab but brought up in a house just like the one he now parked in front of. Brian Mee practically opened the car door for him, and was trying to shake his hand while Rebus was still emerging from his seat.

'Let the man catch his breath!' Janis Mee snapped. She was still standing by the gate, arms folded. 'How have you been, Johnny?'

And Rebus realised that Brian Mee had married Janis Playfair, the only girl in his long and trouble-strewn life who'd ever managed to knock him unconscious.

The narrow, low-ceilinged living-room was full to bursting – not just Rebus and Janis and Brian, but Brian's mother and Mr and Mrs Playfair. Introductions had to be made, and Rebus guided to 'the seat by the fire'. The room was overheated. A pot of tea was produced, and on the table by Rebus's armchair sat enough slices of cake to feed a football crowd.

'He's a brainy one,' Janis's mother said, handing Rebus a framed photo of Damon Mee. 'Plenty of certificates from school. Works hard. Saving up to get married. The date's set for next August.'

The photo showed a smiling imp, not long out of school. 'Have you got anything more recent?'

Janis handed him a packet of snapshots. 'From last summer.'

Rebus went through them slowly. It saved having to look at the faces around him. He felt like a doctor, expected to produce an immediate diagnosis and remedy. The photos showed a man in his early twenties, still retaining the impish smile but recognisably older. Not careworn exactly, but with something behind the eyes, some disenchantment with adulthood. A few of the photos showed Damon's parents.

'We all went together,' Brian explained. 'Janis's mum and dad, my mum, Helen and her parents.'

Beaches, a big white hotel, poolside games. 'Where is it?'

'Lanzarote,' Janis said, handing him his tea. In a few of the pictures she was wearing a bikini – good body for her age, or any age come to that. He tried not to linger.

'Can I keep a couple of the close-ups?' he asked. Janis looked at him. 'Of Damon.' She nodded and he put the other photos back in their packet.

'We're really grateful,' someone said. Janis's mum? Brian's? Rebus couldn't tell.

'Does Helen live locally?'

'Practically round the corner.'

'I'd like to talk to her.'

'I'll give her a bell,' Brian Mee said, leaping to his feet.

'Damon had been drinking in some club?'

'Guisers,' Janis said, handing round cigarettes. 'It's in Kirkcaldy.'

'On the Prom?'

She shook her head, looking just the same as she had that night of the school dance ... shaking her head, telling him so far and no further. 'In the town. It used to be a department store.'

'It's really called Gaitanos,' Mr Playfair said. Rebus remembered him, too. He was an old man now.

'Where does Damon work?' Careful to stick to the present tense.

Brian Mee came back into the room. 'Same place I do. I managed to get him a job in packaging. He's been learning the ropes; it'll be management soon.'

Working-class nepotism; jobs handed down from father to son. Rebus was surprised it still existed.

'Helen'll be here in a minute,' Brian added.

'Are you not eating any cake, Inspector?' said Mrs Playfair.

Helen Cousins hadn't been able to add much to Rebus's picture of Damon, and hadn't been there the night he'd vanished. But she'd introduced him to someone who had, Andy Peters. Andy had been part of the group at Gaitanos. There'd been four of them. They'd been in the same year at school and still met up once or twice a week, sometimes to watch Raith Rovers if the weather was decent and the mood took them, other times for an evening session in a pub or club. It was only their third or fourth visit to Guisers.

Rebus thought of paying the club a visit, but knew he should talk to the local cops first, and decided that it could all wait until morning. He knew he was jumping through hoops. He didn't expect to find anything the locals had missed. At best, he could reassure the family that everything possible had been done.

Next morning he made a few phone calls from his office, trying to find someone who could be bothered to answer some casual questions from an Edinburgh colleague. He had one ally – Detective Sergeant Hendry at Dunfermline CID – but only reached him at the third attempt. He asked Hendry for a favour, then put the phone down and got back to his own work. But it was hard to concentrate. He kept thinking about Bowhill and about Janis Mee, née Playfair. Which led him – eventually – guiltily – to thoughts of Damon. Younger runaways tended to take the same route: by bus or train or hitching, and to London, Newcastle, Edinburgh or Glasgow. There were organisations who would keep an eye open for runaways, and even if they wouldn't always reveal their whereabouts to the anxious families, at least they could confirm that someone was alive and unharmed.

But a twenty-three-year-old, someone a bit cannier and with money to hand ... could be anywhere. No destination was too distant – he owned a passport, and it hadn't turned up. Rebus knew, too, that Damon had a current account at the local bank, complete with cashcard, and an interest-bearing account with a building society in Kirkcaldy. The bank might be worth trying. Rebus picked up the telephone again.

The manager at first insisted that he'd need something in writing, but relented when Rebus promised to fax him later. Rebus held while the manager went off to check, and had doodled half a village, complete with stream, parkland and school, by the time the man came back.

'The most recent withdrawal was from a cash machine in Kirkcaldy. One hundred pounds on the twenty-second.'

'What time?'

'I've no way of knowing.'

'No other withdrawals since then?'

'No.'

'How up-to-date is that information?'

'Very. Of course a cheque – especially if post-dated – would take longer to show up.'

'Could you keep tabs on that account, let me know if anyone starts using it again?'

'I could, but I'd need it in writing, and I might also need Head Office approval.'

'Well, see what you can do, Mr Brayne.'

'It's Bain,' the bank manager said coldly, putting down the phone.

DS Hendry didn't get back to him until late afternoon.

'Gaitanos,' Hendry said. 'I don't know the place personally. Locals call it Guisers. It's a pretty choice establishment. Two stabbings last year, one inside the club itself, the other in the back alley where the owner parks his Merc. Local residents are always girning about the noise when the place lets out.'

'What's the owner's name?'

'Charles Mackenzie, nicknamed "Charmer". He seems to be clean. A couple of uniforms talked to him about Damon Mee, but there was nothing to tell. Know how many missing persons there are every year? They're not exactly a white-hot priority. God knows there are times I've felt like doing a runner myself.'

'Haven't we all? Did the woolly suits talk to anyone else at the club?'

'Such as?'

'Bar staff, punters.'

'No. Someone did take a look at the security video for the night Damon was there, but they didn't see anything.'

'Where's the video now?'

'Back with its rightful owner.'

'Am I going to be stepping on toes if I ask to see it?'

'I think I can cover you. I know you said this was personal, John, but why the interest?'

'I'm not sure I can explain.' There were words – community, history, memory – but Rebus didn't think they'd be enough.

'They mustn't be working you hard enough over there.'

'Just the twenty-four hours every day.'

III

Matty Paine could tell a few stories. He'd worked his way round the world as a croupier. Cruise liners he'd worked on, and in Nevada. He'd spent a couple of years in London, dealing out cards and spinning the wheel for some of the wealthiest in the land, faces you'd recognise from the TV and the papers. Moguls, royalty, stars – Matty had seen them all. But his best story – the one people sometimes disbelieved – was about the time he'd been recruited to work in a casino in Beirut. This was at the height of the civil war, bomb sites and rubble, smoke and charred buildings, refugees and regular bursts of small-arms fire. And amazingly, in the midst of it all (or, to be fair, on the edge of it all), a casino. Not exactly legal. Run from a hotel basement with torchlight when the generator failed and not much in the way of refreshments, but with no shortage of punters – cash bets, dollars only – and a management team of three who prowled the place like Dobermanns, since there was no surveillance and no other way to check that the games were being played honestly. One of them had stood next to Matty for a full forty minutes one session, making him sweat despite the air-conditioning. He'd reminded Matty of the gaffers casinos employed to check on apprentices. He knew the gaffers were there to protect *him* as much as the punters – there were professional gamblers out there who'd psych out a trainee, watch them for hours, whole nights and weeks, looking for the flaw that would give them an edge over the house. Like, when you were starting out, you didn't always vary the force with which you span the wheel, or sent the ball rolling, and if they could suss it, they'd get a pretty good idea which quadrant the ball was going to stop in. Good croupiers were immune to this. A really good croupier – one of a very select, very highly thought of group – could master the wheel and get the ball to land pretty well where *they* wanted.

Of course, this might be against the interests of the house, too. And in the end, that's why the checkers were out there, patrolling the tables. They were looking out for the house. In the end it all came down to the house.

And when things had got a wee bit too hot in London, Matty had come home, meaning Edinburgh, though really he was from Gullane – perhaps the only boy ever to be raised there and not show the slightest interest in golf. His father had played – his mother too, come to that. Maybe she still did; he didn't keep in touch. There had been an awkward moment at the casino when a neighbour from Gullane days, an old business friend of his father's, had turned up, a bit the worse for wear and in tow with three other middle-aged punters. The neighbour had glanced towards Matty from time to time, but had eventually shaken his head, unable to place the face.

'Does he know you?' one of the all-seeing gaffers had asked quietly, seeking out some scam against the house.

Matty had shaken his head. 'A neighbour from when I was growing up.' That was all; just a ghost from the past. He supposed his mother *was* still alive. He could probably find out by opening the phone book. But he wasn't that interested.

'Place your bets, please, ladies and gentlemen.'

Different houses had different styles. You either did your spiel in English or French. House rules changed, too. Matty's strengths were roulette and blackjack, but really he was happy in charge of any sort of game – most houses liked that he was flexible, it meant there was less chance of him trying some scam. It was the one-note wonders who tried small, stupid diddles. His latest employers seemed fairly laid back. They ran a clean casino which boasted only the very occasional high roller. Most of the punters were business people, well enough heeled but canny with it. You got husbands and wives coming in, proof of a relaxed atmosphere. There were younger punters too – a lot of those were Asians, mainly Chinese. The money they changed, according to the cashier, had a funny feel and smell to it.

'That's because they keep it in their underwear,' the day boss had told her.

The Asians ... whatever they were ... sometimes worked in local restaurants; you could smell the kitchen on their crumpled jackets and shirts. Fierce gamblers, no game was ever played quickly enough for their liking. They'd slap their chips down like they were in a playground betting game. And they talked a lot, almost never in English. The gaffers didn't like that, never could tell what they might be scheming. But their money was good, they seldom caused trouble, and they lost a percentage same as everyone else.

'Daft bastards,' the night manager said. 'Know what they do with a big win? Go bung it on the gee-gees. Where's the sense in that?'

Where indeed? No point giving your money to a bookmaker when the casino would happily take it instead.

It wasn't really on for croupiers to be friends with the clients, but sometimes it happened. And it couldn't very well not happen with Matty and Stevie Scoular, since they'd been in the same year at school. Not that they'd known one another well. Stevie had been the football genius, also more than fair at the hundred and two hundred metres, swimming and basketball. Matty, on the other hand, had skived off games whenever possible, forgetting to bring his kit or getting his mum to write him notes. He was good at a couple of subjects – maths and woodwork – but never sat beside Stevie in class. They even lived at opposite ends of the town.

At playtime and lunchtime, Matty ran a card game – three-card brag mostly, sometimes pontoon – playing for dinner money, pocket money, sweets and comics. A few of the cards were nicked at the corners, but the other players didn't seem to notice and Matty got a reputation as 'lucky'. He'd take bets on horse races too, sometimes passing the bets on to an older boy who wouldn't be turned away by the local bookmaker. Often though, Matty would simply pocket the money and if someone's horse happened to win, he'd say he couldn't get the bets on in time and hand back the stake.

He couldn't tell you exactly when it was that Stevie had started spending less breaktime dribbling past half a dozen despairing pairs of legs and more hanging around the edges of the card school. Thing about three-card brag, it doesn't take long to pick it up and even a moron can have a stab at playing. Soon enough, Stevie was losing his dinner money with the rest of them, and Matty's pockets were about bursting with loose change. Eventually, Stevie had seemed to see sense, drifted away from the game and back to keepie-up and dribbling. But he'd been hooked, no doubt about it. Maybe only for a few weeks, but a lot of those lunchtimes had been spent cadging sweets and apple cores, the better to stave off hunger.

Even then, Matty had thought he'd be seeing Stevie again. It had just taken the best part of a decade, that was all.

When Stevie Scoular walked into the casino, people looked his way. It was the done thing. He was a sharp dresser, young, usually accompanied by women who looked like models. When Stevie had first walked into the Morvena, Matty's heart had sunk. They hadn't seen one another since school and here Stevie was, local boy made good, a hero, picture in the papers and plenty of money in the bank. Here was a schoolboy dream made flesh. And what was Matty? He had stories he could tell but that was about it. So he'd been hoping Stevie wouldn't grace his table, or if he did that he wouldn't recognise him. But Stevie had seen him, seemed to know him straight off and come bouncing up.

'Matty!'

'Hello there, Stevie.'

It was flattering really. Stevie hadn't become big-headed or anything. He took the whole thing – the way his life had gone – as a bit of a joke really. He'd made Matty promise to meet him for a drink when his shift was over. All through their conversation, Matty had been aware of gaffers hovering and when Stevie wandered off to another table one of them muttered in Matty's ear and another croupier took over from him.

He hadn't been in the plush back office that often, just for the initial interview and to discuss a couple of big losses on his table. The casino's owner, Mr Mandelson, was watching a football match on Sky Sports. He was well-built, mid-forties, his face pockmarked from childhood acne. His hair was black, slicked back from the forehead, long at the collar. He always seemed to know what he was about.

'How's the table tonight?' he asked.

'Look, Mr Mandelson, I know we're not supposed to be too friendly with the punters, but Stevie and me were at school together. Haven't clapped eyes on one another since – not till tonight.'

'Easy, Matty, easy.' Mandelson motioned for him to sit down. 'Something to drink?' A smile. 'No alcohol on shift, mind.'

'Ehh ... a Coke maybe.'

'Help yourself.'

There was a fridge in the far corner, stocked with white wine, champagne and soft drinks. A couple of the female croupiers said Mandelson had tried it on with them, plying them with booze. But he didn't seem upset by a refusal: they still had their jobs. There were seven female croupiers all told, and only two had spoken to Matty about it. It made him wonder about the other five.

He took a Coke and sat down again.

'So, you and Stevie Scoular, eh?'

'I haven't seen him in here before.'

'I think he only recently found out about the place. He's been in a few times, dropped some hefty bets.' Mandelson was staring at him. 'You and Stevie, eh?'

'Look, if you're worried, just take me off whatever table he's playing.'

'Nothing like that, Matty.' Mandelson's face broke into a grin. 'It's nice to have a friend, eh? Nice to meet up again after all these years. Don't you worry about anything. Stevie's the King of Edinburgh. As long as he keeps scoring goals, we're all his subjects.' He paused. 'Nice to know someone who knows the King, almost makes me feel like royalty myself. On you go now, Matty.'

Matty got up, leaving the Coke unopened.

'And don't you go upsetting that young man. We don't want to put him off his game, do we?'

IV

It had taken a couple of days to get the tape from Gaitanos. At first, they thought they'd wiped it, and then they'd sent the wrong day's recording. But at last Rebus had the right tape and had watched it at home half a dozen times before deciding he could use someone who knew what he was doing ... and a video machine that would freeze-frame without the screen looking like a technical problem.

Now he'd seen all there was to see. He'd watched a young man cease to exist. Of course, Hendry was right, a lot of people disappeared every year. Sometimes they turned up again – dead or alive – and sometimes they didn't. What did it have to do with Rebus, beyond the promise to a family that he'd make sure the Fife police hadn't missed something? Maybe the pull wasn't Damon Mee, but Bowhill itself; and maybe even then, the Bowhill of his past rather than the town as it stood today.

He was working the Damon Mee case in his free time, which, since he was on day shift at St Leonard's, meant the evenings. He'd checked again with the bank – no money had been withdrawn from any machines since the twenty-second – and with Damon's building society. No money had been withdrawn from that account either. Even this wasn't unknown in the case of a runaway; sometimes they wanted to shed their whole history, which meant ditching their identity and everything that went with it. Rebus had passed a description of Matty to hostels and drop-in centres in Edinburgh, and faxed the same description to similar centres in Glasgow, Newcastle, Aberdeen and London. He'd also faxed details to the National Missing Persons Bureau in London. He checked with a colleague who knew about 'MisPers' that he'd done about all he could.

'Not far off it,' she confirmed. 'It's like looking for a needle in a haystack without knowing which field to start with.'

'How big a problem is it?'

She puffed out her cheeks. 'Last figures I saw were for the whole of Britain. I think there are around 25,000 a year. Those are the *reported* MisPers. You can add a few thousand for the ones nobody notices. There's a nice distinction actually: if nobody knows you're missing, are you really missing?'

Afterwards, Rebus telephoned Janis Mee and told her she might think about running up some flyers and putting them up in positions of prominence in nearby towns, maybe even handing them out to Saturday shoppers or evening drinkers in Kirkcaldy. A photo of Damon, a brief physical description, and what he was wearing the night he left. She said she'd already thought of doing so, but that it made his disappearance seem so final. Then she broke down and cried and John Rebus, thirty-odd miles away, asked if she wanted him to 'drop by'.

'I'll be all right,' she said.

'Sure?'

'Well ...'

Rebus reasoned that he was going to go to Fife anyway. He had to drop the tape back to Gaitanos, and wanted to see the club when it was lively. He'd take the photos of Damon with him and show them around. He'd ask about the candyfloss blonde. The technician who had worked with the videotape had transferred a still to his computer and managed to boost the quality. Rebus had some hard copies in his pocket. Maybe other people who'd been queuing at the bar would remember something.

Maybe.

His first stop, however, was the cemetery. He didn't have any flowers to put on his parents' grave, but he crouched beside it, fingers touching the grass. The inscription was simple, just names and dates really, and underneath, 'Not Dead, But at Rest in the Arms of the Lord'. He wasn't sure whose idea that had been, not his certainly. The headstone's carved lettering was inlaid with gold, but it had already faded from his mother's name. He touched the surface of the marble, expecting it to be cold, but finding a residual warmth there. A blackbird nearby was trying to worry food from the ground. Rebus wished it luck.

By the time he reached Janis's, Brian was home from work. Rebus told them what he'd done so far, after which Brian nodded, apologised, and said he had a Burns Club meeting. The two men shook hands. When the door closed, Janis and Rebus exchanged a look and then a smile.

'I see that bruise finally faded,' she said.

Rebus rubbed his right cheek. 'It was a hell of a punch.'

'Funny how strong you can get when you're angry.'

'Sorry.'

She laughed. 'Bit late to apologise.'

'It was just ...'

'It was everything,' she said. 'Summer holidays coming up, all of us leaving school, you going off to join the army. The last school dance before all of that. That's what it was.' She paused. 'Do you know what happened to Mitch?' She watched Rebus shake his head. 'Last I heard,' she said, 'he was living somewhere down south. The two of you used to be so close.'

'Yes.'

She laughed again. 'Johnny, it was a long time ago, don't look so solemn.' She paused. 'I've sometimes wondered ... ach, not for years, but just now and then I used to wonder what would have happened ...'

'If you hadn't punched me?'

She nodded. 'If we'd stayed together. Well, you can't turn the clock back, eh?'

'Would the world be any better if we could?'

She stared at the window, not really seeing it. 'Damon would still be here,' she said quietly. A tear escaped her eye, and she fussed for a handkerchief in her pocket. Rebus got up and made towards her. Then the front door opened, and he retreated.

'My mum,' Janis smiled. 'She usually pops in around this time. It's like a railway station around here, hard to find any privacy.'

Then Mrs Playfair walked into the living-room.

'Hello, Inspector, thought that was your car. Is there any news?'

'I'm afraid not,' Rebus said. Janis got to her feet and hugged her mother, the crying starting afresh.

'There there, pet,' Mrs Playfair said quietly. 'There there.'

Rebus walked past the two of them without saying a word.

*

It was still early when he reached Gaitanos. He had a word with one of the bouncers, who was keeping warm in the lobby until things started getting busy, and the man lumbered off to fetch Charles Mackenzie, *aka* Charmer. It seemed strange to Rebus: here he was, standing in the very foyer he'd stared at for so long on the video monitor. The camera was high up in one corner with nothing to show whether it was working. Rebus gave it a wave anyway. If he disappeared tonight, it could be his farewell to the world.

'Inspector Rebus.' They'd spoken on the phone. The man who came forward to shake Rebus's hand stood about five feet four and was as thin as a cocktail glass. Rebus placed him in his mid-fifties. He wore a powder-blue suit and an open-necked white shirt with suntan and gold jewellery beneath. His hair was silver and thinning, but as well-cut as the suit. 'Come through to the office.'

Rebus followed Mackenzie down a carpeted corridor to a gloss-black door with a sign on it saying 'Private'. There was no door handle. Mackenzie unlocked the door and motioned for Rebus to go in.

'After you, sir,' Rebus said. You never knew what could be waiting behind a locked door.

What greeted Rebus this time was an office which seemed to double as a broom-cupboard. Mops and a vacuum cleaner rested against one wall. A bank of screens spread across three filing cabinets showed what was happening inside and outside the club. Unlike the video Rebus had watched, these screens each showed a certain location.

'Are these recording?' Rebus asked. Mackenzie shook his head.

'We've got a roaming monitor, and that's the only recording we get. But this way, if we spot trouble anywhere, we can watch it unfold.'

'Like that knifing in the alley?'

'Messed up my Mercedes.'

'So I heard. Is that when you called the police? When your car stopped being a bystander?'

Mackenzie laughed and wagged a finger, but didn't answer. Rebus couldn't see where he'd earned his nickname. The guy had all the charm of sandpaper.

'I brought back your video.' Rebus placed it on the desk.

'All right to record over it now?'

'I suppose so.' Rebus handed over the computer-enhanced photograph. 'The missing person is slightly right of centre, second row.'

'Is that his doll?'

'Do you know her?'

'Wish I did.'

'You haven't seen her before.'

'She doesn't look the sort I'd forget.'

Rebus took back the picture. 'Mind if I show this around?'

'The place is practically empty.'

'I thought I might stick around.'

Mackenzie frowned and studied the backs of his hands. 'Well, you know, it's not that I don't want to help or anything ...'

'But?'

'Well, it's hardly conducive to a party atmosphere, is it? That's our slogan – "The best party of your life, every night!" – and I don't think a police officer mooching around asking questions is going to add to the ambience.'

'I quite understand, Mr Mackenzie. I was being thoughtless.' Mackenzie lifted his hands, palms towards Rebus: no problem, the hands were saying.

'And you're quite right,' Rebus continued. 'In fact, I'd be a lot quicker if I had some assistance – say, a dozen uniforms. That way, I wouldn't be "mooching around" for nearly so long. In fact, let's make it a couple of dozen. We'll be in and out, quick as a virgin's first poke. Mind if I use your phone?'

'Whoah, wait a minute. Look, all I was saying was ... Look, how much do you want?'

'Sorry, sir?'

Mackenzie reached into a desk drawer, lifted out a brick of twenties, pulled about five notes free. 'Will this do it?'

Rebus sat back. 'Am I to understand you're trying to offer me a cash incentive to leave the premises?'

'Whatever. Just slope off, eh?'

Rebus stood up. 'To me, Mr Mackenzie, that's an open invitation to stay.'

So he stayed.

The looks he got from staff made him feel like a football fan trapped on the opposition's turf. The way they all shook their heads as soon as he held up the photo, he knew word had gone around. He had a little more luck with the punters. A couple of lads had seen the woman before.

'Last week, was it?' one asked the other. 'Maybe the week before.'

'Not long ago anyway,' the other agreed. 'Cracker, isn't she?'

'Has she been in since?'

'Haven't seen her. Just that one night. Didn't quite get the nerve up to ask for a dance.'

'Was she with anyone?'

'No idea.'

They didn't recognise Damon Mee though. They said they never paid much attention to blokes.

'We're not that way inclined, sweetie.'

The place was still only half full, but the bass was loud enough to make Rebus feel queasy. He managed to order an orange juice at the bar and just sat there, looking at the photo. The woman interested him. The way her head was angled, the way her mouth was open, she could have been saying something to Damon. A minute later, he was gone. Had she said she'd meet him somewhere? Had something happened at that meeting? He'd shown the photo to Damon's mates from that night. They remembered seeing her, but swore Damon hadn't introduced himself.

'She seemed sort of cold,' one of them had said. 'You know, like she wanted to be left alone.'

Rebus had studied the video again, watched her progress towards the bar, showing no apparent interest in Damon's leaving. But then she'd turned and started pushing her way back through the throng, no drink to show for her long wait.

At midnight exactly, she'd left the nightclub. The final shot was of her turning left along the pavement, watched by a few people who were waiting to get in. And now Charles Mackenzie wanted to give Rebus money.

At three quid for an orange juice, maybe he should have taken it.

If the place had been heaving, maybe he wouldn't have noticed them.

He was finishing his second drink and trying not to feel like a leper in a children's ward when he recognised one of the doormen. There was another man with him, tall and fat and pale. His idea of clubbing was probably the connection of baseball bat to skull. The bouncer was pointing Rebus out to him. Here we go, Rebus thought. They've brought in the professionals. The fat man said something to the bouncer, and they both retreated to the foyer, leaving Rebus with an empty glass and only one good reason to order another drink.

Get it over with, he thought, sliding from his bar stool and walking around the dance floor. There was always the fire exit, but it led on to the alley and, if they were waiting for him there, the only witness would be Mackenzie's Mercedes. He wanted things kept as public as possible. The street outside would be busy, no shortage of onlookers and possible good Samaritans. Or at the very least, someone to call for an ambulance.

He paused in the foyer and saw that the bouncer was back at his post on the front door. No sign of the fat man. Then he glanced along the corridor towards Mackenzie's office, and saw the fat man planted outside the door. He had his arms folded in front of him and wasn't going anywhere.

Rebus walked outside. The air had seldom tasted so good. He tried to calm himself with a few deep breaths. There was a car parked at the kerbside, a gold-coloured Rolls-Royce, with nobody in the driver's seat. Rebus wasn't the only one admiring the car, but he was probably alone in memorising its number plate.

He moved his own car to where he could see the Roller, then sat tight. Half an hour later, the fat man emerged, looking to left and right. He walked to the car, unlocked it and held open the back door. Only now did another figure emerge from the club. Rebus caught a swishing full-length black coat, sleek hair and chiselled face. The man slipped into the car, and the fat man closed the door and squeezed in behind the steering wheel.

Like them or not, you had to admire Rollers. They carried tonnage.

V

Back in Edinburgh he parked his car and sat in it, smoking his eleventh cigarette of the day. He sometimes played this game with himself – I'll have one more tonight, and deduct one from tomorrow's allowance. Or he would argue that any cigarette after midnight came from the next day's stash. He'd lost count along the way, but reckoned by now he should be going whole days without a ciggie to balance the books. Well, when it came down to it, ten cigarettes a day or twelve, thirteen, fourteen – what difference did it make?

The street he was parked on was quiet. Residential for the most part with big houses. There was a basement bar on the corner, but it did mostly lunchtime business from the offices on neighbouring streets. By ten, the place was usually locked up. Taxis rippled past him and the occasional drunk, hands in pockets, would weave slowly homewards. A few of the taxis stopped just in front of him and disgorged their fares, who would then climb half a dozen steps and push open the door to the Morvena Casino. Rebus had never been inside the place. He placed the occasional bet on the horses, but that was about it. Gave up doing the football pools. He bought a National Lottery ticket when opportunity arose, but often didn't get round to checking the numbers. He had half a dozen tickets lying around, any one of which could be his fortune. He quite liked the notion that he might have won a million and not know it; preferred it, in fact, to the idea of actually having the million in his bank account. What would he do with a million pounds? Same as he'd do with fifty thou – self-destruct.

Only faster.

Janis had asked him about Mitch – Roy Mitchell, Rebus's best friend at school. The more time Rebus had spent with her, the less he'd seen of Mitch. They'd been going to join the army together, hoping they might get the same regiment. Until Mitch lost his eye. That had been the end of that. The army hadn't wanted him any more. Rebus had headed off, sent Mitch a couple of letters, but by the time his first leave came, Mitch had already left Bowhill. Rebus had stopped writing after that ...

When the Morvena's door opened next, it was so eight or nine young people could leave. The shift changeover. Three of them turned one way, the rest another. Rebus watched the group of three. At the first set of lights, two kept going and one crossed the road and took a left. Rebus started his engine and followed. When the lights turned green, he signalled left and sounded his horn, then pulled the car over and wound down his window.

'Mr Rebus,' the young man said.

'Hello, Matty. Let's go for a drive.'

Officers from other cities, people Rebus met from time to time, would remark on how cushy he had it in Edinburgh. Such a beautiful place, and prosperous. So little crime. They thought to be dangerous a city had to look dangerous. London, Manchester, Liverpool – these places were dangerous in their eyes. Not Edinburgh, not this sleepy walking-tour with its monuments and museums. Tourism aside, the lifeblood of the city was its commerce, and Edinburgh's commerce – banking, insurance and the like – was discreet. The city hid its secrets well, and its vices too. Potentially troublesome elements had been moved to the sprawling council estates which ringed the capital, and any crimes committed behind the thick stone walls of the city centre's tenements and houses were often muffled by those same walls. Which was why every good detective needed his contacts.

Rebus took them on a circuit – Canonmills to Ferry Road, back up to Comely Bank and through Stockbridge into the New Town again. And they talked.

'I know we had a sort of gentleman's agreement, Matty,' Rebus said.

'But I'm about to find out you're no gentleman?'

Rebus smiled. 'You're ahead of me.'

'I wondered how long it would take.' Matty paused, stared through the windscreen. 'You know I'll say no.'

'Will you?'

'I said at the start, no ratting on anyone I work with or work for. Just the punters.'

'Not even many of them. It's not like I've been milking you, Matty. I'll bet you've dozens of stories you haven't told me.'

'I work tables, Mr Rebus. People don't place a bet and then start yacking about some job they've pulled or some scam they're running.'

'No, but they meet friends. They have a drink, get mellow. It's a relaxing place, so I've heard. And maybe then they talk.'

'I've not held anything back.'

'Matty, Matty.' Rebus shook his head. 'It's funny, I was just thinking tonight about that night we met. Do you remember?'

How could he forget? A couple of drinks after work, a car borrowed from a friend who was away on holiday. Matty hadn't been back long. Driving through the town was great, especially with a buzz on. Streets glistening after the rain. Late night, mostly taxis for company. He just drove and drove and, as the streets grew quieter, he pushed the accelerator a bit further, caught a string of green lights, then saw one turning red. He didn't know how good the tyres were, imagined braking hard and skidding in the wet. Fuck it, he put his foot down.

Just missed the cyclist. The guy was coming through on green and had to twist his front wheel hard to avoid contact, then teetered and fell on to the road. Matty's foot eased off the accelerator, thought about the brake, then went back on the accelerator again.

That's when he saw the cop car. And thought: I can't afford this.

They'd breathalysed him and taken him to St Leonard's, where he'd sat around and let the machinery chew him up. Would it come to a trial? Would there be a report in the papers? How could he keep his name from getting around? He'd worked himself up into a right state by the time Detective Inspector John Rebus had sat down across from him.

'I can't afford this,' Matty had blurted out.

'Sorry?'

He'd swallowed and tried to find a story. 'I work in a casino. Any black mark against me, they'll boot me out. Look, if it's a question of compensation or anything ... like, I'll buy him a new bike.'

Rebus had picked up a sheet of paper. 'Drunk driving ... in a borrowed car you weren't insured to drive ... running a red light ... leaving the scene of an accident ...' Rebus had shaken his head, read the sheet through one more time and then put it down, and looked up at Matty. 'What casino did you say you work for?'

Later, he'd given Matty two business cards, both with his phone number. 'The first one's for you to tear up in disgust,' he'd said. 'The other one's to keep. Have we got a deal?'

'Look, Mr Rebus,' Matty said now, as the car stopped for lights on Raeburn Place, 'I'm doing the best I can.'

'I want to know what's happening behind the scenes at the Morvena.'

'I wouldn't know.'

'Anything at all, it doesn't matter how small it seems. Any stories, gossip, anything overheard. Ever seen the owner entertain people in his office? Maybe open the place for a private party? Names, faces, anything at all. Put your mind to it, Matty. Just put your mind to it.'

'They'd skin me alive.'

'Who's they?'

Matty swallowed. 'Mr Mandelson.'

'He's the owner, right?'

'Right.'

'On paper at least. What I need to know is who might be pulling his strings.'

'I can't see anyone pulling his strings.'

'You'd be surprised. Hard bastard, is he?'

'I'd say so.'

'Given you grief?' Matty shook his head. 'Do you see much of him?'

'Not much,' Matty said. Not, he might have added, until recently at any rate.

Rebus dropped him at the foot of Broughton Street, headed back up to Leith Walk and along York Place on to Queen Street. He passed the casino again and slowed, a frown on his face. At the next set of lights, he did a U-turn so he could be sure. Yes, it was the Roller from Gaitanos, no doubt about it.

Parked outside the Morvena.

VI

'Mind if I join you?'

Rebus was eating breakfast in the canteen and wishing there was more caffeine in the coffee, or more coffee in the coffee come to that. He nodded to the empty chair and Siobhan sat down.

'Heavy night?' she said.

'Believe it or not, I was on orange juice.'

She bit into her muffin, washing it down with milk. 'Harry tells me you had him working a tape.'

'Harry?'

'Our video wizard. He said it was a missing person. News to me.'

'It's not official. The son of an old schoolfriend of mine.'

'Standing at a bar one minute and gone the next?' Rebus looked at her and she smiled. 'Harry's a great one for gossip.'

'I'm working on it in my own time.'

'Need any help?'

'Handy with a crystal ball, are you?' But Rebus dug into his pocket and brought out the still from the video. 'That's Damon there,' he said, pointing.

'Who's that with him?'

'I wish I knew. She's not with him. I don't know who she is.'

'You've asked around?'

'I was at the club last night. A few punters remembered her.'

'Male punters?' She waited till Rebus nodded. 'You were asking the wrong sex. Any man would have given her the once-over, but only superficially. A woman, on the other hand, would have seen her as competition. Have you never noticed women in nightclubs? They've got eyes like lasers. Plus, what if she visited the loo?'

Rebus was interested now. 'What if she did?'

'*That's* where women talk. Maybe someone spoke to her, maybe she said something back. Ears would have been listening.' Siobhan stared at the photo. 'Funny, it's almost like she's got an aura.'

'How do you mean?'

'Like she's shining.'

'Interior light.'

'Exactly.'

'No, that's what your friend Harry said. It's the interior lighting that gives that effect.'

'Maybe he didn't know what he was saying.'

'I'm not sure I know what *you're* saying.'

'Some religions believe in spirit guides. They're supposed to lead you to the next world.'

'You mean this one's not the end?'

She smiled. 'Depends on your religion.'

'Well, it's plenty enough for me.' He looked at the photo again. 'I was sort of joking, you know, about her being a spirit guide.'

'I know.'

He met with Helen Cousins that night. They spoke over a drink in the Auld Hoose. Rebus hadn't been in the place in quarter of a century, and there'd been changes. They'd installed a pool table.

'You weren't invited along that night?' Rebus asked her.

She shook her head. She was twenty, three years younger than Damon. The fingers of her right hand played with her engagement ring, rolling it, sliding it off over the knuckle and then back down again. She had short, lifeless brown hair, dark, tired eyes, and acne around her mouth.

'I was out with the girls. See, that was how we played it. One night a week the boys would go off on their own, and we'd go somewhere else. Then another night we'd all get together.'

'Do you know anyone who was at Gaitanos that night? Apart from Damon and his pals?'

She chewed her bottom lip while considering. The ring came off her finger and bounced once before hitting the floor. She stooped to pick it up.

'It's always doing that.'

'You better watch it, you're going to lose it.'

She pushed the ring back on. 'Yes,' she said, 'Corinne and Jacky were there.'

'Corinne and Jacky?' She nodded. 'Where can I find them?'

A phone call brought them to the Auld Hoose. Rebus got in the round: Bacardi and Coke for Corinne, Bacardi and blackcurrant for Jacky, a second vodka and orange for Helen and another bottle of no-alcohol lager for himself. He eyed the optics behind the bar. His mean little drink was costing more than a whisky. Something was telling him to indulge in a Teacher's. Maybe it's my spirit guide, he thought, dismissing the idea.

Corinne had long black hair crimped with curling tongs. Her pal Jacky was tiny, with dyed platinum hair. When he got back to the table, they were in a huddle, exchanging gossip. Rebus took out the photograph again.

'Look,' Corinne said, 'there's Damon.' So they all had a good look. Then Rebus touched his finger to the strapless aura.

'Remember her?'

Helen prickled visibly. 'Who is she?'

'Yeah, she was there,' Jacky said.

'Was she with anyone?'

'Didn't see her up dancing.'

'Isn't that why people go to clubs?'

'Well, it's one reason.' All three broke into a giggle.

'You didn't speak to her?'

'No.'

'Not even in the toilets?'

'I saw her in there,' Corinne said. 'She was doing her eyes.'

'Did she say anything?'

'She seemed sort of ... stuck-up.'

'Snobby,' Jacky agreed.

Rebus tried to think of another question and couldn't. They ignored him for a while as they exchanged news. It was like they hadn't seen each other in a year. At one point, Helen got up to use the toilet. Rebus expected the other two to accompany her, but only Corinne did so. He sat with Jacky for a moment, then, for want of anything else to say, asked her what she thought of Damon. He meant about Damon disappearing, but she didn't take it that way.

'Ach, he's all right.'

'Just all right?'

'Well, you know, Damon's heart's in the right place, but he's a bit thick. A bit slow, I mean.'

'Really?' The impression Rebus had received from Damon's family had been of a genius-in-waiting. He suddenly realised just how superficial his own portrait of Damon was. Siobhan's words should have been a warning – so far he'd heard only one side of Damon. 'Helen likes him though?'

'I suppose so.'

'They're engaged.'

'It happens, doesn't it? I've got friends who got engaged just so they could throw a party.' She looked around the bar, then leaned towards him. 'They used to have some mega arguments.'

'What about?'

'Jealousy, I suppose. She'd see him notice someone, or he'd say she'd been letting some guy chat her up. Just the usual.' She turned the photo around so it faced her. 'She looks like a dream, doesn't she? I remember she was dressed to kill. Made the rest of us spit.'

'But you'd never seen her before?'

Jacky shook her head. No, no one seemed to have seen her before, nobody knew who she was. Unlikely then that she was local.

'Were there any buses in that night?'

'That doesn't happen at Gaitanos,' she told him. 'It's not "in" enough any more. There's a new place in Dunfermline. That gets the busloads.' Jacky tapped the photo. 'You think she's gone off with Damon?'

Rebus looked at her and saw behind the eyeliner to a sharp intelligence. 'It's possible,' he said quietly.

'I don't think so,' she said. 'She wouldn't be interested, and he wouldn't have had the guts.'

On his way home, Rebus dropped into St Leonard's. The amount he was paying in bridge tolls, he was thinking about a season ticket. There was a fax on his desk. He'd been promised it in the afternoon, but there'd been a delay. It identified the owner of the Rolls-Royce as a Mr Richard Mandelson, with an address in Juniper Green. Mr Mandelson had no criminal record outstanding, whether for motoring offences or anything else. Rebus tried to imagine some poor parking warden trying to give the Roller a ticket with the fat man behind the wheel. There were a few more facts about Mr Mandelson, including last known occupation.

Casino manager.

VII

Matty and Stevie Scoular saw one another socially now. Stevie would sometimes phone and invite Matty to some party or dinner, or just for a drink. At the same time as Matty was flattered, he did wonder what Stevie's angle was, had even come out and asked him.

'I mean,' he'd said, 'I'm just a toe-rag from the school playground, and you ... well, you're SuperStevie, you're the king.'

'Aye, if you believe the papers.' Stevie had finished his drink – Perrier, he had a game the next day. 'I don't know, Matty, maybe it's that I miss all that.'

'All what?'

'Schooldays. It was a laugh back then, wasn't it?'

Matty had frowned, not really remembering. 'But the life you've got now, Stevie, man. People would kill for it.'

And Stevie had nodded, looking suddenly sad.

Another time, a couple of kids had asked Stevie for his autograph, then had turned and asked Matty for his, thinking that whoever he was, he had to be somebody. Stevie had laughed at that, said something about it being a lesson in humility. Again, Matty didn't get it. There were times when Stevie seemed to be on a different planet. Maybe it was understandable, the pressure he was under. Stevie seemed to remember a lot more about school than Matty did: teachers' names, the lot. They talked about Gullane, too, what a boring place to grow up. Sometimes they didn't talk much at all. Just took out a couple of dolls: Stevie would always bring one along for Matty. She wouldn't be quite as gorgeous as Stevie's, but that was all right. Matty could understand that. He was soaking it all up, enjoying it while it lasted. He had half an idea that Stevie and him would be best friends for life, and another that Stevie would dump him soon and find some other distraction. He thought Stevie needed him right now much more than *he* needed Stevie. So he soaked up what he could, started filing the stories away for future use, tweaking them here and there ...

Tonight they took in a couple of bars, a bit of a drive in Stevie's Beamer: he preferred BMWs to Porsches, more space for passengers. They ended up at a club, but didn't stay long. Stevie had a game the next day. He was always very conscientious that way: Perrier and early nights. Stevie dropped Matty off outside his flat, sounding the horn as he roared away. Matty hadn't spotted the other car, but he heard a door opening, looked across the road and recognised Malibu straight off. Malibu was Mr Mandelson's driver. He'd eased himself out of the Roller and was holding open the back door while looking over to Matty.

So Matty crossed the street. As he did so, he walked into Malibu's shadow, cast by the sodium street lamp. At that moment, though he didn't know what was about to happen, he realised he was lost.

'Get in, Matty.'

The voice, of course, was Mandelson's. Matty got into the car and Malibu closed the door after him, then kept guard outside. They weren't going anywhere.

'Ever been in a Roller before, Matty?'

'I don't think so.'

'You'd remember if you had. I could have had one years back, but only by buying secondhand. I wanted to wait until I had the cash for a nice new one. That leather smell – you don't get it with any other car.' Mandelson lit a cigar. The windows were closed and the car started filling with sour smoke. 'Know how I came to afford a brand new Roller, Matty?'

'Hard work?' Matty's mouth was dry. Cars, he thought: Rebus's, Stevie's, and now this one. Plus, of course, the one he'd borrowed that night, the one that had brought him to this.

'Don't be stupid. My dad worked thirty years in a shop, six days a week and he still couldn't have made the down-payment. Faith, Matty, that's the key. You have to believe in yourself, and some-times you have to trust other people – strangers some of them, or people you don't like, people it's hard to trust. That's the gamble life's making with you, and if you place your bet, sometimes you get lucky. Except it's not luck – not entirely. See, there are odds, like in every game, and that's where judgement comes in. I like to think I'm a good judge of character.'

Only now did Mandelson turn to look at him. There seemed to Matty to be nothing behind the eyes, nothing at all.

'Yes, sir,' he said, for want of anything better.

'That was Stevie dropped you off, eh?' Matty nodded. 'Now, your man Stevie, he's got something else, something we haven't discussed yet. He's got a gift. He's had to work, of course, but the thing was there to begin with. Don't ask me where it came from or why it should have been given to him in particular – that's one for the philosophers, and I don't claim to be a philosopher. What I am is a businessman ... and a gambler. Only I don't bet on nags or dogs or a turn of the cards, I bet on people. I'm betting on you, Matty.'

'Me?'

Mandelson nodded, barely visible inside the cloud of smoke. 'I want you to talk to Stevie on my behalf. I want you to get him to do me a favour.'

Matty rubbed his forehead with his fingers. He knew what was coming but didn't want to hear it.

'I saw a recent interview,' Mandelson went on, 'where he told the reporter he always gave a hundred and ten per cent. All I want is to knock maybe twenty per cent off for next Saturday's game. You know what I'm saying?'

Next Saturday ... An away tie at Kirkcaldy. Stevie expected to run rings around the Raith Rovers defence.

'He won't do it,' Matty said. 'Come to that, neither will I.'

'No?' Mandelson laughed. A hand landed on Matty's thigh. 'You fucked up in London, son. They knew you'd end up taking a croupier's job somewhere else, it's the only thing you know how to do. So they phoned around, and eventually they phoned *me*. I told them I'd never heard of you. That can change, Matty. Want me to talk to them again?'

'I'd tell them you lied to them the first time.'

Mandelson shrugged. 'I can live with that. But what do you think they'll do to *you*, Matty? They were pretty angry about whatever scheme it was you pulled. I'd say they were furious.'

Matty felt like he was going to heave. He was sweating, his lungs toxic. 'He won't do it,' he said again.

'Be persuasive, Matty. You're his friend. Remind him that his tab's up to three and a half. All he has to do is ease off for one game, and the tab's history. And Matty, I'll know if you've talked to him or not, so no games, eh? Or you might find yourself with no place left to hide.'

VIII

Rebus searched his flat, but came up with only half a dozen snapshots: two of his ex-wife Rhona, posing with Samantha, their daughter, back when Sammy was seven or eight; two further shots of Sammy in her teens; one showing his father as a young man, kissing the woman who would become Rebus's mother; and a final photograph, a family grouping, showing uncles, aunts and cousins whose names Rebus didn't know. There were other photographs, of course – at least, there had been – but not here, not in the flat. He guessed Rhona still kept some, maybe his brother Michael had the others. But they could be anywhere. Rebus hadn't thought of himself as the kind to spend long nights with the family album, using it as a crutch to memory, always with the fear that remembrance would yield to sentiment.

If I died tonight, he thought, what would I bequeath to the world? Looking around, the answer was: nothing. The thought scared him, and worst of all it made him want a drink, and not just one drink but a dozen.

Instead of which, he drove north back into Fife. It had been overcast all day, and the evening was warm. He didn't know what he was doing, knew he had precious little to say to either of Damon's parents, and yet that's where he ended up. He'd had the destination in mind all along.

Brian Mee answered the door, wearing a smart suit and just finishing knotting his tie.

'Sorry, Brian,' Rebus said. 'Are you off out?'

'In ten minutes. Come in anyway. Is it Damon?'

Rebus shook his head and saw the tension in Brian's face turn to relief. Yes, a visit in person wouldn't be good news, would it? Good news had to be given immediately by telephone, not by a knock at the door. Rebus should have realised; he'd been the bearer of bad news often enough in his time.

'Sorry, Brian,' he repeated. They were in the hallway. Janis's voice came from above, asking who it was.

'It's Johnny,' her husband called back. Then to Rebus, 'It's all right to call you that?'

'Of course. It's my name, isn't it?' He could have added: again, after all this time. He looked at Brian, remembering the way they'd sometimes mistreated him at school: not that 'Barney' had seemed to mind, but who could tell for sure? And then that night of the last school dance ... Brian had been there for Mitch. Brian had been there; Rebus had not. He'd been too busy losing Janis, and losing consciousness.

She was coming downstairs now. 'I'll be back in a sec,' Brian said, heading up past her.

'You look terrific,' Rebus told her. The blue dress was well-chosen, her make-up highlighting all the right features of her busy face. She managed a smile.

'No news?'

'Sorry,' he said again. 'Just thought I'd see how you are.'

'Oh, we're pining away.' Another smile, tinged by shame this time. 'It's a dinner–dance, we bought the tickets months back. It's for the Jolly Beggars.'

'Nobody expects you to sit at home every night, Janis.'

'But all the same ...' Her cheeks grew flushed and her eyes sought his. 'We're not going to find him, are we?'

'Not easily. Our best bet's that he'll get in touch.'

'If he can,' she said quietly.

'Come on, Janis.' He put his hands on her shoulders, like they were strangers and about to dance. 'You might hear from him to-morrow, or it might take months.'

'And meantime life goes on, eh?'

'Something like that.'

She smiled again, blinking back tears. 'Why don't you come with us, John?'

Rebus dropped his hands from her shoulders. 'I haven't danced in years.'

'So you'd be rusty.'

'Thanks, Janis, but not tonight.'

'Know something? I bet they play the same records we used to dance to at school.'

It was his turn to smile. Brian was coming back downstairs, patting his hair into place.

'You'd be welcome to join us, Johnny,' he said.

'I've another appointment, Brian. Maybe next time, eh?'

'Let's make that a promise.'

They went out to their cars together. Janis pecked him on the cheek, Brian shook his hand. He watched them drive off then headed to the cemetery.

It was dark, and the gates were locked, so Rebus sat in his car and smoked a cigarette. He thought about his parents and the rest of his family and remembered stories about Bowhill, stories which seemed inextricable from family history: mining tragedies; a girl found drowned in the River Ore; a holiday car crash which had erased an entire family. Then there was Johnny Thomson, Celtic goalkeeper, injured during an 'Old Firm' match. He was in his early twenties when he died, and was buried behind those gates, not far from Rebus's parents. *Not Dead, But at Rest in the Arms of the Lord.*

The Lord had to be a bodybuilder.

From family he turned to friends and tried recalling a dozen names to put to faces he remembered from schooldays. Other friends: people he'd known in the army, the SAS. All the people he'd dealt with during his career in the police. Villains he'd put away, some who'd slipped through his fingers. People he'd interviewed, suspected, questioned, broken the worst kind of news to. Acquaintances from the Oxford Bar and all the other pubs where he'd ever been a regular. Local shopkeepers. Jesus, the list was endless. All these people who'd played a part in his life, in shaping who he was and how he acted, how he felt about things. All of them, out there somewhere and nowhere, gathered together only inside his head. And chief among them tonight, Brian and Janis.

That night of the school dance ... It was true he'd been drunk – elated. He'd felt he could *do* anything, *be* anything. Because he'd come to a decision that day – he wouldn't join the army, he'd stay in Bowhill with Janis, apply for a job at the dockyard. His dad had told him not to be so stupid – 'short-sighted' was the word he'd used. But what did parents know about their children's desires? So he'd drunk some beer and headed off to the dance, his thoughts only of Janis. Tonight he'd tell her. And Mitch, of course. He'd have to tell Mitch, tell him he'd be heading into the army alone. But Mitch wouldn't mind, he'd understand, as best friends had to.

But while Rebus had been outside with Janis, his friend Mitch was being cornered by four teenagers who considered themselves his enemies. This was their last chance for revenge, and they'd gone in hard, kicking and punching. Four against one ... until Barney had waded in, shrugging off blows, and dragged Mitch to safety. But one kick had done the damage, dislodging a retina. Mitch's vision stayed fuzzy in that eye for a few days, then disappeared. And where had Rebus been? Out cold on the concrete by the bike sheds.

And why had he never thanked Barney Mee?

He blinked now and sniffed, wondering if he was coming down with a cold. He'd had this idea when he came back to Bowhill that the place would seem beyond redemption, that he'd be able to tell himself it had lost its sense of community, become just another town for him to pass through. Maybe he'd wanted to put it behind him. Well, it hadn't worked. He got out of the car and looked around. The street was dead. He reached up and hauled himself over the iron railings and walked a circuit of the cemetery for an hour or so, and felt strangely at peace.

IX

'So what's the panic, Matty?'

After a home draw with Rangers, Stevie was ready for a night on the town. One–one, and of course he'd scored his team's only goal. The reporters would be busy filing their copy, saying for the umpteenth time that he was his side's hero, that without him they were a very ordinary team indeed. Rangers had known that: Stevie's marker had been out for blood, sliding studs-first into tackles which Stevie had done his damnedest to avoid. He'd come out of the game with a couple of fresh bruises and grazes, a nick on one knee but, to his manager's all too palpable relief, fit to play again midweek.

'I said what's the panic?'

Matty had worried himself sleepless. He knew he had several options. Speak to Stevie, that was one of them. Another was not to speak to him, but tell Mandelson he had. Then it would be down to whether or not Mandelson believed him. Option three: do a runner; only Mandelson was right about that – he was running out of places to hide. With *two* casino bosses out for his blood, how could he ever pick up another croupier's job?

If he spoke with Stevie, he'd lose a new-found friend. But to stay silent ... well, there was very little percentage in it. So here he was in Stevie's flat, having demanded to see him. In the corner, a TV was replaying a tape of the afternoon's match. There was no commentary, just the sounds of the terraces and the dug-outs.

'No panic,' he said now, playing for time.

Stevie stared at him. 'You all right? Want a drink or something?'

'Maybe a vodka.'

'Anything in it?'

'I'll take it as it comes.'

Stevie poured him a drink. Matty had been here half an hour now, and they still hadn't talked. The telephone had hardly stopped: reporters' questions, family and friends offering congratulations. Stevie had shrugged off the superlatives.

Matty took the drink, swallowed it, wondering if he could still walk away. Then he remembered Malibu, and saw shadows falling.

'Thing is, Stevie,' he said. 'You know my boss at the Morvena, Mr Mandelson?'

'I owe him money, of course I know him.'

'He says we could do something about that.'

'What? My tab?' Stevie was checking himself in the mirror, having changed into his on-the-town clothes. 'I don't get it,' he said.

Well, Stevie, Matty thought, it was nice knowing you, pal. 'All you have to do is ease off next Saturday.'

Stevie frowned and turned from the mirror. 'Away to Raith?' He came and sat down opposite Matty. 'He told you to tell me?' He waited till Matty nodded. 'That bastard. What's in it for him?'

Matty wriggled on the leather sofa. 'I've been thinking about it. Raith are going through a bad patch, but you know yourself that if you're taken out of the equation ...'

'Then they'd be up against not very much. My boss has told everybody to get the ball to me. If they spend the whole game doing that and I don't do anything with it ...'

Matty nodded. 'What I think is, the odds will be on you scoring. Nobody'll be expecting Raith to put one in the net.'

'So Mandelson's cash will be on a goalless draw?'

'And he'll get odds, spread a lot of small bets around ...'

'Bastard,' Stevie said again. 'How did he get you into this, Matty?'

Matty shifted again. 'Something I did in London.'

'Secrets, eh? Hard things to keep.' Stevie got up, went to the mirror again, and just stood there, hands by his sides, staring into it. There was no emotion in his voice when he spoke.

'Tell him he can fuck himself.'

Matty had to choke out the words. 'You sure that's the message?'

'Cheerio, Matty.'

Matty rose shakily to his feet. 'What am I going to do?'

'Cheerio, Matty.'

Stevie was as still as a statue as Matty walked to the door and let himself out.

Mandelson sat at his desk, playing with a Cartier pen he'd taken from a punter that day. The man was overdue on a payment. The pen was by way of a gift.

'So?' he asked Matty.

Matty sat on the chair and licked his lips. There was no offer of a drink today; this was just business. Malibu stood by the door. Matty took a deep breath – the last act of a drowning man.

'It's on,' he said.

Mandelson looked up at him. 'Stevie went for it?'

'Eventually,' Matty said.

'You're sure?'

'As sure as I can be.'

'Well, that better be watertight, or you might find yourself going for a swim with heavy legs. Know what I mean?'

Matty held the dark gaze and nodded.

Mandelson glanced towards Malibu, both of them were smiling. Then he picked up the telephone. 'You know, Matty,' he said, pushing numbers. 'I'm doing you a favour. You're doing *yourself* a favour.' He listened to the receiver. 'Mr Hamilton, please.' Then, to Matty, 'See, what you're doing here is saving your job. I overstretched myself, Matty. I wouldn't like that to get around, but I'm trusting you. If this comes off – and it better – then you've earned that trust.' He tapped the receiver. 'It wasn't all my own money either. But this will keep the Morvena alive and kicking.' He motioned for Matty to leave. Malibu tapped his shoulder as an incentive.

'Topper?' Mandelson was saying as Matty left the room. 'It's locked up. How much are you in for?'

Matty bided his time and waited till his shift was over. He walked out of the smart New Town building like a latterday Lazarus, and found the nearest payphone, then had to fumble through all the rubbish in his pockets, stuff that must have meant something once upon a time, until he found the card.

The card with a phone number on it.

*

The following Saturday, Stevie Scoular scored his team's only goal in their 1–0 win over Raith Rovers, and Mandelson sat alone in his office, his eyes on the Teletext results.

His hand rested on the telephone receiver. He was expecting a call from Topper Hamilton. He couldn't seem to stop blinking, like there was a grain of sand in either eye. He buzzed the reception desk, told them to tell Malibu he was wanted. Mandelson didn't know how much time he had, but he knew he would make it count. A word with Stevie Scoular, see if Matty really *had* put the proposition to him. Then Matty himself ... Matty was a definite, no matter what. Matty was about to be put out of the game.

The knock at the door had to be Malibu. Mandelson barked for him to come in. But when the door opened, two strangers sauntered in like they owned the place. Mandelson sat back in his chair, hands on the desk. He was almost relieved when they introduced themselves as police officers.

'I'm Detective Inspector Rebus,' the younger one said, 'this is Chief Superintendent Watson.'

'And you've come about the Benevolent Fund, right?'

Rebus sat down unasked, his eyes drifting to the TV screen and the results posted there. 'Looks like you just lost a packet. I'm sorry to hear it. Did Topper take a beating, too?'

Mandelson made fists of his hands. 'That wee bastard!'

Rebus was shaking his head. 'Matty did his best, only there was something he didn't know. Seems you didn't know either. Topper will be doubly disappointed.'

'What?'

Farmer Watson, still standing, provided the answer. 'Ever heard of Big Ger Cafferty?'

Mandelson nodded. 'He's been in Barlinnie a while.'

'Used to be the biggest gangster on the east coast. Probably still is. And he's a fan of Stevie's, gets videotapes of all his games. He almost sends him love letters.'

Mandelson frowned. 'So?'

'So Stevie's covered,' Rebus said. 'Try fucking with him, you're asking Big Ger to bend over. Your little proposal has probably already made it back to Cafferty.'

Mandelson swallowed and felt suddenly dry-mouthed.

'There was no way Stevie was going to throw that game,' Rebus said quietly.

'Matty ...' Mandelson choked the sentence off.

'Told you it was fixed? He was scared turdless, what else was he going to say? But Matty's *mine*. You don't touch him.'

'Not that you'd get the chance,' the Farmer added. 'Not with Topper *and* Cafferty after your blood. Malibu will be a big help, the way he took off five minutes ago in the Roller.' Watson walked up to the desk, looming over Mandelson like a mountain. 'You've got two choices, son. You can talk, or you can run.'

'You've got nothing.'

'I saw you that night at Gaitanos,' Rebus said. 'If you're going to lay out big bets, where better than Fife? Optimistic Raith fans might have bet on a goalless draw. You got Charmer Mackenzie to place the bets locally, spreading them around. That way it looked less suspicious.'

Which was why Mackenzie had wanted Rebus out of there, whatever the price: he'd been about to do some business ...

'Besides,' Rebus continued, 'when it comes down to it, what choice do you have?'

'You either talk to us ...' the Farmer said.

'Or you disappear. People do it all the time.'

And it never stops, Rebus could have added. Because it's part of the dance – shifting partners, people you shared the floor with, it all changed. And it only ended when you disappeared from the hall.

And sometimes ... sometimes, it didn't even end there.

'All right,' Mandelson said at last, the way they'd known he would, all colour gone from his face, his voice hollow, 'what do you want to know?'

'Let's start with Topper Hamilton,' the Farmer said, sounding like a kid unwrapping his birthday present.

It was Wednesday morning when Rebus got the phone call from a Mr Bain. It took him a moment to place the name: Damon's bank manager.

'Yes, Mr Bain, what can I do for you?'

'Damon Mee, Inspector. You wanted us to keep an eye on any transactions.'

Rebus leaned forward in his chair. 'That's right.'

'There've been two withdrawals from cash machines, both in central London.'

Rebus grabbed a pen. 'Where exactly?'

'Tottenham Court Road was three days ago: fifty pounds. Next day, it was Finsbury Park, same amount.'

Fifty pounds a day: enough to live on, enough to pay for a cheap bed and breakfast and two extra meals.

'How much is left in the account, Mr Bain?'

'A little under six hundred pounds.'

Enough for twelve days. There were several ways it could go. Damon could get himself a job. Or when the money ran out he could try begging. Or he could return home. Rebus thanked Bain and telephoned Janis.

'John,' she said, 'we got a postcard this morning.'

A postcard saying Damon was in London and doing fine. A postcard of apology for any fright he'd given them. A postcard saying he needed some time to 'get my head straight'. A postcard which ended 'See you soon.' The picture on the front was of a pair of breasts painted with Union Jacks.

'Brian thinks we should go down there,' Janis said. 'Try to find him.'

Rebus thought of how many B&Bs there'd be in Finsbury Park. 'You might just chase him away,' he warned. 'He's doing OK, Janis.'

'But why did he do it, John? I mean, is it something *we* did?'

New questions and fears had replaced the old ones. Rebus didn't know what to tell her. He wasn't family and couldn't begin to answer her question. Didn't *want* to begin to answer it.

'He's doing OK,' he repeated. 'Just give him some time.'

She was crying now, softly. He imagined her with head bowed, hair falling over the telephone receiver.

'We did everything, John. You can't know how much we've given him. We always put ourselves second, never a minute's thought for anything but him ...'

'Janis ...' he began.

She took a deep breath. 'Will you come and see me, John?'

Rebus looked around the office, eyes resting eventually on his own desk and the paperwork stacked there.

'I can't, Janis. I'd like to, but I just can't. See, it's not as if I ...'

He didn't know how he was going to finish the sentence, but it didn't matter. She'd put her phone down. He sat back in his chair and remembered dancing with her, how brittle her body had seemed. But that had been half a lifetime ago. They'd made so many choices since. It was time to let the past go. Siobhan Clarke was at her desk. She was looking at him. Then she mimed the drinking of a cup of coffee, and he nodded and got to his feet.

Did a little dance as he shuffled towards her.

No Sanity Clause

It was all Edgar Allan Poe's fault. Either that or the Scottish Parliament. Joey Briggs was spending most of his days in the run-up to Christmas sheltering from Edinburgh's biting December winds. He'd been walking up George IV Bridge one day and had watched a down-and-out slouching into the Central Library. Joey had hesitated. He wasn't a down-and-out, not yet anyway. Maybe he would be soon, if Scully Aitchison MSP got his way, but for now Joey had a bedsit and a trickle of state cash. Thing was, nothing made you miss money more than Christmas. The shop windows displayed their magnetic pull. There were queues at the cash machines. Kids tugged on their parents' sleeves, ready with something new to add to the present list. Boyfriends were out buying gold, while families piled the food trolley high.

And then there was Joey, nine weeks out of prison and nobody to call his friend. He knew there was nothing waiting for him back in his home town. His wife had taken the children and tiptoed out of his life. Joey's sister had written to him in prison with the news. So, eleven months on, Joey had walked through the gates of Saughton Jail and taken the first bus into the city centre, purchased an evening paper and started the hunt for somewhere to live.

The bedsit was fine. It was one of four in a tenement basement just off South Clerk Street, sharing a kitchen and bathroom. The other men worked, didn't say much. Joey's room had a gas fire with a coin-meter beside it, too expensive to keep it going all day. He'd tried sitting in the kitchen with the stove lit, until the landlord had caught him. Then he'd tried steeping in the bath, topping up the hot. But the water always seemed to run cold after half a tub.

'You could try getting a job,' the landlord had said.

Not so easy with a prison record. Most of the jobs were for security and nightwatch. Joey didn't think he'd get very far there.

Following the tramp into the library was one of his better ideas. The uniform behind the desk gave him a look, but didn't say anything. Joey wandered the stacks, picked out a book and sat himself down. And that was that. He became a regular, the staff acknowledged him with a nod and sometimes even a smile. He kept himself presentable, didn't fall asleep the way some of the old guys did. He read for much of the day, alternating between fiction, biographies and textbooks. He read up on local history, plumbing and Winston Churchill, Nigel Tranter's novels and National Trust gardens. He knew the library would close over Christmas, didn't know what he'd do without it. He never borrowed books, because he was afraid they'd have him on some blacklist: convicted housebreaker and petty thief, not to be trusted with loan material.

He dreamt of spending Christmas in one of the town's posh hotels, looking out across Princes Street Gardens to the Castle. He'd order room service and watch TV. He'd take as many baths as he liked. They'd clean his clothes for him and return them to the room. He dreamt of the presents he'd buy himself: a big radio with a CD player, some new shirts and pairs of shoes; and books. Plenty of books.

The dream became almost real to him, so that he found himself nodding off in the library, coming to as his head hit the page he'd been reading. Then he'd have to concentrate, only to find himself drifting into a warm sleep again.

Until he met Edgar Allan Poe.

It was a book of poems and short stories, among them 'The Purloined Letter'. Joey loved that, thought it was really clever the way you could hide something by putting it right in front of people. Something that didn't look out of place, people would just ignore it. There'd been a guy in Saughton, doing time for fraud. He'd told Joey: 'Three things: a suit, a haircut and an expensive watch. If you've got those, it's amazing what you can get away with.' He'd meant that clients had trusted him, because they'd seen something they were comfortable with, something they expected to see. What they hadn't seen was what was right in front of their noses, to wit: a shark, someone who was going to take a big bite out of their savings.

As Joey's eyes flitted back over Poe's story, he started to get an idea. He started to get what he thought was a very good idea indeed. Problem was, he needed what the fraudster had called 'the start-up', meaning some cash. He happened to look across to where one of the old tramps was slumped on a chair, the newspaper in front of him unopened. Joey looked around: nobody was watching. The place was dead: who had time to go to the library when Christmas was around the corner? Joey walked over to the old guy, slipped a hand into his coat pocket. Felt coins and notes, bunched his fingers around them. He glanced down at the newspaper. There was a story about Scully Aitchison's campaign. Aitchison was the MSP who wanted all offenders put on a central register, open to public inspection. He said law-abiding folk had the right to know if their neighbour was a thief or a murderer – as if stealing was the same as killing somebody! There was a small photo of Aitchison, too, beaming that self-satisfied smile, his glasses glinting. If Aitchison got his way, Joey would never get out of the rut.

Not unless his plan paid off.

John Rebus saw his girlfriend kissing Santa Claus. There was a German Market in Princes Street Gardens. That was where Rebus was to meet Jean. He hadn't expected to find her in a clinch with a man dressed in a red suit, black boots and snowy-white beard. Santa broke away and moved off, just as Rebus was approaching. German folk songs were blaring out. There was a startled look on Jean's face.

'What was that all about?' he asked.

'I don't know.' She was watching the retreating figure. 'I think maybe he's just had too much festive spirit. He came up and grabbed me.' Rebus made to follow, but Jean stopped him. 'Come on, John. Season of goodwill and all that.'

'It's assault, Jean.'

She laughed, regaining her composure. 'You're going to take St Nicholas down the station and put him in the cells?' She rubbed his arm. 'Let's forget it, eh? The fun starts in ten minutes.'

Rebus wasn't too sure that the evening was going to be 'fun'. He spent every day bogged down in crimes and tragedies. He wasn't sure that a 'mystery dinner' was going to offer much relief. It had been Jean's idea. There was a hotel just across the road. You all went in for dinner, were handed envelopes telling you which character you'd be playing. A body was discovered, and then you all turned detective.

'It'll be fun,' Jean insisted, leading him out of the gardens. She had three shopping bags with her. He wondered if any of them were for him. She'd asked for a list of his Christmas wants, but so far all he'd come up with were a couple of CDs by String Driven Thing.

As they entered the hotel, they saw that the mystery evening was being held on the mezzanine floor. Most of the guests had already gathered and were enjoying glasses of cava. Rebus asked in vain for a beer.

'Cava's included in the price,' the waitress told him. A man dressed in Victorian costume was checking names and handing out carrier bags.

'Inside,' he told Jean and Rebus, 'you'll find instructions, a secret clue that only you know, your name, and an item of clothing.'

'Oh,' Jean said, 'I'm Little Nell.' She fixed a bonnet to her head. 'Who are you, John?'

'Mr Bumble.' Rebus produced his name-tag and a yellow woollen scarf, which Jean insisted on tying around his neck.

'It's a Dickensian theme, specially for Christmas,' the host revealed, before moving off to confront his other victims. Everyone looked a bit embarrassed, but most were trying for enthusiasm. Rebus didn't doubt that a couple of glasses of wine over dinner would loosen a few Edinburgh stays. There were a couple of faces he recognised. One was a journalist, her arm around her boyfriend's waist. The other was a man who appeared to be with his wife. He had one of those looks to him, the kind that says you should know him. She was blonde and petite and about a decade younger than her husband.

'Isn't that an MSP?' Jean whispered.

'His name's Scully Aitchison,' Rebus told her.

Jean was reading her information sheet. 'The victim tonight is a certain Ebenezer Scrooge,' she said.

'And did you kill him?'

She thumped his arm. Rebus smiled, but his eyes were on the MSP. Aitchison's face was bright red. Rebus guessed he'd been drinking since lunchtime. His voice boomed across the floor, broadcasting the news that he and Catriona had booked a room for the night, so they wouldn't have to drive back to the constituency.

They were all mingling on the mezzanine landing. The room where they'd dine was just off to the right, its doors still closed. Guests were starting to ask each other which characters they were playing. As one elderly lady – Miss Havisham on her name-tag – came over to ask Jean about Little Nell, Rebus saw a red-suited man appear at the top of the stairs. Santa carried what looked like a half-empty sack. He started making his way across the floor, but was stopped by Aitchison.

'*J'accuse!*' the MSP bawled. 'You killed Scrooge because of his inhumanity to his fellow man!' Aitchison's wife came to the rescue, dragging her husband away, but Santa's eyes seemed to follow them. As he made to pass Rebus, Rebus fixed him with a stare.

'Jean,' he asked, 'is he the same one ...?'

She only caught the back of Santa's head. 'They all look alike to me,' she said.

Santa was on his way to the next flight of stairs. Rebus watched him leave, then turned back to the other guests, all of them now tricked out in odd items of clothing. No wonder Santa had looked like he'd stumbled into an asylum. Rebus was reminded of a Marx Brothers line, Groucho trying to get Chico's name on a contract, telling him to sign the sanity clause.

But, as Chico said, everyone knew there was no such thing as Sanity Clause.

Joey jimmied open his third room of the night. The Santa suit had worked a treat. Okay, so it was hot and uncomfortable, and the beard was itching his neck, but it worked! He'd breezed through reception and up the stairs. So far, as he'd worked the corridors all he'd had were a few jokey comments. No one from security asking him who he was. No guests becoming suspicious. He fitted right in, and he was right under their noses.

God bless Edgar Allan Poe.

The woman in the fancy dress shop had even thrown in a sack, saying he'd be wanting to fill it. How true: in the first bedroom, he'd dumped out the crumpled sheets of old newspaper and started filling the sack – clothes, jewellery, the contents of the mini-bar. Same with the second room: a tap on the door to make sure no one was home, then the chisel into the lock and hey presto. Thing was, there wasn't much in the rooms. A notice in the wardrobe told clients to lock all valuables in the hotel safe at reception. Still, he had a few nice things: camera, credit cards, bracelet and necklace. Sweat was running into his eyes, but he couldn't afford to shed his disguise. He was starting to have crazy thoughts: take a good long soak; ring down for room service; find a room that hadn't been taken and settle in for the duration. In the third room, he sat on the bed, feeling dizzy. There was a briefcase open beside him, just lots of paperwork. His stomach growled, and he remembered that his last meal had been a Mars Bar supper the previous day. He broke open a jar of salted peanuts, switched the TV on while he ate. As he put the empty jar down, he happened to glance at the contents of the briefcase. 'Parliamentary briefing ... Law and Justice Sub-Committee ...' He saw a list of names on the top sheet. One of them was coloured with a yellow marker.

Scully Aitchison.

The drunk man downstairs ... That was where Joey knew him from! He leapt to his feet, trying to think. He could stay here and give the MSP a good hiding. He could ... He picked up the room-service menu, called down and ordered smoked salmon, a steak, a bottle each of best red wine and malt whisky. Then heard himself saying those sweetest words: 'Put it on my room, will you?'

Then he settled back to wait. Flipped through the paperwork again. An envelope slipped out. Card inside, and a letter inside the card.

Dear Scully, it began. *I hope it isn't all my fault, this idea of yours for a register of offenders* ...

'I haven't a clue,' said Rebus.

Nor did he. Dinner was over, the actor playing Scrooge was flat out on the mezzanine floor, and Rebus was as far away from solving the crime as ever. Thankfully, a bar had been opened up, and he spent most of his time perched on a high stool, pretending to read the background notes while taking sips of beer. Jean had hooked up with Miss Havisham, while Aitchison's wife was slumped in one of the armchairs, drawing on a cigarette. The MSP himself was playing ringmaster, and had twice confronted Rebus, calling for him to reveal himself as the villain.

'Innocent, m'lud,' was all Rebus had said.

'We think it's Magwitch,' Jean said, suddenly breathless by Rebus's side, her bonnet at a jaunty angle. 'He and Scrooge knew one another in prison.'

'I didn't know Scrooge served time,' Rebus said.

'That's because you're not asking questions.'

'I don't need to; I've got you to tell me. That's what makes a good detective.'

He watched her march away. Four of the diners had encircled the poor man playing Magwitch. Rebus had harboured suspicions, too ... but now he was thinking of jail time, and how it affected those serving it. It gave them a certain look, a look they brought back into the world on their release. The same look he'd seen in Santa's eyes.

And here was Santa now, coming back down the stairs, his sack slung over one shoulder. Crossing the mezzanine floor as if seeking someone out. Then finding them: Scully Aitchison. Rebus rose from his stool and wandered over.

'Have you been good this year?' Santa was asking Aitchison.

'No worse than anyone else,' the MSP smirked.

'Sure about that?' Santa's eyes narrowed.

'I wouldn't lie to Father Christmas.'

'What about this plan of yours, the offender register?'

Aitchison blinked a couple of times. 'What about it?'

Santa held a piece of paper aloft, his voice rising. 'Your own nephew's serving time for fraud. Managed to keep that quiet, haven't you?'

Aitchison stared at the letter. 'Where in hell ...? How ...?'

The journalist stepped forward. 'Mind if I take a look?'

Santa handed over the letter, then pulled off his hat and beard. Started heading for the stairs down. Rebus blocked his way.

'Time to hand out the presents,' he said quietly. Joey looked at him and understood immediately, slid the sack from his shoulder. Rebus took it. 'Now on you go.'

'You're not arresting me?'

'Who'd feed Dancer and Prancer?' Rebus asked.

His stomach full of steak and wine, a bottle of malt in the capacious pocket of his costume, Joey smiled his way back towards the outside world.

Tell Me Who to Kill

Saturday afternoon, John Rebus left the Oxford Bar after the football results and decided that he would try walking home. The day was clear, the sun just above the horizon, casting ridiculously long shadows. It would grow chilly later, maybe even frost overnight, but for now it was crisp and bright – perfect for a walk. He had limited himself to three pints of IPA, a corned beef roll and a pie. He carried a large bag with him – shopping for clothes his excuse for a trip into the city centre, a trip he'd known would end at the Ox. Edinburgh on a Saturday meant day-trippers, weekend warriors, but they tended to stick to Princes Street. George Street had been quieter, Rebus's tally finally comprising two shirts and a pair of trousers. He'd gone up a waist size in the previous six months, which was reason enough to cut back on the beer, and for opting to walk home.

He knew his only real problem would be The Mound. The steep slope connected Princes Street to the Lawnmarket, having been created from the digging out of the New Town's foundations. It posed a serious climb. He'd known a fellow cop – a uniformed sergeant – who'd cycled up The Mound every day on his way to work, right up until the day he'd retired. For Rebus, it had often proved problematical, even on foot. But he would give it a go, and if he failed, well, there was a bus stop he could beat a retreat to, or taxis he could flag down. Plenty of cabs about at this time of day, ferrying spent shoppers home to the suburbs, or bringing revellers into town at the start of another raucous evening. Rebus avoided the city centre on Saturday nights, unless duty called. The place took on an aggressive edge, violence spilling on to the streets from the clubs on Lothian Road and the bars in the Grassmarket. Better to stay at home with a carry-out and pretend your world wasn't changing for the worse.

A crowd had gathered at the foot of Castle Street. Rebus noticed that an ambulance, blue lights blinking, was parked in front of a stationary double-decker bus. Walking into the middle of the scene, Rebus overheard muttered exchanges of information.

'Just walked out ...'

'... right into its path ...'

'Wasn't looking ...'

'Not the first time I've seen ...'

'These bus drivers think they own the roads, though ...'

The victim was being carried into the ambulance. It didn't look good for him. One glance at the paramedics' faces told Rebus as much. There was blood on the roadway. The bus driver was sitting in the open doorway of his vehicle, head in his hands. There were still passengers on the bus, reluctant to admit that they would need to transfer, loaded down with shopping and unable to think beyond their own concerns. Two uniformed officers were taking statements, the witnesses only too happy to fulfil their roles in the drama. One of the uniforms looked at Rebus and gave a nod of recognition.

'Afternoon, DI Rebus.'

Rebus just nodded back. There was nothing for him to do here, no part he could usefully play. He made to cross the road, but noticed something lying there, untouched by the slow crawl of curious traffic. He stooped and picked it up. It was a mobile phone. The injured pedestrian must have been holding it, maybe even using it. Which would explain why he hadn't been paying attention. Rebus turned his head towards the ambulance, but it was already moving away, not bothering to add a siren to its flashing lights: another bad sign, a sign that the medics in the back either didn't want or didn't feel the need of it. There was either severe trauma, or else the victim was already dead. Rebus glanced down at the phone. It was unscathed, looked almost brand new. Strange to think such a thing could survive where its owner might not. He pressed it to his ear, but the line wasn't open. Then he looked at it again, noting that there were words on its display screen. Looked like a text message.

TELL ME WHO TO KILL.

Rebus blinked, narrowed his eyes. He was back on the pavement.

TELL ME WHO TO KILL.

He scrolled up and down the message, but there wasn't any more to it than those five words. Along the top ran the number of the caller; looked like another mobile phone. Plus time of call: 16.31. Rebus walked over to the uniformed officer, the one who'd spoken to him.

'Larry,' he said, 'where was the ambulance headed?'

'Western General,' the uniform said. 'Guy's skull's split open, be lucky to make it.'

'Do we know what happened?'

'He walked straight out into the road, by the look of it. Can't really blame the driver ...'

Rebus nodded slowly and walked over to the bus driver, crouched down in front of him. The man was in his fifties, head shaved but with a thick silvery beard. His hands shook as he lifted them away from his eyes.

'Couldn't stop in time,' he explained, voice quavering. 'He was right there ...' His eyes widened as he played the scene again. Shaking his head slowly. 'No way I could've stopped ...'

'He wasn't looking where he was going,' Rebus said softly.

'That's right.'

'Busy on his phone, maybe?'

The driver nodded. 'Staring at it, aye ... Some people haven't got the sense they were born with. Not that I'm ... I mean, I don't want to speak ill or anything.'

'Wasn't your fault,' Rebus agreed, patting the man's shoulder.

'Colleague of mine, same thing happened not six months past. Hasn't worked since.' He held up his hands to examine them.

'He was too busy looking at his phone,' Rebus said. 'That's the whole story. Reading a message, maybe?'

'Maybe,' the driver agreed. 'Doing something anyway, something more important than looking where he was bloody well going ...'

'Not your fault,' Rebus repeated, rising to his feet. He walked to the back of the bus, stepped out into the road, and waved down the first taxi he saw.

Rebus sat in the waiting area of the Western General Hospital. When a dazed-looking woman was led in by a nurse and asked if she wanted a cup of tea, he got to his feet. The woman sat herself down, twisting the handles of her shoulder bag in both hands, as if wringing the life out of them. She'd shaken her head, mumbled something to the nurse, who was now retreating.

'As soon as we know anything,' were the nurse's parting words.

Rebus sat down next to the woman. She was in her early thirties, blonde hair cut in a pageboy style. What make-up she had applied to her eyes that morning had been smudged by tears, giving her a haunted look. Rebus cleared his throat, but she still seemed unaware of his close presence.

'Excuse me,' he said. 'I'm Detective Inspector Rebus.' He opened his ID; she looked at it, then stared down at the floor again. 'Has your husband just been in an accident?'

'He's in surgery,' she said.

Rebus had been told as much at the front desk. 'I'm sorry,' he said. 'I don't even know his name.'

'Carl,' she said. 'Carl Guthrie.'

'And you're his wife?'

She nodded. 'Frances.'

'Must be quite a shock, Frances.'

'Yes.'

'Sure you don't want that tea?'

She shook her head, looked up into his face for the first time. 'Do you know what happened?'

'Seems he was starting to cross Princes Street and didn't see the bus coming.'

She squeezed shut her eyes, tears glinting in her lashes. 'How is that possible?'

Rebus shrugged. 'Maybe he had something on his mind,' he said quietly. 'When was the last time you spoke to him?'

'Breakfast this morning. I was planning to go shopping.'

'What about Carl?'

'I thought he was working. He's a physiotherapist, sports injuries mostly. He has his own practice in Corstorphine. He gets some work from the Bupa hospital at Murrayfield.'

'And a few rugby players too, I'd guess.'

Frances Guthrie was dabbing at her eyes with a tissue. 'How could he get hit by a bus?' She looked up at the ceiling, blinking back tears.

'Do you know what he was doing in town?'

She shook her head.

'This was found lying in the road,' Rebus said, holding up the phone. 'There's a text message displayed. You see what it says?'

She peered at the screen, then frowned. 'What does it mean?'

'I don't know,' Rebus admitted. 'Do you recognise the caller's number?'

She shook her head, then reached out a hand and took the phone from Rebus, turning it in her palm. 'This isn't Carl's.'

'What?'

'This isn't Carl's phone. Someone else must have dropped it.'

Rebus stared at her. 'You're sure?'

She handed the phone back, nodding. 'Carl's is a silver flip-top sort of thing.'

Rebus studied the one-piece black Samsung. 'Then whose is it?' he asked, more to himself than to her. She answered anyway.

'What does it matter?'

'It matters.'

'But it's a joke, surely.' She nodded at the screen. 'Someone's idea of a practical joke.'

'Maybe,' Rebus said.

The same nurse was walking towards them, accompanied by a surgeon in green scrubs. Neither of them had to say anything. Frances Guthrie was already keening as the surgeon began his speech.

'I'm so sorry, Mrs Guthrie ... we did everything we could.'

Frances Guthrie leaned in towards Rebus, her face against his shoulder. He put his arm around her, feeling it was the least he could do.

Carl Guthrie's effects had been placed in a large cardboard box. His blood-soaked clothes were protected by a clear polythene bag. Rebus lifted them out. The pockets had been emptied. Watch, wallet, small change, keys. And a silver flip-top mobile phone. Rebus checked its screen. The battery was low, and there were no messages. He told the nurse that he wanted to take it with him. She shrugged and made him sign a docket to that effect. He flipped through the wallet, finding banknotes, credit cards, and a few of Carl Guthrie's business cards, giving an address in Corstorphine, plus office and mobile numbers. Rebus took out his own phone and punched in the latter. The silver telephone trilled as it rang. He cancelled the call, then nodded to the nurse to let her know he was finished. The docket was placed in the box, along with the polythene bag. Rebus pocketed all three phones.

The police lab at Howdenhall wasn't officially open at weekends, but Rebus knew that someone was usually there, trying to clear a backlog, or just because they'd nothing better to do. He got lucky. Ray Duff was one of the better technicians. He sighed when Rebus walked in.

'I'm up to my eyes,' he complained, turning away to walk back down the corridor.

'Yes, but you'll like this,' Rebus said, holding out the mobile. Duff stopped and turned, stared at it, then ran his fingers through an unruly mop of hair.

'I really am up to my eyes ...'

Rebus shrugged, arm still stretched out. Duff sighed again and took the phone from him.

'Discovered at the scene of an accident,' Rebus explained. Duff had found a pair of spectacles in one of the pockets of his white lab coat and was putting them on. 'My guess is that the victim had just received the text message, and was transfixed by it.'

'And walked out in front of a car?'

'Bus actually. Thing is, the phone doesn't belong to the victim.' Rebus produced the silver flip-top. 'This is his.'

'So whose is this?' Duff peered at Rebus over the top of his glasses. 'That's what you're wondering.' He was walking again, heading for his own cubicle, Rebus following.

'Right.'

'And also who the caller was.'

'Right again.'

'We could just phone them.'

'We could.' They'd reached Duff's workstation. Each surface was a clutter of wires, machines and paperwork. Duff rubbed his bottom lip against his teeth. 'Battery's getting low,' he said, as the phone uttered a brief chirrup.

'Any chance you can recharge it?'

'I can if you like, but we don't really need it.'

'We don't?'

The technician shook his head. 'The important stuff's on the chip.' He tapped the back of the phone. 'We can transfer it ...' He grew thoughtful again. 'Of course, that would mean accessing the code number, so we're probably better off hanging on to it as it is.' He reached down into a cupboard and produced half a dozen mains adaptors. 'One of these should do the trick.'

Soon the phone was plugged in and charging. Meantime, Duff had worked his magic on the keypad, producing the phone number. Rebus punched it into his own phone, and the black mobile trilled.

'Bingo,' Duff said with a smile. 'Now all we do is call the service provider ...' He left the cubicle and returned a couple of minutes later with a sheet of numbers. 'I hope you didn't touch anything,' he said, waving a hand around his domain.

'I wouldn't dare.' Rebus leaned against a workbench as Duff made the call, identified himself, and reeled off the mobile phone number. He placed his hand over the mouthpiece.

'It'll take a minute,' he told Rebus.

'Can anyone get this sort of information?' Rebus asked. 'I mean, what's to stop Joe Public calling up and saying they're a cop?'

Duff smiled. 'Caller recognition. They've got a screen their end. IDs the caller number as Lothian and Borders Police Forensic Branch.'

'Clever,' Rebus admitted. Duff just shrugged. 'So how about the other number? The one belonging to whoever sent that message.'

Duff held up a finger, indicating that he was listening to the person at the other end of the line. He looked around him, finding a scrap of paper. Rebus provided the pen, and he started writing.

'That's great, thanks,' he said finally. Then: 'Mind if I try you with something else? It's a mobile number ...' He proceeded to reel off the number on the message screen, then, with his hand again muffling the mouthpiece, he handed the scrap of paper to Rebus.

'Name and address of the phone's owner.'

Rebus looked. The owner's name was William Smith, the address a street in the New Town. 'What about the text sender?' he asked.

'She's checking.' Duff removed his hand from the mouthpiece, listening intently. Then he started shaking his head. 'Not one of yours, eh? Don't suppose you can tell from the number just who is the service provider?' He listened again. 'Well, thanks anyway.' He put down the receiver.

'No luck?' Rebus guessed. Duff shrugged.

'Just means we have to do it the hard way' He picked up the sheet of telephone numbers. 'Maybe nine or ten calls at the most.'

'Can I leave it with you, Ray?'

Duff stretched his arms wide. 'What else was I going to be doing at half past six of a Saturday?'

Rebus smiled. 'You and me both, Ray.'

'What do you reckon we're dealing with? A hit man?'

'I don't know.'

'But if it is ... then Mr Smith would be his employer, making him someone you might not want to mess about with.'

'I'm touched by your concern, Ray.'

Duff smiled. 'Can I take it you're headed over to that address anyway?'

'Not too many gangsters living in the New Town, Ray.'

'Not that we know of,' Duff corrected him. 'Maybe after this, we'll know better ...'

The streets were full of maroon-scarved Hearts fans, celebrating a rare victory. Bouncers had appeared at the doors of most of the city-centre watering holes: an unnecessary expense in daylight, but indispensable by night. There were queues outside the fast-food restaurants, diners tossing their empty cartons on to the pavement. Rebus kept eyes front as he drove. He was in his own car now, having stopped home long enough for a mug of coffee and two paracetamol. He guessed that a breath test might just about catch him, but felt OK to drive nonetheless.

The New Town, when he reached it, was quiet. Few bars here, and the area was a dead end of sorts, unlikely to be soiled by the city-centre drinkers. As usual, parking was a problem. Rebus did one circuit, then left his car on a double yellow line, right next to a set of traffic lights. Doubled back on himself until he reached the tenement. There was an entryphone, a list of residents printed beside it. But no mention of anyone called Smith. He ran a finger down the column of names. One space was blank. It belonged to Flat 3. He pushed the button and waited. Nothing. Pushed it again, then started pressing various bells, waiting for someone to respond. Eventually the tiny loudspeaker grille crackled into life.

'Hello?'

'I'm a police officer. Any chance of speaking to you for a minute?'

'What's the problem?'

'No problem. It's just a couple of questions concerning one of your neighbours ...'

There was silence, then a buzzing sound as the door unlocked itself. Rebus pushed it open and stepped into the stairwell. A door on the ground floor was open, a man standing there. Rebus had his ID open. The man was in his twenties, with cropped hair and Buddy Holly spectacles. A dishtowel was draped over one shoulder.

'Do you know anyone called William Smith?' Rebus asked.

'Smith?' The man narrowed his eyes, shook his head slowly.

'I think he lives here.'

'What does he look like?'

'I'm not sure.'

The man stared at him, then shrugged. 'People come and go. Sometimes they move on before you get to know their names.'

'But you've been here a while?'

'Almost a year. Some of the neighbours I know to say hello to, but I don't always know their names.' He smiled apologetically. Yes, that was Edinburgh for you: people kept themselves to themselves, didn't want anyone getting too close. A mixture of shyness and mistrust.

'Flat 3 doesn't seem to have a name beside it,' Rebus said, nodding back towards the main door.

The man shrugged again.

'I'm just going to go up and take a look,' Rebus said.

'Be my guest. You know where I am if you need me.'

'Thanks for your help.' Rebus started climbing the stairs. The shared space was well maintained, the steps clean, smelling of disinfectant mixed with something else, a perfume of sorts. There were ornate tiles on the walls. Flats 2 and 3 were on the first floor.

There was a buzzer to the right of Flat 3, a typed label attached to it. Rebus bent down for a closer look. The words had faded but were readable: *LT Lettings*. While he was down there, he decided he might as well take a look through the letter box. All he could see was an unlit hallway. He straightened up and pressed the bell for Flat 2. Nobody was home. He took out one of his business cards and a ballpoint pen, scribbled the words *Please call me* on the back, and pushed the card through the door of Flat 2. He thought for a moment, but decided against doing the same for Flat 3.

Back downstairs again, he knocked on the door of the young man with the dishtowel. Smiled as it was opened.

'Sorry to bother you again, but do you think I could take a look at your phone book ...?'

Rebus went back to his car and made the call from there. An answering machine played its message, informing him that LT Lettings was closed until ten o'clock on Monday morning, but that any tenant with an emergency should call another number. He jotted it down and called. The person who answered sounded like he was stuck in traffic. Rebus explained who he was.

'I need to ask about one of your properties.'

'I'm not the person you need to speak to. I just mend things.'

'What sorts of things?'

'Some tenants aren't too fussy, know what I mean? Place isn't their own, they treat it like shit.'

'Until you turn up and sort them out?'

The man laughed. 'I put things right, if that's what you mean.'

'And that's all you do?'

'Look, I'm not sure where you're going with this ... It's my boss you need to speak to. Lennox Tripp.'

'OK, give me his number.'

'Office is shut till Monday.'

'His home number, I meant.'

'I'm not sure he'd thank me for that.'

'This is a police matter. And it's urgent.'

Rebus waited for the man to speak, then jotted down the eventual reply. 'And your name is ...?'

'Frank Empson.'

Rebus jotted this down too. 'Well, thanks for your help, Mr Empson. You heading for a night out?'

'Absolutely, Inspector. Just as soon as I've fixed the heating in one flat and unblocked the toilet in another.'

Rebus thought for a moment. 'Ever had cause to visit Gilby Street?'

'In the New Town?'

'Number 26, Flat 3.'

'I moved some furniture in, but that was months back.'

'Never seen the person who lives there?'

'Nope.'

'Well, thanks again ...' Rebus cut the call, punched in the number for Lennox Tripp. The phone was answered on the fifth ring. Rebus asked if he was speaking to Lennox Tripp.

'Yes.' The voice hesitant.

'My name's John Rebus. I'm a detective inspector with Lothian and Borders Police.'

'What seems to be the problem?' The voice more confident now, an educated drawl.

'One of your tenants, Mr Tripp, 26 Gilby Street.'

'Yes?'

'I need to know what you know ...'

Rebus was smoking his second cigarette when Tripp arrived, driving a silver Mercedes. He double-parked outside number 26, using a remote to set the locks and alarm.

'Won't be long, will we?' he asked, turning to glance at his car as he shook Rebus's hand. Rebus flicked the half-smoked cigarette on to the road.

'Wouldn't imagine so,' he said.

Lennox Tripp was about Rebus's age – mid fifties – but had worn considerably better. His face was tanned, hair groomed, clothes casual but classy. He stepped up to the door and let them in with a key. As they climbed the stairs, he said his piece.

'Only reason William Smith sticks in my head is that he pays cash for the let. A wad of twenties in an envelope, delivered to the office on time each month. This is his seventh month.'

'You must have met him, though.'

Tripp nodded. 'Showed him the place myself.'

'Can you describe him?'

Tripp shrugged. 'White, tallish ... nothing much to distinguish him.'

'Hair?'

Tripp smiled. 'Almost certainly.' Then, as if to apologise for the glib comeback: 'It was six months ago, Inspector.'

'And that's the only time you've seen him?'

Tripp nodded. 'I'd have called him a model tenant ...'

'A model tenant who pays cash? You don't find that a mite suspicious?'

Tripp shrugged again. 'I try not to pry, Inspector.' They were at the door to Flat 3. Tripp unlocked it and motioned for Rebus to precede him inside.

'Was it rented furnished?' Rebus asked, walking into the living room.

'Yes.' Tripp took a look around. 'Doesn't look like he's added much.'

'Not even a TV,' Rebus commented, walking into the kitchen. He opened the fridge. There was a bottle of white wine inside, open and with the cork pushed back into its neck. Nothing else: no butter, milk ... nothing. Two tumblers drying on the draining board the only signs that anyone had been here in recent memory.

There was just the one bedroom. The bedclothes were mostly on the floor. Tripp bent to pick them up, draping them over the mattress. Rebus opened the wardrobe, exposing a dark blue suit hanging there. Nothing in any of the pockets. In one drawer: underpants, socks, a single black T-shirt. The other drawers were empty.

'Looks like he's moved on,' Tripp commented.

'Or has something against possessions,' Rebus added. He looked around. 'No phone?'

Tripp shook his head. 'There's a wall socket. If a tenant wants to sign up with BT or whoever, they're welcome to.'

'Too much trouble for Mr Smith, apparently.'

'Well, a lot of people use mobiles these days, don't they?'

'They do indeed, Mr Tripp.' Rebus rubbed a thumb and forefinger over his temples. 'I'm assuming Smith provided you with some references?'

'I'd assume he did.'

'You don't remember?'

'Not offhand.'

'Would you have any records?'

'Yes, but it's by no means certain ...'

Rebus stared at the man. 'You'd rent one of your flats to someone who couldn't prove who they were?'

Tripp raised an eyebrow by way of apology.

'Cash upfront, I'm guessing,' Rebus hissed.

'Cash does have its merits.'

'I hope your tax returns are in good order.'

Tripp was brought up short. 'Is that some kind of threat, Inspector?'

Rebus feigned a look that was between surprise and disappointment. 'Why would I do a thing like that, Mr Tripp?'

'I wasn't meaning to suggest ...'

'I would hope not. But I'll tell you what.' Rebus laid a hand on the man's shoulder. 'We'll call it quits once we've been to your office and checked those files ...'

There was precious little in the file relating to Flat 3, 26 Gilby Street – just a signed copy of the lease agreement. No references of any kind. Smith had put his occupation down as 'market analyst' and his date of birth as 13 January 1970.

'Did you ask him what a market analyst does?'

Tripp nodded. 'I think he said he worked for one of the insurance companies, something to do with making sure their portfolios didn't lose money.'

'You don't recall which company?'

Tripp said he didn't.

In the end, Rebus managed a grudging 'thank you', headed out to his car, and drove home. Ray Duff hadn't called, which meant he hadn't made any progress, and Rebus doubted he would be working Sunday. He poured himself a whisky, stuck John Martyn on the hi-fi, and slumped into his chair. A couple of tracks passed without him really hearing them. He slid his hand into his pocket and came out with both phones, the silver and the black. For the first time, he checked the silver flip-top, finding messages from Frances Guthrie to her husband. There was an address book, probably listing clients and friends. He laid this phone aside and concentrated on the black one. There was nothing in its memory: no phone numbers stored, no messages. Just that one text: *TELL ME WHO TO KILL*. And the number of the caller.

Rebus got up and poured himself another drink, then took a deep breath and pushed the buttons, calling the sender of the text message. The ringing tone sounded tremulous. He was still holding his breath, but after twenty rings he gave up. No one was about to answer. He decided to send a text instead, but couldn't think what words to use.

Hello, are you a hired killer?

Who do you think I want you to kill?

Please hand yourself in to your nearest police station ...

He smiled to himself, decided it could wait. Only half past nine, the night stretching ahead of him. He surfed all five TV channels, went into the kitchen to make some coffee, and found that he'd run out of milk. Decided on a walk to the corner shop. There was a video store almost next door to it. Maybe he'd rent a film, something to take his mind off the message. Decided, he grabbed his keys, slipped his jacket back on.

The grocer was about to close, but he knew Rebus's face and asked him to be quick. Rebus settled for a packet of sausages, a box of eggs and a carton of milk. Then added a four-pack of lager. Settled up with the grocer and carried his purchases to the video store. He was inside before he remembered that he'd forgotten to bring his membership card; thought the assistant would probably let him rent something anyway. After all, if William Smith could rent a flat in the New Town, surely Rebus could rent a three-quid video.

He was even prepared to pay cash.

But as he stared at the rack of new releases, he found himself blinking and shaking his head. Then he reached out a hand and lifted down the empty video box. He approached the desk with it.

'When did this come out?' he asked.

'Last week.' The assistant was in his teens, but a good judge of Hollywood's gold dust and dross. His eyes had gone heavy-lidded, letting Rebus know this film was the latter. 'Rich guy's having an affair, hires an assassin. Only the assassin falls for the wife and tops the mistress instead. Rich guy takes the fall, breaks out of jail with revenge in mind.'

'So I don't need to watch it now?'

The assistant shrugged. 'That's all in the first fifteen minutes. I'm not telling you anything they don't give away on the back of the box.'

Rebus turned the box over and saw that this was largely true. 'I should never have doubted you,' he said.

'It got terrible reviews, which is why they end up quoting from an obscure radio station on the front.'

Rebus nodded, turning the box over in his hands. Then he held it out towards the assistant. 'I'll take it.'

'Don't say I didn't warn you.' The assistant turned and found a copy of the film in a plain box. 'Got your card?'

'Left it in the flat.'

'Surname's Rebus, right? Address in Arden Street.' Rebus nodded. 'Then I suppose it's OK, this one time.'

'Thanks.'

The assistant shrugged. 'It's not like I'm doing you a favour, letting you walk out with that film.'

'Even so ... you have to admit, it's got a pretty good title.'

'Maybe.' The assistant studied the box for *Tell Me Who to Kill*, but seemed far from convinced.

Rebus had finished all four cans of lager by the time the closing credits rolled. He reckoned he must have dozed off for a few minutes in the middle, but didn't think this had affected his viewing pleasure. There were a couple of big names in the main roles, but they too tended towards drowsiness. It was as if cast, crew and writers had all needed a decent night's sleep.

Rebus rewound the tape, ejected it, and held it in his hand. So it was a film title. That was all the text message had meant. Maybe someone had been choosing a film for Saturday night. Maybe Carl Guthrie had found the phone lying on the pavement. William Smith had dropped it, and Guthrie had found it. Then someone, maybe Smith's girlfriend, had texted the title of the film they'd be watching later on, and Guthrie had opened the message, hoping to find some clue to the identity of the phone's owner.

And he'd walked out under a bus.

TELL ME WHO TO KILL.

Which meant Rebus had wasted half a day. Half a day that could have been better spent ... well, spent differently, anyway. And the film had been preposterous: the assistant's summary had only just scratched the surface. Starting off with a surfeit of twists, there'd been nowhere for the film to go but layer on more twists, deceits, mixed identities, and conspiracies. Rebus could not have been more insulted if the guy had woken up at the end and it had all been a dream.

He went into the kitchen to make some coffee. The place still held the aroma of the fry-up he'd amassed before sitting down to watch the video. Over the sound of the boiling kettle, he heard his phone ringing. Went back through to the living room and picked it up.

'Got a name for you, sorry it took so long.'

'Ray? Is that you?' Rebus checked his watch: not far short of midnight. 'Tell me you're not still at work.'

'Called a halt hours ago, but I just got a text message from my friend who was doing some cross-checking for me.'

'He works odder hours than even we do.'

'He's an insomniac, works a lot from home.'

'So I shouldn't ask where he got this information?'

'You can ask, but I couldn't possibly tell you.'

'And what is it I'm getting?'

'The text message came from a phone registered to Alexis Ojiwa. I've got an address in Haddington.'

'Might as well give it to me.' Rebus picked up a pen, but something in his voice had alerted Ray Duff.

'Do I get the feeling you no longer need any of this?'

'Maybe not, Ray.' Rebus explained about the film.

'Well, I can't say I've ever heard of it.'

'It was news to me too,' Rebus didn't mind admitting.

'But for the record, I do know Alexis Ojiwa.'

'You do?'

'I take it you don't follow football.'

'I watch the results.'

'Then you'll know that Hearts put four past Aberdeen this afternoon.'

'Four–one, final score.'

'And two of them were scored by Alexis Ojiwa ...'

Rebus's mobile woke him an hour earlier than he'd have liked. He blinked at the sunshine streaming through his uncurtained windows and grabbed at the phone, dropping it once before getting it to his ear.

'Yes?' he rasped.

'I'm sorry, is this too early? I thought maybe it was urgent.'

'Who is this?'

'Am I speaking to DI Rebus?'

'Yes.'

'My name's Richard Hawkins. You put your card through my door.'

'Did I?'

Rebus heard a soft chuckle. 'Maybe I should call back later ...'

'No, wait a sec. You live at Gilby Street?'

'Flat 2, yes.'

'Right, right.' Rebus sat up, ran his free hand through his hair. 'Thanks for getting back to me.'

'Not at all.'

'It was about your neighbour, actually.'

'Will Smith?'

'What?'

Another chuckle. 'When he introduced himself, we had a laugh about that coincidence. Really it was down to me. He called himself "William", and it just clicked: Will Smith, same as the actor.'

'Right.' Rebus was trying to gather himself. 'So you've met Mr Smith, talked to him?'

'Just a couple of times. Passing on the stairs ... He's never around much.'

'Not much sign of his flat being lived in, either.'

'I wouldn't know, never been inside. Must have something going for him, though.'

'Why do you say that?'

'Absolute cracker of a girlfriend.'

'Really?'

'Just saw her the once, but you always know when she's around.'

'Why's that?'

'Her perfume. It fills the stairwell. Smelled it last night, actually ...'

Yes, Rebus had smelt it too. He moistened his lips, feeling sourness at the corners of his mouth. 'Mr Hawkins, can you describe William Smith to me?'

Hawkins could, and did.

Rebus turned up unannounced at Alexis Ojiwa's, reckoning the player would be resting after the rigours of the previous day. The house was an unassuming detached bungalow with a red Mazda sports car parked in the driveway. It was on a modern estate, a couple of neighbours washing their cars, watching Rebus with the intensity of men for whom his arrival was an event of sorts, something they could dissect with their wives over the carving of the afternoon sirloin. Rebus rang the doorbell and waited. A woman answered. She seemed surprised to see him.

He showed his ID as he introduced himself. 'Mind if I come in for a minute?'

'What's happened?'

'Nothing. I just have a question for Mr Ojiwa.'

She left the door standing open and walked back through the hall and into an L-shaped living area, calling out: 'Cops are here to put the cuffs on you, baby.' Rebus closed the door and followed her. She stepped out through French windows into the back garden, where a tiny, bare-chested man stood, nursing a drink that looked like puréed fruit. Alexis Ojiwa was wiry, with thick-veined arms and a tight chest. Rebus tried not to think about what the neighbours thought. Scotland was still some way short of being a beacon of multiculturalism, and Ojiwa, like his partner, was black. Not just coffee-coloured, but as black as ebony. Still, probably the only question that would count in most local minds was whether he was Protestant black or Catholic black.

Rebus held out a hand to shake, and introduced himself again.

'What's the problem, officer?'

'I didn't catch your wife's name.'

'It's Cecily.'

Rebus nodded. 'This is going to sound strange, but it's about your mobile phone.'

'My phone?' Ojiwa's face creased in puzzlement. Then he looked to Cecily, and back again at Rebus. 'What about my phone?'

'You do have a mobile phone, sir?'

'I do, yes.'

'But I'm guessing you wouldn't have used it yesterday afternoon? Specifically not at 16.31. I think you were still on the pitch at that time, am I right?'

'That's right.'

'Then someone else used your phone to send this message.' Rebus held up William Smith's mobile so Ojiwa could read the text. Cecily came forward so she could read it too. Her husband stared at her.

'What's this all about?'

'I don't know, baby.'

'You sent this?' His eyes had widened. She shook her head.

'Am I to assume that you had your husband's phone with you yesterday, Mrs Ojiwa?' Rebus asked.

'I was shopping in town all day ... I didn't make any calls.'

'What the hell is this?' It appeared that the footballer had a short fuse, and Rebus had touched a match to it.

'I'm sure there's a reasonable explanation, sir,' Rebus said, raising his hands to try to calm Ojiwa.

'You go spending all my money, and now this!' Ojiwa shook the phone at his wife.

'I didn't do it!' She was yelling too now, loud enough to be heard by the car-polishers. Then she dived inside, producing a silver mobile phone from her bag. 'Here it is,' she said, brandishing the phone. 'Check it, check and see if I sent any messages. I was shopping all day!'

'Maybe someone could have borrowed it?' Rebus suggested.

'I don't see how,' she said, shaking her head. 'Why would anyone want to do that, send a message like that?'

Ojiwa had slumped on to a garden bench, head in hands. Rebus got the feeling that theirs was a relationship stoked by melodrama. He seated himself on the bench next to the footballer.

'Can I ask you something, Mr Ojiwa?'

'What now?'

'I was just wondering if you've ever needed physio?'

Ojiwa looked up. 'Course I need physio! You think I'm Captain Superman or something?' He slapped his hands against his thighs.

If anything, Rebus's voice grew quieter as he began his next question. 'Then does the name Carl Guthrie mean anything to you ...?'

'You've not committed any crime.'

These were Rebus's first words to Frances Guthrie when she opened her door to him. The interior of her house was dark, the curtains closed. The house itself was large and detached and sited in half an acre of grounds in the city's Ravelston area. Physios either earned more than Rebus had counted on, or else there was family money involved.

Frances Guthrie was wearing black slacks and a loose, low-cut black top. Mourning casual, Rebus might have termed it. Her eyes were red-rimmed, and the area around her nose looked raw.

'Mind if I come in?' he asked. It wasn't really a question. He was already making to pass the widow. Hands in pockets, he walked down the hallway and into the sitting room. Stood there and waited for her to join him. She did so slowly, perching on the arm of the red leather sofa. He repeated his opening words, expecting that she would say something, but all she did was stare at him, wide-eyed, maybe a little scared.

He made a tour of the room. The windows were large, and even when curtained there was enough light to see by. He stopped by the fireplace and folded his arms.

'Here's the way I see it. You were out shopping with your friend Cecily. You got to know her when Carl was treating her husband. The pair of you were in Harvey Nichols. Cecily was in the changing room, leaving her bag with you. That's when you got hold of her phone and sent the message.' He paused to watch the effect his words were having. Frances Guthrie had lowered her head, staring down at her hands.

'It was a video you'd watched recently. I'm guessing Carl watched it too. A film about a man who cheats on his wife. And Carl had been cheating on you, hadn't he? You wanted to let him know you knew, so you sent a text to his other phone, the one registered to his fake name – William Smith.' Smith's neighbour had given Rebus a good description of the man, chiming with accident victim Carl Guthrie. 'You'd done some detective work of your own, found out about the phone, the flat in town ... the other woman.' The one whose perfume had lingered in the stairwell. Saturday afternoon: Carl Guthrie heading home after an assignation, leaving behind only two glasses and an unfinished bottle of wine.

Frances Guthrie's head jerked up. She took a deep breath, almost a gulp.

'Why use Cecily's phone?' Rebus asked quietly.

She shook her head, not blinking. Then: 'I never wanted this ... Not this ...'

'You weren't to know what would happen.'

'I just wanted to do something.' She looked up at him, wanting him to understand. He nodded slowly. 'What ... what do I do now?'

Rebus slipped his hands back into his pockets. 'Learn to live with yourself, I suppose.'

That afternoon, he was back at the Oxford Bar, nursing a drink and thinking about love, about how it could make you do things you couldn't explain. All the passions – love and hate and everything in between – they all made people act in ways that would seem inexplicable to a visitor from another planet. The barman asked him if he was ready for another, but Rebus shook his head.

'How's the weekend been treating you?' the barman asked.

'Same as always,' Rebus replied. It was one of those little lies that went some way towards making life appear that bit less complicated.

'Seen any good films lately?'

Rebus smiled, stared down into his glass. 'Watched one last night,' he said. 'Let me tell you about it ...'

Saint Nicked

The man dressed as Santa Claus took to his heels and ran, arms held out to stop the branches scratching his face. It was night, but the moon had appeared from its hiding place behind the clouds. The man's shadow stretched in front of him, snared by the car's headlights. He dodged left, deeper into the woods, hoping he would soon outrun the bright beams. There was laughter at his back, the laughter of men who were not yet pursuing him, men who knew his flight was doomed.

'Come back, Santa! Where do you think you're going?'

'You're not exactly in camouflage! Got Rudolph tied to a tree, ready for a quick getaway?'

More laughter, then the first voice again: 'Here we come, ready or not ...'

He didn't pause to look back. His red jacket was heavy, its thick lining padding out a frame that was stocky to begin with. Funny thing was, he'd been stick thin until his thirties. Made up for it since, though. Chips, chocolate and beer. He knew he could ditch the costume, but that would leave a trail for them to follow. They were right: no way was he going to outrun them. He was already down to a light trot, a stitch developing in his side. The baggy red trousers kept snagging on low branches and bracken. When he paused at last, catching his breath, he heard whistling. *'Jingle Bells'*, it sounded like. The light over to his right was wavering: his pursuers had brought torches. He could hear their boots crunching over the ground. They weren't running. Their steps were steady and purposeful. He started moving again. His plan: to get away. There was a road junction somewhere not far off. Maybe a passing car would save him. The sweat was icy on his neck, steam rising from his body, reminding him of the last horse home in the 2.30.

'You're going to get a kick in the fairy lights for this!' one of the voices called out.

'There won't be enough of you left to fill a Christmas stocking!' yelled the other.

They were still a hundred, maybe two hundred yards behind him. He started picking his way over the ground, trying to muffle any sound. Something scratched his face. He wiped a thumb across his cheek, feeling the prickle of blood. The stitch was getting worse. His heart was pounding in his ears, so loud he feared they would hear it. As the pain grew worse, he remembered someone telling him once that the secret to beating a stitch was touching your toes. He paused, bent down, but his hands didn't even make it to his knees. He fell into a crouch instead, resting his forehead against cold bark. There was a piney smell in the air, like those air fresheners you could get for the car. His clenched fists were pushing against the frozen ground. There was something jagged there beneath his knuckles: a thin slice of stone. He prised it from the earth, held it as he would a weapon. But it wasn't a weapon, and never would be. Instead, he had an idea, and started working its edge against the tree trunk.

The movement behind him had stopped, torchlight scanning the night. For the moment, they had lost him. He couldn't make out what they were saying: they were either too far away, or keeping their voices low. If they stayed where they were, they would hear him scratching. Sure enough, the beam from at least one torch was arcing towards him. He had a sudden, ludicrous image from films he'd devoured as a kid: he was escaping from Colditz; he'd tunnelled out and now the searchlights were tracking him, the Nazis in pursuit. *The Great Escape:* that was the one they'd always shown at Christmas. He wondered if it would be shown this year, and whether he'd be around to see it.

'Is that you, Santa?' The voice was closer. But he'd finished now, and was back on his feet, moving away from the light, sweat stinging his eyes. It was the smoking that had taken its toll. Time was, he wasn't a bad athlete. At school he'd sometimes come runner-up in races. OK, so that had been forty years ago, but were his pursuers any fitter? Maybe they would be tiring, thinking of giving up. Was he worth all this effort to them, when the snug warmth of the BMW was waiting?

Of course! The BMW! He could circle back, nick the car from beneath their noses. If only he could keep going. But his sides were burning, his legs buckling. And the truth was, he didn't even know which direction he was headed. He'd been doing anything but run in a straight line. The car could be anywhere. Chances were he was heading further into the middle of nowhere. Even if he got away, he might end up freezing to death on the hills. There were pockets of habitation out here; he'd spotted the lights during the drive south. But they were within shouting distance of the roadside, and he felt suddenly he was a long way from any road. He was an achingly long way from home.

He knew now that he would give them what they wanted, but only on his terms. It had to be on his terms, not theirs. And he didn't want a kicking. Didn't deserve it. He'd done everything just the way he'd been told ... well, almost everything.

His head felt light, but his body was a dead weight. It was like wading through waist-deep water, and he was slowing again. Did he want to escape, to end up alone in this wilderness? The sky was darkening again, clouds closing over the land. Sleet might be on its way. How could it be that he was floating and drowning both at the same time?

And falling to his knees.

Stretching out, as if on crisp sheets. His eyes closing ...

And then the glare of the searchlights. The guards with their torches. Hands pulling at him, grabbing him by the hair. The silver wig came away. He'd forgotten he'd been wearing it.

'Sleeping on the job, Santa?'

They had him now, both of them. He didn't care. He didn't feel well enough to care.

'Tell us where it is.'

'I ...' His chest was ablaze, as if he'd fallen asleep too close to the fire. He started pulling at the front of his costume, trying to shed it.

'Just tell us where it is.'

'I ...' He knew that if he told them, they might leave him here. Or punish him. He knew he had to play for time. Blood pounded in his ears, deafening him.

'No more fun and games.'

'Scratched it,' he blurted out.

'What's that?'

He tried to swallow. 'Scratched it on a tree.'

'Which tree?'

'I'll ... show you.'

They were trying to pull him to his feet, but he was too heavy, altogether too large for them. Which was how he'd broken away from them in the first place.

'Just tell us!'

He tried shaking his head. 'Show you.'

They dropped him then, arguing with one another.

'He's having us on,' the taller one said.

The stocky one shrugged. 'Tells us or shows us, what's the difference?'

'Difference is ...' But the tall one didn't seem to have an answer. He sniffed instead. 'He's caused us enough grief as it is.'

'Agreed, which is why I want this over with.'

'So why don't I persuade him?' The tall man slapped his torch against the palm of his hand.

'What do you say, Santa?' The stocky one shone his own torch against Santa's face. The eyes were open, but staring. The face seemed to be going slack. The stocky man knelt down.

'Don't tell me ...' the tall man groaned.

'Looks like.' The stocky man made a few checks, and stood up again. 'Heart gave out.'

'Don't tell me ...'

'I just did tell you.'

'So what do we do now?'

The stocky man waved his torch around. 'Said he'd scratched the answer on one of the trees. Can't be too far. Let's start looking ...'

But after twenty minutes, they'd found nothing. They reconvened at Santa's cooling body. 'So what now?'

'We'll come back in the morning. The tree's not going anywhere. Plenty of daylight tomorrow.'

'And him?' The torch picked out the prone figure.

'What about him?'

'We can't just leave him. Think about it ...'

The stocky man nodded. 'You're right. Can't have the kids finding out Santa's not around any more.' He tucked his torch under his arm. 'You take the feet ...'

Detective Inspector John Rebus was in a bad place, doing a bad thing, at his least favourite time of year.

Which is to say that he was Christmas shopping in Glasgow. It had been his girlfriend's idea: everyone, she'd explained, knew that Glasgow boasted better shops than Edinburgh. Which was why he found himself traipsing around busy stores on the last Saturday before Christmas, carrying more and more bags as Jean consulted the neatly typed list she'd brought with her. Each purchase had been selected carefully beforehand, something Rebus was forced to admire. He, after all, shopped from what some would call instinct and others desperation. What he couldn't work out was why the process took so long: even though Jean knew what she was looking for, and where to find it, they still spent half an hour in each shop.

Sometimes – when she was buying something for him – he had to stand outside, shuffling his chilled toes and trying not to look like a man with an impatient wait ahead of him.

It was when they stopped for lunch that Jean, noticing his slumped shoulders, patted his cheek.

'A good impersonation of the condemned man,' she told him. 'You're not exactly entering into the spirit.'

'I'm not the festive sort.'

'I'm beginning to realise.' She smiled. 'The words "retail" and "therapy" don't coincide in your world, do they? Maybe we should go our separate ways this afternoon.'

Rebus nodded slowly. 'That would let me buy a few things for you – without you knowing.'

She studied him, seeing through the lie. 'Consider yourself off the hook,' she said. 'Do you want to meet up later?'

Rebus nodded again. 'Give me a bell when you're finished.'

They parted outside the restaurant, Jean pecking his cheek. Rebus watched her go. Fifty yards down Buchanan Street, she disappeared into an arcade of small, expensive-looking shops. Rebus let his nose guide him to the Horseshoe Bar, where he sat at a corner table, nursing a first and then a second whisky, perusing a newspaper. Thursday's theft from the First Minister's residence in Edinburgh was still causing plenty of amusement. Rebus had already heard two hardened Glaswegian accents joking about it at the bar:

'Looks like Christmas came early, eh?'

'Only Santa was the one on the receiving end ...'

It was all grist to the mill, and rightly so. Doubtless Rebus would have laughed had a man dressed as Father Christmas walked into a reception in Glasgow and wandered out again with a priceless necklace tucked beneath his costume. No ordinary piece of jewellery, but once the property of Mary, Queen of Scots, brought into the light just one day each year so it could be shown off at a party. With the First Minister of the recently devolved Scottish Parliament as victim, Rebus's police station had been a hive of activity, which was why he intended enjoying what was left of today.

Finishing his drink, he asked at the bar for a Yellow Pages, jotting down the addresses of local record shops. He was going to find a small gift for himself, a rarity or some new album, something he could play on the big day. Something to take his mind off Christmas. The third shop he tried was a second-hand record specialist, and Rebus was its only customer. The proprietor had frizzy greying hair tied in a ponytail, and was wearing a Frank Zappa T-shirt that had shrunk in the wash at some point in the 1970s. As Rebus consulted the racks, the man asked if he was looking for anything in particular.

'I'll know it when I see it,' Rebus told him. On an overcast day, it was easy enough to start a conversation. Five minutes in, Rebus realised he knew the man from somewhere. He pointed a finger. 'You were in a band yourself once.'

The man grinned, showing gaps between his teeth. 'That's some memory you've got.'

'You played bass for the Parachute Game.' The man held up his hands in surrender. 'Ted Handsome?' Rebus guessed, eyes narrowed in concentration.

The man nodded. 'The name's Hanson, actually. Ted Hanson.'

'I had a couple of your albums.'

'Almost as many as we made.'

Rebus nodded slowly. The Parachute Game had appeared on the Scottish scene in the mid seventies, supporting headliners such as Nazareth and Alex Harvey. Then things had gone quiet.

'Your singer did a runner, didn't he?'

Hanson shrugged. 'Bad timing.'

Rebus remembered: the band had crept into the lower reaches of the Top 30 with a single from their second album. Their first headlining tour was looming. And then their singer had walked out. Jack ... no, Jake, that was it.

'Jake Wheeler,' he said out loud.

'Poor Jake,' Ted Hanson said. He was thoughtful for a moment, then checked his watch. 'You look like a drinking man, am I right?'

'You've got a good eye.'

'Then I reckon this could be my early-closing day.'

Rebus didn't like to say, but he got the feeling Ted had a few of those each week.

They hit a couple of bars, talking music, bands from the 'old days'. Hanson had a fund of stories. He'd started the shop with stock ransacked from his own collection.

'And my flat still looks like a vinyl museum.'

'I'd like to see that,' Rebus said with a smile. So they jumped in a taxi, heading for Hillhead. Rebus called Jean on his mobile, said he might be late getting back to Edinburgh. She sounded tired and unbothered. Hanson's Victorian tenement flat was as promised. Albums lay slumped against every wall. Boxes of them sat on tables, singles spilling from home-made shelves that had warped under the weight.

'A little piece of heaven,' Rebus said.

'Try telling that to my ex-wife.' Hanson handed him a can of beer. They spent a couple of hours on the sofa, staring into the space between the loudspeakers and listening to a shared musical heritage. Finally, Rebus plucked up the courage to ask about Jake Wheeler.

'You must have been gutted when he walked out.'

'He had his reasons.'

'What were they?'

Hanson offered a shrug. 'Come to think of it, he never said.'

'There were rumours about drugs ...'

'Rock stars and drugs? Surely not.'

'A good way to meet some very bad people.' Rebus knew of these rumours too: gangsters, dealers. But Hanson just shrugged again.

'He never resurfaced?' Rebus asked.

Hanson shook his head. Then he smiled. 'You said you had a couple of our albums, John ...' He sprang to his feet, rummaged in a box by the door. 'Bet this isn't one of them.' He held out the album to Rebus.

'I did own it once upon a time,' Rebus mused, recognising the cover. *The Oldest Tree,* recorded by the remaining trio after Wheeler had walked out. 'Lost it at a party, week after I'd bought it.' Examining the cover – swirly late-hippy pencil drawings of dells and hills, a broad oak tree at the centre – Rebus remembered something. 'You drew this?'

Hanson nodded. 'I had more than a few pretensions back then.'

'It's good.' Rebus studied the drawing. 'I mean it.'

Hanson sat down again. 'Back at the shop, you said you were after something special. Could this be it?'

Rebus smiled. 'Could be. How much do you want?'

'Compliments of the season.'

Rebus raised an eyebrow. 'I couldn't ...'

'Yes you could. It's not like it's worth anything.'

'Well, OK then, thanks. Maybe I can do you a favour some day in return.'

'How's that then?'

Rebus had lifted a business card out of his wallet. He handed it over. 'I'm in CID, Ted. Never know when you might need a friend ...'

Studying the record sleeve again, Rebus failed to notice the look of fear and panic that flitted across his new friend's face.

Sunday morning, Neil Bryant woke up and knew something was wrong. He was the stockier of the two men who'd spent much of the previous evening chasing an overweight, unfit Santa to his death. He was also supposed to be the brains of the outfit, which was why he was so annoyed. He was annoyed because he'd asked Malky Bunker – his tall, skinny partner in crime – to wake him up. It was past ten, and still no sign of Malky. So much for his dawn wake-up call. He phoned Malky and gave him a good roasting.

Twenty minutes later, the BMW pulled up at Bryant's door. Malky's hair was tousled, face creased from sleep. He was yawning.

'You got rid of the deceased?' Bryant asked. Malky nodded. Good enough: the fewer details Bryant knew, the better. They drove out of Glasgow, heading east and south. Different route from last night, and a map neither of them knew how to read.

'Be easier if we drove into Edinburgh and out again,' Malky suggested.

'We're late as it is,' Bryant snapped. The thing was, as you headed towards the Border country, it all started to look the same. Plenty of forests and crossroads. It was early afternoon before they started to recognise a few landmarks. Passing a couple of flatbed trucks, Bryant sensed they were getting warm.

'Working on a Sunday,' Malky commented, glancing out at another truck.

'Run-up to Christmas,' Bryant explained. Then his heart sank as he saw what the trucks were carrying.

'This has got to be it,' Malky was saying.

'Aye,' Bryant agreed, voice toneless.

Malky was parking the car, only now realising that the forest they'd run through the previous night was not a forest. It had been denuded by chainsaws, half its trees missing. Not a forest: a plantation. A fresh consignment of Christmas firs, heading north to Edinburgh.

The two men looked at one another, then sprinted from the car. There were still trees left, plenty of them. Maybe, if they were lucky ... maybe Santa's tree would still be there.

Two hours and countless arguments later, they were back in the car, heater going full blast. The foreman had threatened to call the police. They'd threatened violence if he did.

'They're all the same,' he'd shouted, meaning the trees.

'Just call us particular,' Bryant had snarled back.

'What are we going to do?' Malky asked now. 'We go back there without the necklace, our goose is well and truly stuffed.'

Bryant looked at him, then got out of the car, marching towards the nervous-looking foreman.

'Where are they headed?' he demanded.

'The trees?' The foreman watched Bryant nod. 'Edinburgh,' he said.

'Where in Edinburgh?'

'All over.' The foreman shrugged. 'Probably be sold within the day.'

'Addresses,' Bryant said, his face inches away from the older man's. 'I need addresses.'

Rebus and Jean ate Sunday lunch at a hotel in Portobello, surrounded by families pulling crackers and wearing lopsided paper crowns.

'Basic training for the big day,' Rebus commented, excusing himself from the table as his mobile started ringing. It was his boss, Detective Chief Superintendent Gill Templer.

'Enjoying a lazy Sunday?' she enquired.

'Up until now.'

'We're looking at fences, John.' Meaning people who might be able to shift an item as hot as the necklace. 'You know Sash Hooper, don't you? Wondered if you might pay him a visit.'

'Today?'

'Sooner the better.'

Rebus glanced back in Jean's direction. She was stirring her coffee, no room for dessert. Rebus had promised to go and buy a Christmas tree.

'Fine,' he said into the mouthpiece. 'So where can I find Sash?'

'Skating on thin ice, as usual,' Gill Templer said.

Ever the entrepreneur, Sash – real name Sacha, courtesy of a mother with a thing for French crooners – had opened an outdoor skating rink on Leith Links.

'Just trying to make an honest dollar,' he told Rebus, as they walked around the rinks perimeter. 'Licences in place and everything.' He watched two teenagers as they shuffled across the slushy ice, the rink's only customers. Then he stared accusingly at the sun, cursing its liquefying powers. Music blared from a faulty loudspeaker: Abba, *Dancing Queen*.

'No interest in stolen antiquities, then?'

'All in the past, Mr Rebus.' Hooper was a big man, with clenched fists. What was left of his hair was jet black, tightly curled. His thick moustache was black too. He wore sunglasses, through which Rebus could just make out his small, greedy eyes.

'And if someone came to you with an offer ...'

'The three wise men could knock on my door tonight, Mr Rebus, and I'd give them the brush-off.' Hooper shrugged a show of innocence.

Rebus looked all around. 'Not rushed off your feet, are you?'

'The day's young. Besides, Kiddie Wonderland's doing all right.' He nodded at the double-decker bus decorated with fake snow and tinsel. Mums and young children were lining up for entry. Rebus had passed the bus when he'd first arrived. It promised 'A visit you'll never forget – one gift per child.' 'Santa's *grotto on wheels,'* had been Hooper's explanation, rubbing his hands together. The interior looked to have been decorated with white cotton and sheets of coloured crêpe paper. The queuing parents appeared dubious, but Kiddie Wonderland was the only show in Leith. Still, to Rebus's mind, there was something missing.

'No Santa,' he said, nodding towards the bus.

'Soon as you're gone there will be.' Hooper patted his own stomach.

Rebus stared at him. 'You realise some of these kids could be traumatised for life?' Hooper didn't reply. 'Let me know if Christmas brings you anything nice, Sash.'

Hooper was rehearsing his *ho, ho, ho*s as Rebus walked back to the car.

He knew that there was a place off Dalkeith Road that sold Christmas trees. It was a derelict builders' yard, empty all year round except for the run-up to 25 December. When he arrived, two men were doing a good impression of taking the place apart, studying each tree before dismissing it, while the proprietor watched bemused, arms folded. One of the men shook his head at the other, and the pair stormed out.

'I got a call half an hour back,' the proprietor told Rebus. 'They did the same thing to a friend of mine.'

'Takes all sorts,' Rebus said. But he watched the men get into their rusty BMW and drive off. The elder and shorter of the two – his face was familiar. Rebus frowned in concentration, bought the first five-foot fir offered to him, and took it out to his car. It stretched from boot to passenger seat. He still couldn't put a name to the face, and it bothered him all the way to St Leonards police station, where he made his report to Gill Templer.

'Could do with clearing this one up, John,' she said.

Rebus nodded. She would have the brass on her back, because the First Minister was on theirs.

'We can but try, Gill,' he offered, making to leave. He was driving out of the car park when he saw a face he recognised, and this time the name came easily. It was Ted Hanson. Rebus stopped and wound down his window. 'This is a surprise, Ted.'

'I was in town, thought I'd look you up.' Hanson looked cold.

'How did you find me?'

'Asked a policeman,' Hanson said with a smile. 'Any chance of a cuppa?'

They were only five minutes from Rebus's tenement flat. He made two mugs of instant coffee while Hanson flicked through his record collection.

'A pale imitation of yours, Ted,' Rebus apologised.

'A lot of the same albums.' Hanson waved a copy of Wishbone Ash's *Argus*. 'Great cover.'

'It's not the same with CDs, is it?'

Hanson wrinkled his nose. 'Nothing like.'

Rebus handed over the coffee and sat down. 'What are you doing here, Ted?' he asked.

'Just wanted to get out of the shop – out of Glasgow.' Hanson blew across the surface of the mug, then took a sip. 'Sorry, John. Got any sugar?'

'I'll fetch some.' Rebus got to his feet again.

'Mind if I use your loo meantime?'

'Be my guest.' Rebus pointed the way, then retreated to the kitchen. Music was playing in the living room: the Incredible String Band. Rebus returned and placed the sugar beside Hanson's mug. Something was going on. He had a few questions for his new friend. After a couple of minutes, he walked back into the hall, knocked on the bathroom door. No answer. He turned the handle. There was no one inside. Ted Hanson had done a runner.

'Curiouser and curiouser,' Rebus muttered to himself. He looked down on to the street from his living room window: no sign of anyone. Then he stared at his record collection. It took him a couple of minutes to work out what was missing.

The last Parachute Game album, the one Hanson himself had given him. Rebus sat in his chair, thinking hard. Then he called Jean.

'Not found a tree yet?' she asked.

'It's on its way, Jean. Could you do me a favour?'

'What?'

'Something I'd like for Christmas ...'

Christmas itself was fine. He'd no complaints about Christmas. There was the slow run-up to Hogmanay, Gill Templer growing less festive as the necklace failed to turn up. New Year's Day, Rebus nursed his accessory of choice: a thumping head. He managed to forgo any resolutions, apart from the usual one to stop drinking.

His Christmas present finally arrived on 4 January, having been posted in Austin, Texas, on 24 December. Jean handed it over, having taken the trouble to wrap it in second-hand paper.

'You shouldn't have,' he said. Then he kissed her, and took the album home for a listen. The lyrics were on the inside of the gatefold sleeve. The songs tended to the elegiac, each seeming to refer to Jake Wheeler. Ted Hanson had taken over vocal duties, and though he didn't make too bad a fist of it, Rebus could see why the band had folded. Without Wheeler, there was something missing, something irreplaceable. Listening to the title track, Rebus studied the drawing on the front of the sleeve – Ted Hanson's drawing. An old oak tree with the initials JW carved on it, enclosed in a heart, pierced by an arrow that wasn't quite an arrow. Holding the sleeve to the light, Rebus saw that it was a syringe.

And there beneath the oldest tree, Hanson sang, *you took your last farewell of me* ... But was it the bassist talking, or something else? Rebus rubbed a hand across his forehead and concentrated on other songs, other lyrics. Then he turned back to the sleeve. So detailed, it couldn't just be imagined. It had to be a real place. He picked up his phone, called Jean's number. She worked at the museum. There were things she could find out.

Such as the location of Scotland's oldest tree.

On the morning of the sixth, he let the office know he'd be late.

'That's got to be a record-breaker: the five-day hangover.'

Rebus didn't bother arguing. Instead, he drove to Glasgow, parking on the street outside Ted Hanson's shop. Hanson was just opening up; he looked tired and in need of a shave.

'Amazing what you can find on the internet these days,' Rebus said. Hanson turned, saw what Rebus was holding: a near-mint copy of *The Oldest Tree*. 'Here's what I think,' Rebus went on, taking a step forward. 'I think Jake's dead. Maybe natural causes, maybe not. Rock stars have a way of hanging around with the wrong people. They get into situations.' He tapped the album sleeve. 'I know where this is now. Is that where he's buried?'

The ghost of a smile passed across Hanson's face. 'That's what you think?'

'It's why you had to get the album back from me, once you knew what I did for a living.'

Hanson bowed his head. 'You're right.' Then he looked up again, eyes gleaming. 'That's exactly why I had to get the album back.'

He paused, seemed to take a deep breath. 'But you're wrong. You couldn't be more wrong.'

Rebus frowned, thinking he'd misheard.

'I'll show you,' Hanson said. 'And by the way, happy new year.'

The drive took them over an hour, north out of Glasgow, the scenery stretching, rising, becoming wilderness. They passed lochs and mountains, the sky a vast, bruised skein.

'All your detective work,' Hanson said, slouched in the passenger seat, 'did you notice where the album was recorded?' Rebus shook his head. Hanson just nodded, then told him to pull over. They were on a stretch of road that would fill with camper vans in the summer, but for now it seemed desolate. Below them lay a valley, and across the valley a farmhouse. Hanson pointed towards it. 'Owned by our producer at the time. We set up all the gear, did the album in under a month. Braepath Farm, it was called back then.'

Rebus had spotted something. On the hillside behind the farmhouse, the tree from the album sleeve. The tree Jean had told him was the oldest in Scotland: the Braepath Oak. And behind it, a small stone bothy, little more than a shelter for shepherds, outside which a man was splitting logs, watched by his sheepdog.

'Jake fell apart,' Hanson was saying, voice low. 'Maybe it was the company he was keeping, or the industry we were supposed to be part of. He just wanted to be left alone. I promised him I'd respect that. The drawing ... it was a way of showing he'd always be part of the band, whatever happened.' He paused, clearing his throat. Rebus watched the distant figure as it picked up the kindling, taking it indoors. Long-haired, ragged-clothed: too far away to really be sure, but Rebus knew all the same.

'He's been out here ever since?' he asked.

Hanson nodded. His eyes glistened.

'And you've never ...?'

'He knows where I am if he wants me.' He angled his head. 'So now you know, John. Up to you what you do about it.'

Rebus nodded, put the car into gear and started a three-point turn.

'Know what I'd like, Ted?' he said. 'I'd like you to sign that album for me. Will you do that?'

'With pleasure,' Hanson said with a smile.

*

Back at St Leonards, Rebus was passing the front desk when he saw the duty sergeant emerging from the comms room, shaking his head in disbelief. 'I'm not that late,' Rebus said.

'It's not that, John. It's Mother Hubbard.'

Now Rebus knew: Edwina Hubbard from down the road. Two or three times a week she would call to report some imagined mischief.

'What is it this time?' Rebus asked. 'The peeping postmen or the disappearing dustbins?'

'Christmas trees,' the sergeant said. 'Being collected and taken away.'

'And did you explain to her that it happens every year, courtesy of our caring, sharing council?'

The sergeant nodded. 'Thing is, she says they're early. And using a double-decker bus.'

'A bus?' Rebus laughed. 'Firs, please.'

The sergeant laughed too, turning to retreat into the comms room. 'It gets better,' he said. 'The bus is covered in Christmas decorations.'

Rebus was still laughing as he climbed the stairs. After the morning he'd had, he needed something to cheer him up. Then he froze. A Christmas bus ... Kiddie Wonderland. Collecting Christmas trees ... Two men running around Edinburgh, looking for a tree ... The name flashed from brain to mouth.

'Neil Bryant!' Rebus took the stairs two at a time, sat down at a computer and typed in Bryant's name. Ex-bouncer, convictions for violence. Clever with it. The other man, the taller one, had looked like bouncer material too. And hadn't Sash Hooper run a nightclub a few years back? Sash ... ready to take an unlikely turn as Santa on the bus.

'Santa,' Rebus hissed. Then he was back downstairs and in the comms room, grabbing the sergeant's arm.

'The bus with the trees,' he said. 'Where did she see it?'

Rink.

The bus was full of trees, both decks. But finally they'd found one with that single word scratched on its trunk.

Rink.

The way Bryant had explained it to Sash Hooper, they needed the bus so they could collect as many trees as possible, as quickly as possible. Eventually Hooper had seen the wisdom of the plan. He had got a buyer for the necklace, but the sale had to be quick.

Rink.

Well it didn't take a genius, did it? They'd turned the bus round and headed for Leith Links. The costume had been Bryant's idea too, when he'd heard that the First Minister was throwing a party. Send someone in there dressed as Santa, they could walk out with anything they liked. He'd gone to Sash with the idea, and Sash had suggested Benny Welsh, a pretty good housebreaker in his time, now down on his luck. Benny had been good as gold – until he'd found out how much the necklace was worth. After which he'd tried upping out. Wasn't going to hand it over until they had a deal.

Three of them now – Sash, Malky and Bryant – slipping and sliding across the ice. Looking for the telltale dark patch, finding it. Benny had cut himself a hole, stuffed the necklace in, then poured in some water, letting it freeze over again. Sash had his penknife out. It took a while, the day darkening around them.

'Give me the knife,' Malky said, chipping away with it.

'Watch the blade doesn't snap,' Sash Hooper warned, as if the knife were somehow more precious than the necklace. Eventually all three men clambered to their feet, Hooper holding the necklace, examining it. A string of shimmering diamonds, embracing a vast blood-red ruby. He actually gasped. They came off the ice and back on to solid earth. They were almost in the shadow of the bus before they noticed Rebus. And he wasn't alone.

Two uniforms could be seen through the upper-deck windows. Two more were downstairs. Another was outside, circling the bus.

'Nice little stocking-filler,' Rebus said, motioning towards the necklace.

'You got a warrant?' Hooper asked.

'Do I look as if I need one?'

'You can't just go trampling all over my bus. That's private property.' Hooper was attempting to slide the necklace into his pocket.

Malky tugged at Bryant's sleeve. His eyes had widened. They were on the policeman who'd been circling the bus, the policeman who was now turning the handle that would open the vehicle's luggage compartment. Bryant saw his friend's look, and his own mouth dropped open in dismay.

'Malky, for the love of God, tell me you didn't ...'

Hooper was still concentrating on protesting his innocence. He knew this was the most important speech he would ever make. He felt that if he could just get the words right, then maybe ...

'DI Rebus,' the constable was saying. 'Something here you should take a look at ...'

And Hooper shifted his gaze and saw what everyone else was

seeing. Benny Welsh, still dressed in the telltale red suit, lying at peace on the floor of the luggage bay.

Rebus turned to face the three men.

'I'm guessing that means you're Saint Nicked,' he said.

Atonement

'They're dropping like flies.'

The man collapsed into another fit of coughing, doubling over in the tattered armchair. Rebus looked around him, but no one in the large, overheated room was paying the slightest attention. Some were watching a daytime nature programme, others dozing or staring out of the window. It was a large sash window – three windows actually, forming a bay. The paintwork looked new. Rebus thought he could smell fresh paint, its aroma not quite exhausted. There were other smells, too: the remains of a fish lunch; talcum powder and perfume; perished rubber. The redecorating did not stretch as far as the cornices and ceiling. The cornicing was elaborate, the design almost Celtic. The ceiling was pale green, a few veined cracks radiating from the central light fitting.

At one time, this would have been a fine private home, enjoyed by a bank manager and his growing family. Edinburgh had no shortage of these detached Victorian mansions. Some had been divided into flats, of course. Others were business HQs, or owned by large institutions and charities. Renshaw House, however, had become a care home for the elderly, which meant that the man in the armchair must be elderly. His name was Ken Flatley. When Rebus had first joined the police, Flatley had been a mentor of sorts. Not that the word 'mentor' would ever have been used between them: Rebus was a detective, Ken Flatley the uniform who manned the police station's front desk. All the same, the older man had looked at the younger and understood – understood that tips and hints would be appreciated.

This had been in the early 1970s, the era of boot boys and pub rock: Rod Stewart in his tartan scarf, and Elton John telling teenagers that it was all right to fight on a Saturday night. One such altercation had put Ken Flatley behind the desk: suedeheads clashing after a football derby, Flatley between them quickly becoming their shared target, leaving him with a limp. He used a walking frame these days. His thick brown hair had never gone grey, so that strangers sometimes mistook it for a wig. The face below the low fringe was creased but resolute. Take away the walking frame, Rebus reckoned, and his friend would seem younger than himself.

They had lost touch for a number of years, reunited briefly at the funeral of Flatley's wife Irma. But when Rebus had learned that Flatley had sold the bungalow in Prestonfield and moved to a nursing home, he'd arranged to visit. That first meeting had not started well, Ken asserting that he needed no pity.

'I'm not here for that,' Rebus had told him.

'What then?'

'Maybe I'm just on the lookout,' Rebus had replied, scanning the room. Flatley had caught his meaning and laughed.

'Aye, not too long till you'll be joining me.'

It was a thought Rebus had been pushing away ever since. After all, he was in his late fifties, maybe only fifteen years younger than Flatley. And he lived alone. If anything happened ... if his faculties started to fail or went into reverse ... He had no family nearby, and though he would try to cope, try to do everything for himself, there was always the possibility that he would not succeed. When he had first married and moved into the tenement flat where he still lived, there'd been a man on the top floor who'd lived alone. Rebus had always been slightly wary of this man, especially when his daughter Sammy had been young; hadn't even bothered to attend the neighbour's funeral. And yet now ... now there were students and young couples in his tenement, and he himself had become the oldest inhabitant.

'Dropping like flies,' Flatley repeated, clutching the arms of the chair. It was his own chair, one of the few possessions he'd been allowed to bring with him from home. Much of the rest had been disposed of at auction, a daughter in Bristol taking only a few mementoes – photograph albums and some bone china. Asked if he had thought of going to stay nearer his daughter, Flatley had shaken his head vigorously.

'Got her own life now,' he'd insisted.

Now Rebus watched him as he wiped the back of one tremulous hand across his mouth. 'How do you mean?' he asked.

His friend leaned forward, inviting Rebus to do the same, until their heads were inches apart.

'Faces in here,' Flatley muttered, 'they don't last long.'

Rebus nodded as if he understood, but Flatley gave him the same hard gaze he'd given the young detective whenever Rebus had made some tiro's error.

'I don't mean they just get old and peg it.' He nodded towards an empty chair by the fireplace. 'Mrs Edwards used to sit there. Sprightly, she was, when she came in here. Family said she couldn't cope – what they meant was, *they* couldn't cope. So in she comes and lights the place up ... until last week. Ambulance came for her, and three days later they tell us she's dead.'

'Ken ...'

'She's not the only one, John.' Flatley's voice was insistent, knowing the objection Rebus had been about to make. 'Dot Parker took ill one day, died the next. Same with Manny Lehrer.'

'You're saying they're being bumped off, one by one?'

'It's no joke, John.'

Rebus's smile faded. 'No, I'm sure it's not. So what are we talking about here?'

'I'm not sure ... There was something in the paper recently about staff in care homes letting people die.'

'Benign neglect?'

'I don't think "benign" enters into it.'

'Are you saying they don't feed you?'

'Oh, they feed us all right ... after a fashion.'

'What then?'

'You hear about it all the time, don't you? Nurses who're secretly poisoning their patients.'

'Ken ...' The tone of warning had returned to Rebus's voice. Flatley just stared at him and Rebus sighed, sitting back in his chair. 'What is it you want me to do?'

'I just thought someone should ...' The words trailed off.

'You know, when someone dies unexpectedly, even if they're old, there's an autopsy.'

'What if it's not unexpected, though? They've been ill or frail ... a pathologist is going to find what he expects to find. He's not going to be as thorough as with a corpse with a knife in its back.'

Rebus held his hands up, palms towards his tormentor. He glanced around him, but no one seemed to have heard the outburst. 'If it will help put your mind at rest,' he said, 'let me see what I can do.'

Some of the tension left Flatley's face. He shifted his gaze floorwards. 'Why do you keep coming here, John?'

'Maybe I'm a fan of conspiracy theories.'

'I'm serious.' Flatley fixed him with a stare. 'I mean, it's good to have a visitor now and then ... I just don't see what you get out of it.'

'Could be I've got a guilty conscience, Ken. All those years I never kept in touch.'

'We have to share the dock then – I'm as guilty as you are.'

Rebus patted his friend's leg. 'Let me do some digging, see if someone really is doing a bit of drastic bed-clearing.' He got to his feet. 'And if I don't find anything, will your mind be at rest?'

'My mind gets too much bloody rest these days,' Flatley snorted.

Rebus nodded slowly: maybe that's the trouble, he thought to himself ...

'What exactly is it we're being accused of, Inspector?'

Donald Morrison sat back in his black leather office chair. Rebus was seated at the other side of the desk. Diplomacy had never been his strong point, but all the same, he felt he'd presented the case fairly. Morrison, however, the owner of Renshaw House, was riled. Rebus could tell this because of the way the blood had risen to the man's cheeks.

'As I said, sir, I'm not here in any official capacity ...'

'But you *are* a police officer?' Morrison waited for Rebus to nod agreement. 'And you're here to visit someone who was also a policeman.' He forced the beginnings of a smile. 'It seems Mr Flatley is finding it hard to give up his old job.'

Morrison rose from his chair and turned to face the window – a replica of the one in the communal sitting room. He clasped his hands behind his back and stared out at the expanse of mown lawn, broken only by a sundial at its centre. There were benches around its periphery, shaded by mature trees. He was broad-shouldered, had probably played rugby in his younger days. His hair was greying at the ears and temples, thinning on top. There were horizontal creases above the vents of his suit jacket.

'He's free to leave, you know,' he said, patting one hand against the other. 'Our waiting list is substantial.'

'Of people wanting to leave?'

Morrison turned back to Rebus, tried out another smile on him. 'Wanting to get in, Inspector. Time was, there were plenty of care homes, but not any more. So if Mr Flatley really isn't happy here ...'

'Nobody's saying he's unhappy. He's just worried.'

'Of course he is.' Morrison pulled out his chair and sat down again. 'He's surrounded by people who are not exactly in the first flush of youth. I'm afraid it's part and parcel of the way of things, Inspector. People don't come here to get younger and flourish – I only wish that were the case.' He gave a slight shrug. 'Mrs Edwards and Mrs Parker ... Mr Lehrer ... they were in their eighties, and hardly in the most robust health to begin with.'

'Ken's description of Mrs Edwards was "sprightly".'

Morrison pondered this. 'He saw what he wanted to see.'

'You're saying he fancied her?'

'Age doesn't always blinker the heart.'

'And that's why her death has hit him so hard?'

Morrison gave another shrug. 'Do you think you can put Mr Flatley's mind at rest, Inspector?'

'I can try.'

Morrison bowed his head a little, satisfied at this outcome. 'Mortality is sometimes a difficult concept even for the elderly.'

'I don't think it's the concept that's bothering Ken.'

'You're right, of course.' Morrison had risen, indicating that the meeting was at its end. 'It may not help that he doesn't get many visitors.'

'His daughter lives in England.'

'He must have friends ... ex-colleagues like yourself?'

'I'm not sure he wants them to see him in a care home.'

Morrison chose not to see this as a further slight. Instead he nodded slowly. 'Self-reliance ... it's something we see a lot of: people too proud to ask for help, even when it's needed.' He held out his hand for Rebus to shake. Rebus took it.

'Just out of curiosity,' he asked, 'what did they die of?'

Morrison's face darkened a little, the blood threatening to return to his cheeks. 'Old age, Inspector, nothing more than that.'

'Ken seemed to think they were taken to hospital.'

'Yes?'

'So they all died in hospital?'

'That's right. When a patron weakens dangerously, we're duty-bound to seek medical attention for them.'

'And I'm sure you do so conscientiously.'

'We'd be closed down otherwise.' Morrison reached out to open the door. 'I wish I could feel that I've allayed your concerns, Inspector.'

'I don't have any concerns, Mr Morrison. Thanks for your time.' Rebus was on the other side of the threshold when he stopped and turned. 'I parked my car next to a silver Merc. Is it yours, by any chance?'

'It's mine.' Morrison seemed to be waiting for something more, but Rebus just nodded thoughtfully. 'Nice motor,' he said, turning to leave.

Flatley was waiting for him at the main door. It stood open, letting some much-needed air into the place. Flatley was leaning heavily against his walking frame, but straightened up when he saw Rebus.

'Keeping tabs on me, Ken?' Rebus asked.

'Just contemplating a nice long stroll.'

'Anywhere in mind?'

'Nearest pub's in Marchmont.'

'That's a good half-mile. Maybe I'll join you.'

Flatley's mouth twitched. He looked down at the metal frame against which he leaned. 'Maybe another time, eh? Did you get any joy from the commandant?'

'You're not a fan?'

Flatley wrinkled his nose. 'He's in it for the money, same as the rest of them.'

'I think there's probably better money out there somewhere.'

'Maybe so, but something tells me he's not giving himself the same minimum wage the rest of the staff have to swallow.'

'Steady, Ken, you're choking the life out of that thing.'

Flatley followed Rebus's gaze to the frame's rubber hand-grips, then smiled and relaxed his knuckles a little. 'Did you ask him about the body count?'

'I did.'

'Mention my name at all?'

'Hard not to.'

'So that's me on half-rations.'

'No hardship – you don't like the food anyway. I'll bring you a couple of pies next time I visit.'

There was silence between them, punctuated only by the sounds of the TV set in the room opposite.

'You think I'm turning gaga, John?' Flatley's eyes bored into Rebus's.

'No.'

'Maybe I am at that.'

'Maybe you could leave here … try making do with a home help.'

'My home's not there any more.'

'Then you've got to make the best of it.' Rebus hated himself for saying the words. They sounded hollow, clichéd. *Make do … mustn't grumble …* He felt his old mentor deserved more.

There was sudden movement behind them. An elderly man, stick-thin and with a pale, skeletal face, was shambling in their direction, eyes wide at the sight of the open door.

'Oh Christ, it's—' The rest of the sentence went unfinished as Ken Flatley was barged aside by the old man. He stumbled into the wall, dislodging a framed painting. The frame fell apart as it hit the parquet floor, Flatley sliding down after it. A care assistant's head appeared around a doorway.

'Mr Waters!' she called. But by this time, Mr Waters was through the door. Rebus, crouching to help Ken Flatley back to his feet, saw the man waddle down the wheelchair ramp outside the entrance to Renshaw House.

'Mr Waters!' the woman called again. She was striding down the hall now, drying her hands on the front of her sky-blue uniform. Flatley was nodding that he was all right. Rebus made sure his friend had a good grip on his walking frame, then turned his attention to the fleeing man. Waters was wearing neither shoes nor socks. His upper body was covered only by a white cotton vest, accentuating his thinness. His trousers had slipped down far enough to reveal that he was wearing some sort of incontinence pad beneath.

'Need a hand?' Rebus asked the assistant as she passed him.

'I'll manage,' she muttered.

'She won't,' Ken Flatley said, jerking his head to let Rebus know he should follow her. Waters's gait was that of a walker in the Olympics. He seemed to take what weight he had on the balls of his feet, and his arms were pumping, elbows jutting out to either side. He was heading in a straight line across the lawn, towards an eight-foot stone wall. There was dew on the grass, and the care worker's rubber soles went from under her. There was a banana-skin inevitability to her slow, graceless fall. She snatched at a wrenched ankle and let out a roar that brought Mr Waters to a halt. He turned, arms dropping to his sides. Rebus leaned down to help the woman up.

'Any damage?' he asked her.

'Just twisted it.'

An arm around her waist, he brought her to her feet. Mr Waters was standing directly in front of them.

'I can't remember,' he said, voice high-pitched, false teeth missing.

'Remember what?' the woman asked angrily.

'Where the body's buried.'

'Not that again.' She gave a loud hiss. 'There's nobody dead, Mr Waters,' she told him, as if explaining something to a stubborn child.

'She buried the body. I'm not what you think I am.'

'We know who you are, Mr Waters. Your name's Lionel.' She turned to Rebus and rolled her eyes. His fingers were around the bare flesh of her arm. She eased away from him slightly, and he let her go.

'My treasure's all gone ... The fishing boat ... the castle ... all gone.'

'That's right, Mr Waters, all gone.' She was talking to the man but her eyes were on Rebus, and she was shaking her head slowly, to let him know this was a regular exchange. 'Now let's get you back to the house.'

'I need to see Colin, to tell him I'm sorry. You believe me, don't you?'

'Of course I do.'

But Waters wasn't looking at her. Rebus was his focus. The old man's eyes narrowed, as if trying to place the face. 'Nobody believes me,' he stated.

'You're a bloody nutcase, Waters!' The voice was Ken Flatley's. He was standing in the doorway, while a carer started tidying up the picture frame. 'About time they sectioned you again!' A hand patted Flatley's shoulder, and he turned towards his comforter: Donald Morrison.

Rebus insisted on accompanying the care assistant back to Lionel Waters's bedroom. As she gave the old man a blue tablet and a glass of water, Rebus looked around. The room was bare. He got the feeling all the furnishings belonged to Renshaw House itself. Waters was seated on a chair by his bedside. A tattered magazine was lying open on the bed, showing a half-finished word puzzle.

'What's your name?' Rebus asked the assistant.

'Annie.'

'Sure that ankle's OK?'

'I'll manage.' She was tucking a tartan travel rug around Waters's legs.

'I'd say you've probably got a good case for a day or two on the sick.'

'Maybe so.'

'But you'll manage?'

She turned to him. Her eyes were a deep hazel. 'It's tough enough working here; one goes sick, that just makes it tougher.'

'You're short-staffed?'

'Lousy wages for back-breaking work ... what do you think?'

'I think I couldn't do it.' His eyes shifted over the walls. 'He didn't bring much with him, did he?'

Annie turned her attention to Waters. He was mumbling, but his eyes had gone glassy, the lids drooping. 'Poor sod was in a mental institution before this. Locked away since his twenties. Never really right in the head, according to the family. Eventually they couldn't cope. He was aggressive, you see.'

'And he killed someone called Colin?'

She smiled at the mistake. 'Colin's his brother. Colin Waters?' Her eyes were on Rebus's again.

'The car dealer?'

'Biggest on the east coast – isn't that what the advert says?'

Rebus nodded slowly. 'He comes from a rich family, then. They're paying for this place?'

'I suppose so.' Waters's eyes had closed now. Annie motioned with her head for Rebus to leave. Out in the corridor, she left the door ajar a few inches. The unconscious figure of Lionel Waters could be seen through the gap.

'Why did they let him out of the other place?' *The other place* – because Rebus didn't know what the current term was for a nut-house, a loony bin, an asylum.

'Said he no longer posed a threat. If you ask me, it's been a long time since he did. All he wants to do is run away.'

'To see his treasure.'

She wrinkled her nose. 'Aye, right.'

'And to tell Colin he's sorry ... sorry for what?'

'Sorry he killed him.' She started walking down the corridor, trying hard not to limp. 'He thinks he killed his brother.'

'But Colin must have visited?'

'A few times, yes.'

'Only a few?'

She stopped again, turned to face him. 'How would you feel if every time your brother saw you, he thought you were a ghost?'

Rebus could think of no reply, so gave a shrug. Satisfied with this, she went a few more paces, then stopped at a swing door, ready with her palm against its surface.

'Thanks for your help,' she said.

'My name's John.'

She nodded at this information. 'You're a friend of Mr Flatley. Did he tell you his theory?'

'He thinks people are dying.'

'And what do you think, John?'

'I think you get lousy pay for back-breaking work.'

'And?' Her face was almost breaking into a smile.

'And you do the best you can for your patrons.'

She nodded slowly, pushed open the door and disappeared through it into what seemed to be the kitchen.

*

The painting had been removed from the entrance hall. There was no sign of either Ken Flatley or Donald Morrison. Outside, Morrison's Merc had gone from the car park. As Rebus manoeuvred his own rusting Saab down the driveway, slowing for the speed bumps, each one a potential nail in his car's coffin, he had to pull on to the verge so that a delivery van could pass him. His eyes sought the driver's, expecting some gesture of thanks at the show of courtesy, but the man stared resolutely ahead. The side of the white transit bore the legend 'Pakenham Fresh Fleshing'. Rebus stayed on the verge and watched in his rear-view as the van rattled towards its destination. He knew the driver from somewhere; seemed to recognise the face. It was the jawline, the set of the mouth. Maybe from a butcher's shop, but he didn't know the name Pakenham. All the same, he was reminded that he needed something for dinner. Steak pie maybe, and a tin of marrowfat peas. Or he could always eat out, provided he could find a dinner partner. He thought again of Annie and those deep hazel eyes. Shame she wore a wedding ring. His mobile started ringing. He fished it out of his pocket and checked the display, then held it to his ear.

'How do you fancy dinner tonight, my treat?'

'And will there be any solids involved?' a voice replied.

'Some,' he promised, knowing that Detective Sergeant Siobhan Clarke had already taken the bait.

Diners in the Oxford Bar needed no menu. There was the Cambridge Bar further along Young Street if you really wanted a meal. The Ox, on the other hand, served pies and bridies (until they ran out), and filled rolls – corned beef and beetroot a speciality. Snacks consisted of crisps, nuts and pork scratchings.

'Yummy,' Siobhan Clarke said.

'We can hit a chip shop later if you're not replete,' Rebus responded, placing her vodka and lemonade on the table. She'd settled for a ham and tomato roll. The barman had gone to some lengths to also supply a crusty jar of French mustard. Rebus pulled out a chair and settled himself. Two inches were already missing from his pint of IPA. A macaroni cheese pie sat on the plate before him. 'It was the last hot thing they had,' he explained now.

'I can imagine.'

He took a bite and shrugged. Siobhan spread mustard thinly across the roll, and closed it up again. 'How was Ken?' she asked, lifting it to her mouth.

'He says the inmates are dropping like flies – his exact words.'

'Meaning?'

'Meaning a few of his fellow codgers have caught the last train.'

'Isn't that what happens when you get old?'

Rebus nodded his agreement. 'Something else happened while I was out there.'

Siobhan ate in silence as Rebus told her the story of Lionel Waters. By the end of it, he'd finished his first pint. He raised the empty glass. She shook her head, letting him know she didn't yet need a refill.

'I mean it's your shout,' he said. When she made to get up, he beat her to it. 'Only kidding: you're my guest, remember?'

By the time he returned from the bar, she had finished her roll and was swirling the ice cubes in what was left of her drink.

'I bought my car from Waters Motors,' she told him.

'So did half the city.'

'I'd never heard about a brother, though.'

'Me neither.'

'He's lucky he wasn't lobotomised – they used to do that, you know.'

'You mean they don't any more?'

She saw that he was teasing. 'John F. Kennedy's sister ... I was reading about her only the other day.'

'He had a sister?'

'She died recently. Locked up for sixty years ...'

'And given a lobotomy?'

'That's right.'

'Well, we don't do that any more.'

They sat in silence for a moment, concentrating on their drinks. Siobhan was first to speak. 'What is it?' she asked.

'How do you mean?'

'Something's bugging you. I hope it's not gold fever.'

'What are you talking about?'

'Tales of hidden treasure.' She widened her eyes theatrically. 'They've sent many a man mad before you.'

'Sod off, Siobhan.'

She laughed. 'But there *is* something, isn't there?'

'It's what he said when he was standing in front of me.'

'What?'

'"I'm not what you think I am". He said "what" rather than "who".'

Siobhan snapped her fingers. 'They've swapped places! Lionel is Colin and vice versa – that's how it would work in a film.'

'I'm warning you ...' Rebus stared into his beer. 'And he said "she" – "she buried the body". He wanted to say sorry to his brother.'

Siobhan leaned across the table. 'We're not psychiatrists, John.'

'I know that.'

'We're *detectives*.'

'That's right.' He looked up at her. 'You're absolutely right.'

His tone alerted her. She sat back again, hands resting around her empty glass. 'What are you going to do?'

'For now, I'm going to get you a refill.' He pushed himself to his feet.

'And after?'

'You said it yourself, Shiv: I'm a detective.'

'You're going to see the car man, aren't you?'

A smile flitted across Rebus's face. 'If nothing else, maybe he'll do me a trade-in on the Saab ...'

The main Edinburgh showroom for Waters Motors was just off Calder Road. Rebus headed there next morning, the rush-hour traffic numbing his senses, so that he happily accepted the secretary's offer of caffeine.

'Instant OK?' she asked apologetically.

'Instant's fine.' Colin Waters had yet to arrive from his home in Linlithgow, but that didn't bother Rebus. He had a call to make: to the Scottish Criminal Records Office. During part of the crawl here, he'd stared at the blacked-out windows of the van in front, and this had triggered a memory – a name, which in turn had brought another name into play. He gave both to his SCRO colleague, along with his mobile phone number.

'How soon till you call me?' he asked. He was seated on the showroom's mezzanine level, its smoked-glass walls giving a view of the business area below. The cars on display gleamed. Their very tyres sparkled, picked out by well-positioned halogen bulbs suspended from the ceiling. The salesmen were young and wore commission-bought suits, which made it easy to spot the most successful ones. When the revolving door spat out a newcomer, those who had been sitting leaped to their feet, eyes seeking an acknowledgement from the elderly man in the sagging jacket and slacks.

Colin Waters.

He was in his seventies, much the same age as his brother, but there the similarity ended. Colin Waters was about a foot shorter than Lionel, and boasted a thick head of hair and a face grown pink and round from indulgence. Ignoring the greetings from those around him, he started climbing the open-sided glass staircase, a busy man with a crowded schedule ahead. He glanced at Rebus as he passed him, perhaps mistaking him for a rep of some kind. He closed the office door after him, and Rebus thought he could hear the muffled conversation that followed. When the door opened again, Colin Waters gestured with a crooking of his finger. Rebus thought about staying put – just to see how the man would react – but decided against it. He followed Waters into the office, accepted the mug from the secretary, and watched her leave, closing the door quietly behind her.

There were two desks: one for the secretary, one for her boss. Rebus decided that the proximity had to be for one of two reasons: either Waters liked looking at her, or else he didn't want to miss anything going on around him. Waters was gesturing again, this time for Rebus to sit, but Rebus stayed standing. There was a full-height glass wall here, again looking down on to the sales floor. Rebus pretended to be watching from it, mug cupped in front of him.

'Elaine says you're a police officer,' Waters barked, landing heavily on his own leather-upholstered chair and pulling it in towards his desk.

'That's right, sir. CID.'

'You wouldn't tell her what it's about. All very mysterious.'

'Not really, sir. Just didn't think you'd want me discussing family matters in front of the staff.' When Rebus turned his head, the blood was draining from Waters's face.

'Lionel?' he gasped.

'Don't worry, sir, your brother's fine.' Rebus decided finally to sit down.

'Then what's ... Not Martha?'

'Martha?'

'My sister.' Waters caught himself. 'Obviously not, since you don't know who I'm talking about.'

Rebus was remembering Lionel's words: *she buried the body.* 'Actually, sir, it is about your brother. I happened to be at Renshaw House yesterday, and had to help the staff restrain him. Seems he wanted to walk out of there, so he could find you and say sorry.'

'Oh Christ.' Waters bowed his head, pinching the skin at the bridge of his nose.

'You know he thinks he killed you?'

Colin Waters nodded. 'Right from when he was a kid, we knew there was something that wasn't right about him. He was a lot of fun, though ... boisterous, you know?' He seemed to expect some response, so Rebus produced a slow nod. 'But he never seemed to

have any sense of when he was taking things too far. He'd bite ...
lash out ... even at strangers on the street. Our parents decided he
needed to be kept home, at least for as long as they were able.' He
took a deep breath. 'Martha and I ... we tried to pretend he was
just like anybody else.' He broke off, flicked at something invisible
on the arm of his jacket. 'Special needs is the term these days; back
then, the local children had other ways of putting it. Keeping Lionel
at home became problematic.'

'It couldn't have been easy,' Rebus acknowledged. Waters gave
the briefest of smiles.

'We were wrestling one day,' he said. 'Middle of July – teenagers,
the pair of us – out on the lawn. Lionel loved to wrestle ... probably
fell on me a bit too solidly – he was well built in those days.'

'What happened?'

'I think I passed out. When I came to, he was up to high doh ...
reckoned he'd done me in. We couldn't make him see sense.'

'By "we" you mean ...?'

'Martha and me. She's younger than us. The way he was carrying
on, it scared the hell out of her – roaring like a wild beast, almost
foaming at the mouth. As far as Lionel was concerned, I was a
ghost ...'

Waters paused, lost in memory. His fingers had stretched out to
touch a photo frame on his desk. Rebus could see only the back of it.

'Is that ...?' He pointed to the frame.

'This is afterwards. Me and Martha.'

'Do you mind if I take a look?'

Waters's shoulder twitched as he turned the photo round. It was
black and white, and showed Colin Waters still not quite out of
his teens. His sister looked four or five years younger, breasts just
beginning to appear, hair still held in pigtails. They were seated on
the staircase of what appeared to be a grand house – probably not
dissimilar to Renshaw House. They were peering through the iron
banisters. There was a painting on the wall behind them. Neither
looked particularly happy, and the photographer had failed to get
their faces in sharp focus. There was a ghostly quality to the whole.
Rebus couldn't help wondering why the photo was so important. To
him, it seemed a daily reminder of something lost: the hopes and
dreams of youth.

'Interesting painting,' he said, as Waters turned the photo back
towards himself.

'It's still in the family.'

'Is it a loch or a river?'

'I think the artist invented it, whatever it is. Not too many cliff-top castles in Scotland.'

'Not that I know of.' Rebus made to rise to his feet, Waters following suit.

'I'm still not sure why you came, Inspector,' he commented.

'Me neither,' Rebus told him. Then he slid his hands into his pockets. 'Your brother just seemed so confused and lonely. I take it a visit from you would upset him?'

Waters shrugged. 'I'm a ghost, remember.'

'And your sister? Does she see him much?'

Waters shook his head. 'It upsets her too much to see him like that.' He gestured with an expansive right arm. 'Now, if there's nothing else ...'

'I appreciate your time, sir.' Rebus didn't bother mentioning the Saab; reckoned it would do him another year.

He decided that a further visit to Renshaw House was in order, but first drove towards his home in Marchmont, stopping at the local butcher's shop. He was a known face here, and as with a good barman, the butcher knew what his regulars liked.

'Steak pie, Mr Rebus?' he was asking as Rebus walked over the threshold.

'No thanks, Andy.'

'Couple of nice pork chops, then?'

Rebus shook his head. There was sawdust on the floor – for show rather than anything else. Andy wore a striped apron and a straw boater. Photos on the white-tiled wall showed his father in the self-same get-up. Rebus was struck again by what the photo on Waters's desk must have meant to the car dealer.

'Just a question actually, Andy,' he said.

'Is this me becoming a police informer? The Huggy Bear of Edinburgh?'

Rebus answered the laugh with a smile of his own. He'd never seen the butcher at rest. Even now, with no order to fill, Andy was sorting the display of various hams and sausages. 'I was wondering if you knew about a butcher called Pakenham.'

'Pakenham?'

Rebus spelled it for him. 'They'd be local, I think. "Fresh Fleshing" is what it says on their van.'

'Have they got a shop?'

'I've only seen the van. It was delivering to an old folk's home'

Andy pursed his lips.

'What is it?' Rebus asked.

'Well, it's not always top-grade, is it?'

'Cheap cuts, you mean?'

'Cheapest possible.' Andy held his hands up. 'I'm not saying they're all like that ...'

'But some are?' Rebus nodded to himself. 'Got a phone book, Andy?'

The butcher fetched one from the back of the shop. Rebus checked, but there was no Pakenham Fresh Fleshing.

'Thanks, Andy,' he said, handing it back.

'Sorry I can't be more help. More Yogi Bear than Huggy, eh?'

'Actually, you've been a big help. And maybe I will take one of those steak pies.'

'Family size, as usual?'

'As usual,' Rebus confirmed. He would drop it home before his visit to Renshaw House.

He rang the bell and waited. It was late afternoon now, the sun low in the sky. The detached villa sat on Minto Street, a busy thoroughfare on the city's south side. The house had a faded elegance, its stonework blackened by time and traffic. Most of the houses around it had become bed and breakfasts, but not this one. The name on the unpolished brass door plate was Waters, the letters picked out in verdigris. The sister, it seemed, had never married.

She opened the door herself. No pigtails now, the hair grey and thin, scraped back from the forehead and tucked behind both ears. Her eyes were sunken, as were her cheeks. Colin Waters, it seemed, had stolen all the heartiest genes from his parents.

'Martha Waters?' Rebus said, realising that he was pitching his voice a little louder than was probably necessary – she was only ten or so years older than him.

'Yes?'

He held open his warrant card. 'I'm from the police, Miss Waters. Do you mind if I come in?'

She said nothing, her mouth forming a crumpled O. But she held the door open so he could pass into the hall. It wasn't the same one as in the photograph. The banisters were wooden, darkly varnished. The only natural light came from a window on the upstairs landing. The carpet was ornate but as worn as its owner. She closed the door, adding to the pervasive gloom. Rebus noted an alarm panel on the wall beside the umbrella stand. The panel looked new, with a digital display. A sensor blinked in the far corner of the ceiling.

'Would you care for a cup of tea?' She spoke quietly, pronouncing each syllable. She had yet to ask him why he was here.

'Is there somewhere we can sit, Miss Waters?'

She shuffled in her carpet slippers towards another door, opening it to reveal what she would probably call the parlour. It was like stepping back in time: antimacassars on the sofas, an empty three-tiered cake stand on a large embroidered doily. Little ornaments and knick-knacks covered every surface. A grandfather clock had ceased to work some time back, frozen for ever at one minute to twelve.

'Did you say you wanted tea?' she enquired.

'No thanks.' Rebus had strode over to the fireplace, admiring the large painting framed above the mantel. A bus sped past outside, causing some of the ornaments to rattle. Martha Waters sat herself down. Before his arrival, she'd been listening to the radio: a classical station, the sound barely audible. Nothing much wrong with her hearing, then ... or she was just saving batteries.

'This is a grand painting,' Rebus told her.

'I used to like it,' she said. 'I hardly see it any more.'

Rebus nodded his understanding. Nothing wrong with her eyes either; she meant something else entirely.

'Who's it by?' he asked.

'My brother says it's a Gainsborough.'

'Explains the alarm system ... I take it Colin had that fitted?'

'Do you know about art?'

Rebus shook his head. 'But I know the name. It must be quite old, then.'

'Seventeen eighties.'

'As old as that? And worth a bit, I dare say?'

'Six figures, so Colin tells me.'

Rebus shook his head again, this time in apparent wonder. 'I saw that photograph of it. You know the one I mean?' He turned to her. 'Colin keeps it on his office desk. It stares back at him every working day.'

Her eyes seemed to regain their focus. 'What is it you want here?'

'Me?' He shrugged. 'I just wanted to see it in the flesh. I thought maybe you'd've sold it or something.'

'We could never sell it.'

'Not even after what you went through to get it?'

'I don't know what you mean.'

'I think you do, Miss Waters. I think it's been your little secret all these long years. I've just come from Renshaw House, had a nice long chat with Lionel.'

At the mention of her brother's name, Martha stiffened, clasping her hands on her lap in front of her.

'All those crazy stories he tells ... about his treasure and how he killed his brother ... and how *you* buried him. He keeps rambling about a boat and a castle.' Rebus pointed to the painting. 'And there they are: a castle on a hilltop, fishing boat on the water below it – Lionel's treasure. My bet is, he loved that painting and your parents had decided he could have it. Maybe they were going to will it to him, I don't know. But Colin wanted it, didn't he? And you, young as you were, you wanted it too. Two greedy little kids.' Rebus was standing in front of her now. He crouched so that she couldn't escape his eyes. 'Two brothers having a wrestle. Colin told me Lionel loved to wrestle, but Lionel says he never did: the wrestling was Colin's idea.' Rebus paused for effect. 'And then one of them's not moving, and he's covered in blood. What was it, Martha – ketchup? Paint? Whatever it was, it did the trick, sent Lionel over the edge. Especially when you told him you'd buried Colin.' Rebus stayed in a crouch, but Martha's eyes had drifted to the painting.

'We could never sell it, not after that. We never meant ...' She broke off, took a deep breath. 'We didn't stop to think.'

'You were just a girl, Martha. How were you supposed to know it wasn't a game, some sort of joke? But Colin was that bit older than you ... old enough to know exactly what he was doing. More than half a century Lionel's been kept shut up.'

'It would have happened anyway,' she said in a whisper, a tear trickling from one eye. 'We couldn't have coped. He was driving our parents demented ... nice as ninepence one minute, flying off the handle the next. Schizophrenic, the doctors said. He was turning us into pariahs.'

'You mean the local kids called him names?'

'Not just Lionel ... all of us. We were "the weird ones", "the loonies".' She wiped a hand across her face. 'Do you know how much he's cost us? All the family money, soaked up by care for Lionel.'

'Soaked up by guilt, if you ask me. That's why neither of you could let the painting go.' He rose to his feet. 'All these years ...' He let the words hang in the dusty air. His whole body felt dried out by this house, as if the life were being drained from him.

'What will happen to us?' she asked, her voice trembling.

'Lionel's not going to be in that home much longer – nobody is. So you'll offer him a room here, with his painting above his bed. And if you die before him, you'll make sure the painting goes to him.'

She looked up. 'That's all?'

Rebus offered a shrug. 'Anything you've just told me, Colin will deny – he's got too much to lose. I'd be delighted to see the pair of you in court, but I don't think that will happen. I could dig into your parents' wills, any changes in them, see if the painting was to be Lionel's at any stage, but I'm not sure I'd get anywhere. So ... yes, Miss Waters, that's all.' He started to walk towards the door, but paused.

'You *could* own up, of course, tell Lionel what the two of you did. But I wouldn't, if I were you. It might be too much for him. So don't think of letting Colin near him ... and pray Lionel stays in good health, because if I hear otherwise ... well, I might have to do that digging after all.'

The Suruchi restaurant was Rebus's idea – and his treat.

'Felt I short-changed you last night,' he explained to Siobhan.

After ordering their starters and main courses, they snapped off pieces of poppadom from a central shared plate, dipping them in chutney and biting down on them.

And Rebus told his story.

'Amazing,' she said as he finished. He was drinking lager for a change, while she stuck to mineral water. 'But you're not going to explain it all to Lionel?'

'Even if I got through to him, would it change anything?'

'His whole life's been ...' She couldn't quite find the right words.

'How does that old song go? "If I could turn back time ..." If I could, believe me, I would.'

'It would be handy,' she conceded. 'We'd solve the crimes before they were ever committed.'

'Didn't do Tom Cruise much good in that film.' Their waiter had appeared at the table to clear away the empty plate. Siobhan brushed crumbs from her lap. 'Something else I did today,' Rebus was adding.

'What?'

'Solved Ken Flatley's little mystery.'

She looked at him. 'Who's been a busy boy then?'

He shrugged. 'Easy enough once I remembered the face driving the meat van. Belongs to a guy called Bernie Cable. I arrested him once at Ingliston Market.'

'A Trading Standards bust?'

Rebus nodded. 'Cable was selling dodgy meat from a van.'

'Is this something I should be hearing prior to dinner?'

'Chicken breasts past their sell-by ... that sort of stuff.'

'And now he's selling meat to care homes?'

'Until today he was. I've been on to Environmental Health ... the council ... Trading Standards.'

'You *have* been busy.'

'That's not the half of it. When I asked the Records Office to look up Cable, I gave them Donald Morrison's name too.'

'That suspicious mind of yours.' Siobhan leaned back as a clean plate was placed before her. Another waiter stood ready with orders of pakora and kebab.

'It was the way Morrison addressed me,' Rebus explained. 'He kept calling me "Inspector", even though I'd made it clear I wasn't there in any official capacity.'

'And that got your antennae clicking?'

'Made me think I might not be the first cop he'd ever had dealings with.'

'And?'

'And his name's not really Morrison – that's one of his many aliases. Real name's Charles Kirkup. He's been done for fraud.'

'You reckon he was in cahoots with Cable?'

'I contacted the hospital about those poor old sods who died. Food poisoning didn't show up on the original autopsies, but they're going to check again. It's like Ken said: the pathologists aren't always so rigorous when the corpse was on its last legs anyway.'

'So he was right, after a fashion?'

Rebus nodded.

'And you've told the council this?' Another nod. 'So now he'll be closed down?'

'Bound to be.'

'And where will Ken go?'

'I told him you had a spare room.' Rebus bit into a kebab.

'I've got a better idea,' Siobhan said, spooning sauce over her pakora. 'Colin Waters will know an investment when he sees one. He could keep the place open, maybe just promote one of the staff to manage it.'

Rebus saw those hazel eyes again. 'And why would he do that?'

'You could tell him there's a Gainsborough resting on it,' Siobhan said coyly. 'And after all, if he owns Renshaw House, he won't have to pay for Lionel's care any more. I'm sure you could get Martha to argue your case for you.'

Rebus was thoughtful. 'Maybe I could at that.'

'Atonement, I think it's called.'

'Whatever it's called, I'll drink to it,' Rebus said, raising his glass.

Not Just Another Saturday

It had taken Rebus longer than usual to get to the barber's shop on Rose Street. He'd known about the Make Poverty History march, of course; just hadn't reckoned with the barriers going up so early. Melville Drive had been filling with buses from all over: church congregations from Derbyshire; anti-nuclear pensioners; African drummers; Fair Trade and Christian Aid and Water Aid and Farm Aid ... everything but the one thing Rebus needed – Lucozade. He'd only drunk four pints the previous night, but one of them must have been bad.

There was a stage erected on the Meadows, along with tents and vans preparing to sell food to the hungry masses. Someone was doling out Palestinian flags. The *Sunday Mail* had provided placards saying 'Drop the Debt'. People were dropping the placards instead, then tearing off the newspaper's name before picking them up again. Maybe they were southerners, confusing the Scottish paper with its near-namesake. Rebus was handed a plastic carrier bag. Inside he found a Help the Aged T-shirt. First kid he saw, he passed the bag along. He knew George IV Bridge would be impossible, so headed for South Bridge instead, feeling like a salmon swimming against the prevailing current. Families passed him, the kids with their faces painted. People were smiling in the sun, ready to be seen if not heard. At Fettes HQ, the High Hiedyins had guessed 175,000, but to Rebus it looked likely there'd be more: 200, maybe 250. A quarter of a million people, more than half the city's population. Scale it up, it became four million on the streets of London. Maybe that was why everyone was smiling. They had no need to shout. Their very presence would be louder than that.

Teams of uniforms milled around. Rebus didn't recognise any of them. Their accents were foreign. One sported Metropolitan Police insignia; others were from Cardiff, Liverpool, Middlesbrough ... every bit as varied as the marchers. Rebus didn't stop to say hello. He looked the way he felt: like a civilian. When the cops bothered to meet his eyes, he saw no recognition there. Just mistrust, mixed with controlled adrenalin. They'd been warned to expect trouble. Looked to Rebus as though a few of them might even welcome it. A couple of police motorbikes were controlling traffic on Buccleuch Street, making sure drivers followed the diversions. Not much for them to do, the roads unnaturally quiet for a Saturday. But then this wasn't just another Saturday. He did a double-take when he saw what was written on the back of one yellow protective jacket: London Transport Police. Nice overtime, but he couldn't help feeling the officer would be more use on his own patch, chasing muggers and fare-dodgers. More diversions, more police checkpoints. Some of his colleagues were loving it, looking forward to the whole week. They'd get to tear around the city like they owned it. Courts and cells had been cleared, ready for action. Everyone was poised.

'You'll have to go back that way, sir,' a uniform was explaining now, as Rebus tried to squeeze through the gap between one metal crash barrier and a tenement wall. The accent was English.

Rebus made show of looking back in the direction the man was pointing.

'You mean, cut along the Meadows, through the hordes and the coaches, and take a right at Tollcross, then make a sudden stop at the first barricade on Lothian Road, where I'll be politely told to "go back that way, sir"?'

The officer's eyes narrowed. When Rebus moved a hand towards his inside pocket, he even took a step back.

'Easy, pal, easy,' Rebus said, bringing out his warrant card. 'We're supposed to be on the same side.'

The officer studied the ID for longer than Rebus felt necessary. 'CID,' he said, handing it back. 'Something going down?' He hauled at the barrier, giving Rebus more room.

'Could be a close shave,' Rebus answered, heading on his way.

A close shave it was. Barber's shop on Rose Street. An occasional Saturday treat: hot towels, unguents, the works. Even a splash of cologne afterwards. They didn't use cut-throat razors these days: fear of hep B and HIV. Little disposable blades instead. Still gave a good shave, even though Rebus missed the sliding of the cut-throat against the leather strap. As a kid, he'd watched his father get a regular wet shave, the barber winking at him as he honed the gleaming blade.

'Might call it a day,' the barber told Rebus now. 'Most of my bookings have cancelled.'

'Wimps,' Rebus said.

'Half the shops on Princes Street are shut. Some with the boards up. That fellow Geldof, he wants a million marchers.'

'He won't get them,' Rebus said. 'Man runs a decent concert, but that's about it. He'll get his moment in the sun, shake hands with George W even, and that'll be about it.'

The barber snorted. 'We're maybe cynical old buggers, John.'

'I marched in the sixties.'

'But not now?'

Rebus just shrugged. It was different then, he wanted to say. But he wasn't sure that was true. *He* was different then; no doubt about that. He'd always assumed ideals were for the young, but the people he'd seen heading for the march ... they'd been all ages. Probably all backgrounds and creeds, too. The sun was out, and forty miles up the road at Gleneagles, eight men would sit down to make decisions affecting the whole planet. Not that there was any pressure. Edinburgh's own Chief Constable would be there too, shuffling around in the background, usurped by spooks and Special Branch, bodyguards and Marines. Jack McConnell kept saying how great it was for Scotland, putting the place on the map. Rebus wondered how close Jack would get to the real power; suspected he'd be little more than a meeter and greeter, positioned front-of-house while the real work went on elsewhere.

'Off to the Ox?' the barber said.

'As per,' Rebus acknowledged. A wee Saturday afternoon session: racing on TV and a filled roll to feed the soul. The Live Eight concert would be on later. He'd probably watch The Who and Pink Floyd – especially the Floyd; had to see it with his own eyes. If Dave Gilmour let Roger Waters back on stage with him, anything was possible ... maybe even world peace, an end to hunger and a cure for global warming.

'Might shut up shop and follow you,' the barber said.

'I'll wait,' Rebus offered. The man nodded and began to sweep up. Rebus stepped outside for a cigarette, watching through the window as towels were dumped in a laundry bag, cutters cleaned, the basin rinsed. There was something comforting in observing a person's routine. It was a ritual that placed a full stop at the end of a working day, and it showed pride, too. Combs and clippers went into a little leather pouch, which was rolled up and tied shut. They'd go home with the barber: his talisman.

At last he turned off the lights and switched on the alarm, locking the door behind him. He looked up at the sky. Rebus nodded to let him know he could hear it too: a cacophony of chants, whistles and drums in the near distance. The march had reached Princes Street.

'Fancy a quick look-see?' the barber asked.

'Sure,' Rebus said.

They walked down together. More barricades separated the slow parade from bemused shoppers. Policemen stood with arms folded, legs slightly parted. This was ritual, too. Rebus didn't doubt there'd be troublemakers dotted about the place. Something like this would be a magnet for the city's tearaways, never mind the international brotherhood of anarchists. But right now it all looked as innocuous as a cavalcade.

'Think anyone's listening?' the barber asked. But Rebus couldn't answer that. He noticed that the windows of the shops behind them were covered with protective boards.

'Even the Ann Summers shop,' the barber said with a laugh. 'Can you see the good folk of Edinburgh looting a few bits of cheeky lingerie?'

Rebus shook his head. 'It's the Basque separatists they're afraid of,' he said, lighting another cigarette.

Just for a moment, as he smoked and watched the march, there was the temptation to join in, to add another particle to the mass. But he knew he lacked the passion and the faith. He could try comforting himself with the thought that it wouldn't change anything. The rules of the game were well established, the cards already dealt. But doing nothing wouldn't change anything either. In the end it was the barber who broke the spell, offering up a shrug of his own, that most Scottish of gestures. As if synchronised, the two men turned away from the march.

They wouldn't have let you smoke anyway, Rebus told himself. But he knew he would spend the rest of the day wondering. Wondering, and maybe even regretting.

Penalty Claus

They even had a name for themselves: the Holly and Ivy Gang.

It was Debby's idea. 'They're our aliases.'

Her mother, Liz, wasn't so sure. 'Why do we need aliases? And which one am I?'

'You're Ivy.'

Liz snorted at this. 'Why can't I be Holly?'

'The name's just something they can use about us on the news.'

'But that's my whole point – we're good at this, and that means we don't get anywhere *near* the news.'

'But just in case ...'

'Besides which, there's only the two of us, so we're not technically a "gang".'

'Bandits, then. The Holly and Ivy Bandits ...'

Liz was in the electric wheelchair. Debby was on a hard plastic seat next to her. They were at a table in a fast-food restaurant on Princes Street. Debby's chair was bolted to the floor, meaning she couldn't get comfortable. They were having a bit of a rest. Edinburgh wasn't a place they knew well. They'd come by train, booking off-peak to make it worthwhile. Liz had her head screwed on about such things. No point making money on the day if your outgoings added up to more.

'Harsh economic realities,' she'd explained, nodding slowly at her own wisdom.

Debby was in her early twenties, Liz her mid forties. They lived in a scheme on the outskirts of Glasgow. Glasgow's shopping streets had given them their first taste of success, three years back. The run-up to Christmas, that was their season. They'd get want-lists from friends and would always say, 'We'll see what we can do.' But the lists had to be specific: electrical goods were usually too bulky and well guarded. Clothes and perfumes were what it came down to. Dresses and tops; posh underwear; Paris brands. Liz in the wheelchair, shopping bags hooked over its handles, a travel rug on her lap. Debby light-fingered and shrewd, eyes in the back of her head.

There'd be security staff, but they could be blindsided or distracted. CCTV wasn't always the all-seeing eye. The clothes would carry security tags, but that was where the wheelchair came in. Exiting each shop, Liz would get a bit clumsy and barge into the alarm rail, setting it off. There'd be apologies from Debby as she helped her mother manoeuvre the chair past the obstacle. The staff would be helpful, might even say that the security measures were a pain. No one, so far, had ever stopped them and asked for a rummage.

There was a big 'but', though. It wasn't the sort of stunt you could pull time and again. If you went back to the same shop and set the alarm off a second time, there'd be a bit more suspicion. So they'd moved the operation from Glasgow to Dundee last year, and now it was Edinburgh's turn. Princes Street: big names ... department stores and fashion chains ... easy pickings. They'd already done three shops, and after the burger and fizzy drink would try at least two more.

'Need the loo?' Debby asked. Her mother shook her head. The stuff they'd lifted so far, Debby had gone into Princes Street Gardens with it and found a hiding place in a clump of bushes. Always a worry: you never knew if it would be waiting for you at the day's end. But you couldn't risk the tags setting off alarms as you entered other shops – a lesson learned after their very first attempt. Besides, they needed the shopping bags on the back of the wheelchair nice and empty, the travel rug unbulging.

Their next port of call was all of twenty yards further along the street. Liz had felt it worth pointing out that Princes Street was good for wheelchairs: ramped pavements, helpful pedestrians. Waverley Station had been more of a challenge, sunk as it was beneath street level. All the same, the day was shaping up. They'd even discussed going further afield next time – Carlisle or Newcastle or Aberdeen. Debby wasn't sure about England: 'we'd stand out a mile with these accents'. But her mother had added that maybe they didn't need to wait a whole year. Their friends were always after clothes and make-up and other bits and pieces.

'This operation could go global,' was the seed she planted in her daughter's head.

Their chosen shop turned out to be less than brilliant. The better stuff was kept under glass. The available accessories looked cheap because they were cheap. It was a question of weighing up the risks. The guard was in a uniform of sorts and prowled the floor like he was pacing a cage, just waiting to pounce. The music was too loud for Liz's taste. The place was packed with customers, too. There was a sort of ideal midway point: you didn't want it to be dead, but neither did you want too many pairs of eyes on you. That was one thing about the wheelchair: it drew attention. You had to be careful.

On their way to the exit, Liz did some clumsy reversing. The alarm rang out, the red light on the sensor flashing. Debby started to chide her and the security guard came over. She told him she was sorry.

'One too many sherries,' she explained. 'Lucky there's nobody with a breathalyser.'

'It happens,' the guard said with a smile. He was resetting the alarm as Liz trundled the chair out through the doors. Her way was blocked by a pair of legs. She looked up and saw that the man had his arms folded. He was smiling too, but she sensed there was nothing friendly about it.

'Aw, no,' was all she said.

'So who does the wheelchair belong to?'

Liz and Debby were seated in one of the interview rooms at Gayfield Square police station. Detective Inspector John Rebus was standing, arms folded again.

'It was my gran's,' Debby answered.

Rebus nodded slowly. Even he – though he would never admit as much – had been surprised when Liz Doherty had opted for a patrol car over a van with a ramp at the back. She had risen from the wheelchair with what might have passed for a sheepish look and walked to the car unaided.

'And where's your gran now?' he asked.

'Buried her four years back. Nobody ever came for the wheelchair ...'

Liz asked for a cup of tea. Rebus told her she'd get one in a minute.

'Before that,' he said, 'I need you to tell me where the rest of the stuff is.'

The silence was broken by Debby. 'What stuff?'

Rebus made a tutting sound, as though disappointed in her. He dragged the empty chair out from under the table and sat down so he was facing both women.

'You're not as smart as you think you are. Store detectives tend to share gossip about their day. They'd start telling each other about the clumsy woman in the wheelchair. Glasgow two years back and Dundee last. So you might say alarm bells were ringing across the country. First shop you were in today, they got on the phone. You'd done two more by the time I could get to the scene. We've got CCTV going back three years. It was just a matter of time ...'

'Don't know what you're talking about,' Liz muttered.

Rebus tutted again. 'Christmas in the cells for the pair of you. Is there a Mr Doherty?'

'Aye,' from the mother. A shake of the head from the daughter.

'Best tell him he'll be doing his own cooking.'

'Couldn't boil an egg,' Debby blurted out. Then, turning towards her mother, 'And he's *not* Mr Doherty. He's just a fat guy you brought home one night.'

'That's enough from you,' her mother snapped back.

Rebus let them bicker for a few more minutes, biding his time by checking messages on his phone. Debby kept looking at the device greedily. Her own mobile had been taken from her at the booking desk. Half an hour had passed, and she was suffering the texting DTs.

'What did we ever do without these?' Rebus asked out loud, twisting the knife.

'So when do we get out?' Liz Doherty was fixing him with a look.

'When the process says you can,' Rebus assured her. 'But I'm still waiting to hear where the rest of the stuff is. Hidden up a lane somewhere? Or how about Princes Street Gardens? Me, I'd probably say the Gardens. Edinburgh's not your turf. Laziest option's probably the one you went for.' He turned his attention back to his phone's screen.

'Am I warm?' he asked into the silence. 'Toasty warm,' he decided.

He gave it a couple more minutes, then got up, stretched, and left the room. Liz Doherty was reminding him about the tea as he closed the door on her. He went to the machine and got one for himself, then took it outside so he could smoke a cigarette. He had half a mind to phone his colleague, Siobhan Clarke. She was on a surveillance operation and hadn't replied to the dozen or so mischievous texts he'd sent her over the course of the past twenty-four hours. It was mid afternoon, but dark and damp in the car park. A metal No Smoking notice on the brick wall had seen so many butts stubbed out on it that its message had been all but obliterated. Rebus stood next to it and tried not to think about Christmas. He would be on his own, because that was how he liked it. There were a couple of pubs he could visit on the day itself. He'd buy himself something decent for dinner, and a better-than-usual bottle of malt. Maybe a few CDs and a DVD box-set. Sorted. Then, mid evening would come the phone call or the door buzzer. Siobhan Clarke, feeling sorry for him and maybe a little for herself, though she would never admit it.

She'd want them to watch a soppy comedy, or go for a stroll through the silent streets. He had already considered his options, but felt he couldn't let her down, couldn't scurry out of town for the day or unplug his phone.

'Humbug,' he said, stabbing the remains of his cigarette against the sign.

Back indoors, a couple of officers were discussing the bag-snatcher. He'd gone and done it again, the little sod. His targets were the elderly and infirm, walking frames and wheelchairs a speciality. There'd be a handbag hanging from one or the other, and he'd have his hand in and out of it in a flash, hurtling from the scene with bus passes, purses and keepsakes, none of which ever turned up, meaning he was either dumping them intelligently or else keeping them as trophies. Description: denims and a dark hooded top. The local evening paper had been having a go at the police for their inability to stop him, interviewing victims and potential targets.

Shopping centres were what he liked. The Gyle, Waverley, Cameron Toll.

'Got to be the St James Centre one of these days,' one of the officers was saying. Yes, that was Rebus's feeling, too. The St James Centre, sited at the east end of Princes Street. Plenty of exits. All on one level, meaning it was popular with the walking frames and wheelchairs.

Walking frames and wheelchairs ...

Rebus ran a finger from his chin to his Adam's apple, then made his way back to the interview room.

There had obviously been a bit of a falling-out. The daughter was up on her feet, standing in one corner with her back to the room. The mother had decided to turn away from her in her chair. Rebus cleared his throat.

'All out of tea,' he said. 'But I've brought something else instead.'

Both women turned their heads towards him. Both asked the same question: 'What?'

'A deal,' Rebus said, retaking his seat and motioning for Debby Doherty to do the same.

Siobhan Clarke had another two hours left of her shift. She was seated in an unmarked car alongside a detective constable called Ronnie Wilson. The small talk had run out of steam almost before it had begun. Ronnie had no interest in football or music. He built models – galleons and racing cars and the like. There were blobs of glue on the tips of his fingers, which he took delight in picking clean.

And he had a cold, a persistent sniffle. Siobhan had tried the radio, but he only seemed to like the classical station, and then proceeded to hum along to the first three tunes, causing Siobhan to switch the sound off. There was a faint aroma in the car: the cheese and onion sandwich Wilson had brought with him from home; the chive and sour cream crisps he'd bought from a petrol station. Every now and then he would attempt to dislodge a morsel from between his teeth with his tongue or a fingernail, making sucking noises throughout.

They were parked in a suburban street. It was lined with cars and vans, meaning they stood out less. They were sixty yards shy of John Kerr's bungalow. The family was at home – wife Selina and teenage son and daughter. Everyone but John Kerr himself. Kerr had gone on the run from prison two days ago. He'd been done for fraud, tax evasion and a dozen or so further money-related crimes, but all without landing his employer in it with him. Kerr was the accounting brain behind Morris Gerald Cafferty's operation. Cafferty had more or less run Edinburgh these past several decades. If money was to be made from anything illegal, you'd usually find his name linked to it somewhere. But despite a lengthy court appearance and a slew of questions and inferences, Kerr had kept his trap shut. Then, on a community work placement to the west of the city, he'd simply walked off the job and not come back.

Siobhan had the files with her. They took up half the back seat, and every now and then she would reach for one and flick through it. Kerr had been sentenced to two and a half years, but with good behaviour and incentives would serve only nine or ten months. A model prisoner, it said in the report. Helping inmates on a literacy programme; working in the library; keeping himself to himself. Of course, no one was going to have a pop at him – he was protected by his employer's reputation. So why did he do a runner? As far as anyone could see, the answer had to be Christmas. He wasn't due to be released until March. There were photos in one of the folders. Kerr playing Santa Claus at an old people's home; Kerr – again dressed as Santa – donating a Christmas tree to a city hospice; Kerr with a sack of toys as he arrived at a special needs school ...

Siobhan stared through the windscreen. The bungalow was unassuming. The car in the driveway was a five-year-old mid-range Jaguar. The wife worked behind the desk at a health centre. The kids went to a private school, but that was far from unusual in Edinburgh. It didn't appear to be a lavish lifestyle for a man who'd had two million pounds in his various accounts at the time of his arrest. Siobhan studied his photograph again. Kerr was fifty, short and overweight. That was why they were guessing he'd use the front door. An eight-foot-high fence went around the rest of the property, disguised by leylandii. Nobody could envisage Kerr shinning his way into his garden. He would use front gate, path and door.

Because of Christmas. Because Christmas obviously meant something to him. Siobhan had already asked Wilson what plans he had for the big day. He was travelling to see his parents, who lived in Peterhead. He'd catch up with old pals from school. Boxing Day would see a schedule of visits to members of what seemed to be a hugely extended family. Siobhan just had her mum and dad, and they were in England. She could surprise them, turn up out of the blue, but she knew she wouldn't. She had to visit Rebus, make sure he wasn't sinking. Keep his spirits up. He would miss her if she didn't.

She looked at the clock on the dashboard. An hour and forty minutes till the changeover. She felt muzzy from inactivity. She'd taken a couple of breaks, walking around the block. Christmas trees in most of the windows, lights sparkling. One householder had gone a bit further, adding an outdoor display: reindeer and sleigh on the roof; a waterfall effect cascading down the walls and past the windows; polystyrene snowman next to the front step. Her own decorations hadn't been put up yet. They were still in their box in the hall cupboard. She was wondering whether it was worth going to all the trouble when no one would see them but her.

Wilson was whistling through his teeth. Sounded vaguely like a carol. There was a newspaper on his lap, crossword and other puzzles completed. He was drumming his fingers against the newsprint. Ten seconds he'd been at it, and she was already irritated. But he stopped and jerked his head around as the car's back door flew open. Files and folders were shoved aside. Someone had climbed in and was slamming the door shut again. Siobhan looked in the rear-view mirror.

'Evening,' she said. Then, for Wilson's benefit: 'Don't panic. He's with us. DC Wilson, meet DI Rebus.'

Wilson had had a shock and was slow to recover. He stretched out a trembling hand, which Rebus met with his own.

'Smells like a chip shop in here,' Rebus stated.

'My fault,' Wilson owned up.

'Don't apologise, son. I'm quite liking it.'

'What brings you here?' Siobhan asked.

'You never got back to me.' Rebus was trying to sound aggrieved.

Siobhan's eyes met his in the mirror. 'No, I didn't,' she said. 'So you thought you'd come and gloat in person?'

'Who's gloating? Nice warm car. Bit of a chinwag and a read of the papers ... not a bad way to spend a shift. Some of us are out there on the front line.'

Siobhan's face creased into a smile.

'I haven't heard any reports,' Wilson said in all seriousness.

'Princes Street's a war zone, son. Those Christmas shoppers are like something out of a video game.' Rebus made show of peering in the direction of the bungalow. 'No sign of Al Capone? Do we think he's armed and dangerous?' He had opened one of the files. He knew about John Kerr, knew all about him. Cafferty had been top of Rebus's hit list for most of his professional life. He was picking up the photos Siobhan had been looking at, the Christmas shots.

'I doubt he'll be armed,' Wilson said into the silence, having given the matter some thought. Rebus and Siobhan shared a look. 'Nothing in his profile suggests violent tendencies.'

'Violent tendencies?' Rebus was nodding slowly. He patted Wilson on the shoulder. 'With insights like that, son, you're headed to the top. Wouldn't you agree, DS Clarke? Young officers like Wilson here are the future of the force.'

Siobhan Clarke managed the slightest of nods. Wilson looked as if his name had just been announced at school prize-giving.

'Let me ask you this,' Rebus went on. He had Wilson's full attention now. 'What makes you think Kerr'll come back here? Won't he know we're waiting for him to do just that?'

'No sign of the family shipping out elsewhere for Christmas,' Siobhan felt obliged to respond.

Rebus was shaking his head. 'They don't need to. But tell me this ...' She saw that he was holding up one of the photos of Kerr dressed as Santa Claus. 'Where's St Nick going to go when his sledge lands in our fair city?'

'Rooftops?' Wilson guessed. 'Chimneys?' He even looked out towards the bungalow, as if scanning the skies above it.

Siobhan kept silent. Rebus would tell them eventually. Tell them what he'd gleaned in two minutes that they'd been unable to work out over the past two days. But instead he posed a further question.

'Where do *all* the jolly Santas go?'

And then, for the first time, Siobhan knew the answer.

Two in the afternoon, a couple of hours of daylight left, and Princes Street Gardens was filling up. The Festival of Santas drew locals as well as tourists to watch a couple of hundred Father Christmases running for charity. Some participants were changing into their costumes; others had arrived suited and bearded. As usual, there were some flourishes: a tartan suit instead of the archetypal red; a long blue beard in place of white ... It was a well-organised event. Each runner had raised money by sponsorship. They'd registered beforehand and were given numbers to attach to their costumes, just like any other athlete. Registration was a bonus for Siobhan: made it easy to check the alphabetised list of runners to ensure there was no one called John Kerr on it.

'Could be using an alias,' Wilson had proposed.

But it was much more likely he would just turn up, hoping to blend in with the other runners. Except he wouldn't quite blend in. He'd be the Santa with no number on his back.

'Bit of a long shot?' Wilson had suggested.

No, not really; just annoying that Rebus had thought of it first. A chance for Kerr to spend time with his family without the fear of being apprehended as he entered his home. Siobhan rubbed her hands together, trying to put some feeling back into them. She and Wilson had watched the taxi pull to a stop outside the bungalow. They'd watched Selina Kerr and her son and daughter come out of the house. They had stayed a couple of cars back from the cab as it headed for the city centre.

'Bingo,' Siobhan had said as the cab signalled to a stop on Princes Street.

But then there had been a slight glitch. The son, Francis, had begun a conversation on the pavement with his mother. She had seemed to remonstrate with him. He'd touched her arm, as if to reassure her, then had turned and walked away, sticking his hands into the front of his jacket. His mother had called after him, then rolled her eyes.

'Should we split up?' Wilson had suggested to Siobhan. 'I'll tail him, you stay with mother and daughter?'

Siobhan had shaken her head.

'What if he's off to see his dad?'

'He's not. I think that's what's got his mum narked.'

As Francis Kerr melted into the crowd of shoppers, Selina Kerr and daughter Andrea crossed the street towards the Gardens. They weren't the only ones, of course. Probably a thousand or more spectators would be on hand to watch the runners. But Siobhan and Wilson had no trouble keeping them in view, thanks to Andrea's bright-pink knee-length coat and matching bobble hat.

'Not exactly subtle,' was Rebus's comment when they caught up with him. He was finishing a mug of glühwein from the German market, and a garlicky sausage smell was wafting up from his fingers.

'Getting in the spirit?' Siobhan asked.

'Always.' He smacked his lips and glanced towards mother and daughter. 'Was I right or was I right?'

'Well, they're here,' Siobhan commented. 'But that could just be family tradition.'

'Aye, right.' Rebus took out his mobile phone and checked the screen.

'We keeping you from something?' Siobhan asked.

'Bit of business elsewhere,' Rebus stated. People were milling around. Some had started taking photographs of the Santas, or of the glowering Castle Rock, acting as background scenery to this performance. A DJ had been installed on the Ross Bandstand and was playing the usual favourites, between which he doled out instructions to the runners and interviewed a few of them. One Santa had run from Dundee to Edinburgh, collecting money all the way. There was a cheer from the crowd and a round of applause.

'They don't seem to be on the lookout for anyone,' Wilson commented, watching the mother and daughter.

'Don't seem that excited either,' Siobhan added.

'This was probably Kerr's idea,' Rebus suggested. 'They'd much rather be meeting him in the Harvey Nicks café, but Kerr needs his wee annual dressing-up fix.' He paused. 'Where's the son?'

'Francis came as far as Princes Street,' Siobhan explained, 'but then went his own way.'

Rebus watched Selina Kerr check the time and then turn to peer in the direction of the gates. She said something to her daughter, who glanced in the same direction, gave a shrug, then did some texting on her phone.

'Can we get any closer?' Wilson asked.

'If Kerr sees us, we lose him,' Siobhan cautioned.

'Always supposing he's coming. What if he's meeting them one at a time? The son comes back and the daughter heads off?'

'It's a fair point,' Rebus agreed. 'We can only wait and see.' He looked at his own phone again.

'This bit of business ...' Siobhan began. Rebus just shook his head.

'Think he'll actually do any running?' Wilson was asking.

'Not without a number. The organisers are pretty strict.'

Rebus's phone was ringing. He held it to his ear.

'Ten minutes left until the start,' the DJ was announcing. 'Get those limbs warmed up. Can't have any Santa cramps ...'

'Yes?' Rebus asked into the phone.

'We didn't get him.' It was Debby's voice. She was calling from the St James Centre. Rebus could hear noises in the background: bystanders, trying to comfort Liz.

'He got away?' Rebus guessed.

'Aye. Fast as a ferret. Maybe if you'd been here ...'

'What about security?'

'The guy's right here. Ferret shot past him. Got away with the purse.'

The purse with nothing in it. The purse sitting in a tempting position at the top of the shopping bag on the back of the wheelchair.

The bait.

The bait that had so nearly worked.

'Description?' Rebus asked.

'Same one you gave us. Just another hoodie with trackie bottoms and trainers ...'

'Hey, look,' Wilson was saying. There was a Santa standing just behind Selina Kerr and her daughter. Behind them and between them. Talking to them. Andrea Kerr spun round and gave him a hug.

'That him?' Wilson was asking.

'We tried, though,' Debby was telling Rebus. 'We did what you told us to. So the deal's still good, eh? You'll still put in a word?'

'I have to go,' Rebus told her. 'Be at the police station in an hour. I'll meet you there.'

'And you'll put in a word?'

'I'll put in a word.'

'We're the Holly and Ivy Bandits, remember ...'

Rebus slid the phone back into his pocket.

'Is it him?' Siobhan was asking. There were so many heads between them and the Kerrs, and the light was already fading.

'Got to be.' Wilson was sounding agitated, ready to barge in there.

'Is there a number on his back? Let's get a bit closer.' Siobhan was already heading off. Rebus clasped a hand around Wilson's forearm.

'Nice and slow,' he cautioned.

They took a wide curve around and behind the three figures. The three figures in animated conversation.

A young man brushed past Rebus, and the three were suddenly four. Francis Kerr had his hands stuffed in his pockets. Black hooded top ... tracksuit bottoms ... dark blue trainers ... He was sweating, breathing hard. Nodded at Santa without taking his hands from the pouch on the front of his jacket. Santa gave him a playful punch on the shoulder. Rebus decided it was time to move, Siobhan and

Wilson flanking him. The competitors were being called to the starting line.

'All right, John?' Rebus said, tugging down the elasticated beard and staring into the face of John Kerr.

'Leave him alone,' Selina Kerr snarled. 'He's not done anything.'

'Oh, but he has. He's led young Francis here astray.' Rebus nodded in the son's direction. John Kerr's brow furrowed.

'How do you mean?'

'Might not be your influence,' Rebus allowed. 'Might be your employer's. But something's rubbed off, hasn't it, Francis?' Rebus turned towards the youth. 'Private school and plenty of money ... makes me wonder why you'd take the risk.' He held out his hand. 'Still got the purse, or did you ditch it already? Bit miffed that it was empty, I dare say. But there's plenty of CCTV. Plenty of witnesses, too. Wonder what the search warrant'll turn up in your bedroom ...'

'Francis?' John Kerr's voice was shaking. 'What's he talking about?'

'Nothing,' the son muttered. His shoulders were twitching.

'Then take your hands out and show me.' When his son made show of ignoring this, Kerr took a step forward and hauled both hands out from their hiding place. The purse dropped to the ground. Selina Kerr clamped a hand to her mouth, but Andrea didn't seem surprised. Rebus thought to himself: she probably knows; maybe he told her, proud of his little secret and desperate to share.

'Well now,' Rebus said into the silence. 'There's good news as well as bad.' John Kerr stared at him. 'The bad news,' he went on, 'is that the two of you are coming with us.'

'And the good?' John Kerr asked in a voice just above a whisper.

'Courts won't be sitting until after Christmas. Means the two of you can share a cell at the station for the duration of the festivities.' He looked towards mother and daughter. 'I don't suppose a visit's out of the question either.'

There were whoops and screams from the spectators. The race had begun. Rebus glanced in Siobhan's direction.

'Don't say I never give you anything,' he told her. 'And this year,' gesturing towards Kerr's Santa outfit, 'it even comes gift-wrapped ...'

The Passenger

'She was from Edinburgh.'

'The victim?'

Siobhan Clarke shook her head and gestured towards the book Rebus was holding. 'Muriel Spark.'

It was a slim paperback, not much more than a hundred pages. Rebus had been looking at the blurb on the back. He placed the book on the bedside table where he'd found it.

'How much does a room like this cost?' he asked.

'Got to be a few hundred.' Clarke saw his look. 'Yes, that does mean per night.'

'With breakfast extra, I dare say.'

Clarke was opening the last drawer, checking it was every bit as empty as the others. The small suitcase lay on the floor under the window, unzipped and mostly unpacked. The victim had changed just the once. A toilet bag sat next to the sink in the bathroom. She had showered, made up her face, and brushed her teeth. Clothes lay rumpled on the floor next to the bed – short dress, slip, tights, underwear. A pair of black high-heeled shoes. Jewellery on the bedside table next to the book, including an expensive watch.

'Her name's Maria Stokes,' Clarke said. Rebus had picked up the woman's handbag. It had already been taken apart by the scene-of-crime team. Cash and credit cards still in her purse, meaning they were probably ruling out robbery as a motive.

'Where's she from?' Rebus asked.

'We don't know that yet. I've got someone going through her phone.'

'She didn't give an address when she checked in?'

'Not needed. Just signed her name and turned down the offer of a newspaper or wake-up call.'

'And this was Friday?'

'Friday afternoon,' Clarke confirmed. 'Do Not Disturb sign on the door, meaning it wasn't until lunchtime today that anyone bothered to knock.'

'And they knocked because ...?'

'Checkout's eleven. They needed to get the room ready. Called up from reception but of course she didn't answer. Just assumed she'd left, I suppose.'

'Maid must have got a fright.' Rebus was staring at the unmade bed. He thought Maria Stokes's outline was still there, contoured into the sheets and pillows.

'Doctor reckons she was probably killed the night she got here. Whoever did it, they were clever to put the sign on the door.'

'I suppose we're lucky she didn't pay for a week. How do you think he got in?'

'Either he had a key card, or he just knocked.'

Rebus nodded. 'Someone knocks, you'll assume it's staff. Hotel's the easiest place to walk in and out of, as long as you look like you belong.'

'We'll be asking the manager if there have been any problems.'

'Stuff going missing from rooms, you mean? Not the sort of thing they'd want to broadcast.'

'I wouldn't think so.'

Rebus was studying a card on the dressing table. 'There's a list here of all the different pillows you can request with your turndown service. Doesn't say if strangulation comes extra. What time's the autopsy?'

Clarke glanced at her watch. 'Just under an hour.'

'Staff are being questioned? CCTV?' Rebus watched her nod. 'Not much more for us to do here, then.'

'Not much,' she agreed.

He took a final look around. 'A better place to die than some, but even so ...'

'Even so,' Clarke echoed.

Maria Stokes had reverted to her own surname after the divorce. Her ex-husband's name was Peter Welburn. They had been separated for four years and divorced for one. No children.

Welburn sat in one of the small office cubicles at Gayfield Square police station. He was holding a mug of tea, focusing all his attention on it. He had just been explaining that Maria and he lived on opposite sides of Newcastle but were still friendly.

'Well, sociable, anyway. No nastiness.'

'The separation was amicable?' Clarke asked.

'We just sort of drifted apart – busy lives, usual story.'

'Where did she work?'

'She owns a graphic design business.'

'In Newcastle?' Rebus watched the man nod. 'Doing OK, is it?'

'Far as I know.' Welburn lifted one hand from the mug long enough to scratch the side of his head. He was in his late forties, a couple of years older than his ex-wife. Rebus reckoned they'd have made a good-looking couple – same sort of height and build.

'What do you do, Mr Welburn?' Clarke was asking.

'Architect – currently between projects.'

'Any support from Ms Stokes? Financially, I mean?'

The man shook his head. 'I hardly ever saw her – maybe a phone call or a text once a week.'

'But no nastiness?' Rebus asked, echoing Welburn's own words.

'No.'

'Did you know she was coming to Edinburgh?'

Another slow shake of the head.

'Did she have any friends in the city? Any connection to the place?'

'We visited a few times – years ago now. It's quick on the train. Used to book a B and B, hit a few of the pubs, maybe catch some music ...' Welburn's voice cracked as the memories took hold. He cleared his throat. 'It was terrible, seeing her like that.'

'Formal identification is always difficult on the loved ones,' Clarke offered, trying to sound sympathetic, though she had trotted out the same words so many times before.

'When was the last time you were in Edinburgh?' Rebus broke in. 'Before today, I mean?'

'Couple of years, probably.'

'And this past weekend ...?'

Welburn lifted his eyes to meet Rebus's. 'I was at home. With my girlfriend and her kid.'

Clarke lifted a hand. 'I'm sorry, but these things have to be asked.'

'Why would I want to kill Maria? It's insane.'

'Did she have anyone she was seeing? Someone she might have wanted to spend the weekend with?'

'No idea.'

'And I'm guessing no enemies that you'd know of?'

'Enemies?' Welburn's face crumpled. 'She was a sweetheart, an absolute angel. Even when we were splitting up, there wasn't any drama. We just ... got on with it.' He placed the mug on the desk and let his head fall into his hands, shoulders spasming as he sobbed.

*

'What do you reckon?' Clarke asked. She drummed her fingers on the steering wheel as she waited for the lights to change.

'Seemed genuine enough. Did the deceased take the train this time, or did she drive?'

'She didn't leave a car at the hotel. It's a five-minute walk from the station.'

'I didn't see a return ticket in her bag. Maybe her coat or jacket?'

'Don't think so.'

'Meaning she only bought a single. Does she strike you as the impetuous type?'

'We really don't know much about her.'

'Are you on to CID in Newcastle?'

Clarke nodded. 'They'll give her flat a look. See if there's a diary, or maybe something useful on her computer. You think she was meeting someone? Returning to Newcastle not uppermost in her mind?'

'Or she left in a hurry.'

'She'd taken some care packing that case. Didn't look thrown together in a panic.'

'Then we're not much further forward, are we?'

'Not much. But whoever did it, they've had three days to make themselves scarce.'

'And arrange an alibi.'

'That too,' Clarke agreed.

The general manager's name was Kate Ferguson. She met them in the airy reception and asked if anyone had offered them something to drink.

'We declined,' Clarke replied.

'Well then. This way.'

Ferguson led them to an office on the mezzanine level. Her sizeable desk had been cleared of everything but a laptop computer. Two chairs awaited, both with a view of the screen.

'Two of your officers have already viewed the footage,' she said, in a tone that told them she was busy and important and wanted the whole business consigned to history.

'Just need to see for ourselves.'

'I'm sure we could have forwarded you a copy.'

Clarke offered a professional smile. 'We appreciate the hotel's cooperation.'

Realising that she had lost the skirmish, Ferguson used the mouse to start the film. Four onscreen squares, all in colour and of high quality: the outside steps, reception desk, lift and bar.

'This is her checking in,' she said. She was standing just behind the two detectives, her hand reaching between them to point to the top left square. 'Just the one overnight case, meaning she didn't need help with luggage and didn't want to be escorted to her room.'

'How long ago did she book?'

'Ten days.'

'By phone? Email?'

'It was an online booking.'

'She didn't say if it was business or pleasure?'

'She arrives dressed for business,' Clarke interrupted. 'Two-piece, neutral, flat shoes.'

The clothes that had been left in a pile on the bathroom floor, prior to her shower.

'She didn't hang anything up,' Rebus commented.

The action moved to the lift, Maria Stokes pushing the button. Then pushing it again a couple of times.

'She's in a hurry,' Clarke said.

'No calls that needed connecting to her room?' Rebus asked.

'Everyone has their own phone these days.' The general manager seemed every bit as irritated by this as by the intrusion of the police into her life.

'We're asking her service provider for a breakdown,' Clarke added for Rebus's benefit.

They watched as the lift doors opened and Maria Stokes got in. 'No cameras in the corridors?' Rebus enquired.

'No.'

'So someone could try the doors on every floor and not be spotted?'

'As I told your colleagues, that sort of thing has *never* happened here.'

'Why not?' Rebus turned to meet Ferguson's stare. 'It's a genuine question – seems to me you've left the place wide open.'

'Staff are rigorously vetted. They're also trained to tell a guest from someone who doesn't belong.'

'So what happens now?' Clarke interrupted. 'With Ms Stokes, I mean.'

Ferguson dragged the cursor along the timeline at the bottom of the screen.

'Seven twenty-three p.m.,' she said. 'As you can see, she's changed her outfit.'

Stokes was emerging from the lift, dressed in the clothes they had seen next to her bed. She looked nervous, scanning the lobby.

'A rendezvous?' Rebus offered. He watched as she made her way to the bar. She stopped at the threshold, a member of staff smiling a greeting.

'She's looking for someone, isn't she?' Clarke asked, to herself as much as anyone else.

'And not finding them,' Rebus added. Because now Stokes was shaking her head at the offer of a table. There seemed to be only two couples in the whole place. Friday night was happening elsewhere.

Back in the lobby, she stopped to talk to someone.

'That's one of our concierges,' Ferguson offered. 'Daniel. *Very* knowledgeable.'

'So what's he telling her?' Clarke asked.

'She wanted to know where to eat, where to drink.' Daniel was nodding in the direction of the bar. 'Of course,' Ferguson went on, sounding proud, 'he told her that our own bar and dining room couldn't be bettered.'

There was a little laugh from Maria Stokes, and she even touched the concierge on the arm.

'Friendly sort,' Rebus commented.

'His patter didn't seal the deal, though.' Clarke leaned in a little towards the screen, where Stokes was walking out of the hotel – the door held open by Daniel. She looked to right and left, until the obliging concierge emerged to point her in the right direction. Then off she went, slightly hesitantly, as though the height of her heels were a new and daunting experience.

'Which brings us to ...' Ferguson again used the mouse, dragging the cursor along the screen. 'Ten twenty-six.'

'So she was out and about for almost exactly three hours.' Clarke added the numbers to a small notepad. The sky was dark but the front of the hotel was brightly illuminated. The bar area was at last doing good business, and a middle-aged couple laden with luggage were checking in at the reception desk. There was no one to hold open the door for Maria Stokes, and she struggled a little. Tipsy strides across the floor to the lift, whose button she needed to press just the once, its doors sliding open immediately. A half-glance behind her as a man arrived from outside. She entered the lift and he hurried forward, squeezing in as the doors slid shut.

'Another guest?' Clarke asked.

'Or the person she was meeting?' Rebus added.

'Did she look as though she knew him?'

'Hard to say?' Rebus turned towards Ferguson. 'We need as clear a printout of his face as we can get. Then all the staff need to be shown it.'

'I assumed he was staying here,' Ferguson blurted out. 'Are you saying he could be the one who ...?' She lifted the palm of one hand to her mouth.

'As of right now, we're saying precisely nothing,' Rebus said in a warning tone. 'But we do need that printout.'

'Yes, of course. Anything while you're waiting? A tea or coffee maybe?'

'Tea would be fine,' Clarke said.

'Of course.'

'And one more thing,' Rebus said. 'Get Daniel to fetch it, please.'

'I only spoke to her that one time,' the concierge protested.

'Easy, Daniel. No one's accusing you of anything.'

They were in Ferguson's office, with the general manager on the other side of the door. Clarke was seated behind the desk and Daniel Woods opposite her, with Rebus standing off to one side, feet apart and arms folded. Woods was in his late twenties, lean and sharp-faced. His uniform consisted of charcoal waistcoat and tie, white shirt, dark trousers. Only the shoes really belonged to him, and they were scuffed and cheap.

'Actually,' Rebus broke in, '*I'm* accusing him of something.' He had Clarke's attention, while his was on the concierge. 'Faking your application, for a start. Ferguson's vetting's not as hot as she thinks. Been a while, though, hasn't it, Daniel? Since you did time, I mean.'

Woods's mouth opened but then closed again soundlessly.

'Don't know what it is that changes a man when they're put away,' Rebus ploughed on. 'But it sticks to them. Either that or I'm just receptive. Young Offenders, was it? Fighting or break-ins?'

Woods was running a finger along the edge of his gold-coloured badge, the one that identified him as Concierge. 'Drugs,' he eventually muttered.

'Wee bit of dealing? Probably grassed up by the competition. Clean since?'

'Ever since.' Woods tightened his jaw. 'So do I lose my job now or what?'

'Management hold you in high regard, Danny. I just wanted you to know how things lie, here in this room, between the three of us.'

'Right.'

'So tell us again.'

Woods took a deep breath. 'Just like I said. She looked dressed for a bit of fun, said she was after a wine bar or similar, somewhere she could maybe get a bite. She'd put on too much perfume and lipstick – trying that bit too hard. I wondered if she'd already had a drink, either that or a wee bit of powder or a tab.'

'Nothing out of the minibar,' Clarke interjected. 'No sign of drugs in her handbag.'

'Maybe it was just excitement, then. She was like one of those ... cougars, is it?'

'An older woman out for a good time?'

'And a bit of male company,' Woods added with a nod.

'You didn't offer?' Rebus enquired.

'Not at all.'

'Don't tell me it hasn't happened in the past.'

'Not once.' The fixing of the jaw again. 'I mean, sometimes guests ask me to sort them out ...'

'With an escort?'

Another nod. 'But I didn't get the feeling she was in the market.'

'So where did you send her?'

'The Abilene, on Market Street.'

Clarke looked to Rebus, who knew pretty much every pub in the city, but he just offered a twitch of one shoulder. 'Why there?' she asked Woods.

'It's not too raucous. They do bar food that's edible and pretty good cocktails.'

'You know anyone who works there?'

'Doddy works the door, but he wouldn't have been on duty till later.'

'What sort of crowd is it?'

'Office drones. Ties off and jackets over chairs while they work up a sweat on the dance floor. Tunes the ladies can sing along to. It can be a fun night.'

'Ms Stokes was back here by ten thirty.'

'Do we know she even went there? Plenty of other places in the vicinity.'

Clarke turned the laptop around so it was facing Woods. The CCTV footage had been paused. 'This man here,' she said, 'the one making for the lift.'

'What about him?'

'A guest?'

'Might be.'

'You don't recognise him?'

Woods shook his head. 'Has he got something to do with it?'

Clarke didn't answer. Instead she swivelled the laptop back around again.

'One way to tell if he's a guest,' Woods offered.

'What's that?'

'Keep watching. See if he leaves ...'

With Clarke supplied with another pot of tea and the fast-forward function, Rebus stepped outside for a cigarette. He'd just missed a shower and the pavement glistened, the evening crowd hurrying past, some with hair still dripping. The doorman knew he was a cop and didn't have anything to say. He was in his sixties and had the thickset build and squashed nose of a one-time boxer. Pale blue eyes sinking into puffy red-veined flesh. He held a rolled umbrella, ready for any taxi that might arrive.

Someone had died a few windows up, strangled in their bed, the last moments of their life filled with horror and terror. Rebus doubted any of the pedestrians would care. They had worries of their own and not half enough time. As he headed back inside, the doorman cleared his throat.

'Papers have been sniffing,' he said.

'Make sure they cough up for anything you give them,' Rebus advised. As reward, the door was held open for him, as if he were a regular and cherished guest, the kind that always tipped.

At reception, Rebus showed his ID and asked for the key to 407. He shared the lift with a young couple who didn't look as if they were going to make it fully clothed to their room. Rebus slid the key card into 407's lock, stepped inside and switched on the light. Everything deemed potential evidence had been removed by the forensics team since his last visit – sheets and pillowcases, Stokes's bag and belongings. But the book was still there. Maybe someone had decided that it belonged to the hotel or a previous guest. Maybe it did at that. Rebus picked it up and sniffed it. It smelled faintly of perfume. It was called *The Driver's Seat* and had obviously been turned into a film – the cover showed a heavily made-up Elizabeth Taylor. It had cost £1.25 when first published, but had been bought second-hand for twice that, according to a pencilled price on the inside cover. The author's biography was there, too: born and educated in Edinburgh ... spent time in Africa ... became a Roman Catholic ... Rebus nodded to himself when he came to the title of another of her books: *The Prime of Miss Jean Brodie*. He'd gone to see the film when it had come out. Had it been on a double bill with something else Scottish ...? *The Wicker Man*, maybe? Closing the book, he rubbed his thumb over Elizabeth Taylor's face, removing a light dusting of fingerprint powder. Then he stuck the book in his jacket pocket, went over to the chair in the corner, and sat down to think.

'Quarter past four,' Clarke said, sounding satisfied.

Rebus walked around the desk so she could show him what she'd found. The lift doors opening and the man emerging, moving briskly across the floor. No one around at all.

'There's a night manager,' Clarke explained. 'But he's in an office somewhere. If you're late back, there's a bell you can press and he'll come let you in. But if you're already in, you just push the bar on the door and you're gone.'

Which was what the visitor had done. Walking out of shot into what remained of the night, hands digging into his pockets. The other cameras showed a silent reception desk and a closed bar.

'Half past ten till quarter past four,' Rebus commented, lifting a photocopied still from next to the laptop – the general manager had provided half a dozen, all showing the clearest shot of the man. 'Doesn't take that long to throttle someone.'

'Well,' Clarke replied, as though she'd given it some thought, 'first you've got to get good and angry.' She picked up another of the photos and studied it.

'Because things aren't turning out as planned?' Rebus guessed.

'Maybe.' She stretched her spine, rolling her shoulders and neck.

'It's been a long day,' Rebus sympathised. 'Can I buy you a drink?'

'I've got to go home. Bills to open, plants to water. Need me to give you a lift?'

Rebus was shaking his head. 'I'll walk,' he said.

'Without your course deviating at any point into some pub or other?'

'Oh ye of little faith,' Rebus tutted, his smile eventually matching hers.

'Are you Doddy?'

Time was, all that was required of a bouncer was that he look scary. But these days they had to be smartly dressed too. The man giving Rebus a hard stare wasn't tall, or especially broad, but there was plenty of muscle beneath the black woollen coat and polo neck. An earpiece coiled down past his collar, and an embossed photo ID was strapped high up on one arm.

'Anything wrong, officer?'

Rebus had been about to dig his warrant card from his pocket, but smiled instead. 'Guilty as charged,' he said. The doorman shook his head when Rebus offered a cigarette. He got his own lit and blew the smoke upwards. 'Quiet tonight,' he commented.

'Usual Monday. Money's all spent.'

'That explain the half-price drinks?' Rebus nodded towards a poster to one side of the door.

'Might be an extra reduction for members of the constabulary.'

'Fruit-flavour shots, though – which rots first, the liver or the teeth?'

Doddy dredged up a thin smile. 'So that's the ice broken. Now what do you want?'

'The tourist strangled in her hotel room – I assume you've heard.'

'It was on the news.'

'Friday night around half past seven, we think she came by here.' Rebus described Maria Stokes and Doddy nodded slowly.

'I remember,' he said. 'We get a few single women coming here, but not too many.'

'Did she say anything?'

'Just asked if it cost anything to get in.'

'Did you see her come out again?'

'No.'

'Might have been just before ten thirty.'

'There was a bit of an altercation. Stag party trying to get in. Two of them could barely stand.'

'There'll be CCTV inside, yes?' As Doddy nodded, Rebus held up the photo of the man from the hotel foyer. 'Recognise him?'

'Might have seen him.'

'To talk to?'

'Don't think so.'

'Is he a regular?'

'No. Just looks familiar. Should I tell the boss you want a chat?' The doorman held up his wrist, showing Rebus the mic secreted there.

'I think so,' Rebus said.

Inside, the Abilene was a single room, a long rectangle with a dance floor at one end and a raised dining area at the other, with a shiny chrome bar separating the two. There were about thirty people in the place, only four of them dancing to piped music. Rebus didn't recognise the singer and couldn't make out the words. It was the kind of thing he only heard being pumped from cars, usually driven by young men with carburettor problems.

'Let me get you a drink,' the manager said. 'I'm guessing you're either whisky or beer.'

'An IPA, thanks,' Rebus said. The manager's name was Terry Soames. He was in his late twenties and dressed in a suit that looked made for him. Open-necked shirt and an unadorned silver chain around his throat. They perched on stools at the bar while their drinks were fetched.

'I'd like to see the footage from Friday night,' Rebus said, having explained about Maria Stokes.

'I wish I could help,' Soames apologised, sipping orange juice. 'But we record on a loop. Every forty-eight hours there's a refresh. We only store the pictures if there's been a problem.'

'There was a problem Friday night.'

Soames thought for a moment. 'The stag party? Doddy dealt with that. They didn't get in.'

'This is someone we'd like to talk to,' Rebus went on, placing the photo on the bar. 'Doddy says he's a known quantity.'

'Not to me.' Soames was peering at the face. He gestured for the barman to join them. 'Any ideas, James?'

'He's been in a few times.'

'Got a name?' Rebus asked.

The barman pursed his lips, then shook his head. 'He paid with a card, though.'

'He did?'

'I remember because the first two tries at his PIN, he got it wrong. Couple of drinks too many. He managed on the third go. We had a little joke about it.'

Rebus turned his attention to Terry Soames.

'My office,' Soames said. 'We keep the receipts in the safe . . .'

Clarke was already at her desk when Rebus got into Gayfield Square next morning.

'Autopsy and forensics,' she said, gesturing towards the paperwork in front of her.

'Anything useful?'

'Plenty of prints in the room – too many, in fact. Seems housekeeping didn't do a great job with a duster.'

'How about the Do Not Disturb sign?'

'Just the victim's prints on that.'

Rebus ran a hand along his jawline. 'They sure?'

'Positive.'

'So our notion that the attacker put the sign up to stop anyone going in ...'

'May need rethinking. Victim had downed a fair few gin and tonics and eaten nothing but salted peanuts. No drugs. Signs of sexual intercourse – traces of the lubricant from a condom.'

'No condom in the room, though.'

'And no wrapper either. So the assailant either pocketed both or else flushed them. And we can't be sure if penetration was pre- or post-mortem. No signs of trauma.'

Rebus rubbed at his jaw again. 'We're saying this is all the one guy? She picks him up in a bar and takes him to her room. Instead of saying thank you, he then strangles her?'

'It's the simplest explanation, no?'

Eventually Rebus nodded.

'There are some strands of hair that don't seem to match the victim ...' Clarke was skimming the pages. 'Et cetera, et cetera.' She paused, holding up one final sheet. 'And then there's this.'

Rebus took the piece of paper from Clarke and started to read as she spoke.

'A team from Newcastle went to her flat. Everything neat and tidy, but there was stuff next to her computer, including correspondence from her GP and a couple of hospitals ...'

'Brain tumour,' Rebus muttered.

'Shelf in her bathroom stacked with strong painkillers, none of which she brought to Edinburgh – unless *he* lifted them.'

Rebus placed the sheet of paper on top of the others. 'She was dying.'

'Maybe Edinburgh was on her bucket list.'

'Maybe.'

'Ironic, though, isn't it? You head north to let your hair down. You want to feel something, so you maybe don't bother deadening the pain with drugs. And you end up meeting the one man you shouldn't.'

'Ironic, yes,' Rebus echoed, though he didn't really believe it. 'And his name's Robert Jeffries, by the way.'

'What?'

'The man who went up to her room with her. I'm in the process of getting an address.'

'You better take a seat and tell me.'

Rebus nodded his agreement. 'But can we make it quick?'

Clarke just stared at him.

'I have a book I need to read,' he explained.

*

That evening, Rebus and Clarke sat in the office, listening to the recording that had been made of their interview with Robert Jeffries. A lawyer had been present throughout, but Jeffries had made it clear that he had nothing to hide and wanted to explain.

'That's good, Mr Jeffries,' Clarke had said. 'And we appreciate your help.'

'I hate my voice,' she said to Rebus as she listened.

'Hush,' he chided her.

'I was in the Abilene,' Jeffries was saying. 'It's a nightclub on Market Street. I don't go often, but sometimes the boredom gets to me. Ever since Margaret passed away, I've found my life ... not withering away exactly. Squeezed into a box maybe. Just the telly and the computer, you know. Used to go to the football, but I lost interest. Stopped returning friends' calls. Bit pathetic really.'

Rebus's voice: 'Why the Abilene in particular?'

'I suppose it's handy for the train back to Falkirk. You can sit at the bar and sometimes people talk to you. Even if they don't, you can watch them enjoying themselves. I used to reminisce about clubs me and Margaret went to. Duran Duran was her thing. Simon Le Bon. Even in the living room, I'd come home and find her shimmying around the place.'

There was a pause. A plastic cup of water was being lifted, sipped from, placed with care back on the table. A chair creaked as the lawyer shifted slightly, trying to get more comfortable.

'I only meant to have a couple of drinks that night, but then she was standing beside me. I told her I liked her perfume. She laughed. Really nice white teeth. So then we got talking. Gin and tonic she was drinking. With a slice of lime rather than lemon, and not too much ice. After the third round, they brought us some peanuts and pretzels. She didn't like pretzels.'

Clarke: 'What did you talk about?'

'My job ... her job. She'd dumped her husband – that was the word she used, "dumped" – and found herself a nice flat near the river in Newcastle. I said I'd been through it on the train to York and London but never stopped. She said I should. "It's full of life." *She* was full of life. It was like sparks were coming off her. Deep dark eyes and a nice husky voice. A couple of times I thought she was losing interest – she would scan the room, smiles for everybody. But then she would turn her attention back to me. I was ... flattered.'

Rebus: 'Whose idea was it to leave?'

'Hers. I think she saw me glance at my watch. Horrible thing to say, but I was thinking of last trains. "You're not leaving?" she said. She sounded aghast that I might be. "It's Friday night, you need to live!" Then she mentioned her hotel and how it had a bar that would be getting lively. I honestly thought that was where we were heading.'

Another pause.

'No, I'm lying. I *hoped* that after the bar there'd be an invite to her room. I was tingling all over. Feelings I hadn't had in years. But as it turned out, the bar wasn't the destination she had in mind.'

Clarke: 'You paid for the drinks like a gentleman?'

'I nearly didn't, though. I got my PIN wrong twice.'

Rebus: 'Footage from the hotel entrance shows you a few seconds behind Ms Stokes ...'

'Yes. I thought I'd lost my phone. I stopped to check my pockets. By the time I caught up, she was already in the lift. So that was that.'

Rebus: 'But you'd come prepared? A condom, I mean?'

'That was hers. She had it in her bag.'

'You flushed it afterwards?'

'Yes.' Another pause for water. 'After I'd got dressed. We'd fallen asleep. I mean ... I was sure she was asleep. I woke up feeling awful. Pounding headache and everything.'

Clarke: 'We need you to tell us what happened, Mr Jeffries. Not just the before and the after.'

'Oh God ...'

There was a short interjection by the lawyer, but Jeffries started to make noises. Then: 'No, I *need* to say it. I need to!' Sniffling, nose-blowing, throat-clearing.

'I need you to know it wasn't me. I'm not the adventurous sort. I'd never even heard of it. I know now, though – auto-erotic asphyxiation. She said she liked it, said she wanted it. My hands around her throat while we had sex. "Squeeze tighter. Keep squeezing. Your thumbs. Harder ..." Oh Christ.' Another loud sob. 'And this look on her face, her eyes tight shut, teeth clenched. I thought she was enjoying it, getting into it. So I kept pressing down, pressing, pressing. And then I collapsed on her, rolled off, even said a few sweet nothings ... And passed out.'

Clarke: 'And when you woke up?'

'I got dressed as quietly as I could. Didn't want to wake her. I thought ... well, cold light of day and all that. She might hate herself or me.'

Rebus: 'You didn't check she was breathing?'

'She looked so peaceful. I still can't believe she was dead. It was an accident. A terrible, terrible accident ...'

Clarke: 'Why didn't you come forward, sir? Why did we have to fetch you?'

'I knew how horrible it would sound. The whole thing. And I didn't think.' A further pause. 'Just that, really – I didn't think ...'

Clarke stopped the recording and leaned back in her chair, staring across the desk at Rebus.

'You've had a chance to read it?' he asked.

She nodded and took the copy of *The Driver's Seat* from her drawer, flicking through its pages.

'It's a sort of nightmare,' she said. 'A woman travels to a strange city looking for someone to kill her. Not because she has cancer, but ... well, I'm not quite sure why. To create a sensation at the end of a mundane life?'

'Maybe.'

'The book gave Maria Stokes the idea?'

Rebus shrugged. 'The story doesn't turn out the way Maria's life did.'

'She *was* in the driving seat, though – is that what we're saying? With Robert Jeffries as her passenger – meaning we should feel sorry for him.'

'You don't sound as if you do.'

Clarke started gathering up all the loose sheets of paper on the desk, as if putting them in some sort of order were suddenly important.

'A single ticket,' Rebus said into the silence.

'Sorry?'

'She didn't buy a return because she wasn't going home. Yet she paid for three nights at the hotel – three shots at getting it right.'

'Her head was pretty messed up.'

'And she's messed up Robert Jeffries' head pretty good now too.' Rebus rose to his feet. 'Let me buy you a drink,' he said, reaching across the desk for the book.

'Anywhere but the Abilene.'

'Anywhere but the Abilene,' Rebus agreed.

Clarke placed the paperwork in a drawer, stood up and lifted her jacket from the back of her chair. She crossed to the window as she slipped it on. There was a whole city somewhere out there, waking to another night of possibility and accident, chance and fate, pity and fear.

A Three-Pint Problem

The missing man's car was found on the third day.

It was a gloss-black Bentley GT, parked in a bay two floors up at Edinburgh airport's multi-storey car park – a businessman had recognised it from the description on the news. When police arrived, they found the Bentley unlocked. No key, no parking chitty.

'So we've no idea what time it was left there,' Siobhan Clarke explained to Rebus on the way to the man's home.

'He took a flight?'

'We're checking.'

'Was the business in trouble? That's why people usually run.'

'According to the wife, things had picked up after a lean couple of years.'

'P.T. Forbes – I've been past the showroom many a time.'

'Me too. There was a red E-type in the window one time ...'

'You were tempted?'

'Until I saw the price tag. Plus: no power steering in those old models.'

'What does the P stand for, by the way?'

'Philip. The wife's name is Barbara. Twenty-six years married.'

Rebus had seen the photos of P.T. Forbes in the *Scotsman* and the *Evening News* – a head of thick silver hair, a bit of heft filling out a pinstripe suit. Always posing with one of his cars. He dealt in 'cherished' high-end automobiles, meaning second-hand but pricier than most new models.

'Was the Bentley his?' Rebus asked as Clarke slowed to a stop at a set of traffic lights. They were heading out of town down the coast, towards Musselburgh. The Forbes home was part of a small modern estate backing on to a newish golf course. Rebus reckoned the developer would have called it 'bespoke', like one of P.T. Forbes's motors.

'Not as such,' Clarke was answering. 'According to Mrs Forbes, he came home with a different car every week.'

'Must have been confusing when she came out of the supermarket looking for it.'

'She drives a Mini,' Clarke said.

The disappearance of Philip Forbes was out of character. He had left the house as usual at 9.30 on Monday morning, headed for his glass-fronted South Gyle premises. His wife hadn't begun to fret until 7 p.m. She had called her husband's right-hand man, but found him driving back from Carlisle, where he'd spent the day negotiating the purchase of an Aston Martin DB5. He in turn had called the showroom's receptionist, but she'd been at home all day with a migraine, having texted her boss to apologise.

Forbes had never replied. The showroom had remained closed all that day, mail sitting unopened on the floor.

Philip Forbes was what was known as 'a weel-kent face' in the city. He had been part of a group that had dug deep to try to keep one of the local football teams afloat, and he was photographed at plenty of charity balls and black-tie events. The local MPs and MSPs knew him, as did many councillors and the Lord Provost. Consequently, there was media interest, though no one had gone to the lengths of doorstepping the family home or setting up camp nearby.

Clarke signalled off the main road into Musselburgh and headed down a long straight lane. The modern two-storey golf club was visible in the near distance, the houses bordering it forming a wide crescent. They were constructed predominantly of brick, with feature windows, and garages big enough for three or four vehicles. Each house boasted a name rather than a number. The Forbeses lived at Heriots.

'They're all named after private schools,' Rebus pointed out as Clarke parked her car on the driveway.

Barbara Forbes was already at the door, one hand clasped in the other. She was dressed soberly, and hadn't bothered with her hair or make-up. There were tired cusps under her eyes.

'You've found the Bentley?' she said.

Clarke nodded her agreement, before identifying herself and Rebus.

'Come in,' Mrs Forbes said, backing up a couple of steps into a huge entrance hall. Polished wood underfoot, cream-coloured walls, and a wide central staircase. The space was flooded with light from a glass cupola.

'You know about the car?' Rebus was asking. 'We thought we were here to break the news ...'

'A reporter phoned me. He said it was at the airport.'

'I'm assuming your husband had no plans to fly anywhere?' Clarke enquired.

'Not that I know of.'

'Did he carry his passport with him?'

'It's kept in one of the drawers in the bedroom.'

'You've checked?'

The woman hesitated. 'I don't remember,' she finally admitted. 'Should I go and look?'

'Please,' Clarke said.

They watched her as she headed upstairs. Rebus walked across the hall to a set of double doors and opened them, entering a well-appointed living room. There was a flat-screen TV attached to one wall. French windows led to an enclosed patio beyond which stretched a professionally tended garden. Behind a further set of doors was a formal dining room. One more door and he was back in the entrance hall. Clarke had gone in the opposite direction and was emerging from the kitchen.

'Worth a look,' she informed him.

'Ditto,' he replied, gesturing over his shoulder.

The kitchen offered all mod cons, several of which Rebus failed to recognise. There was a table where he reckoned husband and wife took most of their meals. He nearly tripped over a narrow Persian rug, smoothing it back into place with the heel of his shoe. Off the kitchen was a smaller room, probably originally intended for laundry or as a walk-in pantry but converted into a home office. There were shelves crammed with paperwork, car brochures stacked on the floor, and a laptop computer on the wooden desk. It was currently in sleep mode, a green light on the side of the keyboard pulsing slowly. Rebus lifted a framed snapshot from the far corner of the desk. Voices were approaching, Clarke and Mrs Forbes entering the kitchen.

'No sign of it,' Clarke explained for Rebus's benefit.

'But why would he take a sudden notion to fly anywhere?' Barbara Forbes was asking, voice trembling a little.

'Your son?' Rebus asked, holding up the photo.

'Until five years ago,' she replied. Then, into the questioning silence: 'He took an overdose. In Thailand.'

Clarke was looking at the photo with its three smiling faces. 'I'm sorry,' she said.

'That picture was a couple of years before. Rory was twenty-two when he ...'

'Just the one child?' Rebus asked. The woman nodded. She seemed dazed, pinching the bridge of her nose and screwing shut her eyes for a moment.

'I hate to ask,' Rebus said, 'but is Rory buried here or in Thailand?'

She took a deep breath. 'We brought him home.' She suddenly saw what he was getting at. 'Why would Philip go to Thailand?'

Rebus could only shrug.

'We're checking with the airport anyway,' Clarke offered. 'Still no sign of him using his credit cards or withdrawing money?'

'It's been a few hours since I checked. I know he hasn't switched his phone on.'

'Oh?'

'He was very proud of some tracking thing he has on it. The phone's been off since Monday.' She paused. 'Should I look at the bank stuff again?'

'Might be an idea,' Clarke said. 'Maybe while I put the kettle on ...?'

Barbara Forbes went through to her husband's study and woke up the computer. Rebus followed her, placing the photo back where he'd found it.

'A terrible blow, losing your son like that,' he offered.

'Yes,' she agreed. She had taken a pair of spectacles from a pocket and was peering at the screen.

'Your husband must trust you,' Rebus added.

'In what way?'

'Allowing you to see all his finances.'

'This only lets me into our joint account.'

'He has others in his own name?'

She nodded. 'I've applied for access. Apparently it takes time. You think he's using those to fund his ... well, whatever it is he's doing or done? I mean, nobody's kidnapped him, have they?' She looked up at Rebus.

'There's no evidence of it.'

'Archie probably knows more about the company money than I do.'

'Archie being your husband's business partner?'

'Not partner, no – Archie works *for* Philip.'

'An employee, in other words. But he'd still know if Mr Forbes had dipped into the till, as it were?'

'I suppose so.'

'What about the receptionist?'

'What about her?'

'In my experience, they often know more about the place where they work than anyone else.'

'Then ask her.'

Rebus stayed silent for a moment, watching over her shoulder. 'Is this the only computer in the house?'

'We have laptops, too.'

'I'm guessing you've looked at Mr Forbes's emails?'

'Your lot told me to – there was nothing out of the ordinary.'

'How about stuff he deleted?'

'I'm sorry?'

'When you press delete, stuff doesn't just vanish.'

She was studying a list of recent transaction details. 'His cards still haven't been used,' she muttered.

'The ones you're able to check,' Rebus added.

'What were you saying about emails?'

'Even deleted ones will be stored somewhere, unless your husband really wanted them gone.'

She had closed the banking website and clicked on the email account.

'See where it says "deleted"?' Rebus reached past her so his finger nearly touched the screen. If you click on that ...'

She did so, and a long list appeared.

'I'd no idea,' she said.

Rebus's eyes were running down the items. They were mostly rubbish – offers for insurance and Canadian medicines. But one caught his attention, the one right at the top – received on the Sunday, the eve of Forbes's disappearing act. The subject line consisted of only the one word – Philip – followed by three exclamation marks. The sender was marked as Unknown.

'Can you open that?' Rebus asked.

Barbara Forbes did as she was asked, then gave a little gasp.

WE NEED TO MAKE A RUN FOR IT! THEY KNOW!!!

Nothing else. It didn't look as if Philip Forbes had replied. He had just deleted the message and followed the instruction.

'What does it mean?' Barbara Forbes's voice was shaking. Clarke was standing in the doorway, a carton of milk in her hand.

'You might want to offer Mrs Forbes something stronger,' Rebus said, gesturing towards the screen.

'It's called forensic computing,' Clarke told Rebus. They were in her car again. The laptop had spent the afternoon at the forensic science facility at Howdenhall. Now night had fallen and Rebus was holding his fifth or sixth takeaway coffee of the day.

'So just because it says "Sender Unknown ..."?'

'There's information tucked away for a lab coat to work with.'

'Like a deleted file that isn't actually deleted?'

'Exactly.'

Rebus drained the last of his drink. 'No news from the airport?'

'No record of P. T. Forbes as a passenger with any carrier.'

'But he did take his passport.'

'Airport might be a red herring. Plenty of other ways to leave the country.'

'It would help if we knew the why.'

'Fingers crossed Archie Sellers has some answers.'

They parked on a wide residential street near Inverleith Park. The houses were substantial. Archie Sellers's top-floor flat had been carved from one of them. The windows were small but gave views south across the city, the castle and Calton Hill silhouetted against the darker sky.

'Is this about Philip?' Sellers had asked when he'd answered the door. In place of an answer, Clarke had suggested they go in.

'Lovely view, Mr Sellers,' Rebus said as he stood by one of the living room's three windows. Sellers had lowered himself into a leather armchair. The room had a distinct bachelor feel to it: car magazines, a dartboard on the back of the door, untidy stacks of CDs on the floor next to a hi-fi system. 'Better than from the police station anyway.' With a smile, Rebus settled on the sofa beside Clarke.

'It was DS Rebus's opinion,' Clarke explained to Sellers, 'that Gayfield Square police station should be where we're having this little chat.'

Sellers's eyes widened a fraction. He hadn't shaved in a day or two and his collar-length hair was unruly. A generation younger than his employer, but maybe still too old for the distressed denims and Cuban-heeled boots.

'Why? What have I done?'

'How was business, Mr Sellers? Anything untoward that an audit might be about to throw up? VAT in order?'

'Things were fine.'

'Then how do you explain this?' Clarke unfolded the sheet of paper and held it up towards him, the message printed there clear to see. 'You sent this,' she stated.

'Did I?'

'We have proof that you did. Identifiers lead more or less straight back to your Hotmail account.'

'There must be a mistake.'

'Must there?' The two detectives sat side by side in silence, while Sellers twisted in his chair, looking as though it were made of drawing pins rather than cowhide. He sprang to his feet, but couldn't think what came next.

'Sit down,' Rebus ordered, glowering until Sellers obeyed.

Clarke turned the sheet of paper round again so she could recite the words. '"We need to make a run for it! They know!!!"' Sent by you to Philip Forbes on Sunday afternoon at half past three. What was it the pair of you had to be scared of, Mr Sellers? And why are you still here?'

'It was a joke!' Sellers blurted out, clasping his hands around his knees.

'A joke?'

'A prank. I sent it to half a dozen people. Just to see what their reaction would be.'

'Who else got one?'

'A mate I play squash with ... couple of old school friends ... a cousin ... plus Philip and Andrea.'

'Andrea being ...?'

'She works for us.'

'On reception?'

'Reception, secretary, you name it. I was going to go into work on Tuesday and see what they said. It was supposed to be a bit of fun.' He paused. 'You don't know the story?'

'Enlighten us,' Clarke said, no emotion in her voice.

'Arthur Conan Doyle – Sherlock Holmes and all that. It was in an article I was reading about him. He sent an anonymous telegram to a few of his friends. It said something like "We've been rumbled! What will we do?"'

Sellers was grinning, with the eager-to-make-amends look of a schoolkid caught red-handed.

'And?' Rebus asked.

The grin vanished. Sellers licked his lips, eyes towards the floor. 'Apparently one of them did a runner. He was never seen again. That's what's happened, isn't it? Philip *did* have something he didn't want rumbled.'

'Any idea what that might have been?'

The man shook his head.

'Do you have a number for Andrea, Mr Sellers?'

'Andrea?'

'To verify your story.'

The man's face sagged further. 'She's going to be furious with me.' Then he thought of something. It was obvious in his eyes, in the way his spine stiffened.

'Yes?' Clarke nudged.

But Sellers shook his head.

'We'll need the other names, too,' Rebus stated. 'Your friends, your cousin ...'

'Can't I tell them myself?' Sellers begged.

Clarke eventually nodded. 'If you let us speak to them first, just so we hear it from them. After that, we'll hand the phone back to you and you can come clean.' She was gesturing towards Sellers's mobile. It was sitting on the coffee table, half hidden under the magazine he'd been reading only ten minutes ago, before his world started to go wrong.

'How funny is that joke looking now?' Rebus decided to enquire, as Sellers reached towards the phone.

They were seated in the back room of the Oxford Bar, having found a parking space right outside. That had been the deal: no convenient place to park, no stopping for a drink. Instead of which, Rebus was starting on his third pint while Clarke nursed a soda water and lime.

'I can take a taxi home if you want a proper drink,' Rebus had offered.

'And leave the car outside to be towed in the morning?'

'Right enough.'

There was an open packet of crisps in front of them, but neither had turned out to be hungry enough. The back room was midweek empty. Only four regulars in the front bar, and some European football game on the TV.

'So what have we got?' Clarke asked, playing with one of the beer mats.

'Maybe nothing at all. That email might not have anything to do with it.'

'Bit of a coincidence, though.'

'A bit, aye.' Rebus took another mouthful of beer.

'Is this your version of the three-pipe problem?' Clarke nodded towards Rebus's glass.

'The what?'

'Sherlock Holmes – when he was stuck, he smoked three pipes.'

'Not at the same time, I hope.'

She shook her head. 'And probably not tobacco either.'

'This might be the opposite.'

'Meaning?'

'Maybe we're thinking *too* hard.'

'So there's a nice simple explanation, and you're just about to provide it?'

'We should talk to Andrea.'

'The secretary?'

'You saw it, didn't you? Sellers was thinking how mad she was going to be with him ...'

'He froze for a second.'

'He did, didn't he? And someone like Andrea – working the phones, making appointments, doing the paperwork ...'

'Might know what the big bad secret was?'

Rebus was nodding slowly, his glass halfway to his mouth.

'First thing tomorrow then,' Clarke decided. 'Reckon her migraine will have gone?'

'You think that's why she stayed home Monday?' Rebus asked. His eyes were twinkling behind the pint as he tipped it towards him.

They sat in Clarke's car and watched the receptionist unlock the showroom. Through the plate-glass window they saw her walk briskly to a keypad on the wall behind her desk and disarm the alarm. Her phone was already ringing and she answered it, pushing stray locks of hair back behind one ear.

'Ten sharp,' Rebus commented, tapping his wristwatch.

'Much the same time the boss usually arrives.'

'I'd say Archie Sellers then slopes in a bit later. Not quite as dedicated.'

'Not like us.'

No, because they'd already had to brief their own boss on the case – half past eight in his office. For once he'd seemed apologetic – pressure bearing down on him from above; all those politicians who considered P.T. Forbes a friend, an ally, a contributor.

Having dealt with the call, the receptionist shrugged off her coat. Rebus judged her to be in her late twenties or early thirties. Good-looking. Seated at her desk, she suddenly seemed at a loss what to do next. She got up and walked over to one of the gleaming cars, ran a finger along its paintwork.

'Maserati,' Clarke stated.

'I knew that,' Rebus said, opening the passenger door.

'Liar,' Clarke retorted, removing the key from the ignition.

'She didn't drive,' she added as they crossed the empty forecourt.

'So I noticed.' Rebus was pushing open the showroom door, a

smile on his face. 'Nice Maserati,' he said, gesturing towards the car.

'Can I help you?'

'You're Andrea ...?'

'Mathieson,' she obliged. 'Are you the detectives I spoke with last night?'

They both opened their warrant cards for an inspection that never came. Mathieson had retreated back behind her desk, pulling the seat in.

'You don't drive?' Rebus asked.

'What makes you think that?'

'You arrived on foot.'

'Sometimes I take the bus.'

'Better for the environment, eh?'

She stared at him, unblinking. 'Is there something I can help you with?'

'Must have come as a shock,' Rebus began. He saw that Clarke was either taking a keen interest in the contents of the showroom or else pretending to, so as to give him a clear run. He took the chair opposite Andrea Mathieson. Her eyes were red-rimmed.

'Philip, you mean?'

Rebus shook his head. 'Well, that too. But I was thinking of the email.'

'Bloody Archie!' She spat out the words, causing Clarke to turn away from a sleek BMW.

'Likes to think of himself as a bit of a joker,' Rebus sympathised. 'For what it's worth, the friends he sent the message to were every bit as pissed off. He might be in the market for new drinking buddies.' He paused. 'Did you know he was going to Carlisle on the Monday?'

She eventually nodded. 'I've a good mind to slap him when I see him.'

'He sent you the email Sunday afternoon – when did you open it?'

'That night. I nearly jumped out of my clothes. Ran to the door and made sure it was locked. I was scared half to death. Your imagination starts running away with you ...'

'Same for everyone. But only Mr Forbes seemed to take any action.'

'Is that what you think happened?'

'Did you really have a migraine on the Monday?'

'What?'

'Or was it that you couldn't bring yourself to come to work? Maybe because you'd been fretting about that email all night.'

'Well, yes, maybe.'

'Who did you think had sent it?'

'I'm not sure.'

'No?'

She shook her head, without making eye contact.

'Not Archie? Not Philip Forbes?'

'I'm not sure what it is you're getting at.'

'So everything was fine between the three of you? A happy ship and all that?'

'Why wouldn't it be?'

'Business doing OK?'

Clarke had wandered over from her tour of the showroom. She had a question of her own. 'What car do you drive, Ms Mathieson?'

'A BMW Z4.'

'Oh, those are nice.' Then, as if for Rebus's benefit: 'Sporty. Two-seater. I'd have mine in red ...'

'Same as mine,' Mathieson conceded.

'They drink the fuel, though, don't they? Probably not a hit with the environmental lobby ...'

Mathieson's head collapsed into her hands. She mumbled something they struggled to make out.

'Sorry?' Clarke asked.

Mathieson lifted her face. Tears were streaming down either cheek. 'It was a present from Philip!'

'Nice of him,' Clarke said quietly.

'Is that why you've not been able to drive to work, Andrea?' Rebus asked, dropping his own voice. 'Every time you see your car, you think of him?'

'He loved me.'

Rebus and Clarke shared a look.

'You were having an affair?' Clarke enquired.

Andrea Mathieson shook her head violently. 'Not now. *Then.*'

'Then being ...?'

'Two years ago. It didn't last long – "a fling", he called it. But I knew what it really was.'

'And what was that?'

'He was still grieving for his son. After Rory died, Philip felt crushed. His wife didn't help – that whole part of his life was just dust. He could talk to me – *did* talk to me. Poured everything out. And that's when it started. Just long enough for some healing. But not a "fling". He was wrong about that.' She took in gulps of air, trying to regain some composure. Clarke offered a tissue, which she accepted with a nod of thanks.

When enough time had elapsed, Rebus threw out another question.

'So when Mr Forbes opened that email ...?'

'Yes?'

'He might have thought the affair was about to come to light?'

When Mathieson didn't answer, Clarke asked a question of her own.

'He phoned you, didn't he?'

'He tried.'

'Because the message said *we* need to flee. So if it was to do with your affair, it could only have come from you?'

'I was out early evening. He left a voicemail. I texted him back.'

'On Sunday night?'

'I'd seen the email for myself by then.'

'You must have wondered ...'

'What?'

'Well, suddenly it's not a creepy anonymous message sent out randomly. As far as you knew, only the two of you received it.'

Rebus cleared his throat. 'It had to be someone who knew you both, whether it was about the affair or not.'

'I didn't really think about it,' Mathieson admitted. 'My head was ... You're right, of course. Maybe if I'd had the chance to speak to Philip.'

'Did you think he'd come to your home on Monday?'

'I hoped he would.'

'He knew the place from back in the day?'

'Yes.'

'But instead of that, he disappeared. Andrea, do you think he's run away?'

'I don't know.'

'Is there anything that could have panicked him? Anything at all?'

'Maybe he just wanted to be free from that bloody woman.'

'His wife, you mean?'

'Who else?'

'Did she know about the affair ...?'

There was a soft tapping from the other side of the glass door. Archie Sellers stood there, attempting to look contrite.

'You bastard!' Mathieson shrieked. She was up out of her chair, marching towards confrontation, eyes suddenly steely. Sellers had already started to retreat. The Aston Martin DB5 was parked on the forecourt. He unlocked the driver's side with an old-fashioned key.

'This is all your fault!' Mathieson was yelling as she pulled open the showroom door. Rebus noticed the large welcome mat she'd had to cross. Various marques were listed on it, but what caught his eye were the runs of tape fixing it firmly to the floor.

Health and safety.

Couldn't have anyone taking a tumble.

'Should we do something?' Clarke was asking.

Sellers had gunned the engine and was reversing on to the carriageway. A white van had to brake hard, its horn rasping. Her anger spent, Mathieson's face was in her hands again, shoulders heaving.

'Maybe make her a cup of tea,' Rebus suggested.

'And then?'

'Then we pay another visit to Heriots ...'

'You again,' was all Barbara Forbes said when she opened the door.

'Sorry to trouble you,' Rebus managed.

'I suppose you want to come in.'

'You'll be wondering if there's news.'

'What?'

'Would we drive over here if there wasn't news,' Rebus explained. They were in the entrance hall by now, Clarke pushing the door closed.

'Has he been sighted, is that it?' Mrs Forbes had her back to the detectives as she headed in the direction of the kitchen. But she paused when she reached its threshold, and turned towards the living room instead.

'I'm parched,' Rebus said, holding his hand to his throat for effect. 'Water or a cup of tea wouldn't go amiss.'

'I'll make tea,' Mrs Forbes said.

'Very grateful.' Rebus even gave a small bow.

'If you'd like to wait in there.' She was gesturing towards the living room.

'Fine,' Rebus agreed.

'I might just use the ...' Clarke held up a thumb, indicating one of the closed doors behind her.

'On the left behind the stairs,' Barbara Forbes said with a sigh. Then she turned and entered the kitchen. Rebus gave Clarke the nod and made sure he was filling the kitchen doorway as she started making her way noiselessly up the stairs.

'It's very quiet out here, isn't it?' Rebus asked.

'Comparatively,' Mrs Forbes agreed, filling the kettle and switching it on. 'I did say you could wait in the—'

'You're not anxious to hear what we've learned?'

'All right then.' But rather than stop to concentrate, she got busy with mugs, teapot, sugar bowl and milk. Rebus said his piece anyway – as much of the story as she needed to hear. By the time he had finished, Clarke was back. He felt the pressure of her hand on the small of his back and turned his head. She nodded gravely. So the passport was in the drawer in the bedroom, and Barbara Forbes had lied to them.

'I've never thought much of Archie Sellers,' she was saying as she stared at the kettle, willing it to come to the boil. 'He's like an adolescent in many respects. Bloody irresponsible of him to send that message. I hope he feels a measure of guilt.'

'Interesting phrase,' Rebus said.

'What?'

'"A measure of guilt". Meaning there's more to be apportioned elsewhere.'

'I'm not sure I understand.'

'I think you do, Mrs Forbes. And if we were to go upstairs, I think we'd find your husband's passport just where he left it. You saw an opportunity to muddy the water and you took it. But that means you were trying to mislead us, and that looks bad. Almost as bad as that rug.'

'The rug?' She looked down at it.

'Not something you often see in a kitchen. On a stone floor, I mean. It's too slippy. Could lead to a nasty accident. A rug like this is more the sort of thing you'd find in a room like your husband's den. So what is it doing here?' He had placed one foot on the rug and was starting to move it.

'Don't touch that!' she implored. But Rebus had already revealed the stained surface beneath. A series of blotches and splashes of a dull rust colour.

'Will Forensics tell us that's blood, Mrs Forbes?' Rebus enquired quietly. Clarke had stepped past him to switch off the kettle, and to stand guard near the display of chef's knives. But Barbara Forbes had gone very still, one hand clasped in the other as when they'd first set eyes on her.

'So here's what I think,' Rebus intoned. 'Either you saw the original email, in which case you were maybe the one who deleted it, not knowing it would linger on the machine. Or else it was the text you saw, the one Andrea Mathieson sent to your husband's phone. Was he maybe asleep by then? Or in a different room? You'd known about the relationship but he'd promised it was in the past. Now here was proof to the contrary. She still had her talons in him, and you were furious. Furious enough to grab one of those big solid knives. Furious enough to stab at him. The blood wouldn't shift, so you covered it up as best you could in the meantime.'

Her eyes were closed but she seemed at peace – the ordeal over now that her secret was out. No tears, her breathing slow and steady.

'What happens next?' was all she said, after a few seconds of silence, a silence deeper than any Rebus could remember.

'You need to show us – show us or tell us.'

She nodded, understanding exactly.

'The Mercedes Benz in the garage,' she said quietly. 'It was the only one with a boot big enough. Anyway, I wanted to drop the Bentley at the airport; that's the one he would have taken.' She opened her eyes again and seemed to be staring into some distance far beyond the walls of her kitchen and her home.

'After Rory died,' she began. But then she decided that those three words were maybe enough. Enough to her mind, certainly.

'After Rory died,' she repeated in a whisper, closing her eyes again as if for the last time.

The Very Last Drop

'And this is where the ghost's usually seen,' the guide said. 'So I hope nobody's of a nervous disposition.' His eyes were fixed on Rebus, though there were four other people on the tour. They had wandered through the brewery in their luminous health-and-safety vests and white hard-hats, climbing up flights of steps, ducking for low doorways, and were now huddled together on what seemed to be the building's attic level. The tour itself had been a retirement present. Rebus had almost let the voucher lapse, until reminded by Siobhan Clarke, whose gift it had been.

'Ghost?' she asked now. The guide nodded slowly. His name was Albert Simms, and he'd told them to call him 'Albie' – 'not alibi, though I've provided a few in my time'. This had been said at the very start of the tour, as they'd been trying the protective helmets for size. Siobhan had made a joke of it, warning him that he was in the presence of police officers. 'Officer singular,' Rebus had almost interrupted.

Almost.

Simms was currently looking uncomfortable, eyes darting around him. 'He's usually only seen at night, our resident ghost. More often it's the creaking of the floorboards the workers hear. He paces up and down ... up and down ...' He made a sweeping gesture with his arm. The narrow walkway was flanked by rectangular stainless-steel fermentation tanks. This was where the yeast did its work. Some vats were three-quarters full, each topped with a thick layer of brown foam. Others were empty, either clean or else waiting to be sluiced and scrubbed.

'His name was Johnny Watt,' Simms went on. 'Sixty years ago he died – almost to the day.' Simms's eyes were rheumy, his face blotchy and pockmarked. He'd retired a decade back, but liked leading the tours. They kept him fit. 'Johnny was up here on his own. His job was to do the cleaning. But the fumes got him.' He pointed towards one of the busier vats. 'Take too deep a breath and you can turn dizzy.'

'He fell in?' Siobhan Clarke guessed.

'Aye,' Simms appeared to agree. 'That's the story. Banged his head and wasn't found for a while.' He slapped the rim of the nearest vat. 'They were made of stone back then, and metal-lined.' His eyes were on Rebus again. 'A fall like that can do some damage.'

There were murmurs of agreement from the other visitors.

'Two more stops,' Simms told them, clapping his hands together. 'Then it's the sample room ...'

The sample room was laid out like a rural pub, its brickwork exposed. Simms himself manned the pumps while the others removed their safety-ware. Rebus offered a brief toast to the guide before taking his first gulp.

'That was interesting,' Siobhan offered. Simms gave a nod of thanks. 'Is it really sixty years ago? Almost exactly, I mean – or do you tell all the tours that?'

'Sixty years next week,' Simms confirmed.

'Ever seen the ghost yourself, Albie?'

Simms's face tightened. 'Once or twice,' he admitted, handing her a glass and taking Rebus's empty one. 'Just out the corner of my eye.'

'And maybe after a couple of these,' Rebus added, accepting the refill. Simms gave him a stern look.

'Johnny Watt was real enough, and he doesn't seem to want to go away. Quite a character he was, too. The beer was free to employees back then, and no limits to how much you had. Legend has it Johnny Watt could sink a pint in three seconds flat and not be much slower by the tenth.' Simms paused. 'None of which seemed to stop him being a hit with the ladies.'

Clarke wrinkled her nose. 'Wouldn't have been a hit with me.'

'Different times,' Simms reminded her. 'Story goes, even the boss's daughter took a bit of a shine to him ...'

Rebus looked up from his glass, but Simms was busy handing a fresh pint to one of the other visitors. He fixed his eyes on Siobhan Clarke instead, but she was being asked something by a woman who had come on the tour with her husband of twenty years. It had been his birthday present.

'Is it the same with you and your dad?' the woman was asking Clarke. 'Did you buy him this for his birthday?'

Clarke replied with a shake of the head, then tried to hide the fact that she was smiling by taking a long sip from her glass.

'You might say she's my "companion",' Rebus explained to the woman. 'Charges by the hour.'

He was still quick on his toes; managed to dodge the beer as it splashed from Siobhan Clarke's glass ...

The next day, Rebus was back at the brewery, but this time in the boardroom. Photos lined the walls. They showed the brewery in its heyday. At that time, almost a century ago, there had been twenty other breweries in the city, and even this was half what there had been at one time. Rebus studied a posed shot of delivery men with their dray horse. It was hitched to its cart, wooden barrels stacked on their sides in a careful pyramid. The men stood with arms folded over their three-quarter-length aprons. There was no date on the photograph. The one next to it, however, was identified as 'Workers and Managers, 1947'. The faces were blurry. Rebus wondered if one of them belonged to Johnny Watt, unaware that he had less than a year left to live.

On the wall opposite, past the large, polished oval table, were portraits of twenty or so men, the brewery managers. Rebus looked at each of them in turn. The one at the end was a colour photograph. When the door opened and Rebus turned towards the sound, he saw the man from the portrait walk in.

'Douglas Cropper,' the man said, shaking Rebus's hand. He was dressed identically to his photo – dark blue suit, white shirt, burgundy tie. He was around forty and looked the type who liked sports. The tan was probably put there by nature. The hair showed only a few flecks of grey at the temples. 'My secretary tells me you're a policeman ...'

'Was a policeman,' Rebus corrected him. 'Recently retired. I might not have mentioned that to your secretary.'

'So there's no trouble, then?' Cropper had pulled out a chair and was gesturing for Rebus to sit down too.

'Cropper's a popular name,' Rebus said, nodding towards the line of photographs.

'My grandfather and my great-grandfather,' Cropper agreed, crossing one leg over the other. 'My father was the black sheep – he became a doctor.'

'In one picture,' Rebus said, 'the inscription says "workers and managers" ...'

Cropper gave a short laugh. 'I know. Makes it sound as if the managers don't do any work. I can assure you that's not the case these days.'

'Your grandfather must have been in charge of the brewery when that accident happened,' Rebus stated.

'Accident?'

'Johnny Watt.'

Cropper's eyes widened a little. 'You're interested in ghosts?'

Rebus offered a shrug, but didn't say anything. The silence lengthened until Cropper broke it.

'Businesses weren't so hot on health and safety back then, I'm afraid to say. Lack of ventilation ... and nobody partnering Mr Watt.' Cropper leaned forward. 'But I've been here the best part of twenty years, on and off, and I've never seen anything out of the ordinary.'

'You mean the ghost? But other people have?'

It was Cropper's turn to shrug. 'It's a story, that's all. A bit of shadow ... a squeaky floorboard ... Some people can't help seeing things.' He sat back again and placed his hands behind his head.

'Did your grandfather ever talk to you about it?'

'Not that I remember.'

'Was he still in charge when you started here?'

'He was.'

Rebus thought for a moment. 'What would have happened after the accident?' he asked.

'I dare say the family would have been compensated – my grandfather was always very fair. Plenty of evidence of it in the annals.'

'Annals?'

'The brewery's records are extensive.'

'Would they have anything to say about Johnny Watt?'

'No idea.'

'Could you maybe look?'

Cropper's bright blue eyes drilled into Rebus's. 'Mind explaining to me why?'

Rebus thought of Albie Simms's words: *Johnny Watt was real ... and he doesn't seem to want to go away ...* But he didn't say anything, just bided his time until Douglas Cropper sighed and began getting to his feet.

'I'll see what I can do,' Cropper conceded.

'Thank you, sir,' Rebus said.

'You're supposed to be retired,' Dr Curt said.

In the past, the two men would normally have met in the city mortuary, but Rebus had arrived at the pathologist's office at the university, where Curt maintained a full teaching load between autopsies. The desk between them was old, ornate and wooden. The wall behind Curt was lined with bookshelves, though Rebus doubted the books themselves got much use. A laptop sat on the desk, its cover closed. There was no paperwork anywhere.

'I am retired,' Rebus stated.

'Funny way of showing it ...' Curt opened a drawer and lifted out a leather-bound ledger. A page had been marked. He opened the book and turned it to face Rebus.

'Report of the post-mortem examination,' he explained. 'Written in the finest copperplate lettering by Professor William Shiels.'

'Were you ever taught by him?' Rebus asked.

'Do I really look that old?'

'Sorry.' Rebus peered at the hand-written notes. 'You've had a read?'

'Professor Shiels was a great man, John.'

'I'm not saying he wasn't.'

'Contusions ... fractured skull ... internal bleeding to the brain ... We see those injuries most days even now.'

'Drunks on a Saturday night?' Rebus guessed. Curt nodded his agreement.

'Drink and drugs. Our friend Mr Watt fell eleven feet on to an inch-thick steel floor. Unconscious from the fumes, no way to defend himself ...'

'The major damage was to the base of the skull,' Rebus commented, running a finger along the words on the page.

'We don't always fall forehead first,' Curt cautioned. Something in his tone made Rebus look up.

'What is it?' he asked.

Curt gave a twitch of the mouth. 'I did a bit of digging. Those vats give off carbon dioxide. Ventilation's an issue, same now as it was back then. There are plenty of recorded cases of brewery employees falling into the vats. It's worse if someone tries to help. They dive into the beer to rescue their friend, and come up for air ... take a deep breath and suddenly they're in as much trouble as the other fellow.'

'What a way to go ...'

'I believe one or two had to climb out and go to the toilet a couple of times prior to drowning,' Curt offered. Rebus smiled, as was expected.

'OK,' he said. 'Carbon dioxide poisoning ... but what is it you're not saying?'

'The vat our friend fell into was empty, John. Hence the injuries. He didn't drown in beer – there was no beer.'

Finally Rebus got it.

'No beer,' he said quietly, 'meaning no fermenting. No carbon dioxide.' His eyes met the pathologist's. Curt was nodding slowly.

'So what was it caused him to pass out?' Curt asked. 'Of course, he could have just tripped and fallen, but then I'd expect to see signs that he'd tried to stop his fall.'

Rebus glanced back at the ledger. 'No injuries to the hands,' he stated.

'None whatsoever,' Professor Curt agreed.

Rebus's next stop was the National Library of Scotland, where a one-day reader's pass allowed him access to a microfiche machine. A member of staff threaded the spool of film home and showed him how to wind it to the relevant pages and adjust the focus. It was a slow process – Rebus kept stopping to read various stories and sports reports, and to smile at some of the advertisements. The film contained a year's worth of *Scotsman* newspapers, the year in question being 1948. I was one year old, Rebus thought to himself. Eventually he came to news of Johnny Watt's demise. It must have been a quiet day in the office: they'd sent a journalist and a photographer. Workers had gathered in the brewery yard. They looked numbed. The manager, Mr Joseph Cropper, had been interviewed. Rebus read the piece through twice, remembering the portrait of Douglas Cropper's grandfather – stern of face and long of sideburn. Then he spooled forward through the following seven days.

There was coverage of the funeral, along with another photograph. He wondered if the horse pulling the carriage had been borrowed from the brewery. Warriston Cemetery was the destination. Watt and his family had lived in the Stockbridge area for umpteen generations. He had no wife, but three brothers and a sister, and had served a year in the army towards the end of World War Two. Rebus paused for a moment, pondering that: you survived a war, only to die in your home town three years later. Watt was twenty years old, and had only been working at the brewery for eleven months. Joseph Cropper told the reporter that the young man had been 'full of energy, a hard worker with excellent prospects'.

In the photo showing the procession into the cemetery, Cropper was central. There was a woman next to him, identified as his wife. She wore black, her eyes to the ground, her husband gripping her arm. She was skinny and slight, in contrast to the man she'd married. Rebus leaned in a little further towards the screen, then wound the film back to the previous photo. Twenty minutes later, he was still looking.

Albert Simms seemed surprised to see him.

Simms had just finished one of his brewery tours. Rebus was sitting at a table in the sample room, nursing the best part of a pint of IPA. It had been a busy tour: eight guests in all. They offered Rebus half-smiles and glances but kept their distance. Simms poured them their drinks but then seemed in a hurry for them to finish, ushering them from the room. It was five minutes before he returned. Rebus was behind the pumps, topping up his glass.

'No mention of Johnny Watt's ghost,' Rebus commented.

'No.' Simms was tidying the vests and hard-hats into a plastic storage container.

'Do you want a drink? My shout.'

Simms thought about it, then nodded. He approached the bar and eased himself on to one of the stools. There was a blue folder lying nearby, but he tried his best to ignore it.

'Always amazes me,' Rebus said, 'the way we humans hang on to things – records, I mean. Chitties and receipts and old photographs. Brewery's got quite a collection. Same goes for the libraries and the medical college.' He handed over Simms's drink. The man made no attempt to pick it up.

'Joseph Cropper's wife never had a daughter,' Rebus began to explain. 'I got that from Joseph's grandson, your current boss. He showed me the archives. So much stuff there ...' He paused. 'When Johnny Watt died, how long had you been working here, Albie?'

'Not long.'

Rebus nodded and opened the folder, showing Simms the photo from the *Scotsman*, the one of the brewery workers in the yard. He tapped a particular face. A young man, seated on a corner of the wagon, legs dangling, shoulders hunched. 'You've not really changed, you know. How old were you? Fifteen?'

'You sound as if you know.' Simms had taken the photocopy from Rebus and was studying it.

'The police keep records too, Albie. We never throw anything away. Bit of trouble in your youth – nicking stuff; fights. Brandishing a razor on one particular occasion – you did a bit of juvenile time for that. Was that when Joseph Cropper met you? He was the charitable type, according to his grandson. Liked to visit prisons, talk to the men and the juveniles. You were about to be released; he offered you a job. But there were strings attached, weren't there?'

'Were there?' Simms tossed the sheet of paper on to the bar, picked up the glass and drank from it.

'I think so,' Rebus said. 'In fact, I'd go so far as to say I know so.' He rubbed a hand down his cheek. 'Be a bugger to prove, mind, but I don't think I need to do that.'

'Why not?'

'Because you want to be caught. You're an old man now, maybe only a short while left, but it's been plaguing you. How many years is it, Albie? How long have you been seeing Johnny Watt's ghost?'

Albert Simms wiped foam from his top lip with his knuckles, but didn't say anything.

'I've been to take a look at your house,' Rebus continued. 'Nice place. Semi-detached; quiet street off Colinton Road. Didn't take much searching to come up with the transaction. You bought it new a couple of months after Johnny Watt died. No mortgage. I mean, houses were maybe more affordable back then, but on wages like yours? I've seen your pay slips, Albie – they're in the company files too. So where did the money come from?'

'Go on then – tell me.'

'Joseph Cropper didn't have a daughter. You told me he did because you knew fine well it would jar if I ever did any digging. I'd start to wonder why you told that particular lie. He had a wife, though, younger than him.' Rebus showed Simms a copy of the photo from the cemetery. 'See how her husband's keeping a grip on her? She's either about to faint or he's just letting everyone know who the boss is. To be honest, my money would be on both. You can't see her face, but there's a photo she sat for in a studio ...' He slid it from the folder.

'Very pretty, I think you'll agree. This came from Douglas Cropper, by the way. Families keep a lot of stuff too, don't they? She'd been at school with Johnny Watt. Johnny, with his eye for the ladies. Joseph Cropper couldn't have his wife causing a scandal, could he? Her in her late teens, him in his early thirties ...' Rebus leaned across the bar a little, so that his face was close to that of the man with the sagging shoulders and face.

'Could he?' he repeated.

'You can't prove anything, you said as much yourself.'

'But you wanted someone to find out. When you found out I was a cop, you zeroed in on me. You wanted to whet my appetite, because you needed to be found out, Albie. That's at the heart of this, always has been. Guilt gnawing away at you down the decades.'

'Not down the decades – just these past few years.' Simms took a deep breath. 'It was only meant to be the frighteners. I was a tough kid but I wasn't big. Johnny was big and fast, and that bit older. I just wanted him on the ground while I gave him the warning.' Simms's eyes were growing glassy.

'You hit him too hard,' Rebus commented. 'Did you push him in or did he fall?'

'He fell. Even then, I didn't know he was dead. The boss ... when he heard ...' Simms sniffed and swallowed hard. 'That was the both of us, locked together ... We couldn't tell. They were still hanging people back then.'

'They hanged a man at Perth jail in '48,' Rebus acknowledged. 'I read it in the *Scotsman.*'

Simms managed a weak smile. 'I knew you were the man, soon as I saw you. The kind who likes a mystery. Do you do crosswords?'

'Can't abide them.' Rebus paused for a mouthful of IPA. 'The money was to hush you up?'

'I told him he didn't need to – working for him, that was what I wanted. He said the money would get me a clean start anywhere in the world.' Simms shook his head slowly. 'I bought the house instead. He didn't like that, but he was stuck with it – what was he going to do?'

'The two of you never talked about it again?'

'What was there to talk about?'

'Did Cropper's wife ever suspect?'

'Why should she? Post-mortem was what we had to fear. Once they'd declared it an accident, that was that.'

Rebus sat in silence, waiting until Albert Simms made eye contact, then asked a question of his own. 'So what are we going to do, Albie?'

Albert Simms exhaled noisily. 'I suppose you'll be taking me in.'

'Can't do that,' Rebus said. 'I'm retired. It's up to you. Next natural step. I think you've already done the hard part.'

Simms thought for a moment, then nodded slowly. 'No more ghosts,' he said quietly, almost to himself, as he stared up at the ceiling of the sample room.

'Maybe, maybe not,' Rebus said.

'Been here long?' Siobhan Clarke asked as she entered the Oxford Bar.

'What else am I going to do?' Rebus replied. 'Now I'm on the scrapheap. What about you – hard day at the office?'

'Do you really want to hear about it?'

'Why not?'

'Because I know what you're like. Soon as you get a whiff of a case – mine or anyone else's – you'll want to have a go at it yourself.'

'Maybe I'm a changed man, Siobhan.'

'Aye, right.' She rolled her eyes and told the landlord she'd have a gin and tonic.

'Double?' he asked.

'Why not?' She looked at Rebus. 'Same again? Then you can make me jealous by telling me stories of your life of leisure.'

'Maybe I'll do that,' said Rebus, raising his pint glass and draining it to the very last drop.

Cinders

The Fairy Godmother was dead.

Rebus had had to fight his way through the throng of rubber-neckers outside the Theatre Royal. It was early evening, dark and drizzling, but they didn't seem to mind. He showed his warrant card to a uniformed officer at the cordon, and then again as he entered the red-carpeted foyer. The doors to the auditorium were open, the remaining audience members grumbling in that Edinburgh way as they queued to give their contact details before being allowed to leave. The curtain had been raised for the show's second act, revealing the kitchen of some grand house or castle, all fake stone walls and glowing fireplace.

'Apparently,' a voice next to Rebus announced, 'there's a bit of slapstick with Buttons as he tries baking a cake.'

'Shaving-foam in the face?' Rebus guessed.

'That sort of thing.' Detective Inspector Siobhan Clarke managed a thin smile.

The youngest members of the audience were setting up cries of protest, their annual panto treat ruined. Parents looked numbed, some of the mothers dabbing away tears.

'They know?' Rebus said.

'Second half doesn't start, police arrive – I'd say they've guessed there's no happy ending.'

'So what happened?'

'Easier if I show you.' She turned back into the foyer and pushed open a door marked Private. Stairs up, a narrow corridor, then another door, more stairs, and turns to left and right.

'Should we be leaving a trail of breadcrumbs?' Rebus inquired.

'Wrong story,' Clarke answered.

She had to knock at a final door. It was opened by a uniformed officer. They were in another corridor with doors off.

'Make-up, wardrobe, dressing rooms,' Clarke intoned.

'The business of show.' Rebus peered into some of the rooms as they passed them. Rails festooned with gaudy clothing, strip-lit mirrors, props and wigs. There were loudspeakers set into the walls, broadcasting the sounds from the auditorium. The Scene of Crime crew were bagging and tagging.

'We're not worried about contamination?' Rebus checked.

'Twenty or thirty people pass this way a dozen or more times per show. Maxtone doesn't think we'd be adding much to the mix.'

'Doug Maxtone is in charge?'

'How do you not know that?' Clarke stopped in her tracks.

'I was just passing, Siobhan.'

'Just passing?'

'Well, maybe I heard something at the station...'

'But you're not on the team?' She rolled her eyes at the stupidity of her own question. 'Of course not – Doug Maxtone's hardly in your fan club.'

'I can't understand it – we've got badges and everything.'

'This is a murder inquiry, John. You don't just walk in.'

'Yet here I am.' Rebus gave a shrug. 'So why not show me where it happened?'

She sighed as she made up her mind, then led the way. 'We can't go in, not without being suited up.'

'Understood.'

So they stood at the threshold instead. The interior seemed frozen in the moment. Vases of flowers and good luck cards. Bottles of water and blackcurrant cordial. A bowl of fruit. A small suitcase, lying open. A chair tipped over. A dark stain on the pale blue carpet.

'I smell smoke.'

'Not quite enough to set off the alarm,' Clarke said. 'A metal waste-bin.' She nodded to where it had once sat. 'Off to the lab.'

'Was she a smoker?'

'It was paper of some kind – plus sandwich wrappers and who knows what else.'

'A blow to the head, I heard.'

'Probably when she was seated, facing the mirror. She didn't have the biggest of roles – pops up with the gown and glass slippers, then the coach. Comes on again near the end – or would have.'

'So it's the interval and she's changed out of her sparkly gown and wings?' Rebus mused. 'Meaning the costume department would have been lurking.'

'We're interviewing them.'

'How long is the interval?'

'Twenty minutes.'

'Lots of people backstage?'

'Lots.'

'She would have seen them.' He nodded towards the mirror. 'She'd have seen whoever walked in.'

'Baron Hardup has the next dressing room along. Didn't hear any screams. Then again, he had the radio on, listening to some horse race.'

'And through the other wall?'

'Stairwell.'

'No security cameras?'

'Not here, no.' Clarke paused. 'Did you know her?'

'How do you mean?'

'She was on TV in the 70s and 80s. A couple of sitcoms, even a few films.'

'I saw her face on the poster outside. Didn't ring any bells.'

'And the name? Celia Jagger?' She watched Rebus shrug. 'You've not asked about the weapon.'

Rebus scanned the dressing room but came up empty. 'Enlighten me,' he said.

'The glass slipper,' Clarke said. 'The one left behind at the Ball...'

Not that it was a real glass slipper. It was Perspex or something similar. And it wasn't the one from the performance. The production kept two spares. One of these had been removed from the props department and used in the attack, its stiletto heel piercing Jagger's skull and killing her instantly.

The props department was basically a large walk-in cupboard with shelves. The door had a lock, but was always open during performances. There were storage boxes bearing the name of each character along with a list of contents. Rebus held one of the remaining slippers in his hand. It was heavier than he had anticipated. Nicely made, but scuffed from use. Not that an audience would notice, not with a spotlight making it shine.

Clarke had gone off somewhere, with a warning that he should 'keep his head down'. Some of the chaos had subsided. Fewer headless chickens as the inquiry found its rhythm. Twelve dressing rooms, three of them to accommodate the chorus (who doubled as dancers). The theatre had no orchestra pit – the music was pre-recorded. Two technicians ran everything from a couple of laptops. Everyone would be asked about their movements during the interval. Statements would have to be verified. As yet, no one seemed to be asking the most basic question of all: who would want Celia Jagger dead? Her killing was the end of a story, and for stories you went to people. Which was why Rebus placed the shoe back in the box marked Cinders, and walked towards the exit.

The sign said Stage Door, and that was where he eventually found himself. There was an antechamber of sorts, with a list of actors and crew fixed to its wall. Like clocking in to some old-fashioned factory job, when you arrived you slid a wooden slat along to show you were IN. From behind a glass partition, the man in the security booth watched Rebus.

'I like this,' Rebus said, pointing to the wall.

'It's been here almost as long as the building.'

'And what about you?'

'I used to build the sets. Everything was custom-made in those days.'

'And now?'

'Mostly from stock. Newcastle or somewhere does Cinderella one year, we'll take what we need from them the next, while our Aladdin might head to Aberdeen. We built the tram from scratch, mind.'

'The tram?'

'Director's idea – instead of a carriage. Big puff of smoke and there's an Edinburgh tram. Pretty clever really – means we don't need any horses. Couple of the stage hands use a pulley and Cinders is off to the ball.' The man's smile faded. 'How long will we be closed?'

'Hard to say.'

'Theatre can't go on without it. Same for a lot of these old places – a full house for a few months means you can afford to run the rest of the year.'

'Is that what happens?'

The guard nodded. He was in shirt-sleeves, a mug of tea on the desk next to him. CCTV screens showed the alleyway outside, empty auditorium, and front of house.

'I'm Detective Sergeant Rebus, by the way,' Rebus said.

'Willie Mearns.'

'How long have you been doing this job, Mr Mearns?'

'Fifteen years.'

'Ever since you retired from the workshop?' Making Mearns seventy-five, maybe even eighty. He looked sprightly though. Rebus reckoned the man's memory would be sharp. 'Have you been questioned yet?'

'Not formally – just asked if I'd seen anyone suspicious.'

'I'm guessing you said no.'

'Quite right.'

'And Celia Jagger – did you know her to talk to?'

'Oh aye. I had to remind her that I built the set when she appeared in a play here back in her heyday.'

'Did you use the word "heyday"?'

'I'm not that daft.'

'She had a bit of an ego then?'

'Most of them do. Don't get me wrong – they're lovely with it. But Celia was miffed she didn't get one of the big dressing rooms.'

'They all looked much the same to me.'

'A few inches can make all the difference.'

'You say she was "miffed" – is that as far as it went?'

'More or less.'

Rebus studied the man for a few seconds. 'There's a pub across the street. Do you know it?'

'I might have passed through its door on occasion.'

Rebus smiled. 'Well, tonight we've got half a dozen of Police Scotland's finest keeping watch on the Theatre Royal. I think you can maybe call it a day, Mr Mearns.'

The man made show of considering his options, then started rising to his feet. 'I'll drink to that,' he said.

The interviews were taking place at St Leonard's police station. Rebus found Clarke pacing a corridor, scanning transcripts.

'Who have we got?' he asked her.

She nodded in turn towards four doors. 'Tracy Sidwell, John Carrier, Robert Tennant, Jamie Salter.'

'So that's Cinderella, Baron Hardup, Prince Charming and Buttons.'

'You're well informed.'

'I just spent an hour in a pub with a man who likes to talk. Hardup's a bit too fond of the horses apparently. Always needing to borrow a few quid to tide him over. Meantime, Prince Charming left his wife and two kids for Cinderella – not quite a fairy tale.'

Clarke stared at him. 'Anything else?'

Rebus shrugged. 'There are whispers about Buttons and the Wicked Stepmother. Giggles and whispers behind closed dressing-room doors. Who else have we got?'

'They're waiting in the office until we're ready for them.' They walked together to the MIT suite. The Ugly Sisters – panto stalwarts Davie Clegg and Russell Gloag – had changed out of their costumes but still bore traces of make-up. They were seated alongside the show's writer/director Maurice Welsh, who was visibly trembling as he spoke with another man. Rebus guessed this would be Alan Yates, producer and owner of the Theatre Royal. Seeing the two detectives, Yates leapt to his feet. He was in his sixties and looked to have dined out for most of them.

'Any news?' he asked.

'Not yet, sir,' Clarke assured him.

'We need to offer refunds...prep an understudy. The show must – '

'Sorry to disillusion you, sir,' Rebus butted in. 'But the theatre remains a crime scene. It doesn't open again until we say so.'

'And even then, Alan,' Welsh added tiredly, 'who's going to be in the mood? I mean the audience rather than the cast. We'll have nothing but ghouls...'

'Run's finished,' Davie Clegg agreed. 'Can't sit in that dressing-room and not think of Celia.'

Yates ran a hand through what hair he had left. 'But without the panto there *is* no Theatre Royal! It's our banker!'

'Sorry, Alan.' Clegg offered a shrug of sympathy.

'Ruined,' Yates muttered, falling back on to his seat. Maurice Welsh patted his arm.

'That's all very well,' Russell Gloag piped up, 'but it doesn't tell us who killed poor Celia. And if I find out it was any one of you...'

'Actually that's our job,' Clarke informed him. She broke off as an exhausted-looking detective filled the doorway. He checked his notepad.

'Maurice Welsh?' The director stood up, looking as if a gust might topple him. 'If you'll follow me, sir.' The detective locked eyes with Clarke and shook his head: nothing to report.

Rebus gestured for Clarke to follow him into the corridor. He checked they were out of earshot. 'Where's everyone else? The crew and chorus, plus Dandini and the Stepmother?'

'One of the other offices. Otherwise they'd have been like sardines.' She studied him. 'What else did your friend in the pub tell you?'

'Bits and pieces. I'm not sure yet what they – '

'What in God's name is *he* doing here?'

They both turned in the direction of the approaching voice. DCI Doug Maxtone seemed to fill the corridor as he strode towards them.

'I was just passing,' Rebus explained slowly. 'Happened to bump into DI Clarke and she was just singing your praises.'

Maxtone ignored Rebus, his attention fixed on Clarke. He brandished a sheet of paper ripped from a pad. 'Forensics played a blinder,' he told her.

'The waste-bin?'

'Salient contents: one promotional photograph of Celia Jagger. Not quite done to a cinder...'

'And?'

'It was signed.' Maxtone checked his note. '"To my darling Ed with all my love".'

'Ed?' Clarke narrowed her eyes. 'Edwin Oakes?'

'AKA Dandini. Is he inside?' Maxtone was gesturing towards the MIT room.

'He's with the chorus and crew.'

Maxtone's face hardened. 'I've just come from there.'

Clarke's lips formed an O. 'No Dandini?' she surmised.

'They thought he must be here.'

Rebus made show of clearing his throat. 'Maybe he found the trap-door.'

'You're as useful as last year's turkey,' Maxtone snarled, before barrelling his way back along the corridor, Clarke at his heels.

Rebus stayed where he was. Then he took out his phone and a scrap of paper, reading Willie Mearns' number from it as he got busy on the keypad.

'I need everything there is to know about Edwin Oakes,' he said. As he listened, his eyes began to narrow and his brow furrow. *Curiouser and curiouser...*

The following morning, Rebus was at St Leonard's early. He went through the interview transcripts, gleaning bits and pieces. There was no love lost between the Ugly Sisters apparently – they worked together for the sake of the pay cheque, each privately confiding his loathing of the other to various stagehands. Wardrobe department, make-up, deputy stage manager...all had sung for the detectives. The show's director had a history of substance abuse, as did Prince Charming. Buttons was notoriously lazy, and had almost come to blows with both director and producer while attempting to cut back on his lines so he wouldn't have to remember them. He would also ad lib weak jokes, meaning more arguments after each and every performance.

But there was plenty of gossip about the crew, too. Assignations and affairs, minor misdemeanours and fallings-out. As the show's director had said: *it's a pressure cooker, but if you try turning the heat down sometimes the production suffers.* And in the end, it was all about the show, its run sold out weeks before opening.

'Quite the drama,' Siobhan Clarke said, reading over Rebus's shoulder. She was carrying a cardboard coffee-cup and a leather satchel. 'Maxtone not in yet?'

'Think I'd be here if he was?'

'Fair point.' She put down her things and started removing her long woollen coat. 'I meant to ask you – what are you doing for Christmas?'

'Probably not going to the panto.'

'I mean the day itself – you know you'd be welcome at mine.'

'Thanks, Siobhan, but I have my own traditions to stick to.'

'Meaning finding a pub that's open? Maybe a meal from the freezer after?'

'I'm old-fashioned that way.'

'I feel bad about us shutting down *Cinderella*.'

'We're not the villains here, remember that. Though sometimes all Doug Maxtone lacks is a moustache to twirl.' Rebus looked at his watch. 'Shouldn't have bothered taking your coat off.'

'Is the heating playing up or something?'

Rebus shook his head. 'But we're going out again.'

'We are? Why's that?'

'Because Edwin Oakes is a creature of habit,' he said, rising to his feet.

They decided on Rebus's car so Clarke could continue drinking her coffee, but as they turned out of the car park, they were blocked by a man, his arms outstretched. He wore a flapping coat and was wide-eyed and unshaven.

'Isn't that one of our Ugly Sisters?' Clarke asked.

Rebus was already out of the car. 'Mr Gloag, isn't it?' he was saying.

'I know what he told you and it's not true! Not one word of it!' There were flecks of foam at the corners of the actor's mouth.

'Just calm down.' Rebus held up the palms of both hands. 'I know everyone's a bit on edge...'

'He told you I'd slept with Celia, didn't he?'

'Are we talking about your colleague Davie Clegg?' Clarke inquired.

'Last time I work with that wretched piece of...' Gloag looked at his hands, willing them to stop shaking. 'He told you about *Earnest*? It's true, I was in the same play as her, but nothing ever happened. I mean...she flirted a bit. You know – all touchy-feely, and maybe I picked up the signals wrong.'

'You'd have been accommodating?' Rebus guessed.

'But if you think that was going to make me jealous of Ed...'

'You knew about them though?' Clarke probed.

'We all *knew*.'

'But it didn't make you angry?' Rebus asked. 'The same anger you're feeling right now?'

'I'm not angry.' Gloag tried to laugh. 'I just can't believe Davie would have said anything.'

'Rest easy then, Mr Gloag – Davie Clegg didn't tell tales.'

Gloag looked as if he'd been hit. 'Wh-what?'

'He's been winding you up, sir,' Rebus confirmed. 'Telling you he did something he didn't.'

Colour rose to Gloag's cheeks. 'That does it!' he spat. 'If he thinks we're working together again, he can bloody well whistle. That's our divorce papers right there!' He spun away, hurtling down the pavement.

'Think we should warn Clegg?' Clarke asked, getting back into the car.

'We need to be elsewhere.' Rebus started the car. After a minute of silence, he asked about Oakes.

'Shares a flat in the Grassmarket with Buttons. Though apparently they don't see much of one another.'

'Because Buttons is shacked up with the Wicked Stepmother?'

'Reading between the lines, yes. Bit awkward, with both flatmates carrying on their little liaisons. Oakes's actual home is in Glasgow but he hardly gets back there during the season.'

'Officers have been to both?'

'Camped outside through the night,' Clarke confirmed. 'We've also interviewed Prince Charming's ex-wife plus our esteemed director's partner – he's gay, by the way. And the substance abuse?' She shook her head. 'I don't buy it – he's just naturally hyper.' She peered from the window. 'Where are we headed?'

'The Meadows.'

'Is this your security guy again?'

'He's like a priest – they all tell him their story at some point.'

'Stagehands mostly knew about Oakes and Celia Jagger.' Clarke took another sip from her cup. 'I mean, they knew or they'd had an inkling. Seems she had a bit of history in that department – every production she was in, she managed an affair with someone in the cast. Doesn't seem to matter that she was old enough to be Oakes's mother – actually, maybe even his grandmother.'

'But she decides he's not the one – maybe has her eye on someone else. So he burns the photo and then whacks her over the head.'

'It's a fairly classic set-up.'

'You may be wiser than you know.'

'How so?'

'The relevant phrase is "set up".'

She stared at him as he stopped the car kerbside. They were on Melville Drive. The Meadows was an expanse of playing fields criss-crossed by paths. A lot of students used it as a route to the university. In summer, they would host barbecues and games of

Frisbee, but there was an icy wind today and the few pedestrians were well wrapped up.

'I wish you'd tell me what's in that head of yours,' Clarke complained. Rebus just winked and got out of the car. She followed him to where he had come to a halt, next to a line of trees. There was a circuit of bare earth, the grass worn away by a generation of joggers. Two young women passed them, managing to hold a conversation while they ran. From the opposite direction came an older man, headphones on, steam rising from his singlet. And then, fifty yards or so back, a figure that seemed out of place. He was dressed in cream chinos and a zip-up jacket, below which was an open-necked shirt. Yes, because Edwin Oakes hadn't felt able to return to his digs or to the theatre. He was wearing the same outfit as when he'd walked out of the police station. And Rebus guessed he hadn't slept either. Despite which, he had come for his morning run.

A creature of habit, just as Willie Mearns had said.

Rebus stepped on to the trail, blocking him. Oakes came to a stop, leaning forward to catch his breath.

'Morning, Mr Oakes,' Rebus said.

'You're the police?' Oakes guessed.

'We need you at St Leonard's, sir.'

Oakes straightened his back. 'I didn't do anything.'

'You ran away,' Clarke corrected him.

'I knew you'd think...' He broke off and shook his head. 'I just needed some time.'

'To come up with a story?'

'To *grieve*.' His eyes bored into Clarke's. 'I loved her. I mean, I knew her reputation and everything – once the show ended, we'd be history. But all the same...'

'She gave you a photo,' Rebus said. 'We found it in the waste-bin in her dressing-room.'

Oakes frowned. 'Nobody knew about that.'

'You're saying you didn't set light to it?' Clarke demanded.

'I kept it in a drawer in my own dressing-room, tucked away where it wouldn't be seen.'

'Somebody found it,' Rebus stated. He half-turned towards Clarke. 'No raised voices from behind Celia Jagger's door – someone from the crew would have heard an argument, they all seem to have pretty good ears.'

'I could never have hurt her,' Oakes was saying. 'Never in a million years.'

'Yet you did a runner.'

'I knew you'd find out about us – either that or I'd have to tell you.' Oakes rubbed at his hair. 'I've a girlfriend – sort of – back in Glasgow. Someone I'm fond of. She's got a daughter who dotes on me. It was the look on her face I couldn't stand, finding out I'd cheated on her mum...'

'You need to come back with us,' Rebus said quietly. 'We know you didn't do anything. Talking to us means taking us a step closer to finding whoever did.'

Oakes nodded slowly. Clarke's eyes were on Rebus. He knew what she was thinking: *How can we be sure?* As they escorted Oakes to the waiting car, she asked the actor when he had last seen the photo.

'A few days back. Maybe longer than that. It actually hurt me a little.'

'Why was that?'

'It's the sort of thing you hand to a fan at the stage door. I mean, the message was personal but not *that* personal. And that was actually the real message – none of this means anything except in the moment. Soon as the production ends, we go our separate ways.' Oakes angled his head back, as if to stop the tears coming.

Just as well someone usually writes your lines for you, Rebus thought, before inquiring whether Oakes had ever walked into his dressing room and found someone from the cast or crew there.

'All the time – it's an open house. I've usually got chocolate biscuits or cans of cola. Jamie's a demon for the sugar.'

'Jamie meaning Buttons?'

Oakes nodded. 'And John's always wandering in with some sure-fire bet he wants to share. They're like family...' His face darkened. 'It can't be any of them. There must be someone else.'

'Maybe so, Mr Oakes. Maybe so.' Rebus pulled a slip of paper from his pocket and handed it across for Siobhan Clarke to take.

'See if you can track down this guy,' he said. 'He's the one we probably need to talk to now.'

She read the name. 'Howard Corbyn? Who the hell is Howard Corbyn?'

'You're a detective,' Rebus told her. 'You'll work it out.'

They installed Oakes in the back of the car. But before getting in, Clarke grabbed Rebus by the arm.

'Maxtone needs to know you're the one who did this.' She gestured towards the actor.

'I don't mind you grabbing the good reviews, Siobhan.'

She narrowed her eyes. 'It's not over, is it? There's another act coming?'

Rebus nodded towards the slip of paper. 'Depends what comes from that,' he said, making his way round to the driver's seat.

*

Rebus stood alone on the stage of the Theatre Royal. A stage-hand had raised the curtain and put on a few lights. The scene was still set for the opening of the panto's second half – the kitchen of Baron Hardup's castle. Close up, the set and props looked tired, paint fading or flaking, edges chipped – not unlike the building itself. He knew that council officials had ordered expensive modifications (yet to be carried out). The roof needed repairs and the carpets were fraying or threadbare.

None of which would have mattered to each day's audience, primed with sugary snacks and drinks, pockets emptied in the purchase of glo-sticks, magic wands and glossy programmes. Each year's twelve-week panto run just about made up for nine months of loss-making. The box office next door had been handing out refunds when Rebus arrived. The apology taped over the poster for Cinderella said that the show had been cancelled 'until further notice'.

'Is there any news?' Alan Yates asked, coming on to the stage from the wings.

'Isn't that bad luck?' Rebus said. Yates looked confused. 'You entered stage left. Lighting director told me the show was cursed from the moment Celia Jagger made the mistake of entering stage left during the first rehearsal. Stage left is for villains. Goes back to the medieval mysteries or something.'

Yates forced a smile. 'Stage left is hell, stage right heaven – I know the story, but it's only actors who are superstitious that way. Theatre owners live in the real world – we're even allowed to say the word Macbeth, as long as none of the cast is in earshot.'

'You might have just jinxed yourself then, Mr Yates. You asked if there's news and there is – we've got Russell Gloag in a cell at St Leonard's.'

'Russell?' Yates sounded disbelieving.

'He gave Davie Clegg a bit of a battering – so it looks like you've lost your Ugly Sisters, too. The real world you live in isn't doing you any favours, eh?' Rebus paused. 'Bit of a blow to your ego, I dare say, when your Fairy Godmother decided on Edwin Oakes.'

Yates's face creased. 'I'm not sure I follow.'

'She played here seven years ago in The Mousetrap. Then again three years later in an Oscar Wilde play...'

'Yes?'

'And both times you enjoyed what Wilde might have called "a dalliance".'

Yates's face was colouring. 'We most certainly did not.'

'Oh yes, you did. Crew at the time knew it. *Everyone* knew it. So you reckoned it would be the same again this year. Must have hurt your pride to be rebuffed.' Rebus took a step closer. 'In the lane outside the stage door – the lane covered by CCTV. Willie Mearns saw you. Trying for a clinch, being pushed away. A pointed finger, a slap, a few angry words.'

'This is preposterous.' Yates made to lean against the table, but it creaked, reminding him that it was not solid. 'You're suggesting I killed Celia because she was seeing Oakes?'

'Not at all.' Rebus paused again. 'You killed her out of simple greed, more than anything. You're like Baron Hardup with a castle that's going to ruin you.' Rebus gestured to the set. 'Just the single solitary panto run each year keeping the creditors from your door. But all the renovations and improvements that need to be made… It'd be years before you saw any return. If the panto could be stopped from spinning gold, you'd have the perfect excuse to sell the place off – no one would blame you or paint you as the villain. That's why you started talking to Howard Corbyn.'

'Who?'

'Howard Corbyn,' Rebus repeated.

'I've never heard of him.'

'Is that right? Well, he's a property developer.' Rebus turned towards the auditorium and raised his voice a little. 'Aren't you, Mr Corbyn?'

He was seated in the front row of the Grand Circle, Siobhan Clarke next to him, the pair of them just about visible beyond the stage lighting. Corbyn nodded and waved, and Alan Yates swallowed a gulp. Perspiration made his face gleam.

'Willie Mearns watched the pair of you,' Rebus went on, turning towards Yates again. 'Three visits when you knew the theatre would be empty. A handshake in the lane at the end of the third. Flats, commercial use, maybe a super-pub – Mr Corbyn wasn't sure what he would do with the place, but he wanted it if the price was right. You just had to shut down *Cinderella*. A real-life tragedy would do the trick. You could get back at Celia Jagger for her snub, and maybe even put her lover in the frame – all you had to do was take that photo from his dressing-room and place it in hers – just singed enough to look the part. You think we can't lift fingerprints from a half-burned picture, Mr Yates? You'd be surprised what we can do these days with anything less than cinders.'

Yates was looking at the floor, as if willing it to reveal an escape route.

'No disappearing act for you,' Rebus warned him. 'But you might want to take one last good look around. Because you know where your reputation's going to be from now on?'

'Where?' Yates couldn't help asking, his voice cracking.

Instead of answering, Rebus looked up to where Siobhan Clarke was sitting.

'Behind you!' she called down.

'Behind you,' Rebus repeated quietly, leading Alan Yates from the stage.

Further Copyright Information

'Dead and Buried' © John Rebus Limited 2013

'Playback,' 'The Dean Curse,' 'Being Frank,' 'Concrete Evidence,' 'Seeing Things,' 'A Good Hanging,' 'Tit for Tat,' 'Not Provan,' 'Sunday,' 'Auld Lang Syne,' 'The Gentleman's Club,' 'Monstrous Trumpet' from *A Good Hanging (And Other Short Stories, Featuring Inspector Rebus)* © 2002 by Ian Rankin. Reprinted by permission of Minotaur Books, an imprint of St. Martin's Press. All rights reserved.

'My Shopping Day' © Ian Rankin 1997 (first published in *Herbert in Motion and Other Stories* in Great Britain in 1997 by Revolver)

'Facing the Music' © John Rebus Limited 2002 (first published in *Beggar's Banquet,* 1992)

'Trip Trap' © Ian Rankin 1992 (first published in *1st Culprit* by Chatto & Windus, 1992)

'Talk Show' © Ian Rankin 1991 (first published in *Winter's Crimes* 23 by Macmillan, 1991)

'Castle Dangerous' © Ian Rankin 1993 (first published in *Ellery Queen Mystery Magazine,* October 1993)

'In the Frame' © Ian Rankin 1992 (first published in *Winter's Crimes* 24 by Macmillan, 1992)

'Window of Opportunity' © Ian Rankin 1995 (first published in *Ellery Queen Mystery Magazine,* December 1995)

'No Sanity Clause' © Ian Rankin 2000 (first published in the *Daily Telegraph,* December 2000)

'Death Is Not the End' © Ian Rankin 1998

'Tell Me Who to Kill' © Ian Rankin 2003 (first published in *Mysterious Pleasures,* Little, Brown & Company)

'Saint Nicked' © Ian Rankin 2002 (first published in the *Radio Times,* 2002)

'Atonement' © John Rebus Limited 2005

'Not Just Another Saturday' © John Rebus Limited 2005

'Penalty Claus' © John Rebus Limited 2010 (first published in the *Mail on Sunday,* 2010)

'The Passenger' © John Rebus Limited 2014

'A Three-Pint Problem' © John Rebus Limited 2014

'The Very Last Drop' © John Rebus Limited 2010 (written to help the work of Royal Blind)

'Cinders' © John Rebus Limited 2014 (first published in the *Mail on Sunday*)

About the author

Ian Rankin is a #1 internationally bestselling novelist and the recipient of an Edgar Award, a Gold Dagger for fiction, and the Chandler-Fulbright Award. He lives in Edinburgh, Scotland, with his wife and their two sons.

...and the return of Detective Inspector John Rebus

In *Even Dogs in the Wild,* Rebus comes out of retirement...to save his nemesis Malcolm Fox. Following is an excerpt from the book's opening pages.

Eventually the passenger ejected the tape and tossed it on to the back seat.

'That was the Associates,' the driver complained.

'Well they can go associate somewhere else. Singer sounds like his balls have been trapped in a vice.'

The driver thought about this for a moment, then smiled. 'Remember we did that to . . . what was his name again?'

The passenger shrugged. 'He owed the boss money – that's what mattered.'

'Wasn't a lot of money, was it?'

'How much further?' The passenger peered through the windscreen.

'Half a mile. These woods have seen some action, eh?'

The passenger made no comment. It was dark out there and they'd not encountered another car for the last five or so miles. Fife countryside, inland from the coast, the fields shorn and awaiting winter. A pig farm not too far away, one they'd used before.

'What's the plan?' the driver asked.

'Just the one shovel, so we toss to see who breaks sweat. Strip off his clothes, burn them later.'

'He's only wearing pants and a vest.'

'No tattoos or rings that I saw. Nothing we need to cut off.'

'This is us here.' The driver stopped the car, got out and opened a gate. A churned track led into the forest. 'Hope we don't get stuck,' he said, getting back in. Then, seeing the look on the other man's face: 'Joke.'

'Better be.'

They drove slowly for a few hundred yards. 'There's a space here where I can turn,' the driver said.

'This'll do, then.'

'Recognise it?'

The passenger shook his head. 'It's been a while.'

'I think there's one buried somewhere in front of us, and another over to the left.'

'Maybe try the other side of the track, in that case. Torch in the glove box?'

'Fresh batteries, like you said.'

The passenger checked. 'Right then.'

The two men got out and stood for the best part of a minute, their eyes adjusting to the gloom, ears alert for unusual sounds.

'I'll pick the spot,' the passenger said, taking the torch with him as he headed off. The driver got a cigarette lit and opened the back door of the Mercedes. It was an old model, and the hinges creaked. He lifted the Associates cassette from the seat and slipped it into his jacket pocket, where it hit some coins. He'd be needing one of those for the heads-or-tails. Slamming the door shut, he moved to the boot and opened it. The body was wrapped in a plain blue bedsheet. Or it had been. The trip had loosened the makeshift shroud. Bare feet, pale skinny legs, ribcage visible. The driver rested the shovel against one of the tail lights, but it slid to the ground. Cursing, he bent over to retrieve it.

Which was when the corpse burst into life, emerging from sheet and boot both, almost vaulting the driver as its feet hit the ground. The driver gasped, the cigarette flying from his mouth. He had one hand on the shovel's handle while he tried to haul himself upright with the other. The sheet was hanging over the lip of the boot, its occupant disappearing into the trees.

'Paul!' the driver yelled. 'Paul!'

Torchlight preceded the man called Paul.

'Hell's going on, Dave?' he shouted. The driver could only stretch out a shaking hand to point.

'He's done a runner!'

Paul scanned the empty boot. A hissing sound from between his gritted teeth.

'After him then,' he said in a growl. 'Or it'll be someone else's turn to dig a hole for us.'

'He came back from the dead,' Dave said, voice trembling.

'Then we kill him again,' Paul stated, producing a knife from his inside pocket. 'Even slower than before . . .'

Malcolm Fox woke from another of his bad dreams.

He reckoned he knew why he'd started having them – uncertainty about his job. He wasn't entirely sure he wanted it any more, and feared he was surplus to requirements anyway. Yesterday, he'd been told he had to travel to Dundee to fill a vacant post for a couple of shifts. When he asked why, he was told the officer he'd be replacing had been ordered to cover for someone else in Glasgow.

'Isn't it easier just to send me to Glasgow, then?' Fox had enquired.

'You could always ask, I suppose.'

So he'd picked up the phone and done exactly that, only to find that the officer in Glasgow was coming to Edinburgh to fill a temporary gap – at which point he'd given up the fight and driven to Dundee. And today? Who knew. His boss at St Leonard's didn't seem to know what to do with him. He was just one detective inspector too many.

'It's the time-servers,' DCI Doug Maxtone had apologised. 'They're bunging up the system. Need a few of them to take the gold watch . . .'

'Understood,' Fox had said. He wasn't in the first idealistic flush of youth himself – another three years and he could retire with a solid pension and plenty of life left in him.

Standing under the shower, he considered his options. The bungalow in Oxgangs that he called home would fetch a fair price, enough to allow him to relocate. But then there was his dad to consider – Fox couldn't move too far away, not while Mitch still had breath in his body. And then there was Siobhan. They weren't lovers, but they'd been spending more time together. If either of them was bored, they knew they could always call. Maybe there'd be a film or a restaurant, or just snacks and a DVD. She'd bought him half a dozen titles for Christmas and they'd watched three before the old year was done. As he got dressed, he thought of her. She loved the job more than he did. Whenever they met up, she was always ready to share news and gossip. Then she would ask him, and he would shrug, maybe offer a few morsels. She gulped them down like delicacies, while all he saw was plain white bread. She worked at Gayfield Square, with James Page for a boss. The structure there seemed better than at St Leonard's. Fox had wondered about a transfer, but knew it would never happen – he would be creating the selfsame problem. One DI too many.

Forty minutes after finishing breakfast, he was parking at St Leonard's. He sat in his car for an extra few moments, gathering himself, hands running around the steering wheel. It was at times like this he wished he smoked – something to occupy him, to take him out of himself. Instead of which, he placed a piece of chewing gum on his tongue and closed his mouth. A uniform had emerged from the station's back door into the car park and was opening a packet of cigarettes. Their eyes met as Fox walked towards him, and the other man gave the curtest of nods. The uniform knew that Fox used to work for Professional Standards – everyone in the station knew. Some didn't seem to mind; others made their distaste obvious. They scowled, answered grudgingly, let doors swing shut into his face rather than holding them open.

'You're a good cop,' Siobhan had told him on more than one occasion. 'I wish you could see that . . .'

When he reached the CID suite, Fox gleaned that something was happening. Chairs and equipment were being moved. His eyes met those of a thunderous Doug Maxtone.

'We've to make room for a new team,' Maxtone explained.

'New team?'

'From Gartcosh, which means they'll mostly be Glasgow – and you know how I feel about *them*.'

'What's the occasion?'

'Nobody's saying.'

Fox chewed on his gum. Gartcosh, an old steelworks, was now home to the Scottish Crime Campus. It had been up and running since the previous summer, and Fox had never had occasion to cross its threshold. The place was a mix of police, prosecutors, forensics and Customs, and its remit took in organised crime and counterterrorism. 'How many are we expecting to welcome?'

Maxtone glared at him. 'Frankly, Malcolm, I'm not expecting to *welcome* a single one of them. But we need desks and chairs for half a dozen.'

'And computers and phones?'

'They're bringing their own. They do, however, request . . .' Maxtone produced a sheet of paper from his pocket and made show of consulting it, '"ancillary support, subject to vetting".'

'And this came from on high?'

'The Chief Constable himself.' Maxtone crumpled the paper and tossed it in the general direction of a bin. 'They're arriving in about an hour.'

'Should I do a bit of dusting?'

'Might as well – it's not as if there's going to be anywhere for you to sit.'

'I'm losing my chair?'

'And your desk.' Maxtone inhaled and exhaled noisily. 'So if there's anything in the drawers you'd rather not share . . .' He managed a grim smile. 'Bet you're wishing you'd stayed in bed, eh?'

'Worse than that, sir – I'm beginning to wish I'd stayed in Dundee.'

Siobhan Clarke had parked on a yellow line on St Bernard's Crescent. It was about as grand a street as could be found in Edinburgh's New Town, all pillared facades and floor-to-ceiling windows. Two bow-shaped Georgian terraces facing one another across a small private garden containing trees and benches. Raeburn Place, with its emporia and eateries, was a two-minute walk away, as was the Water of Leith. She'd brought Malcolm to the Saturday food market a couple of times, and joked that he should trade in his bungalow for one of Stockbridge's colony flats.

Her phone buzzed: speak of the devil. She answered the call.

'You off up north again?'

'Not at the moment,' he said. 'Big shake-up happening here, though.'

'I've got news too – I've been seconded to the Minton enquiry.'

'Since when?'

'First thing this morning. I was going to tell you at lunchtime. James has been put in charge and he wanted me.'

'Makes sense.'

She locked her car and walked towards a gloss-black front door boasting a gleaming brass knocker and letter box. A uniformed officer stood guard; she gave a half-bow of recognition, which Clarke rewarded with a smile.

'Any room for a little one?' Fox was asking, trying to make it sound like a joke, though she could tell he was serious.

'I've got to go, Malcolm. Talk to you later.' Clarke ended the call and waited for the officer to unlock the door. There were no media – they'd been and gone. A couple of small posies had been left at the front step, probably by neighbours. There was an old-style bell pull by the pillar to the right of the door, and above it a nameplate bearing the single capitalised word MINTON.

As the door swung open, Clarke thanked the officer and went inside. There was some mail on the parquet floor. She scooped it up and saw that more was sitting on an occasional table. The letters on the table had been opened and checked – presumably by the major incident team. There were the usual flyers too, including one for a curry house she knew on the south side of the city. She didn't see Lord Minton as the takeaway type, but you never could tell. The scene of crime unit had been through the hall, dusting for prints. Lord Minton – David Menzies Minton, to give him his full name – had been killed two evenings back. No one in the vicinity had heard the break-in or the attack. Whoever had done it had scaled a couple of back walls in the darkness to reach the small window of the garden-level laundry room, adjacent to the locked and bolted rear door. They had broken the window and climbed in. Minton had been in his study on the ground floor. According to the post-mortem examination, he had been beaten around the head, then throttled, after which his lifeless body had been beaten some more.

Clarke stood in the still, silent hall, getting her bearings. Then she lifted a file from her shoulder bag and began to reread its contents. Victim had been seventy-eight years old, never married, resident at this address for thirty-five years. Educated at George Heriot's School and the universities of St Andrews and Edinburgh. Rising through the city's teeming ranks of lawyers until he reached the position of Lord Advocate, prosecuting some of Scotland's most high-profile criminal trials. Enemies? He would have had plenty in his heyday, but for the past decade he had lived out of the lime-light. Occasional trips to London to sit in the House of Lords. Visited his club on Princes Street most days to read the newspapers and do as many crosswords as he could find.

'Housebreaking gone wrong,' Clarke's boss, DCI James Page,

had stated. 'Perpetrator doesn't expect anyone home. Panics. Game over.'

'But why strangle him, then start beating him again once the victim's deceased?'

'Like I say: panic. Explains why the attacker fled without taking anything. Probably high on something and needing money for more. Looking for the usual – phones and iPads, easily sold on. But not the sort of thing someone like the noble lord would have in his possession. Maybe that annoyed our man and he took out his frustration then and there.'

'Sounds reasonable.'

'But you'd like to see for yourself?' Page had nodded slowly. 'Off you go then.'

Living room, formal dining room and kitchen on the ground floor, unused servants' quarters and laundry room below. The window frame of the laundry room had been boarded up, the window panel itself removed, along with all the shards of glass, to be taken away and examined by forensics. Clarke unlocked the back door and studied the small, well-tended private garden. Lord Minton employed a gardener, but he only visited one day each month in winter. He had been interviewed and had expressed his sadness, along with his concern that he hadn't been paid for the previous month.

Climbing the noiseless stone staircase to the ground floor, Clarke realised that, apart from a toilet, there was only one further room to check. The study was dark, its thick red velvet curtains closed. From the photographs in her file, she could see that Lord Minton's body had been found in front of his desk, on a Persian rug that had now also been taken away to be tested. Hair, saliva, fibres – everyone left traces of some kind. The thinking was: the victim was seated at his desk, writing out cheques to pay his gas and electricity bills. Hears a noise and gets up to investigate. Hasn't got far when the attacker bursts in and smacks him on the head with a tool of some kind – no weapon recovered yet; the pathologist's best guess, a hammer.

The chequebook lay open on the antique desk next to an expensive-looking pen. There were family photos – black and white, the victim's parents, maybe – in silver frames. Small enough to be slipped into a thief's pocket, yet untouched. She knew that Lord Minton's wallet had been found in a jacket over the back of the chair, cash and credit cards intact. The gold watch on his wrist had been left too.

'You weren't that desperate, were you?' Clarke muttered.

A woman called Jean Marischal came in twice a week to clean. She had her own key and had found the body the following morning. In her statement she said the place didn't really need that much attention; she just thought 'his lordship' liked a bit of company.

Upstairs there were too many rooms. A drawing room and sitting room that looked as though they'd never seen a visitor; four bedrooms, where only one was needed. Mrs Marischal could not recall a single overnight guest, or a dinner party, or any other kind of gathering, come to that. The bathroom didn't detain Clarke, so she headed downstairs to the hall again and stood there with arms folded. No fingerprints had been found other than those belonging to the victim and his cleaner. No reports of prowlers or out-of-place visitors.

Nothing.

Mrs Marischal had been persuaded to revisit the scene later on today. If anything *had* been taken, she was their best hope. Meanwhile, the team would have to look busy – it was expected that they would *be* busy. The current Lord Advocate wanted twice-daily updates, as did the First Minister. There would be media briefings at midday and four, briefings at which DCI James Page had to have something to share.

The problem was: what?

As she left, Clarke told the uniform outside to keep her wits about her.

'It's not true that the guilty always come back, but we might get lucky one time . . .'

On her way to Fettes, she stopped at a shop and bought a couple of newspapers, checking at the counter that they contained decent-sized obituaries of the deceased. She doubted she would learn anything she hadn't already read on a half-hour trawl of the internet, but they would bulk out the file.

Because Lord Minton was who he was, it had been decided to locate the major incident team at Fettes rather than Gayfield Square. Fettes – aka 'the Big House' – had been the headquarters of Lothian and Borders Police right up to April Fools' Day 2013, when Scotland's eight police regions vanished to be replaced by a single organisation called Police Scotland. In place of a Chief Constable, Edinburgh now had a chief superintendent called Jack Scoular, who was only a few years older than Clarke. Fettes was Scoular's domain, a place where admin took precedence and meetings were held. No CID officers were stationed there, but it did boast half a corridor of vacated offices, which James Page had been offered. Two detective constables, Christine Esson and Ronnie Ogilvie, were busy pinning photos and maps to one bare wall.

'We thought you'd like the desk by the window,' Esson said. 'It's got the view if nothing else.'

Yes, a view of two very different schools: Fettes College and Broughton High. Clarke took it in for all of three seconds before draping her coat over the back of her chair and sitting down. She placed the newspapers on the desk and concentrated on the reporting of Lord Minton's demise. There was background stuff, and a few photographs dusted off from the archives. Cases he had prosecuted; royal garden parties; his first appearance in ermine.

'Confirmed bachelor,' Esson called out as she pushed another drawing pin home.

'From which we deduce nothing,' Clarke warned her. 'And that photo's squint.'

'Not if you do this.' Esson angled her head twenty degrees, then adjusted the photo anyway. It showed the body *in situ*, crumpled on the carpet as if drunkenly asleep.

'Where's the boss?' Clarke asked.

'Howden Hall,' Ogilvie answered.

'Oh?' Howden Hall was home to the city's forensic lab.

'He said if he wasn't back in time, the press briefing's all yours.'

Clarke checked the time: she had another hour. 'Typically generous of the man,' she muttered, turning to the first of the obituaries.

She had just finished them, and was offering them to Esson to be added to the wall, when Page arrived. He was with a detective sergeant called Charlie Sykes. Sykes was normally based at Leith CID. He was a year shy of his pension and about the same from a heart attack, the former rather than the latter informing practically every conversation Clarke had ever had with the man.

'Quick update,' Page began breathlessly, gathering his squad. 'House-to-house is continuing and we've got a couple of officers checking any CCTV in the vicinity. Someone's busy on a computer somewhere to see if there are any other cases, within the city and beyond, that match this one. We'll need to keep interviewing the deceased's network of friends and acquaintances, and someone is going to have to head to the vaults to look at Lord Minton's professional life in detail . . .'

Clarke glanced in Sykes's direction. Sykes winked back, which meant something had happened at Howden Hall. *Of course* something had happened at Howden Hall.

'We also need to put the house and its contents under a microscope,' Page was continuing. Clarke cleared her throat loudly, bringing him to a stop.

'Any time you want to share the news, sir,' she nudged him. 'Because I'm just about ready to assume you no longer think this was a panicked housebreaker.'

He wagged a finger at her. 'We can't afford to rule that possibility out. But on the other hand, we also now have this.' He took a sheet of paper from the inside pocket of his suit. It was a photocopy of something. Clarke, Esson and Ogilvie converged on him the better to see it.

'Folded up in the victim's wallet, tucked behind a credit card. Shame it wasn't noticed earlier, but all the same . . .'

The photocopy showed a note written in capital letters on a piece of plain paper measuring about five inches by three.

I'M GOING TO KILL YOU FOR WHAT YOU DID.

There was an audible intake of breath, followed by a few beats of complete silence, broken by a belch from Charlie Sykes.

'We're keeping this to ourselves for now,' Page warned the room. 'Any journalist gets hold of it, I'll be sharpening my axe. Is that understood?'

'Game-changer, though,' Ronnie Ogilvie offered.

'Game-changer,' Page acknowledged with a slow, steady nod.